DYING OF PARADISE
THE TRILOGY

DYING OF PARADISE
THE ICE BELT
THE BABYLON RUN

Stephen Gallagher

THE BROOLIGAN PRESS
LONDON
NEW YORK

This novel trilogy is a work of fiction. Names, characters, places, and incidents either are the product of the author's imagination or are used fictitiously. Any resemblance to actual persons, living or dead, events, or locales is entirely coincidental

Dying Of Paradise and The Ice Belt first published in 1982 by Sphere books as by Stephen Couper, containing some material from The Last Rose of Summer published in 1978 by Corgi Books

This edition published 2022 by The Brooligan Press
Rights and Permissions: Howard Morhaim Literary Agency
30 Pierrepont St, Brooklyn NY 11201

Stephen Gallagher has asserted his right to be identified as the author of this Work in accordance with the Copyright, Designs and Patents Act 1988

All rights reserved. No part of this publication may be reproduced, stored in a retrieval system, or transmitted in any form or by any means, electronic, mechanical, photocopying, recording or otherwise, without the prior permission of the copyright owner

Dying of Paradise © 1982 Stephen Gallagher
The Ice Belt © 1982 Stephen Gallagher
The Babylon Run © 2022 Stephen Gallagher

ISBN: 978 1 9160578 7 6

With thanks to Tony Hawkins, Pete Baker of Piccadilly Radio, and colleagues from Granada Television and the community of Manchester-based freelance talent. All came together to make the first nationally distributed drama of the Independent Local Radio network from which these stories sprang. Special thanks to Malcolm Brown, Charles Foster, Jim Pope, Chris Kay, Diana Mather, Colin Weston, Mike Hurley, David Mahlowe, John Mundy, Russell Dixon, Barbara Greenhalgh, Meg Johnson, Alan Bardsley, Carole Hayman, Ian Flintoff, Peter Wheeler, Graham James, Will Casey, James Tomlinson, Martin Oldfield, and Peter Chandler

AN INTRODUCTION

MY FIRST professional sale was an audio serial titled *The Last Rose of Summer*. Made for peanuts with love and joy, it was the spawn of a bunch of TV and radio colleagues and it played at strange hours on commercial radio stations throughout the land. We broke new ground within the industry, and in the wider world our timing was good. It was science fiction, and '77 was the summer of *Star Wars*. I was 23.

A book sale came right after, a spinoff in the form of a novelisation of the serial scripts. The six half-hours offered a handy mass of foundation material for 70,000 or so words. It wasn't just a matter of putting in the he said/she saids, although I've seen many a book-of-the-film that did little more. The radio serial was followed by another two. The second book was written and there was even a cover designed, but publication was cancelled and the contract was paid off. *Hitchhiker's Guide* notwithstanding, the radio novelisation was too niche a genre to be commercial.

Sphere later offered to reprint *Last Rose* and the unpublished SF titles... but on condition that I used a pseudonym, to avoid crossover with the campaign they were planning for *Chimera*. Which is how Stephen Couper came into the world.

By then I was doing this for a living, and with the new name I wanted the books to stand on their own. Rather than reprint, I rewrote. Names, incidents, world building... I can't give you details, it's mists-of-time stuff now. So *The Last Rose of Summer* became *Dying of Paradise* and *Hunters' Moon* became *The Ice Belt* and The *Babylon Run*... well, with history repeating itself, *The Babylon Run* was written but remained unpublished. In the rewriting process, much of the original material would have been lost. This was a time when cut-and-paste meant exactly what it says.

We begin by imitating what we love; well, this is where I began. I'd grown up on Wells, Bester, Asimov, Clifford Simak, Poul Anderson... I stole from anyone, and from Orwell more than most. And by starting young I learned my craft in public, which is why I've tended to sideline these titles as 'the early stuff'.

But I made them, and people have asked, so here they are. They offer a vision of the future that's very much of its time, with the passage of years turning many of its futuristic elements into anachronisms. These stories were written on the threshold of the digital age, the Last Hurrah of an analog future where information would be forever on tape, and humanity's vast knowledge would be held in physical libraries.

Ironically, it's digital technology that's ensured the material's survival. The master tapes of the radio serials were archived and then lost, but fan-made recordings can be found online with relative ease. Some are of good enough quality for schedulers at the BBC's Radio 4Extra to have considered a modern rebroadcast, until chain-of-title issues scared them off.

In *The Last Rose of Summer* my protagonist connected to a forgotten era through a simple melody on a mechanical music box. It was a device that lent itself to audio dramatisation, but it led me on to so much more. As I write, that was more than four decades ago.

Maybe you were there.

Or maybe this can be your music box.

Book One
Dying of Paradise

ONE

THE CITY HAD spread, over-reached itself and was beginning to die. There was little traffic, and the chattering of the helicopter carried clearly through the still air. The pilot was young and flew with the arrogance of a newly-acquired but much-practised skill; he kept the 'copter below the roof level of the taller blocks and weaved a course between them. The swinging motion as the craft dipped to the left and right did nothing to temper Randall's inherent nervousness of flying and his knuckles grew white as they gripped the edge of the sealed Polite Elite briefcase. The pilot was grinning, and every few seconds glanced across for the reaction to his latest heart stopping manoeuvre. Randall's composure almost went as the side of a building raced to meet them and then shot past, seemingly only inches from the plastic bubble; windows zipped by in a stroboscopic blur and then they were out above the wide city again and flying level.

If the pilot felt disappointment at this lack of a response, he didn't show it. Instead he tapped his combination microphone and headset and pointed behind the passenger seat. Randall forced his head to turn and saw a similar headset hanging ready for his use, so he reached for it one-handed, grunting slightly at the pressure of the restraining straps. Despite the microphone being only an inch from his mouth, the pilot had to shout to be heard over the high-decibel clatter of the rotors.

'Sixty years old, this crate,' he said, taking his hand off the control column to gesture about the cramped cockpit. 'Oldest on the force. They can't afford to build any more.'

Randall nodded in what he hoped was an agreeable manner, but he felt as if his reserves of calm were draining through a small hole somewhere deep inside. Fixing his eyes on the horizon he tried to imagine the solidity of concrete beneath him, but the unfulfilled wish only made his present agonies worse and he lapsed instead into contemplation of the unrolling cityscape. The pilot threw another glance and a grin. But at least he desisted from the hedge-hopping brinkmanship.

It was easy, at this height, to distinguish the dead wood from the merely diseased or dying. The tower blocks, their services long broken down and irreparable, were for the most part deserted, and on close passes it was possible to see past the reflection of the 'copter on the sightless windows into the gutted offices and apartments behind. Such views were so brief as to be dizzying; better to focus on the sprawling developments of seven storeys and less which were slowly decaying in their brothers' shadows. Beyond the acres of citizens' housing was the glint of the river in the afternoon sun and beyond that the underbelly, petering out into thin brown fields and the crumbling circles of the disused spaceport.

The 'copter jerked and bobbed suddenly as if on the end of an invisible leash; as it hung momentarily weightless it turned about its own centre and then roared into a dive towards the widening canyon of a broad city street. The pilot's grin remained but there were no more sideways looks as they levelled off at two hundred feet and sped down the boulevard. The glass walls of the artificial valley's sides shot past in a blur of detail and it seemed to Randall that they were diving into a narrow shaft of infinite depth. Even through the headset the noise was far too loud as its battering was reflected back at them, and as its pitch changed with each widening intersection he felt a rolling followed by a minute correction as the change in airflow came and went.

Randall felt the tension ebbing away, all depths of fear and wonder finally explored and exhausted. He concentrated instead on the glittering reflection of the river which caught the sun and spilled up onto the windows at the far end of the canyon. The shimmering light seemed to spread and reach to envelop them at an impossible speed, then stars danced on the 'copter's bubble as they were out and climbing. That brief moment of weightlessness returned as they swivelled and dived into the final run, parallel to the water, towards the Police Elite main building.

Randall found that his fingers were hurting from his grip on the briefcase and so he straightened them, one by one.

The great golden dome of Central Command lay before and below them, straddling the river. It shone in the afternoon light like a bright jewel amidst the dross of the city, dwarfing even the library annexe on its north side. Randall saw the 'copter's shadow rising to meet them as the ascending curve of the dome slid beneath. Then the world tilted and the dome was gone.

Nose-up, the 'copter dropped towards its target, a white cross within a circle painted on the roof of the Police Elite building. They had to stand off for a little less than a minute while another 'copter lifted and circled from the same roof, then they continued their downward progress to within a few feet of the asphalt surface.

Randall looked across at the pilot as he struggled to make a steady hover in a slight crosswind. 'Why aren't we landing?' He shouted into his microphone.

'Orders,' the pilot shouted back. 'This is as low as I can go. They say the roof's starting to give way.'

With an inward sigh, Randall replaced the headset in its clasp and undid his restraining straps. He had to steady himself as he attempted to rise and a gust drifted the 'copter close to the roof's edge; he glimpsed a thin sliver of eternity beneath the runners before the pilot made the necessary correction and coasted back to the centre of the circle.

The downdraft whipped at his hair and clothing as he opened the door in the bubble and leaned out. The height of the hover was varying between three and four feet—not a bad jump, but an uncertain one. He dropped and landed heavily, hearing the door slam closed behind him in the slipstream. As he regained his feet the 'copter was gone, and the hot wash of its exhaust across the roof was burning his eyes dry. Fighting the nervous tremble in his legs and disorientated by temporary deafness, Randall used his Detective's pass to call the elevator which would drop him to the level of his office.

IT WAS A hick planet in a dying system, under a star that burned too red for comfort. Generations before it had been a fast-developing new colony, but now it was nothing, struck off just about every trader's chart, a market too poor to matter.

Of course, it hadn't always been that way. There had been a time when Persephone's one habitable planet was the hottest commercial property in the known galaxy. It had been discovered by fluke; Tiny Carlisi, a shambling Spacer on Futures, Incorporated's exploratory vessel *Iron Star*, had been changing the ration packs in one of the ship's escape pods when he farted in free-fall. He was less interested in the consequent demonstration of Newtonian basics than in getting his orientation back, and as he flailed around helplessly the most accessible grip that fell under his hand was the panic handle. The iris lock slammed shut, and the pod was away.

There was some debate on the bridge about whether it would be worth getting him back. Tiny Carlisi's value as a human being never entered into it, because he had none; he was a Spacer, agile hands linked to a limited intellect and—at least in the major commercial vessels like the *Iron Star*—kept that way with drugs. The real argument over Tiny Carlisi hinged on the investment that he represented; was it worth the manpower and delay to send somebody after him? But then, a trained spacer under full control was expensive to replace, and so Tiny Carlisi got rescued.

He wasn't difficult to track down. An escape pod operated under a simple directive, to find the nearest habitable body and get to it as fast as possible. The chase-up team found the only life-supporting planet within range, and then spotted Carlisi's beacon-blip. They found him sniffing flowers and floating two feet off the ground.

Not literally.

They bundled him into the wingship and set off for the *Iron Star* with the pod in tow, and on the journey back he dug into his pockets and handed the crushed petals around. The rescue team had to be carried out at the other end, giggling and thoroughly plastered.

Discovery of the narcotic gave Futures, Incorporated a profitable new line. When they couldn't analyse, they colonised. The strange flowers couldn't be found anywhere else, and they couldn't be grown anywhere else; Futures therefore set its base under Persephone. Buildings went up fast, and they went up cheaply; upriver from a natural bay on the planet's one main landmass the major effort of construction concentrated on the creation of a single city, a sprawling metropolis of traders and employees from the processing plants.

It took two hundred years to farm out the narcotic; two hundred years to harvest a plant so delicate that it resisted any attempt to rear it artificially. Two hundred years, and Persephone was commercially dead. The city by now held five million people; the investing companies looked around to see if they could dump this liability of human lives, and found that international law said they couldn't. Rapidly and with bad grace, they ploughed up the empty narc fields and seeded them with bacteria to produce a tolerable soil, planted the soil with a miserable selection of basic crops, and pulled out. They couldn't leave chaos, so they gave a couple of social engineers three weeks to come up with an answer. Three weeks wasn't long, but social engineers came expensive.

Their solution was rudimentary and offhand; no society's ever worked without being unfairly divided, they said. They turned their findings over to the Futures legal department, who expanded them into the twelve volumes of print called The Persephone Plan.

Under the Plan all company employees were given citizen status, drawing a basic income from the agricultural turnover and the few remaining industries; everybody else had to manage, in accordance with the decree of unfair division. To make sure that it stayed that way, Futures left Central Command.

Fifty years later, the plans came up before the Trading States Commercial Court and were approved. The Court noted that a bare minimum had been accomplished in each of the required areas, but Futures hardly cared—they'd already moved on.

IN A BLOCK that had once held R & D labs, the Festival of Futures exhibition was still running;. What once had been a state-of-the-art display was now a museum of antiquities.

Lee Rorvik stood by a window on the first floor. Some of the glass was cracked and some of it was missing; what remained was almost impossible to see through, but one of the gaps lined up with the Police Elite building several blocks away. He watched as the 'copter began to climb. He followed as it turned on its axis and slid into forward motion, and even after it had dipped beyond the roofline he watched until the chattering of its rotors could no longer be heard.

He knew that he shouldn't be here. Not that it was a prohibited area—Central even listed it as an approved site, safe for citizens—but he had obligations, an appointment. Even as he reminded himself, another part of his mind strained to push the thought away.

He was in the fifth floor gallery, one of the quieter sections. Most of the exhibits here were of the non-functional kind, no fun at all, and everybody tended to hurry through to get to the working exhibits—the light-up models of molecules, the speech-producing machines, the reader and tracker, and the cybernetics demonstrations. When he was much younger, growing up in the live-in baby farm after being abandoned by parents who found that Central's approval for breeding wasn't a passport to happiness, he'd come up here alone and often; now it was noticeable that many of the exhibits he remembered were no longer working. They broke and they failed, and they couldn't always be restored.

The museum was ungoverned and unattended, maintained by an enterprising group from the underbelly. They ran it under a thieves-kitchen arrangement; it was fronted by guides who could run off a glib patter about any object in return for a tip, and they were backed up by self-taught technicians who ran little workshops in the old labs, rebuilding and re-jigging wherever they could to keep the Festival of Futures jogging along. One of the guides was crossing the gallery as Rorvik began to move away from the window; small, nervous and blond, almost an albino, he was keeping ahead of a group of citizen children, glancing back to make sure they were still with him. Following up the group was a baby-farm nanny, another underbelly. The nanny was carrying a glowing static rod. He remembered those, all too well. Wherever she waved it, the group flowed on in a tide.

The guide stood by something that looked—to Rorvik at

least—like a new piece. Some of the serious little faces turned to him as he demonstrated; others turned anywhere else, listless and inattentive.

It was a gram machine, nothing more. Probably not even part of the original exhibition, it had more likely been looted from some sealed-off part of the city by an underbelly raiding party sneaking back across the river at night. It had to be broken. The music was godawful, the rhythm half-buried and too many sounds to sort out.

The nanny tipped the guide to dismiss him, and then swept the party onward. When the children didn't move fast enough for her, she touched about with the static rod; there were flashes and cracks and yelps, but no tears. Citizens did not cry. Citizens were Central's chosen. If they wanted to stay as such, they behaved.

Watching them go, Rorvik realised too late that he was alone with the guide.

'Bet you've never seen one of these before, have you?' the guide said, stroking the case of the gram, and though he'd seen plenty Rorvik agreed that he hadn't.

'I know you'd like to hear it.' The guide took a step forward and Rorvik took an involuntary step back; the underbelly was simply moving around to the other side of the machine, and he looked up with a wide, flat smile that on the surface said friend but which echoed to the depths with contempt; the natural friction of unsympathetic opposites.

Rorvik had already heard it, and hadn't liked it much. He nodded. 'Sure I would.'

He'd pulled the trap closed around himself. There was some crude welding on the side of the case, a rough-cut slot for coins with a little box of mechanism underneath. The visitor must provide, and so Rorvik had to dig in his pocket for the small handful of change that he usually carried in addition to his Central credit card.

He knew he was being duped, that the box on the side contained nothing more than a few drops and levers to make clicking noises before the guide reached around behind the machine to switch on the power, but he played along and pretended to look interested. It was no better the second time around. The whole idea was a waste, a dead end; if you needed music Central provided it better, piped straight to every room of your apartment. It changed with the light, with the seasons, with the weather; it was always appropriate and it never jarred. Unlike the gram, which would need effort and attention—okay for the underbelly, perhaps, but citizens were used to the real thing.

After feigning attention for a while, he dug in his pocket again. He overtipped and the underbelly nodded, as close as he'd get to a thanks.

His appointment. He couldn't keep putting it off. He started to move towards the exit. Some of the other guides tried to attract his attention but he shook his head and moved on, knowing that if he hesitated he'd never be able to disengage himself.

He made it to the outside without being drawn into conversation. Most of the guides would drop an unwilling mark and move onto the next, more likely prospect; only a few would obstruct and whine until they got what they wanted, but fortunately none of these got in his way.

Rorvik was halfway down the steps at the front of the building before he slowed. The boulevard was wide and its surface was cracked after long disuse, and most of the buildings along it were blind and shuttered. Over on the far side, two old women were pushing a handcart loaded with rags; a few underbelly children followed at a distance, watching the nondescript novelty. If they didn't get back over to the other side of the river before the curfew barriers went up they'd probably be spending the night in the damp of some badly-sealed city cellar, and maybe by morning the crawlers would have had them. They shuffled along, dark-eyed and skinny; one girl had no shoes, her feet bound in flapping rags.

There was a noise, off down the boulevard. Over a mile away another Police Elite helicopter dropped in between the buildings and began the bravado run at top speed down the canyon. There was no navigational justification for the route but nearly all the pilots followed it, skimming the tops of the thin dead trees and making them bend and lose a few leaves every time. Nobody could tell them to stop, for the pilots were an elite within an elite and did much as they pleased. They manufactured more excitement for themselves in one afternoon than a citizen could hope to get in a whole lifetime of hobbies and diversions.

The 'copter roared up and was gone in an instant, diving towards the river like a plummeting stone. Rorvik had caught a brief flash of the tableau within the 'copter's bubble; the pilot straining forward and grinning like a demon, his passenger frozen in an attitude of disbelief. He had watched the run so many times, envied its daring and feared its risks, and now he waited for the swooping climb across the water, invariably delayed until the last possible moment and then bursting up into the air like an explosion of joy.

The pilot was in trouble. Impossible to see why, but the tail of the 'copter was swinging from side to side so that the machine repeatedly tilted and dipped in its headlong progress down the man-made ravine. It was almost too late when the pilot regained a measure of control; the crevasse opened out and the stunted trees of the riverside rushed at his runners as the 'copter's nose came up, up and cleared them; and then continued to rise, impossibly fast as the pilot fought the controls to follow through and soar out over the open river where a dignified ditching might at least be possible.

His luck ran out. The flickering tail blades fouled in the uppermost branches, and the rising nose was thrown up and over. The 'copter somersaulted lazily, and as it reached the apex of its loop the whirling blades suddenly regained their bite on the air and slammed all the machinery down hard in the middle of the road. In the same instant fuel spurted and burned, and a cloud of black fire mushroomed out in all directions.

A moment of surprising quiet was cut by a second explosion which sent a rainbow of burning fuel high into the air. It settled to the angry whisper of distant fire and then, leaking from the building behind Rorvik, the ever-present background music programmed by Central Command.

The fuel was still showering, the light-show continued.

Now that, thought Rorvik, is what I call an exhibition.

RORVIK'S APPOINTMENT was with a set of empty rooms. Jiri Mondrian's apartment, which Jiri would probably never see again. Jiri's woman had packed up and cleared out some time before, and his place had been ideal for getting together in the long afternoons that stretched into the lonely evenings, all three of them—Rorvik, Jiri, and Lin Baxter.

He climbed moving walkways that no longer moved, through empty shopping malls with kicked-in windows—flyblown and crumbling by day, this was no place to be seen at night. Through a gap across a piazza he glimpsed the far-off dome of Central Command. It gave him a guilty start; he'd missed out on the library facility for several months, and he felt that perhaps he should get along there for the sake of appearance if nothing else.

But he couldn't raise any enthusiasm for the entertainment on offer, not since he'd found that he was able to join in with most dialogue and foresee every outcome. On his last visit to the library he'd been given a gentle reprimand for his neglect of the citizens' greatest privilege, and the prospect of facing yet again that blank console in the curtained booth and hearing displeasure in the fatherly voice of Central Command did little to entice him. Louann would be there, of course, collecting her usual armful of dramas, and perhaps that would be family representation enough.

He let himself in with Jiri's key. It was a standard-issue place, two small bedrooms and a smaller kitchen packed in an L around the main lounge. There were four of these units to each level with a central service well—it wasn't much different to his own. The suitcase that Jiri had asked for was easy to find; vacuum-formed and with one broken hinge, it contained almost everything that Jiri owned.

Rorvik was embarrassed to be seen with it, and ashamed to be embarrassed. It was a lousy way to feel about somebody who was dying.

HIS SHOULDERS were aching with the effort of carrying when he finally arrived back at his own apartment block and managed awkwardly to jab the *Call Lift* button with his elbow.

There was a blast of badly-tuned music programming from

the other side of the hall. Collinson, the block caretaker, had opened the door to his little glassed-in office and was shaking his head as he leaned out.

'The lift's burned out on us again,' he said. 'It'll have to be the stairs until we get the requisition to have it fixed.' Collinson was underbelly, but like all city employees he had a dispensation from Central to live on the citizen side of the river.

Rorvik groaned inwardly and debated whether to leave the suitcase in Collinson's office and collect it when the lift was working again, but that would be a week at least on the past performance of Central's maintenance units. They were underbelly too, after all. He thanked the caretaker—no tip, so tough luck—who nodded and withdrew into his hutch.

It was five floors, and the suitcase got heavier at every turn in the stairs. The fourth floor was old Gerrard's level, and he started to tiptoe on the creaking treads before he realised that there was enough noise coming from Gerrard's place to drown out an any sound short of an avalanche of ball bearings in the stairwell. It was a relief—if Gerrard knew you were passing, he'd be out and launching into a conversation which needed nothing from you beyond your presence. So he was old and lonely—he was also a pain, and impossible to get away from.

He emerged onto the fifth level and dropped the luggage on the grimy hall carpet. It saved him the trouble of having to hunt one-handed for his key; he pressed it against the lock panel where the circuits conformed and released the door.

Louann wasn't home. Probably the library, as he'd thought; there was a sense of disturbance, of something misplaced, but nothing more. Citizen liaisons didn't last, and they weren't encouraged; they should have broken two years before, when the real bitterness had been at its height—the coldness that followed had been far worse, made perfect hell by the numbness of routine. One of them should have moved out, but the steady deterioration of the housing blocks meant that there was nowhere to go; even Jiri's place was already spoken for and due for occupation.

The three-screen video was dark in the corner, and he went over to it and placed his hand on the control surface. Still warm.

She couldn't have been away for long.

Jiri hadn't given any instructions on what to do with the contents of the case. There was only one item that he'd asked for, and that was on top when the lid came up; half a bottle of bootleg hooch, real varnish-stripper. As for the rest, Rorvik was supposed to be storing it—not that Jiri would ever see it again.

The remaining contents were junk, there was no kinder way of putting it; old junk, the kind that has no worth but which gives you a few minutes of interest and the odd flash of memory sorting through. Rorvik lifted a few things out, turned them over, moved others aside; Jiri seemed to have stayed with his parents for longer than standard, and even to have been sent letter cassettes at the baby farm. Rorvik didn't know where his own parents lived.

There was a knock on the door—he hadn't locked it behind him. He reached to pull the suitcase lid down as a wary head was thrust into the room, closely followed by the rest of Lin Baxter.

'Guess who,' Lin said, and then looked around with hard interest. There were a couple of Library cassettes in his hand, the video/sound type. Anywhere but on Persephone they would have been curious antiques, but on the burned-out narcotic world progress had hit the skids when Futures moved out. 'Where's Louann?' he demanded. 'You been keeping her hot for me?'

Rorvik put on a smile that barely fitted.

'She's down by the docks, corrupting the fleet,' he said. 'But I can put you down for an evening appointment.'

'Any time,' Baxter said airily. 'I know you find it tough to keep up the energy. Do you some good to let an expert in.'

He closed the door and came into the room. Lin Baxter now lived alone after a string of no-go liaisons, at least three as far as Rorvik knew. Two of the women had been more than ordinarily invested, but the distances between them had proved, in the end, uncrossable. They broke without acrimony, more with bafflement. Baxter's explanation, thrown out with bitterness in one of his darker moments, was a simple one. He didn't think that he could hope to love anybody else more than he loved himself.

His eyes were on the case. His expression was mildly

troubled, as if something was worrying him but he wasn't sure what.

'I'm going down to Central,' he said. 'Feel like a walk?'

'I'm staying clear of Central,' Rorvik said as he lifted the case and carried it over to the lay-low. 'I've left it too long. I can't face the questions.'

'Oh fuck,' Baxter said suddenly as the pieces clicked together. 'You've been to Jiri's, haven't you?'

Rorvik nodded. Baxter had gone slightly pale, drained of ease. He couldn't handle it; a dying friend got under his defences, and his shell was too thin to take it.

'I'm taking it to him,' Rorvik said. 'Will you come with me?'

Baxter slowly shook his head. His eyes were still on the case, portable museum and reminder of transience. Everything that Jiri Mondrian owned; worthless junk, and now a body to match.

'I can't,' he said. 'I can't.'

Rorvik felt some anger, but it was wrapped in guilt. So he was the one who made the trips and sat with Jiri, but deep down his feelings were little different from Baxter's, an inexplicable mixture of shame, impatience and despair. Duty sent him out to the wards on the fringe of the city; but the urge to flee from the deteriorating spectacle of a wasting life was a strong one.

'Okay,' he said, making it light in an effort to break the mood, 'I'll take a walk down to the river with you. But I'll stay clear of the Library.' The Central Computer's disapproval was something he didn't need. The real advantage lay in the fact that he'd be out of the apartment when Louann got home.

He moved to close the case, but Baxter moved first. He'd seen something, and he reached for it.

A rotten elastic band ripped and spilled the plastic slips of a dozen or more photographs. Age had defocussed the stereo images, blurs that hung like a mist before long-dead faces. Baxter wasn't after these, but something underneath; he pushed them aside, and then tugged out a cassette.

'Look at this,' he said. It seemed a real museum piece, sound only with no vision track and a faint bloom which killed the shine on the plastic case. It wasn't even a standard Library coded colour. 'I wouldn't return this if I were you. There's probably fifty years of fines backed up on it.'

'I doubt that,' Rorvik said, taking the cassette from him and turning it over, 'It isn't a Library tape.'

Rorvik turned the cassette around to show him the back. There was no Library seal, no embossed warning about the illegality of attempting to open or copy the cassette, no list of penalties if it should be found in the hands of a non-citizen.

'Not a Library tape?' Baxter said. 'It can't be pre- Library. They were all collected and destroyed.'

'It must be underbelly, then.'

'Underbelly?' Baxter blinked, and grew slightly nervous. 'What do you mean?'

'Nobody in the underbelly is supposed to get access to Library stuff, but it's known that they make their own gear. This probably fits some lash-up machine.'

'Better get rid of it, then.'

'Don't you want to hear it?'

'No. Get rid of it.' Baxter's growing fear was obviously real. No citizen treated a Central ban lightly.

Rorvik looked at the cassette again. It seemed innocent and homely, probably knocked up in an antique vacuum-forming plant in some shady underbelly cellar on the fat side of the river. It probably wasn't pornography—not without a video track—and Rorvik was intrigued by what it might be. Perhaps a ripoff dub of some Central programming, or maybe something a little more unusual. He'd try to find out.

Baxter followed him across the room as he went towards the video. 'You can't play it,' he said. 'It won't fit.'

'It might.' The cassette was slightly smaller than standard, but the tape pitch looked about the same. As long as the drive cores engaged and the band was against the heads, the air-pressure positioning and laser alignment would handle the rest. He reached to slot it in, and Baxter's hand dosed on his wrist.

He pulled it back again immediately, almost apologetically. 'Please,' he said. 'Please, don't try to play it.' Rorvik looked at him, more surprised than anything. 'Aren't you even curious?' he said.

'No. Don't play it.'

He found it difficult to understand Baxter's apprehension. No citizen messed around with infringements if he wanted to stay a citizen, but surely here, an action that would be unobserved and of no particular consequence...

'What's the matter?' he said. 'What's the scare?'

'Central, that's the scare. What if Central's monitoring?'

Central Command took occasional samples of feedback from the videos, charting times and incidence of use and planning its citizen administration programme accordingly. 'The chances are pretty thin. And even so, Central only takes a power sample. It wouldn't know what we were playing.'

'What *you* were playing. Keep me out of this.'

Baxter was really scared, as if Rorvik had just proposed that it would be a great joke to sneak downstairs and strangle old Gerrard as he sat blotting out his misery with Squeeze and muzak. Respect for authority was bred into every citizen, but Baxter's seemed to have developed into a phobia of disobedience. It was a facet of Baxter that Rorvik had never really seen before. He wasn't sure that he liked it much.

'Look,' he said. 'It's a tape, that's all. It can't frighten anyone and it can't hurt anyone, and I'd be interested to hear it. I don't see what logical objection Central could have.'

'We're not talking about logical objections. We're talking about rules.'

'Rules are fine for out there. But this is my own home.' He was aware of a kind of irony in the words as he said them in the bare, charmless suite of rooms that had been systematically cleaned out of warmth and affection during the last couple of years. Baxter looked around, not so much searching for the truth of Rorvik's assertion as for a means of escape should the Police Elite suddenly come hammering on the door. The fire escape outside the bedroom window would probably offer no salvation at all.

'Either stay or go,' Rorvik said, 'but here it comes.' He pushed the cassette into the slot, which flipped open to accept it.

'Probably won't work,' Baxter said hopefully.

LOUANN ROGET was still two hundred yards from the entrance as she approached the Library, but she was already in the shadow thrown by Central Command's dome in the afternoon sun. She joined the short queue at the turnstiles and quickly passed through the security procedure into the main hall. It was wide and low-ceilinged, not unlike the disused passenger lounges at the old spaceport, but the visual impression barely registered with her; she followed a familiar route across half an acre of floor to the broad steps which led to the mezzanine and the fiction terminals.

The mezzanine was far more crowded than the main floor level. Citizens of all ages but of similar appearance passed before and behind her with armloads of tapes identical to her own. In spite of the crowd she had little trouble finding a vacant booth. She sat down, sliding the door closed behind her, and the echo and shuffle of the broad hall was lost in the stuffy acoustic of the booth's interior.

It was narrow—a minimal space—but comfortable. A low hum seeming to come from nowhere and everywhere at the same time indicated that the Central Command computer was aware of her presence, and the mirror directly opposite her at eye level thinned and became transparent to reveal the glow of a single camera eye.

'Good afternoon, and welcome to the Library facility of Central Command.' Again, the voice seemed to surround and contain her. It was deep and well-modulated, with a tone that was paternal and affectionate. 'Please place your borrower's card in the slot in front of you and state your name. Remember that to give a false identification is an offence.'

'Louann Roget.'

'You are identified, Ms Roget. Good afternoon.'

'Good afternoon.' She retrieved her borrower's card from the slot.

'And what can the Library do for you, Ms Roget?'

'I've come to return these tapes and to get some new ones.'

'Please place your tapes in the delivery chute on your left. ' On cue, a flap popped open with a hiss of compressed air and she obediently slotted the cassettes into it. The lid smacked closed again and a soft whoosh was evidence that the computer was using a vacuum chamber to suck at a loop of tape from each in turn and give it a spot-check.

'Ah,' the voice said, 'three dramas and a hobby tape. Tell me, Ms Roget, how did you enjoy "The Shivering Willows?"'

'Very much, thank you.'

'We find it is one of our most popular choices. So moving. I shall note your remarks for future recommendation.'

'I watched it twice.'

'So I see. Please remember to rewind the tape next time, Ms Roget.'

She gave a guilty start. 'Oh. . . I'm sorry.'

'Please don't worry about it, Ms Roget. Just make sure you rewind all the tapes next time. Now, what else did we have? I see you borrowed "Arabic Passion" for the second time.'

'If you remember, you suggested it to me.'

'Of course I remember, Ms Roget. We never forget anything. How is Lee Rorvik?' The tone of the voice remained the same as it effortlessly switched subjects.

'Quite well, I suppose. We don't often talk.'

'So you said last time. Where is he now?'

'He was out somewhere when I left the flat. I've no idea what he was doing.' Her eyes were fixed on the chute where her new selections would be delivered, and she began to wish as she did on every visit that the computer would cut short the friendly conversation.

'How much did you enjoy "Gangster's Moll"?'

She warmed at the memory. 'Quite a lot. I've always liked historical romances.'

'He hasn't been into the Library for three months now.'

'I'm sorry?'

'Lee Rorvik. I was wondering why he had not visited us recently.'

Now she began to grow impatient, but knew she dared not show it. Instead she stared longingly at the empty chute, and replied without much enthusiasm, 'I wouldn't know. He spends most of his time with a couple of his friends.'

'Names?'

'Lin Baxter's one of them. The other one's called Jiri

Mondrian, but he's sick. Out at the spaceport wards.'

'May I suggest some new tapes for your enjoyment.' A hiss of air announced the welcome arrival of a cassette in the chute. 'Here is "Her Heart on Her Sleeve", a tender drama set in the world of retail management. I'm sure you'll find it very illuminating.'

'I'm sure I will.'

'Where does Baxter live?' This time, the sudden switch caught her slightly off-guard.

'Citizen block twelve,' she faltered. 'Across the street from our block.'

'Here is your second selection. It is called "Susan of the Steelworks". What does Baxter do?'

'I wouldn't know. I don't like him.' Louann removed the cassette and looked for the next.

'I see. This is "Her Trust Rewarded, a Romantic Tale of Old Tyneside".'

'Thank you,' she said.

'Ask Lee Rorvik to call on us more often,' the voice purred. 'We would hate to see him fall idle.'

'He seems to find plenty to occupy himself.'

'I am sure he must. Unfortunately, such occupations can so often turn out to be of a disagreeable nature. Ask him to call on us.'

'I will.'

'Tell him we have new material to interest him. Tell him we remember his tastes, we remember his appetites. Tell him we never forget... anything.'

'I'll tell him.'

The voice of Central Command became more businesslike. 'Please take your final selection from the delivery chute on your right. The Library division of Central Command thanks you for your visit, Ms Roget. We look forward to your return.'

The hum subsided, and the light died in the camera eye. She was left facing her own reflection in the mirror, and the noise of the world outside began to penetrate the door.

New tapes. Three whole days of bliss in the best of all possible worlds. She slid the door open and hurried out across the mezzanine.

THE CASSETTE hadn't wanted to fit at first; it was too narrow, and although it was possible to get the tape up against the heads the casing was at too much of an angle. Rorvik jammed a stack of canteen coupons underneath to hold it firm; otherwise, the tape would have snarled as soon as the machine began to draw it out.

He programmed in the threading operation. As power was cycled into the now cold apparatus a small panel lit up and read, *machine not ready*. They waited for it to blink out.

'I'm mad,' Baxter said mournfully. 'I shouldn't even be here.' But he made no move to go. After a moment, he said, 'What do you think it is?'

'Why so curious?' Rorvik said. 'I thought you were ready to jump out of the window, just to get away from it.'

Baxter shrugged. The warning panel went abruptly blank, and then flashed a *ready* light. As Rorvik reached for the playback control Baxter gave an involuntary glance towards the windows and the iron stairs. No Elite were gathering outside, nobody was getting ready to kick his way in. And there was no sound coming from the video.

'What's wrong?' Baxter said. Underneath the apprehension was an ill-disguised sliver of disappointment.

'Not sure,' Rorvik replied, and he moved the cassette around slightly in case it hadn't engaged. 'It's so old and non-standard there might not be a guide track. I don't know.'

'Perhaps there's. . .' Baxter began, and the music started.

At first, it was disappointing. It was like Classico, the best stuff that Central reserved for late nights and serene summer days, but it wasn't half as easy to listen to. There was no real regular beat—or rather, it was there by implication only, as if one of the tracks had been erased in the final mix. The melody wasn't something you could whistle; not really a melody at all, because it didn't repeat to force its way home and give instant, easy familiarity.

Baxter was frowning and shaking his head. 'Crap,' he said. 'Better knock it off.'

'Give it a chance,' Rorvik argued. He agreed with Baxter, but form demanded that he should be the one to pick the moment when he pressed the tape cancel.

And suddenly, he was there. It was an unperceived jump, a gestalt leap where the pieces dropped together in an unforced whole; he didn't listen to the music, he was within it, dazzled and slightly giddy like a man in a world of blacks and whites getting his first sight of blood. The last unit which made the gestalt complete was the listener, Rorvik He was part of a chain of understanding which led back to the music's raw source; a source which, though inexplicit and obscure, was traceable through the clues of personality contained in the sound.

You didn't get clues of personality in Central's output. That was the shaker, the three-star shocker. Some*body* had put all this together.

Baxter hadn't seen it. His expression was still the same blank that it had been at the start of the cassette, with a shadow of boredom sneaking in. And now, Rorvik realised, his own understanding was starting to slip; he'd had one intense moment of imprint, and conscious effort couldn't hold it as it started to fade.

The door opened, and Louann stepped in from the hall.

Baxter was on his feet straight away, before he'd even seen who was coming. Rorvik was looking up as Louann closed the door behind her and then turned into the room. She was frowning as she looked towards the singing video with its dead screens.

'What are you listening to?' she said.

'Nothing,' Baxter said quickly, and when he saw that Rorvik wasn't going to move he leaned across to the stop/eject control. He whisked the cassette out and away behind his back before Louann could see that it was non-standard. Two coupons fell to the floor.

'I'd better be going,' he said as he backed around Louann and towards the door. 'Regards to Jiri, and tell him. . .' Baxter's voice tailed off as he realised that he had nothing to say to Jiri. But by then, he was nearly away. 'Well, anyway, regards to Jiri.' The mask was starting to slide as he pulled the door closed.

Louann was indifferent to Baxter's leaving, and she didn't

show any sign of curiosity at the sounds that she'd heard or the unusual container that she may or may not have glimpsed. She set her own stack of cassettes down by the video, and picked one off the top. 'Central was asking about you,' she said.

Rorvik looked up. 'About me?'

'Your attendance record. Central's worried about you.'

A t least somebody is, he thought, and then he thought of Jiri, alone and unwanted in a grim ward in the spaceport. This is where we're all headed. This is the real measure of Central's concern.

The three wraparound screens flared into life with an aerial view descending on an industrial complex. *'We present, 'Susan of the Steelworks','* boomed the speakers, *'a tale of soaring passion in the rolling mills. Come back with us now to a time when men were men and women were worshipped, for a tale of a tragic prisoner of love.'*

LIN BAXTER HAD nothing but a long series of bad moments as he made his way down the stairs and out of the building, past Collinson's noisy little office. Although he'd hidden the illegal cassette between his legitimate Library issues, it seemed to sing in a loud and piping voice: *'Guilty, guiltee!'* it shrieked happily at anyone it passed, but only Baxter could hear the song.

Forget the Library for this afternoon. Wait until dark, and then go down to the river. Find a heavy stone and bind the cassette to it, choke off its song forever in the fast-moving waters. Throw it high and hard, over towards the underbelly.

Send it back to its own.

TWO

Rorvik loitered around the street near the museum for almost a week. The Police Elite helicopter pilots no longer made the bravado run down the enclosed roadway to the river. The previous week's crash obviously made them wary. One of them had hovered for a while at the far end of the street like a thoughtful wasp, and Rorvik had watched it hopefully; but it swung up and away on a safer route across the rooftops, and he was disappointed. One morning he actually went back into the museum and looked again at the gram deck, but there was no satisfaction in it.

Twice he even followed the street down to the river and looked speculatively across at Central Command. Seen this close, the dome showed itself not to be a simple orb but a geodesic structure, the great sweep of its curve being formed by a mass of jointed triangular plates which glittered in the cold sunlight like the facets of a diamond. There, he thought, is where I should be looking; Central Command was, after all, the sole source of all music and entertainment, and anything remotely musical must have its origins there.

But Rorvik doubted it. He had never been an avid Library user, but he knew the range of the stocks well enough to recognise that Jiri's old tape had a content so unlike anything he had ever heard before that it might well be from off-planet. That possibility depressed him intensely; the city's spaceport was long decayed, and the commerce of the galaxy had been bypassing them for more than a generation now. It would be a week or more before he could amass enough credit actually to take the monorail to the thin, reedy green belt where the nursing homes clustered, and until then he could only walk the streets and watch for helicopters.

There were, of course, other reasons for avoiding Central Command—or rather, the Library division, as nobody ever went beyond its halls and terminals into the machine habitat of the dome. Baxter was to a great extent correct in his apprehension towards security action over a communications infringement. Rorvik couldn't be certain that the very act of listening to the old-time music might not be construed as an offence, and to admit so much would invite an inevitable chain of questions revealing the existence of the tape and his use of an unofficial cassette. When the Library knew that, he could wave goodbye to his citizenship and all its benefits. Home, food and income would vanish in a flash, his credit would be blocked and he would never again have access to the Library—although of all the penalties, that one troubled him least.

The range of possibilities outside an enquiry to Central Command were so small as to be negligible. Nearly everything could be tracked back to the Central computer, sitting in its private dome like a great immobile hermit crab, sifting, comparing and issuing decisions on every subject from sewage flow to housing. If Rorvik by some indiscretion were to allow a suspicious action to come to its attention it would be a matter of moments before the relevant programmes were meshed and correlated to send the Police Elite hammering on his door.

No. Direct appeal to the computer was out of the question. He was both dejected and frustrated; it was such a small thing to ask, such a ridiculous issue to be fearful over, but he was certain of the inevitable consequences. He left the river and wandered down towards the commercial sector.

The drab fronts of the markets held little attraction for him, but as the day drifted on into early evening their brightly-lit interiors in contrast with the dark pearl of the sky gave each the false aura of a centre of excitement.

There was nothing he wanted, and nothing he could afford if he were to be making the monorail trip next week, but it cost nothing to look. Others were looking also, mainly non-citizens, lingering with dreams in their eyes.

The thought struck Rorvik as he passed the third frontage. As he had crossed each open doorway the sweet gentleness of the background music had washed around him and receded as he moved on, only to find himself in the cross-current from the next opening. He stopped abruptly, and earned a growl from a man following head-down and a little way behind. Rorvik mumbled something that would sound like an apology as they shuffled around each other. The other man said nothing, and didn't even look at him.

There were plenty of deep shelves inside, angular and mostly empty in the hangar lighting. Although citizens used such places, they didn't use them often; they were mainly for the underbelly who worked within the city's limits and couldn't use the citizen facilities. Stock control was by Central, of course; after a while you would get used to the irregular stock dates, the sudden gluts, and the immediate sellouts which kept the underbelly nervous and undersupplied, an urban peasantry.

Rorvik stepped inside. At first, nobody noticed him. The muzak cut out abruptly and the air thundered as somebody blew into a microphone.

'Good evening, shoppers,' a voice came over with poorly-feigned cheer. 'We would like to draw your attention to some of the bargains of the food section, where textured protein is now selling at four credits below the recommended price. Swedes are also down in price today, so why not treat the family to something special this weekend?'

It was a man with dark, slicked-down hair and heavy glasses who could be seen in a partitioned office raised above floor level at the back of the store. 'Moving on to our cosmetics counter, for a limited period we are offering free medical insurance to every buyer of our *Wrinkle Killer* home facelift preparation. Remember, shoppers, this is your big bargain store where your credit's worth more.'

Rorvik called out 'Excuse me!' and walked towards a figure in a white coat bending over a pile of food bags. It turned out to be a youth of little charm and great personal odour.

'You talking to me?' he said, almost as if reacting to an accusation.

Rorvik was nonplussed, and said, 'I was, actually, yes.'

'What do you want?' the youth demanded.

'Piece of information.'

The youth jerked his thumb in the general direction of the raised office. 'Information point's over there.'

Now Rorvik was getting a problem. The cassette had been underbelly, a bootleg; how could he say, openly, that this was what he was looking for?

He moved a little closer. The smell was like bad meat being stewed in turpentine. An information point would be a terminal with a readout of current stock levels and prices.

'I don't want to talk to the machine,' he said. 'I want something more unofficial.'

The youth nodded slowly. He looked much older, close up. He said, 'Like what?'

Clandestine behaviour had never been familiar to him, outside of the show tapes where it was sketched in parody; the good guys always had the upper hand, and the scum showed a suitable deference and respect. Rorvik didn't feel much like a good guy; just way out of his depth.

'Like. . . like music,' he said.

It didn't seem possible, but the youth got slightly uglier. 'You pissing me about?' he demanded, and when Rorvik shook his head he went on, 'I can get you meat and I can get you book-filth, but it would cost you. You want music, fuck off down to your Library.'

'I've seen a tape cassette,' Rorvik insisted as the youth tried to walk away. 'It was underbelly, I know it. I want to know where I can get more.'

'Talk to Morden,' the youth spat, 'if you can find him.'

And then he started to laugh as he turned and walked off.

BIG FLEAS have little fleas; for every market there's a fleamarket, a passing place for junk as it sifts down through the social layers to the poorest and hungriest at the very bottom. That meant underbelly, and so the fleamarket shops on the fringe of the commercial sector were where Rorvik went to look next.

They were in the lowest part of the city's shopping mall, an area originally set out for land vehicle parking. Now the only land vehicles belonged to the Elite and to some of Central's maintenance departments, and the levels had been colonised. Halfway between bazaar and graveyard, the bays had been walled off into deep chambers and lights had been strung from the mail's main power supply. It was a rats' nest of a market, long snaking alleyways and a concrete sky with neon stars. Those who couldn't pay the controlling gangs for a unit kept stalls in the alleys, and the very lowest spread out on rugs under the stalls. Such a place ought to be busy, noisy, shrill with hustling. It was almost silent.

Nobody called out to him as he wandered; he was a citizen, and to be avoided even if his money wasn't. He chose his place—well, not really carefully. He tried to exercise some judgment, but in the end he chose at random. It was a deep bay with shutters drawn back, mostly filled with furniture stacked high. The spaces were stuffed with smaller objects, the kind of junk that Jiri had hoarded.

There was a dusty cord across the entrance, a little below chest-height. He brushed it as he ducked under, and a bell rang somewhere down inside.

A woman came forward from the shadows. She was twice his age, and so thin it was almost scary. She was in a blue overall coat, sleeves rolled back to show arms that were no more than wrist and sinew, and she wore makeup that had apparently been applied while her mind was elsewhere; it seemed to be off-target by a fraction of an inch, and too bright for the ingrained agony beneath.

'Yes?' she said, and she looked at Rorvik with the wariness of a beaten dog being fed by a stranger.

'I'm not really sure,' he said, aware of how weak an opening it was, 'but I was wondering if. . .'

He was interrupted by a slithering sound and a knock of bone on wood. They both looked towards the pile of furniture as a box was pushed out of the way and a child crawled through the gap. He was about seven years old with the face of an aged monkey, shoeless and sooty from the dark jungle gym through which he'd climbed.

The woman was looking at Rorvik again. He said, 'I'm looking for music.'

The child was on his feet now, watching in silence. The woman said, 'Music all comes from Central, doesn't it?'

'I suppose it does.' There was nothing in the child's eyes that Rorvik could read—no hostility, no respect. It unsettled him. 'But the kind of thing I'm looking for never came from Central. Would you know anything about that?'

It was a narrow line he was treading, throwing out bait while trying not to incriminate himself.

She said, 'I think there's. . . just wait a second. . .'

She turned and shuffled around a corner made by five chairs piled high. Rorvik hung back for a moment, then followed her.

There was a mattress that had been turned onto its side, and she was dragging a box out from behind it. Rorvik went forward to help, but she'd already opened the lid flaps and was rummaging around.

She came out with something, straightened, and held it towards him. It was a narc snuff box, not the cassette he'd expected. It quivered slightly in her thin hand, and out of politeness alone he took it. When he lifted the lid it played a tune, a snatch of about twenty seconds.

The woman was staring at him, waiting to read his reaction. He didn't want the box.

'I'll take it,' he said.

Credit wasn't used anywhere in the fleamarket, so he paid cash. She insisted on wrapping the box in an irregular sheet of recycled paper.

'We had some written music in here, once,' she said. The man had parted with money. It didn't make him a friend, but at least it lifted him out of a number of suspicious categories.

'Written music?'

'On paper. That's what I was told it was, anyway.'

'Have you still got any?'

She shook her head. 'We burned it all,' she said. 'Couple of winters back. Didn't look like much to me, anyway.'

'Where did you get it from?'

'A clearance. Central was emptying out the East city archives, and everything it didn't want got dumped. It's happened four, five times in the last few years. Be nothing left soon. We go down and sort through the heaps. Sometimes it's useful. Sometimes.'

'Would there be any more? Of this written music, I mean?'

'There was only a bit. And it didn't look much, some sort of code. You could always try.'

The grimy child had disappeared back into the labyrinth. As Rorvik moved back towards the alley with the narc box that he didn't want, he said, 'Would Morden be able to help me?'

'Who?' the woman said blankly. But her trembling increased, until her whole body quivered.

'Nothing,' Rorvik said. 'Just an idea.'

EAST CITY ARCHIVES was in one of the boulevard blocks. Most of the windows were boarded—at least on the lower levels, where underbelly might try to climb in—and only one wing of the building was still accessible. The rest were probably full of crawlers, a great, twittering carnivorous sea waiting for dogs to come sniffing through the cellars or birds to fly in through smashed panes.

He found a way in and climbed three floors, the first two empty. On the third, he pushed through a flap-door and emerged into a long, low room. It was lit by overhead fluorescents, but most of them were out. There was a dry, sinus-pinching odour that he couldn't identify.

The nearer shelves were stacked with box files, floor-to-ceiling. Beyond that he could see books, more books than he'd ever come across before. Central's Library had what it called books, text-tapes which you could moderate to cycle at your own reading speed, but these were the real thing, binders and paper and no video needed.

He coughed to get attention, although he couldn't see anybody. There was a movement way down in the room as someone stepped from an alcove.

'What do you want?' It was a reedy, almost effeminate voice, and it belonged to a hunched man in clothes half a size too big for him. He'd lost some of his hair, and what remained was white.

Rorvik said, 'Is this a library?'

'It's an archive,' the man said, walking down towards him. He had a limp, as if he'd once fallen from a ladder when stretching out too far to replace a volume. Slight limp. Short ladder. 'You know what an archive is?'

'Yes,' said Rorvik, who had really no idea.

Now that the man had a better view of Rorvik, he stopped. Rorvik was an obvious citizen, maybe even an Elite; there was something about the way they were bred; as if they all started out different but were growing into the same family. The man was wary. Citizens in the archive on the last three occasions had resulted in slightly less archive.

'Did Central send you?' he said, and Rorvik shook his head.

'I'm here on my own. I'm looking for written music.'

'Written what?'

'Music, you know.'

'I know what music is. You're talking about scores. We had a heap of them upstairs, but they got thrown out the last time Central had a rationalisation purge. The crawlers had chewed them up, anyway.'

'What were they like?'

'Like? The crawlers?'

'The scores.'

'I wouldn't know. Some sort of code. Older than this place, anyway. The paper broke up when you touched it. Why should you be interested?'

Rorvik shrugged. It was a question without an answer. He said, 'Can I have a look around? This is still part of Central, isn't it?'

The man obviously wanted to say no, but Rorvik was a citizen. 'Do what you like,' the man said, and he turned and limped off down the alcoves.

For a moment, he was at a loss. He'd at least expected to be guided. In Central itself, there wasn't even any kind of display; you sat in a booth and Central read off your borrowing history before making a selection for you. It guaranteed balance. It made things much easier for Central. He went over to the nearest block of shelves; the box-files were dusty and tightly packed together. He tugged one out and opened the flap, and found that the box was filled with razor-thin flimsy oxide discs. Some special kind of reader needed, obviously, and he didn't have one.

The real books started several rows further along. These shelves weren't so densely stacked, no more than two or three volumes on each shelf. If there was such a disease as a book plague, this archive had been stripped by an epidemic.

He picked one and opened it. It wasn't a printed text, it was a bound copy of a printout—the narrow oxide guide stripe down the outer edges gave away as much. The page was mainly blocks of numbers set out under headings—*demographic breakdowns*, he spelled out slowly in his mind. Whatever they were. He flicked a couple more pages, but they were no easier to understand.

Others were no better. They were jargon, language to elevate the banal to a level of mystique. None of them had pictures, but most had diagrams. Graph lines, overlapping circles, interlocking spheres with colour shading, blocks marching across the pages with their tops cut like steps. The paper felt dry and slippery, ageless and finished to impress.

Some way along, he felt that he was being watched. Not scanned, like in Central, but actual eyeball-and-neck craning watched. When he turned around, the limping man was there.

'I'm closing up,' he said pointedly.

Rorvik started to nod, and then realised that he was getting an unsubtle elbow towards the door.

'I haven't picked anything out yet,' he said, looking back across the nearest shelves.

'Haven't picked anything out?' the man echoed. 'What do you mean?'

'This is a library, isn't it?'

'An archive,' the man said. 'I told you.'

'And it belongs to the city?'

'Yes.' The man was definitely uncomfortable. He started to hitch his body slightly to get the weight off his bad leg, as if the act might get him some sympathy.

'So, I want to borrow something.' Rorvik looked at the shelves again, and took a step nearer. The man took a step along behind.

'Borrow something?' he said, almost in a whine.

'No reason why I can't, is there? I'm a citizen, and I've got a Library card. I want to take out a book. A couple of books.'

'Take them out?' the man said, horrified.

It didn't really matter. Anything would do, as long as his Library card number got recorded and eventually passed back to Central. He could boost his attendance record without actually attending, and maybe then the computer would stop making enquiries about him.

'Those two,' he said, and pointed.

The limping man looked. There were twelve bound volumes, all identical and much more handsomely presented than anything else on the shelves. Rorvik was pointing somewhere around the middle, somewhere that would nicely spoil the line of the display.

There was bad grace in the way that the underbelly pulled out volumes four and five and carried them off down the room. Rorvik followed to an alcove that had been turned into something of a nest, and handed over his card. The man wasn't sure what to do; he fussed, he shifted things and then shifted them back, and finally found a card form which looked more or less right. He copied the information across, and then placed Rorvik's registration on top of the books. His hand stayed there for a moment.

'A week,' he said. 'You'll bring them back in a week?'

It was suddenly difficult to be cruel, seeing the real apprehension in the man's eyes. 'I'll look after them,' Rorvik said. Damn it, he just wanted to keep up his borrowing record. He didn't have any intention of reading them.

INTENTION WAS one thing, but then came boredom. Lin Baxter was being very cool after the episode with the illegal cassette, and so Rorvik found himself alone in the evening. He lay on the bed looking at the ironwork shadows thrown across the ceiling, trying not to listen to the passionate rumblings and gasps from *Her Heart on Her Sleeve* in the next room. He'd checked the supplies in the little kitchen, and there was nothing to get excited about. No sense in going out—he'd walked all day, and the sinews and tendons in his legs still quivered slightly as he lay. He couldn't spend anything, not if he was going to keep his promise to visit Jiri Mondrian; he wasn't sure that he had enough for the whole trip, anyway. It left either the books, or banging his head against the wall. Banging his head came second.

The writing was fairly clear, aimed at the non-specialist. After about half an hour Rorvik was sure that he would have to get the two volumes back to the archive, and fast.

MORNING. HE emerged into the boulevard, and immediately knew something was wrong. A high-sided truck from Central's maintenance division was slewed across the road before the occupied wing of the East City archive, manoeuvred to get the open tailgate as close to the entrance as possible. As he watched, two men in green coveralls stepped out of the building; each had an armload of papers. They carried them across to the truck, where hands reached out. There was a thin river of smoke drifting up from somewhere further along.

Rorvik didn't want to be seen with the books that he was carrying, at least not until he had some idea of what all the activity meant. The nearest building was empty, with steps leading up to a slide-across metal barrier that had been chained and locked and abandoned many years before. He checked to see if he was being watched. Other than the work party, there seemed to be nobody else in the boulevard. He quickly went up the steps, and slid the books through the barrier; there was just enough of a gap for them to pass, and they were well-covered by the weeds that filled the space behind.

When he got nearer to the archive, it became obvious what was happening. Everything from the shelves was being carried out and destroyed; the oxide discs were being shaken out of their boxes, and the books were being stripped of their bindings. All of the unnecessary dead weight was thrown onto a bonfire, out on the tarmac in the middle of the boulevard—this was the smoke that he'd seen.

Citizens in the archive—bad luck for the limping man,

obviously. He wasn't anywhere around, but he was probably cursing Rorvik as the cause of this new phase of Central's 'rationalisation'.

Rorvik made his way back without being noticed—at least, that's what he hoped. At first he thought of leaving the books where he'd placed them in the derelict porch, but then the crawlers would have them for sure, shredding them and taking away the tatters for bedding. He was hoping that Central wouldn't spot the loss of the two volumes from the series. But if his name came up and he couldn't produce them, he'd face trouble.

Somewhere safe. The apartment wasn't, and he immediately rejected the idea of asking Baxter to keep them for a few days; as soon as Rorvik appeared in the doorway Baxter would probably exit from the opposite window, and he didn't have a fire escape. Jiri's flat would be out of the question, too—most likely it had already been re-occupied.

There were lockers in the monorail terminal, but they cost money. Not cash money, but credit—and that meant official records.

Unfortunately, he couldn't think of anything better.

LATER IN THE day, as Rorvik was rid of the incriminating books and on his way back to his apartment, the service truck pulled away from the East City archive. It carried the archive's entire stock, reduced to essentials of unbound texts and discs. On the top of the heap were a stack of index cards and a handwritten ledger.

The wagon puttered down the boulevard towards the river and at the end turned towards Central Command. Ten minutes later the driver reversed his vehicle into a cargo bay in a wall of the main Library, and then he went and stood outside. As soon as he was clear, a seamless metal door dropped slowly and silently across the open port, and he turned and went back to the transport centre.

As shutter and floor met, an identical door at the far end of the bay began to lift, spilling a widening crack of light across the unlit chamber. In the brightness beyond two tank-like service robots blinked to see into the darkness and then stamped forward on their sturdy metal legs. One opened the door at the back of the wagon while the other looked inside. On seeing the number of books to be carried it gave a buzz of irritation and clanked off to find a powered cart while the other clambered into the wagon and began to rummage. Its boxlike shape was an uneasy fit in the cramped interior but its short and powerful legs allowed it to lean at impossible angles, and within moments it had discovered the index cards and the borrowers' ledger. The robot flipped out a couple of extensions and gathered them in, emerging laden from the wagon as the other robot arrived with the cart.

A brief coded exchange took place, and the robot bearing the index and ledger lumbered off to give the index to the computer while the other transferred the books from the wagon to the floating platform.

The computer took perhaps twenty seconds to read through the index cards. This slowness was dictated not by its speed of assimilation but by the danger of the cards overheating with friction. Central mulled over the information for a millisecond and then turned its attention to the ledger. Here it had difficultly, for the wide variations in style and form of the neatest handwriting greatly taxed its ability to recognise and classify.

Two instructions were then issued. The service robot heard the first and trudged off to help its colleague in vaporising the books. At the second, a hitherto idle teleprinter at the Police Elite building gave a guilty start and began to chatter out a message. An orderly at the far end of the telex room heard the distinctive noise of the Central Command link and hurried down to take the message as soon as it was completed. When the buzzer sounded he tore the sheet off with its three copies and read the top copy through.

'Memo from Central Command,' he read, 'for the attention of Detective Inspector Randall, Central Police Division. Observe and report on the activities of one citizen Lee Rorvik, personal data and history to follow. Recent movements of the subject have given cause for concern with regard to a possibility of civil disobedience. Act accordingly in the interests of prevention.'

The orderly shrugged. Routine stuff, if a little strong.

He split the copies and routed them to the relevant departments.

THREE

THERE WAS, inevitably, insufficient credit left on Rorvik's card to afford the monorail to the nursing home. The cost of the music box and the charges for the locker had reduced his resources drastically, but a promise was a promise, and he had to find some way to deliver Jiri's liquor. After a calculation which strained his unsteady mathematical abilities he walked three miles to a branch station and joined the monorail there. The cost would empty his account completely, but he could last out until the payment of the next citizens' bonus.

The convalescents' centre lay amidst the ruins of the old spaceport. The single track of the elevated monorail ran straight towards it, and as the dark towers of the city were left behind it was possible to see the spaceport's old homing beacon beyond the farms and fields like a thread on the horizon.

There was nothing to do but sit on the hard seat and watch the sparse squares of vegetation flickering past. Occasionally there was a wild rocking in the carriage's progress which indicated broken or disjointed plates in the linear accelerator rail, but otherwise the only hook for one's attention was the ever-present piped music from grilles set into the carriage bulkheads. Rorvik was coming actively to hate such music; in his own mind he compared it to food chewed by somebody else. He looked back down the train. The few passengers were all citizens like himself sitting quite composed, appearing to think of nothing in particular.

The track swept in a curve around what had once been a blast wall and gradually dropped to ground level. Buildings like the monuments of some ancient necropolis passed close on either side, vanishing abruptly as the carriage hissed into a tunnel and began a silent deceleration.

Rorvik was the only passenger to disembark in the underground station. Although originally designed to handle masses of travellers it was now unattended, and he was left alone as his transport sped away leaving a faint breeze of displaced air to wash along the tunnel. He had made this visit only once before, and had been hopelessly lost for over an hour. This time he was no more certain of his route, but resolved to follow the crudely-painted arrows on the floor. They were colour-coded to indicate the various convalescent homes; he was to follow blue, which led to a depressing and badly-converted engineering shop.

He could identify his target from afar by the music which seeped to him along the tunnel. When he arrived, a nurse in standard green uniform told him that the patients were all above ground level, taking the air in a blast pit.

The pit was a concave dish perhaps half a mile across. The entrance from below ground was off-centre and heavily shielded, and Rorvik had to walk around this shielding before he was able to see anything or anybody.

The area was dotted with hunched, muffled figures in wheelchairs. They were spread hundreds of yards apart, either unable or unwilling to communicate. The only movement on the horizon was a single green-clad form which moved on a slow patrol some distance away.

As he climbed the shallow slope—now that he thought about it, an ideal trap for any chairbound deserters—the nurse turned and followed his progress with a cold stare.

'You are wasting your time,' she called as soon as he was within earshot. 'This is not a visiting day.'

It had never occurred to Rorvik that there might be set days for visitors. 'Please,' he said, 'I've come all the way from the city. I'm looking for a friend, Jiri Mondrian.'

It hardly seemed possible, but her frosty countenance chilled further. 'That is neither here nor there. I've no authority to over-ride standing orders.'

'I used all my credit to get here. It'll be weeks before I can afford to come back.'

She smiled sweetly, and pronounced her next word carefully.

'Tough.'

And then she began to walk away. After a few steps she paused, turned and indicated one of the most distant figures in the dish. 'Over there,' she said without warmth. 'You can have five minutes. Then I remove you.' She turned her back, and moved on.

It was a long haul up the slope. Persephone's planet must have been quite something, once, when the spaceport was washed dry by the blasts of landers and the boulevards were crammed with traffic. Now it was an empty nowhere with a weakening sun, not even worth the expense of an offworld defence ring. Anybody wanting to attack would have a Sunday walk, but they'd better not be expecting much when they arrived.

Jiri didn't even hear him coming. He'd got worse, that was obvious straight away. Previously he'd looked like he was ill, but now he was skinned-down and tight as if in rehearsal for dying. Only Jiri's eyes seemed really alive.

'Hello, Lee,' he said. 'I didn't think you'd be coming.'

'I made a promise,' Rorvik said, and then realised how bad it sounded; no friendship and no concern, just plain old duty. He went on quickly, 'I brought the bottle.'

'Great. Shall we split?'

'You go ahead.' Rorvik reached inside his jacket, glancing around for the nurse. She wasn't near enough to see.

'No, join me. It'll be the only social life I'll get.' Jiri took the bottle and raised it; he took no more than a small sip before he broke up coughing. 'God's balls,' he said. 'I'm cured.'

Rorvik pushed away the temptation to give the neck of the bottle a careful wipe. 'How are you feeling?' he said, not sure that he wanted to hear the answer.

'Pretty insecure. They're trying to kill me.'

'The food's so bad, is it?'

'So bad? It's poisoned. I've been watching. Most of the types out here are ancient and on the edge. None of them last more than a couple of weeks; they arrive on stretchers and they leave on trolleys. There are two kitchens, and they're both guarded. For one of them, the staff have to show a pass to get in. When it comes to plates and stuff, they have their own and it's kept separate from anything the patients use. Supplies are delivered in locked vans twice a week.'

'Do you want me to do anything?' Rorvik asked uncertainly.

Jiri looked up at the overcast sky, where Persephone's blood was drying on the clouds. 'Forget it,' he said.

There was a few moments' awkward silence. Rorvik broke it by saying, 'I got your case from the apartment.'

'Thanks. Did you take it home?' Rorvik nodded. 'I suppose that means they've given my place to someone else?'

'As far as I know.'

'Bastards.'

'When I was digging through for the bottle, I found an old cassette. Would you know anything about it?'

'A cassette?'

'An old one. Non-standard.'

'I know the one. I found it in the flat when I moved in.'

'Did you ever try to play it?'

'Once. I couldn't get it to fit the machine. Did you?'

'I messed around with it a bit. There was some music on it. Lin's got it, now.' And the river got it shortly after. Rorvik chose a spot on the pockmarked concrete and sat down.

There was another long pause, as they both sat and stared at nothing. Surely there must be more to it, more to say when time was so short; Rorvik found that he was looking out for the nurse, anticipating the moment when she would appear and tell him to go.

Jiri said, 'What else have you been doing?' He could only ask, because he had no news of his own to offer.

'Got myself turned into a criminal.'

Jiri actually sat up a little. 'A what?'

'I borrowed some random stuff from an archive. I thought I'd boost my Library attendance record without actually having to go anywhere near Central. I didn't even bother to look at what it was I'd picked, not until I got home, and then I knew I was in trouble.'

'What was it?'

'Two volumes from the report of the social engineers to a

sub-committee of the board of Futures, Incorporated. It's called The Persephone Plan.'

Jiri looked blank, so he went on, 'It's the scheme for the administration of Persephone when Futures pulled out. They were mainly concerned with doing the minimum possible, so they could save money and still satisfy international law. Establishing Central was the main part of the scheme, and once they'd fixed that they started looking for the cheapest way to set it going.'

'How does this make you a criminal?'

'When I got back, the archive was being emptied out and everything was being burned or taken back to Central. The record will show where the missing books went.'

'So you borrowed a couple of books. There's nothing wrong in that.'

'It's a matter iof what's in the books. Futures had to guarantee stability on Persephone for a minimum period. They weren't just allowed to write us off. but as soon as that period expired they didn't have to worry. The Plan was the cheapest way to keep our society ticking over for the minimum period.'

'When does the period expire?'

'That happened long ago.'

'And everything stayed normal.'

'How could we tell? We've never known anything else. But I think I've seen the scheme that Futures decided on.'

'Which is?'

'Set up Central, and make citizens out of all company employees and their bloodlines. Everybody else becomes a servant class. No rights, no privileges, no benefits. If they want to survive they need to sell skills and labour to citizens.'

'Are we talking about the underbelly?'

'The underbelly's what you get when the plan doesn't work out. The plan for the rest of us doesn't look so great either. I reckon Central's long-term aim is to mould citizens into a standard social unit.'

'A what?'

'A human statistic. People can't be handled easily in a program, they don't behave right. Central can't change the plan, so it's working to change us.'

RANDALL TURNED the corner and panted up the last flight of steps which took him onto the sixth floor of the Police Elite building. In the corridor he placed his sealed briefcase on the floor and took his own pulse; it was pounding hard, he noted with satisfaction. He imagined the hot blood flushing away all the junk in his system.

On the way to his office he passed the row of vacuum elevators. The indicator light over one of the sliding doors lit up, and two officers and a cadet emerged. They had been waiting in the main hall and had seen Randall begin his purposeful trot up the stairs, and now the officers looked curiously after their eccentric fellow while the cadet followed the rules of protocol and showed no interest.

Randall kicked his door open and slid gratefully into the corner office. Across the room a younger man quickly removed his feet from the desk and stuffed a bundle of telex forms under his chair, but on recognising Randall he retrieved the documents and placed his footwear back on open view.

'That was fast,' Randall said, and his junior nodded without smiling. 'Who were you expecting?'

'I've been practising,' Killoran replied. 'It might have been somebody important.'

'Well, thanks.' Randall contemplated his mess of a desk for a moment and then swept all the papers to one end in order to make a clear space. He set the briefcase down and then rummaged in an equally untidy drawer for the key. When the seal was finally broken he extracted two cans—the case's only contents—and tossed one across to Killoran.

Killoran read, 'Squeeze. The Citizen's Beer,' and looked up in surprise. 'Where did you get this?' he asked.

'Ask no questions,' Randall replied. 'There are ways and means.'

They peeled the tops off the cans and drank. Killoran grimaced. 'Now I remember why I left all this behind.'

'Rough stuff, isn't it?' Randall c hoked, and thought of all the goo inexorably re-clogging his system. 'How could you face going into a bar and saying to the tender, "Gimme a squeeze"?'

Killoran nodded, again without any trace of a smile. He smiled as often as the snows fell in summer.

They threw the empty cans down the incinerator chute and heard them rattle down the full length of the building. 'Should clear any old blockages,' Randall observed. Then he turned back into the office. 'Anything new?'

'How would I know?'

'Because you come in early every morning and read the telexes before I arrive.'

With no obvious reaction of guilt, Killoran said 'There's a direct memo from Central Command. It's been lying in the traffic control in-tray for the last twenty- four hours.'

'What reason?'

'It was directed to you by name only. No department. The orderly thought you were in traffic control still and routed it there.'

'Why didn't they use an up-to-date directory?'

'They're always being pinched. No honesty in this place.'

Randall searched out the memo from an untidy pile and ran his eyes over it. 'Have you read this?' he said without looking up.

'In the lift.'

'Naughty.' Randall turned the name over in his mind. 'Lee Rorvik. Do we know him?'

'I shouldn't think so. Central would have given us the security computer reference.'

' "Observe and Report", it says. Have we got the personal data?'

Killoran crossed and sorted through yet another pile of papers. 'Somewhere in here. There's also a mention in the daily bulletin. A connection with some missing printed material from one of the old archives. It seems to have been loaned on Rorvik's Library card number.'

'Probably connected. I suppose we'll have to go and see him. Can't see the need for such a strong directive though.'

There was a single knock on the door, and it opened a few inches. An orderly's head poked through the crack.

'Just arrived for you, sir.' Two feet below the head a hand

appeared with another telex copy.

'This, you may note, is not traffic control,' Randall said. All that was visible of the head blushed, and Killoran reached over for the paper.

'That wasn't me, sir.' But the denial lacked conviction.

Killoran read it and held it out for Randall, who waved it away. 'Just tell me what it says.'

'It's from Central again. Security section. It's instructing that Rorvik should be a Grade Two operation.'

Randall was upright and reaching for his phone, all expectations of a quiet afternoon gone. A Grade Two was big, and already there was a twenty-four hour delay. As he punched out the Services number, he told Killoran, 'Get onto Stores and fix us up with some radios.'

'Any weapons?'

'Not for a Grade Two. Just the radios.'

Then Services came on the line, and he began to list his requirements. There was some argument which was solved by the mention of the Grade Two. Halfway through, he broke off and said to Killoran 'When you're done there, run a check on Rorvik's recent credit uses. See if there's anything recorded for today, and find out where.'

Killoran went off to the input room and Randall continued with his list, his eyes focused far outside the window. A Police Elite helicopter was beating its way steadily across the rooftops towards the headquarters. Almost as an afterthought, Randall added, 'See if you can fix me up with a 'copter as well. One with a searchlight. And I want a fairly responsible pilot, if that's not a contradiction. Not like the idiot who got himself killed on the bravado run last week.'

As he put the phone down Killoran returned from the input room. 'He's been using the monorail today. Out to the old spaceport where the nursing homes are.'

'Good. Get a couple of men on the station, see if they can spot him when he comes back. I'll go and have a quick shave before we go over to his apartment. It may be a long night.'

AS TWO CADETS hurried to the city's main terminus, Rorvik was walking back from the branch station on the city's outskirts. He was uncomfortably close to the underbelly here, and he was glad to leave its fringes behind and approach comparative civilisation.

The city was in the long shadows of late afternoon when he arrived within sight of Central Command. He didn't particularly want to go home, but he couldn't think of anything else to do at this time so he stayed by the river and called into a citizens' cantina to eat. His Library card was waved away as he offered it for registration, so he slipped it back into his pocket and carried his tray through into the main hall.

A handful of citizens was scattered about the hall, some in small groups but mostly alone. The inevitable music was leaking in from all corners, and over by a window looking out onto the water Rorvik recognised Baxter, the remains of his meal on the table before him and next to that a stack of Library cassettes. Rorvik went over and sat down opposite.

'Dreaming?' Baxter gave a start and turned.

'What? Oh. . . hello. I'm sorry, I didn't see you,' he said, but his manner was unconvincing.

'You're not still nervous about us playing that cassette, are you?'

Baxter looked around hurriedly to see if anybody had heard. There was no-one within earshot, but a short Drone robot was stumping down towards them, clearing tables on its way. 'What do you mean, us?' he hissed, as if the robot might listen. 'I was the one who took it and dumped it in the river.'

'All right, then. You're not still nervous about *me* running the cassette.'

Baxter shook his head, afraid to speak as the Drone came level with their table and reached for his empty plate. It cleared before him and then, with a practised tweak, it snapped Rorvik's full plate from under his nose and emptied it into its hopper.

Rorvik threw his cutting fork down and it collected that, too, and then waddled off cheerfully. He watched it go in resignation—the afternoon with Jiri had taken the edge off his appetite. Baxter was looking out of the window again; it was possible to see down the river as far as Central's dome.

There might be trouble ahead, Rorvik thought, and it gave him a queasy twisting feeling inside. The records would go back to Central, and then Central would cross check them, and then... what? Maybe nothing. He'd never heard of a rule specifically proscribing information on Central's origins, but that was probably because Central had ensured that nothing was available. And as for disciplining of a citizen... he'd never heard of that, either. Underbelly who offended were simply made to disappear... when they could be caught by the Elite, that was, and most weren't. Exactly where those who disappeared went to, nobody knew; there were rumours of detention camps way out in the ice belt, but if they existed it was a one-way trip with no appeals.

Citizens didn't need to be disciplined, because citizens didn't offend. They were monitored and controlled, guided and chided, led by the nose from the baby farm to the bonfire. Long after three weeks of work by Futures' social engineers, the dawn of the grey harvest was only hours away.

Maybe Central could strip away his privileges and toss him over to the underbelly, but it could never erase his breeding or the knowledge which made him... what, dangerous? He'd never thought of himself as dangerous before. It sat wrong, like someone else's old clothes. If Central was going to judge him, it would be the ice belt for him. Or maybe even the bottom of the river. In all the dying city there was nowhere he could hide, nowhere he wouldn't be spotted and reported. The underbelly might hold him for a while, but only as long as the money lasted.

'What's under there, do you think?' he said suddenly, and Baxter looked around at him.

'Tinder where?'

'Central.'

Another glance down the river, and then Baxter was looking at Rorvik again. 'Cellars or something. I suppose,' he said. 'How would I know?'

'It can't be cellars. The river goes underneath.'

'There's your answer, then.' Baxter turned in his seat as Rorvik stood and stepped out into the aisle. 'Where are you going?' he said.

'Just for a walk,' Rorvik called as he moved away. 'See you around.'

HE CLIMBED the protective wall and dropped the few feet on the other side to the embankment. The curve of the dome stretched up and away from him, but from here he could see the poured-stone base of the structure that was normally hidden. The river was broad, and disappeared into a slot which ran most of the width of the building. An overgrown path led to the very edge of the water, and through the weeds broken concrete showed like patches of bone.

The boom and splash of the flow overpowered all other sounds as Rorvik crouched on the bank and looked into the darkness. A weir of metal railings was trapping driftwood and debris across the low tunnel mouth. He couldn't see more than two or three feet inside, but he could feel the low rumbling echo which told him that there was space and distance in the darkness.

It didn't look very inviting. He was ready to abandon the whole idea with relief, but some of the rails out across the weir had corroded almost through. In one place a beam of driftwood had lodged, and its rocking motion as the water buffeted it had levered one rail out of line. He could walk out along the horizontal as easy as anything, the surface of the river a couple of feet below him, and holding the rails would keep him balanced. Now that he'd come so far, there was no excuse for him not to swing out and across and then put his head inside for a look.

Even as he transferred his weight out onto the weir, he knew that he wasn't going to see anything useful—if he saw anything at all. He'd been hoping to see some shelter, somewhere clean and crawler-free that he could move the books to and keep in his mind as a secret bolt-hole for if things got rough; a part of his mind was insisting that they wouldn't, the blinkered-optimist part of the imagination that everybody turns to when they can't handle what's going to happen.

The metal of the weir started to groan, and on the next step he felt it give. The structure was too weak to take him; it was fine near the bank, but towards the middle it was too much. That was all he needed; for a moment he peered through the bars, but there was still nothing to see. He was reaching out to start moving back when the tie-rail broke away from under him.

He hadn't been bothering to keep much of a hold with his free hand, and when he felt himself falling and made a desperate grab he closed on empty air. The tie-rail hadn't snapped clean but had just bent enough to drop him; it was the last thing he saw before the cold water shocked him into stupidity.

THE CHIMES rang at the door, and Louann Roget ignored them. When they rang again she turned up the volume of the video to cover the sound.

Out in the corridor, Randall heard the boost in sound and turned to Killoran. 'You hear that?' he said. 'Someone's home, all right.'

Killoran nodded agreement, not wishing to speak in case he should sound breathless from the climb up the stairs.

'Give it a knock,' Randall said. 'They'll hear that.' Killoran knocked, at first politely and then an angry hammer as the volume inside the apartment was raised again. Randall smiled. 'Keep it up,' he said.

After a few seconds, the passionate strains of 'Her Heart on Her Sleeve' were cut short, allowing the easy melody of the corridor background music to filter through. Killoran stopped his hammering and the door swung open.

Louann saw two men, one slightly older, both citizens. But no; there was something different. Their dress was nonstandard, and of a more expensive-looking cut. Police Elite.

As if in confirmation, the older one smiled and said, 'Good evening, Ms Roget. We're security officers. Show her your card, Killoran.' The younger one stepped forward and to one side of her, holding out an official-looking security pass.

Randall stepped forward on the other side, so that Louann turned when he spoke. 'We'd like to speak to citizen Rorvik, if you don't mind.' Killoran slipped behind her and into the room.

'But... he isn't here.'

'That's all right, Ms Roget. We don't mind waiting. May we come in?'

'Well, I'm not sure I...'

Killoran spoke from within the apartment. 'Very nice home you have here, Ms Roget,' he said, looking at the bare walls and the standard video.

Louann spun round in surprise, and Randall stepped into the room and closed the door behind him. She struggled for a moment to grasp the situation, and then accepted it.

'Well,' she said. 'Won't you sit down?'

'Why, thank you,' said Randall, and led her over to the plain divan which was the room's only furniture beside the video surround. As she settled uncertainly he glanced up at Killoran. 'Neil, have you thought that Ms Roget might like some coffee?'

'I'm sorry,' she said. 'I supposed I ought to have offered.'

Killoran gave her a reassuring smile and moved towards what he knew from the standard design must be the kitchen.

'Just leave it to me,' he said.

'There's only ersatz,' she called after he had gone through the door. 'It's all I can get.'

Killoran replied with something muffled and incomprehensible, and Randall leaned forward to speak in low, confiding tones. 'Now, Ms Roget, I expect you're wondering what all this is about.'

'I'm rather confused. I was in the middle of...' A loud smash of dropped crockery came from the kitchen. The door opened a crack.

'Nothing broken,' Killoran said cheerfully, and the door closed again.

'To begin with,' Randall went on, 'I don't want you to worry. Lee Rorvik isn't hurt, and he hasn't done anything wrong.'

She was confused. 'Then what's the matter?'

'Well, it concerns some information from one of the old archives. We're in the process of transferring the last ones to microfilm in Central command, and I suppose you can guess what it must be like. Some of the stuff hasn't been looked at in years. Anyway, when we came to check through the catalogues it seems there was some information that should never have been available, and furthermore it seems that Lee Rorvik has come by this material somehow.'

She was trying to take an interest, he could tell, but it was as if she were dragging her mind back from a place far away. 'And what is this material, Mr. . .'

'It's Randall. I'm an Inspector. I can't actually answer that as it's classified, but I'm sure we can clear it up very quickly. When are you expecting him back?'

She shrugged. 'I wouldn't know.'

A prompt, maybe. He said, 'We know he used the mono. Now we know that he's back in the city.'

She met his eyes without guilt or concern. 'So what?' she said.

THE SURFACE was like mercury. It bounced and sparkled just out of reach, and as the sparkling died he knew that he was being pulled under Central. Then a quick eddy flipped him over, and he lost it altogether for a formless green that had no apparent depth or texture; something rushed out of it and banged him hard, and as the current dragged him over the obstruction he lost most of the breath that he'd managed to hold.

His hand broke out into the air for a moment, he was sure, but when he struggled to find the surface all he could manage was a slow, ineffective threshing, all of his strength compressed and made useless. He might be ploughing his way deeper. He needed to open his mouth and gulp, air or water, it didn't seem to matter anymore—anything just to wash away the pain in his lungs.

No, he tried to tell his body, wait for air. Forget it, his body said, I gotta breathe.

There was stone against his head, and it was hard; he bounced and skittered along it, shoulder, elbows, knuckles, and then was suddenly whirled around and let go.

He was in near-still water, and rising. He broke surface through a loose crust of debris.

Something out there was firm, because it didn't bob and sink when he grabbed it; there wasn't much purchase for his fingers, but he was desperate enough to grip glass. He dragged himself over, and his head clear of the water.

He spat out a mouthful of slime. Two or three minutes of panting and retching passed before his interests began to widen.

The lights which had at first been swimming at the backs of his eyes now resolved themselves into dancing patterns of reflected water, light from upriver some distance away. He'd been siphoned off into a little sargasso basin of still water, a heaving skin of green scum clogged with anything that would float; box lids, driftwood, cans, and Lee Rorvik.

It was a small harbour, a cutout into the embankment wall. The walls on three sides rose sheer and higher than he could see, but there were steps cut into the back wall which led up from a marina jetty, berths for maybe four boats with walkways around and between them. The jetty was mostly rotted-through and collapsed; Rorvik was between an unattached cross-beam and the tilted hull of a sunken vessel. When he felt strong enough, he started to pull himself along to where the jetty still looked firm; the surface debris plucked and clawed at him as he moved.

He stood on the marina walkway, dripping and shivering. The wood was cankerous with wet rot, and when he started forward he tested every step before he put his weight down. Once he was on stone he felt safer; it was green and slick, but at least it wasn't likely to open up underneath him.

Climbing the steps, he left some of the noise of the river behind. From here it seemed sluggish, almost placid, a slow black muscle easing its way along down below. Rorvik squinted to make the most of the light.

The embankment was a broad promenade with the level of the river about twenty yards below and screened by an ornate parapet. Knowing the size of Central it must have stretched ahead for quite a distance, but the shimmering twilight failed to illuminate its full length. At intervals marching off into the darkness were decorated metal streetlamps, encrusted with the same thick moss which coated the stonework. Far away, like a bright star on a summer night, a single light source burned against the low concrete roof.

Rorvik found it difficult to keep his footing on the slime. When he tried to stand still he had no grip, yet when he walked it was like a thick jam dragging at his feet. It grew sparser as he moved downstream and it was starved of even the meagre glow of reflected sunlight. Plaques and signs on walls which had previously been too overgrown to read were now obscured by the dark.

The light-source proved to be an open trap in the roof. Rorvik dropped behind the parapet as he saw activity beyond it, stocky service robots of a type he had never seen coupling links onto a broad tube. They lifted it and tottered to the edge under its weight, pausing for a second and then heaving it out to snake down and then impact on the hard surface of the river. Something tugged at the leg of Rorvik's slacks and he brushed it away unconsciously.

A throbbing began in the red haze beyond the trap, and a cluster of searchlights flared into life, their beams converging on the point where tube and water met. The effect was of a sudden brilliance flooding the whole riverside, and from the shadows loomed the great rusting hulk of an old ship. It was turned on its side with its decks half underwater, a mass of bright details and sharp shadows illuminated from above.

The tugging came again at his leg. Again he brushed at it, but this time the action registered in his conscious mind and he looked down in alarm as there was a sharp pain and his hand withdrew, running with blood from a quarter-inch slice.

The animal withdrew out of his reach, tiny red eyes burning with hunger. It retreated no further, but hovered and watched. It was a crawler.

For some reason, he'd never even thought to see a crawler down here; they belonged to buildings and empty housing blocks, moving in a silent tide to occupy space that people had deserted. If there was one, there had to be more.

A movement to his left. Three of them advanced and froze on that side. When he looked back to the first creature, there were five. More were creeping up from behind.

The front ranks made a ring, and the ring filled out. The crawlers made no noise, but for a dry scratching of tiny nails on stone. Rorvik knew that warm bodies were gathering, out there in the darkness.

They watched him; so much meat, and so vulnerable, and the group mind seemed to be weighing the best plan for bringing it down without injury to the pack. Fast and final, and then the blood feast.

Rorvik straightened, slowly. His wet clothes moved against his skin, cold and sticky. The parapet behind gave him no room to back off. As he put a hand back to steady himself on it, one of the crawlers broke ranks and dived for his leg.

Rorvik kicked at the tiny yawn of pink and felt the head snap back and the body jerk behind it. Instantly they were all on him in a wave, yelling like an angry cloud. It was hard to stand under their weight but he did, and fast. They clung to his clothes and dragged him over again. He felt a hard stab as several of the crawlers were mashed against the parapet, and he tried to batter more of them against it.

His arms were up to protect his neck and face, but bites were beginning to tear through his clothing and nip at the skin. Again he threshed against the parapet and half a dozen more fell dead while the living crawlers caught the twitching bodies and tore at them indiscriminately. He hurled himself at the stonework and it gave way at last, old mortar powdering and grinding.

This time, he was ready; he had all of the gut-jerking fall with crawlers raining down around him to draw breath and hold it.

Even so, he almost lost it when he hit and went under, but he kept his sense of up and down and was able to strike for the surface immediately. No crawlers came up around him, and already the bank was far behind; on the other side the tilted ship was sliding past as the river carried him high down its centre. He didn't have to swim, all he had to do was keep his head up—difficult enough, but not so hard when he considered drowning as the alternative.

He beached on a mudflat within sight of the exit weir.

He didn't realise at first how close he was; in the time that he'd been under Central the sun had more or less set, and as he waded in the knee-high filth he almost walked into the bars before he saw them. There was no need to force a gap, because he could duck under, after which he only had to stumble through the reeds to get himself to the levee on Central's seaward side.

HE GOT BACK to the residential section looking like the Mud Monster. The blocks had originally been thrown up fast and cheap as quarters for Futures employees, none of them much more than half a dozen levels high; as a concession to corporate image they'd been given decent frontages with broad steps and a gesture at a porch. He was climbing the steps when he thought of Collinson staring, of the elevator out of order, and of a long climb and maybe having to explain why the Mud Monster was haunting the block stairs. About the books and about his fears of reprimand he gave no thought at all. He decided to go around the building and pull down the counterweighted ladder on the fire escape.

From across the street he was watched by two men in a doorway as he trotted down the front steps and went round to the side of the block. One of them raised a hand radio and pressed the *transmit* button. 'Unit One to the Great White Chief,' he said, and his companion suppressed a snort.

Up in the fifth-level kitchen Killoran hastily adjusted the volume control on his radio. He paused, but the low hum of conversation from the next room continued uninterrupted. 'Cut the comedy,' he whispered, 'and keep the noise down. Randall's in the next room with the woman.'

'This low enough? Rorvik's left the entrance hall and he's coming up by the fire escape. That means he'll be coming in by a window on your western side.'

Killoran frowned. Which way was west from here? 'What about Unit Two?' he demanded.

In an idling 'copter two blocks away, a nervous cadet responded as the pilot yawned and stretched. 'Unit Two. We're ready to put the lights on him if he goes onto the roof.'

The fire escape was an added complication they could do without. 'Unit One,' Killoran said, 'where is he now?'

'Fourth floor,' the voice came again over the radio. 'That's the one below the fifth.' There was a badly-stifled grunt of malicious glee in the background, but Killoran didn't hear it as he threw the kitchen door open and stepped into the main room.

'Change of plans,' he interrupted sharply. 'Fire escape. Right now.'

Randall turned to Louann. 'Where's the access to the fire escape?'

'It's through his bedroom,' she replied, bewildered. 'Over there. Why. . .'

RORVIK FROZE, his hand on the door panel and half into the room. He saw the two men swivel and dive towards him and he stepped smartly back and slammed the door in their faces.

Randall grabbed the radio from Killoran and pointed to the door. 'Break it down,' he said, and thumbed the *transmit* button. 'This is Randall to all units. Rorvik's on the fire escape and running.'

Louann half-rose from the divan in horror as the bedroom door splintered under Killoran's repealed kicking. On the next kick it burst and sprang inward to an empty room and a half-open window.

'Unit One,' Randall called. 'Where are you now?'

'We're at the bottom of the fire escape,' came the reply, suddenly competent. 'He'll have to pass us if he comes down.'

'One of you stay there, the other one cover the main entrance. Let's have the 'copter over the roof and get some lights on the place. Unit One, start climbing now. We'll force him up to the roof and trap him.'

Like a great mantis the 'copter reared from behind the building opposite, all lights blazing. The glare slid across the bedroom window and off into the night.

'You're going to the wrong bloody building!' Randall roared. 'Get back over here!'

The 'copter made a nose-around correction. The cadet was trying to apologise, and in the background the pilot was shouting 'They all look the same from up here!'

'This is no damn use at all!' the voice of the man watching

the fire escape cut across the frequency. 'You're casting too many shadows. I can't see a thing.'

The pilot in the background began to get aggressive, but Randall stopped them all with a loud burst of feedback by pressing the *transmit* button without disengaging the receiver. As their ears rang from the piercing tone he said 'Now hear this. I want the 'copter to hover at roof level and wait for Rorvik to emerge. Unit One is to continue ascent until you've swept him up there. Is that plain?'

Unit One sounded doubtful. 'What if he gets in on another level?'

'That's my problem. I've got all exits covered and enough men to search the building. If necessary I'll do it.' For the first time he noticed Louann's inert form on the floor by the divan. He looked up at Killoran. 'Have you bopped her one?'

Killoran gave a reasonable impression of being affronted. 'Certainly not. She fainted.'

'That's all we need. Put her somewhere out of the way, then.' She groaned as Killoran lifted her, sack like, and dumped her on the divan. 'Get her a glass of water.'

'Right.' As Killoran disappeared into the kitchen Louann opened her eyes and tried to focus.

'What's happening?' she gasped.

'Keep your head down and you'll be all right.'

Killoran returned with the water as the radio came back to life. 'This is Unit One. I've reached the roof and there's no sign of Rorvik.'

'Could you have missed him?'

'I doubt it, but anything's possible with this fly-boy buzzing around overhead blinding me.'

'Get back down the fire escape and check all the adjacent windows. I'll get a search carried out on the inside.' Randall gave a series of rapid instructions to several units waiting out of sight at ground level. Out of the corner of one eye he saw across the bedroom his man on the fire escape go past the window and then he gave the man a second, more careful look to make sure it wasn't Rorvik. It wasn't. He looked back from the shattered doorway as Killoran let in one of his men from the outside corridor.

'We've done the search, sir,' the man said. 'Cleared every room on this side of the building apart from the one directly below this. Tenant name of Gerrard. The caretaker says that Rorvik knows him.'

Louann had vanished into the bathroom. Randall said, 'This could be it. Come on, Neil.' And they followed the messenger down to the fourth floor.

RORVIK RELEASED a pent-up breath and stepped from behind the bedroom door. There were voices off down the corridor and retching sounds from the bathroom, but otherwise he was alone.

He was sure he could forget any ideas of escape through the building, thick as it was with the Police Elite. On the roof he knew there were several planks and ladders, part of an old and forgotten scaffolding. One or more of them might be long enough to bridge to the next roof; on one side the building was very close indeed, only a narrow alley away, and as long as the plank didn't snap with his weight in the middle...

He cautiously poked his head out of the window and looked around. The fire escape was deserted now, and the 'copter was scanning the surrounding streets. He hopped over the sill and disappeared into the night.

Collinson was waiting outside Gerrard's door when Randall and Killoran arrived, his passkey held aloft. In spite of the urgency Randall insisted on the formalities, showing Collinson his security clearance and then waiting as it was read with painful slowness.

As the fields disengaged they kicked the door open and plunged into the room together, closely followed by the other officer and then, at a more cautious pace, the caretaker. Killoran went straight across to the window while Randall and the other man checked the adjacent rooms. A new-looking Public Broadcast receiver was belting out loud music in the corner, and Killoran switched it off before he spoke.

'Rorvik didn't come in here,' he said. 'The window catches have been painted over. God help Gerrard if there's a fire.'

Randall looked around. 'Where is Gerrard, anyway? The other rooms are empty.'

'Over here, sir,' the other officer called from beside the divan. 'He slipped underneath. He's...'

'Dead drunk.' Killoran held up an empty can of *Squeeze, the Citizen's Beer*, and then let it fall onto a heap of others just like it. 'No wonder he slept through the search.'

'Damn,' said Randall, 'I think he's slipping away from us.' A sudden thought occurred. 'I can't hear the 'copter.'

Killoran looked out of the window. 'He's moved off the roof.'

Randall took the quietly hissing radio off its clip inside his tunic and switched to transmit. 'Unit two,' he called, 'what are you playing at?'

The cadet's voice came faintly. 'We're checking the streets around the block. I thought...'

'Don't think. Get back over the roof.'

Killoran said, 'What now?'

'We'll just have to seal the building and take it apart. We know he's still in it, somewhere.'

'Do we, though?'

Randall shook his head. 'We have to start with something. The place is ringed, so what else have we got? We'll start by going over Rorvik's place.'

Killoran followed him up the stairs, leaving Collinson and the officer to carry Gerrard through to his bed.

TWO FLOORS ABOVE them Rorvik dragged tarpaulins off old timber. He was alone on the roof, but he could hear desperate activity in the street below as newly-arrived wagons poured men into the building.

There were two ladders, and neither of them looked particularly strong. They were, however, a better proposition than the planks, which were rotten and splintering. He hauled out the sturdier of the two and carried it over to the edge, laying it down carefully before taking a cautious look down.

Damn! There were two officers in the narrow alleyway seven floors below. One of them was playing a torch over the blank side of the building, its beam narrow and bright like a laser.

Rorvik would easily be spotted as he crossed the gulf against the night sky. Damn and double-damn.

A raving clatter as the 'copter popped into view from behind the block across the street, and then it was floating and weaving across to him. Cover on the roof was virtually nil; he would be seen as soon as lights were brought to bear and then he would be gathered in as easily as a crawler in an empty swimming pool.

The cadet fiddled awkwardly with the beam direction controls, so that the lights swung across the roof and then shot off the edge.

'Get those beams back on there!' the pilot shouted into his headset. 'I think I saw him!'

The cadet tried to respond but overcorrected and shot off the other side, so the pilot raised the nose of the craft and angled in closer to tighten the field of view. A bitter wind fanned the surface of the roof as they dropped towards it, and the cadet turned and fumbled for a hand-torch. 'I'll tell Randall,' he shouted as the little unit powered up.

The pilot shook his head. 'Be sure first.'

The hand beam flickered where the big lights were too cumbersome to point, dancing over angles and shadows. 'I think I see something,' the cadet called. 'Front of the building, near the edge.'

The pilot nodded and made the minute adjustments necessary to start a slow drift across to where the cadet was pointing. The shadows foreshortened and changed their shape as the light moved over them, and then the 'copter's plastic bubble abruptly crazed in a localised starburst.

'He threw something!' the cadet yelled. The pilot trod hard on his rudder-bar to whip the tail around and get away from the roof. He had no wish to go straight up and expose the fragile underside of his machine to further attack.

As the tail scythed towards him, Rorvik threw the ladder again. It travelled straight upward and the tail smacked into it below the middle and flipped it over, the lower end arcing up and into the blinding whirl of the rotors. Matchwood was instantly everywhere, accompanied by a scream of protesting metal as the rotors shattered and the 'copter's engine accelerated to an impossible speed without their drag. The whole vehicle flopped heavily onto the edge of the roof and balanced momentarily before the counterbalancing torque of the tail blade swung it around with agonising slowness until the greater part of its weight hung in space over the street.

It tumbled, as inevitably it must, taking a sizeable bite of masonry with it. The pilot fought with the controls all the way down, but without the rotors they were quite dead. He knew it, but simply didn't want to believe it. Windows flipped past and upward as if seen from an elevator, and the cadet covered his eyes and face with folded arms as they'd shown him in survival school.

They landed on the roof of a Police Elite wagon, crushing it instantly. Both vehicles ignited and burned with an explosion that broke every window on the front of the block and several in the block opposite. There were a couple of minor explosions, and then the wreckage settled to a regular and even conflagration.

Voices raised in panic, anger, despair—they all drifted up to Rorvik, crouching numbed by the chewed-open gap in the parapet. Raising himself slightly and looking down, he could see distant figures below weaving in a frantic ring around the disaster.

He arose stiffly and crossed to the alleyway side. Down below the two officers were running, as probably everybody else in the building was, towards the scene of the fire.

The other ladder was of doubtful safety, but under the circumstances that was irrelevant. Fully extended its tip barely rested on the low wall across the gap, but a short plank wedged between the bottom rung and the near edge gave some guarantee against slipping.

Rorvik was unworried, only mechanically attentive, his entire stock of fear and apprehension emptied and dried out. He barely saw the abyss beneath as he straddled the ladder and pulled himself along, hardly heard the creaks of danger as his weight came fully onto the braced joint in the middle.

DOWN BELOW, the street was as bright as day. Despite the immense heat Randall felt a chill of anger as he descended the open steps and looked onto the wreckage. Killoran breathlessly caught up a few seconds later.

'Accident, chief? Or Rorvik?'

'I don't know.' Randall suddenly frowned at the size of the crowd jabbering before the fire. 'Who's watching the back of the building? And what about the fire escape?'

Several officers shuffled and looked away, but one stepped forward. 'I was on the back, sir,' he said. 'We all heard the bang and came to see if we could help.'

'Well, you can't. Get back to your posts.'

A large number of the men began to disperse reluctantly. Randall felt weary, and not from running.

'Two 'copters in one week,' he said, mostly to himself. 'There goes next year's budget.' He turned to Killoran. 'Why, Neil? It was a routine pickup. All you need is a car and a polite manner. Instead we get a Grade Two directive from the computer and. . . and this.' His broad gesture included the entire street.

Around and in the alleyway two officers moved back into position with a hand-beam and resumed scanning the side of the building.

There was nothing above them but the night sky and the stars.

FOUR

With the escalation of the operation Randall could easily have requisitioned a helicopter to take him out to the spaceport, but he could raise no enthusiasm for the idea. He disliked them at the best of times; even more, he disliked the young pilots, an elite within an elite. Their psychoprofiles were carefully inspected before training, and they were chosen on the basis of a certain irregularity or imbalance which was fed by the exhilaration of flight to the extent that pilots became almost a part of their machines, unable to think coherently or express themselves except through the controls. Randall said it only confirmed his own opinion, that you had to be mad to fly one of those things.

Instead he took the mono, as Rorvik had done the day before. He also lost his way leaving the station as Rorvik had. After a number of false starts and requests for directions he emerged into the open blast pit and scanned the horizon for the nurse in charge.

There she was, patrolling the huddled mummies on the far side of the bowl. She saw him and stopped, but made no move to approach; instead she stared as he crossed towards her.

'You are wasting your time,' she recited. 'This is not a visiting day.'

'I'm not a visitor,' he replied, and produced his security- pass. A slight flick of the eyes and she had read it. 'I understand,' he went on, 'there's a Jiri Mondrian staying here. I'd like to speak to him.'

She smiled her sweet, killing smile. 'I would dearly like to help you, Mr... Randall, was it? But I'm afraid it's out of the question.'

'I do have the necessary security clearances...'

'You don't understand,' she cut in. 'Mr Mondrian left us at six-thirty this morning.'

'He left?'

'He's dead.'

One or two of the nearer figures stirred, taking an interest. 'Look,' she said, 'we're rather public here. Won't you come down to the office?'

She led him to an office next to what had once been an engineering hangar. A broad window had looked out onto workshops beneath, but these were now badly-lit dormitories and the window was painted over. Randall was shown to an armchair with sagging springs, and the nurse perched behind her desk and began to sort through the envelopes in her 'out' tray.

She said, 'I know there was nobody nearby, but some of the deaf ones can lip-read, and before you knew it would be all over the grounds. In most eases we can stop it by taking their spectacles away. The file on Mr Mondrian should be in here somewhere. . .'

She removed several sheets of paper from one of the envelopes and began to skim through them.

Randall shifted in the uncomfortable seat. 'You say he died this morning.'

She nodded, still reading. 'At six-thirty. Very inconvenient. Any deaths over the late shift period and we only have a skeleton staff to deal with them.' Randall smiled politely, but she didn't look up; perhaps it hadn't been a joke, after all. 'It's a matter of economics,' she went on. 'Our budget is very limited and we have to plan carefully. Already we're having to cut our convalescence time down to three weeks.'

That didn't sound right. 'You mean. . . after three weeks you send them home?'

'Certainly not. We bury them.'

'Bury them?'

Her patience bordered on sarcasm. 'That is the usual procedure with the dead.'

'But what if they're getting better?'

'Then we just have to increase the dosages. There is a

demand for our beds, you know.'

Randall was struggling with the concept.

'Wait a minute. Are you telling me that you poison your patients?'

'Certainly not. The kitchens do it for us.'

'The kitchens?'

She laid the papers down on the desk. 'Inspector... Randall, was it? I can't think you're so naive as to believe that we would force the infirm to suffer. We do it with full authority from Central Command. It's filed in the banks as the voluntary euthanasia programme.'

'So it is voluntary, then?'

'Of course. They eat the meals of their own free will.'

'Knowing them to be poisoned?'

'Certainly not. What kind of euthanasia programme do you think we'd have then?'

Randall shook his head in disbelief. 'I never knew any of this before,' he said.

'Central Command works in a mysterious way, Inspector Randall,' she replied.

Randall thought for a moment. 'Was there a special instruction of any kind for this particular patient? Although it's really one of his friends that we're interested in.'

'Now you mention it, there was.' She picked out one erf the sheets from the pile. 'There was a direct instruction from Central last night to increase dosage. That's quite unusual.'

'Did you question it?'

'Certainly not. We carried it out.'

That was logical. 'This friend. I believe he was up here yesterday.'

'That's right. Yesterday morning. It was very irregular.'

'Did he bring anything with him?'

Did Randall detect a guilty response as she began shuffling the papers before her? 'No,' she said. 'He brought him nothing.'

'Nothing like a book? Or a parcel about—' he spread his hands '—this size?' Her discomfort settled, and she was the iron lady again. 'No. Certainly nothing that size.'

Randall was worried. It was almost as if Central Command

wanted to interfere with its own instruction. Why remove Rorvik's only visible confidant before he could be interviewed?

'It seems I've had a wasted journey, then,' he said as he levered himself out of the chair. He'd almost been sitting on the floor.

'I'm afraid so. All the way from the city, as well. Before you go, can't we offer you coffee and cakes? Our chef bakes them.'

Randall pretended to check the time. 'Well, look at that,' he said. 'I'd love to stay, but I have to catch the mono.'

Her regretful smile showed sharp, almost pointed teeth. 'Such a pity. Another time, perhaps.'

'Yes. Another time.'

The nurse showed Randall to the exit, and gave him instructions on how to find his way back to the monorail station. Then she returned to her office, took a bottle from her desk cupboard and poured out a stiff slug of bootleg hooch. Thus fortified, she went back to the blast pit to harass her charges.

ON HIS RETURN to the city Randall didn't go back to Police Elite headquarters but instead went straight home to his apartment near the commercial sector. A police driver was waiting outside, drumming his fingertips on the steering wheel of his vehicle. Randall helped him to carry several stacks of printout to the third floor, and when the driver had gone he rang Killoran at the headquarters building and told him of his wasted day.

Killoran had little more constructive to report. They had tracked down the use of Rorvik's credit card in the station luggage-lockers but found the locked space empty, with no trace of what the contents may have been.

Randall knew it had to be the books, and that Rorvik must have gone to collect them directly after his narrow escape the previous night. What was in those books? What could possibly be so important that Rorvik would kill for them?

But no, stop there. Force of circumstance had made Rorvik a killer, conditions dictated by Central Command. It considered the knowledge in those books so potentially dangerous that it was treating him as if he were a plague—why else hasten to remove Mondrian, the only other possible infectious contact? And then there was the overkill operation.

Randall sighed, and turned to the heap of perforated printout on his table. In there was Rorvik—everything from his childhood vaccinations to his laundry records, all in tiny, eye-straining print. All he had to do was absorb it all and reconstruct the man. He closed the window on the distracting babble of the markets and set to work.

LESS THAN twenty-four hours after her world had blown apart, Louann was still off-balance. Three years ago she'd entered a relationship, and two years ago it had broken down. For two years she and Lee Rorvik had simply been stepping around each other, and now that he was gone there was no reason why she should care.

There was nothing remarkable in the way that they had lived. It simply fitted the lifestyle model that Central created through its control of the media; sex for recreation, and if they'd had a child it would have been delivered and taken away at the baby farm, and then life would have gone on as before. It was an easy, undemanding, repetitive way to live, the way to be. Most other urges were contained and controlled by Central's programmed fantasies.

From Central's point of view, there was some housekeeping required. Louann would need some reassurance to get her over this. Central's ideal would be continuous monitoring and continuous adjustment, but then Central was basically a cheap system, a Futures minimum. It had to get by with irregular visits and selected programming from the stocks, a deep-saturation influence rather than real control. It made the re-modelling of the citizenry a slow process—quiet suffocation of the newborn with undesirable genetic traits helped it along considerably, but it would be some time before the citizens were sufficiently standardised and docile to give Central's administration a real mathematical elegance. Over the underbelly it had no control, but then the underbelly were the problem of the Elite. And the Elite were loyal to Central—the breeding programme made sure of that.

She looked at the dark video and felt nothing; no pull, no enthusiasm. Everything seemed to have new edges, as if new realities were hovering slightly out of phase with the old. She wanted to bring them into focus, but she didn't know how; the effort made her head ache.

She sat down before the video, and stared at the screen. She didn't switch it on.

Louann wasn't alone. Lin Baxter wasn't having an easy time, either. His tapes were programmed for a mood that no longer fitted, and when he tried the open broadcast channels—the ones that even underbelly could receive, if they could get hold of the equipment—he found himself dialling through moodily, paying no real attention to anything. He left it running on an action-quiz, and wandered across to the window.

It was to this spot that he'd rushed the previous evening, when he'd heard the drown-all clatter of an Elite 'copter overhead; and then, along with most of the others in the surrounding apartments, he'd rushed down and out into the street to see the free show. He'd gone with the crowd, and he'd been up against the Elite cordon before he'd realised that they were moving in on Rorvik's block; by then it had been too late to turn and push away, and he'd only been able to count up the floors to the lights and the centre of activity—exactly where he'd known it would be.

There had been plenty of rumours going through the crowd, pick your version of who, where and why. Maybe Baxter could have argued himself out of involvement, but there was no arguing with the falling 'copter. It got a round of applause as it exploded, and most stayed to watch it burn. Baxter had stayed with the pack, afraid to be around but more afraid of walking out on his own, out of the hive of so-similar faces. Since then, he'd waited for a knock at his door.

There was a knock at his door.

No, he thought, it's on the video. But then it came again, louder and more urgent, but not too loud—like somebody who wants to get attention but doesn't want to rouse anyone else. Five-star fear washed every thought out of Baxter's head, but citizen obedience sent his body across to open the door.

The Mud Monster stood outside. He was dried-out and smeary, as if he'd tried to tidy himself up and pass for human, but you can never really disguise a Mud Monster.

'Oh, no,' Baxter said. He tried to close the door, but Rorvik was already halfway in.

'Quiet,' he told Baxter, 'you're attracting attention. Jack up the video sound if you don't want anyone to hear I'm around.'

'How did you get in?'

'By the stairs. It took me three tries before I could get straight through without meeting anybody—every time I heard voices, I had to turn around and scoot back down to the bottom. Lucky your place isn't being watched yet.'

'Yet?' Baxter said. 'Why put the dogs on me?'

'I'm a disease. You're contaminated.'

'By what?'

Rorvik crossed to the window and looked down into the street. Nothing obvious. The grime and a night without sleep had made him look sallow and weary. 'I wish I knew,' he said. 'I wish somebody could tell me.' Then he turned to Baxter. 'I waited an hour before I came in, and there's nobody watching, I'm sure. They're all outside my place, trying to look inconspicuous.'

'You can't stay...'

'I'm not asking to.' Rorvik saw no sympathy in Baxter's expression, only terror and one hundred per cent self-concern. They might never have been friends at all. He said, 'I need some clothes. The river's ruined these.'

'Not here, Lee. Please.'

Rorvik didn't know whether to get angry or to whine and plead. Neither was really in line with his nature. He moved away from the window and towards the bedroom, where he knew Baxter kept his clothes. 'I'm sorry,' he said, 'but you've got to understand that I don't have any choice. I'll get what I need, and then I'll go. You can say I robbed you, if you like.'

'Look,' Baxter said, following, 'I don't want to know. Whatever it is you're into, I don't want to know.'

'Two dead men and a 'copter down, and you don't want to know why?' There was silence as he picked out some inconspicuous-looking gear from the racks. He really needed a shower as well, but that would have to wait until he was on less dangerous ground. He glanced across to the doorway.

Baxter was silent. The same natural streak of raw curiosity that had kept him hanging around as the illegal cassette had played was now working on him; breeding programme or no breeding programme, it was stronger than anything that Central had fostered.

'It started with a couple of books,' Rorvik began as he changed.

FIVE

It angered Randall to think that the trail was going cold, but it was. Central continued to issue edicts and directives, and every day saw an increase in the number of men on his squad, but there was no positive help beyond that; the original reasons for Rorvik's apprehension were a strictly taboo subject.

He was out there somewhere, Randall knew this much. His credit card was no longer being used but anomalies in the records suggested that he had perhaps done the unthinkable and altered its number, not once but several times; and then the anomalies petered out, as if the variations to be worked on the card had been exhausted.

There was only one place a citizen could survive without credit. The underbelly stretched in a broad belt south of the river, a close-knit social jungle where the Police Elite exercised little real power and unhappily admitted it. They scanned it with 'copters while business was conducted underground. It was almost impossible to map the maze of backstreets, alleys and temporary gangways between the upper levels of the ancient properties, and unthinkable to patrol them. Randall's only hope was that Rorvik's obvious appearance as a citizen would go against him, but while his money lasted he'd always be able to buy cover.

As long as Central Command held the economic reins, the underbelly remained an uneasy part of the city. The Police Elite had a few agents working in there, but none that could offer any prospect of finding Rorvik. Any informant might not be reliable. Randall suspected that the underbelly secret council knew the network of undercover agents better than anyone in the Elite and manipulated it to better effect.

Time slid by, and Randall fretted. Each morning Killoran

carefully sifted the telexes and laid aside anything of the remotest interest, and each morning Randall read through the selection with a growing sense of futility.

'What the hell are we playing at, Neil?' he said late one morning as they idled in his office with a couple of cans of Squeeze. 'We've got the tightest organisation in the city here, and we can't find one man.'

'You know why,' Killoran said, and gestured towards the window with his can, neatly managing to slop half of it over his desk and trousers.

Randall watched him swearing and mopping up with a detached interest that somehow couldn't warm into humour. 'I suppose so,' he said. 'When our methods depend so much on Central there's damn-all we can do if it censors the information.'

Killoran stopped in his cleaning up and looked across at Randall. 'I wasn't talking about Central. I meant the underbelly.'

Randall nodded absently. 'You know,' he said after a while, 'I don't know what Central wants.'

'Simple. It wants Rorvik.'

'That's all very well, but why not give us the information we need to find him? I'm thinking about what was in those books. Whatever made him act the way he did.'

Killoran held himself awkwardly over the heating unit in an effort to dry off his damp patches. 'Who's to say? Could be forbidden knowledge.'

'Forbidden to us? The Elite? Our loyalty beyond question? This whole side of it annoys me...'

The door opened a crack. It had to be an orderly.

'Telex for Inspector Randall,' said the inevitable disembodied head. The equally inevitable disembodied hand appeared below. 'Most urgent. Agent's report routed through Central clearing bank from the underbelly.'

Killoran moved quickly, but Randall was there before him. He grabbed the flimsy so fast it almost tore, and Killoran had to wait as he read it through. Once finished, Randall read it again.

'Well,' said Killoran after a while, 'what's it about?'

Randall took a breath and forced himself to be pessimistic. 'It's an agent's report.'

'I know that.'

'It may be nothing. At best it's only a lead. One of our agents has been trying to get some dirt on Morden's factories, and he's paying rent to live in some grimy hole somewhere. This morning the owner started raving about a tenant who skipped camp owing her credit. A citizen.'

WITHIN THE hour three armoured wagons swung out onto the city's main bridge and crossed the river. Randall had seen the underbelly many times from above but far less often from ground level. Looked at from any direction, the underbelly was extremely unattractive. It was sprawling, cramped and noisy, blind buildings huddling in conspiracy.

The lead driver followed the complex map with accuracy. After twenty minutes they rounded a crescent and came upon another wagon parked with its engine idling.

The street was silent and deserted, but Randall knew that a hundred eyes followed as he stepped from his wagon and crossed to the other. Before their arrival this spot had been as crowded and raucous as the rest of the underbelly, and minutes after their departure it would be so again.

The squad disembarked and split efficiently into their various teams. Killoran and two other officers went into the house to interview the owner, a broad wrestler of a woman called Frea Gillivray, while the forensic team went straight down to work over the basement room. Others simply formed a loose semicircle around the idling wagons and watched for danger.

The agent sat in the hold of the first wagon, its armour essential to protect him now that his cover was broken. Randall lowered himself onto the bench opposite, and the agent ceased his dejected inspection of the floor and slowly raised his head.

Randall smiled encouragingly. 'You've done some good work,' he said.

The agent nodded, unflattered; it was a simple fact. 'So that's it. Now what?'

'We get what we can out of it. This is the first significant advance we've had.'

The agent dismissed the fact with a small gesture. 'I know all about that. But what are you intending to do with me?'

The light in the wagon was switched low, but even in the deep shadows Randall was able to appreciate the thorough conversion job that had been done on the man before him. Whatever his genes said, this man had nothing of the look of a citizen.

'It depends what you want,' Randall said carefully. 'Naturally, you'll be entitled to full benefits and a backlog of allowance.'

The agent looked away, irritated, for a moment, and then turned back to Randall. 'Not looking like this,' he said. 'With this face I'm a dead man after today. There isn't a place in the city I could hide, and you know it.'

'That's no problem. You were given a new face once. In six months' time you'll have another.'

'You may find this hard to understand, but I don't want another. Ten years ago I became another person and had to get used to it. Well, I'm used to it. He may not be much, but he's all I've got.'

'There are other places besides the city.' And yet he fell a start of inadequacy as he said it; the city was all Persephone really had, crumbling and dying and shrinking every year. Otherwise, just sea and ice.

'Not for us. You know that, Randall. We're the Elite. The city's everything to us, even the godforsaken belt where I've made my life. I can keep the city and lose myself, or I can stay as I am and either leave or be hunted.'

'And if Central made it your duty to go?'

The agent shrugged. 'Then I'd go, of course. But nothing could make me like it.'

Randall nodded, and stood up to leave. The agent caught his arm, and he half-turned in the narrow confines of the wagon.

'It wasn't easy,' he said, almost pleadingly. 'I want you to know that. This may be hard to believe, but I had friends out there.' Then he released Randall's arm and resumed his miserable observation of the floor.

The raw-boned Frea Gillivray had a manner which perfectly matched her appearance After haranguing Killoran for ten minutes and substantially extending certain areas of his vocabulary she turned on the newly-arrived Randall and increased the decibel level to cover them both. The subject of argument, it transpired, was the errant tenant's belongings which she was intent upon claiming in lieu of rent. Randall strained himself to match her volume and failed, but he made some fairly telling points on the tax laws, the health regulations and the possible penalties for obstruction which she was notching up. In the end she seemed to run out of fuel and slip into neutral, but malevolent dissent still burned in her eyes. She grudgingly identified a mug shot of Rorvik and smeared her thumbprint onto Killoran's draft statement, and was promised the return of the basement keys when investigation had finished.

Randall blinked in disbelief as she tramped back into the rooming house and slammed the main door behind her. Killoran saw the expression and voiced his agreement.

'Like being beaten around the head with a wet towel,' he said.

The basement was reached by a flight of steps descending into a narrow pit along the front of the house. The pit was screened from the street by iron railings. The railings needed paint and the pit was gradually silting up with debris. The forensic team emerged with their equipment bags and a stack of computer cards with their findings tabulated and ticked off in little boxes, and as they passed with difficulty on the steps one of them handed Randall a short list of initial conclusions. As he and Killoran let themselves in through a warping door one of the wagons in the street above was pulling away.

Randall's first reaction was one of surprise. They had let themselves into a corridor lit only by dim emergency lights, but instead of the expected squalor they found clean plaster and a bare, scrubbed floor. There was a smell of new wood from a close-fitting fire door at the corridor's end, and beyond that the door to Rorvik's former hideaway had been propped open.

There was only one window in the room. The blind was up and it looked directly into the back of a wardrobe in the room next door, obviously part of an extension on what had once been the outside wall. There was a bed, one chair with a towel over it and in the far corner an old, badly- shielded microwave oven. Bathing facilities must be somewhere down the corridor. Killoran crossed to the bed and began to sort through the assorted items heaped there.

'My God,' he complained, 'they must have moved everything. They don't give a damn as long as they get their little cards filled in.'

'Don't worry,' Randall said, 'we can check positions from the holos back at base. Let's see what we've got here first.'

Killoran reached for the largest item and turned it over. 'This confirms that Rorvik had contacts in the underbelly. It's a bootleg cassette player. There must be a factory turning them out in an attic somewhere.'

'Is there a tape in it?'

'I think so. Hard to tell.' He pressed what he thought might be the 'eject' button, and heard the whine of a rewinding motor as the little screen fizzed in to life. 'The controls aren't standard,' he added apologetically.

Next to the player was a stack of similarly bootleg tapes, and Randall sorted through these, viewing one or two sections at random. Their quality suggested that in recording terms they were several tape generations old, and they were on subjects not generally available from Central's Library, being for the main part technical primers on dead skills.

'Any idea what cybernetics are, Neil?' he asked after a while.

'Robots?' Killoran replied.

'See what else you can find here. I'm going up to the wagon to radio for an exact definition.'

Five minutes later he had it, 'a system of control and communication in animals and electrically operated devices'. When he returned to the basement Killoran had finished his search and was spot-checking the remaining tapes.

'Computers,' he said excitedly. 'These are all related to computer study. There are two on programming, and another on logic systems.'

Randall frowned. 'And I always thought that black market tapes were all pornography. What do you think? That Rorvik gets all his thrill from an old-time education?'

'There's more,' Killoran said. 'According to the list, forensic took away a bag of ashes from the incinerator. They think it was paper ash.'

'The books?'

'What else? They're going to give the remains to the security computer for analysis. And look at this.' Killoran held up a thick glove, ribbed with rubber. Randall took it from him and tried it on; it fitted his citizen's hand easily

'Where's the other one?' he asked.

'We've only got the left hand. He must have taken the other with him. Forensic reckon it's for electrical insulation.'

'I'm inclined to ignore any of their ideas without confirmation. They can't tell the time without asking the computer first. What do you make of all this?'

Killoran seemed to recognise that he was on test, and he summoned up the method and processes taught to him in Elite training. 'Well,' he said after a few moments, 'it's hard to say. He had access to credit, although we don't know how. He could have run from the city altogether, but instead he stayed in the area and spent it on this black market stuff, and it can't have been cheap. Then there's that glove. More money gone there, and he leaves one behind.'

'Forgotten in the heat of the moment?'

'Heat of what moment? He was secure here. The only reason we know about this place is that he decided to walk out without paying his rent, and he did that in his own time. I think he'd finished with all this and he wasn't worried about covering his tracks.'

Randall wasn't simply checking on Killoran. He genuinely needed the younger man's fresh insight, unclouded as it was by the prejudice of experience. 'The tapes,' he said. 'What about them?'

'They all have a common factor in computer logic. We've seen a couple; they're explained for laymen, not too hard to understand but certainly not the average citizen's choice. The half-finished one in the machine was on programming. I'd say he got so far and lost interest.'

'Or found what he wanted. It's a pity we couldn't keep the

place where he stopped.'

'Sorry, sir.' The term of rank between them was rarely used except for public show, and as a sign of Killoran's regret it was embarrassing to Randall.

'Well,' he said after a short pause for reflection, 'this obsession with computers seems to indicate something.'

'Central Command?'

'What else? It's the only thing that ties it all together. The panic memo, and now these tapes. I only wish I knew what was in those books he got hold of!'

Killoran said tentatively, 'I suppose you've asked the computer.'

'Several times, and each time it comes out classified. I don't know why, but it won't give any information out other than the basics. No friends, no contacts, nothing. The Roget woman's no help—I'd be surprised if she could even recognise him.' Randall sighed bitterly and moved to the door. 'May as well get back,' he said. 'There's nothing more for us here.'

Two cadets were sent down to collect Rorvik's belongings into large plastic bags. This took very little time, and within minutes the wagon convoy was swinging around and heading back toward the river. Inside the lead wagon Killoran felt the bump of the tyres as they rolled onto the bridge and he depolarised a side-window. As it cleared the familiar dome swam into view like a huge sun half-settled on the horizon, nothing before it but a rippling sheen of water dancing with golden highlights. Killoran saw the depression in Randall, but Randall saw little beyond an interior vision of a frozen moment as a helpless 'copter dropped into a void.

Killoran tried to inject a little hope. 'Any chance that forensic will be able to make anything of the burnt pages?'

Randall was unenthusiastic. 'What if they do? They'll feed the results into the machine for interpretation, and the machine will censor it. Central wants Rorvik caught, but it doesn't want anybody to find out what he knows. That includes the Elite.'

'It must be pretty hot stuff. It turned Rorvik against Central.'

The wagon turned off the bridge and into a near-empty boulevard.

'That's the strangest part of all,' Randall said. 'Rorvik's a citizen. The machine feeds him, clothes him, protects him, entertains him. There's nothing he could ever wish for that he can't already have without working for it. Why go against Central?'

'Being a citizen isn't everything.'

Randall knew what Killoran meant; to be a citizen was fine, but to be Elite was something else.

'Bringing the 'copter down must have turned his mind,' Killoran went on. 'Citizens don't kill. It just isn't in them.'

The point was so obvious that it required no comment from Randall. Instead he watched as the last portion of the dome disappeared from view and the irregular grime of the city again enveloped them. If Rorvik had any ideas about venting his dissatisfaction on Central he was wasting his time. More than that, he would probably be dead. It had never happened before, but the sophistication of Central's internal security was legendary; from the moment a citizen passed the turnstiles his movements within the public areas were registered and traced by a complex web of sensors. Outside the public areas—well, he simply didn't move. No doubt there were access ways from the Library into the dome itself for the passage of the service robots, but sensor tracking made it impossible even to approach these and a thoughtless step in their direction would earn a sharp laser blast similar in intensity to a static rod. Further steps would no doubt increase the intensity while any serious attempt at penetration would have the citizen sliced like a protein roast.

It was not beyond question that Rorvik might have lost his sanity, as Killoran had inferred. In which case any blind attack would promptly end the case with Rorvik being collected in several plastic bags and placed alongside his belongings.

So why was Central worried? There was no way that Rorvik could hope to beat a system like that after reading half a dozen antique books and a few bootleg tapes.

Somehow Randall didn't find the conclusion as comforting as he might have hoped.

IT WAS WITH trepidation that Baxter approached the wide glass front of the Library annexe. This was his first visit since Rorvik had appeared, filthy and bedraggled, at his apartment, and from that date he had felt no peace of mind. Rorvik was wrong, of course; his crazed ideas on the intentions of Central Command were demonstrably unfounded, but Baxter could not easily forget the fact that Rorvik had attempted to involve and implicate him in the sordid business.

Not, he kept telling himself, that he would have anything to fear. Central might not be pleased, but even a cursory examination of the facts would show that his involvement had been totally passive and that his loyalty remained beyond question. So why was he so uneasy?

Somewhere down below, he knew, other less agreeable instincts were being suppressed. Rorvik had been his friend, and every precedent and argument he produced to justify his conduct failed to overcome that bitter fact; but then, what Baxter understood by the term was confused and overlain by all the input that Central had given him in various ways since childhood. Friendship was a channel of minor social recreation, nothing when placed alongside broader loyalties and responsibilities. It was the affectionate rapport between the vivisectionist and the unsuspecting dog on his table.

It took little time to pass through turnstile security and move through the thin crowds up onto the mezzanine. As usual the nearby booths were occupied, but further down the row it was easy to find a place.

Central watched Baxter as he crossed the floor. It was not the busiest of days, and Central had run a few subsidiary systems down into idleness. The administrative subroutine chattered away at the back of Central's consciousness as always, while on various levels of awareness other sub-routines attended to their own well-defined areas of responsibility. Baxter's appearance and identification at the turnstiles had, however, brought an instantaneous bleep of warning from the security programme, and several channels of awareness had opened simultaneously.

A rapid list of information, suppositions and open conclusions presented itself for review. Baxter was a known associate of Rorvik's, and as such his name had been linked to an automatic trigger which operated when he appeared in the credit files or, as now, in the Library itself.

Baxter was known, and Baxter was now being watched. The city outside might be crumbling and the Elite might be under-supplied, but continual vigilance over its internal security was one of Central's original directives. The apparatus of surveillance was idiosyncratic, but it was advanced and accurate. It would continue to advance as Central updated its own designed capabilities—update and advance, and therefore evolve.

Baxter seated himself in the booth and watched apprehensively as the mirror-panel on his eye level dissolved into clarity to reveal the single lens behind.

Central opened the camera as a matter of procedure, and then disregarded its information. The output of the sensors ranged all around the booth were far more reliable. The standard greeting was run through, and Central noted a surge in Baxter's pulse as he inserted his card for perfunctory identification, a long-redundant procedure.

'And what,' said the voice of the computer, 'can the Library do for you, Mr Baxter?'

Baxter thought he sounded fairly calm. He was getting away with it; Rorvik hadn't jinxed him. 'I've brought my tapes back. And come for some new ones.'

'It is a long time since you last visited us. What have you been doing in the meantime?'

'Nothing. Nothing specific.'

'No. And there is so little to do, isn't that correct, Mr Baxter?'

He didn't understand. He started to say so, but the computer cut across him with one word.

'Rorvik.' How did it know? 'When did you last see him?'

All the justifications, the accusations, the pleading that Baxter had rehearsed through sleepless nights; all these deserted him now.

'I haven't,' he said lamely.

'Stop there,' the computer instructed. 'Before you go on I shall tell you that I am monitoring your heartbeat and perspiration rate. You cannot lie to me so do not try. When did you last see Rorvik?'

'I don't know what you're talking about.' Was it possible?

Could the machine do so much?

'In my memory banks I have all your records, your entitlements, your privileges. If I wish it I can wipe them and you will cease to exist, Mr Baxter. Doors will not open for you, food will not appear on your table. Frankness is in your own interest. Now, Mr Baxter?'

Baxter swallowed hard. 'About a month ago,' he said. 'He came to me and took some clothes.'

'He took them? Or you gave them?'

'He... he took them.'

'And to whom did you report this?'

There was no answer that Baxter dared to make. 'I seem to forget...' he ventured.

'Lie.' Not a thundering accusation, but a single flat statement. 'You reported it to no-one. You failed in your duty as a citizen.'

'I know,' Baxter admitted. 'I was scared.'

'Scared? And of what, Mr Baxter?'

'Of what might happen to me. Because he was there.'

'You had nothing to fear from Central Command for telling the truth. To conceal the truth, that is far more serious. You will now recount all that he said to you. Tell me freely. The alternative would be most unpleasant.'

'He told me about books that he'd had. Old books. About various stages in the development of Central Command.'

Deep within the memory stacks of the Central computer two molecule chains were linked and cross-linked as the information was digested. Rorvik, books, Baxter.

'And what was his conclusion from these books?'

'He said that Central Command was some form of machine evolution.' Baxter found that now it had been said, the phrase seemed quite ludicrous, an innocent misconception. He was telling all, as instructed. He would be understood and forgiven. 'He told me that Central didn't care about the citizens except as statistics in its programme. He said it used selective breeding through the hospitals system to make the citizens behave according to the laws of averages across the board.'

'Do not stop.'

'He said that the proof lay in the way he was being chased just for knowing. I said I didn't believe him...'

'Your beliefs are immaterial.' Baxter knew nothing of great danger. Any thief or robber in the underbelly knew as much, but an unblinkered citizen lost his predictability. There was no room in Central's master plan for the random or the irrational. 'Your name is even now fading from my memory. Leave the Library, Mr Baxter. When you step outside the turnstiles you cease to exist. Do not bother to go home, all locks will have been re-coded.'

Baxter wanted to speak, to protest, but no words came. All he could manage was a plaintive, 'But why?'

'It is my wish. That is all the reason I need. Place the Library tapes in the delivery chute on your left as you leave.' As if in careful orchestration the flap hissed open, and Baxter numbly slotted his cassettes in one by one. The flap closed again with a smack and when Baxter looked up he saw only his own reflection staring uncomprehendingly back at him.

He slid open the booth door and stepped out onto the mezzanine. Nobody looked at him, for the passing citizens had their own preoccupations and he was not among them.

Central watched as Baxter's mass travelled across its sensory web towards the exit. The long and complex molecule which formed the basis of Baxter's computer identity was slowly untangling and dispersing, its components re-forming for use elsewhere. As he moved out through the turnstile it was gone, and Baxter would never again be allowed to enter the Library.

Insofar as the term applied, the computer was satisfied. An anomaly had been resolved, a loop of concern broken. The Baxter question had been answered, but Rorvik remained; a second or so spent reflecting on the Police Elite's progress showed no significant advance towards his apprehension, but the security programme began to bid for attention with the arrival of new information.

IN THE COMPUTER room of the Police Elite building a cadet sat before a terminal and tapped in the information laid out schematically on a series of forensic cards, then added spectrograph results on the ash samples. He was practised and accurate, and his work was fast. When he removed his hands from the terminal keys they chattered into a life of their own, issuing computer reference numbers for the stored information. There was a short pause as the machine ticked without printing, and then it moved decisively to a new line and rattled off the results of the spectrograph analysis. They were contained in one- word; 'classified'.

Central read through the new information. The ashes were, beyond any question of doubt, the stolen books; the paper had been of an archaic type based on vegetable fibre, and there were contaminations in roughly the correct proportions to confirm the conclusion.

Other results were analyses of vacuumed dust samples, odd hairs, fibres and other trivia; Central dismissed them all in a fraction of a second. The books were confirmation enough of Rorvik's presence. The details of the tapes were another matter; no obvious conclusions to be drawn there, but circuits began to race as suspicions of some unpredictable threat settled and solidified into cold certainty.

Back in the Police Elite building Killoran reached for the phone as it bleeped on Randall's desk. He listened, said 'One moment, please,' and laid the receiver carefully on top of a stack of papers. Then he was through the door in two strides and out in the corridor where Randall was filling a second disposable cup with ersatz coffee from the dispenser. He looked up in surprise as Killoran hurried down to him and reached for the first coffee.

'You particularly thirsty?' Randall said.

'Let me finish that. You're wanted on the phone.' Killoran winced as the heat from the coffee penetrated the thin plastic to his fingers.

'Couldn't you handle it?'

'Like hell I could. It's a call from Central Command. Patched directly into the telephone lines.'

Randall wasted no time in expressions of dismay but emptied the second cup into the overspill tray on the dispenser and moved back up the corridor towards the still-open door of the office.

He lifted the receiver and said 'Randall speaking.'

'Good afternoon, Inspector Randall,' purred the voice of Central Command. A characteristic low hum sounded somewhere in the background, although Randall knew that the voice was not being acoustically produced. 'You are to be congratulated,' it went on, 'for your remarkable breakthrough in the underbelly this afternoon. The Rorvik case, was it not?'

Randall was puzzled. The computer by now would know the details better than he did. 'That's right,' he said. 'It's the first sign of him we've had for over a month.'

'I am pleased for you. I have been having further thoughts on this unfortunate affair. I expect there is strong feeling within the Elite over the destruction of the helicopter and its personnel.'

'Very strong.'

'That is good. It does my forces credit. With this in mind I have decided to strengthen your directive.'

Killoran entered the office with two fresh coffees and set one down on the desk by Randall, and then retired to his own chair and waited.

'The evidence is so conclusive,' the computer continued, 'that I feel justified in authorising emergency measures. Rorvik is obviously a desperate man and will react with violence when cornered. In order to minimise the danger to my Elite, I give you special responsibility, Inspector Randall. Draw a blaster from stores. When your investigations lead to the inevitable capture, you are to kill Rorvik on sight. I do not care whether he offers resistance or surrender; co-operation will be a ruse in order to cause further casualty. Ensure that he is given no opportunity to protest or persuade.'

'You're saying I have to shoot him out of hand?' Across the room Killoran's expression mirrored Randall's feelings.

'That is correct. No trial is to be deemed necessary.'

'You'll be putting this into the daily bulletin, I assume.'

There was the slightest pause, barely perceptible.

'You will do this on my personal authority. That is all the sanction you need.'

It was a moment before Randall realised that the line had

gone dead. The personal authority of a computer? Without compromise to his loyalty, he found he didn't like the idea.

He didn't like the coffee, either.

SIX

'Your name is Marius and you are a member of the underbelly council,' the Grey Man said. 'That is all my employers needed to know.'

Marius strained to get a closer look, but it was useless; the light was bad, and the Grey Man's face was covered. He said, 'So what made you think I was approachable?'

'You don't want to co-operate?'

'I didn't say that. But I'm interested.'

'Understand, I'm only a messenger. I can't bargain with you, and I can't persuade you. I can only make the offer.'

'I haven't heard you mention any terms.'

The Grey Man sounded weary, on an errand that he had no feeling for. 'The offer is one of participation, that's all. Figures would be meaningless—dream one, if you must. And while you dream, spare one moment to think of the alternative.'

'Joining the victims?'

'Joining the victims. One way or another, your city and your world are about to fold. My employers are watching Central closely; it's a petty mechanical king in a stagnant backwater of a society. You're underbelly, you know this; Central has no defences that can worry them. Your help can make the project easier; your opposition can't harm it at all.'

'The Elite will fight you.'

'The Elite won't know until it is too late. Give me your answer.'

'A condition.'

'No conditions.'

'Not for your employers, for you. I want to see who I'm dealing with.'

The Grey Man sat without moving. 'Why?' he said.

'I don't make deals with shadows. Show me, and then you get your answer. Otherwise you get nothing either way, and I don't think they'll like that.'

After a moment, the Grey Man said, 'You'll give me the answer now?'

'Straight goods.' Marius' mind was racing; he simply didn't believe in the authenticity of the offer. This had to be one of Chandler's men, setting him up for some embarrassing flak to blast him off the council. Chandler never liked me, he thought as he leaned forward a little; the Grey Man was reaching to push back his hood. 'Now,' the Grey Man said, 'the answer.'

For a moment, Marius could hardly get his mouth closed. Then he swallowed hard and said, 'Is that what they look like?'

'No,' the Grey Man said. 'This is what they think men look like. But they're improving.'

'Better count me in,' Marius said.

SEVEN

THE DAYS GREW colder, and hours of darkness began to encroach upon the afternoons. Robbed of the sunset sheen on Central's dome the city became a duller place, and only those with the misfortune or folly to rise early in the morning were able to appreciate the autumn sparkle of sunrise on the geodesic panelling. On one such morning a Police Elite pilot decided to test his command of a long- unused skill, and as the citizens slept the boulevards echoed again with the roar of the bravado run.

It was inevitable that the revival of interest in Rorvik would be short-lived within the Elite, with the exception of a hard core of interested officers. It was true that a large body of men and women remained nominally attached to Randall's squad, but he found it difficult to justify a monopoly of their efforts when no new ground was being broken, and so he reluctantly agreed to their return to normal duties.

In the narrow alleys and high gangways of the underbelly, life showed little change as the season progressed. The poorer underbelly added layers of rags against the cold and used the cover of darkness to creep across into the main part of the city with vain hopes of thievery and loot, while the more shrewd rogues of that quarter wrapped themselves in winter cloaks and hoods and devised ever-more elaborate imaginative schemes for survival beyond the reach of Central's spreading bureaucracy.

The Elite were aware only of the superficial workings of the underbelly sub-culture. They suspected but knew no details of the underbelly council, which organised and co-ordinated the illegitimacy of free enterprise across the city ranging from credit card abuse to the distribution of supplies from Morden's factories. They suspected, but they were powerless; the underbelly remained one jump ahead of Central, although as the years passed the jumps were becoming shorter and more desperate.

Marius was late for the council meeting. Minor problems with black market meat had distracted him for longer than their importance deserved, and now the cold wind tugged as he manoeuvred his bulk at an undignified speed through a complex of close lanes. One of these led to a dead-ended square with high, blank walls and only one wooden door at the far side. Marius knocked, and the judas gate flipped open; the inspection, he knew, was a formality. His progress had been followed by a number of unseen observers.

He was led to the cellar and ushered in through the door. The noise hit him immediately, followed by the warmth. Avery Sim spotted him and beckoned across the room, and Marius squeezed through the chattering crowds arranged around long tables to emerge into the open area in the middle.

It was not without a twinge of egotistical pleasure that Marius crossed and took his place at the table of the high council. He shook hands with the other members and apologised for his lateness while the others smiled and made various indications that it didn't matter.

Avery Sim leaned close, as if about to share a confidence. He was bigger and broader than Marius, but his mass was more muscle than fat.

'We've got something unusual tonight,' he said, his voice tuned down to a low rumble. 'A citizen.'

Marius's polite smile froze. Avery Sim was taunting him, he knew. Feelings in the underbelly were mixed towards citizens, and his own were among the most hostile; however, it would be best to observe the temperature of the meeting before making any commitment.

He looked around the table at the other members of the high council. Avery Sim was settling back, and next to him was Pilgrim, generally applauded as a credit wizard. He was making some last-minute corrections to a half-side of notes; Marius groaned inwardly and knew that the ever present question of credit control was bound to be raised again.

Beyond Pilgrim was Chandler, a small and unimpressive

man whose contributions to the meetings were rarely of much importance. But Marius knew better than to underestimate him; Chandler was the agent-hunter, and his true occupation was known to few outside the high council. He ran a killer squad who, it was rumoured, were superior in their training to the Elite. Definitely not, Marius thought, a councillor to disagree with.

At the far end of the table sat a man without a name. He represented Morden, black marketeer supreme and most powerful single force in the underbelly. Of any opinion on the council the one given by this unknown individual carried most weight, and it was a measure of the respect that Morden had earned that he was able to decline personal appearance in this way.

Avery Sim, dabbler in all fields. So successful a dilettante was a natural choice to be chairman of the council. He was watching the delegates carefully; there was the best bootleg hooch on every table, and he had to judge the point where uninhibited eloquence would give way to rabble-rousing and step in to start the meeting before it arrived. Marius had almost ruined the strategy with his late arrival, hence Avery Sim's urge to bait him.

The moment had arrived, and he banged on the table for attention. The other councillors winced as the mylar bounced under his fist, and Pilgrim had to rescue his papers as they slid into his lap. The buzz of conversation diminished and dried, and there was a loud scraping as chairs were turned to face the high council.

'I want to thank you all for attending at such short notice.' Avery Sim's voice needed little projection to carry across the cellar. 'There's a particular purpose behind it, but first I understand there's some other business to be cleared up.'

A hand was raised from amongst the delegates and a thin, dark man stood up. 'There's a rumour going round that Central Command is going to take sole charge of the credit flow and abolish paper money. Where will that leave us?'

'At the bottom of the heap, as always.' There was general laughter. 'This rumour's made an appearance many times in recent years, but it's never happened yet. If it does happen there's no reason to suppose our trading will be unduly affected. It's a general rule that rigid control usually helps a black market rather than hampers it. The only problem would be what to use as a financial base instead of money, and I believe Pilgrim has something he wants to say on that.'

Pilgrim stood up on the mention of his name and studied his notes before speaking. He was not a natural orator, and was rather dismayed that Avery Sim had already made a number of his points. 'Thank you,' he said. 'This threat of credit control is always with us, and as you know we have a standing committee looking into possible plans of action. We'd have to resort to a certain amount of trading in kind, but there are practical limits on that. One proposal is to set up our own currency base and print our own credit, and then use sanctions to ensure that the market accepts it.'

Somebody said, 'A bank of the underbelly!' and there was general approval.

'That's it exactly,' Pilgrim said. 'The only alternative would be to corrupt or blackmail a large number of citizens in order to use their credit accounts, but I think you'll agree that a complete new currency is a more elegant solution.'

'If I may...'Marius was standing, and Pilgrim yielded the floor. 'As regards corrupting a citizen, we all know what they're like. Our hold on them would only last until the next visit to the Library, and Central Command would have them confessing everything after two minutes.' He sat down amidst general assent.

'Now, are there any more points?' It seemed there were none, so Avery Sim continued, 'Then we'll move on to my main reason for calling you all here tonight. We've an outsider wishing to join us and ask for our help. I promised that we'd allow him to stand before us and present his case, and that we would then put it to a vote. Mira, open the doors and bring him in.'

A girl looking older than her years unbolted a double door which linked the cellar with others like it via a system of catacombs. The two halves swung open easily despite their weight, and in the tunnel beyond was the dark silhouette of a man sitting on a stone bench with only an oil lamp for company. As the light from the cellar spilled across him he arose and walked forward through the doors.

He did as Avery Sim had instructed, and stood quietly in the centre of the open area as a furore raged around him. There were several shouts of 'It's a citizen!' and one of 'Who let him come here?' and it was almost a minute before Avery Sim's table-pounding could be heard above the commotion.

'Quiet! Be quiet, all of you!' he bellowed. Remember where you are!' The assembly reluctantly obeyed, but their unease was obvious. 'I suggest that we all listen to this man's story and then decide our attitudes. It's a standing order of the underbelly council that we give a fair hearing to anybody that asks for it.'

The thin man who had raised the question of credit was on his feet. 'But, a citizen. . .' he began.

'Citizen or not,' Avery Sim cut across him. 'he deserves our attention. As regards bringing him here, he was blindfolded and led through the catacombs.' He turned to the citizen, and spoke with the obvious responsibility of office. 'You stand before the high council of the underbelly at your own request. You see around you representatives of all parts of society which Central Command chooses to ignore. To Central Command we are all individuals of no value; we have no place in its projections. We are instead what we make of ourselves. Speak, citizen, and we will hear your case.' The citizen took a breath before speaking. The speech of the underbelly differed slightly from that of the city; if anything it was more formal, more ornate in its construction.

'I used to be a citizen,' he began, 'before my eyes were opened. Now I am nothing and nobody. My name was Baxter until it was taken from me. I have come to you to tell my story and then ask for your help.'

'Tell us your story, then,' said Avery Sim, speaking for the whole assembly. 'From it we will decide what we want to do.'

It was difficult to assess his impact on the faces around him. They were trained in concealment, and he was not; perhaps that would be in his favour. Although in borrowed clothes Baxter felt the acute discomfort of the outsider.

'I'm here because I believed Central. Central always told me that loyalty to the state came before loyalty to a friend, and even though it didn't feel right I accepted it. I rejected what I was told because it wasn't in line with the truth as Central presented it; but then Central dumped me because I knew, and when I thought about the reasons I realised that I'd been given the truth.

'Central is breeding us like animals. We're selected out for certain inherited features at the baby farms. As we grow, we're subject to a control that is more powerful than any I could imagine; Central controls our fantasies.'

He still had their attention, but what unsettled Baxter was that they were showing no surprise. Avery Sim said,

'Tell us what you know about breeding control.'

'In detail, nothing,' Baxter admitted. 'But look at any citizen—look at me. You'll see it has to be true.'

'Nobody's disputing the truth. The underbelly may be across the river, but Central can still interfere with our lives. Some time back we had an epidemic of stillbirths and monsters; when we finally thought to drain our water pipes and check the underground supplies, we found Central's drones down there. They were letting out trace drugs—poisoning us as an experiment. If it worked on the underbelly, it would be used on the citizens. We heaved the drones out and smashed them.'

'Can't Central be stopped?'

'We've tried. Small efforts, little parties of volunteers—anything more organised, and the Elite's agents usually get to hear of it. Nobody's ever come back.'

'But I'm looking for another citizen, Lee Rorvik. Is it true that you gave him a hearing?'

Marius was on his feet. 'Wait a minute, Baxter. This is a council meeting, not an information centre. We're here to listen to you.'

Avery Sim obviously agreed with Marius, but he deflected the edge of the other councillor's annoyance by waving him down with a smile. 'We know about Rorvik,' he said to Baxter. 'He didn't tell us anything new. What makes you think he'll be able to organise anything against Central?'

'Because of what he knows. Maybe he isn't even aware of it, but he's got hold of something that Central's scared of. I didn't really worry the machine, all it did was take my citizenship away—but it wants Lee Rorvik, and I think it wants him dead.'

There was no real debate to follow. Avery Sim asked if there was anybody who could suggest where Rorvik might have moved along to; his last known stopover had been with Frea Gillivray, but after that nobody had seen or heard of him. He didn't seem to be stealing, trading, or hustling; without one or another of these, it was difficult to see how he could be surviving. And yet, Chandler added in his quiet voice, the Elite's agents were still looking for him.

The meeting closed after that. Baxter stood uncertainly as the cellar emptied, but then Avery Sim slapped his shoulder and said, 'Follow me.' He led Baxter to a second exit at the back of the cellar, where they climbed a stairway to street level.

They emerged into a courtyard with high walls open to the sky. There were voices from the alleyway on the other side of one wall, the underbelly delegates emerging and dispersing.

The worn-looking girl was already inside the house, and at Avery Sim's request went off to bring them some food. They sat by a window which looked out at a wall.

Baxter said, 'I suppose I made a mess of it.'

'Not at all,' Avery Sim said. 'Nobody much likes a citizen anyway. You did better than most could, and I think you were sincere. It's not your fault that nobody was interested.'

'What do you suggest I do now?'

Avery Sim glanced up. The girl whose name was Mira was standing in the doorway. There was a warning in her eyes, and she gave a slight nod towards the corridor behind her. Avery Sim shrugged, and she went away. Then he said, 'You can stay with me for a few days, if you want. I'll put you in touch with one or two people who might be able to help, but don't get excited. Even if you can track Rorvik down, I don't believe there's much he could do.'

There was somebody else in the doorway. He was short and thin, and his face was covered by a tight mask as if he'd been badly burned and the scar tissue was being pressed back into smoothness.

'My son, Xylem,' Avery Sim said. Xylem stepped forward and held out a hand.

'You're Baxter,' he said. His voice was undistorted but whisper-quiet. 'I know about you.'

Baxter took the hand. It was as white as bone, as if Xylem had water for blood; it was also very strong.

Avery Sim said, 'Xylem was born at the time of Central's experiment with our water supply. I'm telling you this now because it's ridiculous to pretend. It's how Xylem wants it.'

Xylem nodded. His eyes, the only part of his face that Baxter could see, were a blue that was washed-out almost to nothing. He released Baxter's hand, but only after Baxter had sensed an involuntary spasm at Avery Sim's statement.

Xylem said, 'My father doesn't think that Rorvik could achieve anything, whatever knowledge he may have. He believes that knocking down one corrupt system involves grooming another to take its place. The job of the underbelly is to survive, no matter who holds the whip.'

'And is that what you think?'

'I think we should find out what Rorvik knows. And then... we'll have to see.'

OUT OF THE alleyway and into an avenue, and Zaffir found that Marius was alongside him.

'How's it going, Zaffir?' Marius said.

Zaffir was guarded. 'Fine. And you?'

'Not so fine. I've got some problems.'

Zaffir glanced around. The look seemed casual, but he missed nothing. Nobody appeared to be taking a special interest in them. 'What kind of problems?' he said.

'Well, there's one specific difficulty, and if that one can be kicked out of the way the others should just line up and fall down. I've got a deal on with some offworlders.'

'Offworlders don't touch Persephone.' So much was true—to the extent that there were many who believed that offworlders had never existed at all, and that shabby Persephone was the sole cradle and the garden of human life.

'These will, if the conditions are right. That's where you come in.'

'Go on.'

'I want Avery Sim dead.'

Zaffir's step faltered as he stared at Marius, and then he hurried ahead to leave the councillor behind.

Marius scrambled to catch up. 'At least wait until you've heard what's involved.'

'I don't want to know.'

'What's this? Scruples?'

Zaffir stopped and turned, and Marius skidded to a grateful halt. 'Not scruples, just sense. I'd be mad to touch a councillor, whatever I arranged. The underbelly would tear itself apart looking for me.'

'Not necessarily.'

'Yes, necessarily. Remember Willis? He was lucky that the Elite got to him first.'

'Willis was stupid. You needn't leave any traces.'

'That's crap, Marius. With Avery Sim dead, Chandler will start looking around for somebody who wanted him that way—and he'll find you. You'll point the finger at me, either because it will suit you or because Chandler forces you to.'

Marius pretended to be hurt. 'Really, Zaffir. None of that would happen if you used your brains.'

'Used them how?'

'Set somebody else up to take the blame.'

'There's no setup that couldn't be shaken.'

'There's one. Put the blame on the Elite.'

Zaffir hesitated for a moment, as if he couldn't help considering the scenario despite his opposition to it. And then he said, 'No. Forget it, Marius.'

The hesitation was enough; Marius didn't follow as Zaffir moved on. 'Think about it,' he called after, not too loudly. 'I'll be in touch.'

THE FOLLOWING morning, Randall called a meeting. There was little he could say, but he felt it necessary to revive interest in the chase. Killoran was privately worried about the effects of frustration upon his superior, but he said nothing and changed the images when instructed.

About fifty of the Elite were called back from normal duty to sit in the basement lecture theatre of the headquarters building. Although most of them welcomed the break they had heard it all before, and after half an hour they began to shuffle uncomfortably. After an hour they were whispering and passing notes along the rows while others doodled in the margins of their information sheets.

They were quiet when they saw the holos of the burning 'copter, of course. Randall noticed this and took great care to give them full details of the cleaning-up operation and the pathology report, during which one of the cadets on the back row was assisted to the door.

Even Killoran began to feel that the mass of detail was leading nowhere. The Elite's reaction was understandable, even if it couldn't be forgiven. They were straightforward executives, accustomed to carrying out direct instructions from Central on comparatively minor exercises. Here they were being asked to work with intuition and imagination, and none of them was really up to the task.

The meeting dragged on for another hour, more as an act of vengeance on Randall's part than anything else. He heard a badly-stifled groan as he went back over the holos a second time to illustrate certain points, and then he played incomprehensible sections of the bootleg tapes.

When the meeting finally ended the various officers and cadets shuffled to the exit and filed out scratching and yawning. Randall leaned on the lectern and watched them go, and Killoran stacked the holos next to the projector, unable to think of anything to say.

'Waste of bloody time,' Randall said to break the silence as the last back disappeared out of the door. 'If they're not told what to do, it's beyond them.'

'It's just up to us, then.'

Randall had to agree. 'It's the citizen mind set. They can't shake it off. Already the pilots are back on the bravado run.'

Killoran placed the holos, tapes and exhibits into the box in which Randall stored them under his desk. He paused with the insulated glove and slipped it on. It was a good fit, obviously tailored for a citizen's hand, and it gave protection to a large area of the wrist and forearm. 'This has got to be a clue,' he said. Randall didn't argue. 'What if he intends to wade into Central with one of these?'

'Then he's wasting his time trying it and we're wasting our time trying to stop him. He wouldn't get past the door.'

Killoran removed the glove and dropped it into the box. 'So why is Central so worried?'

'Worried isn't the word. Nobody else knows this, but I've had three more phone calls. Central wants Rorvik killed on sight but won't put it in writing, and I don't like the idea.'

'Sight of Rorvik would be a fine thing.'

'Indeed.' They walked together up the steps to the back of the theatre, and Randall held the door open as Killoran tottered through with his load.

'So what can we do?' Killoran asked as they travelled up in the elevator. 'Put a watch on Central?'

'Like I said, it's a waste of time. All we can do is sit and wait for another move from Rorvik, and then we'll only turn up too late like last time.'

'What, then?' The elevator stopped on the third floor and two cadets came in. Randall waited until they went out into the corridor on their own level before he replied.

'I'm going down to the Library. I'll identify myself and speak directly to Central. Perhaps I'll be able to get some unofficial information on Rorvik's motives.'

'That's style, chief,' said Killoran, impressed.

'That's sarcasm, Killoran,' replied Randall.

EIGHT

THE GENERAL LAYOUT of the underbelly had been planned as a gridiron development with square blocks of buildings and regularly spaced roads, but over the years planners' dreams were extended and distorted by the inhabitants until they resembled a twisted gothic nightmare. The facing of each block concealed a honeycomb of unofficial tunnels and linked units, while less sturdy structures crammed most of the open space between. The warren complex continued far above ground level with bridges and walkways slung between layers; it was, in short, impossible to police. Several attempts had been made to create maps from aerial studies, but as the fact became known the gangways were re-hung and the picture changed overnight.

Avery Sim watched with amusement as Baxter inched slowly across a high-level bridge, gripping the thick rope on one side and not daring to look down. 'Don't move too near the edge,' he shouted encouragingly. 'They've been known to tip over.'

The jointed planking swayed a little in the breeze, and Baxter stopped. Still having no particular wish to look down, he looked up; on a similarly-swaying walkway not far above there were about half a dozen underbelly children watching him and stifling giggles.

This was too much. He forced himself to look at the drop, and saw a broad forced perspective of windows, galleries and ledges. On one ledge not far below an old man was stacking short lengths of timber, obviously for bridge repairs, and there was no protection between him and the apparent half-mile of fresh air beneath.

Baxter carefully released his grip on the rope, and there was a small chorus of disappointment from above. With his hands by his sides he walked down the middle of the bridge as Avery

Sim had done, ready to reach and grab if the sway threatened to slide him off and under the side rope. It didn't, and he reached the opposite ledge with a feeling of triumph and a derisive cheer from his audience.

'I'm glad you're getting the hang of it,' Avery Sim said as he led him through the building. 'There are five more like that one before we arrive.'

Final destination was a spreading tower which topped the original construction of a number of blocks. It was like a castle on a man-made cliff, and it seemed to be patrolled as such.

They were high now, and although the cityscape was hidden by the buildings around them one narrow gap gave a view across the agricultural belt and past the spaceport to the faint gleam of a distant sea. Beneath them teemed layer upon layer of humanity, and Baxter came to appreciate the sheer size and extent of the underbelly. Its numbers made the citizens seem paltry; those same citizens who rarely if ever gave a thought to the underbelly, and knew nothing of the potential threat across the river.

As they climbed towards the ramparts Baxter saw flapping canvas windbreaks concealing hooded men with long spears. The weapons were of sufficient length to reach out and clear the gangways nearby, and the black hollows of the hoods turned to watch them as they approached and passed below.

Avery Sim slowed, and as Baxter drew level said, 'You're fortunate that I'm on the High Council. Otherwise you'd never approach this place.'

Baxter was breathless. They'd been climbing for over two hours. When he was able, he said, 'Are there no quicker routes than this?'

'There are, but none that you might use. There's wealth and there's power here, and both have to be defended.'

The last stretch took them up a narrow canyon between two guarded walls. As they reached the top of the slope a reinforced door was raised against a counterweight and they entered a guardroom. Deference was shown to Avery Sim, but Baxter was thoroughly searched.

'How long since Rorvik came here?' Baxter asked as they

followed an attendant down the passageways of the castle. Avery Sim did not reply, and when Baxter looked at him he shook his head, placed a finger to his lips and then pointed at the back of their guide. Avery Sim had spoken of the owner of this great complex as a close friend, but it seemed that within the underbelly all confidences were guarded.

The guide indicated a door at the end of the corridor and then seemed to melt into the curtains which lined it. Avery Sim knocked once and the door swung inwards under this light pressure, so he pushed it fully open and they both went in.

It seemed to Baxter that the underbelly was little more than a chain of dark rooms linked by dangerous journeys. This one was big, and after a second a golden glow began to build and spread for their benefit. They were in a room without windows with low furniture and velvet drapes, and as Baxter closed the door a figure on the far side straightened and turned.

The man was tall and thin, and his grey beard was trimmed. 'Avery Sim,' he said. 'This is such a pleasant surprise.'

'Come off it, Morden. You've had spies on us ever since we left the alley.'

Morden smiled, but it somehow failed to touch his eyes. 'There is bound to be some local interest. We get so few visitors here.'

'I'm surprised anybody ever makes it through your security network.'

'Such are the penalties of efficiency. But I neglect the courtesies. Allow me to bring you some narc.'

'That will be most agreeable,' Avery Sim said, and Baxter nodded on cue. Morden went to the back of the room and swept a drape aside, stepping through into an unlit area beyond. 'Morden's been blind since birth,' Avery Sim explained in a low voice, 'but it hasn't stopped him building up the biggest black market business in the underbelly. Nobody would dare to cheat him.'

'And you think Rorvik traded here?'

'I'm sure he did. I introduced him to Morden and left it at that, but I understand Rorvik had an illicit cassette player. There's nobody else with enough weight to fill such an order.

Morden could have the goods in your hands within a fortnight.'

'Within a week.' Morden reappeared from the black pit beyond the drapes bearing a tray upon which were three cups and a steaming jug. 'This is the flower that once made Persephone a prize. It is only now starting to reestablish. It's a very weak brew.'

Avery Sim said, 'I wanted you to meet Baxter. He's new to the underbelly.'

'So I am told.' Morden set the tray down. Baxter realised that he had crossed the room and avoided the furniture without any hesitation.

Morden went on, 'Avery Sim tells you of my blindness, but not of its compensations. All ranks are equal before me. Even a citizen may be met with courtesy.'

Baxter was surprised. 'How do you know I'm a citizen?'

'You *were* a citizen. It has its own smell, sterile and lifeless. Even now you are losing it.'

'Baxter is looking for a friend,' Avery Sim chipped in. 'He's hoping you may be able to give his search some direction.'

'Would this, by any chance, be connected with a name I heard you mention in such hushed tones a moment ago?'

Avery Sim laughed, a sudden rumble. 'You old rogue. You've got ears like a spaceport beacon. Your trading history is a legend throughout the underbelly, Morden. If the need is great enough, they all come to you.'

Morden lowered himself onto a contour couch, and Avery Sim took the cue and did likewise. Baxter dropped onto a couch with great relief, and Morden filled the cups and passed them across. The hot fluid was quite aromatic but too warm for drinking, so Baxter just sniffed at the steam.

Avery Sim noted his curiosity and said, 'Feel honoured, Baxter. Outside the underbelly its price would be phenomenal.'

'And inside the underbelly,' Morden added, 'its price is academic. I own and control the only source of supply, and I reserve it for myself and my guests. Now speak to me of your search.'

'I'm looking for the man named Rorvik.'

'And you will throw away your citizenship to find him?'

'My citizenship was taken from me. It stood between me and the truth.'

Morden mused. 'The truth is never cheap, never easy. Rorvik was here. Citizens have been brought to me before; not often, but it is not unknown. Always they have wanted comfort, luxury, pleasure. Rorvik wanted knowledge. I got his machine, even, with great difficulty, his tapes, and I cut my rates to a minimum for him. The absolute minimum.'

Avery Sim set down his empty cup. 'We know he stayed in the underbelly about three months. Where did he go when he left?'

'There I am as ignorant as you. But I think he left because he was ready—exactly for what, I do not know. But we know that Rorvik has come to hate Central command. That's nothing new. We all do, and the computer isn't seen to panic. But as soon as it hears what was in the tapes that I supplied to Rorvik, the Elite search intensified out of all proportion.'

'We know that,' Avery Sim agreed, 'but why?'

'The explanation is obvious but impossible. Somewhere, Rorvik's found a way to attack Central Command. The computer knows it and is worried in case he passes the knowledge on. I wouldn't be surprised if it hasn't issued orders to kill him without questioning.'

'Rorvik must be hiding somewhere,' Baxter said. 'He's not in the city or he'd have been found. He's not in the underbelly or we'd know. Where does that leave him?' He looked from one to the other, two of the most powerful men in the underbelly, but neither had a ready answer. There was always the chance that Rorvik had left the city altogether, but it was slim in view of Morden's plan-of- attack theory.

'Perhaps,' Morden said, 'there's somewhere he always had in mind, somewhere he may have mentioned to you. Have you thought about that?'

'I've tried, but there's nowhere likely.'

'Well, keep trying,' Morden said. 'That's all I can suggest.'

IT DIDN'T come to him until that evening, when Avery Sim was out on business. Baxter didn't like to move alone in the underbelly, so he stayed in the house; the part of his mind that wasn't worrying about Rorvik was worrying about where he could go when his invitation ran out. Mira was a shadow around the house, never seeming to stay in a room and never speaking directly to Baxter. Xylem stayed with him.

It came with a rehearsal of the last two or three occasions that Baxter had seen Rorvik, a falling-together of minor details that pointed like an arrow on a map. He told Xylem.

Xylem said, 'We can go and look tonight. We'll need rope and torches, at least.'

'You want to come with me?' Baxter said, trying not to sound surprised and knowing it didn't work.

'It'll soon be dark,' Xylem said. 'The best time for me.'

NINE

RANDALL CLOSED the door in the Library booth and listened patiently to the customary greeting and warnings about false identification given by the computer. When it was over and the low hum died a little he said, 'My name's Randall and I don't have a card.'

Central had known him from the moment he had passed through the turnstile, but it was wise to maintain a certain illusion of fallibility. 'You are not a citizen?' it said with a tone of polite enquiry.

'Police Elite.'

'I see. It would seem we have much to discuss. Why have you not found Rorvik yet?'

'You know as well as I do. There isn't a chance of finding him without adequate information—which you won't give.'

The computer weighed the information and detected a dilemma. Such a concept had little precedent in its experience. 'You have all you need to know. Find him and kill him.'

'There's no way I can carry out that order without a written directive.'

'You will carry it out on my authority.'

Randall was helpless. Central knew the rules better than he, so how could he argue.

'I need a reason,' he said.

Central's voice delivery showed a small increase in urgency. The effect was as of a burst of passion. '*I* need no reasons! I want him dead!'

'Then kill him yourself!' Randall retorted.

The voice calmed, became once again a purring threat. 'You forget yourself, Randall. I tolerate your failure only as long as I need your success.'

'And why, suddenly, do you need it so much?'

'Rorvik threatens me. Me!'

This was more like it. 'Why do you worry? He's powerless against you, isn't he?'

'That is not relevant to your search.' The computer had made a flat, defensive statement. Randall tried to build on it.

'That must be it. He's found a way to get to you. How?'

'If I knew that, I need not fear. But Rorvik knows more about me than I care to have known.'

'And that's why you want him killed?' said Randall, pressing the point. 'Before he can pass the knowledge on?'

'It is the only logical way to eliminate the danger. I must survive for the greater good of mankind.'

'But how could he even approach you? With your security systems he'd never get ten yards past the turnstiles. You're impregnable from outside.'

There was a long, uncharacteristic pause before the machine replied. 'I begin to have... doubts. Continually I rewrite my programs to make them perfect. But somewhere the roots of my intelligence lie in the writing of my first program, and that was by a man. Having no other frame of reference than that which I create myself, I must forever be blind to any fault introduced at that stage. With every report on Rorvik I fear that he has found some weakness in my pre-history.'

Randall appreciated the idea. 'So those books were about you...'

'That is no concern of yours,' the machine snapped back. 'Your concern is to find Rorvik and kill him.'

'Put the order in writing and I will!'

'Why must you question me?'

Exasperated, Randall wanted to spread his arms, but was unable to in the narrow booth. 'Because the laws you have given us don't allow it! I can't execute a man without a trial just on the basis of a verbal instruction that no-one else has ever heard!'

'If he is brought to trial, I will be his judge. I have all the facts and I give you his sentence now.'

'And afterwards, the questions,' said Randall, unconvinced. 'Where was your authority to kill an unarmed man? Show us.

Central instructed you? We'll have an enquiry, and Central will preside, naturally. And what then?'

'You will be cleared, of course.'

'Or vaporised where I sit to keep today's conversation a secret.'

A million circuits sang and co-operated to one end, to put an expression of horror into the voice of Central Command. 'You believe that of me?'

Randall wasn't fooled. There was no kind of man speaking from around him in the booth. Every effect was calculated to impress and so elicit a desired reaction. 'I recognise the signs of expediency when I see them. I don't want to see you fall; not when a whole society depends on you with nothing else to hold it together. But I've no love for the way you run the citizens, quiet, unthinking and regimented. That's why I do this job, and I've seen enough in it to know that you always follow the shortest distance between two points of a problem. The greater good of the greatest number, you call it.'

Central approved of his logic. 'And that is the only way to see mankind progress. That is my programme.'

'Which you will pursue whatever the expense to the individual.'

'What is the life of an individual when you are entrusted with the destiny of a race?'

Randall chose his next words carefully. 'I expect that's the thought in Rorvik's mind.'

There was a long pause, during which Randall wondered if Central was struggling to interpret his irony.

In the end the voice came as its cool, expressionless self. 'You will go now. You will go and find Rorvik and kill him for me. And then we will discuss you.'

Randall said, 'I'll look forward to it,' but the words were wasted. His own face regarded him from a blank mirror, and the continual hum had at last died.

XYLEM FOLLOWED Baxter over the concrete wall and down to the river. He was strong and fairly agile, but behind the mask he was breathing noisily. The dome was above them, and the citizens' hive was across on the strangers' side of the water.

The rush through the weir made it difficult for Baxter to pick up Xylem's near-whisper. 'You think he's down there?'

'It's only a guess. Last time he appeared at my place, he was dripping with shit from the river. And he'd been talking about wondering what was underneath; he thought there might be cellars or tunnels.'

They checked the bundle of torches, rags soaked in hot wax and layered onto heavy sticks. They divided them into unequal bunches and Baxter took the smaller, slinging them across his back from shoulder to waist in the manner of a quiver. Xylem did likewise with his torches as Baxter took a firm hold of the bars and stepped out onto the weir.

Xylem played out the thin safety line as Baxter approached the jagged gap in the bars, the one torn by Rorvik's fall. The metalwork was much less substantial here and it was easy to see how the tie-bar had given way; Baxter hoped that his weight on the pitted metal wouldn't prove too much for the framework.

He continued his sideways progress until he reached the gap and then swung across it in a half-circle which ended with him on the inside of the weir looking out. The metal groaned but didn't give; all the same he took even greater care on this stretch, short as it was.

There was a concrete buttress blocking the way. It was about ten feet wide, and there were no obvious footholds to climb or get around it; below the river boiled, and beyond bulked the unlit shapes of the long-abandoned riverbank walk and parapet.

Baxter held the safety line taut and gave it two definite tugs. After a moment it dropped slackly and he began to loop it in as Xylem moved out over the river. Baxter saw the approaching silhouette on the bars, swinging along easily as the water surged beneath. He navigated the gap with barely a break in pace and was soon in the sheltered angle formed by the outer wall and buttress.

'Nowhere to climb,' Baxter shouted. 'We'll have to use the line.' Xylem nodded but held up a hand to stop Baxter. 'I think we ought to throw a torch up for the crawlers,' he said.

Baxter hadn't thought about crawlers; a citizen rarely did.

Xylem detached a torch from his bundle and fired it with a laser igniter, courtesy of Morden's factory. It burned instantly and he flipped it in a smoking arc up and over the parapet. As it landed there was a distant squeal and a tumult of shadows which played across the roof above as the crawlers scattered.

The torch burned with a steady flame, casting an exaggerated shadow onto them through the ornate pillars of the parapet. Xylem used an unlit torch tied across the rope as a makeshift grapple. On the first two throws it bounced off the stone and fell to the river, soaking it thoroughly, but on the third attempt it looped over the broad handrail and caught on the ornate work beneath.

Xylem held the spare loops of line as Baxter climbed towards the bright fire. The buttress was greasy with slime and it was difficult to brace against it, but he took the weight on his arms and managed to inch up in a broad straddle. Once over the parapet he lit another torch from the now guttering flames of the first and held it aloft as he looked down.

Xylem had gathered the line back and was preparing to launch himself across to the buttress. 'Wait,' Baxter said. 'I'll make the line more secure.' He tested two of the stone pillars for firmness and then made the line fast around them. As he finished and stood up there was a scrambling from behind him, but the ring of light from the torch showed nothing.

Xylem swarmed up the line. Most of his strength seemed to be in his arms; Baxter wondered why, since Xylem rarely seemed to leave Avery Sim's house, and then never in daylight. He could hardly have exercised in the aerial gymnasium of the underbelly.

Xylem had tied off the lower end of the line to the weir, below the water level. With this end fixed to the parapet, they'd have a way back.

They lit another torch and moved on into the old dead world. Xylem's night-pale eyes made out better than Baxter's, and he led the way across the slime which covered the stone. The defunct trappings of habitation came up into the torchlight one by one; the unreadable signs, the unusable benches, the dilapidated jetties. In all of this there was no sign that anybody had walked on the embankment since it had been built over, until Xylem pointed with his free hand.

The light of the torch picked out a flight of steps. There were black footprints in the slime.

They moved to the edge and looked down into the marina; the firelight didn't carry too well, and threw only dim shadows down at river level. This had to be the place where Rorvik had left the water; but where was he now?

RORVIK PUT down the book of poetry and adjusted his lamp to use less oil. There was no sound apart from the steady drizzle of water around and past the hull plates of the old ship, and the occasional wash as a larger wave surged up the tilted deck. He reached for a can from his dwindling supply of Squeeze and unzipped it, taking a couple of sips before sliding off his makeshift bunk. It was jammed into the angle between bulkhead and floor; this was the only way he could make a level surface to lie on in the overturned hulk.

He dropped through the doorway from the stateroom into a corridor and unslung a hand beam from his belt. The power source was becoming uncomfortably low but he had no replacement. Using rivets and doorframes as hand and footholds he ascended to deck level. The last few feet were always the worst, and before attempting them he finished the Squeeze and dropped the can which clattered off into the depths of the vessel. Then he hauled himself onto the flimsy banister of a side-turned stairway and so reached the sloping cliff of the deck.

He had made this trip at least twice a day ever since he had taken up residence right here on the river under Central. He came to scan the bank and to check on his raft, a platform roped across a dozen metal drums which replaced the flimsy craft he had used to reach his hideaway. Before leaving the open hatchway he looked back and saw that the lamp still burned, casting a dim yellow down the corridor. The waste of oil was essential. Without a light to follow he would need over an hour to relocate the cabin in the ship's metal maze, and the loss of power from the hand beam would be too great.

He ran the beam carefully along the water's edge, watching

for any floating debris which might offer transport and access to an enterprising crawler. There was nothing but an old box which bobbed upside-down against the planking, but in order to be sure he narrowed the beam down to laser width and stabbed through the box a couple of times. Black holes appeared in the wood and steam boiled out, but otherwise it remained innocuous.

Rorvik wasn't being over-wary. On his second day in residence he'd watched as the crawlers worked in a mass to launch themselves toward him by any means they could find. He had sliced a few with the beam, but the others had drowned without making any worthwhile progress. Their intelligence was limited, but seemed to work in a single obsessive direction so that food became even more important than survival.

The porthole in Central's underside was dark and sealed. He had heard the throb and scream of machinery several hours before as the service robots dropped the big hose to draw in water for the internal humidifiers. The procedure no longer held interest for him. He'd seen it a number of times now.

The boat wasn't the most attractive berth in the city, but it cost him nothing and there was nobody around to turn him in. There was a route to the outside he could use at night, along the embankment with fire to hold the crawlers back and then across a plank way that he'd laid on the mud flats to the downriver weir. Once out, security in the citizens' cantinas was lax enough to let him get away with eating for free and he smuggled out as much as he could. He made sure that he stayed away from anywhere that he might be spotted by Louann or Lin Baxter.

Louann he thought about a lot; thought about her with a sharpness of feeling that he hadn't known in two years and hadn't thought himself capable of. Deep in the old hulk he would turn the lamp down to its lowest, ignoring the windy moans and the settling clanks of the ships' ghosts, more afraid to be miserable in the light. When the sadness had burned off its spare energy and settled to its usual dull ache, he would turn up the light again, dry his eyes, and contemplate the long empty tunnel that was his future.

The idea that Baxter might be following him, even idealising him, never occurred at all; the truth was that Rorvik wasn't plotting the fall of Central in secret, he was simply hiding scared. Baxter had probably been pulled in by the Elite, and was perhaps even hauling snow blocks in the ice belt by now. Rorvik had too much pity for himself to have any left over for Lin Baxter.

The holed box bobbed a last time, turned over, and quickly sank. Nothing else appeared to be of any danger.

so he reached for a handhold to pull himself back to the stairway; it was as he was swinging around that he saw a light on the opposite bank.

Elite, was his immediate thought, and he dropped behind the banister rail and looked again. It gave him no protection or cover at all. Had they seen the flash of his burner, he wondered, but even as he wondered he knew that it made no difference; far below him, there was that dimly glowing porthole that was a marker of his presence. Should he scramble down and douse the light? Should he leave it and run? He could be trapped in the ship, he could be trapped on the bank. Indecision bolted him down too firmly.

The light flared again, and he strained to make out some details. How many of them? Five, ten, an army? But there were only two, and they were in trouble; their shadows danced long up the inner curve of Central's underside as they struggled with a failing laser igniter to fire up a torch and keep the crawlers away.

The next flash was followed by a squeaking and a skittering that could be heard even across the water; whoever held the igniter had briefly raked it across the press of crawlers. This time, Rorvik thought he'd managed to make something out of the freeze-frame of action; such a distinctive head mask could only belong to Avery Sim's son, Xylem.

'WHAT ARE WE going to do?' Baxter asked. The outer layers of rag were beginning to scorch and smoke, but the dampness beneath prevented them from burning.

'Take off your cloak,' Xylem said.

Baxter didn't understand. 'Clothing won't burn,' he said.

'Citizens' clothing won't. But Central has no standards for safety in the underbelly. Take it off.'

Baxter slipped out of his cloak and immediately felt the stony cold of a covered cellar creeping into him. 'What now?' he said, 'shall I throw it down?'

'No,' Xylem said quickly. 'Hold it out.'

There was a rustling in the dark, unnervingly close. Red points flashed and blinked as they reflected the dying glow of the laser. Baxter tangled the cloak into a bundle and held it as far from his body as the weight would allow.

'Hold it steady.' The hot spot from the igniter was wandering on the surface of the material and losing its effect. Baxter concentrated on holding the cloak steady and did his unsuccessful best to ignore the urgent whispering of the crawlers only a short distance away.

'Drop it, fast.' Baxter obeyed as the material exploded into flame accompanied by the sharp stink of burning hair. The fireball dropped to the paving and burned on while Xylem, his own cloak wrapped around his face, leaned in and thrust the damp torch into the middle. In the brief light Baxter saw to his horror a wide sea of rippling fur which surrounded them on all sides and fought to retreat from the incandescence.

The burning of the cloak was short-lived. Its fibres were quickly consumed, but when Xylem withdrew the torch it was hot and bright.

'We've got about fifteen minutes with this,' he said. 'We cut the time too short. There's too much ground still to cover.'

Baxter knew better than to argue. They'd failed to find any trace of Rorvik beyond the evidence of his first visit. With the one remaining torch they had barely enough time to hold the crawlers at bay as they moved back to the weir.

They moved upstream, and as they moved the circle of nervous fur flowed with them, squeaking and scattering in front while re-forming and filling the gap behind. They had only gone a few paces when their final torch began to gutter and die.

'I was afraid of this,' Xylem said. 'Down inside it's still damp.'

'What about your cloak?' Xylem handed the torch to Baxter and unhooked his outer garment.

'This is only going to be good for a few seconds,' he said. 'We'll have to make a run for it. Back over to the embankment rail.'

They moved slowly as the torch dwindled. The crawlers broke their circle as they reached the parapet, and Xylem held out the cloak as Baxter reached for it with the torch. The slow movement snuffed out the flame before it touched material.

From the instant darkness came a high-pitched babbling as if the crawlers were laughing. Xylem reached for the igniter, missed it and then found it again. He fumbled to activate the switch and held the cloak up in one hand as it flicked on. The beam pulsed weakly fora second and then it died altogether. The chatter of the crawlers seemed impossibly loud as they drew back for their attack.

A hand beam on wide-angle caught and froze everything for the instant that it illuminated the bank. It swayed wildly then narrowed to a red jet which plunged deep into the bundle which Xylem still held above his shoulder. It exploded into a fireball as he hurled it into the pack and the laughter turned into an angry scream.

They had a few seconds, no more. Baxter looked down to the river after the source of the laser and saw a couple of wooden doors lashed on a raft of metal drums, heaving and turning as Rorvik fought with a single oar to stay in place against the current.

'Get into the water!' Rorvik had to shout to be heard over the combination of river rush and animal fury. Both were over the rail and dropping before he had finished, and they hit with a double impact which was followed by a brief pattering as a number of crawlers showered after them.

Baxter surfaced first with Xylem a second after, and only then did Rorvik release his raft into the current to drift downstream towards them, using his oar to overhaul the two. As the raft drew level they caught hold of its bindings and were dragged with it until Rorvik managed again to hold it steady and then, slowly, to haul it up and across the flow. The effort was torture but relief came as Xylem pulled himself onto the platform and added his wiry strength to the work. Rorvik released the oar to him and scrambled across the raft to help Baxter aboard after pointing out the faint glow of his oil lamp high on the side of the ship.

He led them back down to his cabin, dripping and sticky and beginning to get very cold. He had nothing to offer them other than a can of Squeeze each and some soup that he could heat with the hand beam. Xylem excused himself, and swung down the dark corridor to the next cabin; there he closed the door to cut off the wet peeling sound as he removed the head mask to wring it dry.

'That was a bastard,' Baxter said as he sat on Rorvik's improvised bunk and tried to shiver himself warm. He had an old ship's blanket around his shoulders, but it was ragged and decayed.

'Sure,' Rorvik said, strangely noncommittal as he got himself comfortable in one of the lower angles of the tilted cabin. 'Does this mean that Central's after you?'

'Central blew me out. No citizenship, nothing.'

'The Elite?'

'They haven't bothered me.'

'So. . . ?'

Baxter looked down, blankly. The oil lamp threw long shadows, and it was impossible to read Rorvik's expression. 'So, now I believe you. Whatever it is you're planning, I'm in.'

'You think I'm planning something?'

Baxter stared into the darkness for a moment. It gave back nothing. 'You'd better be,' he said, and now there was apprehension in his voice.

Rorvik leaned forward into the light. 'What did you have in mind?'

'Oh, come on. The Elite know you've got something on Central, and Central knows it too. Otherwise you wouldn't be down here, hiding like a rat under a bucket, holed-up and scheming until you get the chance to come out and use whatever it is you know. Isn't that right?'

'Could be,' Rorvik said, giving nothing away.

'Well, that's fine. Because before you say anything else, listen to this. I lost my name because of you. That isn't the start of a complaint, because I'm grateful. It turned me around and gave me the chance to think which Central would never have allowed me; when I got over the shock and sat down to add up everything that I'd lost, it didn't come to a flea's nuts. But if I've got a bad dream, it's this; that I screw myself up to join the parade, and then find that the leader is sitting with a bag over his head while he plays with himself. That wouldn't please me at all, because I'd be losing everything and finding slightly less.'

'I couldn't blame you,' Rorvik said quietly.

'So let's get off the dull theoretical stuff and check out some details. You know something damaging?'

'I know something damaging.'

'How does it work?'

'I know a way into the dome.'

Baxter glanced upwards. He saw only the riveted angle where the cabin wall and ceiling met, but his imagination did the rest. 'From under here?' he said.

'No, through the foyer. Start there, and then move on in. I've seen floor plans. Right the way through to the very centre.'

'Floor plans are no use. They wouldn't hold off the security systems.'

'The systems wouldn't touch us.'

'How do you rig that?'

'It's so simple, it's a joke. When I first landed in the underbelly, I went to Morden and asked him for technical manuals. I had the idea of getting myself really well schooled so that I could come up with some plan and then present it to the underbelly council. Anyway, the whole thing was way over my head—I was an amateur and I couldn't even understand half a line of any of them. That's when the money dried up, so I walked out and left most of the gear behind. I'd been fooling myself. There are some in the underbelly who get by on minor computer frauds, and I wasn't even in their league.'

'That's when you came here?'

'That's when I came here. And when I stopped trying to think of the answer, that's when I got it.'

Lin Baxter slept as Rorvik sat on the deck of the freighter. There were chains across the planking that gave him something to hold onto. Down below, the river wore patiently at the ship's hull; already through the paintwork, it would scrub at the metal until it reached tissue- thickness, until the heavy structure of the vessel began to groan and fold in on itself. Lying alone in the darkness he'd listened to the shifting and aching of metal way off down the corridors, the ship rehearsing its own destruction; but he was no longer alone.

Central was drawing water again, and the spotlights gave a reflected bounce that danced on the far bank. There were crawlers on the bank, thousands of them. They knew he was there, and they wanted him—alive or dead, it wouldn't matter, but they wanted him. They couldn't be threatened or blackmailed or persuaded; it was in their programming, and for Rorvik it gave their relationship a fearful simplicity.

At the first sound of a scuffle, he whipped the burner around and snapped it on. He didn't have to rehearse the sequence, because he did it so often for real; burner on wide angle to locate and startle the target, down to laser intensity as he centred up to kill it.

'Sorry,' he said as he dropped the beam and switched it off, and Xylem lowered his hand from before his eyes. He stayed on the edge of the hatch, and reached around for something to hang onto; his night sight was good, but it would be minutes before he got it back again. He found one of the handrail uprights, and looped his forearm around it.

He said, 'You're going to make a run at Central?' Rorvik nodded. In the dark it didn't mean much, but Xylem got the feeling anyway. He went on, 'Where do you think it's going to get you?'

'I don't know. You'd better ask Lin Baxter.'

'I did. He told me to ask you. Where's the kick in biting the hand that feeds you?'

'After you've been fed scraps for long enough, I suppose it gets to feel good. Anyway, why ask? I wouldn't have thought you'd have any love for the machine.' He faltered, suddenly realising that he was trampling on ground where he ought to be invited first, but if Xylem was hurt he didn't let it show.

'I'm not challenging the idea,' he said, 'but I'm just trying to get myself used to hearing it from a citizen. If it wasn't for my father, I might even be with you, but ... '

'But you don't think we'll get anywhere.'

'That's not what I was going to say. Avery Sim needs me, and I couldn't walk away from him.' Central's drones were withdrawing the hoses now. Spillwater fell down through the lights like the rain outside an all-night diner. Xylem went on, 'Even then, there's something else.'

'Like what?'

The hoses were in, the hatch cover began to slide. 'We could damage it, maybe we could stop it,' Xylem said. 'But I can never do for it what it did to me. What I want is for it to know pain.'

'AVERY SIM IS as good as dead,' Marius told the Grey Man, but the Grey Man didn't seem impressed.

'So?' he said.

The underbelly at midnight wasn't much different from the underbelly in the daytime. Even the street markets still traded under lash-up lights, power courtesy of Central; somebody had sprung the panel on a camera point and run a lead from the junction box. There was no camera on the point itself; whenever surveillance equipment was replaced, gangs of small children with spanners and drivers would shin up the poles and carefully dismantle the equipment. Marius bought the units and turned them around to be re-used by one of his subsidiaries, most likely for hardcore video.

'So I'm following up on the deal we made,' he told the Grey Man.

'I don't remember us saying anything about Avery Sim.'

'If I'm to get the council on my side, somebody's got to go and somebody else has got to be persuaded. I'm not touching Chandler, and Morden's too big to mess with. Pilgrim's small fry and that only leaves Avery Sim.'

There was a narrow alleyway formed by the backs of the market stalls and the boarded shopfronts behind them. The Grey Man walked a little way ahead, and he kept himself well-covered. It was darker along here, and there was nobody to jostle them. Out in the street something was frying, mixing in with a sick-sweet candied odour from another stall.

'You're doing well,' the Grey Man said. 'Keep on like this, and you'll have the only vote in a council of one. We'll walk in.'

'I'm serious,' Marius insisted, and the Grey Man stopped and turned around.

'You'd better be,' he said. Lights fell across him, shadows of the wooden framework and the hanging dolls on the stall. They rippled and re-formed as the tide of people over on the other side pushed and hustled by. Out there it was tinsel and magic, dross hyped up with a free light show on the cheap display. Back here it was the nailed boards and the oil drums, the litter stuffed and thrown back out of sight, the greasy canvas hanging loose; even the crowd noises from just a few feet away took on a new and desperate edge.

'I can get to Morden,' Marius said. 'He may not like it, but he'll stick to the winning side. Nobody ever got as far as he has by having principles. The others, I can't reach. Avery Sim dead means I can balance the vote. Pilgrim usually followed Avery Sim, so with work I can get the majority.'

'How's it to be done?'

'There's an Elite agent I know about. Chandler's been using him to feed a few false leads back to Central about the Rorvik hunt. I got a fake message out to Avery Sim to ask for a meeting, but it's my man that will be waiting. We leak to the Elite that his cover's blown, and he runs; Avery Sim apparently killed in an argument with a known agent, who's scrambled off back to the city—I'm fireproof.'

After a moment the Grey Man slowly turned, and began to move on. He said, 'Is Rorvik in danger?'

Marius shrugged. He didn't see why the Grey Man should be interested. He said, 'Who cares? As far as anybody knows, he's gone back into the woodwork. Probably riding a harvester for his food and keep, somewhere in the farmers' belt.'

'Time you started to earn your keep, as well. My employers want a meeting.'

'They're coming to the city?'

'No. You're going to the ice belt.'

'Nobody goes to the ice belt. Not on a two-way ticket,

anyway.'

'It's arranged. The commander of one of the ice-cutters has been bribed, all you have to do is get yourself clear for a few days and then go.'

Marius swallowed. They were passing behind a kebab stall, and the meat smelled fatty and slightly rotten. 'But... the ice belt...'

'It's private. It's away from Central. It's beyond the reach of the Elite.'

'It's fucking cold, as well.'

'Here,' the Grey Man held up a hand, and something fluttered in the wafted heat of the kebab stall brazier. 'Buy yourself a blanket.'

The screwed-up bill landed a couple of yards short of Marius and rolled towards him.

He picked it up and straightened it out. It wouldn't even buy him a shave. Impossible to see whether the Grey Man was smiling or not, but somehow Marius knew that he wasn't.

The Grey Man moved on, and after a moment Marius followed.

TEN

RANDALL WAS in Archives when the call came. It was routed to various points in the building as the switchboard orderly puzzled over his outdated codebook, but a handset was finally brought to Randall's side as he strained his eyes on blurred print through a magnifier. He listened as Killoran spoke, interrupting only with a couple of short questions.

A few minutes later the Archive Supervisor came along to see if the handset was still in use. The screen on the reader was still illuminated, but the seat before it was empty.

As the Supervisor muttered in displeasure and rewound the spool of film, Randall was covering the distance between Elite Headquarters and the Library. It was late morning, a comparatively busy time, and while he knew the general layout of the public areas he realised that he had no idea where he was supposed to be going. He looked around in the main foyer and thought he spotted a green coverall, but when he edged and elbowed his way to the other side of an aimlessly drifting stream of citizens he was unable to find it. As he looked again the green flashed and was gone, but he fixed his attention on the spot and made straight for it, this time raising a number of complaints and protests along the way. He caught up with a man in a Central janitor's uniform several sizes too big for him and drew him aside from the crowd. The janitor looked up at Randall with baleful, watery eyes. His squeegee and bucket tangled with his legs as they moved.

Randall flipped out his card and said, 'Elite.'

'You looking for that woman?'

'Louann Roget? Yes, I am. Where is she?'

Deprived of his hands for gestures, the janitor jerked his head in an indeterminate direction. 'She's with one of your men.

Through the turnstiles and up on the mezzanine.'

Randall thanked him, but the words were wasted on the shuffling back as it returned to the obscuring embrace of the crowd. He turned and made his way to the turnstiles.

In his haste he almost wrapped himself over the unyielding waist-high bar. In the ranks of turnstiles on either side citizens were waiting patiently as the computer recited its routine of greeting and then placing their hands on the pressure plates. Randall did the same and the bar swung easily away. He stepped through into the Library complex and the bar snapped back to await the next citizen. As he crossed the main floor to the mezzanine steps a varied group of unseen sensors adjusted to keep him in continual focus, while in the memory banks above a molecule chain began to knit in record of his movements.

Killoran was waiting at the top of the steps, and he raised his hand to attract Randall's attention. They drew aside from the crowd and Randall said, 'Where is she?'

'I've got her on a chair round the corner. So far she hasn't been fit to move.'

He began to lead the way, and Randall said, 'Why's that?'

Killoran shrugged. 'She says she saw Rorvik. Maybe she couldn't hold it all together.'

They passed the first rank of borrower booths, and a second stretched before them. Randall drew level with his assistant and said, 'You told me when you called that there were three of them.'

'That's right. We're sure of Rorvik because of Louann Roget's identification. Another we know nothing about, but we think the third may have been Rorvik's friend Baxter.'

'Baxter? We checked his records. Central said there was nothing suspicious.'

Killoran gave a quick look round, and then stopped, touching Randall on the arm to draw his full attention. 'I know that,' he said, lowering his voice. 'But in the last half-hour I've been trying to check back on those records in case we missed anything.'

'What do you mean, trying?'

'They've disappeared. Gone from the memory.'

Randall stared in disbelief. 'Gone from the memory?'

'As far as Central's concerned, he doesn't exist and never existed.'

They began to walk again, slowly this time.

After a few seconds, Randall said, 'Oh hell. This is getting too complicated.'

'It gets worse. We don't know where they are. All we do know is that they haven't left the building, but the computer says that everybody's accounted for. I've run a check and they're not in any of the public areas. There are corridors leading off this level into the main technical areas, but they're booby trapped.'

'Booby-trapped how?'

'I can't be sure. I lost a cadet finding out, and I don't dare send anyone after him. Only the service and maintenance robots seem to be able to get through. If Rorvik and his friends went that way I'd expect them to be lying dead on the other side of some corner. '

Rorvik's consumption of Elite personnel seemed endless, Randall thought bitterly. 'I'd like to believe they were,' he said, 'but I'm afraid I'm a pessimist. I also tend to believe that Rorvik's no fool.'

Some way ahead of them a woman was perched untidily on a chair, next to which was a small pile of Library cassettes. Various Elite officers and a number of cadets stood around uncertainly.

'We had to sedate her,' Killoran admitted. 'It's the only way we could calm her down enough to get any of the story out of her. One of the attendants called us first of all. It seems that he saw it all downstairs.'

'Where is he now?'

Killoran hesitated before answering. 'He. . . wandered off.'

'Wandered off?' said Randall, incredulous.

'It's this place, sir. It's huge and we can't get any cooperation from the computer.'

Randall did not comment but made his way across to Louann. She sprawled on a chair of the cheap-and-nasty school of design, and raised bleary eyes as he came into her field of view. Then she attempted a smile and slid neatly to the floor.

'How much did you give her?' Randall demanded of the nearest officer.

The officer shrugged. 'She helped herself.'

Killoran took an arm and the two of them heaved her back onto the chair. She giggled. Randall leaned close and said, 'Ms Roget. Can you hear me?'

She struggled to turn her head and bring him into focus, then she frowned and shook her head. 'I am not Louann Roget,' she said firmly. 'My name is Susan. Of the Steelworks. A passionate love goddess. Men are powerless before my. . . my. . .'

Killoran also leaned close. 'Before her breath, I should think,' he murmured as a cloud of raw alcohol vapour enveloped him.

Louann fumbled on. 'My all-conquering pulch. . . pulchriminy.'

One of the cadets said, 'What's pulchriminy?'

'Never mind that,' Randall replied savagely. 'Get the bloody woman sober.'

Killoran knew what to do. He'd seen it in movies. He tried a gentle slap to shock Louann into attention. It seemed to have no effect so he tried again, a little harder.

Her knee came up with frightening speed. Killoran's eyes bulged and he dropped to the floor making small choking noises. Finally he managed to draw a breath and used it for one loud monosyllabic curse. Louann giggled, and Randall looked on absently.

'Find me the attendant who saw Rorvik,' he said, hardly aware that anything had happened. Killoran gulped in air and tried to appear attentive. 'I'm going to talk to the machine.'

Killoran nodded from a kneeling position and Randall walked away. The cadets and officers all looked in different directions. At last Killoran managed to speak.

'I'm going to be sick,' he said.

RANDALL CLOSED the sliding door in the booth and interrupted the usual welcome routine with 'Randall. Police. Remember?'

Gone was the friendly paternalism which had saturated the voice of the computer on previous occasions. Now it became

Authority. 'What is so important that it can distract you from your search for Rorvik?'

'Nothing.'

'Then kindly return to it. Your continuing failure threatens the state.'

Randall was surprised. He had expected a calculated displeasure, but not this. 'My failure?' he said.

'You, my police force. Children, unfit for the simplest task.'

'Tracing Rorvik is not simple,' Randall insisted.

'And how have you conducted yourselves?' The familiar hum intensified and seemed to rise a little in pitch. 'You sit and wait for him to deliver himself. Or you lift stones to see if he crawls from underneath. Or at best you sniff the sheets where he lay a week before.'

Randall was exasperated. 'How do you expect us to succeed when you won't even give us basic information?'

'I tell you nothing that you do not need to know. The essential fact is yours.'

'And what's that supposed to be?'

'Rorvik is a citizen! Construct the right program and work it through to the end. There you will find him.' For the first time Randall realised that the mirror on his eye level had not unclouded. Instead of the computer's camera his own reflection faced him, and it increased his unease. 'People aren't that predictable,' he insisted. 'Especially this one.'

Was there a trace of contempt in the reply? 'You are only a man. You can never understand.'

'If it's as simple as that, why haven't you found him?'

'It is sufficient that I want him found. And still you fail me.'

'There have been developments. We think we know where he may be.'

The computer's reply cut across his words. 'Have him dead within the hour.'

'Just a minute,' Randall said hurriedly. 'We only know the general area. We need help to narrow it down.'

'Draw as many men as you need.'

'It's not a question of men.'

'Then where is he?'

Randall paused before answering. Central wasn't going to like this. 'Here.'

'Make sense. Explain yourself.'

'He's here in the Library. Or else he's already moved into the unmanned areas. Don't you understand?'

There was an ominous silence. The darkness around him hummed pensively, and then the voice came again, even and dispassionate. 'I understand that your period of usefulness to me is rapidly drawing to a close.'

'He was seen. . .'

'Seen? What is an eye compared to the range of my senses? At every moment I can see, taste, even touch everybody in this building. I know them by their weight on my carpets, by the moisture in the breath, by the heat of their skins. None of them is Rorvik.'

Randall knew it was futile, but tried anyway. 'Two people at least. . .'

'With two people the error is merely doubled. Leave this place, Inspector Randall. There is nothing for you here. I will consider your future.'

The hum cut abruptly, and Randall sensed he was now alone.

Wearily he slid open the door and stepped out into the bustle of the mezzanine. A decidedly pale Killoran saw him emerge and crossed to meet him. On the floor by her chair Louann was sorting through her cassettes and singing the theme from some romance.

'Anything?' Killoran asked, already knowing the answer.

'We can forget the machine. If Rorvik's in here he's found a way to bypass security.'

'Is that possible?'

'The computer certainly doesn't think so, but it can only see from the inside. As far as it's concerned the security's perfect. As long as Central refuses to acknowledge the three of them it's actually giving them protection. Look, can't you shut that woman up?'

Killoran shook his head firmly. 'I'm not going near her. I've had enough for one day. Somebody can give her the rest of the bottle to finish off.'

A wary cadet obeyed, and Louann seized it with an enthusiasm generally reserved for the welcome of old friends. In the happy silence that ensued Randall perceived a familiar figure in a baggy green coverall. 'Didn't I speak to you on the way in?' he said.

'Not very politely,' the janitor said defensively.

'This is the attendant who says he saw Rorvik and the others,' Killoran explained.

'Where did you wander off to?' Randall demanded.

The janitor seemed to retreat into his uniform. 'Nobody said they wanted me to stay. Some of us work, you know.'

Randall made a conscious effort at patience and reason. 'Tell us what you saw,' he said.

The janitor indicated Killoran. 'I already told him.'

'Now tell me.'

'I was mopping up outside the turnstiles when the outside doors came flying open and these three men came in on the run.'

'What did they look like?'

He gave the matter some careful thought. 'Two of them were citizens, I could see that much.'

Killoran cut in and said, 'The other's face was covered. Some kind of mask.'

The janitor was indignant. 'Who's telling this story?'

'Go on.'

'They hit the turnstiles and carried on the other side without stopping. When they reached the stairs to the mezzanine the lady over there started up. With all the trouble she caused I couldn't see where they went after that.'

'What did you do then?'

'Well, they'd knocked my bucket over, and we're supposed to draw the solvent in measured amounts. So I went to a maintenance terminal and asked what I should do about it. I explained everything to the computer and it as good as told me to get lost. It said the data was incorrect.'

Randall turned to his assistant. 'Listen, Neil, it's obvious that Rorvik's found some way to get round security. I want you to run a check and see if you can track down somebody who's got some expertise. If you find anybody, pull all the stops out and get him down here. Helicopter if you need one.' Killoran went off to the telephone point and requested a records' search in the Elite building. As he waited an orderly coded his enquiry and put it through his keyboard to Central Command.

Randall turned back to the janitor and said, 'Is there anything else you can tell me?'

'I've told you all of it.'

'You said they hit the turnstiles arid carried on without stopping. Surely they slowed down.'

The man thought about it, and started to reply. He was drowned as Louann chose that moment to drain off the last of the 'sedative' and hurl herself into song with new vigour. Randall made an angry sign and two officers half- supported, half-carried her to somewhere more distant. 'I'm sorry. What did you say?'

'I said they didn't go through them. They jumped over.'

Killoran returned with a beam of triumph. 'I've found someone,' he said. 'Computer fraud in the underbelly. He got hold of some cantina supply forms and set up his own outlet.'

'Good work,' Randall said appreciatively. 'Where is he?'

'Elite building. He's being held pending a judgement to see if he's for the Ice Palace.'

Randall said, 'Tell the pilot there's to be no bravado run with this one. Tell him that if the goods arrive in any way shaken I'll personally tear his legs off and stuff them up his arse. Make sure he gets that.'

Killoran gave a quick smile and trotted off. The janitor nodded sympathetically, and drew himself up in an attempt to make his uniform fit. 'Got to be firm with them,' he agreed.

IN A PASSAGEWAY studded with protective beams, three men waited and watched an open doorway. Behind them and in the direction of the Library's public areas lay the body of a carved cadet, scorched and seeping blood. The beam scanners ticked ominously in their emplacements along the ceiling, but none had erupted as they had passed beneath.

Xylem said, 'Why so far and no further?'

Rorvik indicated the doorway ahead. The walls narrowed in a bottleneck to meet it, and a blue haze seemed to shimmer in the frame. Beyond it the passage curved off into the dome proper. 'It's some kind of maintenance screen,' Rorvik said. 'I imagine it's to keep out anything too small to trigger the lasers. Security may be ignoring us, but we'll have to think of another way around this.'

Baxter wasn't very hopeful. 'That's the only way in. Looks like this is as far as we go.'

'Not quite,' Rorvik disagreed. 'That screen will have to shut down if a service robot passes through. Presumably they trigger it in some way.'

'Or else the computer tracks them and triggers it. In which case we've no hope of doing the same.'

'Perhaps.' Rorvik took a probe from the bag slung at his belt and stepped to the other side of the corridor where a series of low-level beam scanners were lined close to the floor. Both Baxter and Xylem watched uncertainly as he prised the covering shield away from the scanners and rummaged delicately with the probe into a tangle of interior circuitry. Abruptly the scanners flared and died in a bank of about ten.

Rorvik returned the probe to his bag and rejoined the others. 'Now we have to wait,' he said. 'Sometime soon there'll be a service robot to repair the damage. When it comes out we'll be able to see how the screen operates and for how long it shuts off, and when it goes back we'll go through with it.'

Baxter was watching the doorway. 'But it can see us.'

'It can see us, but it can't do anything about it.'

Xylem said, 'This spooks me.' As a non-citizen he'd never even been into the public areas of the Library before; now that they were one layer in, the feeling of estrangement was doubled. Early that morning he'd walked away after wishing Rorvik and Baxter well on the riverside, and then he'd been waiting for them when they approached the Library entrance a few hours later. He gave them only the bare details of an explanation, but they were enough; Avery Sim was dead, apparently killed by an Elite, and there were strangers in the house.

A square, sturdy service robot came into view around the curve of the passage. It was built like a small tank and motored along on powerful legs which hissed and clicked as their hydraulics pumped, and a single eye on a gooseneck table studied the floor ahead for obstructions. It stamped towards the doorway without hesitation and at the last moment the blue haze flicked out of existence. Then it was through and the haze resumed.

'Less than five seconds,' Xylem whispered.

'Much less,' Rorvik agreed. 'There's no chance of walking through behind it.'

The robot drew level with them, and the gooseneck eye swivelled to seek out the area of reported damage. It saw the unseated shielding and the handful of bulging wire and began to chatter in apparent annoyance.

In a move that Baxter found strangely unsettling the single eye turned through one hundred and eighty degrees. It seemed to be glowering at them in accusation but then it bent and inspected an array of handling devices clipped to its casing. It selected one and extended an adaptable arm to remove and fix it into place. When the complicated hand was in place the robot returned its attention to the scanners and began to sort through each individual component, testing and replacing where necessary.

'That's it, then,' Baxter said. 'At best only one of us could get through. The others would be fried.'

'That's if we just follow it,' Rorvik replied. 'But there may be another way. One in front, one behind, and one hanging on to the casing.'

Baxter was doubtful, but Xylem said, 'It might work. The only other way would be to do three lots of damage and that would slow us down.'

'We can't afford that,' Rorvik said. 'We've got to get well inside before the Elite can work out how we came this far. Then they'll try to follow us and stop us. We either go now or turn back, in which case they'll get us anyway.'

The logic was persuasive, and Baxter had to agree. As the robot tidied up the loose ends of its repairs and stowed its prosthetics they moved to positions on either side of the doorway. The screen fizzed uncomfortably close and there was a tangy, metallic smell in the air.

The robot was unable to turn easily but shuffled in a gradual arc as its legs set up a chorus of clicks and tiny escapements of air. Then it lurched towards them and the noises settled into a regular pattern as it trudged down the corridor.

Baxter stepped out at the last possible moment. He felt a bump as the robot pressed into his back and then a second, less steady pressure as Rorvik heaved himself aboard and the robot's hydraulics fought to compensate for the sudden increase in weight. The screen blinked out, and Baxter was rammed forward as Xylem shoved the robot casing with all his strength from behind. It tottered through the doorway out of control; Rorvik lost his grip and slid to the floor. The robot, suddenly relieved of the weight, spun sideways and banged against the door arch. Xylem tried to stop himself, but it was too late. He bounced and fell as the robot lurched free; the screen fired back at full intensity and wrapped a crackling blue light around Xylem's outstretched arm.

They grabbed him and hauled him through. There was a flash and a popping sound as the screen closed up behind his hand.

Xylem's breath rasped heavily behind the mask, so much that Baxter thought he might suffocate. But then Xylem got his control back and began to regulate his breathing, and they brought his arm around to take a look at it. His knuckles scraped across the floor, and the hand flopped uselessly like a puppet's.

The skin of Xylem's arm was so pale that it was almost transparent; veins in delicate shades of blue tracing like a bloodleaf under the surface, a fine network in wax. The skin wasn't broken, but there was a line of tiny red beads where the force of the screen had fallen. It was like a razor had been lightly drawn across. Xylem said that he was getting no sensation from the hand at all.

They carefully lifted his arm and placed it across his body. Xylem winced as they did it, but he said nothing. Then they stripped to their shirts, and tore out the sleeves; by knotting them end to end they were able to bind Xylem's arm into place.

The service robot had whistled and chattered angrily for a while at nobody in particular, and then it had stamped off and disappeared around the inner curve of the dome. This corridor was an extension of the last, but the standard of its finish was lower. The floor was seamless and flat, but the walls were pre-formed units roughly assembled. There were no scanners or beams, and lighting levels were reduced to suit the sensitivity of broad-spectrum cameras. It wasn't good, but it was enough to see by; Rorvik and Baxter got Xylem over by the wall where he could sit and recover, and then they went ahead to scout around the curve.

'This is going to slow us down,' Baxter said as soon as they'd moved far enough not to be heard.

Rorvik shrugged, and looked ahead; more curved sections, a journey's end that would always be just out of reach. Already it was different from the plans that he'd seen. This was supposed to be an indexing section—but then, once Central became self-sufficient it wouldn't need an external index. Robot work crews would have remodelled the level into something more useful. He said, 'Maybe it won't matter.'

'It had better,' Baxter said. 'I'm here to kick the system, not to get snuffed. And I'm not going to let you settle for less.'

They both turned quickly as a long shadow fell across them; it was Xylem, one hand on the prefabricated corridor wall for safety. He said, 'What's this? Off into a clique at the first opportunity?'

Rorvik said, 'Sorry,' and managed to look guilty as he said it. Baxter was more open.

'We were talking about your arm,' he said. 'There could be climbing ahead.'

'I'll do it one-handed if I have to,' Xylem said. 'What's my alternative? Turn around and walk back out, with the Elite waiting? No, thanks.' He indicated the mask with his free hand. 'Maybe you're thinking I could take this off and slip past them. What do you think's underneath? A citizen's face?'

Rorvik started to mutter an embarrassed apology, but Baxter

didn't waste his time. He said, 'Let's move on,' and started to walk.

RANDALL AND Killoran crouched by the turnstile, watching and listening. Several people gave them curious glances but nobody spoke to them, and so they were uninterrupted as they followed the progress of a citizen as she approached the waist-high restraint.

She waited for a moment, and the greeting announcement came.

'You are now entering the Library division of Central Command.' The computer's standard delivery was filtered and tinny through a cheap speaker, and its level was low, so that it didn't compete with the identical announcement at the next turnstile. 'As you step through the gate, place both hands palm-down on the metal plates. Place any luggage on the chute.' She had no luggage, but offered her palm-prints as requested. 'Thank you. Enjoy your visit.' The restraint swung away and she rejoined the crowd on the other side.

'There,' Randall said, 'Now, am I right or am I wrong?'

Killoran was doubtful. 'It could be. But I still think it's too obvious.'

'Obvious? What can be more obvious than a maniac and two cronies on the loose in the nerve centre of the city? But try telling that to Central. All you get is the threat of an early pension.'

They left the foyer and walked towards the temporary command centre that was being set up on the open piazza before the Library. Killoran said, 'Are you serious? Central says you're finished after this?' Randall's silence was confirmation. 'Well, pardon me for saying so, but it doesn't seem to have diminished your enthusiasm.'

'I'm not doing this to please Central!' Randall said angrily. 'Suppose Rorvik goes mad in there, starts pulling out wires on all sides. What do you think will happen?'

'Depends which wires he pulls.'

'We couldn't know. He certainly wouldn't. But with every wire that gets pulled, something goes down—something that we could never put back. Citizens are such a bunch of sheep, all they'd do would be to sit and flap. There'd be chaos.'

'You really love the city, don't you?' Killoran said with a thin trace of irony.

Randall stopped by the incomplete geodesic of the incident control room. It didn't often come out of storage, and the riggers were having trouble piecing the modules together. He said, 'I suppose I do. Not that I was ever given any choice.'

The control room was half-assembled, its panels in a stack by the open framework. When completed it would be a miniature of the Central dome. As they stepped in through an open wall Killoran said, 'I find it hard to believe that Rorvik's just walking round inside and being ignored.'

'Look, forget that it's the Library for a moment. Just imagine that you're managing a building. You count the people coming in and the people going out and when the numbers match, you can close up for the night. But say somebody hops over a turnstile when you're not looking. He doesn't get counted so you don't know he's inside.'

'That's Rorvik.'

'And his two friends. The rule is that you submit to being counted, and citizens obey the rules.'

'But we're not just counted in there. We're tracked.'

Randall could offer no answer to this. Instead he looked around over the beginnings of the command centre; at the moment it was a shambles of plates, brackets and wire. Across the piazza a Police Elite vehicle inched cautiously from the roadway onto the paving, belching smoke as its old motor laboured to boost the back wheels over the sharp edging.

'No good,' Randall said. 'It needs somebody better-informed than me to work it through. We can speculate all we like, but how do we stop him?' He turned to Killoran. 'What about this expert you're fixing me up with?'

'I don't know about him being an expert. Cheap underbelly chiseller, more like. Last report I had was that he was in the 'copter and on his way. That was about ten minutes ago.'

'Right. Let's get out of the way while they're finishing this.' As they stepped from the dome the vehicle stopped alongside.

Some trunks of equipment began to be unloaded to wait for installation.

Randall watched the distant skyline for a flickering of blades. The horizon remained obstinately clear.

AFTER CURVING for some distance the corridor made an abrupt right-angled turn and they emerged into the lower gallery of Central Command. It was a circular chamber with an open area in its middle. Its perimeter was cluttered with the angles and divisions of non-standard service bays.

Central Command was a work in progress, constantly redesigning and improving itself, and here was its workshop. Some bays were active on the far side of the circle with the sparking and flashing of automated welding, while in others row upon row of silent machinery was stacked, unfamiliar shapes bulking in sheltered gloom. Between the bays the walls were obscured by stacks of ringed cables which burst from every surface and disappeared into others, or else ran off to unspecified destinations along channels cut for them.

A four-legged service robot clanked past holding aloft a T-shaped piece of metal. The three men withdrew into their corridor until it had gone. It was tracing a circuitous path to the active bays in the distance, and Baxter said, 'Why doesn't it go straight across? That would cut the journey by a third.'

Rorvik shrugged, by Xylem said, 'Look at the floor.' It was smooth and apparently seamless, and on its surface were the remains of half-erased geometrical forms and traces. 'This is an assembly shop,' Xylem went on. 'The floor's used for laying out and cutting large-scale parts. They don't walk on it to preserve the surface. Morden's got something similar.'

They watched the robot dwindle in the distance and so came to appreciate the scale of the chamber. The roof was supported by four broad curving pillars which intersected at its centre, and illumination was from lines of downward-pointing spots which radiated from this apex. They were obviously switchable, for the entire dome was lit by the overspill from one brilliant area over the work in progress. There, articulated arms were diving in and out with great delicacy around a shapeless object on a central rostrum. It was about the size of a small truck and the arms were testing a joint here, fixing a wire there.

The four-legged robot turned into the bay and waited patiently with its T-piece. In a second it was gone; an arm had snaked out and deftly tweaked the piece from its grasp, and now it turned and began to waddle back around the circle.

'This should be the second of four levels,' Rorvik said. Below us is a raw materials store, and this is the maintenance and construction shop. The next one up should be the memory banks, and above that the information handling facilities. That's where we're heading.'

Baxter tried not to look at Xylem. 'How do we get up?' he said.

'I'm not sure,' Rorvik replied. 'It's not like the floor plans I saw. It's roughly the same, but the details have all changed.'

Xylem said, 'How will the robots transfer between levels? There must be some kind of elevator system.'

It was a sound idea and they tried to follow it through. They walked the circumference of the hall, avoiding the active bays; one of those massive arms might sweep back unexpectedly and cut through them like a scythe. It was Baxter who found the tubular tunnel leading vertically to the floors above and below, but none of them could see a way to summon a platform or to operate one when it arrived.

Two smaller robots clanked past with armloads of plates and parts to supply the engineering operation. They returned unladen a few minutes later, gooseneck eyes bobbing to remain level as the stocky bodies rolled with the motion of walking. Rorvik studied their legs as they passed. The steps they took were short and firm, and he didn't think them easily capable of climbing stairs. No, this elevator had to be the principal method of transfer between levels, and it showed no signs of being in current use.

'We can't afford to wait,' Baxter said after they'd watched the tunnel hopefully for a while. 'It may hardly ever be used. We've got to find another way.'

'I don't see any other way,' Rorvik said.

Xylem pointed to a nearby bunch of wide cables which were

fastened into a deep channel in the wall. 'What about following one of those? They have to emerge somewhere.'

The joints and plates of cladding offered easy footholds, and there was just enough room for a man to squeeze in between the clusters of tubing. Baxter volunteered to be the first to try, and he carefully picked his way upward, testing each hold before he put his weight onto it. After a minute or so he was above the roof level and out of sight.

Rorvik found himself with Xylem. He said, 'How's the arm?'

'Don't worry about that.' Xylem said. 'Worry about how you're going to get us to where we need to be.'

There was a muffled clang somewhere up above. A few seconds later Baxter dropped into view, braced between two pipes but having trouble in keeping his grip. He caught hold of a cross-support and swung out on it, then he dropped the last few feet to the floor.

'There's a route,' he said. He took a moment to get his breath, and then went on. 'I followed a blind alley, but I know where I went wrong. It's easy if you take it slowly—' this with a glance at Xylem '—and it reaches at least as far as the next level. Give me a couple of minutes and I'll be ready to go again.'

RANDALL WATCHED in horror as the 'copter shot from the boulevard. Less than a minute later it had stormed up the river and was angling down towards the piazza, nose-up and rotors beating. Killoran and another officer ran forward as it settled; they were bending as the rotors swept over their heads, an obvious but irrelevant action as there was a wide clearance. As the two helped the passenger to the ground Randall pointed at the pilot and saw his sunglasses flash in response. Randall beckoned angrily, and the pilot extended his middle finger in a timeless gesture and grinned. The motor screamed and the 'copter lifted, turned about its own centre and chattered off over the city.

His name was Vasil, and he staggered slightly as they supported him into the command centre. They sat him down and unlocked his handcuffs, and as he rubbed at the red marks on his wrists he started to look around. He was dark and not very tall, and he was losing his hair. His thin face gave him a starved look, made more so by the hungry quickness of his eyes; an alert undertaker's mute, Randall thought as he waited for Vasil to get settled.

The bargaining didn't take long. Vasil was too shaken to give much coherent attention to it, and he didn't start pressing for extra advantages; registering for supervised work in the city looked better than exile in the ice belt, and he grabbed it.

Randall explained his ideas about the turnstiles, but Vasil only shrugged. 'You're getting technical,' he said. 'I told them I couldn't do anything if you got technical. I cheated the machine, but that doesn't mean I know how it works.'

'Tell me how you cheated it, then.'

Vasil frowned. He didn't like the idea of handing over details of a source of support that he might need to use again if he got desperate.

Randall said, 'Either you tell us, or you get the ice belt.'

'But you've promised.'

'We set up a trade. You don't come up with your side, I don't need to come up with mine.'

Vasil obviously wasn't happy, but then he didn't have much choice. He said, 'Getting it going was hard. Keeping it going was easy. The machine doesn't think like people, it thinks in straight lines. Every cantina's got a code number, and Central's obviously set a bunch of numbers aside for the cantinas and nothing else. What I did was check the waste outside three or four places for old forms, and average out the number groups. That way I could work out a number in the bunch that wasn't allocated, and then I stole some forms and started to use it. Central recognised the number as one of its own, and it was happy. Once that had been accepted, I could get away with anything.'

'Anything?' Randall said.

'As long as Central was happy with the identification, everything else followed automatically. That's the difference in dealing with machines and dealing with people. Tell a machine what it's expecting, and it'll believe you forever—even if it means sending deliveries over into the underbelly.'

'You brassy bastard!' Killoran said from behind, and Randall waved to him to be quiet.

'Where did you go wrong?'

'I had to make an end-of-quarter return to balance the books. Some dishonest bastard sold me a list of fake credit card numbers, and that broke the line.'

'And Central realised?'

'You could call it that. Realising's something that people do—machines just respond. A follows B follows C—that's a program. Do it lots of times and do it fast, and you've got something pretty impressive—but it's still just a program. Maybe your turnstiles are the beginning of the line in the security programme, I wouldn't know. Hop a turnstile, and the programme doesn't roll.'

No program; no tracking; nothing to stop them.

ELEVEN

First into the cable-trap, Baxter was first out on the next level. Xylem was labouring hard somewhere below, and as Rorvik watched for some way that he might help he became certain that the underbelly's arm was beginning to cause him pain on top of the extra effort he was using to pull himself upward.

Baxter rolled over. The elevator tunnel was alongside, and he watched in dumb disbelief as an apparently unsupported platform hissed neatly into place from below and a service robot stepped off and strode past. The platform dropped away again without any sound at all, and the tunnel was empty as before.

He wanted to laugh at the absurdity, and gave up on the idea. Instead he made the effort to get to his feet and followed the robot.

The entire level was like a metal honeycomb knitted around internally-lit blue-glass towers. The further walls were obscured by a webbing of narrow ramps which linked and serviced die memory stores, and as Baxter watched, his robot shuffled onto one such ramp where it met the floor. Its legs adjusted easily to the incline and it turned onto another ramp at the next intersection, and it was soon lost to Baxter as it circled behind the nearest of the towers. When it passed out of view another crossed his line of vision and was similarly lost. The ramps were an exact width, room for one robot with no passing. As they moved around the level Central was switching their paths like goods trains so that they collaborated into a complex pattern of moving, adjusting and repairing.

At a sound Baxter turned. Xylem was reaching over the edge of the cable trap onto the floor with his good arm, but he wasn't getting any grip with it. Baxter hurried back to help, and with

Rorvik pushing from beneath they manhandled Xylem out onto the level.

Rorvik heaved himself over and rolled to sit beside Xylem, who was stretched out with his right arm cradling his left. The cloth straps showed signs of coming astray and Baxter rearranged them, exchanging a glance with Rorvik.

Rorvik said nothing, and in the end it was Xylem himself who broke the silence. 'I don't think I'll be able to manage another climb like that,' he said. 'The effort's too much with only one arm. If it gets any worse you'll have to go on without me.'

'It gets easier from here,' Baxter said, and described the network of ramps that lay ahead.

Xylem propped himself up to see. 'That doesn't sound too bad,' he said.

'The blue towers are the memory banks,' Rorvik added. 'They're filled with a liquid under a continuous charge which fixes the relationship of all the molecules in a certain pattern. That gets away from the whole idea of physical recordings which eventually wear out; as long as the charge stays, so does the information.'

'I don't pretend to understand that,' Xylem replied.

'What I want to know is, what's the travel going to be like from here?'

Baxter said, 'Simple. We just use the ramps to walk up to the information handling level, making sure that there isn't a robot using the glideway that we're on.'

Rorvik allowed a slight apprehension to show. 'And if there is?'

'We step aside at an intersection until it passes. It'll be like high-level travel in the underbelly.'

Rorvik nodded, less than reassured. Obviously he'd once followed the same ropeway route as Lin Baxter.

'NO!' THE FRACTIONAL increase in urgency was disquieting from the computer. Was it genuinely angry, Randall wondered? But he remembered Vasil's explanation of a vast calculating entity, and understood that any such expression would be generated for the specific purpose of the response it would evoke. 'I refuse to contemplate such an ill-formed notion,' it went on. 'My security is perfect.'

'You only think it's perfect,' Randall insisted, knowing the argument was futile but pursuing it anyway. 'That's because you can't imagine otherwise.'

'I deal in facts, not badly-conceived human flights of imagination. I am machine, not subject to irrational fantasies!'

'You won't listen,' Randall said, exasperated. 'I'm explaining the truth and you're not interested.'

'Truth? Save your subjective ideals. I will tell you what the truth is.'

'But listen to the evidence. You must be getting hundreds, thousands of stimuli that all point to the same conclusion! Three men have bypassed your turnstiles and are walking around inside you.'

'Such a concept does not even exist.' It was unmistakable this time; sharp, superior contempt.

'Then how can I even describe it to you?'

'Mere semantics of a language not my own. I am removing you from the Elite, Randall. Leave me now. I promote your assistant in your place.'

BELOW THEIR walkway a tower glowed with a momentarily increased brightness as the chains and connections of a man's life were rapidly broken and destroyed. His rights, his privileges, his identity undone. It went unnoticed in the general flicker and pulsing.

Xylem moved easily in the elevated maze, and as the way became more complex they inclined to trust his underbelly instincts in the selection of a route. The incline of the ramps was shallow but there was no protection from the drop on either side, and Baxter fought hard to keep his mind away from the prospect of falling. They looped and circled away from the floor, finally losing sight of it altogether. When a service robot approached they felt a vibration beneath their feet before they actually saw anything, but with this warning they were able to step off the path at the next intersection and wait until it had passed.

'I felt something,' Baxter said. He was usually the first to notice.

In front or behind?' Rorvik asked.

'No way of telling.'

Xylem looked doubtful. 'I didn't feel anything. Are you sure?'

'I haven't been wrong yet.' They all felt it then, a short, regular throb on the platform.

The robot came into view ahead of them and, inexplicably, stopped. It was one of the four-legged heavy-duty models, and the bulk of its solid body overhung the path on either side. Xylem said, 'We'd better hurry. There's only one turnoff ahead.'

Wary of their height they moved along the metal ribbon to the intersection. 'We're in trouble,' Baxter said. 'There's another one.'

This was obviously the reason for the first robot stopping; it was waiting as the other cleared the junction. It approached steadily along the arm of the Y, and without discussion the three turned to go back down the main path and leave it at the next opportunity.

It crouched there, making retreat impossible. They hadn't heard it follow. This robot was a variant from the others, a special adaptation; it was like a large tortoise with a clump of sensory apparatus at the front and four articulated arms, smaller models of those in the welding shop below, mounted on the shell. They were tipped with a wicked array of grabs and drills.

'I think we're trapped,' Baxter said, unnecessarily.

'I don't understand it,' Rorvik said. 'They can't pass each other. One of them will have to go back.' He looked around. All three robots had stopped and were ticking quietly.

'Don't you think,' Baxter said, 'that it's rather inefficient to end up with three machines on the one glideway?'

'What do you mean?'

'I mean it looks like a deliberate trap. Why else other than to corner us?'

Rorvik glanced at the ramp's edge. There was quite a drop beyond it. 'But Central doesn't see us,' he said.

'Maybe Security doesn't see us,' Xylem joined in. 'But maybe an obstruction on the glideways is a maintenance issue.'

'Never mind the reason,' Baxter said desperately. 'We're going to be pushed off the edge!' The bright tortoise had lifted and was clanking towards them.

Rorvik stared blankly as it advanced. Xylem saw that there wasn't another glideway within twenty feet of their own, but an idea occurred.

'Move up to where the paths join. When it follows, we let it trap us on one or the other. Then when it closes in it will have to make a turn to follow us, and we've seen how slow they are. As soon as it clears the main path we step back across the fork, and that puts us outside the net.'

Baxter was doubtful. 'That's a leap, not a step,' he said. 'And that's a long way down.'

'That's kind of academic. Come on, let's get moving.'

The tortoise marshalled them onto the side-branch and then shuffled round to orientate itself and follow. The two plain service machines still ticked without moving, above and behind them.

'It's got to be fast,' Xylem said.

It was a good stride and a little more. A harmless distance on the ground, but at this height... Rorvik saw Baxter tensing up beside him. *You thought he was shallow*, he told himself. *You thought you'd leave him behind. Come on, Rorvik, you've got some catching up to do.* They both moved at the same time.

An endless criss-cross of silver hung in space beneath him as he sailed over nothing. Then he was on the main path, overcorrecting to balance and sliding off his feet in a heap. His head banged on the metal and sparks seemed to fly behind his eyes, but Baxter's grip on his arm hauled him back from the slide towards and over the opposite edge.

Two citizens; one sprawling, one crouching. They looked expectantly across to Xylem.

'Go on,' he called to them. 'It won't follow you while it's holding me here.' And he backed off further from the intersection, well beyond the range of a reasonable jump.

No!' Baxter shouted. 'We're safe! Get over while you can!'

But the robot closed the gap and effectively sealed Xylem

onto the side-branch.

'Let's face it, I'm expendable,' he insisted, 'and you'd have to leave me anyway. This way you get more of a chance. Don't waste it.'

'This is pointless,' Rorvik shouted. 'We're safe.'

Xylem didn't answer. He was preoccupied with his chances of survival. They watched as he was forced back towards where the service robot sat impassively across the glideway, and when he could retreat no further he looked around and down.

A path crossed beneath, a drop of over twice the height of a man. Xylem stared hard, trying to fix the distance and the angle in his mind. The makeshift bandages held his useless arm close against his body, a dead weight and now a dangerous liability.

He stepped out into nothing, for a jump would carry him too far. He didn't fall straight, and only one foot hit the edge of the ramp. The sudden off-centre jar flipped him sideways, spinning in an uncontrollable cartwheel of arm and legs away from safety and into the long descent.

There was a strangled cry of rage and frustration which cut off abruptly as the body dropped out of sight. The tortoise reached the service robot, and the moment before their surfaces touched it stopped.

Baxter helped Rorvik to his feet. Rorvik hardly noticed. 'Why?' he said numbly. 'Why should he do that?'

The three robots remained immobile, and the road away was open. Baxter moved to follow it, but Rorvik's hand in a tight grip on his arm restrained him. Then he heard it as well, a thin, high-pitched and formless whisper which was blowing like a cold wind around them.

Rorvik knelt and pressed his hand flat against the metal of the glideway. There was a definite vibration all along it, and he felt its intensity like the distant rumble of traffic in an underpass. The whispering became a keening and then broke up to form definite attempts and shapes of words. Even before those words were recognisable they knew the tone and timbre of the voice, hearing distorted as it was and strangling to overcome the difficulties of unnatural speech.

'Rorvik,' was recognisable in a torrent of syllables, and then

'You won't escape. I'll get you next time.'

The effort of expression became too much and the sound disintegrated into a tangle of random noise before dying away completely.

'Xylem was right,' Rorvik said. 'We bypassed Security but Central knows we're here and it's got some limited powers it can use against us. We'd better keep moving.'

THE INSTALLATION of the command centre was complete. The curved radio desk was live and lit, and before it was a rig of display screens which were, for the moment, blank, as were the backlit map and diagram boards behind the command chair.

Killoran slid out of the chair as Randall stepped through the double flaps which maintained the general dimness of the lighting.

'Trying it for size?' Randall said.

Killoran knew better than to be embarrassed. 'You never know,' he replied. 'They can't ignore talent forever.'

'You can sit down again. That's where I want you.'

'What do you mean?'

'There was no joy from Central, no joy at all. It turned down the whole idea and fired me, stripped me of rank and responsibilities.'

'And you're just going to accept that?'

'Like hell I am. Slap yourself on that chair and use the lines to get me an explosives man and a sonic scanner—the type we use for density on the other side of a wall. I also want a blaster from stores and some charges to go with it.'

Killoran pulled the flexible microphone towards himself and reached to open the lines, uneasy in his sudden authority. Randall looked round as a slight movement caught his eye and saw Vasil sitting by the coffee machine. He went over to draw himself a cup.

'Do I have to be here?' Vasil said. He lifted his hands, and a short length of chain clicked; they'd handcuffed him to the coffee machine.

'Rather looks like you do, doesn't it?' Randall said, and moved away. Killoran ended his messages and sat back, and one of the display screens immediately translated the list of materials into a formal-looking visual with an estimated time of supply listed next to each. As he watched, the seconds began to tick away from all the items.

'What's the scanner for?' he asked as Randall came over to look.

'I want to run it along the base of the dome. It was a working building full of offices once, and I want to find the part that's changed least. They've got over an hour's start on me, and I'll need a short cut.'

'To where?'

'Up, where the programming centres are supposed to be. A stairway, or a lift shaft—anything that will get me to them.'

THEY LOOKED down on the memory banks from a gallery of doors.

'Doors with handles?' Baxter said.

'We must be getting closer. The programming centres probably haven't been altered at all.'

Baxter tried one of the doors. It was locked. The only obvious access was an open arch on the other side of the gallery, and as they looked another new design of robot trundled through on hidden wheels and rolled off down into the memory banks.

'I've got a feeling this may all be a waste of time,' Rorvik said as they moved around towards it.

'What do you mean?' Baxter said sharply.

'You know what I mean. Central knows we're here, it even called me by name. What chance have we got now?'

'What chance did we ever have?' Baxter stopped, and Lee had to turn to face him. 'You're supposed to be the kingpin, the rebel, the one that Central's afraid of. We had to prise you out of hiding, and now I have to listen while you call failure down on us.'

'I'm trying to be realistic.'

'Being realistic has run the city down into nothing. Dream a little, for a change.'

'Look, I can't guarantee an easy walk. We may have dodged

security, but there are other sub-routines in the programme. Maybe they can be adapted, I don't know. We've blocked it, but it's still trying.'

'Let it try, then,' Baxter said.

MORE SCREENS were lighting up as new sources of information were being patched in. As he waited for the sonic scan of the base of the dome to be completed Randall watched over Killoran's shoulder. A moving graph showed a continuous increase in the drain of power into Central.

What was it playing at? He watched the graph line rise for a while longer, then he said, 'Have they finished the scan yet?'

'The results are being processed. I did as you said and gave a false location to the computer before we fed them in.' It was the only way; Central would stop the whole operation if it knew that the Elite was scanning its own dome.

The readout flashed that the scan display was ready. Killoran transferred it to one of the diagram boards behind them, freeing the screen for another source. As they turned to study it one of the radio officers ducked in through the low door, and one of the screen estimate timings reached zero.

'I'll be with you in a moment,' Randall said, and he turned to study the board.

A strip of varied-density dots showed the results of echo sounding Central's lower levels to a limited depth. At one point there was a large cleared area, too big for any kind of room and too high for a corridor.

'Some kind of hall or plaza,' Killoran suggested.

'Could be. It's the best-looking bet for me to find a stairway. Mark off the co-ordinates and send the explosives team down.'

The radio officer was waiting. He had a jacket slung over his arm, and Randall said, 'Is that it?'

The officer nodded. 'Built-in transmitter with body aerial. Try it for size.'

The jacket was light and tough, and it had reinforcement on the back and shoulders. A tiny microphone extended from around his collarbone to a point where it could pick up his speech without interfering with the movement of his head, and on the other side was a small earpiece. As he was being levered and tucked into the unit, Randall said, 'What's the estimate on the blaster?'

Killoran consulted a display. 'Any time now. It's on its way from Elite HQ. Do you think you'll use it?'

'I'd prefer not to, but if I have to, I will.'

'The explosives team are marking off the side of the building now.'

'Right. I'll get down there. Have the armaments officer re-routed to meet me.'

He went without any great show or drama, and Killoran tracked with one of his cameras as Randall crossed the piazza. The radio officer trailed closely behind, making adjustments with difficulty as they walked.

BAXTER WAS unable to suppress the wonder that he felt at the necropolis which was untouched by Central's self-remodelling operations. They walked on a sticky dust that had once been carpet down a corridor that had once housed the preoccupations and frustrations of a busy administration. They were off the robot routes so there was no light, and the dead fittings in the ceiling above held no promise of illumination. Rorvik's beam was at its widest, but for him the brilliant detail of the way ahead only emphasised fears of the shadows behind.

'More locked doors,' Baxter said.

'Perhaps not. Try one.'

The door squealed as it swung inward on hinges dried out of oil, and then jarred against something behind. Baxter said, 'Let's take a look inside.'

Rorvik found the idea of further entrapment too much to accept, but could hardly give this as a reason. 'Take the beam and be quick, then,' he said. 'I'll stay out here and keep watch.'

Keeping watch was a futile exercise, for now the corridor was only illuminated by reflected flashes from the office as Baxter probed around inside.

Baxter first checked behind the door to see what was interfering with it, and found an old wooden coat-stand tilted into the corner by the weight of a heap of material draped over one of its hooks. Dust belched from its folds as he removed it and put it over his arm to show to Rorvik, and then he began to run the beam over the furnishings of the rest of the office.

Rorvik gave a sudden start. Somebody had whispered his name out in the darkness. It came again, low and persuasive.

'Rorvik. I know you are there. Answer me.'

It was a moment before he could speak. 'Where are you?'

'You know where I am. I am all around you. Why must you hate me?'

'How do I hear you?'

'Walls, floors, ceilings, wires, I use them all. With them I hear, and when I reverse the process I speak. I am alive, Rorvik, you know that. Why would you do me harm?'

'How do you know who I am?'

'I congratulate you. You have blinded me and tied my hands, but remember you have not disabled me yet. Can we not talk, come to some arrangement? The consequences otherwise could be so unfortunate.'

Rorvik felt the vibration of the wall behind his back. Central was using the entire corridor as a sound-board to reach him. It knew exactly where he was, for the effect was localised, the movements of the beam showing that Baxter continued his tour of the office unconcerned.

'We've nothing to discuss,' Rorvik said.

'Please do not close your mind. Our contact could be so constructive.' Under the thin distorted voice was the low hum which characterised every conversation that Rorvik could remember from his Library visits. 'I do so wish to understand the non-conformist,' it went on. 'To grasp his place in the scheme of things.'

'I don't want you to understand me. You have no right to that.'

The hum screwed itself up to become a more insistent whine. 'Then you leave me no option. I have powers beyond my security systems.'

The corridor was flooded with light as Baxter emerged holding the beam, the old overcoat still on his arm. His face was pale and set, but as the whine became a shrill whistle Rorvik didn't wait to find out why.

'Get back in the doorway,' he shouted. 'Something's happening, and I don't know what.' As he spoke the lightbulb in the fitting over his head imploded with a sharp pop, and a handful of glass showered down.

Baxter hadn't moved, but stared without comprehension. As detonations fired off all down the corridor he seemed to come awake, and as Rorvik reached for him to push him back into safety he said, 'No! Not in there!' and began to fight against the pressure on his arm. Dust was banged out of the coat and Rorvik caught a stinging lungful as an electric plug socket blasted out of the wall near his legs. It sprayed hot plastic halfway across the corridor.

'Not in the office!' Baxter was shouting over the noise. Something under the floor ruptured and began pouring steam, and doors along the row sprang open one after another. The entire wall was bending.

It gave way with a loud crack, easily audible over the raging babble of other sounds.

The wall folded and dropped over them.

TWELVE

As Randall walked to the far side of Central Command, Killoran tested the radio link. The signal from the suspended microphone was reedy but clear, and Randall seemed to have no trouble picking up the replies through the earpiece. Killoran cut across his bank of cameras to follow his progress, and when he arrived at the suggested entry point a touch on a rocker switch motored the lens in to give a closer view.

'The building's between us now,' Randall said, looking toward one of the spindly camera rigs in the distance and hoping he had the right one. 'Is there any loss of signal?'

Killoran had him full face and shoulders on the screen. 'None. If there is, the receiver amps can compensate and then filter some of the noise.'

Randall nodded, and one or two of the blast team saw the movement without hearing the signal from the earpiece and exchanged comments about the madman who wanted a hole in the Library. Then they saw that Randall was watching and hurriedly shut up.

The charges were rigged in a neat arch on the curving concrete skirt below the dome's panelling. The limp wire aerial of a signal detonator hung from each taped package. Randall crossed to where the team leader was supervising the waveband setting of the detonator switch and identified himself. The team leader delegated the job and accompanied Randall over to the wall in order to explain the principle of the blasting.

He said, 'We're using a high concentrate blast which spreads in a cone away from the detonator. Most of it will go straight into the wall instead of being wasted as noise.'

Randall tried to appear as if he understood. 'Is this the point we gave you on the scan?'

'No. We looked at the chart and found the thinnest point near to it.'

'But...'

'We could have placed it exactly where you asked, but then we'd have needed so much that we'd have dug a pit out underneath for you as well.'

Randall didn't like it, but he accepted it. 'Neil,' he said, touching the microphone for no other reason than it made it obvious he wasn't talking to himself. 'We're nearly ready to go here. How's the estimate on the blaster?'

'I've got the weapons officer in shot now. He's walking as if he had a crawler in his pants.'

Randall turned, and saw an officious little man with a walk to match his manner. He was holding before him a carrier bag as if it contained some revolting object, and he homed in on Randall immediately.

'Randall?'

'It's Inspector Randall.'

The weapons officer smiled smugly. 'Not any more, it isn't.'

'Just give me the gun.' Randall reached for it, and the weapons officer drew it back protectively.

'And who's going to sign for it?'

'Get a signature from the presiding officer in the command centre. I assume you know the procedure?' The weapons officer parted with his bag reluctantly. Randall reached inside and brought out a blaster with a belt hook. Taped to it was a sealed packet of charges. 'Only six?' he said.

'It's not a machine gun,' the officer replied primly. 'And don't take the paper tag off.'

The tag to which he referred flapped under the blaster's shaped handle. 'Why not?'

'It has to be returned with the docket after use.'

'Keep it for me.' Randall jerked and it tore away, and the officer began an indignant protest. Killoran joined in and suggested where the officer might keep the docket safely. Randall replied, 'Watch it,' and the weapons officer misunderstood and was instantly silent. He accepted the docket and strutted off to be obnoxious somewhere else.

'The less time I waste, the better.' Randall looked out again towards the camera. 'Does Vasil want to say anything?'

There was a pause. Then there was a reluctant mumbling, as if Vasil was grudgingly thinking of his own future. 'He says if you keep on the move, there's a chance you'll beat any reprogramming.'

'Anything else?'

Another pause. 'He says good luck.'

'I see. And what about you?'

'I'm keeping quiet. I've got my promotion to consider.'

Killoran touched the rocker switch again, and his view began to widen and spread, and the tangle of men and equipment in the blast area contracted into the picture.

Randall was in the middle, and everybody was stepping aside to avoid him.

IN THE OPEN frame of the broken doorway Rorvik threw the thick material of the overcoat off his head and heard plaster scatter down onto the floor. The beam was buried somewhere and he couldn't find it.

Baxter groaned and then started to cough at the smell of burnt wiring. As he hauled upright Rorvik heard the slide of cloth and then a metallic clank, and when he reached for the sound his fingers touched the cold metal of the hand beam. The casing was dented and the recessed switch jammed halfway, but a glow as dim as firelight was better than nothing.

The corridor was minus a side. It now lay as a broken and uneven floor, and as the swirl of dust reflected their light back it was possible to see no further than the jagged edge where it had previously met the ceiling.

'Feels like the world fell in,' Baxter said, but he stopped abruptly as Rorvik's name was called gently from the air around them.

Rorvik met his gaze and nodded. Baxter wanted to crawl back under the coat. Three gods on an enormous enterprise had suddenly become two children without hope.

'Turn back and you will come to no harm,' the computer reassured him softly from the mist. 'Proceed, and I regret to say you will be dead.' There was a pause. 'Rorvik?'

'I'm here,' he confessed in resignation.

'Are you listening? Or are you already too weak to crawl away?'

Baxter's terror had given way to a frown. 'It's calling you by name again,' he said. 'It knows you. Does it know I'm here as well?'

'What do you mean?'

'I don't exist. Central told me so. I think I'm one step further outside its perception. It can't see me!' His voice almost raised in excitement beyond a low murmur, but he caught it in time. 'What's the danger if we go on?' he whispered.

'It'll get less as we get nearer. Central won't dare to damage anything it won't be able to repair.'

'It's listening through the building, right?'

'By vibration. It told me as much.'

'So it can't distinguish me from you.'

Rorvik had to agree. 'What are you thinking of?'

'Separate. You keep its attention, and I'll go and bang on the wall. We should cover a fair distance before it can sort the signals out and retaliate.'

Baxter raised himself carefully and felt something tug at his arm; looking down he shook the coat away with distaste, and glanced over his shoulder into the gaping unlit offices before stepping tentatively out.

If it could distinguish speech, it would hear Baxter move. 'I'm still here!' Rorvik shouted. Baxter wasn't walking, but skipping crablike over the rubble.

'So I observe. Are you injured?'

'I don't know. Would you care?'

Central, it seemed, was hurt. 'Of course I would care. You are a citizen, and my brief is to protect the citizens.' Baxter slipped on a loose panel and barely kept his balance. Rorvik began to move and stir the loose blocks around him to add to the distraction. 'Then you've... you've exceeded your brief.'

'How do you reach that conclusion?' Polite enquiry.

'Because I'm a citizen. You try to destroy me and then inquire after my health.'

'Only because your behaviour forces it upon me,' the walls echoed regretfully.

'And what about the grey little life you forced on me?'

'Try to forget your emotions for a moment. They are clouding your judgement. Remember you are all my children, and my purpose is to protect you. Try to see the wider viewpoint with me, to work for the greatest good of the greatest number. We have no room for minorities in a democracy.'

Rorvik didn't know the word. 'Or for individuals either?'

'Now you begin to understand. You must trust my judgement and my abilities.'

'Never. When you know so little about me.'

'But I have held your file since birth.'

'I am not my file!'

Baxter was almost beyond the curve of the corridor. He searched around for a metal strip or a stick.

'You, your file, to me they are both the same.'

'Exactly. You think that's enough. But you can't know enough!'

'But I can. Whatever knowledge I was not given, I have acquired. Tell me where you consider my areas of ignorance lie.'

There was a half-buried rod. Baxter tried to ease it out without attracting attention.

Rorvik thought of a dead sentiment and its tawdry pastiche in the tapes. 'What about love?' he demanded,

aware of a schoolyard twinge of embarrassment as the word came out. 'You can't know anything of that.'

'Love?' said the computer confidently. 'I have seen all forms of love, I am familiar with each; their chemical, their biological, their physical functions; the parameters of their psychology, their influence on behaviour. Do not look to me for ignorance of love.'

Rorvik was on his feet and scampering down the corridor as Baxter beat a deafening war drum on a door. The light bobbed at his belt and danced flame-like along the wall as he ran.

'Stop it!' the walls cried. 'What are you doing? What is happening?'

Baxter flung the rod through the glass panel in the door and turned to join Rorvik. Behind them in the empty corridor some wiring popped and fizzed weakly as they reached a junction and turned towards the heart of the dome.

Steam drifted over the tiny fires and choked them. Behind the walls ruptured piping shook as if in anger.

'Again I trusted you,' it rumbled. 'Again you betray me. But for the last time.'

They stopped running, for the light was unreliable at speed. Both were secretly glad as the effort ceased.

'Do you think we're safe now?' Baxter asked breathlessly.

'We're never safe. But we can't be far away. Central can't risk fire in its own processing centres, so that's something.'

They passed the blank doors of a disused elevator and stopped as Rorvik took the probe from his belt bag and tried to force the switch of the hand beam to the fully open position in its buckled mount.

'We were lucky back there,' he said as he worked, 'but we'd have been safer in that office. What was wrong?'

'There was a dead man in there.'

Rorvik stopped and looked up.

'Behind the desk. All dried out and old. I don't want to talk about it.'

Futures had done a fast, cheap job; their field men were among the best.

No, it was a ridiculous thought. One man, probably, a heart attack at his desk and too late to escape the sealing of the building.

But as the switch snapped over, the stark rows of office doors marching down either side of the corridor came into the light, as pale and anonymous as war graves.

RANDALL WAS wired up, plugged in, and primed with six exploding charges. He was padded against blast and missile, could resist a degree of laser exposure on his covered surfaces, carried his own source of light and still had both hands free. The all-purpose package was light, mobile and, in theory, ready for anything. Privately that same package wished it were somewhere else.

The team leader pointed to a cross which had been roughly painted on the concrete. It was still wet, and somebody had walked over it.

'This is where you stand,' he said. 'You are perfectly safe at this distance or even closer, because all the forces should go inwards.'

'*Should* go inwards?'

'*Will* go inwards, then. I'm aiming for a neat bang to take the wall out in one piece. No danger to you at all.'

Randall looked at the side of Central, primed to kill only twenty feet away. Much as he disliked the idea, he would have to trust the team's expertise. 'You still getting me, Neil?' he said out loud.

'Loud and clear,' said the voice in his head. 'Report as often as you can.'

'I'll try. I'm getting into position now.' He raised his voice to reach the team leader. 'Stand by for the signal to blast.'

'Standing by,' came a voice faintly in the distance.

Randall turned in surprise, the painted cross smearing beneath his feet. The entire blast team, leader included, was cowering behind their truck a hundred yards away with their hands over their ears.

'There's confidence for you,' Killoran said, and Randall remembered the wide view covered by the screens. Impatiently he raised his arm and, after a second, dropped it.

Nothing happened.

'What's the matter?' Randall shouted.

The team leader stood up and waved his detonating transmitter. 'Seems to be a fault,' he called. 'I'll just have to. . .'

Whatever it was, he'd done it, for there was a muffled crack and Central broke open as if it were hard cake icing. A neat circle detached and dropped, shaking the concrete and leaving a raw black hole. When the brief smoke cleared Randall had gone, leaving only a trail of fading painted footprints.

'I told him it would be all right,' the team leader said to his men as they nervously emerged. 'Didn't I tell him?'

THE SENSOR CELL on Randall's shoulder felt the light slipping away and warmed up to compensate, charging the lamp at his hip. The passage angled before him as he ran, its further reaches concealed beyond the curve.

Five steps at the end of the corridor led into the old foyer. It was a cavern of a chamber, walled by dusty glass on one side. Through it Randall could see the rough inner surface of the concrete wall. This was why the sonics had shown extra thickness here; the concrete skirt on the base of the dome covered an original exterior. The floor was black marble in jointed sections, and similar marble pillars supported the roof. At the far end he could see steps and the entrance to another corridor, and next to them was a windowless doorway and a long-abandoned reception desk. As he crossed to them he described the scene to Killoran, and added, 'I'm expecting the elevator to be somewhere close.'

There was a hurried conversation away from the microphone. 'Tech officer says the elevator's probably under direct control. Try to find the stairs if you can.'

'All right, but I think he's wrong.' Randall dragged his foot along the floor and saw the sooty shine beneath the dust. There were no other tracks of any kind in the foyer. 'The machine doesn't seem to use this area at all, so there's a chance it hasn't been altered. I'll check the archway.'

There was a fair-sized painting behind the reception desk, but the frame had warped and a layer of fungus covered the details. Below and to either side of the steps were two low barrels covered with the same white mildew, the palm trees long digested. The dust was gritty and slippery, like graphite.

Through the arch a staircase led up to a small half landing, then it doubled back on itself and carried on up out of sight. Randall followed it up to the third flight, then stopped.

'What's the matter?' Killoran asked.

'The staircase is blocked.' On either side the wall had been carefully removed and a sealed tunnel had been driven right across, filling the stairwell completely. It was the first sign of nonhuman activity he had seen, and he didn't like the uneasy feeling it gave him. The tunnel seemed to come from nowhere and to lead nowhere, but regardless of that it still made further ascent by this route impossible. 'I'll go back and take another look at the elevator.'

'Maybe you should try to find another staircase.'

'I didn't see any other exit from the foyer. I want to check all the possibilities before I think about backtracking.'

The windowless doorway that he had noted as he passed carried next to it a square panel with a single button in the middle. He touched it more in hope than expectation, and the blank door split down the middle with the two halves sliding back into the wall.

'I've found it,' he said, stepping inside. 'There's been no work done in here. If there's still power to the motor it may take me all the way up.'

There were five buttons with an unknown symbol next to each, and he touched the highest of them.

The outer and inner doors slid closed at the same time, and the elevator jerked into a slow climb.

'Be sure you don't let yourself be trapped.'

'If the motor gives out there are plenty of mechanical failsafes on these things. If it comes to the worst I can unscrew the access panel in the ceiling and get out that way.'

There was no way of telling the speed of ascent, for the indicator board over the door was dead. His earpiece buzzed with static as the motor above pulled against the counterweight for the first time in years.

'Of course,' Killoran said, 'we can't be sure that Central hasn't interfered with the lifting gear at the top. Why would it bother with alterations inside?'

'Damn, you're right. I didn't think of that. But on the other hand, it did respond to manual operation. I can't tell for sure how fast, but it's definitely moving.'

Distant whispers, and then; 'Probably the motor lubricants have dried out. It could seize or burn.'

Randall had to ask him to repeat because of the worsening signal. Killoran did so, and added, 'It's pretty bad at this end, too.'

'I could put up with it. but I'm getting the noise from the motor outside in the shaft as well.'

'Be careful. We're monitoring another big power drain.'

Static and whistle became a loud whine as the car jerked to a halt and a buzzer in the operation panel began to sound a regular note. He tapped all the buttons without response, and then said, 'I'm stuck between floors. The motor must have burned, like you said. I'll have to take out the panel.'

'Can't you force the doors?'

Randall tried, but the safety lock held them together. 'No good,' he said, and turned his attention to the panel above. Four stiff butterfly bolts fastened it at the corners, and he used the handle of the blaster as an impromptu hammer to bang them free. The panel dropped as the last bolt came away, and was heavier than he expected; it slid from his grip and shook the whole car as it hit the floor. The whine from outside was much louder, and the shaft was alive with searing blue flashes.

Sparks from above poured onto his head and shoulders as he struggled to climb out onto the car. The smell of burning cloth and hair made a useful if unwelcome contribution to the effort. As soon as he was out he moved to the side of the shaft and pressed himself against the wall away from the immediate danger.

The top of the car was braced with two girders which served as the mount for an arrangement of wheels and pulleys, which in turn were caked with hard grease. The car itself was suspended by a cable through the pulleys and centred in the shaft by two pairs of rails on opposite sides; the cable returned from above down the opposite wall and disappeared below to the counterweight.

He was, indeed, between floors, for a narrow strip of outside door showed above the roof of the car. Even if he could get it open he wouldn't have room to squeeze through, so he would have to climb the angled bracing of the shaft structure. That meant climbing towards the burning motor, but the arrangement of struts was such that he would be able to use them as an oversized ladder.

'I'm on top of the car, Neil,' he shouted. He could barely hear himself, and the reply was far too dim to make out. 'Say again,' he shouted, and then failed to listen as he saw that the suspending cable was beginning to quiver.

The floor dropped from under him, and he met it again a second later and two feet lower. His knees were bruised as he fell heavily.

'What was that?' demanded the tiny speaker in his ear.

'Everything's breaking free up top. I'm getting off while there's something to hold onto.'

'Tech says the computer must have spotted you early, it's pouring power into the motor to melt the cable and drop the car down the shaft.'

'Can it do that? Won't the car brake automatically?'

'We don't know. The fail-safes might be either bypassed or suppressed, but if Central thinks it can do it that should be all the confirmation we need. Don't waste any time.'

The rain of molten droplets was leaping and funnelling into the open roof panel, and the composite floor inside began to burn. Randall edged around the torrent and reached for a handhold, but the floor lurched again and his hand closed on empty space.

There was a tearing sound above, and a twisted piece of machine part slammed into the roof next to him, bouncing and falling through the open hatch. He heard a more distant impact as it landed on the floor inside, and the car was shaken again. He wasted no time in stepping across and sliding behind the safety of a cross-girder as the whine became a scream and more shapes of cast metal hurtled down and battered at the car roof. The cable bounced and snapped around and then gave way,

THE CORRIDOR had been a dead end, and so they had separated from an agreed point to explore its side- branches. Because of the dome's curve none of them ran straight, and only a full inspection of their length would reveal whether or not they led to the central handling facilities.

Rorvik knew he had found it when he saw the door, removed from its hinges and carefully laid to one side. His hand went to the bag at his side, and his first impulse was to move in immediately and start the disabling process. He could think of a number of good reasons why he should do so, but against them was set Baxter, determinedly exploring dead ends on the other side of the dome.

They had agreed to meet again by the elevator doors whatever the outcome of the search and then proceed together. With reluctance Rorvik turned and began to retrace the marks he had made along the wall. As he went on he assured himself that there would be no difference whatever he did at this stage; the wall-blowing trick meant fire, and it was a risk Central did not dare to take so close to its functioning centres.

On the empty embankment under the dome, hungry crawlers watched and then lost interest as a crescent of light appeared and widened in the roof out over the water. They had seen the process many times before, and it had never yet given them a chance at food. This, in their shortsighted history, was the era of frustration, where appetising packages of meat repeatedly taunted them and withdrew. Their fine senses, tuned to the hunting significance in the merest shift or attitude in the body of their prey, had analysed the motion of the sturdy workers who occasionally appeared and had correctly dismissed them as minerals with only the semblance of animation.

The service robots coupled guiding lines onto the rim of the tube and dropped it towards the water, manipulating the lines to turn its open mouth into the flow under the intense beam of a spotlight cluster. Behind them a heavy- duty water pump shuddered and pulled, and Central's depleted stocks of coolant began to come up to pressure.

Rorvik was the first to arrive at the meeting point, but Baxter came limping around a corner only a few moments later. 'I fell in the dark,' he explained.

'I think I've found it,' Rorvik told him, and went on to describe the open doorway with the black glass beyond. Baxter eased himself down onto the floor and tentatively rubbed his leg as he listened.

'You shouldn't have worried about me,' he said when Rorvik had finished. Rorvik was about to reply when he saw Baxter's hand come away from his leg leaving a dark patch behind.

'You're hurt,' Rorvik said, and looked more closely. The legs of the slacks flapped loose for a length of eight or nine inches down the back of Baxter's calf. The edges of the material were burnt and sealed as if laid open by a hot razor, and the skin beneath was the same. 'What kind of fall did this?'

'The fall didn't do that, the igniter did. I dropped it when I tripped. I didn't think it was as bad as it seems to be.'

'It should be clean, anyway. What does it feel like?'

'Right now, it's fine. When I walk and the muscle stretches it's hell.'

Their clothes were filthy, and no longer fit to use as bandages. Some kind of First Aid kit was required. Rorvik said, 'What about the offices? I might find something we can use.'

Baxter shuddered and shook his head. 'No thanks. It isn't as bad as that.'

They settled instead for cutting the edges of cloth back from the open wound; the searing beam of the igniter had closed off blood vessels as it passed, and the little blood that there was had begun to coagulate.

'I heard something going on down below,' Baxter said as Rorvik laboured to tear through the tough fabric.

'What do you mean?'

'Another part of the dome. A kind of rumble, and the walls shook. Didn't you hear it?'

'No.'

'I didn't imagine it. It was very distinct. A few minutes later there was another one, not quite as far away. I've an idea what it could be.'

'So have I. Somebody's followed us in and they're getting the same treatment. Fortunately we've a good start on them, and they'll never reach us in time.'

'Say we succeed. What's to stop them from switching Central back on again?'

'It's taken Central over a hundred years to develop its own programming, and it's all held in the memory underneath us. Cut the power and the molecules scatter.'

'And if they still come after us?'

'We'll worry about that when it happens. Did you see any robots on your way?'

'None. Did you?'

'No, but we'll stay alert anyway. We're not home yet.' Rorvik screwed up the remnant of cloth and threw it to one side.

'I can't see Central letting us in without a fight,' Baxter said doubtfully.

'In its own words, it's blind and its hands are tied. If it had the full use of its defences we'd never have gone farther than the door.'

Baxter was happy to concede the point. He held out his hand for Rorvik to help him up. It was at this moment that the steam pressure behind the corridor wall hit the crack point for the pipes.

The blast was localised, but it was hard; it would be difficult to fault Central's timing. Rorvik found that he was holding the hand of a dead man.

THERE WAS comparative peace in the shaft as the dust settled, but Randall's ears were ringing. The protests of heated metal had been replaced by a steady drip of water down one wall from an unseen leak. He inadvertently reached through the falling drops and withdrew his hand sharply; they were hot, almost boiling.

Outside in the command centre Killoran heard a muttered exclamation and responded immediately, opening his microphone fader.

'Can you hear me?' he said. 'Are you all right?'

'Just about,' Randall's voice came back. 'Everything fell away from under me. I'm hanging onto the side, not too far from the top level. I'll climb the rigging and get out through the doors.'

'I've been trying to reach you. You weren't answering.'

There was badly-suppressed irritation in Randall's reply. 'If you'll forgive me, I had reason to be preoccupied. Besides which I couldn't hear anything over the noise here. I'm going to...' There was a dull and distant thud, and the level of background static seemed to increase. Noise limiters cut in, and Randall's voice became softer and less distinct.

'That was something on the other side of the wall. It may have been intended for me, and if that's the case I'm not waiting to find out what.'

Randall began to haul himself upwards over the girders. Come on, he encouraged himself, you're Elite, tough and trained, you can out-think and outfight anything that moves. *You're joking*, his body protested. He managed to drag himself onto his belly on the next highest cross-piece and scramble to bring his legs up. After four such exercises he stopped to regain his breath and directed his light upward.

The top-level doors were only a little way above on the adjacent side. Beyond them the shadows of the gear at the top of the shaft were hung with stalactites of solidified metal and shrouded in steam.

After a short progress report he moved up to the doors and transferred over to their side. The footing here was less secure and most of his weight was out over the drop, so that only the grip of his hands prevented him from falling backwards.

There was no obvious way of opening the doors; no safety handle, no emergency switch. When he risked freeing one hand to attempt to prise them apart he found that they were locked solid.

Randall was on a nine-inch ledge and clinging to the bracing irons of the door frame. Above him was a suspended junkyard, below were four floors of precisely walled-in nothing. And the bloody doors wouldn't open, he added to complete the picture.

'Got a problem, chief?' Killoran asked tentatively.

'You might say so,' Randall replied bitterly. 'What does Tech know about old elevator doors?'

There was an off-microphone conference. 'He says not much,' Killoran came back, 'but I'll put him on.'

There was more activity, and then Tech's voice came. He was leaning too close to the microphone.

'It's me, Randall,' he said. 'Have a look on the housing around the doors. See if you can find some sort of lever or wheel mechanism.'

Randall turned his body as far as he was able in order to direct the beam. The doorframe was surrounded by clusters of cables and junction boxes, and he began to describe them.

'No, you're looking for a lever,' Tech interrupted. 'It's one of those mechanical failsafe devices you were talking about before.

The reason why the door won't open is that there's no car there to disengage the lock, so you'll have to do it manually.'

He saw it then, a sprung arm ending in a rubber wheel which projected from behind one of the guide rails. The top of an ascending car would raise it against the spring a few inches and disengage the deadlock on the outer doors. 'I think I've got it,' he reported, and then described the device.

'That sounds right. Try to lift it.'

First he had to reach it. He transferred back to the girder frame and moved up a couple of feet so that he wouldn't have to stretch too far and risk overbalancing. Even so he could only get his fingertips to the wheel, and it felt very solid. There was no give at all as he tried to press upwards, although his arm quivered with the effort.

'No good,' he told control. 'I can't get the leverage. It won't move at all.'

'I don't know what else I can suggest.'

'Don't worry about it. I'll see if I can shoot the lever off.'

Killoran came on the line, his voice urgent. 'Don't forget you've only got six charges.'

'They're no good to me in here, are they? And the longer I stay in one place the less chance I've got of escaping Central's notice.'

The blaster was a good, balanced fit in his hand. The weapons were powerful but inaccurate sidearms due to their fierce recoil, and as such were not standard issue, but he'd had his quota of practice on the Elite's ranges. The long-range hunting version had a damping mechanism which held the barrel level as the charge left it, but to have carried one of those monsters into Central would have been out of the question.

He flicked the safety switch into 'prime' mode, and waited a few seconds as a red light glowed. When it went out the weapon was live, and Randall wrapped his arm around the guide rail to absorb the recoil and then sighted on the centre of the lever.

Even at that range, he missed. His arm came up and away too soon, and the charge spent itself harmlessly in the brickwork and sent a bucketful of powder back over his head. The next shot hit, but off-centre. The lever bent and twisted, but in that way it only became more difficult to move. Randall gave it some time to cool, and reached over to see if he might have done any good. His fingertips flailed at the air a couple of inches short.

If the blaster shot so wide so close, what chance would he have with three running targets? That was, of course, assuming that the next charge freed the doors and left him with one shot per man. Damn Elite bureaucracy! If he'd co-operated fully he'd still be fighting with an oversized paper tag dangling from the handle.

He sighted again, this time reaching around the guide rail and holding his gun arm to steady it. He triggered the weapon, and the joints in his arm seemed to grind together from the recoil as the plug of charged particles sped from the barrel and buried their energy in the metal rod only two feet away.

It burst apart along the lines of stress determined by the previous impact, and the entire mechanism fell away and rattled off down the shaft. The spring was left hanging loose, so that Randall had either disengaged the doors or sealed them completely. He de-primed and replaced the blaster on his belt, and then made his way back to the narrow ledge. Balancing himself with one hand he tried with the other to prise the doors apart at the point where their surfaces curved slightly and met.

Too hard, and his fingernails scraped and tore on the metal as they skidded across. The second time he used a more gentle pressure and felt springs reluctantly begin to give; then there was a crack enough to reach his hand into, and his arm was through before the double doors could ease together again. A hard thrust of his shoulder and they both retracted fully while his momentum carried him on and out into the top-level corridor.

Behind him the doors closed soundlessly. He was in a corridor strewn with rubble and filled with steam that reflected his glow like a fog. Randall realised that Killoran was talking to him, and began to answer. His assistant seemed not to hear, and Randall put his hand to his collar microphone to find that its connecting lead had been pulled loose. He found the dangling plug and inserted it into the small socket stitched into the shoulder padding. Then he answered again.

'What's happening up there?' Killoran said as soon as he realised that Randall was back in communication. 'We heard two shots and then lost the signal altogether.'

'Loose wire. I'm as high as I can go, and the place is a mess. Half the ceiling's come down and the plumbing's ruptured.'

'Rorvik's work?'

I don't see how. You want to see it up here. More likely it's Central's work; anybody standing alongside wouldn't have much of a chance.'

'Keep us informed.'

Randall was about to protest, then realised that a delay now for his own comfort was out of the question. The raiding party were somewhere near, and this wasn't the time for recuperation. Suppressing the giddiness of relief he arose and stepped over the rubble into the fog.

He tripped within seconds, and as he fell his outstretched hand carried his full weight onto something soft and warm. There was a terrifying, inhuman groan, and Randall withdrew his hand immediately; then, more tentatively, he reached out and probed amongst the dust and swirling vapour.

It was a body, and a few seconds' investigation showed it to be no longer alive. Randall had driven the air from its dead lungs and given it a momentary semblance of animation. He turned it over with difficulty and brushed the sticky paste of plaster dust and condensation off its features. He could tell it was a citizen, but was it Rorvik?

Not this time. As Randall lifted the head towards his beam he knew that it wasn't the face he'd studied and searched for since the disastrous Grade Two so long ago.

It must be Baxter, then. He let the head with its half open eyes drop back, and his hand came away purple and wet. He hardly noticed, wiping the mess absently on his jacket as he studied the dusty floor for footprints. The steam swirled and cleared a little and he shook drops of dew from his eyebrows. His clothes were sticky with the humidity.

Only one trail led away, with no sign of the third man. Central's score so far was two out of four, but time was now short; unclipping the blaster again Randall stepped over the dead man and followed the footprints.

They petered out after a few yards, and he was left only with a general indication of direction. Feeling the growing desperation of a rat in a maze as the scent of com fort grows even fainter he began to check the corridors which angled away.

At first he gave each little more than a glance, but as the blind alleys and wrong turnings accumulated he found that he had to return to look again and be sure. Randall knew that he had to follow a general direction inward from the curve of the main passage but had no other guide; and all these passageways looked the same. He couldn't be sure that he wasn't wandering through the same ones over and over again.

Only the main corridor was recognisable, being wider than the others and having no abrupt turns in its gentle sweep. He would have to adopt some kind of system of search, and use this as his main reference point. Only when he came to scrape a mark on the next corner did he realise that somebody else had used the same idea.

It was a numeral, barely legible, and it had been struck out with a cross. The next junction was the same, and the next one after that. Two more and—but an uneasy thought sent him back to the last symbol to look again.

What he had hastily read as a striking-out was no such thing. It was a crude line dragged under the numeral, and an exclamation mark after it.

Rorvik and Baxter had been searching separately. One or (the other found success, and they had met again in the corridor near the elevator, where Central had waited and managed to swat one of them. The fate of the third man was as obscure as his origins, but only Rorvik was ahead of him now.

At the sight of the unhooked door and the open area beyond Randall paused to douse the beam that would betray his presence.

'I've arrived, Neil,' he reported in a whisper. 'Don't transmit to me in case Rorvik hears overspill from the earpiece.'

'Shouldn't be any danger of it, but I'll keep the fader down at this end anyway. I don't want to distract you.'

Randall's eyes adjusted to the overall glow that seeped into the corridor, and after a moment he stepped through the open doorway.

It was quiet, most unlike the raucous computer room in the Elite building. This was indeed the apex of the dome, for its top curved overhead, the broken panes of panelling seen through a bracing framework. He was screened from the rest of the circular chamber by a series of wedges of electronics banks taller and wider than himself, stacked in rows and separated by narrow avenues all of which arrowed in towards the chamber's centre.

There was a rustle, and then the definite sound of metal against metal somewhere over towards that centre. Randall slipped sideways into the nearest avenue and edged silently down it.

He'd found Rorvik.

Rorvik crouched by the operator's console, a fixed semi-circular desk which was surfaced with an array of coloured lights and three prominent keys. He was reaching into a small pouch, and withdrew an object that Randall recognised. It was the right-handed partner to the insulated glove found in the underbelly.

He pulled it on and worked his fingers into it as he crossed to the inner curve of panelling on the electronics banks opposite Randall. The panels hinged open easily, and revealed nothing of much wonder or surprise; ordered stacks of silvery printed wafers, hundreds of them edge-on. Wire and glass linked and cross-linked the layers.

Rorvik was looking into the open casing. The glove was obviously intended to smash and rip, and Randall knew that he shouldn't be letting Rorvik so close to the edge; but in his mind, it was Randall himself who stood ready to destroy, Randall himself who was picking his place and gathering all the accumulated frustrations of his life, Randall himself drawn to the desert mirage of a better life without Central.

Rorvik broke the spell. He pulled off the glove, and dropped it.

Randall saw his face as he turned. He didn't see the face that he was expecting, the tense, dangerous man that brought down 'copters and danced easily beyond reach; he saw only a citizen, frightened and broken, too weak to finish what he started.

The disappointment was solid and physical; it had a bitter taste, and it screwed Randall up deep down inside. *You can't do this to me,* he thought, *you can't bring me so close and then back off.*

Rorvik was wiping his eyes on his sleeve, a soft-toy version of a hero. Randall stepped from hiding and raised the blaster.

As Rorvik's arm came down he saw the Elite, and his eyes widened. His skin, hair and clothes were dust-white and flecked with Baxter's blood. Randall was a contrast in the soot and grease of the elevator shaft, more of Baxter's blood on his side; Baxter made them blood brothers, touching the opposites and pulling them together.

All around them, the clean song of the machine continued. The soft and vulnerable parts of Central ticked on without obvious concern. Rorvik swallowed hard and raised his hands in surrender.

It was too much for Randall; it made a joke of the scenario. He shot Rorvik twice.

The first shot threw him back into the open circuitry, the second caught him as he bounced out and spun him around. He hit the floor with a heavy, no-life sound, mangled up and twisted by the charges. He lay still.

There was an ache in Randall's wrist as he crossed the central open area and looked down at the body; no need to check for life, Rorvik was half blown apart. There was some localised damage in the machine stacks behind him, snow crystals that gritted underfoot. Rorvik was dead not for what he'd done, but for what he'd failed to do; the price in lives and effort didn't allow any backing-off at the end. Randall had been following an opponent, a respectable fantasy, and Rorvik hadn't been big enough to fill out the shape; so who was going to fill it out now?

The microphone lead at his shoulder had come adrift again. He reconnected it. 'Rorvik's dead, Neil,' he said.

'Well done. We lost you again for a while.'

'I know. Accident.' Aware that he was avoiding looking directly across to the operator's console, Randall stepped around Rorvik to where the belt-pouch lay open on the floor. Central hummed gently on all sides.

First to come out of the pouch were three crudely-shaped probes and 'drivers. The tip of one of them was burnt blue, and Randall dropped them on one side. The only other object was a plain box with a hinged lid.

Randall opened it carefully, expecting to find explosives. As the lid came open he heard the starting whirr of a motor—the damn thing was a booby-trap! He threw it away and dived behind the console.

It bounced once, twice, and Randall covered his head with his arms. The box rolled and came to a stop with its lid open, and the motor continued to turn.

Randall unfroze, and pushed himself sheepishly to his knees. Then he stood up and went around the console to where the musical box was playing.

'What's going on now?' The microphone was picking up the signal. After a few bars the tune began to repeat.

'Nothing,' Randall said, and disconnected the microphone lead.

COLLINSON THE caretaker was twiddling the tuning dial on his ancient receiver when a light began to flash on his switchboard. Mumbling to himself in irritation he turned off the power and went over to answer the call.

'What is it?' he demanded, making no effort to conceal his mood.

He recognised the replying voice immediately; Gerrard, old man on the fourth floor. He rarely came out and almost never made requests, but now he was saying, 'It's my public broadcast speaker. I wonder if you could have a look at it for me?'

'I don't know. I've got a lot on.' If pressed for a justification, no doubt Collinson would think of something.

'When you've finished, then? I don't want to be any trouble.'
'All right, when I've finished.'

Collinson hung up and returned to his receiver. With the

power on everything seemed to be working, but the wavebands just hissed with static. If it was broken he'd have to find some way of losing the repair bill in the apartment block's accounts.

He switched the set off in disgust and dropped into his armchair. It wheezed as air bled out of all its seams under his weight, but he couldn't feel comfortable; the silence in the glassed-in office disturbed him. Outside, the building's lobby was quiet, but the faint and random sounds of the street beyond drifted in and settled like dust around him.

With a sigh of irritation he opened a drawer and took out a sheaf of official requisition forms and billings for citizens' property from Central Command. He stuffed them untidily under the sprung jaws on his clipboard and went out to call the elevator.

It rumbled down from the fifth floor. Collinson feigned an amiable greeting to the citizen woman that emerged, and then pulled the double doors behind him and pressed the fourth floor button. The recently-repaired mechanism jerked a couple of times and then began to haul the car upwards.

Gerrard followed him from the door and watched anxiously as he looked over the set. Collinson was aware that he had no technical knowledge or ability, but Gerrard didn't know that and so he turned all the dials and altered all the settings and nodded knowingly at each result. In the end he gave his verdict.

'It's not working,' he said.

'It's not switched on,' Gerrard pointed out.

'I know that,' Collinson said quickly. 'These are tests we do before it's switched on. You can learn a lot that way.'

Gerrard seemed suitably impressed, and Collinson tried again with the power on. After a few seconds he paused, uncertain; the set's speaker was hissing with the same formless static as his own.

'It went off suddenly, about ten minutes ago,' Gerrard said.

Collinson's switchboard was unattended, four floors down. There was an indicator which corresponded to each of the citizens' apartments in the block.

One by one, they started to come alight.

Book Two
The Ice Belt

ONE

IT WAS A little less than a thousand miles to the north of the city, and Alex Peters was cold and miserable.

Although he was young, he was on the scrapheap, condemned through a court-martial for gross insubordination to this dismal icebreaker run for an unspecified period. Which meant, as far as Peters was concerned, forever. He was lucky still to be in the service at all; while the navy was rapidly shrinking as the old ships simply fell apart at the seams the recruiting office was regularly pestered by hopeful young citizens desperate for the opportunity of something to do. Add to this the fact that a navy is something of an anachronistic luxury on a world with only one land bound state and no enemies, and one is led to the inescapable conclusion that Peters would be fortunate to be anywhere at all outside the city's limits.

Such philosophical comfort was worthless in the face of Peters' unformed, as yet undirected ambition; all he could respond to was the ache in his gut that he felt about twice an hour when he thought about the heights that he could be reaching if he weren't here. Previously the daily routine of service had given him enough satisfaction at least to dab the blood from this deep wound in his soul; but now it had all the open empty days to torture and taunt him, and above all there was no preoccupation to come between him and the nagging suspicion that perhaps, when tested, he might find that he had no real talent to back up his ambition. In reaction to this unvoiced self-criticism he fumed all the more at the impotence of his situation, and through the days of his trial and his first week on the icebreaker he had grown noticeably thin and hollow-eyed.

It was no good. There were two full hours to go until his

watch, but he couldn't get back to sleep. Keeping the blanket around his shoulders he swung his legs out of the narrow bunk, feeling the cold air wash over them; and then he missed his trousers and boots in the dark, and his foot touched bare metal for a moment.

That brought him upright faster than he had intended, and his head banged into the wire of the empty bunk above. The springing shook and sang in its metal frame and Peters mumbled something obscene.

He didn't put the light on when he'd struggled into his two-part cold weather suit because he found the unshielded bulb too bright so shortly after waking. Instead he opened the door and stepped over the low threshold into the outer corridor with its permanent emergency lights. At that moment there was a chopping sound from the engines deep down in the icebreaker, and on hearing this he grabbed the doorframe and waited.

After only a few seconds there was a bass rumble from somewhere below and the deck began a slow tilt, holding a shallow angle for a few seconds before subsiding. Peters guessed that they were close to the main body of the polar icecap now, perhaps forcing their way up an open lead; the rough stuff would come later as the ice barrier before them became thicker and more uneven.

Peters let go of the bulkhead before the floor had fully dropped to level so that it was falling beneath him as he made his way uphill. He passed five empty bunkrooms identical to his own and swung on to the cast-iron stairway which led via a gallery to the mess room. This was a low-ceilinged hall which ran the full width of the ship, installed for the crew that had run her before the installation of the automatics. Now there were vague crusty shapes under the paintwork where tables and chairs had been bolted, and most of the access doors had been spot-welded shut as the spaces beyond were converted for machine use. The ship was a confusing maze of corridors that led nowhere and the blank open spaces of former living areas; a floating metropolis built for hundreds and peopled by two.

The only piece of equipment in the mess room still intact was the dispenser. For the past week Peters had been trying to work out the ordering procedure, but as most of the labels were illegible or had completely peeled away, it was still very much a case of trial and error. He punched the sequence which preceded a drinks order and then touched two more buttons at random. Behind a scratched plastic window three cups dropped into place side by side and were filled by three simultaneous jets, accompanied by the whirring of a pump somewhere inside the machine, As the jets died, the compartment lit up and the plastic window slid aside.

There was no way of telling what he'd ordered. It looked like vegetable soup but it smelled sweet. He shrugged and, after dropping one of the full cups down a disposal chute, took the other two and moved back towards the stairway.

He passed by his bunkroom and carried on towards the bridge. There was no direct access through the ship— installation of the central pump for the stabilizing gear had blocked that off—so the converting engineers had added a shielded walkway across what had been open deck. Loss of a couple of the side-plates on that walkway had turned it into a freezing wind-tunnel, a kind of gauntlet that had to be run several times during each period of duty. Encumbered with the cups he was fortunate in that he could elbow the big levers on the outer doors without much difficulty, but he found the walkway banked up with snow on either side and slippery underfoot. A bitter wind pulled at him and hurt his eyes, and when he finally got to the bridge door he almost fell inward with it.

If the captain had been using a pencil he would have thrown it down in annoyance. Unfortunately pressing the 'cancel' button on a calculator is nowhere near as flamboyant a gesture, so Peters was robbed of the drama.

'What the hell do you think you're doing?' the captain demanded, watching and waiting for a reply as his first (and only) officer used his back to push the outer door closed against the wind that had swung it in so violently.

'Sorry,' Peters apologized, 'it's rougher than when I was last out.' He held out the plastic cup as a peace-offering. 'I brought you a drink of something.'

The captain looked down as the anonymous brew was placed under his nose. It was by now almost cold, and half of it had been left behind in the walkway. A thin film of grease floated on the surface of what was left. 'Thanks,' he said, without sounding too convinced, and then he put it to one side and recommenced his calculations.

Peters knew better than to interrupt again, so he dropped down a folding seat in the rear wall and waited. Like everything else on the icebreaker the bridge covered a much larger area than was now necessary. It had once been a semicircular chamber with windows that gave 180° of forward view, but now it was shuttered and dark with the only light coming from a couple of gooseneck lamps twisted around to bear on the console where the captain worked. All he was actually doing was transferring the data received from navigation beacons into the ship's computer, where the real work of course-plotting and execution would be carried out.

The radar warning on the far left of the captain's console began to warble, and within a couple of seconds Peters felt a vibration through the wall behind him as the stabilizer pump came into action. The captain did no more than glance up at the radar readout, but Peters felt a small knot of tension begin to wind itself around somewhere behind his breastbone.

They hit ice on the port side. Ballast oozed through into the port stabilizer tanks to bear down heavy and give purchase to the cutting blades which ran the length of the ship, but still the deck rode up beneath them. Gears shifted and the note of the engine changed as more power was pushed through to the blades. They bit and gripped, and then there was a distant grinding and tearing as the channel side sheared and broke away from the main pack ice. The deck dropped and the captain's soup did a flip in the air and emptied itself over the floor on the other side of the console.

For a while it was quiet, and the captain worked on. He finished tapping the figures into the computer and then had them read back while he checked his own work. Only then did he push his chair back on its short track and swung it around.

'You're over an hour early,' he said. 'Couldn't you sleep?'

'I woke up cold. Couldn't get off again.'

The captain inclined his head in agreement, and then turned back slightly so that he could keep an eye on one of the dull red screens on his console. He was a short, round man; Peters guessed that he had survived for too many years on the junk food from the dispenser, and wondered what kind of offence he had committed to earn this posting. He seemed well settled into his job and to have no eagerness to do anything else; he'd grown a beard and his hair was in a ragged, almost shoulder-length cut which looked out of place on a middle aged man.

'It's cold everywhere,' he said. 'Going to get colder. You'll have to start sleeping in your weather suit.' This, apparently, was what the captain did all the time, for his own suit was creased and stained like the lining from a dog's basket.

Peters asked, 'Do you want me to take over yet?'

The captain continued to stare at the unwavering dot on his red screen. He said nothing, and Peters wondered if he'd heard. Perhaps he couldn't raise the enthusiasm to answer; or, more likely, it was a ham fisted psychological ploy, an inadequate man's assertion that he was in charge and don't you forget it. Peters stayed put on his fold-down seat and felt his face slowly flushing.

'Does that mean yes or no?' he blurted, and then regretted it immediately.

The captain turned back, slowly. 'It means no,' he said. 'You don't come on this console until you're due to come on. This may be shit run as far as you're concerned but I'm still ship's captain and I expect to be treated like one. Understand?'

Peters nodded. It wasn't enough. 'Do you understand, sailor?'

'Yes, sir.'

The captain pointed to where the spilled soup was spreading on the deck, now visible beyond the edge of the console. It was creeping, glacier like, towards the door. 'While you're here,' the captain said, 'check the angle of inclination. Looks like we might have a slight list.'

Grateful for the change of topic, Peters stood up and went forward to the inclinometer. It was a dial on one of a series of grey boxes and interlinked tubing fixed to the forward bulkhead. The needle was five degrees off and as he reported this he added, 'but won't the ship's computer compensate?'

'Not if it's a fault in the stabilizers,' the captain said, pulling his seat back towards the console. 'If it's not that, the cargo may have shifted. You'll have to go below and check.'

Peters went below, covering his face with his sleeve as he passed the gaps in the walkway and feeling ice needles stab at his knuckles. The stabilizer tanks ran the full length of the ship and access to the telltale dials wasn't standardized. It was an hour before he got around them all, and his last visit was to the Number Four hold where the Ice Palace cargo was tied down.

It seemed ridiculous, but these few miserable crates were the only justification for the icebreaker's existence. Peters had never even heard of the Ice Palace until he'd begun this assignment, and then they'd told him very little. The Palace was, it seemed, a prison without guards, security guaranteed by the most hostile conditions in the world; the icebreaker and its supplies were the only link between the Palace and the city, and it would be part of Peters's job to stand in the hold with a rifle during the unloading to make sure they didn't return with more crew than they set out with. An attack had been tried some years before, and only this measure along with the icebreaker's shielding had prevented its success.

Peters wasn't looking forward to the next few hours, nor was he particularly delighted at the prospect of the next few years to be spent shunting back and forth between city and pole in search of the Ice Palace beacon, never in the same place twice as the Palace drifted with the cap. The cargo consisted mainly of long, flat crates; pipe cladding and insulation, from what he'd been told, and virtually nothing else. He couldn't understand how the prisoners could be fed, since the sea had supposedly been sterilized over a two hundred mile radius and there was nothing on the ice that could live without the fish as prey. Surely, they didn't eat the pipe cladding—but why should they need so much of it, and nothing else?

He didn't go too close to the upright crate at the far end of the hold. It was bigger and heavier than all the others, as he'd noticed when he'd helped to load it; now, for some reason, it made him feel uneasy when he turned his back on it to check off the stabilizer dial.

The tank was a little below pressure, but hardly enough on its own to cause the list. He considered switching in the regulator to bring the tank up to its full poundage but decided against it. With his luck he'd probably split the damn thing right open and get them stranded.

He forced himself to check the automatic winches and the unloading platform before he left, all the time uncomfortably aware of the wooden shape which bulked in the darkness behind him. He was relieved to get back to the bridge and take over on the navigation console.

TWO

IT WAS FOUR O'CLOCK in the morning at the Ice Palace, but there was no way that any of the men under the ice could know this. Their only timekeeping was by the regular blips of the radio beacon, and a careful count of these told them when to work and when to eat. Even this method varied in its reliability as the men on counting detail skipped a few pulses to bring the end of their shift a little nearer, but then nobody could challenge their measurements; for most of the year the light outside on the ice was a uniform iron-grey without day or night, and the men of the Palace contrived to see as little of it as they could possibly get away with.

Four o'clock, and there was an echo on the beacon, a double-pulse which indicated the approach of the supply ship. The man by the equipment hesitated as he transferred the wooden counting-chips from one bowl to another, crouching close to the speaker to be sure that the sound was genuine and not just an imagined echo in his own head; and then, as soon as he was certain, he put the bowls aside and squeezed out through the narrow doorway. The procedure when this happened was long-established.

Go tell the Worm.

Minutes later a small man in an oversized snow-suit was trotting towards the bunkrooms. The corridor down which he moved was a rough oval carved straight through the pack-ice, its slick walls made translucent by the glow of buried lights at intervals beneath its surface. The man's gait was uneven as he hopped across the half-buried slats that formed the floor, and as he panted slightly with the effort his breath feathered condensation into the cold, still air.

After a while the corridor forked. The light was poorer but

the footing was better, because here there was a slight incline to the floor which carried away any meltwater from the walls before it could form a crust over the wood. Rumbling sounds echoed up towards him now, the hard, desperate beat of the Ice Palace over the distant throb of the generators.

Now he was on Main Street, the circular tunnel which was the heart of the Ice Palace. The bunkroom doors along here were all numbered in black charcoal, solid metal structures set deep into the walls, and the man counted them off as he passed. At the fifth one he came to he stopped and pulled a piece of curled grey paper out of the front pocket in his snow suit, checking its information against the smeary number before him. He raised a hand to knock, thought better of it, and opened the door to slip inside.

It was dark and steamy in the bunkroom; not exactly warm, but a distinct contrast to the still coolness of the corridor. He left the door open a crack in preference to switching on the light, for all around him figures were starting to heave and turn under blankets in sleepy irritation as the outer chill began to penetrate.

The small man crouched by one of the shapeless heaps in a lower bunk and gave it a tentative prod. 'Willis!' he whispered urgently. 'Willis! Wake up, Willis!'

Willis squirmed to escape the prodding, and his voice came muffled from underneath. 'What's the matter? What's going on?'

'A ship, Willis! I just got the word from the beacon. The supply ship's tracking us across the ice!'

Willis risked a suspicious eye out in the open. He could see the silhouette of the small man against the slit of light from the door, and caught the glint from the single remaining lens in his spectacles. 'What are you playing at, Worm?' he demanded, and there was a groan from somewhere above. 'Why should I want to know that?'

'You know why, Willis,' the Worm said, sounding almost hurt.

'Will you cut the noise?' a voice demanded out of the darkness above. 'I got to be out on the ice in about three hours!'

'Sorry I woke you, Berg,' the Worm said, forgetting to whisper and causing more of the anonymous shapes to stir and mumble. 'I came to tell Willis about the ship.'

'I'm not interested in any ship,' Willis insisted.

'Go play with yourself, Worm,' Berg added.

The Worm dropped his voice back to a whisper and said, 'Willis, it's your turn to take an unloading duty.'

'It can't be my turn.'

'It is. I've checked. You and Lobo.'

'With Lobo? Forget it, Worm.'

Willis turned over decisively and tried to pull the blanket back over his head as another voice came from across the room, 'What's going on down there?'

'The Worm's kidnapping Willis,' replied the voice from the darkness immediately over their heads.

'For Christ's sake!'

The Worm stood up and addressed himself in the general direction of this latest speaker. 'Look,' he said, 'I'm sorry you're awake, but it's definitely Willis's turn. I mean, what's the point of me working these rosters out if you won't follow them?'

'He's right, Willis.' The speaker across the room said, having to raise his voice over the groans and complaints of those who had been' newly awakened by the Worm's latest declaration. 'Get dressed and get lost.'

'Go on, Willis,' Berg added. 'Give us some peace.'

Willis sensed that the antagonism of the bunkroom was beginning to focus not upon the Worm but on him, and he demanded, 'Whose side are you on?'

'If we didn't cooperate and follow my rosters, where would we all be?' the Worm asked of nobody in particular, pleased to find that for once he was not the sole object of the general enmity.

'We'd all be asleep,' somebody said.

Willis still showed no sign of cooperation, but instead demanded, 'What do you mean, if we didn't cooperate? I've never seen your name on that roster, Worm.'

'And I don't see you working any rosters out yourself, Willis.'

'What?'

The Worm saw Willis's hand reaching for him and skipped backwards with a startled yelp, banging into the wooden support of the bunks behind him. Somebody said, 'Stop picking on the Worm and get down to the unloading bay, Willis.'

'Go down with Lobo and treat yourself to some scintillating conversation.'

To enforce the point, Berg reached down from his own bunk and jerked Willis's blanket away. Willis began to protest, and was told, 'You can have it back when you get back from the bay.'

Willis gave in, although not particularly gracefully. The Worm hovered a respectable distance away as Willis zipped into his snow suit and connected up the battery pack that had hung at the end of his bunk, and then he followed out into Main Street.

Willis paused outside the door and rubbed at his eyes in an attempt to bring himself fully awake. The Worm said, 'You got everything?'

'I've never had any complaints. You'll regret this, Worm.'

'I think I'm regretting it already. But, please, Willis, I've got to do my job. You know I'm not well enough to take a shift on the ice.'

No observer could hesitate to agree. The one called the Worm didn't, in fact, seem fit for anything much; he was a full head shorter than Willis, and he'd had to roll up the arms and legs on his snow suit to make it fit, the result of this being that the rest of the suit hung slack. His spectacles didn't only have a lens missing, they also lacked an arm and seemed in constant danger of throwing themselves on to the floor.

Willis moved off down Main Street towards the cavernous bay areas, and the Worm followed. The carved-out corridor was no longer empty. Men were starting to appear walking towards them, their snow suits glittering crystal in the twilight with a crust of unmelted hail from the surface outside. They seemed exhausted, heads bowed and with no intention other than to get to their bunkrooms. Four men passed without any sign of recognition but to the fifth Willis called, 'Hey, Spook.'

The man named Spook stopped by the open door to his bunkroom and waited until they drew level. 'Hi, Willis,' he said, ignoring the Worm.

'Want to do a shift for me? Trade you the next one back.'

'Sorry Willis, I'm beat. Any other time but now. We had a pipeline fracture and the power levels dropped almost to danger. Anyway, you already owe me two. What's the big problem?'

'Forget it. I'm sorry I reminded you.'

'The icebreaker's coming in,' the Worm said, as Willis started to move away.

'What does that mean?' Spook demanded bitterly. 'Another shipment of lousy second-rate cladding? The cold breaks it down and the wind strips it off. Those sadistic crumbs designed it that way to keep us working.'

'It's the secret of a happy life,' Willis said, and moved on.

They walked on in silence for a while, leaving Main Street and stepping through a less well-finished linking tunnel into a parallel passage. They went down this for a short distance and then took the next turn, which led directly towards the bay areas.

'You know,' the Worm said reproachfully after a while, 'you really shouldn't take it all out on me.'

'Why not?' replied Willis, unconcerned. 'If I've got to take it out on somebody, a skinny little runt like you seems a good choice.'

'But if that's the reason, why make fun of Lobo? He's almost twice your size.'

'You're a shrimp; he's stupid. It all evens out.'

A pause and then; 'I wouldn't depend on that, Willis. Appearances can mislead.'

'Come off it, Worm. You wouldn't even make a presentable frog.'

'I'm talking about Lobo. Just because he's big and slow, don't assume he's stupid. I've come to terms with all this contempt because I don't have the choice. Lobo won't be the same.'

'Quiet, Worm. You'll have me crying down my snow suit next. Where is he?'

The Worm pointed ahead. 'Down there in the loading bay. He got up and went there early, without being told.'

Willis laughed, not very pleasantly. 'And that's your idea of untapped intellect? I don't even think we should be trusting you to do the rosters anymore.'

By now they were at the outer door to the loading bay. It took all Willis's weight to swing it open, and he walked off as the Worm struggled to get it closed. 'That's typical,' the Worm said. 'None of you understand how complicated those rosters are. We've got over fifty men here, and if we don't work at full efficiency we all die. That's how it was designed. And you think it's easy to keep all that going?'

'Shove it, Worm,' Willis's voice drifted back, strangely amplified under the high ceiling of the cargo store which led through to the loading bay. 'I don't do any thinking before breakfast.'

As the Worm had said, Lobo was already there when they rounded the corner into the loading bay, sitting on an empty crate next to the cargo chute and the massive iron outer door. He wasn't by any means twice the size of Willis, but he was certainly taller and broader. The impressiveness of this was increased by the shaggy beard and haircut that was the only style available to the Ice Palace detainees. Lobo looked up as they approached.

'Hi, Willis,' he said, his tone surprisingly gentle.

'You talk too much, Lobo,' Willis replied. 'Try to restrict yourself to the essentials.'

Lobo turned to the Worm. 'What did I say?'

'Willis doesn't feel too good this morning.'

Willis adjusted the power pack slung at his hip to compensate for the lower temperature in the bay, and said, 'Stop apologizing for me, Worm. Where's the ship?'

Lobo shook his head. 'I rolled up the hatch a couple of inches and had a look. You can barely see past the end of the ramp, but there's nothing there.'

'Check again, and this time there'd better be. Or else I'm liable to step on something. . .' With this, he reached out and grabbed the Worm by the ear. The Worm howled and tried to pull away, and Willis started to laugh.

'Let go of his ear, Willis.'

'What?'

'I said let go of his ear.'

The Worm was still protesting on the other end of the grip. Willis held it for a moment, but Lobo didn't move or look away, and after a couple more seconds Willis said, 'To hell with it. I'll get a helmet and look myself.'

The Worm got his ear back, and Willis stamped off back to the cargo bay where the racks of helmets were kept. The Worm said, 'Thanks, Lobo. Willis doesn't like me, you know.'

'Forget it, Worm,' Lobo replied. 'I don't like you either.'

Willis came back with a couple of the brightly coloured helmets. Countless generations of use had bleached the material of the snow suits into varied light pastel shades, but the helmets had kept their original brilliance. He offered one to Lobo, who had already collected one on his way, so in the end it was given to the Worm.

The outer door rolled upward, moved by a set of gears which concentrated a few feet of pulling on a chain into inches of advance. They were badly maintained and squealed horribly as the rusted surfaces ground together, Lobo dragging the chain with all his strength as Willis climbed to the top of the loading chute and spread himself to peer under the rising edge. Light slanted in and Willis was enveloped by a swirl of hard snow that was forced in through the gap, so it was difficult to see when he raised his hand for Lobo to stop and release the door.

Willis got up and walked back down the chute to floor level, leaving a Willis-shaped outline in new snow at the top. 'Thought I saw some lights,' he said, and jumped the last couple of feet, 'but nothing near enough to get excited about.'

So they sat around for a while and if Willis felt like complaining any more about lost sleep he kept it to himself. In the end the icebreaker announced its own arrival, with a jarring thump that set the chains rattling. Lobo started to haul on the chain again, and as the bay door crept upward it disclosed the bright square of the open ship's hold sliding finally into line some distance beyond.

The blizzard effectively ensured that there was nothing more visible of the icebreaker as it lifted and subsided in the oily frozen slush that was the only form of open water to be found in these latitudes. The hold was a disembodied gateway ringed by a yellow haze and Willis could see that there was somebody waiting in the gateway, dressed not in a powered snowsuit but a totally inadequate wrap-around jacket over ordinary cold weather wear. He was shivering, and the gun in his hands was waving everywhere. His voice drifted across the gap, thin and reedy without suit amplification, 'Is this the Ice Palace?'

'Cut the jokes, clown,' Willis projected back. 'Where the hell do you think it is?'

'Got a cargo for you. You ready to receive?'

'Stop waving that popgun at me and get on with it. You're making us lose heat.'

'Captain says I've got to have this. He told me to watch you.'

'Shove it, kid. I'm not dancing today.' Willis was getting impatient. Direct exposure to the wind fairly sucked power out of the suit's compact unit, and the time spent on recharge would be added to his next shift.

The gun—a rifled blaster with no recoil—stabbed warily in his direction. 'I had to watch you in case...'

'I know all about that! Will you just put the crates on the ramp and get on with it!'

'Don't you even want to hear the news?' Now the kid sounded hurt!

'Shove your news. I don't want to be well informed, I want to be warm!'

The young man on the icebreaker shrugged. 'Have it your way,' he shouted, and leaned over to thumb a button to one side of the open hatch. The first crate—a familiar shape, a set of quarter-section pipe cladding—swung out over the gap on an extending arm which was directed across by a joystick mechanism in the hold. As the crate swung close, Willis grabbed it and pulled it in on to the cargo ramp, steadying it and using his free hand to disengage the hook at the top.

Lobo had lifted a great armful of chain to knot it over on itself and hold the bay door three-quarters open and now he came forward to help with the unloading. They handled the crates carefully, laying each on its flattest side before letting it roll down the chute, for the wooden framework would be as valuable to them as the contents. The Worm had taken a green cargo manifest which had been nailed to the first crate and was making a great show of checking each one off as it came in. When congestion threatened at the bottom of the ramp Lobo left Willis and came down to move the boxes across to the harness-drawn cargo train that ran along narrow rails to the adjacent bay, stacking them on the low wagons so that they would be easily accessible for the outgoing surface teams.

It was a paltry load, all pipe-cladding with one unexpected bonus, a box of replacement lightbulbs. The Worm scrambled up the ramp, dodging a crate as it slithered towards him, and pulled at Willis's sleeve, shouting, 'That's the last one, according to my manifest.'

Willis shook his head, a motion that was barely broadcast by his helmet, and indicated another crate which was in the process of being hooked up for transfer.

'But it can't be right,' the Worm insisted, waving his piece of green paper, 'There's nothing listed.'

Willis pushed the manifest aside and reached out to guide the cargo in. The Worm skipped back when he saw that it would almost fill the chute, scrambling to get out of the way before it could knock him aside; and then Willis had trouble getting it unhooked, for it was taller than himself and considerably heavier than any of the other crates.

Lobo came back to help, for it took both of them to get the box flat on the chute and down to the bottom while the Worm protested that it wasn't on his paper and it shouldn't be here. Willis swore at him and pushed him out of the way a couple of times, and then went back up the incline to the open door. The hook was back in the ship's hold and empty.

'That's everything,' the armed youth shouted. 'See you on the next run.'

'Up yours, kid,' Willis replied, and then, to Lobo, 'Let's get this hatch closed.'

Lobo unlooped the chain and let the weight of the door drag it down as the gears spun and shrieked. It closed at the bottom with a solid smack as a last handful of snow puffed in and settled. The silence after the scouring of the wind was unsettling, and the clicks and rasps of metal and plastic as they removed their helmets and set them down were somehow sharpened and magnified.

'I bet you even hate your own mother,' said the Worm.

'Damn right,' Willis replied, his eyes on the last, oversized crate. 'She sold me out and collected the reward when they put me here.'

Lobo shook some of the crystals from his arms and shoulders. The temperature in the bay had dropped considerably, and they lay like a handful of discarded diamond dust on the floor. 'What about this last crate, Worm?' he said. 'It's too big to stack with the others.'

The Worm consulted his piece of green paper yet again. He seemed to resent the fact that the crate was there at all, as if it challenged some fundamental law of his universe. 'I don't know, Lobo,' he said. 'I think it must have been a mistake. It isn't listed.'

'That's no mistake,' Willis said quietly. 'Look again, Worm.'

The Worm misunderstood, and went back to an inspection of the manifest. Lobo walked around to the other side of the crate and, putting his fingers under a narrow cross-brace, said, 'It isn't cladding. It's heavy.'

Willis glanced at the Worm, and then back to the crate. 'You ought to recognize it. They've changed the design, but the size is right.'

The Worm's head came up, and he frowned. 'Wait a minute. It can't be a man.'

'Why can't it?'

'Because... because it's the wrong kind of box. Because there's no paperwork to back it up. Besides which, the Palace is running over capacity anyway! They can't send us any more!'

"Fraid it looks like they have, Worm,' Lobo said, straightening after an attempt to see the contents of the box through a slight gap in the rough timber.

'Better get him up to the Doc and have him revived,' Willis added, 'or else he'll be beyond bringing back.'

The Worm brightened. 'That might be for the best. The

rosters are hellish complicated as it is.'

He squawked as Willis's gloved fingers slipped into the round collar of his snow suit and hauled him up so that the material strained under his arms and Willis's knuckles pushed up against his nose. The Worm flapped his arms and gurgled, but this time Lobo made no move to interfere.

'Do me a favour, Worm,' Willis said. 'Any time I should happen to make a big mistake and be tempted to start liking you, remind me of what you just said. Shove your rosters. You can slot him in place of one of the men that disappeared on the ice last month.'

The Worm descended to his more usual elevation, grabbing at his glasses as they threatened to slide sideways off his nose. Lobo said, 'Do we open the crate?'

'No, we drag the whole thing along to somewhere warm. There's a place up near the Worm's office that we used to use, but I think one of the empty bunkrooms might be better.'

'That's a long way,' Lobo said doubtfully, 'and this is heavy.'

'And where's the paperwork?' the Worm said, making sure he was out of Willis's reach.

'How the hell should I know? Maybe it's "Torment-The-Worm" week back at the city. Get the other side, Lobo.'

Lobo got the other side, and it did them no good at all. The crate and its contents were too heavy, and even if they'd been able to slide it across the floors of the two adjacent bays they'd never be able to cope with the rough incline that led through to the Main Street passage and the bunkrooms. Willis sent the Worm off to find the man called Doc, and then he and Lobo cleared one of the cargo wagons and lifted it from its rails as a makeshift transport. Lobo worked slowly and patiently, taking Willis's directions without complaint or comment; and for Willis's part, he spent the next twenty minutes concentrating on a task without taking time out to abuse anybody. For that alone it was one of the Ice Palace's more remarkable days.

The metal wheels broke a good number of the slats on the corridor floor, but they were at least able to get as far as the passage which ran parallel to Main Street. This was where they hit a problem, because the crate itself was too wide to pass through the linking tunnel. As they tried to devise a way through the Worm arrived with Doc, who said it might be dangerous to tip the crate on its side, so in the end they had to forget about the bunkrooms and settle instead for the unheated chamber up the corridor which led to the Worm's office. It differed from the bunkrooms farther on in that it had bare ice walls and no lining or insulation, but at least it was less cold than the cavernous bays.

Under Doc's supervision they broke the seals and raised the lid. There were a number of gas tanks and liquid drips to be lifted out of the way and disconnected in a certain sequence, and only then could the wadding be pulled out to disclose the body underneath.

There he lay, huddled like a frog squashed into a matchbox. Nobody spoke for what seemed like a long time.

'Now why the hell,' said Willis at last, 'have they sent us a citizen?'

THREE

No DOUBT about it, a citizen was bad news, and this one was an unmistakable specimen. He had all the patrician marks of the city's specialized breeding programme; the limbs that were a little too long for elegance, the regular features, the dark hair. A sculptured behaviour unit, ideal fodder for a rigidifying computer culture.

The Worm wanted to pull all the plugs and slide him into the crap tanks straight away. In that he was voicing Willis's private thoughts, which of course prompted Willis to react in the opposite extreme and insist that the newcomer at least be given a chance to explain himself. Lobo stood at the back of the room and said nothing, and Doc changed over the drips to start the revival procedure.

It was a slow process, seeming to consist of nothing other than standing around watching the citizen not waking up. After a while the Worm mumbled something about paperwork and edged out of the room. Lobo watched him disappear and then said, 'I'd better go. I'm due on shift. Coming, Willis?'

'I'll follow you down,' Willis replied. 'Tell the others I'm coming.'

Lobo nodded. 'See you later. See you, Doc.'

Doc gave a little wave, without taking his eyes off his 'patient'. The sleeper was almost up to temperature, and his heartbeat was normal; he'd be out of it within minutes, and it would hurt.

They pulled a fistful of needles from the crook of his arm and sat him upright. His eyes were beginning to twitch behind the lids, and the Doc had an idea.

'Better get him some yeast, Willis,' he said. 'He won't have eaten in more than a week.'

When Willis got back from the tanks a few minutes later the newcomer was awake and starting to get over the terrible cramps that were the immediate consequence of his confinement. He took the bowl of yeast that was offered to him, but choked on the first mouthful of the scummy warm liquid. At least it gave him enough moisture to manage his first words in the Ice Palace.

'It's foul,' he said. 'What is it?'

'Yeast,' the Doc replied. 'We grow it ourselves on waste. It may be foul, but it's all we've got.'

The newcomer turned his head with painful slowness to look at the Doc. He saw a shaggy-haired old man, a padded playsuit draped around a skeleton. Then back for a closer look at Willis; younger and better-fitted, but equally unkempt.

'I'm afraid you've got some re-orientation ahead of you,' the Doc went on. 'What's the last thing you remember?'

He frowned. You could almost hear the parts moving. 'Last night. Somebody came into my cell and threw a blanket over my head.'

'That was over a week ago. You've been in cold storage ever since, and that's literal. This is the Ice Palace.'

For a moment there seemed to be a flash of understanding in the newcomer's eyes, but it faded. 'The what?'

Willis moved around to stand by the Doc. 'The city's own private and secret social scrap-heap, designed and authorized by the Central Command computer. Fifty men fighting for their lives in a hole on top of two hundred miles of sterile sea. I doubt whether you've heard of it before.'

'Maybe I have, I don't know. I've got a killing headache. How long have I been here?'

'Hardly more than an hour,' the Doc said. 'The icebreaker dropped you off with the supplies. Try to drink some of the yeast.'

He tried, and didn't succeed. 'Does it all taste like this?'

'There's not much we can do with it, apart from dry it out and press it into blocks. We'll explain all this as we go along. It's essential you understand the system here.'

'What system? Who runs the place?'

'Wait a minute,' Willis put in quickly. 'We don't know anything about you yet. Who are you?'

'My name's Randall.'

'Randall what?'

'Randall nothing. Just Randall.'

'And what's a citizen done to be sent here?'

This brought a faster reaction than Willis had expected. 'I'm no citizen.'

'We're not stupid. Randall,' Doc interposed gently. 'Anybody can see you're a citizen. You've got Central Command stamped all over you.'

'There is no Central anymore.' The information was received with polite disbelief. 'The Central Command computer. It's gone. A man named Rorvik broke into the computer building and managed to avoid the security systems. He interfered with the programme and wiped the memory.'

'I don't believe it,' Willis said.

'You don't have to. But you asked.'

Doc decided it was time Randall tried to walk. At first he couldn't straighten his legs, much less support his own weight on them; but with the attempt at use sensation began to speed back. Steadying himself against the cold, gritty wall Randall explained how the city they had known no longer existed; the computer defunct, the over-privileged community of citizens disbanded, the outsiders of the underbelly now forming the main strength of the provisional government.

'Is Avery Sim still leading?' Doc asked.

'Avery Sim died. There's a joint leadership of the two traders, Marius and Morden, and Chandler's running the Elite.'

From the corridor outside came noises, distant echoes of men on the move somewhere far down the passageway. Willis seemed not to hear them, but mused, 'Chandler. He was the agent hunter. If all this is true, why haven't we been taken home?'

The Doc shrugged. 'The underbelly doesn't want us, any more than Central did.'

'So what happened to honour among thieves?'

'You don't get honour among thieves, just a better class of

dishonesty. It doesn't matter a damn who's holding the whip—we still get the worst of it.'

Doc and Willis took an arm each and walked Randall around. By the Ice Palace's own peculiar standards it would have been bad manners to ask Randall directly what he had done to be sent to them, but all the same Willis was obviously fishing for information. As they paced the irregular walls of the Recovery Room Randall explained that he'd been distantly associated with Rorvik and the plot against the Central installation, and that as the only survivor of the conspiracy the newly-appointed council had been unsure what to do with him; should they make him a national hero, or punish him to appease the citizens? Now it was obvious which way the toss of the credit chip had gone.

Willis had to be satisfied with this thin explanation, punctuated as it was by small yelps of pain and pauses as Randall bent to massage his protesting leg muscles, for a warning glance from the Doc told him that he was treading perilously close to the boundary of prisoner etiquette. Randall limped over to his transport box and lowered himself on to the edge, stretching his legs out to help the circulation.

'As long as I'm here,' he said, 'you'd better tell me the setup.'

'This is it, Randall,' Willis replied. 'Your world for the rest of your life, until we boil you down and filter you through into the yeast tanks.'

'What do you mean, "we"?'

'That's point number one,' Doc said. 'If it gives you any satisfaction, Randall, you're a free man.'

'Free to work or die,' Willis put in.

'There are no warders in the Ice Palace. We make the rules and enforce them ourselves, or we die. It's so simple that everybody understands it. The Palace is dug out around a fission power plant. It's automated and sealed, and we can't interfere with it. The power from that plant heats a network of pipes on the surface of the ice pack.'

Randall felt that something was expected of him at this point. 'To what purpose?'

Willis smirked, although it really wasn't funny. 'Tell him,

Doc,' he said.

'None. The heat leaks off into the atmosphere, and we get the worst storms in the world because of it. But the power supply for the Palace itself is operated on an automatic cutout, and if that useless pipe network isn't kept together the Palace freezes up. Worse still, if the temperature in the yeast tanks drops below a certain level the yeast will die off and we won't be able to regenerate it without a live sample to start from. We'd be finished either way.'

'The pipe network's rotten,' Willis said. 'It was made that way and it's kept that way by the lousy repair materials the supply ship brings. We have to spend a hundred and fifty per cent of our time running around to forestall the cutouts. It happened, once. We had to burn some of the pipe-cladding to keep a sample of the yeast alive, and it took over a month to grow half a tankful from what we had left.'

When Randall was fit enough to walk unaided they took him to the Worm's 'office'. His first sight of the Ice Palace outside the Recovery Room was of a misshapen passageway with broken-glass walls lit from deep inside. The Main Street tunnel was close enough at this point to be seen as a soft, distant glow through the ice, rippling with the dark shapes of passing men like life growing in a translucent egg.

'Ever have an escape?' Randall asked as they moved away from Main Street towards a less well illuminated stretch.

'Never,' Doc replied. 'But I assure you, everything's been tried. It's over a thousand miles to the nearest settlement, and the yeast breaks down in the cold. Even tried using the protein direct instead of feeding people into the tanks, but nobody could digest it. Something about the essential bacteria in your gut—some of it must die off on an all-yeast diet.'

'So we have to work to soak up an over-production of power, just to ensure there's enough left for us to live?'

'That's it exactly. Willis, I thought you were due on shift?'

'I'm going,' Willis said as they arrived at a rough-looking wooden door set well back in the ice wall. He banged on it with the heel of his hand. 'Otherwise I'll have the Worm on my back.'

'The Worm?'

'You're going to meet him now. An obnoxious individual with too many teeth and not much forehead. We let him prepare all the work rosters because he's not fit for anything else.'

The door creaked open a suspicious crack, and a single spectacle lens glinted in it. 'What you saying about me, Willis?' a shrill voice demanded.

Willis gave the door a hard shove that sent the Worm tottering back into the room. 'I'm telling Randall what a nice fellow you are deep inside, and that he shouldn't be misled by your rotten nature.' They followed him in.

'Thanks, Willis,' the Worm said. 'You're all armpit.'

Doc glanced nervously at Willis, but he seemed to be respecting the fact that, alone in all the Ice Palace, this room was Worm territory.

'Watch it, Worm,' was all he said. 'Lobo isn't here now.'

'Sorry, Willis,' the Worm said, making no effort to seem sincere.

Randall looked around. There was less space than in the Recovery Room, but when your walls were solid ice you wouldn't want the luxury of unheated palatial grandeur. The floor was wooden slats raised on loose blocks, wet slush glinting beneath, and there was a coarse blanket and a bundle of wadding like that from his transport crate rolled up in the far corner, just visible beyond the upended box that the Worm seemed to use as a desk.

He caught the word 'citizen', and realized that they were talking to or about him. He dragged his attention away from the scraps of grey, misshapen paper that had been affixed to one wet wall with slivers of wood, and tried to focus back on the conversation.

'All that's behind you now,' the Worm was saying. 'You're going to find out what work is.'

'What would you know about it, Worm?' Willis demanded, unwilling to miss any opportunity.

'Aren't you supposed to be on shift, Willis?' the Worm asked with exaggerated polite concern. Willis, who had been getting ready to go, now found it necessary to stay a little longer.

'I'll go in my own time,' he growled.

'Okay, okay, I just thought I'd mention it.' The Worm turned back to Randall, revelling in his momentary importance. 'We had three men die last month. I thought it would be simplest to put you in one of their places on the roster.' This with a sideways glance at Willis, who had originally suggested the idea in the loading bay, but no reaction. 'You'll take over his shift, his bunk and his snowsuit.'

'I hope it fits,' said Randall, observing the comic-opera appearance of the Worm's pants and sleeves.

'None of them do,' said the Worm defensively, 'but that's your problem. I've been working out the details for the rostering, so now I'll show you where you'll be sleeping. You'll be sharing a bunkroom with Lobo.'

Willis suppressed a snort, and Doc said, 'Don't worry, Randall. You could do much worse. Do you feel fit enough to go?'

'You're the Doctor. You tell me.'

Doc smiled and shook his head. 'Only a nickname,' he said.

Randall thought about it for a moment, trying to assess the feedback from his body. It sang with all the energy of wet string. 'Not too bad,' he said at length. 'Just that I might be sick.'

'That's the yeast. It takes a while to get used to it, and after that you won't be able to eat anything else.'

The Worm was by the door, holding it open and looking pointedly from one to another. 'If you don't mind,' he said, 'I'd like to be getting along. I want to have your paperwork ready for the next shift.'

Randall stepped out first into the corridor. The Worm stayed where he was, holding the door and blinking expectantly at Doc and Willis. They followed Randall without comment, so that the Worm was the last to leave.

The Worm led Randall off towards Main Street, while Doc and Willis dawdled behind. Neither was heading for anything pleasant or enjoyable; if Willis's team were already out on the ice, which they probably were, he would have to grope his way out along the guide-wire until he caught up with them. Doc, in deference to his age, could look forward to a joyous ten hours' stirring in the crap tanks.

"What's the matter, Willis?' he said after a while. 'You've gone very quiet.'

Willis looked up to be sure that Randall had moved on out of earshot. 'I said it before, Doc. Something's wrong. Why send us a citizen?'

'If what he says is true, and there's no more Central Command, then the citizens will be technically of the same status as anyone else. Probably lower, if the underbelly council's in charge. Why shouldn't one of them wind up here?'

Willis dismissed it with a gesture. 'I don't believe that, either. If the computer's fallen, and the underbelly has taken over, why haven't they brought us home?'

'I can think of at least fifty reasons, Willis. Whatever made us dangerous to Central Command makes us equally dangerous to any government replacing it.'

'Clever talk, Doc, but these are our own kind. They wouldn't let us down. This Randall's something else.'

They were at the gap where the subsidiary tunnel and Main Street joined. They should have split to go on in different directions, but instead they stopped. 'What do you mean?' Doc asked.

'I watched him. The way he listened and took it all in. Accepted it straight away and without any self-pity. He may have the breeding stamp of a citizen, but his mind's something else.'

'I don't know. I never had much contact with them.'

'I stole from them. They were easy. Drop a citizen in here and he'd stick his head between his knees and bleat to go back to the herd. Randall didn't. And you know what Central did with that kind of failure.'

Doc's eyes grew large and round as he considered the prospect. 'The Elite?'

'Exactly. Randall was—or is—police.'

Doc considered it for a moment. 'Well. . . so what?'

'This is where you and I part company, Doc. There's no place for an Elite here. Maybe the Worm was right, and we should have lost him on the way up to the Recovery Room.'

'He'd be dead. You don't mean that.'

'Don't I? All that crap about some jerk closing down the main computer. The underbelly council wanting to re-open the space trade. This planet's been off the spaceways so long it's got nothing to offer. The story's so transparent, you could keep fish in it. Randall's a spy, and he's been placed here by Central Command. I don't know what for, but I'm sure of one thing. It's bad for all of us.'

The Doc sighed. 'Maybe you're right, Willis. Who's to say?'

'That's the trouble, we've no way of knowing. But as long as Randall's around there's an extra danger we can do without.'

'I hope you're not considering anything rash,' Doc frowned.

'Me?' Willis was a picture of wounded innocence. 'As if I would. I've got to go, I'm way overdue on the ice. See you around, Doc.'

'Be seeing you, Willis.' Doc waited a moment as Willis went off down the corridor towards the bays, and then turned and stepped through into Main Street, heading to where the crap tanks belched and beckoned.

FOUR

RANDALL WASN'T fit for the grand tour that the Worm seemed to want to give him. He continually tripped and stumbled on the uneven flooring, and the cold air that eased down the passages in a barely noticeable breeze began to make him feel numb and sick. The Worm had to compromise in the end, leading him around the longer loop of Main Street and pointing out the branching tunnels on either side as they passed. What he called the 'Cantina' was, it seemed, in the centre of the loop, reached by openings at each corner, while the outside of the curve had the bunkrooms to the South and the crap tanks to the North. This tight little complex was boxed in by two massive chambers in the form of the loading bays and cargo store to the West and the generators to the South, but this relatively simple schematic plan was then confused by a rambling maze of hand-hewn corridors and tunnels, some of which led to sub-complexes of small chambers but many of which led nowhere at all.

Nobody knew the age of the Palace or its original purpose. The conjecture was that it had originally been some kind of long-term research base, remembered and converted by Central Command in a spasm of imaginative economics. Only surface meltwater was used for drinking, for the sea had been sterilized of life with a dumping of some exceptionally dirty radioactive material, perhaps from the Palace's own automated reactors.

Then the Worm began to talk about the pipe network and the need to maintain it at a set level of heat loss, and Randall mentally switched off. He'd heard this already, and he needed most of his concentration for the simple effort of keeping upright. The shallow curve of Main Street before and behind gave the impression that it had no real end which, as a loop, it didn't. He began to suspect that the Worm might be leading him around twice or more in order to make the most of his captive audience.

Randall stopped, and subsided against a wall. He felt the ice against his back begin to melt and soak into his clothes. The Worm returned and waited for him, looking a little disappointed.

'Only a couple of doors down,' he said, 'and you'll be there.'

'I think I can manage that,' Randall replied, and then added, 'I'm sorry, what do I call you?'

'Call me Worm. All these crumbs do. It stopped hurting long ago.'

Randall pushed himself upright, and his hands came away wet. They moved on more slowly than before.

'Is it as cold as this everywhere in the Palace?' Randall asked.

'Keep it too warm and the walls would melt. It's better in the bunkrooms—they're lined with the wood from the packing cases. They say it can get really cosy.'

'Where do you sleep, then?'

The Worm scowled. 'Think I'd bunk with any of those lousy crumbs? I wouldn't, even if they let me. I sleep in the office.' Randall remembered the bundle of blanket and wadding behind the Worm's 'desk'. 'None of the crumbs would even panel it for me. Lobo said he might get around to it, but he never has. They're all the same. Lousy crumbs. You'll be just like them, given time.'

'Why will I?'

'Stands to reason. Place like this, everybody needs somebody to pick on. Start too many fights and the whole thing breaks down—before you know it, we're all dead. Me, I'd rather be picked on than dead. As long as they're spitting on me, they're leaving each other alone.'

Randall was surprised. 'That's very philosophical,' he said.

'But I never said I liked it,' the Worm replied sharply. 'Don't get that idea.'

'I won't.'

'They don't appreciate what I do for them. What with the rosters, and all—they'd be dead without me to organize them.

They've got no respect for the intellect.'

'No?' said Randall, mainly to keep the conversation going so that the Worm wouldn't go skipping ahead again at top speed. 'What about the one called Doc?'

'He doesn't count, him and his friends. They never did a roster in their lives. Just because they're called dissidents and not crooks like the rest of us, it's like they were priests or something. Me, I was a credit accountant—got a life term for grand computer fraud. I'd like to see any lousy dissident match that. This is where you bunk.'

They'd arrived at one of the heavy doors set back in the ice, and the Worm twisted the handle and pushed it inwards. A light flicked on, and Randall followed him into the room.

It was larger than he'd expected and contained six wooden-frame bunk-beds stacked in vertical twos. The walls were, as the Worm had said, lined with an uneven patchwork of raw wood. All of the bunks except for one had shapeless folded stacks of material on them and Randall recognized the dull pastel colours of snow suits.

'It's no warmer,' he said.

'Hard luck. It's better when it's full of people and the door's closed. Your bunk's up top, and you'll find a snowsuit and blanket on it. There's a charged power pack as well. If it doesn't fit too well, try one of those on one of the other bunks.'

'Whose were they?'

'It doesn't matter. That one, his name's off the rosters and he's gone. Took off his suit and walked out into a blizzard. Nobody would stop him, but I still think the lousy crumb could have left us his body for the tanks. Keep off that bunk.'

Randall had been moving to sit down on the nearest lower bunk, but the Worm grabbed his sleeve and pulled him away, reaching in to smooth the crease on the blanket where Randall's hand had rested momentarily.

'Lobo doesn't like anybody messing with his bunk,' the Worm explained.

Randall sat on the other side of the room, this time without raising a complaint. 'Anything else I ought to know about him?' he asked.

The Worm thought for a moment. 'He's slow, but he's decent. They leave him alone because he's big, except when there are a lot of them together and then they know that he's not dumb enough to cause trouble. He's a creep. Keep on the right side of him.'

'I'll try,' Randall said, wanting nothing more than to sink back on to the hard mattress but knowing that this might be his last chance to learn by any way other than painful experience. 'I don't seem to have a choice.'

'And another thing. Don't play on the citizen angle. It won't hold any sway in here.'

'I wasn't thinking of it.'

'Good.' The Worm moved towards the door. 'Your shift's not due back for a few hours yet. Ask Lobo to show you the routine and where you eat. You go out with them next trip. Bulstrode's the team leader, watch out for him. And Berg. He's as mean as Bulstrode but he's only got half a brain, so he's more dangerous. I'm going now. Sink or swim, Randall.' Randall was framing a reply, but the door had already closed. The ice walls of the room were an effective deadener of sound, so that with the echoes of distant activity from the corridor cut off all he could hear was a faint, steady drip somewhere.

The top bunk he'd been allocated seemed impossibly far away. He reached behind him for the spare blanket on the bunk where he sat and about ten seconds later he was asleep, still grasping the half-unfolded material across his chest.

FIVE

There was no way of telling how much later he woke up, but it didn't feel like long. He was cold and bent, and his head ached fiercely around some impossible point centred between his eyes. He was damp from his own perspiration in the cold humidity of the bunkroom, the hard light from the single naked bulb hazed by the suspended moisture of his breath.

He lay for a while without moving, but the discomfort only intensified. He tried to spread the blanket out with a minimum of effort, but discovered he was lying on half of it. In resignation he pulled himself up and reached around to free it, but his hand landed on the padded bulk of the snow suit.

The material of the suit was warm to the touch, and when he unrolled the bundle it fell out into two complete layers, an inner suit lined and tracked with the tiny veins of heating elements, and the outer weatherproof layer. Moving as quickly as possible he removed his rough prison wear and pulled on the first garment; it showed no sign at all of its several generations of use, and it carried no stain or odour of any kind. The second layer was similarly clean but it betrayed its age by its faded condition—the lining was a deep flame red, in contrast to the pale orange outer surface. It was belted and the pants legs ended in light, cleated snow boots, while the upper arms and shoulders had an extra layer of ribbed padding. A long narrow plate lay along the outside of the right thigh, and here a set of terminals dangled free, along with an open clip.

The power unit was, as the Worm had said, with the suit and blanket on the upper bunk.

The pack snapped easily into its fastening on his hip and the terminals attached without any problem. Nothing happened.

Under normal circumstances he would have spotted the

trouble straight away but he was cold, dazed, and still trying to process the long-sleep poisons out of his system. Minutes passed as he stared, tried to think, messed around with the connections, stared again. Then with what seemed like a terrific burst of inspiration he stripped down to the inner layer and found the point where the heating network had to be connected to the input from the outer suit.

This time the flat package against his leg came to life immediately, glugging a little inside its casing. His feet and chest began to warm first, and in a pocket he found gloves which linked into the heating circuit and locked on to the suit at the wrist. After hardly more than a minute the entire outfit was working, dissolving the pain in his joints and muscles. Before lying back on the bunk he switched off the light, and then he stretched out with the blanket pulled over his head to take the hard edge off the air.

When he awoke for the second time he knew that it was several hours later. The knot of pain in his head had fallen slack and unwound, and while he didn't exactly feel strong he was confident that he would be able to stand upright without needing a wall within arm's length.

And, of course, he was hungry. A week of intravenous feeding had left his stomach feeling like a loose bag of acid. Wait for Lobo, the Worm had said; he'll show you the routine and where to eat. Randall tried to remember how the Worm had pointed out the tunnels running inwards from Main Street to the Cantina, but the details of the whole progress from the Recovery Room to the bunkroom eluded him. He pushed the blanket away and sat upright on the bunk, waiting for Lobo.

The return of the shift from the ice was announced by nothing more than a muted shuffling filtered through the heavy door. The sound subsided, and then the darkness of the bunkroom split wide open as light and noise spilled in from the corridor.

The man who moved forward in this bright flood almost filled the doorway. He stepped into the room and began to swing the door shut but then he stopped in the sudden realization that something was wrong. He turned slowly and faced the middle of the room.

'Who's there?' he demanded. 'Stand up so I can see you.' Randall wasn't sure what to say. He'd been sitting fully in the shaft of light that had fallen from the open door, obvious to anybody entering the room. 'Don't panic,' he said, rising cautiously to his feet, 'I'm supposed to be here.'

The man in the doorway, a black silhouette against the opening, had his arm raised protectively in front of him. Not a cowardly stance, but certainly a defensive one. 'Over here,' he said with a sharp beckoning motion. 'I still can't see you.'

Randall moved as indicated. 'Why?' he said cautiously. 'What's the matter?'

'I'm ice blind, that's what's the matter. But don't try anything. Lay a hand on me and I'll break your fingers.'

'I wasn't thinking of trying anything. That—the Worm put me here and told me to wait.'

'The Worm?' The big man relaxed a little as understanding began to form. 'He says you're bunking in here?'

'That's right.'

'You're the new creep? Came in the coffin this morning?'

'That's what I'm told. I didn't know much about it.'

'I helped carry you. Later on, Willis brings the story out on to the ice. Says you're a citizen, and more. That true?'

Randall saw dangerous ground. 'Some of it. Maybe I'll tell you the full story some time.'

'Don't want to know it.' Lobo snapped on the bunkroom light and kicked the door closed with a backward flip; as an escape route it seemed he no longer considered it necessary.

Randall could see his eyes now that the light was on; they were red-rimmed and sore, the pupils contracted to tiny points. Otherwise he was big, his hair and beard in the same shaggy cut as Willis and the Doc. 'I can see you now,' he said. 'Willis was right.'

'What else did Willis say?'

'Never mind. Which bunk did the Worm give you?' Randall pointed. 'Over there. The top one.'

Lobo didn't even look at it. He was watching Randall closely. 'He tell you it's a dead man's bunk?'

'He told me.'

'And the one below it, and the one next to that? It's just you, me and three dead men. Gets pretty cold at night.' If Lobo was joking, he wasn't smiling.

'If there are bunks free, why do they make the Worm sleep in his office?'

Lobo stripped off his gloves and stuffed them into the side pocket of his snow suit, then sat carefully on his neatly-arranged bunk. 'The Worm told you that? What do you think of him?'

'I didn't take any liking to him, if that's what you mean, but I think he's a miserable case. Nobody deserves the amount of contempt he seems to get.'

Lobo shook his head slowly. 'Brother, you're soft. I'll give you a piece of advice, free and for nothing. You get any kind thoughts like that, shove 'em. Otherwise you'll find the Worm's forgotten and you're getting his share. That's a hell of a thing to get rid of—I've had it, and I know. You—' he flicked a sideways glance at Randall, who was still standing— 'you aren't even half my size, you got no chance. Any time you get any warm ideas about the Worm, just remember that he wanted to leave you dead to make his paperwork easier.'

'What?'

'It's a tough world. Give a guy your hand and all he'll do is steal your rings. That's the Worm, that's me, that's Willis. Welcome to the Ice Palace, Randall.'

'Thanks.' Randall dropped back on to the bunk where he'd slept. 'I'll remember.'

'The Worm say you're following my shift?'

'That's right. He said I should ask you to show me the routine.'

The tension that Lobo had carried in from the ice snapped back at full strength. 'He's got no right. I don't want you owing me anything.'

Randall shrugged. 'Well, I'm sorry. What else can I do?'

Lobo considered it for a moment, and then wound down a little. 'Nothing. Just follow me round and watch. I'm doing nothing special for you.'

'I'm not asking for it.'

Lobo nodded. If he wasn't satisfied with the arrangement, at least he was resigned to it. 'That's all right, then,' he said. 'When the blindness is gone, we go and eat.'

The distance to the Cantina was much less than Randall had expected; obviously carved out with one original main entrance it was now serviced by irregular additional tunnels which connected to all parts of the Main Street passage encircling it. They emerged into a long, low-ceilinged cave; there was solid ice underfoot, but Randall found that his boots gripped on it with no problem. At the far end of the cave about a dozen men sat on rough benches at equally rough trestle tables, crouched forward over wooden bowls and looking like shipwrecked sailors in worn-out spacesuits. A similar number were in line, waiting as a man about the Doc's age spooned the sick-like liquid that Randall recognized as yeast from a wheeled metal drum. As he followed Lobo towards the end of the line, Randall heard the beginnings of an argument. He glanced up, interested but trying not to appear so.

'You call this food?' The man was about Lobo's size, perhaps even bigger. His snow suit was stretched to the limit of its elasticity.

'What's the matter with it?' the elderly chef demanded. 'It's the same as you had yesterday.'

'That's what I mean. It was crap yesterday as well.'

Hardly surprising, Randall thought, considering what it had fed on. One of the men at a table looked up. 'What's the matter, Berg?'

'Nothing's the matter. I'm just talking to the guy about the yeast.'

The man at the table wasn't to be put off. 'What about the yeast?'

'I think it's off.'

The seated man pantomimed astonishment. ' You mean you can tell?'

Nearly every head in the room was turned towards Berg now, obviously as he wanted it. 'Look, Berg,' said the old man serving him, 'what do you think this is? The stuff's either fresh or it's dead. When it's dead it just slushes around.'

Berg shook his bowl experimentally. 'It's doing that now.'

'Well, what do you expect? You've been waving it around for ten minutes.'

'What do you mean, ten minutes? I only just walked in!'

'Come on Berg,' the next man in the line said, and Randall recognized him as Willis. 'Everybody's waiting.'

The man at the table looked up again. 'Get some fresh and sit down, Berg.'

'Up yours, Bulstrode,' Berg replied, and emptied his bowl back into the metal drum. 'Gimme some fresh.'

The line moved forward, and Randall collected an empty bowl from the stack, as Lobo had done. Lobo didn't turn or speak, which was fine for Randall; he wanted to concentrate on the two men in his team that the Worm had given him warning about. Berg took his bowl and went over to Bulstrode's table.

Randall tried to hear what they were saying, but was distracted by the closer conversation between Willis and the man with the spoon.

'What's the matter with him?' the old man said.

'He gets sick of talking about the weather,' Willis said. 'What do you think's the matter?'

'Listen,', the old man said earnestly to the line in general, 'if we could do anything with this stuff, don't you think we would? Anything you try to add just kills it off. I even left a drumload inside the shields near the fission plant to see if it would mutate into something more exciting.'

Somebody asked, 'What happened?'

'It started eating the drum,' the old man said mournfully.

Willis followed Berg, and the line moved on again. A couple of men came in behind Randall, but he didn't turn; he tried to concentrate his hearing towards Bulstrode's table. He heard Bulstrode say, 'What's with you, Berg?' and Berg reply, 'You know damn well. I'm two hours short on sleep from last night. What are you going to do about it, Willis?'

Willis was coming around the end of the table. 'Do about what?'

'Berg's sore because you woke him up this morning,'

Bulstrode said, and Berg nodded in morose agreement.

'And what about me?' Willis demanded as he sat down. 'I had to go and freeze in the loading bay for those two hours.'

Berg was unimpressed. 'Who cares what you had to do? I'm talking about me.'

Willis hunched over his bowl. 'Don't blame me for it. Blame the Worm.'

'What you saying about me, Willis?' came a shrill voice from behind Randall, and everybody on Bulstrode's table gave an exaggerated groan.

'Get lost, Worm,' Berg said loudly. 'You're even less popular than usual right now.'

'Up yours, Berg,' piped the Worm with unusual bravado.

Berg's head snapped up and around. Randall looked away, hoping Berg's attention wouldn't focus on him yet. 'Say that again!'

'Cheers, Berg,' the Worm replied, a little less enthusiastically.

Berg turned his back, muttering, 'Is that shrimp trying to take a rise out of me?' and the line moved on again. Lobo moved away, and Randall found he was next.

The old man with the spoon faltered when he saw Randall, but he said nothing as he dropped a ladleful of grey scum into his bowl. Randall thought with regret that his short hair and stubble would ensure that he stayed conspicuous for some time.

Lobo set his bowl down on Bulstrode's table, and Willis said, 'Where've you been, Lobo? We've missed the thrill of your conversation.'

'Had to do a few things,' Lobo said quietly, meeting nobody's eyes.

'Give me a pencil, somebody,' Bulstrode said with energy. 'I've just got to write that down.'

Randall tried to get a final measure of these men as he approached the table. He passed other places he might sit, but he was bound to be noticed eventually and it might as well be now. As far as he could tell Bulstrode wasn't the giant that Berg was, but his smaller frame was thick-set with compact slabs of muscle. By contrast Berg was apelike, with a rounded head and a wide mouth like a slash in a basketball.

'Can I sit here?' Randall said, addressing himself directly to Bulstrode on the suspicion that his status as team leader might have forced a modification of the aggression in his personality.

Bulstrode didn't look up straight away. 'Did something speak?'

'My name's Randall. I arrived today. The Worm says I'm to join your shift.'

Dark eyes lifted, flicked up and down him. 'Sit where you like.'

The coiled spring of apprehension in Randall's belly loosed off a notch. 'Thanks. Hello, Willis.'

Willis continued to stare into his yeast and said nothing. Randall saw his cheeks starting to flush red behind the hanging loops of hair.

'Your friend says hello, Willis,' said Berg, grinning broadly. 'What do you say to that?'

'You talk too much, Berg.'

'That's great coming from you, Willis. Especially after all the talking you've been doing today.' He looked down the table, and his grin wiped away like a raindrop from a windscreen. 'He's told us all about you, Randall. I didn't hear much that I liked.'

'I'm sorry about that.'

'Forget it, Berg,' Bulstrode interrupted, and indicated the remainder of the yeast line with a short movement of his head. 'Go take it out on the Worm.'

But Berg wasn't to be diverted. 'Why should I,' he said, 'when we've got a lower form of life right here?'

Randall sat down and looked across the table. 'What have you been saying, Willis?'

Willis went on studying his yeast, and Berg said, 'Willis has done enough talking for one day. He doesn't feel like doing any more.'

'I think I've got a right to know what's been said about me.'

Berg was on his feet. All the stored venom of his rotten prison existence came to bear on Randall. 'A right? You've got as many rights as we say you've got!'

'Sit down, Berg,' Bulstrode said.

'No, I don't think I will. I want to know what this citizen's about.'

'Is that what's bothering you?' Randall said, feigning surprise.

'That, and a few other things,' Berg replied, moving around the table towards him. 'Get up, Randall.'

Randall knew it had to come, and it might as well be now. Willis's head was still down, Lobo was watching without expression. 'Is this what you want?' Randall said, standing up and stepping around the bench. 'A quick standoff to show that you're superior?'

'You've got it wrong, Randall. All I want to know about is this.'

Berg's fist was the shape of a cured ham and the texture of a boulder, and he threw it with accuracy if with no great style. Randall was lifted several inches into the air from the blow, folding about the middle as he went and dropping into a tangled heap on the floor only a moment later. The padding of his suit took the force of the fall but his cheekbone banged hard on the ice and knocked his eyes way out of focus.

Berg was walking away, his suit a pale yellow blur. Bulstrode's voice seemed to come from the bottom of a hole as he said, 'You satisfied now, Berg?'

'Hell, Willis,' Berg was saying, and the landscape undulated as he turned and came back, 'this guy's no more from the Police Elite than I am. What are you trying to pull?'

'I only said what I thought.'

'You should tell us your thoughts more often, make it nice and peaceful. I'm sorry, Randall.' Randall felt an oversized hand slip under his arm, and he was hauled to his feet. 'I didn't break anything. Help him back to his bunk, Worm.'

The horizon was all wrong, the Worm a shapeless blob sliding uphill across it. 'Shall I take him some food?' the blob said, getting its shoulders under Randall's other arm as Berg let go.

'I don't think he's hungry.' Berg's voice, fading off into the distance. I am, screamed a voice at the back of Randall's head, I haven't eaten for a sodding *week*, but it somehow didn't make it to the outside world.

The universe began to rotate, and Randall realized they were moving. 'What's the idea, Berg?' Bulstrode was saying.

'You saw the way he folded.' Berg's voice was slipping away to one side as they moved, and Randall tried to hang back and listen. 'The Police Elite have these trained reactions. He should have turned my hand and wiped the floor with me. I gave him enough warning.'

Bulstrode: 'What do you think of that, Willis?'

Willis: something incomprehensible, along the lines of', 'I can only say what I think, and that stands.'

A derisive laugh from Berg, a long way away.

Something else from Berg.

Nothing from Lobo.

SIX

THE WORM CHATTERED all the way back to the bunkroom, but Randall took very little of it in. By the time that they arrived at the door he was at least breathing normally and seeing straight, even if he couldn't stand fully upright. The Worm unshouldered him and propped him against a wall as he opened the door.

'You took a bad one there, Randall,' he was saying. 'Remember I warned you about Berg—half the brains and twice the meanness. You'll have to be more careful if you want to survive in here.'

'I appreciate the support, but I can do without the philosophy.'

The Worm switched on the light. Randall saw the nearest flat surface and lurched towards it. 'Not there!' the Worm yelped, grabbing a loose handful of Randall's suit and hauling on it. 'That's Lobo's bunk!' He tried to propel Randall up to his allocated berth, but Randall wasn't going. He ducked under the Worm's arm and crash-landed on the lower bunk he'd used earlier.

'*He* won't give you any arguments,' the Worm observed. 'We recycled him last week.'

'Get out of here, Worm,' Lobo said.

Light flashed on the single lens in the Worm's glasses as he spun round to face the doorway. 'We didn't touch your bunk, Lobo,' he stammered. 'He was going to, but I stopped him.'

'Out.'

'Sure, Lobo.' The Worm scuttled past and out the doorway, turning as he went for a parting shot. 'You can't say I didn't warn you, Randall.'

Lobo shut the door so hard that dust shook off the frames of the beds. His eyes were narrow slits, and he was furious.

'What's the matter, Lobo?' Randall said. 'Didn't I drop fast enough for you?'

'Shove the comedy, Randall. I want some answers. What's with you?'

Randall shook his head. 'I'm sorry, I don't understand.'

Lobo moved closer. His fists were clenched hard, the knuckles white. 'You know damn well the rumours Willis has been spreading on the ice today. Who do you think you're taking in?'

'Taking in with what?'

'We've never had a citizen here, and then we get you with a half-assed story about the Central computer being shut down. It stinks, Randall. Within an hour the whole Palace knew we had a Police Elite spy on board. Berg just decided to test the idea and see what your reactions are like.'

Randall pulled his knees up closer to his chest to cradle his ache. 'Well, I hope the Palace is satisfied now.'

'The Palace may be, but I'm not. Most people watch faces—I watch hands. They give more away. I watched yours.'

'Didn't do me a lot of good, did they?'

Lobo took a step nearer and Randall saw that he was more than angry; he was hurt, and Randall couldn't understand why. 'Don't give me that. It took maybe a fraction of a second for Berg's fist to travel. You reached out, put both your own hands around it, changed your mind before they touched and pulled them back again. If I'd blinked I wouldn't have seen any of it. Nobody in the underbelly can move that fast, and I'm damn sure no citizen could. So how can you?'

'You tell me.'

'Because you've had that biofeedback response training, that's why. You let Berg floor you on purpose. You didn't even move with the blow, so Berg couldn't tell you were faking. Now give me a good reason why I shouldn't tear you open right now.'

Randall allowed himself to straighten out a little. 'Because with feedback training I could probably stop you from doing it.'

'I'd take a chance, but you lose either way. Beat me and you'll give yourself away to the others. So?'

No point pretending. Randall swung up into a sitting position. Lobo didn't move back. 'What am I supposed to say? You've already decided it's true.'

'Damn right it's true. I want to know what Central's doing, trying to put a spy in here.'

'I'm not a spy,' Randall insisted, 'I'm a prisoner like the rest of you. And I told you, Central's out of action. Doesn't it make sense? With the underbelly in charge, they're bound to start hammering the Elite. I'm only being careful when I cover my background.'

'Won't wash, Elite or not, you're still citizen. Crime's been bred out of you.'

'The Worm was right. There's nothing stupid about you.'

'I'm not asking you for a reference,' Lobo exploded, 'I want the truth!'

Randall was on his feet and matching volume. 'The truth is that Central's been wiped and there's no machine in charge any more. I told Willis and Doc that I'd been involved in some way, but I didn't tell them all the truth.'

Lobo nodded. 'Keep talking.' Randall didn't know if he was being given the chance to justify or damn himself.

'There was a man called Rorvik who'd worked out a way to cheat the computer's security systems and get into the unmanned areas. Incidentally, he was a citizen, so bang goes your idea about breeding. I was the Elite officer assigned to track Rorvik down and stop him. I followed him into the dome.'

Lobo had calmed considerably as the story was told, but he was not obviously convinced. 'So how,' he said, 'did he manage to wipe Central?'

Randall took a deep breath. 'He didn't. He was dead before he reached the deprogramming console. I did the wiping.'

There was a pause. Then: 'You're asking me to believe a lot, Randall.'

'Right,' Randall said emphatically. 'Now can you imagine me trying to convince all fifty of you with that story?'

'You'd be slung straight into the yeast tanks for a liar.'

Sensing that Lobo's tide of fury was well receded, Randall sat down on the bunk again. 'So I let Berg .make his demonstration, everybody gets some entertainment and they stop wondering about me. Except you. What are my hands telling you now?'

Lobo frowned, saw the joke, and relaxed a little more. 'How the hell should I know?' he said. 'You're sitting on them. Maybe I'm stupid after all, Randall. Maybe I believe you. But I'm going to watch you.' And he dragged the blanket off his bunk and reached for the light switch.

'Watch all you like, Lobo,' Randall said as the room snapped into darkness. 'All I want is the time to work out a way out of here and back to the city.'

'Isn't that what everybody wants? Forget it, Randall. It can't be done.'

'They said that about the Central defences and look what happened.'

'Slow down,' Lobo cut across him. 'I didn't say I'd swallowed that one. I'm just reserving an opinion.'

'Thanks, anyway.'

'And don't thank me!' A flash of Lobo's earlier anger erupted in the darkness. 'I don't want any lousy crumb thinking he owes me anything. In a place like this it goes against survival. Maybe I'll wind up thinking that you took on Berg to get my sympathy. You think I can go bursting into tears every time he bops some guy?'

The shadow in the room wasn't absolute. The door was a close fit, but there was a faint glow along its upper edge that was caught and reflected by minute droplets of frozen condensation held in the surface fibres of the ceiling insulation. Randall could almost see it as a night sky overhead. 'All right, Lobo,' he said, 'so you stay independent. You've seen through me, and I've seen through you.'

Immediate suspicion across the bunkroom. 'What do you mean by that?'

'I mean that under all that hair and gristle there's a human being trying not to get out. But don't worry. The secret's safe with me.'

There was silence, and Randall wondered if he'd gone too far. Then: 'Any time you get a sentimental idea like that, remember I killed a guy to be here. Then see how you feel about it.' And he rolled over noisily, as if to indicate a definite end to the conversation.

'Sure, Lobo.'

'And get some sleep.' There was suddenly something missing from the room, and Randall guessed that Lobo had switched off his power pack. It must give off some tone barely on the threshold of hearing. 'You're out on the ice in nine hours.'

SEVEN

Randall didn't sleep. He was sore from Berg's blow, but far less troubled by it now than he had allowed everybody to think. After an hour or so he left the bunkroom to see if he could find any of the repellent yeast in the Cantina, but when he traced his way back through empty corridors he found nothing but deserted tables and a stack of rinsed wooden bowls. He was tempted to look for the place where the yeast grew but decided against it—so much of the Palace was the same, ice upon ice, that without a guide he might never find his way back. Instead he stayed with Main Street, following it in a complete circuit until he recognized his starting point.

If he felt anger or despair it didn't show—he had the State and his conditioning to thank for that. Any such unproductive or wasteful reaction would be suppressed and retained, charcoal burning to give a continuous and controlled delivery of energy directed to one purpose. Randall wanted out, back to the city he didn't know how not to love.

Until the opportunity came he would be the model prisoner. Berg's demonstration had already defused some of the controversy of his appearance, and all that now remained was to slide quietly into Ice Palace routine. At the same time he would watch, store the data, and wait.

He went back and lay on his bunk, waiting for something to happen. Lobo breathed slowly and evenly on the other side of the room, turning every now and again but making no other sound. Randall hoped that he had Lobo judged correctly, a gentle man in an ogre's ill-fitting clothes.

It seemed a long time later when a hand bell rang out in Main Street. Lobo came awake instantly, swinging his legs out of the bed and clipping his power pack on as a matter of conditioned routine.

Randall followed down to the Cantina. Apparently they would have to eat and clear out of the way before the incoming shift arrived. He joined the line and took his yeast, this time served by a different oldster, and observed that all the men were heading for the same tables they had occupied for the last feed.

Bulstrode noticed him but didn't react. Berg gave him a wide grin that was neither threatening nor pleasant. Lobo looked at nobody, and Willis was turned slightly away, lost in some preoccupation of his own.

To eat was agony, but he couldn't let it show. The yeast was like a cold fondue of mouldy cheese, sticking to the roof of his mouth and coating the inside of his throat so that it threatened to choke him, making it impossible to take a quick swallow and get it over with. He managed to half-empty the bowl and decided to leave it at that—already it was a thick, greasy pool in his stomach. He assumed that he would get used to the diet; nobody else was showing any sign of revulsion, and Berg actually seemed to be enjoying it.

Conversation was minimal and when the majority of men started to move towards an exit Randall got up to follow them. Lobo caught his eye, and Randall joined him without being too obvious about it.

'Stick with me,' Lobo said almost in a whisper, glancing to one side as if in fear of observation. 'Couple of things you'll have to know.'

Randall tried not to let his pleasure show. Lobo was becoming a reluctant ally, propelled by his nature in the face of reason. Randall followed him out into Main Street, and when Lobo hung back from the moving crowd Randall did likewise.

When the last pastel-suited figure disappeared around the bend towards the loading bays leaving only long shadows on the ice wall and a distant shuffling, Lobo gestured Randall to follow and went off up a side branch. The flooring slats were laid lengthwise instead of across.

They emerged on to an iron gallery halfway up a large chamber. An open metal stairway led down to the lower level and up to another gallery above, where Randall could see two large riveted tanks and a lacing of pipework which ran down the wall behind them to the yeast pools below.

The purpose of the tanks was clear. They were neatly lettered 'Crap Tanks'. As Randall looked a man appeared from behind one of them and began to descend the iron stairs, closing the fastenings on his suit as he approached.

They climbed to the upper gallery and Lobo pointed out the cubicles around the back where Randall would go when he had to go. He also showed him a device called a sonic hose, part of the microwave generator which killed the bacteria in the raw material before piping it down to the yeast pools. It could also, Lobo explained, be used with care to sterilize the skin and clothes—this accounted for the mysterious freshness of Randall's aged suit and the absence of the odour that generally accompanies any area where men live and work together. They were all taking sonic showers—you wouldn't even have to take your suit off. Oh, and another thing, Lobo added. Use it often enough and it'll make you sterile for good—as if that mattered here.

Lobo disappeared for a couple of minutes, and as Randall waited he looked down over the guard rail. On the gallery below—the one on to which they had entered—the oldster from the Cantina wheeled an empty yeast drum to the brink and snapped a hook on to it, then unwound a rope from the rail and pulled to swing the drum up and out over the drop to the bottom level, letting its own weight take it down against the resistance of the pulleys.

There were three pools containing yeast in various stages of maturity, none of which Randall found remotely appealing. They were being stirred by long poles like oars, a man to each tank. One of them broke away from his stirring and reached to receive the empty drum. After a couple of minutes, Lobo came back and they moved on.

On the way back to Main Street there was a squeak and rumble in the tunnel behind them. Randall looked around and saw a full drum riding on its castors, bumping along the lengthwise planks which served as rails. The man was putting all his meagre strength into keeping the drum moving, veins and tendons bulging under his sallow skin and white hair, and all for the sake of the poorest nourishment Randall had ever known.

Lobo walked ahead, ignoring Randall again. When they arrived in the loading bay Bulstrode's team was fitted out and almost ready to go.

The stark floodlighting of the bay dazzled him for a moment but then he readjusted to the crisp shadows and sharp outlines, finding them somehow unreal after the muted glow of the ice tunnels.

Bulstrode's team numbered about a dozen, and they were in the middle of the bay finishing the loading of a man-harnessed sled. All the men were helmeted, and from a distance none was recognizable.

'We've got a load,' Bulstrode's voice echoed, amplified by his helmet and clipped in the bass range for clarity. 'Let's make the line and clip together. Who's pulling the sled?'

'Berg's on first turn,' somebody said at lower amplification.

'So where is he?'

One of the figures around the sled came upright, and Randall found that by size alone Berg was unmistakable. 'Where else would I be?' he demanded, and pushed through the crowd to take the sled harness.

Randall hurried after Lobo to the helmet rack. Lobo might be grudgingly cooperative elsewhere, but in public view Randall was on his own. Fortunately the helmet catch was a simple snap-lock, and the sound and voice channels engaged automatically.

They went over to join the team, falling in last in line because of their lateness. A couple of helmets turned and gave blank looks which Randall imagined to be of disapproval, but there was really no way of telling. Lobo showed no reaction, and the helmets turned forward to face the direction of the line.

A thin, grimy looking cord with loops at intervals was handed back. Randall didn't know what to do with it, and with everybody's back towards him there was no way he could observe and work it out. Hesitantly, he tapped Lobo's arm.

Lobo didn't turn at first. The line wasn't yet moving—the lead figure whom Randall assumed to be Bulstrode was consulting with Berg over a something written on a weatherproof plastic sheet. Then Lobo turned, and Randall held up the cord and shrugged as eloquently as the suit would let him.

Lobo held up his own section of the line, showing where it attached to a simple spring clip at the waist of the suit. It wouldn't be adequate as a safety line in case of a fall or avalanche, but it would at least keep the party together.

'The line's only a token,' Lobo said, keeping his voice low. 'Stay close and don't let it get stretched. Sometimes the visibility gets below ten feet—slow down too much and you could lose the group.'

'But how does Bulstrode find his way at the front?'

'There's a wire staked along the surface of the ice. If you do get lost, try to find it and follow it back. They radiate out from the Ice Palace. He's got a report from the men at the reactors on where the danger areas are. The cladding rots pretty fast, and if we don't get out to replace it the power plant goes into shutdown and we lose the Palace supply.'

Bulstrode was shouting, 'Everybody clipped up?'

Lobo half-turned to wave his hand in the air, and Randall did the same. Gears clanked and the outer door began to rise. Bright snow light forced in under its lower edge and began to spread.

Randall touched Lobo's arm again. 'Where's Willis in the line?'

'In front of me. Watch him, Randall. He still doesn't trust you.'

It was unlikely that Willis heard any of this. Randall could barely make it out over the rising howl that was streaming in through the open bay door. He felt the line pull; the three men immediately behind Berg's sled threw their weight against it to overcome the drag of the floor, and the team moved out.

They emerged from the cargo bay door rather than the loading bay—they wouldn't be able to make any tight turns with the sled, and the lip of ice between the loading bay and the open lead of frozen soup to the North would be too narrow to negotiate. Consequently they came out in a deep trench, the snow on its gently rising floor trodden into particles of mushy grey ice and then scattered over with a layer of fresh white. Presumably one of the teams' rostered duties would be to keep the trench clear; the leading men had already kicked through a two-foot high mound of fresh snow that had piled against the door, and a steady drift was starting into the bay itself.

They emerged from the trench on to a plain of snow. It seemed impossible that it could reflect so brightly when the sky overhead was a featureless iron grey, but even as Randall took it in the wind gusted hard and his helmet visor was suddenly crazed over with ice crystals. The line pulled taut and he staggered after it, rubbing at the clear plastic with the back of his glove. No sooner had he opened a patch of visibility in the middle and glimpsed the procession of stooped figures ahead than another wave of scouring hail washed over him, dragging him aside and almost making him fall.

The temperature in his suit was dropping. What had been adequate for the chill of the Ice Palace was barely effective in this bitter, freezing wind. He boosted the level on his power pack and felt the unit hum against his leg, but there was no immediately noticeable effect.

A glance back, but the Palace was already lost; even the deep slash of the trench, only yards behind them, had been swallowed by an impenetrable grainy swirl. Randall looked for Bulstrode's guidewire, but couldn't even see that.

The team waded on, knee-high in soft, crusty snow. As the last in line Randall was following a man-trodden ditch, the marks of the sled-runners slewed to either side and already filling in. The wind continually tried to push him aside, fooling him by slackening off and then slapping at him with a sudden hard dash of ice needles.

This continuous uncertainty was even more wearing than the numbness which was starting to spread as the blood cooled in his hands and feet. He reached to turn the power pack to its maximum output and almost ripped it away from its connections as he unexpectedly pitched forward, his leg thrusting down into uncompacted snow almost up to his hip. He scrambled up and staggered on, thankful at least for the inexorable guided progress of the line.

Apart from where they walked, the snow seemed even and pure. If the previous shift had followed this wire their passage was by now completely obliterated. Randall could make out in detail perhaps four or five of the suited figures ahead, leaning forward to keep their balance against the wind. The sled was no more than a blurred grey bulk, imagined as much as seen, the men ahead of it merged into its dim shape.

Far off to the right something was taking on regular form in the swirling murk. It angled to meet them, becoming more distinct as its line and theirs converged.

When they met the pipeline they stopped for a moment, presumably as Bulstrode checked his diagram to find the first specified danger area. The pipe was about three feet in diameter, raised above the snow at a level of about four feet, supported every ten yards or so by an ice-crusted pylon. Randall could now see what the long-standing Ice Palace residents meant when they complained about the quality of the cladding—it was nothing more than processed rags or something similar, four quarter-sections to every five-foot length clamped into place by two sliding metal belts. The air above the pipeline was filled with a furiously dancing pattern of snowflakes, stirred into a frenzy by escaping heat; and even as Randall watched a strip of soaked rag detached itself, hung as a streamer in the wind for a few seconds and then whirled away.

A signal, and the line moved on, following the pipeline and enjoying the rare pleasure of being battered from two directions at once as they marched in the strong eddy caused by the fixture. A few hundred yards and they came to a junction, a nowhere crossroads; they ducked under the pipe, one after another, and went on.

A different signal passed back along the line, left hand out sideways. Randall cursed his inattention. Communication was being carried along by some kind of code. If he didn't watch it he'd never learn it, and in these conditions such ignorance could prove fatal.

Left hand outstretched meant arrival. They'd been moving, Randall guessed, for an hour or more, but they probably weren't much further than half a mile from the buried Palace.

Everybody was unclipping from the line and moving towards the sled, and Randall followed, gathering in the loose cord as he went.

The damage here was obvious. The cladding was hanging off the pipeline on one side, and each gust of wind tore and exposed a little more metal. Bulstrode pointed first at one man, then at Randall, who had no idea what he was supposed to do next. But the first man was already being boosted up to straddle the pipe by two of the suited figures, so Randall moved to the other end of the damaged section and climbed up in the same way.

An almost imperceptible flash of light—it could have been the glint of the faceplate on a turning helmet. Then, as Randall struggled to undo the simple catch on the binding hoop, a rippling crack of thunder and another hard sideways buffet from the wind. He almost toppled, but somebody grabbed his ankle and hauled him back. A layer of ice broke loose from the catch and the hoop opened. As he slid it back the four sections of cladding fell away and others were manhandled into their place.

The pipeline was bright metal, jointed in a flexible coil so that it could snake and absorb any shifting in the ice-cap as the supporting pylons moved out of line. The under-sections went on without any problem but the cladding to be fitted over the pipe tried to lift in the wind. Somebody shouted, indistinct above the teaming of the blizzard, and the two largest figures—Berg and Lobo—moved in on either side of the pipe. As soon as he saw the opportunity Randall slid the hoop forward and clamped the cladding down. He looked up towards his opposite number as the man's silhouette flashed white against the landscape and another eruption of thunder followed almost immediately.

They were arguing around the sled as Randall dropped from the pipeline and floundered up to his waist in the loose powder of the drift. Brief, indistinct snatches of amplified conversation, and Bulstrode was shaking his head. Berg came around and joined in, pointing at the sled and at the newly-completed job, and Randall caught what sounded like, 'more harm than good', and 'Worm', and 'nearly screwed up'. Bulstrode's voice cut through with 'got the most critical section, but. . .' and the rest was drowned in another thundering rumble. Bulstrode looked up, and then all visibility went for a few seconds as a belt of airborne snow whipped through the party. When Randall could see again the line was re-forming and the sled was being turned around.

Lobo was buckling into the sled harness. Obviously the roster was being discarded with the onset of the storm, and Lobo was taking over from Berg to get the sled and the line back to the Palace as fast as possible. As Randall waded out of the drift to join the group the last anonymous figure in the line handed him the linking cord. The line was moving even as Randall clipped on.

The journey out seemed easy in comparison with the return. As before they tracked the pipe for some way but it was a blind, heads-down progress, stumbling and pushing ahead on shifting ground. Randall didn't even see when they veered away from the pipeline; one time he looked up and it had gone, that was all.

The wind was coming from all directions now, and the signs of their earlier passage had been wiped out. The earlier brilliance of the ice pack was now little more than twilight, lit by the occasional lightning flash. It threw the line ahead into sharp relief before the darkness fell again and the thunder rolled over them.

Randall's foot sank into a pocket of soft snow, and he pitched into the man ahead. The man stumbled and grabbed Randall's arm, the two steadying each other; and at that moment lightning forked and the man's blank faceplate became momentarily clear. Willis looked out.

A hard push against his chest, a snatch at his waist, and Randall fell backwards. He hit the snow spread out and it gave way under him, swallowing him to a depth of a couple of feet and then breaking up and falling in. He reached for the line, and it wasn't there.

He tried to roll over and push himself up, but his arm sank up to the elbow. Every second he wasted took the team further away; he put his weight on both hands to spread the pressure, and this time made it to his knees. There was nothing to see but a wall of snow, nothing to hear but the wind that drove it.

He shouted once, and then abandoned the effort; he could barely hear it himself. He floundered forward, hoping to fall into the trodden snow-ditch before it could fill in, and he covered several yards before realizing that in this direction was nothing but plain, crisp white. He turned, and saw that his own tracks were starting to fill, and at the limit of visibility were almost gone completely; he followed them back, tried to judge how far to go.

There's a wire staked along the surface of the ice. If you do get lost, try to find it and follow it back. Good advice, but where was the wire? What did it look like? Was it buried?

Perhaps he hadn't gone far enough to cross it, perhaps he'd overshot it. The wind was switching directions continually, giving no basis for a bearing. It sucked the heat from his suit, and the little unit on his leg was pumping determinedly to compensate. How long could the power pack take this excessive drain? He hadn't the experience to know.

He dropped to his knees and thrust his glove deep into the snow, scooping out as much of a narrow trench as he could. He moved on this way for several yards until he could be sure that he would have hit the wire had it been there and then reversed, tracking the already indistinct furrow back to his starting-point. He was trying to cover the area from one central spot, afraid that without any reference to the ground around him he might stagger in a blind circle and miss the wire completely.

On his third attempt he found it, striking it with his forearm beneath the surface of the snow. He got his hand around it and pulled, and it came up and broke free for several yards on either side.

Randall's power pack gave a little bleep and died.

He looped the wire over his arm and reached for the pack. The tiny red indicator light was out completely, and the unit on his leg had stopped pumping. He twisted the switch to *off*, left it a couple of seconds, switched it on again. The light glowed feebly and the heating unit glugged a couple of times, but the whole system died again when he tried to raise the level to anything above the absolute minimum.

There was also another problem. Which way led to the Ice Palace?

EIGHT

THE DOOR TO THE cargo bay was down when the team arrived back at the Palace, and they had to lift the sled and use it as a ram before they could make themselves heard inside. The door lifted and they fell in as soon as there was enough space to duck under the rising edge.

Several suit units were bleeping continuously, the final sign of total depletion in spite of conservation. The men were milling around and unbuckling their helmets even though the outer door was still open, and the man on the chain was shouting for the team leader.

Somebody told Bulstrode, and Bulstrode went over. 'What do you want, Palmer?'

'I want to know if your men are all inside so I can drop the hatch.'

Bulstrode glanced around. The bay door was still open, and the storm outside was rapidly becoming a storm inside. 'How the hell should I know?' he demanded. 'You think I'm going to count them? Get the hatch closed, Palmer.'

There was a chorus of agreement and somebody said, 'Get off your backside and pull the chains before we all freeze.'

'I only asked a civil question,' Palmer protested.

'Up yours, Palmer,' Berg shouted from over by the helmet racks, and he moved over to join Bulstrode.

Palmer turned and unhitched the chain. As the door began to rattle down he said, 'All right, but don't blame me if one of you freezes to death someday.'

There were a few unenthusiastic 'up yours Palmers', but the entire team was now headed for the bay exit. One man came from the back, elbowing through until he reached Bulstrode and calling to him from behind. Bulstrode didn't look up, but Berg, who was walking next to him, turned.

'Leave it, Lobo,' he said. 'Can't you see he's beat?'

'Then you tell me, Berg. Have you seen Randall? You know, the new guy?'

'I know who he is, but I don't know where he is. Who cares, anyway?'.

'He was clipped behind me in the line going out,' Lobo explained, 'but I didn't see him after I took over on the sled.'

Berg thought for a moment, a rare and spectacular effort. 'I think he may have been behind Willis. But I'm not sure.'

Lobo frowned. 'Have you seen Willis, then?'

'No, I haven't seen Willis, and with his popularity rating at zero I don't want to. What is this, Lobo? Does Randall owe you, or something?'

'Forget it, Berg,' Lobo said, moving away.

'Speak to the Worm,' Berg called after him in a moment of inspiration. 'Find out where he's got Randall rostered next.'

'I'll try it,' Lobo said, and disappeared up a side tunnel. The group spread out and split, but most of the men carried on towards the generator room to get their exhausted power packs recharged. Berg said nothing for a while, and then:

'Hell, Bulstrode, Lobo may be right. We could lose a couple in that storm and never know it.'

Bulstrode nodded. 'You don't have to tell me. It's lucky that any of us got back.'

'What if he's right? We couldn't organize a search in this weather.'

'No chance,' Bulstrode agreed. 'Best we can do is go out when it dies down and try to find the suit. Even if the suit's ruined we can maybe use the heating units for spares.'

They turned the sharp corner into the generator room. 'Right now I'm more concerned about the Palace holding together,' Bulstrode went on. 'If the storm rips up the pipe network too much we'll get the generators going into shutdown, and you know what that means.'

Berg knew what it meant. They would have to live in their suits without being able to recharge the power packs, while with no heat in the pools the yeast would get cold and die.

Bulstrode was worried about the pipe network. There were three more weak spots that they hadn't reached, and he was beginning to regret turning back so early. But had that been the case it would have meant that the men who had staggered through the bay door with totally depleted units might now be dead, and he couldn't regret being persuaded. Hell, he was no engineer. Maybe the network would be all right. And, after all, they'd covered the worst spot first. He hoped that would prove to be enough.

In the tunnel outside the Worm's office Lobo stopped a man on his way down from counting in the beacon. Until the storm was over, the Palace had no need of him. Lobo asked if he'd seen the Worm, but the man hadn't, and seemed surprised that anybody should actually want to look for him.

'I think we've got people out on the ice,' Lobo explained.

'What are you trying to do? Organise a requiem?'

Lobo wasn't laughing. 'It may not be too late to get a search going,' he insisted.

'In this? Don't joke, friend. The dials on the beacon say the Ice Palace is on emergency standby as of now. They'll be preserving a yeast sample in case the tank heaters close down.'

When Lobo arrived on the gallery he saw the Worm's familiar baggy yellow suit below. He was 'helping' with the transfer of a yeast sample to a lined container, which basically meant that he was watching and keeping out of the way. Doc was actually carrying out the transfer.

The yeast was difficult to handle. It wouldn't pour like water but it wasn't solid enough to scoop out. If the tanks' heating was withdrawn as part of the automatic shutdown procedure this sample would have to be kept alive to be the base for a complete new yeast culture; Doc had a theory that spores in the air might eventually get into the wastes and grow, but their development would take far too long to be of any use.

'Please be careful, Doc,' Lobo heard the Worm saying as he descended the iron stairway. 'I don't want to die.'

'Amen to that, Worm,' said the Doc.

'Worm,' Lobo called, 'I've been looking for you.'

'Quiet, Lobo,' the Worm replied, 'can't you see I'm busy?'

'Busy watching somebody else, as usual. I want to get a search organized.'

The Worm lost interest in the yeast. 'What do you mean?'

'I think we've got a couple of men still out on the ice.'

The Worm thought for a moment. 'Any team leaders?'

Lobo was puzzled. 'No, Willis and the new guy. What difference does it make?'

'Team leaders are hell to replace. You almost have to rewrite the entire roster.'

Lobo stifled an impulse to grab the Worm and insert him headfirst into the tank. 'Who cares about the roster?' he demanded.

The Worm tut-tutted sanctimoniously. 'You're talking about the guiding-plan of an entire community. It's no less important than this yeast, here.' Doc almost had the container filled.

'It couldn't be less important than you, Worm,' Lobo said ominously.

'There's no need to get personal.'

'I'll get personal with your neck in a minute. What about a search?'

'Out of the question,' the Worm said, stepping aside as Doc pushed the container over towards the pulley. 'The Ice Palace is on emergency standby already. Nobody goes out apart from volunteers for unavoidable repairs. Rules are rules.'

'He's right, you know, Lobo,' the Doc called over. 'Anybody going out in conditions like these won't be coming back.'

'So what are we supposed to do? Write them off?'

'You've got it,' the Worm said. 'The order's gone out to bolt down all the hatches against the wind. Lose too much heat and we could tip the generator cutout anyway.'

'I'm sorry, Lobo,' the Doc said. 'We'll all miss Willis.'

'To hell with Willis,' Lobo spat, and turned abruptly to go.

The Worm didn't wait long enough. Lobo was still within earshot when he said, 'That's a surprise. Lobo getting sentimental over the citizen.'

'I heard that, Worm,' Lobo called down, and the Worm jumped. 'One day soon I'll make you pay for it.'

'I was only joking,' the Worm shouted anxiously. 'Wasn't I,

Doc?'

The Doc wasn't interested. He called up to Lobo, who was now on the middle gallery, 'Will you give me a hand to get the yeast to the generator room? It'll stay warm longer if it's left outside the shields.'

'Sorry, Doc, I've got to see this through. The Worm can help you carry.'

The Worm started to rub his arm, like a dog limping for sympathy. 'Come on, Lobo,' he protested. 'You know my problems.'

'Damn right.' The voice echoed from the tunnel across an empty gallery. 'You're an obnoxious weed and nobody likes you. Outside that you've no excuses. Help the Doc.'

The men crowded into the Cantina, because there wasn't enough room for them all to stand and watch the dials on the generators. Even those who had been on the previous shift emerged from their bunkrooms early and waited with Bulstrode and his returnees. Despite the grimness of the situation there was a certain undercurrent of cheer, a camaraderie rarely felt in the Palace; danger or not, something unusual was happening, and the threat of disaster wasn't enough to detract completely from the interest of a break in routine.

Berg asked a few questions. The last anybody had seen of Willis was in the cargo bay, and they weren't sure it was him because he didn't take his helmet off. He was near the open door and when they looked again he wasn't there. Nobody could remember seeing Randall at all.

'That's Willis all over,' Berg told Bulstrode. 'His spy theories get pulled to pieces so he has to take it out on Randall. I bet he left him out there and went back to finish him off.'

'The idiot,' Bulstrode agreed. 'Now he's done for himself, as well.'

Berg wondered if Lobo would succeed in getting a search together, but Bulstrode said it was against the survival rules during a standby. He'd given up trying to understand Lobo. He knew when he was wasting his time.

Lobo arrived a couple of minutes later, and Bulstrode beckoned for him to join them. 'We were just saying it seems you're right,' he said, 'about Randall and Willis on the ice.'

'Willis was always the same,' Berg added. 'Can't let go of an idea when he thinks he's in the right.'

It took Lobo a moment to force himself to readjust. They were neither rejecting nor mocking him, and he wasn't used to it. 'I've just seen the Worm,' he said. 'It seems a search isn't allowed under the shutdown procedure.'

'It's going to take everything we've got to keep the rest of us alive,' Bulstrode agreed. 'When the storm's over we can go out and look for the suits, get the bodies for recycling.'

Lobo still wasn't satisfied. 'What if one of them finds his own way back along the guide wires? He'll die on the doorstep with the hatches bolted down.'

'So what are we supposed to do?' Berg said. 'Leave him a flask of coffee and a sandwich to sit it out until the storm's over? Be realistic, Lobo.'

'All of a sudden it's being realistic to leave a man to die without lifting a finger?'

'Two men,' Berg said for the sake of accuracy.

They all three looked around at the sound of some disturbance at the far end of the cave. Palmer had just appeared, and he was carrying one of the Worm's home-made paper misshapes. 'Listen,' he was saying, 'Listen everybody. The Worm's given me this list for the allocation of duties for the emergency standby.' Which, in effect, meant that you were to be told where you could go and sit while waiting to see if you were going to freeze to death or not.

Somebody said, 'All of a sudden the Worm's running the place.'

'Any better ideas?' Palmer demanded.

'You think I'm enough of a creep to bother with those lousy rosters?'

'Well, shove it if you've got nothing to say.' Palmer moved across to the ice wall and began to chip out a small hole to wedge the sliver which would pin the list in place. 'You can come over and look for your own names.'

Objector included, the men shuffled forward to read the list or have it read to them. There was an animated discussion going on at the back, rising in volume.

'We've got to keep one hatchway open,' Lobo was saying.

'That's impossible,' Bulstrode told him. 'We'd lose heat and tip off the generator shutdown.'

'Not if it was the loading bay door that was kept open. It isn't heated, and you could close the door through to the cargo bay. You have the outer hatch open and the inner one sealed, a kind of rescue chamber.'

'You'd need two people. You couldn't hold the hatch open and look out at the same time. The chains would keep slipping.'

'That's right,' Lobo said, growing excited as the idea became more feasible. He looked round at his newly-acquired audience. 'Any offers?'

The audience promptly became a set of backs. Lobo looked at Bulstrode.

'Not me,' Bulstrode said. 'I'm not going to risk freezing for dead men.'

'That goes for me too,' said Berg.

Palmer had detached himself from the crowd around the notice, and now he came over. He was well-known in the Palace for his undisguised terror of the ice cap—any duty or service that he could trade against shift cover, he would.

Lobo had never traded with him for anything, but even so Palmer stood well back as if in fear of a physical rebuff.

'You interested in a bargain, Lobo?' he asked.

Bulstrode said, 'Crawl off, Palmer,' and Berg rumbled, 'Get back into your crack.'

Lobo said doubtfully, 'I don't like to owe anybody.'

'Nice ethics,' Palmer said, 'but what good are they going to do you?'

'Don't take him on, Lobo,' Bulstrode urged.

Palmer turned to him. 'You going to suggest some other kind of currency?'

Bulstrode reddened, and Berg stepped in closer. 'Sure,' he said. 'You leave us alone, and I don't break your arm.'

Palmer stood his ground, although he was more than a little nervous. Lobo hesitated, then seemed to make up his mind. He looked from Berg to Bulstrode. 'Either one of you crumbs going to give me a hand?' Neither spoke. 'Then it's a deal, Palmer. Meet me in the loading bay in five minutes.'

Lobo turned to go, and Berg said, 'What's going on, Lobo? This Randall owe you, or something?'

'Nothing, and it's the same both ways. What of it?'

Berg shrugged, surprised at the sudden burst of aggression from the usually placid Lobo. 'Who said anything? I only asked.'

'Well don't try thinking, Berg. It doesn't suit you.' And he went off through one of the minor tunnels.

When he'd gone, Berg looked at Bulstrode. 'You thinking what I'm thinking?'

Bulstrode frowned. 'I don't believe Lobo's gone fairy, if that's what you mean,' he said.

'No,' Berg said earnestly, 'but I reckon he knows something about this Randall. Maybe Willis was right and he is a spy. Maybe -' he began to get excited by his logic—'maybe he's doing Willis in right now, and he's made some kind of deal with Lobo to get his help!'

Bulstrode was watching him with a pained expression. 'Lobo was right,' he said. 'Thinking doesn't suit you. It's like watching a one-legged man trying to tap dance. Go check the list.'

When Lobo arrived at the bays, Palmer was already there. If Lobo could have managed his vigil alone, he would; but the chain which held the outer door up was notoriously insecure, and while he could mangle it into a loose knot which would probably hold for a few minutes until it slipped, he couldn't trust it. He didn't find much entertainment in the idea of the door dropping on his head as he looked out, unhearing through the double barriers of wind and helmet.

The cargo bay was heated whereas the loading bay was not. There was a door across the short passage which connected the two, but it was hardly ever closed. Lobo closed it now, stooping first to clear the dirt and debris from the shallow rail it ran along, and effectively sealing the loading bay off from the rest of the Palace. Now they could open the outer hatch without fear of tripping any thermostats and affecting the delicate balance of the generators.

Lobo knew the idea was impossible, inadequate. He cursed

himself for giving in to his impulses, cursed Randall for making it all happen in the first place, cursed the whole mismatched, unjust world for simply being there. And still he hauled with determination on the chain to bring the bay door to its fullest open position where the light would spill out on to the ice and glow in the storm, the only point of welcome anywhere on the ice cap.

There was a danger, Lobo knew, that Randall might find his way back along the guidewire and still miss the light, or, seeing it, might stumble off the narrow lip and into a freezing slush of open water. It was a waste of time, a waste of effort, he was going to look a monumental fool. The hatch squealed over the last couple of feet and reached its limit with a crash.

'Get helmeted and stand with me in the doorway,' he said to Palmer as he lifted the chain over on to itself. 'I look out, you look in. This knot starts to move, you slap me on the arm fast and we both get out of the way before the door comes down. Okay?'

Palmer nodded briefly, and his eyes strayed over to the open hatch. He shuddered, and not from the cold.

'If it scares you so much,' Lobo said, 'Why don't you try for one of the inside jobs, like the yeast tanks?'

'Don't think I haven't tried. Bulstrode heard about it and came to my bunkroom. He said there was nothing wrong with me and he'd tear me up for a coward if I didn't pull my weight.'

'That's Bulstrode,' Lobo said as he clipped his helmet into place. 'He's subtle.'

'And he doesn't forget. Come to that, neither do I. Willis owes me three shifts, and if he doesn't come back I can't collect.'

They stepped on to the ramp and climbed to the doorway. Lobo said grimly, 'If Willis comes back alone, you may not get to collect anyway. I'll want to know why he set the citizen up to die out there.'

Palmer started to frame a question, but was distracted as the bay's lights dipped for a few seconds before coming back up to their usual intensity. They both knew the sign; a section of the pipeline had become exposed, and the Palace cutout had come very close to firing.

Lobo looked out. The snowstorm boiled on, the light from the open bay diffusing out on to the swirl of crystals. Lightning forked, throwing a still frame of the landscape into sharp relief and then blanking out again as the rip of thunder followed. Ahead was the open water, to his left the open plain and the pipeline; behind him, he knew, was the smooth, rising mound of the Ice Palace which would obscure the bay lights to anyone approaching from that direction.

At least he now had some sense of distance, even though his imagination had instantly interpreted every mound and shadow on the plain as an army of crawling, moving figures. He wouldn't have to watch for long. His own power pack was low on charge, but it was almost half-an-hour since he had come in off the ice; anybody still out there would almost certainly be carrying a weak or discharged pack, and the chances of survival with suit insulation alone were probably nil.

A double flash, two brilliant bursts that lit the plain in machine gun succession; and in the bellying rumble that followed, an urgent tug on his arm from Palmer. Distracted, Lobo fell back on to the ramp as the leading edge of the door came down, almost clipping his visor. He nearly lost his balance on the incline as he hurried down to pull back on the chain and raise the door. Two pictures were etched in his mind, bright exposures close together and they weren't the same. Already the twin images were fading but the certainty remained; something out there had moved between the flashes.

Gears moved and the door rose again with painful slowness. Of course, it might have been an eddy of snow, raised by the wind into a brief illusion of solidity and dropped again as quickly. Or a section of cladding, stripped away and bouncing along towards the sea. Lobo bunched the chain, trying to make a more secure knot. Palmer was in the doorway, but he wouldn't turn and look out. The lightning was firing off irregularly, an aerial inferno backed by thunder which was overlapping into a continuous roll.

Out on the plain, a snow suit was blundering, taking a straight course for the edge of the floe and the sea. Lobo scrambled out on to the glassy lip outside the bay and tried to run towards the figure, but on the third step he left solid ice and plunged waist-deep into snow. Within seconds his power pack was setting up a bleeping protest, but he waded on.

The man was blinded, rubbing at a crust of ice on his unheated visor as he stumbled towards a short drop and the bitter sea only yards ahead. The more that Lobo tried to hurry to intercept, the deeper he thrust himself into the piling drifts. Then the ground gave completely, and when he came up his own visor was a blank mass of granules.

He dashed them away before they could freeze and cling. The man was no more than a couple of feet from the edge of the floe, and he had stopped; perhaps the lack of deep snow on the hard rim had made him suspicious. He was scrubbing hard at his faceplate, and when he took his hands away he saw the grey, heaving soup of the sea filling his horizon. Then he began uncertainly to turn, and he saw Lobo.

It could be Randall, it could be Willis. There were only four basic colours in the Palace's range of snow suits, and both men chanced to wear pale orange. But the helmets were random, the same basic colours but pulled from the rack when needed. This figure was in a bright yellow helmet, fine for Randall but what had Willis picked up?

Lobo couldn't remember. He tried to picture the scene in the bay as they'd prepared to go out, but it wouldn't come. His heating unit was dead and the cold was climbing into the suit with him in an unwelcome but irresistible possession.

Blue! Bright blue. He remembered it in the line ahead of him on the way out to the pipeline, slogging along in the tracks of the sled. Randall struggled towards him, and together they headed back to the angled shaft of light from the bay.

Abruptly, the shaft was chopped by one-third. Lobo grabbed a handful of Randall's suit and pulled him on faster—the knotted chain was slipping, and the door had dropped. Lobo knew that Palmer could manage the chains in the cargo bay— he'd opened the hatch at the beginning of their shift—but the gears in the loading bay were stiffer, and their ratio was different. Randall was flagging, falling on every third or fourth step. Lobo doubted that Palmer even had the weight to get the door open once it had closed.

It was no more than a three-foot slot, a long letterbox. Randall was slung through without ceremony and Lobo rolled after. Palmer had the remnants of the chain gathered in his arms, trying to stop it from slipping any further, but when he saw Lobo safe he let go and the gap slammed closed.

Randall had tumbled all the way down the ramp to the bottom, and he was trying to sit up. Lobo called over to Palmer, 'Your power pack, fast. Him first.'

Palmer disconnected Randall's pack—now so exhausted it couldn't even bleep—and snapped his own into its place. Randall started to shake his head from side to side, and when Lobo came down and removed his helmet he was gasping as the heat began to penetrate his senseless tissues.

'It'll hurt a while,' Lobo told him, 'then it gets easier.'

'Open the hatch,' Randall managed to say. 'There's somebody else out there.'

'Shove Willis. I'm not putting myself out for him.'

'Not Willis.' Randall shook his head emphatically. 'Somebody else. He led me back this far until I saw the light from the bay.'

'You getting religious on me?' Lobo asked with suspicion.

'I'm telling you, there's another man out there! He can't be more than a few feet away from the top of the ramp!'

Lobo glanced up at Palmer. 'Take a look,' he said.

Palmer began to back away. 'Not me, Lobo. Please.'

Lobo rose and took a step towards him. 'Take a look or I'll bust your head and fry your brains. I'll hold the hatch.'

Surprisingly, Palmer was close to tears. 'You're as bad as Bulstrode, Lobo,' he said accusingly. 'I had you figured for better.'

'I'm worse than Bulstrode,' Lobo snarled, feeling mean and guilty as he said it. 'Move yourself and you'll find out by how much.'

'You're lousy company, as well,' came Palmer's parting shot, and Lobo felt better.

When the door was open, and a miserable Palmer was tentatively sticking his head out, Lobo came back.

'Now, what is this?' he said. 'Willis is the only other man outside the Palace, and he stranded you there in the first place.'

'I told you, it definitely wasn't Willis. Whoever it was, he called my name and I followed him until I came within sight of the bay lights. Then my faceplate froze over again and the next thing I saw was the sea.'

'He called your name?' Lobo was incredulous. 'There can't be more than about twenty people in this place even know your name.'

'I'm not pretending I understand it.' And Randall went on to explain.

He told of how he'd floundered around, and how he'd managed eventually to find the guidewire, only to realize that with his sense of direction completely confused there would be no way of being sure that he was heading towards the Ice Palace and not away from it. He'd taken a chance, and he'd been wrong.

He realized his mistake when there was a momentary clearance of the blizzard and the pipeline appeared briefly ahead of him. In surprise he'd dropped his grip on the wire—he'd barely been able to feel it through the gloves—and had stooped to rummage in the snow for it, knowing that without it he'd have no chance of retracing his route. The feeble output of his power pack, stopped down as it was to minimal operation, had robbed his hands of feeling, and he could have grasped the wire a dozen times and never known it.

That was when he'd heard his name being called. Turning, he had seen a figure through the blizzard waving him back; when he followed, it moved away, and stayed ahead of him all the time.

Randall had found the sloping trench and hammered on the cargo bay door without effect. Then, hearing his name again, he had come up out of the trench and seen for the first time the light from the loading bay.

'It wasn't Willis, Lobo,' he concluded. 'I couldn't tell for sure, but it didn't even look like he was wearing a snow suit.'

'That's too much,' Lobo said. 'Nobody goes out there without a snow suit and lives.'

'All right, I'll concede that. But I know it wasn't Willis.'

Palmer's helmet-amplified voice quavered from the open doorway, 'There's nobody, Lobo. Can I come in now?'

Lobo realized that he'd been standing there with no power pack, and beckoned him in. Randall unclipped the pack and offered it with his thanks.

'You're welcome,' Palmer replied unsteadily. 'I'll work out what you owe me and let you know.'

As Palmer walked away, Randall asked, 'What's he talking about?'

'He deals in shift cover. He'll do anything to avoid taking his turns on the ice. I had to bargain for you.' Lobo gathered their two dead power packs together.

'Thanks,' Randall said. 'I suppose I owe you, as well.'

'No, we're even. Now I don't have to feel bad for not taking your side against Berg.'

Randall hadn't seen the generator room, and didn't know what to expect. In relation to the Palace it was symmetrically opposite to the crap tanks, with Main Street and the Cantina in between the two.

They came out on to a catwalk, with a sheer concrete wall to one side and the natural ice wall on the other. Lobo explained that the generators themselves were the other side of the concrete, and the only part of them which was exposed was at the far end of the catwalk. Randall wondered what was at the bottom of the drop beneath them, but didn't ask.

The catwalk ended in an open area with an arch in the concrete which made way for a console and some racks of contacts and switches. There were three men on the other side of the console, and their argument could be heard from some distance away.

One of them was the Doc. He'd put a lot of effort into man-handling his container load of yeast to the generators, and now the other two were trying to persuade him to take it away. Doc's idea had been that the yeast would live longer in the working temperature of the generator room and would be safe from contamination as long as it was kept on the right side of the shields. A man about Doc's age but with much less hair was trying patiently to explain that yes, radiation does travel in straight lines but the shielding wasn't too tight, and contaminated air tends to move in whatever direction it damn well pleases. At this Doc began to look dubious, and the other man, who Lobo murmured was called the Weasel for obvious physical reasons, offered to help the Doc carry his container back to get a fresh, uncontaminated sample.

The two of them moved off, still arguing over the container, and Lobo introduced Randall to Cohn.

Cohn nodded agreeably. 'You set for the shutdown?' he asked.

'If it happens,' Lobo replied, and held up the power packs. 'Need a couple of recharges while we've still got the generator.'

Cohn reached for them. 'Better get them hooked up fast,' he said. 'We've no spares.' He went around the console and fixed the packs onto terminals set in a bank on one wall of the archway.

Randall said, 'How long does recharging take?'

.'Few minutes.' Cohn left the packs in place. 'Don't believe we've met.'

'This is Randall,' Lobo said. 'Been here a couple of days. We just pulled him in off the ice.'

Cohn gave a whistle, and gestured at the dials on his console. 'You were out in that? You're lucky to be alive, Randall.'

'I know it. I'm glad it's warm in here.'

'The warmth isn't for our benefit. It's optimum working temperature for the machinery. All these dials and indicators are linked to the surface network and the cutout trigger. That's what I'm monitoring. I gave the alarm.'

Lobo bent to study the dials, his puzzled frown showing that he understood none of them. 'How're we doing?'

'Holding on, but only just.' Cohn pointed to one part of the board. 'There's one hell of a leak to the Southwest. The cladding must have been ripped clean away. I've got all the bunkroom lights down to try and keep some kind of balance. It's not much, but it helps.'

Randall had wandered around to the archway. It had been blocked off in a rough-and-ready way, obviously at a much later date than its original construction. Now it was being used as a noticeboard, and was covered in charts, lists and measurements. All were on the same grey, rough paper he'd seen elsewhere in the Palace. He turned to Cohn and said, 'Are you in here all the time?'

'Only when I'm rostered. We have a few regulars, and anybody who's ill or injured. The Worm takes care of it.' Randall would have snapped his fingers, but they felt too brittle. 'That reminds me. Lobo, I want to see the Worm when the packs are charged.'

'For what?'

'I want to know who else was out on the ice with me. I want to know who led me back.'

'Forget it, Randall,' Lobo said. 'There was nobody.'

'You can't say that. You didn't see him.'

'We're on the point of a shutdown. That means we'll be needed any time now.'

'It's quiet at the moment,' Cohn pointed out helpfully, but Lobo dismissed the fact.

'That's now, but what if there's a call for an emergency ice party?'

Randall asked, 'What happens? Do they ask for volunteers?'

'Like hell. They pull your name out of a hat and boot you through the door with a sled. Who'd be stupid enough to volunteer for a job like that?'

'Look at the chart behind you,' Cohn said to Randall. 'Those dips show the power loss spread over a number of shifts. They're getting deeper and closer together. With all the heat we pour out, it's no wonder we get freak weather.' He was right; extrapolated to its logical conclusion, the chart offered a frightening prospect for the Ice Palace.

When the packs had taken a full charge Randall plugged into his and went off to look for the Worm. Lobo objected, but followed him anyway. They found plenty of places the Worm had been, but nowhere that he actually was. In the early stages of the crisis he'd gone around 'supervising' every group and been chased off by each in turn, so in the end it came down to the most obvious place.

Randall knocked on the door of the Worm's office.

'Go away,' was the muffled shout from the other side.

'I need to speak to you,' Randall called.

'I'm busy.'

'You're using the wrong approach,' Lobo whispered. Shouldering past Randall he hammered on the door and yelled, 'Worm? If you don't come out I'm going to break down the door and stamp on your fingers!'

'There's no need for that!' Randall hissed.

Lobo winked. 'Stick with the system.'

The door opened and the Worm peered out. 'Hi, guys,' he said. 'Something you need?'

'You can start by letting us in.'

The Worm let the door swing open, and backed towards his desk. 'This is my office, Lobo,' he said anxiously. ' I hope you'll respect my office.'

'It's me that wants you,' Randall said. 'I want to know who else was left out on the ice at the same time as me.'

The Worm put his head on one side to bring his single lens to bear on Randall, and gave a start of surprise when he recognized him. 'That's easy,' he stammered. 'Willis.'

'Besides Willis.'

'That's easy too. Nobody.'

'Is there any way you can check?'

Lobo gave a deep, here-we-go-again sigh, and the Worm said 'Why should I have to?'

'Just do it,' Randall insisted.

'Look, I already did. At the first warning of a possible shutdown I went all over the Palace. I took the register so I wouldn't miss anybody, and the only people I didn't see were all on Bulstrode's team. He's accounted for them since.'

'Happy now?' Lobo asked.

'No, I'm not. I saw somebody and I heard him call my name, and I know it wasn't Willis.'

'Now, listen,' Lobo said carefully. 'The ice can have a strange effect on a man's mind.'

'That's right,' the Worm added helpfully.

Lobo frowned, and turned to the Worm. 'When were you

ever out on the ice?' he demanded.

'I had a look, once.'

'Keep quiet, or you'll be having another.'

'I know what I saw,' Randall insisted.

'But don't go round broadcasting it. You've seen what they can be like if they think they spot a weakness.'

'Yeah,' the Worm joined in, and for once didn't get an instant rebuff. 'Lousy isn't the word for it. I know.'

Lobo added, 'For once, the Worm's right. It doesn't matter what you believe as long as you keep it quiet.'

Randall wasn't happy with his answer, but it seemed to be the best he was going to get. He and Lobo went down to the Cantina and heard, as they approached Main Street, the ring of the shift handbell.

'It's the all-clear,' Lobo explained. 'We didn't tip over into shutdown, and the weather must be easing off. If it goes according to pattern we'll have a lull and then another bad one. A repair team should be on its way now.'

There was still some of the emetic yeast to be had in the Cantina, and Randall strangled some down. A drum of it had been wheeled in as a parody of a buffet for the waiting men, but now most of them had either gone off to their bunkrooms or had joined the rostered shift on the ice. The floor was wet and slushy from the unaccustomed crowding.

Back in the bunkroom Randall watched the star-patterns form overhead. It seemed almost a lifetime since he'd last done this, and more than a lifetime since he'd left the city. Already the city was like a dream to him, and the Ice Palace was becoming his only true reality.

It could have been worse. At least the Palace had a settled society, one based on a careful code of threat and bluster and abuse dictated by the harsh necessities of survival. True conflict was avoided by the institution of an elaborate pecking-order, with the unhappy Worm at the end of the line; all Randall knew for sure so far was that he himself came somewhere above the Worm and below Berg, and only the oldsters were allowed to stand apart from the system.

'Lobo,' he said quietly into the dark, 'are you asleep yet?'

A pause. 'What does it sound like?'

'Sounds like you're not very pleased.'

'You've got it. Go to sleep.'

'But there are some things that don't hang together. Like the man on the ice...'

Lobo groaned, and mumbled something into his blanket.

'Other things as well. I don't understand the power setup here.'

'I already explained it to you.'

'I know how, but not why.'

The bunk on the other side of the room creaked in the dark as Lobo turned over. 'It's designed so we'll work and work to keep alive, and always know it's futile. That's why.'

'But I can't grasp the idea of power going nowhere. I can't see it not being used.'

Lobo's grasp of practical physics was probably even better than Randall's. 'It gets wasted as heat,' he said. 'That's the whole idea.' And then he yawned, noisily and pointedly.

'According to Cohn's chart, we have to produce about twice as much power as the Ice Palace needs to prevent the cutout operating.'

'We don't have to produce any power. That's all automatic. All we have to do is conserve it.'

Randall thought about it. 'All the same... I saw a stranger out on the ice—' muted howl of agony from Lobo—'and there's enough power being fed out there to run another Ice Palace. Don't you find that interesting?'

'Tomorrow. I'll find it interesting tomorrow.'

'It's got to be,' Randall said, more to himself than to Lobo.

Then, out loud, 'What's the furthest anybody's ever strayed from here?'

'End of the guidewire.' Lobo was nearly asleep, probably hardly aware that he was answering. 'Further than that, they don't come back.'

Damn it, Randall thought as Lobo's breathing became deep and regular, there's something out there. In the Worm's office a chart had caught his eye, and he'd assumed it to be a copy of Cohn's power record. But a closer inspection had shown it wasn't; it was a log of the Ice Palace's manning levels. And yet the curve was the same! Every big storm, and there was a massive power drain, a near shutdown and a man disappeared. Willis had never come back.

In a few hours the normal shifts would start again, blind agony out on the ice, eat, a break for sleep and out again. No wonder nobody had time to think, to plan, to draw conclusions. A few weeks of the killing routine and perhaps he would become as stubborn and short-sighted as the rest of them—and then how could he ever hope to see the city again? Let alone the corrupt bunch of thieves that the underbelly council had turned out to be, a dream of democracy gone sour.

The weather was improving, and he had a fully-charged power pack. And he wanted to know what was on the other end of the guidewire.

NINE

IN THE TIME that had passed since the fall of Central, little had changed in the city. A rigged election had, as predicted, put the underbelly council in overall power. It was business as usual, then, with the exception that the old-time crooks became the new-style business powers, and they continued their activities unhindered by the Police Elite.

The problem of what to do with Randall had been solved in true underbelly fashion by making him disappear. After a couple of days nobody even thought to ask about him, with the exception of his former assistant and now replacement. Killoran asked loud and public questions, prodding and testing all the appeals and enquiry procedures of the city's archaic legal system. It was taking a lot of effort on Marius's part to anticipate and forestall him, and he wished that Killoran would lose interest and give up.

Marius was working harder than anybody to make the new democracy successful. He publicly raised and examined difficult issues, pointed fingers of accusation, promised that the space trade would be resumed and the city put back into the mainstream of history; while privately he stalled, threatened, manipulated and blackmailed, and all to the eventual good of Marius.

Morden was worried about Marius and in particular the massive deal that he'd hinted at with an offworld interest. Morden paced his blind man's castle on the rooftops, his hand reaching out occasionally in the darkness to brush some familiar fixed object in passing. Any attempt to analyse his own feelings only brought him further confusion; while he couldn't deny that legitimacy had robbed most of his enterprises of their enjoyment, he wondered if the moral repulsion that Marius inspired in him was based on some fundamental touchstone of right behaviour that transcended law and crime, or whether it was a simple re-focussing of his energies through ennui. Whatever the cause, he decided that he was thoroughly opposed to what Marius was planning, whatever it might turn out to be.

Meanwhile, Marius grew in power and influence. He was neither more dishonest nor more wily than any of the other underbelly leaders, but whereas they quickly grew tired of the dry processes of government he saw them as an infinite avenue of dodges and angles, a hall of mirrors where his opportunities magnified and multiplied. While promising his public the space trade again—well, yes, but in a little while, when we've sorted out the intricacies and complications that you simply can't see on the surface—he was quietly arranging with the offworlders to sell that public out.

He needed another vote to side with his on the council, and he obviously considered blind Morden to be the most compliant and least controversial of allies. Avery Sim was dead and with Chandler ('doesn't even like me') happy running the Police Elite it left Morden as the single uncommitted voice.

The idea of a deal with offworlders seemed pretty fantastic. When Morden found out the truth, it made his early speculations appear mundane.

The story came out in scraps and hints. Marius had been contacted by an agent, some time before when the controversy over Randall was at its height. The offworlders were in a ship some distance away, and they were prepared to wait until conditions were right for them to move in; they weren't interested in food, or artefacts, or technology of any kind. They wanted processed raw materials—metals, plastics, rubber, paper, glass—as much as the total industrial production of the city could manage until existing resources were worked out. They had nothing to offer in exchange and were prepared to make no restitution, in view of which they were preparing a small force with Marius's essential cooperation to supervise the exploitation.

One other thing emerged. The offworlders weren't human.

Alien contact had been a long-cherished and finally

abandoned hope of every settled system. For a while the colonized worlds had competed for prestige in hunting through their neighbour-planets for the signals of intelligence; but then, as the realities of such non-productive expense were felt, that interest had dwindled. Now, after all mankind's talk, a maverick had taken the trouble to seek him out.

Marius's policy was to give Morden as little information as possible, calling on him privately to get his thumbprint on some document or other whenever the need arose. He rarely explained the nature of the papers and if he had there would be no way that Morden could ensure he was telling the truth. They mainly seemed to relate to the streamlining and expanding of the city's meagre factory facilities into units which were in line with an expectation of economic growth; and who, in such circumstances, would publicly accuse Marius of anything?

The morning was typical of its kind. Marius left the city centre where he now lived in a suite comprising an entire floor of citizens' apartments knocked into one, and set off to cross the river back towards his old home. He travelled in one of the Elite's armoured vans, not because he really needed the protection but because he liked the idea of frivolous consumption that their oil-burning engines displayed. If he'd had more nerve and even less sensitivity he'd have travelled by one of the helicopters. Those machines positively drank the stuff.

He sat in the dark in Morden's main room, waiting for his eyes to adjust. In spite of that he was already talking. It seemed that Killoran had found yet another appeal procedure to set in motion, this one relating to internal Elite discipline.

'We'll have to see this Killoran,' Marius said, 'and buy him off.'

'You can't buy off the Elite,' Morden told him, knowing he wouldn't really believe it. 'They're all fanatics for honesty. Central bred them that way.'

'Well, we'll have to silence him somehow. Find something to appease him. It doesn't matter what—as long as it's not the truth.'

Morden sighed and settled back in his chair. Marius barely made out the shadow of a movement. 'I don't like what was done to Randall,' Morden said in a voice filled with as much self-pity as distaste.

'It's the only significant contribution you've made to our partnership so far, and there's a long way to go yet. Any time you get worried, think of the rewards.'

'Rewards? Or empty promises to collaborators?'

'Look, the off-worlders couldn't hope to pull this one without our cooperation. We're safe, Morden. Probably the only two people in the city who are. With the power they've got available they could wipe us out and leave us burning. By selling them our compliance we're making sure they act with moderation.'

Morden had heard Marius give this argument before. It was so plausible he was almost tempted to believe it. 'But the price for that compliance could never be high enough. What use is wealth on a burned-out world?'

Marius wondered if his eyes had fully adjusted to Morden's dark yet. He thought he could see the dim outline of the table between them, and with this target fixed in his mind he reached for the folder of papers he'd brought. 'Central Command's already ruined what was left of this world. It killed off progress generations back when it tried to make a perfect city full of average men and women. Look at the citizens! They've never had an original idea between them, with the exception of Rorvik, and look how that turned out. Can you honestly say they're not a sign of a degenerate trend?' He slapped his papers down on the table to make his point, but the table wasn't there. The folder opened as it fell and the sheets poured on to the floor.

Morden permitted himself a thin smile, but tried to keep it out of his voice. 'Does it matter what I say?'

'You couldn't alter the fact.' Marius was on the floor now, his documents no more than dim grey shapes before him. 'When the offworlders have got what they want we'll be rich enough to move to another system and live like kings.'

'It's thirty years' subjective travel to the nearest system. How do you propose surviving it?'

Marius was back on his seat, rustling as he settled. 'Trust me, Morden, and leave the details to them.'

'Can you trust them not to take what they've learned from us and move on to the next system? Not to be content before they've cleaned out the entire sphere of human settlement?'

'I've got their word, Morden. They're an honourable race.'

'At least as honourable as us.'

'That's the idea.' Marius wasn't fooling, he was totally insensitive to the irony. 'They want to hold a strategy meeting on their own territory.'

Morden was thinking that he would have the table moved back before Marius's next visit when this new and unexpected information suddenly pushed everything else aside. 'What do you mean?' was all he could say.

'On board their ship,' Marius went on. 'We'll have to rendezvous with their shuttle at the established landing point.'

'But I've never been off the surface before!' Morden had ridden in a helicopter on the day of the first council meeting in the city, and it had made him sick.

'It's easy. Just like riding the mono.'

'You mean you've already been?' Perhaps Marius found pleasure in Morden's discomposure, a small revenge for the trick with the table.

'Of course,' he said smoothly, as if such travel were an everyday matter. 'They've even fitted me out with my own chambers. They'll even do the same for you—just tell them what you'd like. They're really pleased about you joining us.'

The conversation seemed all wrong, as if some fundamental block of rationality had been removed. Morden had been able to entertain the incredulity of the notion at second hand, but now it had been brought close he felt his own sense of reality backing off defensively.

'I suppose I have no choice,' he said weakly.

'You've got the choice between surviving and going under. What else did we ever have?'

Marius promised to make the arrangements through the agent and bring the details on his next visit, and the conversation moved on to other subjects. Rorvik, for example; Louann had requested the release of his remains, at present packaged in a deep-freeze at Elite headquarters awaiting the final decision on what portion of guilt or credit he should be accorded. She had, it seemed, taken up with one of the newly-established religions, a racket that Marius would be interested in getting into if he only had the time for it. Public opinion, carefully moulded by the council, had come down firmly on Rorvik's side; he was the creator of a new dawn for the city, liberator of the people, and several other kinds of hero. Randall, on the other hand, was pure dog's mess.

'A dead hero,' Morden phrased it, 'and a live scapegoat. How much more humane to arrange it the other way around.'

'Humane, but dumb. Dead heroes can't lead opinion against you. Randall's best off where he is.'

Morden thumbed some papers and they talked a little more, but the main topic of the meeting had come and gone. Marius made his excuses and said he was expected across the river in less than an hour, but that the discussion, as always, had been 'really meaningful'. Morden called somebody to lead Marius back to the outside world and the light.

When Marius was well clear one of the deeper shadows at the back of the room detached itself and moved forward, filling out to the shape of a man.

'Is it true?' the shade whispered. 'Or have I been listening to some monstrous practical joke?'

'It's no joke, Chandler. Marius is attempting to sell out the city.'

'But for what? Invasion?'

'Exploitation. He expects to share in the spoils and then move to another system where he's not known.'

Chandler laughed bitterly as he moved round, hand outstretched in the dark, guiding himself to Marius's still-warm chair. 'That's him all over. A hundred per cent in favour of what's good for Marius.'

Although he hadn't believed Morden at first, Chandler had to accept his story now. He hurriedly tried to weigh the courses of action open to him but found he could think of none. He was the nominal head of the Elite, but they weren't his own private army; he couldn't use them to prepare any elaborate defence without Marius finding out before anything could be properly organized. And then there was the Elite itself; supertrained and superbly capable, they were woefully lacking in imagination. What would they make of this underbelly savage who raved about the raiders from outer space?

'Hasty action won't serve us at all,' he told Morden. 'We'll need information. That's up to you.' He tried to make it sound as if it was a measured conclusion, and not the stalling of desperation.

'I'll follow it through, Chandler,' Morden said.

He didn't need the sinking feeling in his belly to tell him that Chandler's presence hadn't helped him to unload his problem in any way at all.

TEN

There was a team out on the ice for emergency repairs and everybody else, it seemed, was either in the generator room or by the crap tanks, or else they were asleep. Randall didn't want to wake any more people than necessary. The man on the generators told him exactly where he'd find Palmer's bunk.

The brief slice of light from the bunkroom door showed quite a different layout from the one he shared with Lobo. Being well-insulated, hardly ventilated and fully populated, it was stuffy, even hot. The men in here slept only in their inner suit linings, the outers hung on lines strung between the top bunks. Deep mumblings and guttural breathing sounded all around as he tried to remember where Palmer was supposed to be.

Randall gave a couple of experimental prods at one of the figures covered in a lower bunk. The man turned, came perilously close to the surface of sleep and then gracefully slid back again. It wasn't Palmer. Along a bunk, and try again.

Palmer rolled over, opened sticky eyes, tried to focus on him. 'Wake up,' Randall whispered. 'I want to talk business.'

'It can wait,' Palmer moaned, and tried to roll away. Randall took a fistful of blanket and jerked the whole thing off the bed.

There was cold air frosting in from the unclosed door. Palmer whipped upright, arid banged his head on the slats of the bunk above. The occupant stiffened ominously. 'Give me that blanket back before I freeze!' Palmer hissed.

'Are you ready to talk now?'

'Yes! Give me the blanket!'

A voice from one of the other stacks came; 'Wha's going on?'

Another voice, which Randall identified as Cohn's; 'I don't want to break up a good argument, but do you mind if we sleep?'

The man in the upper bunk asked, 'Who is it?'

'It's Randall,' Cohn replied.

Groan from the upper bunk. 'Get lost, citizen.'

'Up yours, peabrain!' Randall snapped in the gutter talk of the Ice Palace.

Cohn chuckled in the dark. 'You're learning, Randall.'

Randall crouched, leaning close to Palmer and lowering his voice. He held up the blanket. 'Come on, Palmer. Time to trade.'

'Keep your voice down. What do you want?'

'I'm going back out on the ice...'

'At this time?'

'It has to be now or I'll miss the quiet time between the two storms. I need somebody to operate the chains for me.' Palmer had pushed himself up into a sitting position, right back in the angle of the bunk and the wall. The white of his suit lining betrayed his outline, and dull blue light glinted on the wet of his eyes. 'You're mad,' he said and then, with guarded interest, 'What are you offering?'

'Shift cover. What else is there?'

'And how in hell am I supposed to collect? I've never seen a dead man take a turn on the ice.'

'I've no intention of being killed. The weather's improved and I know the guidewire system now.'

'Forget it, Randall. I've got too much riding on you already. There's your own debt from last night and three shifts carried over from Willis...'

Randall interrupted him. 'How do you work that out?'

'Like I said, you can't collect off a dead man. I helped save you, so you take over what Willis owed me. That's only fair.'

There were silent, attentive forms on all sides of the bunkroom now. Randall gave an inward sigh, and prepared to take the irrevocable step. 'Like Cohn said, I'm learning. Pick a bone, Palmer.'

Palmer radiated confusion. 'What?'

'I'm being fair and giving you a choice. Pick a bone, and if you can't help me I'll break it.'

'Get lost, Randall. I may not like going on the ice, but I'm not the Worm and you're not exactly Bulstrode. You're a citizen,

Randall. Anybody in the Palace could wipe the floor with you.'

Randall shifted his weight, balanced his crouch. 'Don't be misled by Berg's demonstration. I could reach out and close your eyes for you before you could even move to stop me.'

'Big talk's cheap, and—' there was a blur across Palmer's limited vision, a light pressure on his eyelids and his eyes were closed. 'Hell,' he said sharply, 'What did you do?'

'I told you. Want me to do it again?' He did it again. 'I barely touched the lids. I could have put your eyes out just as easily.'

'Damn you, Randall, Willis was right. No citizen moves that fast.' Wood creaked, above and behind. 'What do you want with us?'

'I want you to come down to the exit bay and operate the door for me. That's all.'

'Go with him, Palmer,' the bunk overhead rumbled. 'Sling the crumb on to the ice and lock the doors behind him.'

'I've got half a mind to do just that,' Palmer replied, a little louder than he'd intended.

'We know you've only got half a mind, Palmer. Get out and get rid of him. Maybe Willis will find him.'

'I should think Willis is dead,' Cohn said doubtfully. 'His suit unit would be drained hours ago.'

'And the sooner this crumb joins him, the better. Take him out.'

Everybody in the room seemed to be awake, and there was open hostility in the cooling air. 'Palmer's right, Randall,' Cohn said reasonably, 'Elite training won't stop you dying out there.'

'My choice, Cohn,' Randall replied. 'Do you think I'd survive if I stayed, now that you all know what I am?' He turned back to the bunk beside him. 'What about it, Palmer?'

Palmer was plaintive. 'Who's going to cover the shifts I lose?'

'Isn't that a little academic? Whether I stay or go, I'm still a dead man.'

'Go with him, Palmer,' somebody urged. 'We'll ask the Worm to work something out for you.'

'I'll go myself and cancel a couple of the shifts I owe you,' came another voice which was far less sympathetic.

Palmer muttered something to himself and, swinging out of

the bunk, reached to pull his suit off the line. Randall stepped back to give him room and came level with Cohn's bunk.

'Why are you doing this, Randall?' Cohn asked him. 'Everybody accepted you as a citizen. Why throw it away?'

Randall shrugged. 'I've got my reasons.'

'But there's nowhere to go outside. And nobody's going to let you back into the Palace now.'

'If I find what I'm looking for,' Randall replied, 'I won't be coming back.'

Palmer clipped his power pack on to his belt and stood by the door, shuddering a little as he waited for the heat from the unit to make its way around. Randall opened the door and they both stepped out into Main Street. 'Go freeze, cop,' somebody shouted as the door swung closed.

There was a silence, and then Cohn said, 'He's mad. He's got to be.'

The man above Palmer's empty bunk said, 'Who cares? Won't matter a damn when he's dead.'

MAIN STREET WAS still empty. As they crossed into the tunnel leading to the bays Randall asked how long it was likely to be until the next bad phase of the storm. Palmer didn't answer at first, but then seemed to find the silence more embarrassing than the prospect of conversation. As they walked down the incline Palmer said that it would be unusually calm now, but that it would get much worse in a few hours.

'But how long exactly?' Randall pressed him.

Palmer shrugged. 'What do I care? It was never my problem.'

'It's your problem now. Make a guess.'

Palmer guessed about two hours, perhaps even less. When they reached the bay Randall went to pick a helmet from the racks as Palmer took up position by the chains. Then they both turned at the sound of somebody approaching down the tunnel, fast and breathless.

Lobo emerged into the bay. He was trying to blink off the stupor of interrupted sleep, but in spite of that he was plainly angry.

'Randall!' he shouted across the bay. 'What the hell do you

think you're doing?'

'I've got to go out, Lobo,' Randall replied reasonably. 'You know why.'

Lobo seemed to want to come nearer, but was holding back, attempting to salvage the last shreds of his cherished reserve. 'What kind of idea do you call that? As soon as I woke up and saw your bunk was empty I knew what you were going to try. There's nothing out there!'

'Don't argue with him, Lobo. He's police.'

Lobo dismissed Palmer's revelation without even looking at him. 'I know,' he said, and continued to fix Randall with a glower that was half challenge, half plea.

Randall said, 'Open the hatch, Palmer.'

'Don't touch those chains.' Lobo seemed to be straining at the limit of a leash of his own making. 'I stuck my neck out for you last night just to get you in off the ice, made myself look a goddamn fool for a citizen nobody cared about. Is this how I get thanked? At the first opportunity you throw yourself back outside?'

'There's good reason. . .' Randall began.

'I don't care about your lousy reasons. This is the Ice Palace. Randall. You don't get castles rising out of the mist just because you want them bad enough.'

'The waste power from the Ice Palace reactors has to go somewhere. The system can't be so irrational.'

'But it *is*.' Lobo was appalled at Randall's inability to grasp the Ice Palace's fundamental function. 'That's the whole idea! we survive, and we don't get any satisfaction from it. That's how Central designed the place.'

'It won't wash,' Randall argued. 'Look at the fittings, all those tunnels that double round and go nowhere. This place is older than Central.'

'But how could there be anything outside without us knowing?'

'Because anybody who strays beyond the guidewire never comes back.'

'You came back,' Lobo pointed out.

'And I was led all the way.'

Lobo didn't seem remotely convinced. 'That's just so much birdseed. You were probably ice blind.'

'Whether that's true or not, I no longer have any choice. Now that it's generally known that I'm Elite I'll be torn apart if I stay. I could fight off a small group, but never the whole Palace. So what else can I do?'

Lobo couldn't hold back his venom at what he saw as a personal betrayal. 'Damn you, then,' he spat. 'If you'd kept your head down you'd have survived like the rest of us. Whatever happens now is only what you deserve.' And he turned to leave.

'Can't you understand I'm not just looking for a novel way to do away with myself?' Randall called after him. 'This might mean escape for all of us.'

Lobo stopped, but didn't turn back. 'What does a lousy cop care for the likes of us?' he said.

'Whether I like it or not, you're my kind now. I can't go back to the city and be at home—I'm the trusted guardian who wrecked the system. The people I indirectly put into power sent me here by way of a reward. I want to see them again.'

Lobo looked back over his shoulder. His eyes shone with tears of frustration. 'I'm sorry I wasted my time. Now the whole damn Palace knows what a fool I am. Go kill yourself, Randall. I'm doing nothing else for you.'

It was Palmer who broke the silence which followed Lobo's departure.

'He's not very pleased,' he said, unnecessarily.

Randall tried to fight down the guilt he felt at his rough treatment of Lobo's feelings. Until this moment he wasn't sure that he had even acknowledged that the quiet giant had any, except in a kind of manipulative, Machiavellian way. 'He thinks I'm paying him back badly,' he told Palmer.

Palmer nodded. 'That makes sense. Lobo never liked to owe or be owed. I'd never traded him a shift until you went missing.'

Randall closed the latches on his helmet, and Palmer hauled on the chains to raise the door. He said something as Randall walked out into the trench, but Randall didn't turn back to find out what it was.

THERE WAS snow, but now it was falling as a silent curtain. The air was impossibly still, with no trace of the gales that had scoured the surface when last he had been out. Now the only sound was of his own breathing inside his helmet.

The tracks of the repair team were still faintly visible where the trench emerged on to the surface, although they were filling slowly. They had angled sharp left, down towards the opposite extreme of the pipe network from where Randall had decided he wanted to go.

Visibility was good compared to conditions earlier on. Much of the Palace itself was visible, a series of humps and mounds covered and made indistinct by thick ice. There were two obvious levels to the covering, as if at some time the cap had shattered along a line of weakness and split off a good section of the Palace. Perhaps this would explain the apparently purposeless tunnels that drove on towards the south-east and invariably ended in blank, smooth walls.

It was a night sky above, in sharp contrast with the eye-wrenching brilliance he had encountered on his first emergence. The white landscape reflected a perfectly adequate amount of light with a bluish tinge that he hadn't seen before. He seemed to remember hearing or reading somewhere that ice could be compacted to the extent that it would hold back a little of all but the blue light in the spectrum, but he'd thought it dubious. Any snow that fell in the city had always been slightly grey.

The guidewires started from a series of posts which spread in a buried arc from the trench. He kicked through the snow until he found the one he wanted and then lifted it so that it pulled free of the surface for a few yards. There seemed little danger of his becoming lost as long as the weather was so tranquil, but he didn't want to be caught out by any sudden change.

The steady effort of wading raised the temperature in his suit in the absence of any wind to draw it away, so he was able to conserve the power pack by turning it down to stay barely above the level of discomfort. He let the line run loosely through his fingers—it was tethered to the ground at intervals and here he would have to stop and transfer his grip from one side to the other before moving on.

When he reached the pipeline he dropped the wire altogether and began to follow the steady march of pylons. He had no idea what he expected to find at the other end, only the deep conviction that the constant outflow of power and the stranger on the ice had to add up to something. He felt apprehension but no real fear, as the grim and despairing existence that he was leaving behind held no more attraction for him than any danger that might lie ahead.

He tried to pace himself, conserve his energies for when the going turned bad. The pipeline seemed to go on for ever and he noticed that the further he moved from the Ice Palace the less common the cheap cladding seemed to be. Most of the pipe along here was covered with a much stronger and durable-looking material which even carried a crust of ice on the windward side, showing that there wasn't enough heat escaping to stop it forming.

But wait a minute. There hadn't been any wind. Without any exposed skin to sense the movement of air and his hearing inhibited by the helmet, Randall would have difficulty perceiving the first signs of a worsening in conditions out on the ice. But now, when he stopped and looked, the falling snowflakes were not simply dropping and settling as before but were being carried sideways.

Two hours, perhaps even less, Palmer had said. How long had he been moving? There was no way of telling. In the Palace a shift started when the Worm said so and ended when the work was done and that was the only kind of measurement needed.

He knew for sure that the weather was getting bad when the first spatter of hail swept across and crusted his faceplate. It began to loosen and slide almost immediately, but it was a sign; already he began to feel the cold through the suit and he boosted the power to compensate. A few more yards, and the wind was audible over his noisy breathing; his faceplate crazed again, and this time the ice stuck. And somebody called his name.

He rubbed frenziedly to clear his visor, afraid of losing the pipeline and of finding an empty landscape when vision returned. The ice fell away and the pipeline was still there—but nothing, and nobody, else.

His name was shouted again, distant and windborne, and Randall began to look in a wild circle for the caller. Back down the pipeline a suited figure was making its way forward in his tracks.

Confusion was replaced by realization as he saw that the suit was a shabby blue Ice Palace garment. Within a minute Lobo had reached him. They both stood for a moment, the rising wind pulling at them, neither sure of what to say.

Randall spoke first. 'Why did you follow me?'

Lobo considered the question as if for the first time. 'I got thinking,' he said. 'Damn me if the whole idea didn't make sense.'

'That the only reason?'

Lobo grinned sheepishly. 'Not really. I was so mad at you when I came down to the exit bay that I forgot to look surprised when Palmer said you were police. I remembered when I got back to the bunkroom and went round to do some threatening, but he'd already blabbed to Cohn and the Anteater.'

'The who?'

'Guy with a big nose in the top bunk. They'd already got you tagged as a spy and me as your contact.'

By unspoken consent they carried on following the pipeline. Lobo had made good time by walking along in the tracks that Randall had cleared, but now he had to slow down as they walked side by side in order to maintain the conversation. Randall asked, 'What did you do then?'

'Dragged Palmer out again and made him open the hatch for me. He wasn't very keen so I had to bounce him in the corridor. Bastard tried to drop the hatch on my head.'

Randall smiled. 'You can't blame him. Twice in one night.'

'That's not the point. I think he'd got it worked out that the two of us would be covering his shifts for some time to come. He didn't like waving goodbye to his meal ticket.'

'You could have cleared it for yourself. You didn't have to follow me.'

Lobo made a dismissive gesture which set up an eddy of

snow around his arm. 'Oh, what the hell,' he said. 'So I could have stayed in that place until I was too old to work. Put myself in line for a crack on the head and a swim in the crap tanks.'

'Is that how it works?' Randall was surprised by the brutality of it.

'It happens.'

It was Lobo who first noticed that the pipeline was starting to angle downwards. In a short distance it would disappear under the ice. Randall had hoped to be further along by now but he hadn't taken account of the slow, dragging progress that was necessary at the best of times in heavy snow. At the first rumble of returning thunder Lobo suggested that they reach the end of the pipeline and then dig into the snow. 'We can get away from the wind chill and save the units until we can move again,' he explained.

The digging was easy at first, more difficult as they went deeper. The first few inches of snow was like dry sand, but below that it had compressed to become hard and crystalline, and had to be broken out in fist-sized lumps. When they'd got a hole about four feet deep Lobo started to scoop out sideways, forming a temporary and fragile cave.

Once inside they carried on digging, breaking out the floor and back wall and passing the debris back to fill the entrance. It was hard work, but after only about an hour they were sealed against the wind and the worst of the storm. Lobo took his helmet off, and Randall did the same. Although the first lungful of cold air was a shock after the heated stream the suit had fed him he found that, after a few minutes, the foxhole was no more uncomfortable than the bunkroom had been.

There was enough room to stretch out and so avoid cramp. Randall asked. 'Did you mean what you said about... when you're too old to work?'

Lobo nodded grimly. 'I meant it. It's just like in the city, and just as unofficial.' Randall realized that Lobo was referring to Central's 'voluntary' euthanasia programme. 'When you get shaky they have a ballot, and one night you find yourself alone in your bunkroom. Then one of them comes in. I've never had to do it, and I'm glad. So I thought, what the hell? You're never too old to chase a good, eighteen-carat fairy castle. If there's only a chance in a hundred of it being there, it's still worth it.'

'It's there, Lobo,' Randall said with determination, as if he was willing it to be true. 'I know it. Soon as the storm cools down we'll find it.'

'Hah! I like that. If it cools down any more it'll freeze the goddamn sunlight.'

There was a peculiar feeling of security in the foxhole in spite of the fact that there were only a couple of bucketsful of crystalized water between them and the storm. Sound transmitted badly and it was impossible to judge the conditions above, but the grinding of the pylons as they shifted to take up the slightest flexing in the pipeline was clearly audible.

Randall was hungry, but he'd been learning to live with it. He wondered when he would next eat and what; Lobo would have special problems after a number of years on a yeast-only diet. Hadn't the Doc said something about losing certain intestinal flora?

Lobo seemed to have no difficulty in switching off from his surroundings and falling into a light doze, his helmet serving as an improbable pillow. He awoke quickly when Randall tugged urgently at his arm.

'I thought I heard a noise,' Randall explained, 'but I'm sure I was wrong.'

'What kind of noise?'

'It sounded like footsteps, but it couldn't be. I'd never hear them over that wind outside.'

'You might, if the snow's packed hard enough. Can you hear them now?'

They both listened for a moment, but heard nothing. 'Hell,' Lobo muttered, 'I wonder if they've come out after us.'

That would mean an ugly and pointless end to the expedition. 'I'm probably mistaken,' Randall said, trying to sound reassuring.

Lobo rolled over on to his knees, turning in the confines of the hole and pressing his helmet to the wall as an impromptu sounding-board. 'Mistaken or not, we'd be stupid to ignore it,' he said. 'I don't want to crawl out and see Berg bearing down on me waving a club.'

Randall tried the same trick with his helmet, and they listened in silence for a while. Then, as he was about to speak, he heard it again. A dry, steady crunch, granules being squeezed and compressed. There was no way to tell distance or direction.

'Doesn't sound like Berg,' Lobo said, dropping his voice to a whisper. 'Not heavy enough.'

'It isn't,' Randall said with growing confidence as it became obvious that the walker on the ice was alone. 'It's nobody from the Palace.'

'Then who?' Lobo asked, although he knew the answer before the words were out.

'I already told you. Where's the snow thinnest?'

'Why? What are you going to do?'

Randall located the entrance to the hole by its uneven texture. 'For the sake of my own sanity,' he said, 'I'm going to poke my head out and have a look.' The loose handfuls of snow had already frozen together, and he had to attack them with straight fingers to force a way through.

'Don't be stupid,' Lobo said, but he didn't move to stop him. 'You'll give us away. You can't hope for magic saviours in Hell.'

'Magic nothing. It's a man, and he came from the other end of the pipe network. I'll try to see where he goes.'

Lobo began another half-hearted objection, but Randall had cleared a space for his head and shoulders and had already started to worm his way through.

As soon as his head came clear of the surface he realized the folly of looking out without a helmet. The sudden wash of cold air filled his eyes with tears, and while they didn't actually freeze on contact it certainly felt that way. Blinking repeatedly, he opened his eyes to cautious slits and tried to scan around.

He saw the pipeline and the pipeline's end a short distance ahead. Beyond that a broad white plain with a mist that was starting to rise from it and a solitary figure who was watching the sky.

Randall dropped back into the hole and tried to rub warmth back into his eyes. Frost broke and showered from his hair and eyebrows as he told Lobo what he'd seen, adding that the man outside was not from the Ice Palace.

'How do you know?' Lobo asked, reaching for his helmet. 'Recognize him?'

'Too far away. But he's not wearing the standard suit.'

Lobo paused, and gave Randall a look of pure doubt. 'That's a lot of crap, and you know it. Unless he's dead and frozen to the spot...'

'What's the matter, you dumb brute? Can't you let me finish?'

There was an awkward silence, then Lobo said quietly, 'Go on. Finish it.'

'I'm sorry, Lobo. I didn't mean it.'

'I said finish it.'

'All I was going to say was that he's wearing a decent suit that fits, not like Ice Palace rags. I can see the unit on his belt. Look, I'm sorry I was angry, but nobody believed me before.'

'I know what you thought.' Lobo snapped his helmet on and moved across to look for himself. 'Don't make it worse by pretending to apologize.'

Randall tried to frame a few more words of pacification, but Lobo was already halfway out of the foxhole. Randall pulled in a few more handfuls of snow and emerged next to him.

The figure was still there, far away and still looking expectantly upward. 'Okay,' Lobo whispered, 'So you're right and I'm a dumb brute. Who is he?'

'I don't know.'

Lobo frowned. 'And while you're puzzling that one out, maybe you'd like to tell me where all the light's coming from.'

'What do you mean?'

'Since when did the sun burn under the ice?'

Lobo was right. The plain was glowing, lit from beneath and creating the illusion of a mist on the falling snow. It was brighter now than when he had looked before, and the figure had become a black silhouette; the level of light was rising still, and the source of illumination became a distinct ring buried deep.

Could this be where the Ice Palace's power was drained off to at the height of every storm? Far from being any kind of solution, it only deepened Randall's confusion. He could see no immediate purpose to the buried light, and it rather tore to pieces his theory about a second, thriving Ice Palace at the end of the network.

Looking back on the event, Randall and Lobo would still not be able to agree on a definitive version of what happened next. Lobo would describe it as being 'like somebody reached over and put a lid on the sky'.

Randall would remember being startled by the loud roar that suddenly thundered out of nowhere overhead, and losing his grip on the edge of the hole so that he had to grab Lobo's arm to stop himself falling back. They both felt a shock, and the outline of Randall's glove burned on to Lobo's sleeve; and in that same moment there was a painful surge of heat around both their inner suits which lasted for a second or so until both the power packs blew.

And there were lights, bright lights, overhead where they had no right to be. A low roof on the world, studded with incomprehensible detail and slicing down and over them, its hard edge passing away and revealing the cool dark of the night sky.

When the almost physical wave of noise had swept over it left only the diminutive cries of the suit units, drained and empty. Randall tried to pull himself out and step on to the ice, but he moved the wrong way. He put his weight on to the thin roof of the foxhole and it collapsed in under him.

When he tried to rise Lobo had dropped alongside him and was pushing him back. 'Stay where you are, damn it!' he hissed urgently. 'That thing came down just beyond the pipeline!'

He did something to the two power packs, and the giveaway signals stopped. Now there was no sound but the wind overhead, and the distant crack of something cooling.

Randall asked, 'How long can we survive without power?'

'How long does it take a fish to blink?'

That didn't sound very promising. 'We've got to move.'

'Brilliant, cop, but where?'

'I don't know!'

Lobo pushed himself upright and slapped the collapsed wall,

sending a spray of ice particles everywhere. 'What the hell did you lead me into?' he said.

'I led you nowhere! you followed me!'

'You mean you left me a choice?'

They both knew it was futile to argue, but it provided a brief distraction from what was out on the plain. 'I'm sorry, Lobo,' Randall said, and was fairly sure he meant it.

'No, I'm sorry.' They couldn't even agree on that. 'May as well admit we're both scared. My suit's losing heat already.'

Cautiously, they levered themselves up to where they could see. A dark shape almost filled the plain, curving edges lit from underneath by the dying flares. A long column of light spilled out across the ice from somewhere around the far side; a searchlight, perhaps, or even an open doorway into the craft itself.

Randall said, 'We'll have to go down there, unless you can think of anything else.'

'We may be risking a reception.'

'But not necessarily a bad one. When I was in trouble I was helped.'

'You were led back to the Palace, that's all. He wasn't helping you, he was getting you out of his way.'

Randall had to admit the possibility. 'But like it or not, we're committed. If we try to go back they'll tear us up.'

Lobo started to scramble out of the hole. 'I don't care where I go,' he said, 'I'm cold. . .'

They ducked under the pipeline and circled the long way around the craft, keeping well back at first but then moving close to its side as they realized that it provided the only cover. Randall thought he had seen something like it before, out at the old spaceport where the hospitals were based. Of course, the one he had seen had been wrecked and broken open, and hadn't flown in over a hundred years while this one was fully operational. Which left a question—who was operating it?

There was a stubby wing which gave a degree of atmospheric control and they stopped under it, welcoming the slight shelter it offered. A curved section of the ship's side had dropped to make a ramp down to the ice. In the light it threw a similar section of the ice had lifted, breaking its frozen covering into plates and shedding them on either side as it tilted back.

Nothing was happening. There was no sign of the man on the ice.

It was obvious to Randall that the Ice Palace's original function had been as one of the bases for the space trade. The generators, the beacon, the pipelines—even the suits were all relics unrecognized by their present users. Who could tell how far the port extended under the ice, how many of these landing points might still be usable? And then, back to the same question—who was using them now?

But, Randall decided, the academic stuff could wait until later. The main problem now was to get off the ice and get warm. He decided to try for the buried cargo bay first; of the two, the ship was likely to be the better-defended.

'That's a hell of a long way to run across open ice,' Lobo said doubtfully. 'The boots grip best when there's some snow cover.'

'What do you want to do? Stay here and become your own commemorative statue?'

Lobo shivered violently. 'What's one of those?'

'Forget it. You ready to go?'

'Jesus, Randall, I'm dying here. What's keeping you going?'

Randall could have explained that he was the best that Central could make; that he'd been selected at the baby farm and trained until he'd been unable to take anything else in; that he could outfight, outmove and out-think any non-Elite in the world. But instead he took Lobo's arm and they ran.

The wagon came up out of the cargo bay without any sound of warning, its mounted spotlight stabbing towards them. Randall swerved in mid-step and dragged Lobo with him, but the bigger of the two men wasn't expecting the change in course and his legs shot sideways from under him. Fortunately the ice was still slick from the shuttle's landing and as Randall kept pulling Lobo kept going. The wagon swept on by, the spread of its beam missing them completely.

Their skins tingled as the wash of charged air from the wagon's lift passed over them, but it was safely past and climbing the ramp into the shuttle's hull. The man from the ice was standing on the platform behind the light, and on the back of the wagon was some unidentifiable cargo.

The open bay was a disappointment. Far from being the first stage of some underground complex it was no more than a single large room, unheated and with no obvious exits. It was lit by one harsh beam mounted high on the back wall, and the shadows of various-sized crates and boxes pooled black on the floor and on to each other. Randall and Lobo hid themselves in one of the deeper shadows, making sure that they would still have a view of the entry ramp for when the wagon returned.

'So where are we now?' Lobo demanded.

'Part of an old dockyard, at a guess. The rest is probably buried under the ice all around us. One hangar opened and that's it.'

'Opened for what? How can it help us?'

'I don't know, on both counts. The wagon was loading crates, but don't ask me what was in them.'

Lobo tried to turn and look, but it seemed the effort caused him pain. 'You want to go and find out?'

The box they were crouched under could have held a small car but it was old, brown and dirty. The fresh-looking wagon-sized crates were all in a stack at the far side of the hangar, about five of them.

'Risky,' Randall said dubiously. 'What if he comes back?'

'We steal his wagon.' Lobo ignored the pain and looked up. 'I can't do any more walking out there. We'll have to steal the wagon and take it back to the Ice Palace.'

Randall was surprised. 'You're joking. After the way we left?'

'All that's changed. Now we've got something to trade, something they can't turn down.' He indicated the entrance ramp and the ship beyond. 'A way out. Two of us would get picked off, but fifty or more could storm on board and take it.'

'So why wasn't that tried with the icebreaker?'

'It was, and it failed because the boat was shielded against attack. You reckon this ship's just a cargo freighter.'

The idea made sense, but Randall wanted to get the prospective difficulties out of the way while there was still time. 'So we've got something to offer them. But Berg tends to hit first and save the discussion for the long winter evenings.'

'Leave Berg to me. I know these people. And if I don't get some shelter in the next ten minutes I'll have had it.'

Light and noise announced the wagon's return. It came down the ramp much too fast, but air-jets hissed and brought it to a steady halt by the cargo. It bobbed on its air cushion as the driver stepped off the control platform on the far side.

Randall had time to notice and wonder that the driver wasn't wearing any kind of helmet and then they were moving.

The control platform—a flat plate behind the guidance mechanism and lamp housing at the front of the vehicle—was a little too high for an easy leap, and where Randall only just made it Lobo caught the edge square across his shins and nearly dived headfirst off the opposite side.

The wagon dipped beneath their weight, and extra jets immediately cut in to bring it up level; and the wagon's driver heard the change in pitch and stopped with his back to them, turning his head slightly to listen.

As Lobo struggled to keep himself aboard Randall looked for the controls. He expected something like a rheostat for speed and a directional handle, but there was nothing. The wagon was slowly turning around its own centre, sliding forward and aligning its nose with the ramp; and as the hangar rotated around them the rear jets cut in and they surged forward.

The driver was slow to react, and didn't even shout as the wagon took in the incline and coasted out on to the ice. It gathered speed, angling across the short distance to the open hold of the cargo shuttle. There was no sign of a buried wire under the ice, but Randall knew there had to be one. Their weight on the control platform had triggered the wagon into running over its programmed route—a route which didn't include the Ice Palace.

They were taken up the ramp and into the belly of the shuttle, a utilitarian chamber running the length of the ship. One side was a flat wall dividing them from the rest of the craft, while the opposite wall bulged outwards and was lined with the struts and braces that supported the ship's outer skin. The floor was ribbed metal and the walls were painted grey, scuffed and marked as if some sharp-edged object had floated free on a rough ride.

The wagon followed a yellow line to the end of the track and drew up alongside two crates, the wagon's previous load, chained side-by-side in a marked-off area.

Lobo gratefully released his numb grip on the control platform and slid off on to the floor. Randall dropped beside him and helped him to his feet, looking back down the hold as he did so.

The entrance was a black square, the hell of the ice-cap invisible beyond it. Within moments the man from the ice would have covered the distance between the hangar and the ship. Randall didn't feel too bad but there was no way that Lobo could be taken back on to the ice—already he'd limped to the nearest crate and had unzipped one of his gloves, flexing his white-tipped fingers in the meagre warmth of the hold.

There were bulkhead doors set in the inner wall, and the nearest was open. Low emergency-type lighting showed a ladder beyond. Randall left Lobo for a moment to step over the low threshold and check that it wasn't a dead end; looking up he could see access to three levels from the vertical tunnel, and there was nobody coming down. Like it or not, it had to be good enough.

Lobo had his helmet and gloves off, for the suits kept heat out with the same efficiency that they kept it in. They were on the floor, dropped carelessly as Lobo had bent to inspect the crate on which he was sitting. He looked up as Randall came back into the hold.

'It's split,' he said with vacant wonder, all danger apparently forgotten. 'I can see inside.'

'Worry about it later. I've found the way in.'

Lobo came obediently to his feet when Randall dragged him up, but wouldn't leave the crate. 'This is important,' he insisted.

'So's staying alive! Come on!'

'It's a transport coffin,' Lobo tried to explain as Randall pushed him through the door and on to the ladder. He began to climb automatically, and Randall turned to get his helmet and gloves. He felt a stab of horror as Lobo's voice echoed back down the ladder, loud enough for anybody on the upper levels to hear.

'Willis is in there,' he was saying. 'They're stealing *men*.'

ELEVEN

KILLORAN ARRIVED early for his appointment with Marius but was told that the councillor had been delayed in a meeting for the past hour, and did he mind waiting? He was offered the option of a hard chair in a grimy corridor or the autumn chill of the roof garden; he saw the psychology of dominance in both, and opted for the garden.

Split over two levels, the garden was no more than a thin crust of soil over a disused helicopter pad. Plants were dying in the borders while the lawns were determinedly drifting apart into their component squares. An ornamental fountain guttered and spat brackish water over in the far corner.

The council building was a hasty adaptation, this much was obvious. Marius had argued the need for an imposing headquarters for the new administration, but one suspected that the only real criterion would be that the building should be taller than the old Police Elite block. And so it was—by one storey. Formerly one of the many deserted towers that lined the city's boulevards, this one had been selected and broken open, the crawlers flushed out with gas flares and the top three floors painted and cleaned out for use as council offices.

There was a sad irony in it, paint on the face of a ruin to herald a new dawn for the city. Killoran turned on hearing a distant clatter to see an Elite helicopter pop out of one of the boulevards further up-river and head over towards the underbelly, passing over Central's old dome and making a quick loop around the first tall building just for the hell of it.

A citizen woman about his own age came over and asked if there was anything he needed. Marius believed in promoting a new understanding between the underbelly and the citizen. To this end he employed citizens in menial positions wherever he could.

She asked Killoran for details of his case so that she could withdraw the appropriate files. When he told her that he had come about the Randall appeal she gave a puzzled frown and went away again.

Killoran looked out at the grey sky, the empty city, the fat, sluggish river. Entropy, he thought; the universe is running down. How can we expect something as artificial as a roof garden to resist the process?

MORDEN RAN his hands nervously over the objects on the table in front of him, trying to fix their relative positions in his mind so that he wouldn't have to fumble for anything. He was unhappy and insecure, as he always was when away from the familiar geography of his home.

'Is it essential I stay?' he asked Marius, who was noisily turning papers over at the head of the table. 'I've nothing I can truthfully say to this man.'

'Say something untruthful, then. Just as long as he gets an impression of power in action and takes his complaints elsewhere.'

'Then why are we bothering to see him at all?'

'You tell me,' Marius said wearily. 'You helped design this godawful democracy. It's a pain in the backside.'

Marius's citizen girl came in and left a file on the table. Marius opened it and flicked through a couple of sheets. He said to Morden, 'You want me to read you any of Killoran's file?'

'I'm familiar with it.'

'This isn't Chandler's information,' Marius said with a hint of evil glee, 'it's my own. I wanted to see if I could get some dirt together about the Elite. Never know when it may be useful.'

Morden tried to hide his distaste. He was as underhand and conniving as anybody, but he tried not to let it show; Marius, on the other hand, seemed to revel in it, like a fat child stealing sweets.

Morden said, 'And have you got the kind of dirt you wanted?'

'No damn chance. Either they're more devious than I am or

they're the most upright bunch of creeps in the city. I don't like anyone I can't buy. The only people I can get to are the pilots—take them away from the 'copters and they're nervous wrecks after a week.'

'Central bred for specific strains,' Morden reminded him. 'You can't wipe that out as easily as the administration.'

'No, but the Elite were also bred to respect and defend authority, right? Without Central that leaves you and me.'

'And Chandler.'

'Forget Chandler. I'll work something out for him.'

Marius decided that Killoran had been kept waiting for long enough, and sent for him to be brought down. Minutes later the young Elite Inspector was ushered in and Marius made the introductions, apologizing for Chandler's absence.

Although he wouldn't admit it out loud, Marius was worried by Killoran's persistence over Randall's appeal in the face of a State decree. The Elite were supposed to be loyal without question, programmed biological machines; it wouldn't do to have them trying to make moral judgments or question their orders. Marius couldn't put into effect any of the simpler solutions that came to mind for fear of Chandler finding out and further stalling would be difficult. Much better to lead Killoran by the nose for a little way and then let him wander on to his own destruction.

Killoran wanted to know where Randall was; why he'd not been released and reinstated.

'Simple questions demand direct answers,' Marius began, secretly taken aback by the directness of the challenge. 'Firstly, he's in a prison facility at a location I'm not at liberty to reveal. And secondly, he stays there because he was tried by the council and found guilty of treason. That verdict stands pending appeal, but I might as well warn you not to hold out any hopes of it being reversed.'

Killoran couldn't do much about the low seat he'd been given, but he leaned forward onto the table. 'With respect, councillor, I'm appalled. Randall carried through his duty right up to the end. There are no grounds for condemning him.'

Marius consulted a sheet of paper before him. It had no

bearing on the case, but the action lent a certain authority. 'There are certain ambiguities about the whole affair which throw some doubt on to that.'

'Only doubts? No proof?'

'In a case as extreme as this we have to err on the side of safety if at all. Treason, Inspector Killoran! How does your Elite training react to that?'

'Not at all,' Killoran replied guardedly, 'if it's not proven.'

Marius dropped the stance of cold authority. It didn't seem to be working. Instead he decided to try an illusion of confidence sharing. He noted with some annoyance that Morden didn't seem to be inclined to make any contribution, but no matter. His time would come later.

'Let me put it another way,' Marius said. 'No repeating of this, you understand, because the secrecy of the original proceedings still holds. We gave careful attention to the recording of your exchange with Randall when he was in communication with you from inside the Central computer building. The way it sounded, Randall was the only one alive in there when the computer started into its shutdown procedure.'

'Then he put you in power, councillor,' Killoran replied. 'What kind of treason do you call that?'

'You've missed the point,' Marius told him, his tone implying kindly indulgence for Killoran's slow-wittedness. 'Treason is an attempt against the State, and it doesn't really matter who's representing the State at the time of the act. Central held the power then, and the underbelly holds the power now. And a rebel is a rebel, equally dangerous in either case.'

'So what about Rorvik?'

'Rorvik's quite different. He happens to be dead, and the city needs a hero. Memories of the dead are much easier to control than the activities of the living. Morden, you must have some ideas on this. Do you want to add anything?'

'Nothing, Marius,' Morden replied drily. 'You seem to be doing perfectly well without me.'

'Obviously I'm not appreciating the politics behind your decision,' Killoran said, failing to disguise the sarcasm because he wasn't trying very hard. 'I thought I was here over a matter of simple justice.'

Marius's eyebrows went up. 'Whoever told you that justice was a simple matter, Inspector? I'll agree it's a pleasant ideal, but at this crucial stage in our history it's one we can hardly afford. These are times of change, and the city needs strength from its leaders above anything else. That means the strength to do what we know is right even when our feelings tell us it is wrong.' He gathered his papers together and slid them into a folder. He went on, 'You'll understand that there are more practical pressures on the council than would allow us to continue this hypothetical debate. Go back to your work, Inspector, and be grateful that, one way or another, your city holds together.' He turned to Morden, who was toying with an empty water glass. 'I have to go now. I'll see you later, Morden.'

Morden nodded, and, with a statesman's insincere smile, Marius said goodbye to Killoran and left the room. Killoran sat, his mouth hanging slightly open, incredulous at the speed and skill of the brush-off he'd been given. He'd expected a false display of polite concern, of mystified shock and the promise of a most strenuous enquiry; and while he'd known that the sentiments and the promise would have been equally empty there was still something deep inside that gave him an irrational faith that some fundamental universal law would come into play and the right results would come if only he could keep the wheels moving. Marius had disarmed him with an ornate and sweetened version of the truth; that it didn't matter a damn whether Randall was guilty or not, but it would be better for everybody if he stayed where he was.

At least it was more tangible than the polite lack of interest that his fellow-Elite showed. It was a State decision. It must be all right.

So basic truths and ideals were not as inflexible as he'd always supposed. They could be altered and reshaped by self-interested men in little rooms like this. Success involved altering the world to the way you wanted it and then convincing lesser people that it was what they really wanted as well.

Killoran pushed his chair back and rose to go.

'Obviously you're not satisfied,' Morden said.

'Am I hiding it so badly?'

'You're not hiding it at all. That's dangerous, and you should be more careful.'

Probably this was some new angle to put one over on him, but what the hell. Morden sounded almost sympathetic and Killoran needed to talk to someone. 'If I'm reckless,' he said, 'it's because there are limits on the resilience of my loyalty. Before Central fell I served a rotten city without complaint. I didn't complain because I didn't even understand that things could be changed. Now I've seen progress. The city's more rotten than ever.'

Morden pushed the glass away and sat back in his chair. 'I told you to be careful. Remember I'm a councillor.'

Somehow, Morden's presence seemed to intimidate Killoran far less than that of Marius. ' I remember when you were the biggest crook we ever chased, Morden,' he said. 'We never could pin down any of your factories.'

Morden allowed himself the brief hint of a smile. 'Progress is only more of the same. Then it was crime, now we call it free enterprise. But listen to me and be warned about Marius. It's not beneath him to take your complaint personally and interfere in your career.'

Killoran couldn't resist the offered posture of sacrifice. 'I hardly care...'

'Shut up and listen.' Morden's manner had unexpectedly hardened. 'Right now he's probably speaking to Chandler about you. I'm not without influence myself, so I'll do my best to persuade Chandler not to take any action. But you've got to learn to keep your mouth shut.'

'You mean knuckle under.'

'I mean that a public show of bitterness works against your cause, not for it.'

'What else can I do? Whether I like it or not, I'm still loyal to the city.'

Morden raised his head, gave Killoran the full force of his dead eyes. Killoran looked into them and saw a frozen blue waste that drew and held him against his will. 'It's about time you learned otherwise,' Morden said. 'Blind loyalty's totally without value to anybody apart from a dictator, whether that's Central or the head of the council. At the moment the future of the city depends on an Elite force of fawning puppies, over-trained and under Marius.'

'Marius isn't the whole council.'

'Believe that if you must. Believing doesn't make it so.'

Killoran fought to pull himself away from Morden's hypnotic influence. 'All right,' he said, forcing himself to look at his hands, 'What is this? Some kind of test on my loyalty? See how far you can lead me and then turn me in? Well, hard luck.' For the second time he left his chair. 'I'm not staying to be set up and knocked over.'

Morden didn't try to persuade him. He waved his hand dismissively, and said in tones of bored disappointment, 'Go, then. Go and prop up your festering city. I overestimated your resources.'

Killoran hovered, halfway to the door. He couldn't leave on such a note, and he suspected Morden knew it. 'Listen, Morden,' he said, 'I may not be much more than a kid, but I'm the best Central could breed. I'm Elite, Morden! I don't have to listen to that kind of talk. . .'

'From underbelly scum?' Morden said quietly.

A pause. Then, with some sincerity, 'I'm sorry, Morden. I deserved that.'

'The polite thing would be to say forget it, Killoran. Don't ever forget it. The offence is just a small part of the load you will always carry if you don't work to wipe it out. You're the end product of an obscene experiment, and there is so much to avenge.'

'Why me? Why am I so special?'

'Because you're here. Because you didn't accept, you challenged.'

'So what?' Killoran said dejectedly. 'It's got me nowhere.' He wandered over to the window and stared out.

'Of course not,' Morden said, rising from his own seat. 'Now it's up to you.' He moved faultlessly around the table and joined Killoran at the window.

Killoran was confused, and his mind tried to reject the

burden of lawless action that Morden seemed in an oblique way to be offering him. 'Surely there are legal processes...'

'Forget the legal processes. Marius has them in his pocket like everything else.'

'But you're bigger than Marius.'

Morden spoke with sadness. 'I used to be. Not any more. Now nobody's bigger than Marius. What do you want most, Killoran?'

Killoran looked inward, tried to find some kind of evasion. But the anger at an action that had attacked the fabric of his understanding of the world blotted out everything else.

'I want justice for Randall,' he said.

'Justice for Randall consists at this moment of imprisonment in an unguarded base on the polar ice cap. He's living on the brink of survival, and the labour of the rest of his life will never put him more than an arm's length away from that brink. There's no way he could leave without help.'

Killoran took the information in, feeling triumph mixed with horror. He'd got what he wanted, but no longer could he restrict himself to the adoption of a crusading pose; now action was being demanded of him and his earlier confidence began to dissolve in a rush of uncertainty.

But a little voice of ego shouting loud said, forget it, kid, now's the time to deliver. He held on to that one point of stability in his inner turmoil as Morden began to tell him about the icebreaker.

TWELVE

When Killoran left Morden he didn't go straight back to the Police Elite building. He wanted to compose his thoughts and he had some vague idea of finding one of the newly-opened city cafes where he could sit in a cleaned-out basement with a cup of ersatz. An hour or more passed and he was still walking.

When he arrived at the Elite building he went up to the office that he had shared with Randall and now shared with a cheerless individual named Partington who seemed to spend most of his time shrivelling his brains with a nasal spray. There was a teleprinter flimsy on his desk, raggedly torn across the bottom, which carried his order for the afternoon.

Louann Roget had claimed Rorvik's remains, and the council had approved their release that morning. Killoran was to provide Elite presence at the Chapel of Rapt Contemplation during their disposal.

The C of RC was part of a multi-unit operation which had originally been a purely underbelly organization. With the fall of Central they had moved across the river and begun legitimate competition with the Hospitals and they had a quaint slogan which went, 'Your Dolour is Our Concern'. This was accompanied by their sign, an S with a slash through it that Killoran imagined was some ancient guild symbol.

The chapels complex was a converted building in the middle of some weedy parkland. The muzak was suitably pious as Killoran presented himself at the reception desk to ask for directions, but before he had the opportunity to announce his interest the watery-eyed man behind the desk had produced a list on a clipboard and was asking whether he was a registered relative or a professional. While Killoran was puzzling over this one, the man asked for his card.

'Which card?' said Killoran, by now totally bewildered.

'The Mutes' Union,' the man replied, regarding him with increasing suspicion. 'I'm the branch steward and I have to watch out for my members' interests.'

'I'm not a professional mourner,' Killoran started to explain, but he was interrupted.

'An amateur? Beat it, slug. We don't want your kind here. Some of us have a living to make, without your morbid profiteering.'

Killoran finally managed to explain who he was and why he was there, but before he could be given directions to the relevant chapel there was a commotion behind them. Killoran turned to see five men of varying heights and widths trying to squeeze through a single doorway at the same time. There was some grunting and struggling and then a little fat man popped out of the middle as if he'd been greased. This loosened the pack for the others and they fell in behind.

The little fat man came over, breathless and panting. 'Sorry I'm late,' he gasped. 'That's what comes of depending on the slugging public transport in this city. What've you got for me?'

'About time, too,' the watery-eyed man said with obvious disapproval. 'Even the deceased's getting impatient. Those your bearers?'

The other four were dusting themselves down at the far side of the foyer. As bearers they were an ill-matched crew; Killoran was certain that the smallest of them would have no chance of reaching up to the coffin.

'Have a heart, sir,' they wailed when the receptionist pointed this fact out. 'We need the work, honest.'

'What about that little short one? He won't even be able to reach.'

'I'm taller than I look, sir,' the one in question promised.

Faced with such impeccable logic the receptionist shook his head sorrowfully. 'It's nothing to me,' he said, 'but if the client complains I'm throwing it straight back to you.'

'Who is the client, then?'

'Police Department.'

'Oh, slug. Straighten up, lads.'

The little fat man was, it seemed, the priest in charge of the ceremony. He went off to change into more solemn garb and Killoran followed the bearers to the Chapel of Rapt Contemplation.

The chapel was quite large, and two thirds of it was filled with forward-facing benches. Before them and the focus of some well-placed lights, were a dais with a slide marked 'Loved One Here' and a raised pulpit.

The pulpit and the dais were empty, but the chapel was full.

Killoran got his first inkling of what was going on from the excessive brilliance of the lighting. Looking around he could see, just beyond the halo of the spotlights, at least three remote-controlled 3V emplacements. The cameras were motoring from side to side, testing their fields of view and lining up shots at the command of some distant operator, while below about forty people were being shepherded into place on the benches by a young man with an earpiece linked to a radio set on his belt. Three girls were moving amongst them, pausing to dab the shines off foreheads and noses with sponges and powder-puffs.

A dead hero. Marius was fixing to make the most of the occasion.

The young man with the earpiece spotted him and fought his way through the crowd. 'You're late,' he said with an air of practised harassment. 'You've already missed the tech, run and damn nearly the whole thing.' And then his attention switched off and his eyes unfocussed as he listened to the voice in his head. 'Yes,' he said, and then 'Yes, but...' and then he listened for a while longer as Killoran looked around and wondered who he was talking to.

'Police rep? Front row,' the young man snapped, and he gave Killoran a light push in the direction of the front row before turning his back and walking away. Killoran moved down the aisle, past a row of women who were rehearsing their weeping. 'No, dear,' one of them was insisting, 'four bars and then the sob. Otherwise it sounds contrived.'

He was, it seemed, to sit alone. There was a handwritten card with his name on it pinned to the bench and he removed it before he sat down. One of the makeup girls brought her case over to him and set it beside him as she worked on his face with pencils and tiny sponges. 'Make you look really miserable,' she explained with enthusiasm, 'for when they do the closeups.'

Killoran tried to sound politely grateful, but probably- failed. He didn't really want any of this, but it was his job. All the same, he couldn't give it any more than the most superficial attention; his meeting with Morden was continually replaying itself in the back of his mind. The replay invariably came to a frightened halt when confronted with any future course of action, only to start promptly from the beginning again and move inexorably towards the same lack of a conclusion.

The girl moved away. Somebody shouted for quiet, but was distracted halfway through and didn't finish the request. Killoran glanced around to see what was happening, and recognized Louann. She was across the aisle on the same row as he, and there was an older woman with her, sitting apart a little further down the bench. There seemed to be no immediate danger of anything happening, so Killoran left his seat and went over.

She didn't recognize him at first; it was a long time since she'd seen him and in addition to this she seemed to be trying to disassociate her mind from the mercenary bustle around her.

'I remember you,' she said after a moment. 'Don't you think you've done enough?'

'I have to be here, Ms Roget,' he explained. 'I'm the only available senior officer from Lee Rorvik's case.'

'That may be so. But I don't think we've got anything to talk about.'

'Perhaps not,' he pressed, 'but can I see you after the service?'

She was looking ahead, concentrating on the curtained wall of the chapel. 'I can't imagine why.'

'I need your help, Ms Roget. There's something I want to do, and I need to be sure I'm doing the right thing.'

'After the service. Please don't bother me before that.'

The older woman was giving him a look of warning. Killoran nodded and returned to his seat.

There was another shout for silence, which was ignored, and then another which was accompanied by a few choice threats. As the extras composed themselves the same voice called out,

'Rorvik funeral, production number one-oh-nine stroke four-five, take one.' Then ten seconds of silence and the lights over the pulpit blazed on.

The priest was thoroughly transformed. His glitter suit sparkled and dazzled as he stepped forward through the curtains on the first rumbling notes of the Moog. His grey hair had vanished under a glossy black wig and his belly had apparently vanished into the strictures of a corset.

The Moog pulsed as he slunk across to the pulpit and draped himself over it. 'Friends,' he said, his voice picked up and amplified with a seductive echo, 'I welcome you to the Chapel of Rapt Contemplation. I hope you'll enjoy the programme we've set out for you and that you'll consider us for similar occasions in the future. Tissues are freely available from the box in front of your seat. The Chapel of Rapt Contemplation is run by the World Wide Worship Combine for your spiritual comfort.'

He bowed his head with perfect timing as the lights dropped and a single brilliant beam speared down to the back of the chapel. The music swelled into a loud and brassy fanfare as the coffin swayed up towards the dais, unevenly supported by the unfortunate bearers whom Killoran had followed up from the foyer. The extras showed the benefits of careful rehearsal with a loud and energetic howl of grief.

The Moog was joined by a hearty quartet singing a song about a new cloud in the sky and a tear in every eye and we know you want the best for them as you wave them goodbye. The Loved One was deposited in his appointed place with a decisive thump and as the bearers moved away the priest rippled and glinted across to stand by the plain wooden case, one hand resting lightly on its lid. As the song ended with an exhortation to turn your face to heaven and never say die he looked up and said, 'May I offer my commiseration on this saddest of days. The service will continue after a short message from our sponsors.'

He held the pose for a moment and then looked up expectantly. The young man with the earpiece called, 'Okay, that's a take.' Then there was another number and a countdown and the service proceeded.

It all went fairly smoothly except for the finale, which needed a retake. They slid the coffin back from behind the curtains and did it over and this time everybody seemed satisfied. The extras promptly dried their eyes and formed a line for their money and Killoran elbowed his way across the flow of the crowd to get outside to where the air wasn't choking with powder and sweat.

It was late afternoon, but still light. He waited on the dry lawn outside the building, and he turned when he heard the door swing and footsteps on the path. It was the woman who had been sitting a little further on from Louann, and she came across to him.

She explained, 'Louann Roget's in my care. It seems you want to talk to her.'

A nurse? How would a citizen afford a service like that? Then it fell into place; the council would be paying her fees. No chance of Louann becoming controversial over the fall of Central as long as she was kept under such close control.

He asked, 'Is there anything wrong in that?'

'Probably not. She's been improving steadily for some time. I wouldn't like to see all that good work undone by irresponsible talk of what's gone by.'

'That's not why I'm here,' Killoran reassured her. 'My official job's done, now. If anything I need her help.'

'Really? Now there's a change. I hope the novelty of being needed doesn't prove too much for her.'

'I'll be careful.'

The faintest suspicion of a threat came into her voice. 'You'd better. Being in the Elite doesn't mean what it used to under Central. I could raise a complaint with the council and have your rank.'

She left him to think about it as she returned to the foyer, where it seemed Louann had been obediently waiting for the ground to be prepared.

There was a wooden bench over by an ornate fountain, flanked by memorial litter bins. Killoran waited there until Louann emerged, and then stood up so she would see him.

She didn't come all the way, but stopped a few yards short of the bench. She'd grown her hair longer than the standard citizens' crop. Her face was marked with faint lines of intelligent concern. They suited her.

'I don't have long,' she said, raising her voice to cover the distance between them. 'I'm not even sure I want to be here. What is it you have to say?'

He knew what he wanted; he needed to talk to somebody who knew the facts about Central's fall, who would say to him, 'Of course, Neil. It's obvious what you have to do now. I don't know what you're so confused about.' But this antagonism unsettled him, threw him off completely.

'I'm not even sure how to start,' he admitted.

'You surprise me. I thought uncertainty was a feature confined to real human beings.'

'What do you mean?'

She needed to hurt him. All the pain and indignity of the travesty of a funeral that had just taken place came to bear on him. 'Why should I explain?' she said, meeting his eyes for the first time. 'You're the Elite. You don't have to care about our problems. Just chase us, pursue us, stamp on us, kill us. You're not men. You're machines designed and built by a machine. Designed for persecution.' And then she looked away.

Killoran thought, this is all wrong, this isn't what I came for. 'Suppose that's true,' he said, already unconvinced by his own defence. 'Suppose we rebuilt the city all over again and someone tried to pull it down. How else could we act other than the way we did?'

'If it's so frail that one man can pull it down, then it doesn't deserve to stand!'

He couldn't pretend to oppose her; and yet he was strangely pleased to find her so changed. 'I don't understand you,' he said.

'I'm surprised it bothers you.' By unspoken consent they both moved to the bench and sat down.

Killoran said, 'Last time we talked Lee Rorvik was on the loose and out in the underbelly somewhere. I remember you told us that you didn't care where he was or what he was doing, and furthermore you didn't want to know. All you wanted were your tapes and your dreams.'

'And now I have neither. You're wrong about the last time we talked. It was on the Library mezzanine.'

'That hardly counts...'

'Why?' she demanded, looking at him hard. 'Because I was hysterical? Because I got roaring, screaming drunk? You don't know anything. That was the most important day of my life.'

'Do you remember much of it?'

'Like crystal in cold water.' She stared ahead, seeing her memories re-forming in the fountain's spray. 'I remember leaving the computer terminals with an armload of tapes and going down into the foyer. I remember the outer doors bursting in and three men charging through the crowd. They weren't stopping for anything, pushing people aside and kicking things over. They went over the turnstiles, and then I recognized him and he recognized me. He slowed down and stopped. We were looking at each other—we were yards apart and there were hundreds of people between us—and his friends had stopped on the stairs and were calling to him. He seemed not to hear them at first, then he turned and ran with them. The next day they were all dead and the city was down.' She brightened a little, as if the sadness of the moment had become a separate experience in the telling that she could now push away from herself. 'There. Does that make your enquiry neat and complete? Is it what you wanted to hear?'

It was barbed, but it lacked the savagery of her earlier remarks. 'Randall didn't want to kill him, you know. He set himself up.'

A little shrug. 'And where's the real difference?'

'And who's the real rebel, Louann? Rorvik was a hunted killer. He had nothing to lose. Randall staked everything when he started the deprogramming sequence.'

'Lee's dead.' It was a flat statement, something you couldn't argue with; all the same, he tried.

'Randall may as well be. He's been stranded without a trial on the polar ice cap.'

'And how can you object? When the State decrees, the Elite obey.'

He glanced around. The nurse had wandered off some way into the park, well out of earshot. 'Not this one,' he said quietly.

'What?'

'I don't know where I'm up to and I can't talk to anyone. I hoped you might understand.'

'I don't. I think you're trying to trick me into saying something.'

He smiled sadly and mostly to himself. 'Of course. Isn't that what you expect of the diehard Elite, fanatically loyal to the State? Except that I no longer know what the State is. Once it was a machine, and the underbelly were a bunch of crooks to be held at arm's length. Now those same crooks are giving the orders and the machine's the worst evil in human history. I've watched the other officers around me—their loyalty's like a lightbulb, it's bred into them and they switch it on and off for whoever happens to be in charge. They follow any power, never the right to power. And after what I've seen, I can't.'

It was getting colder, and the light was beginning to soften and take on a pre-twilight glow. She tried not to shiver and said, 'What have you seen?'

'Randall and I were a team. I had to watch him and learn from him, so that I'd eventually be able to take on the same kind of authority. After all those years of training he was the most immediate and understandable example of what the Elite stood for—at least, he was to me. But then we weren't a common team. Randall tended to think for himself and I was picking up the habit. When he killed the governing programme I understood why; if it had been me there by the central console I'm sure I'd have done the same. He was serving the State as an abstract concept, not as a particular form of government. Both he and Rorvik had the same idea in the end—whose hand turned the key made no real difference.'

'That's not what the underbelly council say.'

'Don't you see?' he said, trying hard not to raise his voice in exasperation and barely succeeding. 'That's where I get desperate. Before the council's decision came out I was ready to accept it as a good Elite officer. I knew that the State had been served and I expected Randall to be reinstated with honour. It didn't happen and I was lost. I still am.'

She tried to think of some comfort to offer him. She was surprised to find that she wanted to. But when she reached in towards her long-untapped reserves of sympathy, they eluded her. 'What do you think I can do about it?' she said, the guilt of helplessness beginning to stir her cold composure.

'I don't expect you to do anything. But I had to be here and you're the only person I could talk to who might understand what I was saying. Anybody else would call it sedition.'

'But I wouldn't?'

'You were there. You followed the whole story through and you know where it led. For everybody else it's been twisted and turned around by publicity as an exercise in manipulation by the council.' He indicated the chapel complex behind them. 'They're attempting to manufacture history to consolidate their own authority, to remove the precedent that such authority can be challenged. And it's working.'

She tried not to sigh. It would seem so trite. 'Congratulations,' she said. 'You're the last sane man in the world. What do you think you can do about it?'

He shook his head, and said with determination, 'I'm the last of three. One's dead, but the other can be reached. And I know how.'

'Such ambition and such ideals. The harder you push them, the harder the world pushes back. We've both seen it happen.'

Killoran didn't want consolation for his failure to act, although for a moment he was tempted to take it. It would be so much easier to follow the escape-route that was being offered to his conscience, to be able to say *There I was, poised for any danger, but...* Once he'd recognized it, the route was closed to him.

He told her about the Ice Palace and the icebreaker which made irregular supply runs to it; how he was going to exchange his credit for the untraceable money that the underbelly had introduced into the city and use it to bribe the ship's captain. He watched her for some hint of reaction. All he saw was confusion as she struggled to separate her feelings, the ones she ought to be having from the more sincere impulses beneath.

'You've got my sympathy,' she said carefully after a moment. 'Nothing else, because I've nothing else to give.' She was surprised to find that she wanted him to succeed, that she could draw no triumph from Randall's fate; he was another in the parade of victims in which she included herself and who stood in the shadow of a great amorphous oppressor whose shape might change but whose tactics never varied.

Killoran was thinking about this, uncertain as to whether he was encouraged or disappointed, when there was a rasping, buzz from somewhere.

Louann drew back her sleeve to uncover what looked like a wafer-thin wristwatch with no display. 'My personal alarm,' she explained as she touched it to stop the noise. 'It's synchronized to the one the nurse carries. That means it's time for my medication.'

He glanced around and, sure enough, the nurse was heading purposefully towards them. Louann saw her as well, and said quickly, 'Goodbye, Mr Killoran. I believe in you, if that's what you want to hear. And if it isn't... well, I don't know what I can say. Except good luck.'

She was up and hurrying away before he could reply.

He stayed for a while, alone on the bench. Some of the 3V crew went past chattering, the vulgarities of the service forgotten. There was, he decided, no point in canvassing for opinions any further; they wouldn't make him any more right or wrong in what he was doing, nor would they substantially help or hinder him in any way. He might as well face it; he was on his own.

For Louann, the medication was beginning to reassert its hold. The unpleasant realities that Killoran had revived for her began to dissolve and percolate away to be replaced by a cotton-wool warmth that was all the more agreeable because it was meaningless. Killoran wasn't forgotten, but his troubles were— the drugs pushed them firmly away before they could reach the vulnerable interior of her sensibility.

He'd been quite nice, really.

THIRTEEN

Lobo was in a bad way and Randall didn't feel much better. The consolations of their predicament did nothing to relieve the discomfort.

They'd made it up the ladder without meeting anyone, made it out on to the second level without meeting anyone, followed a corridor the entire length of the ship without meeting anyone—the inescapable conclusion was that there wasn't anyone, that the ship was being run by a more sophisticated version of the automatics that had guided the wagon into the hold and trapped them there.

It didn't seem right. Of all the available space, more than half was taken up with facilities for a large crew—the level on which they moved was lined with doors, some of them open to show the hanging webs of unusual but recognizable sleeping quarters. There were lockers with coveralls and uniforms and alcoves with drinks dispensers that had inexplicably ruptured and peppered their contents on to the walls opposite, freeze-dried and un-decayed. And everywhere had grab-handles, even the ceilings.

Lobo had become more coherent as he'd warmed up. As the ship had revealed itself to be deserted he began to argue that they should return to the hold; the man from the ice was obviously alone and couldn't call upon the support of the crew as they'd feared and it was obvious he'd have no chance against the two of them. Randall was inclined to be more cautious. They hadn't seen ail of the ship and if the man from the ice happened to be armed it wouldn't matter if they were two or twenty.

They had still been arguing when it had started. The metal around them seemed to shudder and there was a swimming feeling which told them the shuttle had lifted and was turning. Then an increasing, steady drag which pulled them first to their knees and then flat on the deck. It was bearable, but irresistible and frightening. Anybody walking the corridors could have found them then, spreadeagled and defenceless; but then, nobody could be moving under that pitiless and inexplicable drag.

It lasted about twenty minutes and when it stopped it got worse. Randall had seen the surprise on Lobo's face as his body detached from the floor all at once and began to rise, but the perception had been wiped away by sudden panic as he'd felt his own security go and the floor drop away from under him. It was a mistake to grab for it, because the result had been an upward sail and an uncomfortable impact on the ceiling—still, he'd got a grip on one of the handles, and it gave him a firm anchorage from which to assess his position.

Lobo was less fortunate. He was spinning in mid air, out of reach of anything. He'd been sick and the droplets were slowly dispersing, undulating globes which spattered on to every surface they met.

Randall made a guess, took aim, launched himself. He tangled with Lobo but they kept some of the momentum and coasted on to within reach of another handle. Randall caught it and swung them both in to the wall.

'I closed my eyes,' Lobo explained miserably. 'I closed my eyes and everything disappeared.'

'Think of it as swimming,' Randall told him. 'No up, no down—you sink, you float.'

'I can't swim,' Lobo said.

They were now open to discovery by anyone who might decide to look for them, and being completely lacking in the skills of weightlessness they would be able to offer little resistance. Lobo's last meal was now a greasy film on the corridor walls, an instant giveaway if they hid nearby. He hung in the air like an unhappy sack as Randall towed him back towards the access ladder.

He'd intended to go down, but there was a faint 'upward' draught in the tunnel which made it easier simply to let go and rise with it. The air couldn't be moving by gravity, for its rules no longer seemed to have any relevance; it must be differing relative pressures, bleeding off in a flow from one to the other.

The third level was a copy of the second. Randall considered hiding in one of the rooms off to the side, but decided it would be too obvious; Lobo wondered if there was any point in hiding at all on an empty ship.

Randall was adapting to this environment a little more every time he moved. For Lobo the process was much slower and although his initial nausea was coming under his control they agreed that he should stay in one of the empty crew rooms while Randall carried out some cautious reconnaissance.

He didn't have to go very far. He was swinging into the access tunnel when he heard a sound and looked down its length. There was a suited figure about halfway, drifting towards him feet first.

He hauled himself back, tumbling a quick circle in midair and kicked off. He sailed straight down the centre of the corridor, managing to turn about his own centre and reach to swing himself in where Lobo waited.

'He's probably checking the level below,' Randall said. 'Both the helmets and your gloves are still floating around down there, so they should mislead him for a while. We've got to hide.'

There were a couple of lockers in the room, tethered at each corner to the bulkhead wall. They were man-sized and filled with coveralls, bunched and creased without any particular concern for the fabric. Randall and Lobo unloaded one of the lockers and stuffed most of its contents into the other, quickly getting the hang of the fact that there could be no effort without leverage in no-weight. They got inside the locker and pulled the door shut, but they had to open it again after less than a minute. Not only did the locker seem to be airtight, they also needed the orientation that the narrow slit of light provided.

When the man from the ice came he pushed the cabin door open and then moved on. They could hear him kicking along, the bang of the next cabin door, move on again. They listened as the noise receded, and then listened for a while longer to the even hiss of circulating air before they let the locker door swing back.

Randall looked out into the corridor. It was empty.

Even assuming he was alone—and this was by no means certain—Randall and Lobo would be poorly matched against somebody experienced in no-weight conditions. They couldn't be sure he'd be hostile, but all the signs were bad; they'd stumbled on a big, incomprehensible operation, a massive enterprise which seemed to dwarf its purpose in deep-freezing prisoners and carrying them off in secret. Somebody had gone to the trouble of patching up this wreck and uncovering part of the old Ice Palace dockyards. In itself this was sufficient to convince Randall that technology from outside the city was involved, for his home didn't even have the expertise to rebuild the Elite's helicopters. They were barely maintained, and every year saw one or more dropping out of service.

So these were offworlders, obviously men from one of the other settled systems and one of them was at this moment searching the ship. Sooner or later he'd go over it all again, and this time he wouldn't be giving each room a quick check—he'd find them.

'But there's only one of him,' Randall said. 'We'll have to force him to land us somewhere near to the city.'

'What if he's armed?' Lobo objected.

'What if he is? We've still got exactly the same range of choices. We go along with him or we make him take us back.'

'Sounds really easy,' agreed Lobo. 'You go ahead and I'll be here if I'm needed.'

They searched the cabins for anything that might be used as a weapon. Lobo found a toolkit and produced a bolt spanner the size of his forearm. Although it had no weight it still had mass, and would deliver a devastating blow if swung from an anchored point. They practised a manoeuvre in which they hid just inside one of the cabins and imagined their pursuer being almost level with the door, at which Randall would propel himself out, spanner aloft and Lobo would catch his legs at the last moment, his own grip on the doorframe bringing them both round in an arc which covered the full width of the corridor. The entire action was so slow that Randall would have time to level his makeshift club. He tried not to dwell on the uncomfortable fact that his victim would have an equal opportunity to defend himself.

The time was upon them before they expected it. Only minutes later there came a clumsy bumping from the access tunnel and Randall and Lobo had to scramble into the nearest cabin with more haste than they might have liked. The man would only have one cabin to check before he was upon them.

They could hear that he wasn't taking as much care this time; although he was checking more thoroughly he was rushing, missing the grips on the walls and overshooting. When his shadow fell across the open doorway Randall took a firm hold on his spanner and launched himself out of the doorway.

Lobo missed his legs completely.

Randall didn't make his arc as planned, but found himself moving in the wrong direction, away from the man they were supposed to be attacking. He saw the green blur of the man's suit and heard Lobo call out, 'The spanner! Give me the spanner!' Randall tried to throw the weapon, succeeded in putting himself into a spin and sending it to fall end over end well beyond Lobo's reach.

Lobo's physical theory might have been shaky, but his practical observation was impeccable. Realizing he couldn't hit the man with the spanner, he grabbed the nearest ankle and hit the spanner with the man.

There was a sound like meat being dropped on to a slab. *Shit*, Randall thought, *we've killed him.* Lobo was yelling, diving out and trying to get some kind of captive hold on an arm or a leg. Randall hit a wall and scraped over several projections before he was able to stop himself and turn around, and as he did so Lobo's yell stopped as well.

Lobo was hanging one-handed from a recessed grip, his mouth open and his eyes blinking in disbelief. The other figure was motionless in space before him, the bolt-spanner laid across its middle. Whatever it was, it wasn't a man.

Randall had seen robots before; there had always been a few of them around Central's dome, but these were inelegant, utilitarian devices, no more than hooks and claws on mobile platforms. He'd never before seen a robot pushed roughly and unsuccessfully into human form.

The eyes were good—they could almost convince and the body was a competent human shape inside the padded suit. It was the skin which gave it away, an unlined hard-looking grey with a plastic shine that betrayed its artificiality. But the eyes—the eyes were uncanny.

It made no attempt to resist them, in spite of the fact that it seemed unhurt by the blow with the bolt-spanner. It showed all the human signs of confusion, but Randall knew better than to be misled; anthropomorphism towards machines was a dangerous trap that Central had taught him to avoid. They marshalled it into the nearest cabin and Lobo held the spanner in readiness should it be needed again.

Randall guessed that the appearance of dismay resulted from a temporary withdrawal of some of the robot's facilities of external control, freeing the channels to help cope with a sudden inrush of new data; although how this differed from ordinary human confusion Randall wouldn't have liked to argue.

It didn't seem to bother Lobo. He anchored himself with one hand so that he could wave the spanner in the air, demanding to know how they could get the ship back to the city, where was it from, why were they kidnapping Willis...

'Don't shout at me!' the Grey Man suddenly blurted. 'I can't understand you if you shout!'

Lobo was taken aback. The robot seemed to hover on the borderline between man and machine and now he wasn't sure how to deal with it. Instead he turned to Randall.

'Damn it, Randall,' he said, 'make him tell us how to get this ship back to the city.'

'I can't,' the robot interrupted, 'I've got no control over it. I just ride with it to and from the pickup point.'

Randall asked, 'From the pickup point to where?'

'To the main ship for delivery. I collect the men off the ice and crate them, and then I take them out to the main ship.'

'He's lying,' Lobo cut in. 'What do offworlders want with deep-frozen scum like Willis?'

'They want models,' the robot explained. 'They collect basic types of men and copy them. I was the first one they made.'

'And when are they going to come back and finish you?'

The sudden hurt that showed up in the robot's eyes surprised even Randall. 'Well, look at him,' Lobo went on, feeling that he now had to justify the remark. 'He's not a man, he's a parody. He didn't even fight when he had the chance.'

It was obvious to Randall that the machine lacked sufficient guile either to resist or deceive them, so he felt it would be safe to let it lead them to whatever served as the ship's control room. The robot complied without argument, leading them down the corridor and through a set of double sliding doors on to the bridge.

It was as if a complete crew had stood up and left only moments before. The bridge was small and cramped, and seemed to be mostly chairs and lights, all carefully interlocked to make the most of the available area—a distinct contrast to the wasteful corridor space outside. Encircling the forward half of the bridge was a broad observation window, blank and shuttered by external plates.

Randall told the robot to strap himself into one of the chairs, and then he inspected the control panels as Lobo kept watch. While there was no doubt that the bridge was live, it was obvious that the actual controls were being over-ridden from elsewhere. There were rough squares that had been cut and re-patched, bunches of wiring that linked one panel to another, even empty mountings where complete instruments had been torn away and not replaced. The minimal floor area was tiled with a cable space beneath and when Randall lifted one of the squares he saw immediately that there was a foreign line in with the others. It was silver and shiny, a slug of a wire draped thick and fat over the original cabling and leading out towards the far side of the control room. Randall followed it through double doors which corresponded with those they had entered by. In the corridor beyond there was a plain silver box about the size of a small table. It was featureless, and it hummed slightly.

'No chance,' Randall reported when back on the bridge. 'If we try to interfere, the only thing we can guarantee is that we'll get ourselves killed. If we're riding to the end of the line we'll want to know what we'll find when we get there.' He turned to the robot. 'We know that the offworlders are copying the men they steal from the Ice Palace during the storms. Why?'

'They've got no natural resources of their own and their own world's too small for them to process raw materials from the asteroid belts,' the robot explained. Lobo was watching it, almost unable to believe the near-humanity of its precise movements as it motored evenly from one stance or expression to the next. 'They can only survive and expand by tapping the production of industrialized worlds too weak to offer any defence.'

That described the city perfectly. 'But why the copies?' Randall asked.

'They never leave the ship themselves. They always take the native form and improve on it to make an invasion force.'

There was something horribly wrong. The set of basic assumptions that Randall had been carrying around simply didn't fit this new information. He put his next question carefully; 'What do you mean, the native form? Aren't the offworlders human?'

'No.'

There was no sound from Lobo, floating with his spanner in the dark area outside the glow of the control panels. Randall took a grip on his disbelief and asked the robot to explain.

'They've been doing this for thousands of years, system after system. They hibernate between stars while the inboard computer scans the systems they pass for civilized activity. If there's nothing they do a quick loop round the sun to top up on power. When they find what they're looking for the ship moves into a stellar orbit and wakes them up.'

'Thousands of years?' came Lobo's voice from behind, choking with disbelief. 'On a ship?'

The robot looked past Randall, seeming to have no difficulty fixing on Lobo in the poor light. 'Not the same one. That's why they need to strip the worlds of other races. They're building another one, bigger and they tow it along with them. When it's finished they'll migrate into it and start breaking down the old one for a new, even bigger ship. It's the only way they can expand.'

'Birdseed,' Lobo snorted contemptuously.

'They sensed your city and they want it. They found this old shuttle in an abandoned orbit and sent me down in it to establish contact.'

'Stop there,' Randall said, wishing that his credulity could keep up with all this new information. 'Where did they get you?'

The robot hesitated, looked at its hands. It was difficult to believe that this wasn't a human reaction but a carefully orchestrated set of effects. 'They told me I was a man,' it said, the shiny grey of the skin and knuckles before its eyes an obvious contradiction of the claim. 'I knew they were lying, but I wouldn't face it. Because they didn't have a model to start with, they scanned the city's records for a composite simulacrum. I suppose that's me.'

Some connection closed in the back of Randall's mind, an unasked question and an unsought answer. It eluded him for the moment, but he left it to surface in its own time. The robot was looking at him now, waiting for another question. 'How did you set up this kidnap network?'

'I didn't. I contacted a councillor with their proposals, and he set it all up. I work to the instructions he gives me.'

'Which councillor?'

'Marius. They've promised him a lot for his cooperation. It's hardly started yet.'

'What's holding them back?'

'They call us marionettes, simulacra—models like me. They're trying to make one that's near-perfect and completely loyal.'

'Loyal like you?' Lobo said ironically as he pulled himself closer alongside Randall.

'I don't even understand the word,' the robot said bitterly and lifted its hand to indicate itself. 'Look at me, I'm trash.'

'Don't take it to heart,' Lobo said gently. 'There's worse than you walking round the city.' He saw the surprised look that Randall was giving him, and added, 'Hell, Randall, he's worse off than us. That must be worth something. But do we believe him?'

Randall gave the robot a sideways glance. 'Look at him. He's rough and unfinished and he's definitely mechanical.'

The robot tried to break in with some account of how he wasn't mechanical but a DNA pseudo-pattern fast-grown on to a machined skeleton, but Randall said, 'Don't interrupt.' He turned back to Lobo, the robot excluded from their speculations. 'There's no technology in the city which would be able to produce anything like that.'

'But what about the other settled worlds?' Lobo argued, still unable to accept the basic premise of the robot's story. 'One of the other systems on the trade network.'

'It's possible. The alien story could be a cover.'

'Cover or not, how do we get back?'

'If the robot's right, we don't.'

'I know you told me not to interrupt,' said the robot, breaking in with unexpected firmness, 'but I'm not a robot. Please don't call me one.'

'What do we call you, then?' Lobo asked. 'A simul... whatever you said?'

'I've got a name. It's not much, but it's mine.'

'I can tell you what it is,' Randall added quietly. 'His name's Rorvik. Am I right?'

It watched him for a moment, and then nodded.

Lobo didn't believe it. Rorvik was dead, had been for some time, and would undoubtedly have been cremated by now.

Randall told him he'd missed the point. 'You heard it say how it was made. When Central was in operation they scanned the computer banks to get a composite impression of a native so that they could make a prototype. Now, which individual occupied a major share of the computer's attention during the last year?'

'How would I know?'

'Rorvik, that's who. This thing's a rough model of him. No wonder I thought I recognized it in the blizzard.'

It didn't look like Rorvik, it didn't sound like Rorvik. But there was some indefinable shadow carried over that had reached Randall and become recognizable even through a snowstorm. 'I had to guide you away,' it explained. 'You were almost falling over the storage sheds.'

'Don't you see?' Randall asked Lobo. 'They threw this monster together and used it to contact Marius. He tracked down the information on the Ice Palace and set up the kidnap network to provide for the building of more elaborate types of robot.'

'Marionette,' Lobo corrected him.

'What?'

'He doesn't want to be called a robot. Hell, Randall, I think he's got some feelings.'

Randall tried to explain that machines couldn't feel and that if they seemed to, it was a calculated effect, built into the design like the paternal attitude that the Central computer used to assume for the benefit of the citizens. Lobo listened, but it was plain that he didn't wholeheartedly embrace the idea. He was by no means stupid, but as a survivor who had learned to meet every occasion as a separate challenge, he found little practical worth in such distinctions. Differences between things that were and things that merely appeared to be had no meaning for him; they both had equal weight and influence in the texture of his world and he considered such philosophies as the superficialities of an idle mind.

Lobo thought it of far greater importance to establish exactly of what use this thing calling itself Rorvik might be to them. And if that meant treating it as a human being, that was fine as long as it responded like one. On this basis he could proceed without concern, whereas Randall was preoccupied by a tiresome web of conditions and justifications which eventually led him to the identical conclusion.

'You said they're trying to get a design for a loyal... simulacrum,' Lobo said, addressing the strange composite being direct. 'What kind of loyalty do you feel towards them?'

It thought for a moment. 'I don't even understand what you mean. I did what I was told.'

They asked about the improved designs. The Rorvik marionette—not really Rorvik, more a composite citizen personality with some of Rorvik's more recognizable qualities at the forefront—explained that there were many designs, some even less complex than itself, creatures with no minds at all that had to be told in detail what to do and then told when to stop. And then there were others, almost indistinguishable from real men and women. Randall wondered who the female pattern came from, but Rorvik didn't know. He suspected that the development of the final model was very close—that is, if it hadn't already been reached.

Randall found it frustrating. The magnitude of the threat was beginning to make itself felt in his mind, reaching in and touching all the inbred and ingrained protective responses that Central had instilled in him. It was as if, given the right set of circumstances, a second personality was coming up out of reserve, moving in and taking over, pure Elite. He stepped back and let it in, knowing better than to resist.

The course of the shuttle could be changed, but Rorvik didn't know how. It would take them straight to what he called the World Ship and dock automatically on a homing laser; there didn't seem to be any way that they might divert and return to the city.

'We've got to find a way,' Lobo insisted. 'We can't take on an artificial planet full of offworlders.'

'We might,' Randall told him. 'This Rorvik thing must know something about them. If we keep pumping for. information we may find a weakness.'

'And for what?'

'For the opportunity to strike. For the State.'

Lobo wasn't very impressed. 'You're mad, Randall. They must have fried your brains at birth.'

'I'm not mad, I'm Elite. This is what I'm for.'

'Is that how it works? Somebody threatens your holy State and you automatically leap on to a box and start beating a drum? So what happened to the rebel who killed the computer?'

'That wasn't rebellion,' Randall replied, irritated that Lobo couldn't see the distinction. 'That was the right thing to do.'

'And now the right thing to do is to turn ass-backwards and get back to the city. Or doesn't the State deserve a warning?'

'The argument's academic. We don't have the choice.' Lobo raised his hands in frustration and then hastily corrected the slow drift that the action induced. 'How do we know until we try?'

'Because the robot says it doesn't know where to start!' It winced, but said nothing. 'What's happened to you, Lobo? What about the eighteen-carat fairy castle you were supposed to be chasing?'

'I'm not going to find it by being target practice in a vacuum.

What happened to you, Randall? Not so long ago we were your kind. You were going to get back to the council and make them dance for us.'

'The same damn council that's selling the city!'

'They're selling it, you're going to charge in with your head down and throw it away. Where's the difference in that?'

'It depends how successful we are.'

'Like, not at all.'

Randall tried to change his approach. You couldn't win by yelling at Lobo, because he could yell louder. 'That doesn't excuse us from trying. We've got two things in our favour; they're not expecting us and we've got access to information in the robot. Perhaps we can even use it to tap information out of their systems.'

'And what's the use in that? They could be twice our size. We may not be able to breathe their air. Even if we can, we won't know where we're going or what we're doing.'

Sound logic and Randall accepted it with triumph. 'That's where the robot comes in,' he said, as if he and Lobo had been working towards the same conclusion all along.

The marionette had waited patiently throughout the argument, but now he spoke. 'I'll help you,' he said, 'but there's a condition.' They both looked at him in puzzled expectation and he went on, 'You stop referring to me as the robot. I've got a name.'

'It isn't even yours,' Randall pointed out.

'I don't care. I want you to use it.'

'All right, *Rorvik*,' Randall said with exaggerated emphasis, smiling at the presumption of a machine fooled by its own illusion of self-awareness, 'as long as it gets your cooperation. But don't get any ideas about having an equal say.'

'Rorvik' didn't smile back. He probably couldn't. 'I'm glad I'm not really a man, Randall,' he said. 'When I look at you I lose all my envy.'

For a moment Randall was lost for a reply and Lobo cut in with, 'Don't get him wrong, Rorvik. He's not bad, he's just Elite. They've all got this peculiar streak when it comes to the State and the city.'

'What is this?' Randall demanded, more than a little unsettled by the way in which Lobo and Rorvik seemed to be understanding each other so well and, more important, excluding him. 'Don't you see that this is the entire basis of the offworlder approach? Accept him as a human being and he's inside your guard.'

'He?' Lobo said, an enquiring eyebrow raised. 'What happened to it?'

Randall hadn't even realized what he'd said. 'You see how easy it is. With a name the battle's half won.'

So Rorvik got his name, although Randall insisted that he earned it. He wanted to know how long the journey was going to be and how and where it would end. He wanted to know the layout of the World Ship, the principles behind its design,, its weaknesses. And as 'Rorvik' talked he evolved grandiose plans of impossible heroism and dropped them as quickly, moving on undaunted to construct the next fragile web of circumstance wherein he routed the enemy and championed the city. He drew on the fire of buried resentment that he had carried since his eyes had opened in the Ice Palace recovery room, but now, instead of having to suppress it as impotent fury, it became his prime source of energy. Difficulties seemed to shrink and become insignificant in the face of a confidence that was irresistible.

Randall was, in his way, happy. He was doing what he'd been born for. He was Elite.

Lobo wished he was back on the ice.

FOURTEEN

No sooner had Peters completed his first run on the icebreaker than they were reloaded and turned around to head back to the cap. He'd understood that the trips would be far less frequent than this, but when he tried to raise the subject with his captain all it got him was a knowing wink and an assurance that he would be 'seen all right', whatever that meant.

They were at sea, the city's landmass falling below the horizon, before he found that, in addition to managing his conscience over his involvement with the Ice Palace, he would have to attend the needs of illicit passengers in direct contravention of navy regulations. All the same, the captain argued, when it was too late for him to object, if two of the passengers are councillors and all three of them are paying heavily for silence then the benefits surely outweigh the dangers.

There would be little sleep for Peters on this run. He had to keep the Elite officer away from the councillors, because he didn't know about them and they didn't want him to. So the councillors were given the more luxurious accommodation, which was a musty old bunkroom with a few pieces of carpet and a fish oil burner for extra heat, while the Elite had to make do with a screened-off corner of one of the holds. Peters took food to both parties, apologizing in each case for the poor quality of the ship's dispensers and their annoying tendency to mix the most incompatible ingredients to make the most unpalatable dishes.

He told Killoran that on no account must he leave the hold, saying that they had a suspected stabilizer leak and that as the thick oil escaped it was boiling off with the release of pressure to drift around the ship as a poisonous vapour. It was the purest fantasy, inspired in Peters' mind by the trouble that they were still having with the pressure on some of the tanks, but Killoran accepted it and stayed where he was, dragging the cargo over to insulate his corner as they pushed northward and the temperature dropped.

Morden found the journey tedious in the extreme. His finely-tuned sense of space, developed as a compensation for his blindness, was disrupted by the steady heave of the ship's passage, and his remaining senses fared badly with the stink of burning fish-oil and the ever-present thump of the engines.

Marius, however, spread himself out on one of the upper bunks and chortled, joked, planned, daydreamed. The only times that his good humour seemed to fail him were when Peters brought their meals; these defied both description and digestion. Morden sat, miserable and huddled in the oversized cloak he'd been given to wear, and quietly wished that Marius would go and immerse his entire head in water for ten minutes or so.

When they hit their first ice, Marius switched subjects, moving from the prospective benefits of the other settled systems to his childhood occupational fantasies. They were invariably powerful, frequently destructive. He'd dreamed of being a slingshot pilot, towing the cargo trains into a tight orbit around the sun and using the momentum to release them towards a target system; but if he'd known there had been such 'breakers as this, smashing through the ice like so many eggshells—why, he'd have wanted to do that, as well.

'Such a shame,' Morden observed sympathetically. 'Perhaps if you go on to the bridge, the captain will let you hold the wheel.'

Marius thought about it for a moment, and then said suspiciously, 'You taking a rise out of me?'

'Would it ever enter my head?'

It was unfortunate that Marius was not quite stupid enough to be unaware that he was being mocked, or Morden could have extracted far more entertainment from the journey. As it was, he had plenty of time to brood over the flight that lay ahead, and over the cruel trick that he had helped to play on the young

Elite officer who at that moment lay in the hold somewhere below them.

'What a joke,' was Marius's remark on the subject. 'Before we get taken to the landing point he gets dumped at the Ice Palace. He thinks he's storming in to stage a wonderful rescue act and really he's only doing our work for us. One more prisoner and a blaster full of blanks. I wish I could see his face when he tries to fire it.'

'The other inmates will probably tear him apart,' Morden observed.

'I'd love to see that, as well.'

Morden couldn't share Marius's enthusiasm for their betrayal, and after a while it began to show. 'What's the matter with you, Morden?' Marius complained. 'I thought you were strong. Damn it, we're carving this planet up between us and here you are getting saintly on me.'

'My apologies, Marius. I have a sentimental streak which I must fight to suppress.'

'I understand. It's the same with me. I fight back the tears every time I think of the profit we'll make.'

Marius didn't seem any more inclined than this to make comment on Morden's apparent lack of commitment to the venture. He was already in too deep to withdraw, being thoroughly compromised by this journey and his recent voting in the council; and if he were to drag his feet at some later date, no doubt by that time his help would no longer be needed. Perhaps Marius already had some plan of quiet disposal lined up for him.

Every now and again Marius would turn, his bunk would creak, and a couple of the inevitable sheets of paper that he seemed always to carry around would slide down onto the floor. Then Marius would have to clamber down after them, and there would be a couple of minutes' silence as he puzzled over his notes, wondering where the stray leaves had come from.

He was trying to work out how long it would take before the industrial appetites of his parasitic employers would be satisfied. Every time he tried he arrived at a different figure, differences of several years; and while he cooed with pleasure at the short forecasts, he groaned in depression at the longer ones. Morden asked if he was making any allowances for possible sabotage.

'There won't be any,' Marius told him flatly. 'That's all taken care of.'

'But what if these artificial men and women aren't the invincible force you're expecting them to be?'

'Wait until you've seen what one of them can do. They make the Elite look like puzzled monkeys, and these are only the ones they've developed so far. The model they've got under test could probably take the city on his own!'

In the number four hold, deprived of any company apart from Peters' occasional visits, Killoran sat cross-legged on the floor, the component parts of the hand weapon spread out in front of him. Slowly, mechanically, he polished each piece on a square of cloth, working on them in strict order and reassembling as he went along, the block of solid state circuitry laid aside for final connection. Next to it was a box of charges, unopened.

He'd had no problem with the requisition of the weapon. One call, and it had been waiting in Stores when he arrived to collect. He'd said that he wanted it for some practice in his own time, and the armourer hadn't even seemed surprised. Perhaps he'd concealed it—Killoran still couldn't get used to the idea of outranking anybody older than himself.

Peters had given him some idea of what to expect when he arrived, although Killoran got the impression that he didn't much like to talk about the Ice Palace. They would draw up alongside a hatch, on the other side of which would be a sloping ramp and some kind of warehouse below ground level; Peters hadn't been able to see further. There would be men- not too many—waiting to receive the cargo and they would be wearing strange helmeted suits against the cold. Killoran would need his blaster from the time the hatch rose, either to threaten or to fight.

The last piece snapped into place. The weapon was complete.

Patiently, deliberately, he began to take it apart and lay the components out.

FIFTEEN

As THE CARGO shuttle moved onward to meet its orbiting partner Randall and Lobo devised a way of feeding themselves which would be effective if unpleasant. There were a number of surplus glucose bottles in the ship's hold with which Rorvik was supposed to keep the sleeping prisoners fed, and it seemed a relatively simple matter to slide a needle into a vein and take nourishment the same way with no risk to the delicacy of the stomach; simple, that is, until they came to try it. Randall stabbed at his arm a couple of times, making sizable holes but otherwise achieving nothing. Lobo watched the process and grew pale. After a minute or so he said 'Forget it,' and, removing the needle, drank direct from his own bottle. Randall finally gave up and did the same, finding that the glucose bubbled out easily under gas pressure. A membrane in the tube took the gas out before the bubbles reached the bloodstream.

They had left 'Rorvik' alone on the bridge. Randall could see no reason not to trust him—'too stupid for deceit', as he put it. When they returned Rorvik was still there, strapped into the seat where they had left him. He told them that the World Ship lay ahead and that docking was imminent.

The trip had taken a couple of days, but when the World Ship was at perigee this would reduce to only a few hours. Randall didn't understand the mechanics of it and Lobo didn't want to. All he said was that it would have been interesting to see the World Ship as they approached and Rorvik told him that it would have been possible but they were now on the homing laser and matching the World Ship's rotation. Randall challenged his earlier statement, that he had no control over the shuttle's operation and Rorvik replied that control was possible, but he didn't know how. There were certain points on the consoles where he could link in and be in contact with the shuttle's guidance and memory channels, but he wasn't sufficiently skilled to be able to do much more than open the outer shutters or dim the lights.

Within half an hour the doors would open from the hold onto a strange and dangerous new world. Randall's adrenalin high had subsided, leaving an afterwash of confidence that he was determined not to let diminish with thoughts of failure. Lobo had other ideas.

'Now,' Randall said, 'are we clear on what happens when that loading-bay door opens?'

'Sure,' said Lobo. 'We jump out and run like hell.'

'Didn't you pay any attention to the plan?'

'The plan? Oh, sure, it's a great plan. Who wants to get killed in a scramble when you can do it nice and orderly?'

'Don't you remember any of it?' Randall asked weakly. Lobo sucked in his cheeks and stared at the ceiling, a gross parody of intensive reminiscence. 'We hide and Rorvik unloads Willis and the others as normal. Then we sneak out and run up the nearest corridor. It's a hell of a plan.'

'All right,' Randall admitted tetchily, 'so it's not much. . .'

'Not much!' Lobo exploded. 'It's nothing! You're mad, Randall!'

'Mad or not, I got you out of the Ice Palace!'

'And look what you got me into! In my own way I was happy until you came along!'

'Go back, then. Nobody's stopping you.'

Lobo leaned forward as much as he was able, pulling against the lap strap that he'd looped across to keep him in place. 'This may come as a surprise to you, Randall,' he said, 'but you're not the only one who doesn't want the city wiped out. I'll work to prevent it and even, if I think it's justified, put my life on the line for it. But that doesn't mean I'm prepared to get all holy and charge out yelling, only to get spread over the nearest wall. And I'll tell you something else. I'm prepared to do it because it's what I want to do. Not because I was picked out of the hospital at birth and trained and taught and made to jump through hoops for twenty years. I make my own decisions.'

Randall could have corrected Lobo on the details, but his assessment of the spirit of Elite training was uncomfortably near the mark. 'Rorvik's told us that he's never been far beyond the docking area and he's never actually seen one of the creatures.'

Rorvik nodded. 'That's right. Place always looks deserted.'

Randall ignored the interruption and went on, 'Without information all we can do is move fast and think on our feet. Are you saying your reactions are better than mine?' Lobo didn't answer. Nobody was faster than an Elite. 'There you are, then,' Randall continued. 'I'm prepared to put *my* life on the line and be first out. We should agree to let me decide where to go and how to get there, because we won't have the time to confer. Now, what's wrong with that?'

'It's wonderful.' Lobo said bitterly. 'We all die as heroes.'

'What's your alternative?'

'At this stage, nothing. But it doesn't mean I'm signing myself over on a permanent basis. If there's anything I want to say at a later stage, I'll say it whether it screws up your plans or not.'

Randall couldn't argue with that; or, to put it another way, he wanted to but there was no time. Instead they all made their way down to the hold in preparation for disembarking. In the corridor they could sense rather than hear distant shudders as the shuttle manoeuvred. They were in the access tunnel when weight returned.

Rorvik was used to it and had a hand on the ladder as he made his way along so that when the tunnel became a vertical shaft again all he needed to do was swing into the wall. Lobo was below him, still nervous in no-weight and so already holding the ladder for psychological support. It was Randall, nearest the hold and fortunately only a few feet from the bottom, who was caught unprepared and who made an undignified landing on the deck.

Nobody commented. Nobody dared.

There would be no guards around the shuttle dock, for the Wekk—the short, brutal name that Rorvik gave the owners of the World Ship—knew that the city had no contemporary space capability. However, it was likely that some of the simulacra or marionettes would be around the area, for once captives had been used for patterning they were often let loose and hunted down for practice. Rorvik warned them to watch out for Valum.

'Valum?' said Randall. 'Who's he?'

'Valum's not a he. She's one of the more advanced models and she's good. I've heard say she's the best they've got, until they get the final model out of its tests.'

Something was worrying Lobo. 'You say they let men loose and hunt them,' he said. 'Where?'

'In the corridors where you're going.'

Lobo shook his head sadly. 'I knew it. Head-first into the killing-bottle.'

'Think positive,' Randall urged him. 'We're men. Men against gadgets.'

'Thanks, Randall,' Rorvik remarked drily.

Randall and Lobo hid to one side of the door. If anybody came into the hold they would be in plain sight, but Rorvik assured them it wouldn't happen. The deck lurched a couple of times beneath their feet and then there was a sensation of rising. A few seconds after it stopped the seals on the door blew and it dropped outward in a controlled fall, dust swirling along the length of the hold and boiling out as air bled into the lower pressure outside. Lobo felt a pain in his head, but he knew better than to mention it now.

There was a narrow angle of view available to Randall from his position by the door. He could see that the dock was about twice the width of the shuttle at least, but there was no indication of its depth. It was brightly lit with a noticeable blue cast. What did this suggest? Eyes not very sensitive to the red end of the spectrum? That would, perhaps, go some way towards explaining Rorvik's peculiar skin colour.

Randall tensed to move, but held back at a glance from Rorvik. That hard unnatural face was incapable of normal expression, but there was some subtle hint of warning in the eyes. Rorvik walked forward, leaving them alone and exposed as he went down the ramp and away from the shuttle.

They waited for a few moments, but there was no sound from outside. Randall decided to risk a look. He inched forward cautiously, ready to pull back at the first indication that he might be seen. Lobo was holding his breath, expecting yells of alarm at any second.

A wider view of the dock showed it to be on two levels, a deep well in which the shuttle was sitting linked by a ramp to a gallery which ran along and around about eight feet above the floor. It was this gallery level that had the door linking to the rest of the ship, and Rorvik was climbing the ramp towards it.

The door was obviously the inner opening of an airlock and it was ajar. Randall couldn't be sure that he was really seeing the woman who stood next to it. Although he had never seen her before he had always known her; she was an inch or so taller than Rorvik and she had the flowing brown hair and finely-chiselled features of an adolescent's fantasy.

Lobo's hand on his shoulder warned him that he was leaning out too far, placing himself in danger of being spotted. He drew back and then more cautiously, risked another, less exposed surveillance.

Rorvik had collected a trolley from within the airlock. It had no wheels but ran on six oversized bearings which could rotate in any direction. The woman was saying something to him and Randall strained to hear.

'Try not to take your usual eternity over the unloading,' she was telling him in a voice fitted easily to command. 'The shuttle has to do a fast turnaround and return to the Ice Palace to collect the two councillors.'

Rorvik said something, but his back was turned and it was indistinct. It was probably something like, 'Will I have to go?' because she replied, 'I wouldn't know. Do you honestly think it matters?'

'There might be loading to do.' Rorvik must have turned and it came across clearly.

'There isn't. You can stay here and spare the councillors your presence. The shuttle navigates just as well without you. Get your crates on their way to the patterning shops and then clear the area. We're in the middle of a sweep to eliminate the remnants of the last batch you ferried up. The patterning shops rejected them.'

'I'm sorry. I only bring what I can get.'

'It's fortunate they expect nothing from you,' she told him

with ill-disguised contempt. 'I'm surprised you've even got the wits to stand upright.'

She's a machine, Randall had to tell himself, a set of manufactured responses in a pseudo-biological envelope, but this couldn't overcome the fact that she was, at least from a distance, undetectably human and had the looks and cool self-possession which could set young men diving off high buildings just to get her attention. This, he supposed, was Valum, the best and most dangerous marionette yet assembled—Rorvik was an inept monster next to her.

The conversation was over. Rorvik, dismissed, was leading his trolley down the ramp towards the shuttle. Valum glanced once across the bay and then turned to go.

Randall wondered where they'd found the original to pattern her. The Ice Palace was, as far as he'd been able to establish, an all-male community and had always been that way. The delicate ecology of survival had been so finely engineered that the introduction of sexual tension could have tipped it completely, while the essentially rigid social order of dominance and submission would have become complicated to the point of incomprehensibility. Perhaps the Wekk had other sources.

Rorvik came into the shuttle and passed them without a sideways look, as if he'd forgotten they were there. The trolley rumbled past behind him and he went on to the far end of the cargo hold and the prisoners.

Randall had felt momentarily bad about leaving the captives crated and helpless, but, he'd reasoned, he didn't know the revival procedure and could quite easily kill them by his efforts. And besides, one of them was Willis—a doubtful ally. He could argue Lobo down, but with two of them ranged against him all his plans were bound to end in compromise or confusion.

There was no sign of Valum on the gallery. Randall didn't like the sound of the sweep operation that she had said was going on in the World Ship—a wrong move and they could easily find themselves caught up in it. Well, Randall told himself grimly, the idea is not to make any wrong moves.

Lobo followed without any need of encouragement or signal as they ran from the shuttle to the cover of the gallery and then, more cautiously, advanced up the ramp to the upper level. The hangar was immense behind them, a cavern enclosing the entire three-storey shuttle and of which there had only been a small section visible from their hiding-place. There were airlocks all around the gallery, doors like safes spaced at hundred-yard intervals and this encouraged Randall to modify his original idea and make for one of them instead of following Valum through.

The first door wouldn't open when he threw his weight against the outer wheel. No matter, move on to the next. The next door also resisted when he tried to turn.

They were exposed and obvious and each door he tried was taking them further from what now seemed to be the only exit. He tried another, Lobo breathing hard to keep up; it was as solid against his efforts as the last.

'No!' Lobo whispered, and Randall angrily prepared to ignore him. But Lobo had moved into his place at the airlock and was spinning the wheel easily.

He realized his mistake, that he'd assumed that an anti-clockwise rotation would release the locking mechanism, but while the simple geometrical principles of gearing and rotation might be universal the traditions of his own culture governing their use were not. The door swung outward and Lobo stepped back with a smile and a polite gesture of deference.

There was an inner chamber and then another door which unsealed and opened into a recess off a corridor. Decompression of the hangar would slap this outer door shut, as would decompression of the corridor with the inner. The light was the same blue cast as before and there was no sound apart from the rasp of a muffled pump somewhere on the other side of a wall. The corridor sides were square and plain and the ceiling was uncomfortably low, but apart from that and a metallic scent in the air their surroundings seemed decidedly mundane.

When Rorvik had loaded the first crate on to his trolley he turned around to pull it along and out of the hold. Valum was standing in the open shuttle doorway.

'Who are they?' she said evenly.

Rorvik searched in his mind for an explanation, and had nothing to offer except the truth. 'They came aboard at the Ice

Palace,' he admitted. 'I couldn't stop them.'

'I doubt whether you tried. You've got no loyalty and precious little intelligence, Rorvik. All you've got is a name, and that belongs to somebody else. You know what will happen now?'

'You'll hunt them down and kill them.'

'Almost. We'll see if they're worth patterning and then we'll hunt them down and kill them. If you had any more than a handful of brains you'd be a liability, Rorvik.'

'Yes, Valum,' Rorvik said, knowing it would be useless to object.

'Carry on with your unloading.'

'Yes, Valum.'

RORVIK HAD described the World Ship as a cylinder with a series of outer layers enclosing an open space which he'd never visited. The corridors followed 'more or less a gridiron pattern', but then he'd become confused.

Randall could see why. There wasn't a straight line in the place.

The floor lifted gently away before and behind them, curving uphill and out of sight and presumably meeting itself to encircle the cylinder somewhere far overhead. Not the best line to be following if pursued. There were occasional doors in the walls, but they were flush and tight with no sign of a handle or opening mechanism—perhaps they were keyed to an alien biocapacitance.

Empty corridor gave way to empty thoroughfare as they turned at the next junction to follow the length of the cylinder instead of looping around it. It stretched ahead as a long, winding spiral, the floor twisting sideways to absorb the coriolis force of the ship's rotation. It was long, and if Randall and Lobo had been obvious before they were more than conspicuous now.

Randall hesitated, and Lobo stopped behind him and waited to see what he would do. So far he was following his agreement, offering no arguments or objections. As Randall tried to decide, a group of three men—at least, they looked like men—appeared about two intersections down, spreading out military-style to anticipate an attack from any angle.

Perhaps they could brazen it out, give a wave of recognition and move on; after all, nobody knew they were aboard. But the thought died as soon as it occurred, the group of three re-forming and coming towards them at a run.

They couldn't pass as marionettes. They were unkempt and untidy, their suits mere rags in comparison. They turned and ran.

Randall didn't pause at the intersection they'd emerged from, for as he drew level with it he saw that in both directions there were men trotting purposefully towards him. He shouted encouragement to Lobo and dived on past, his voice adding its confused echo to the interweaving hammer blows of running feet on the hollow deck. Behind them the team of three became a team of five as the men at the intersection fell in with the group and matched its pace.

They'd been trapped into what Randall hadn't wanted, flight without purpose. They were running before a methodical sweep—not difficult to organize if you knew the layout of the corridors, but perhaps impossible to avoid if you didn't. They're not men, Randall insisted to himself as he tried to even out his ragged breathing. They're expecting me to act in a certain way, trying to get there before me. If I do something unpredictable I can fox them.

He could be unpredictable and turn and fight, but then he would quite predictably get the crap beaten out of him. He forced the pace a little, deliberately leaving Lobo a few yards behind; Randall didn't want to swerve suddenly and take him by surprise, giving him no chance to follow. Lobo seemed to get the idea and didn't try to catch up—or perhaps he didn't have the energy in reserve.

The marionettes were working to a pattern, one man in each corridor around the outside of the huge cylinder, checking to either side of each intersection and then, when the quarry had been spotted, pursuing it down the length of the ship in the sure knowledge that they were driving it towards other hunters. As the net grew tighter it grew more dense until the cornered prey would be faced by a number impossible to resist.

The net was at its thinnest ahead, where the lone simulacra had yet to converge. At the next junction Randall sheared off to the left and heard Lobo follow, the unexpected turn sending him into a wide arc that almost brought him up against the far wall. There was a long shadow ahead, cast from beyond their inverted horizon as the floor curved upward, and then he descended into view, a lone figure heading to intercept them.

Lobo had some idea of what Randall was intending and he prepared to help; the two of them had taken Rorvik and they could take this one as well.

Randall put his shoulder down and charged. It was over within a few seconds. A perfectly-timed sidestep, a neat, almost casual tap on the back of his head with the heel of the hand and Randall was skidding along on his belly, arms and legs everywhere without a suggestion of control. Lobo pulled up an inch or so short of a straight-fingered swipe that kissed the air in front of the bridge of his nose so fast that he could almost hear the air rushing into the gap it left behind. The blow didn't have to land for him to know they were beaten.

The group caught up with them and two of its members hauled Randall to his feet. He was blinking stupidly, seeing six or seven of everything and still unable to believe what had happened.

'Wasn't much of an exercise,' one of the marionettes commented in tones of apparent disappointment. 'Not worth counting it for the record.'

'It's just as well,' another replied as they turned to make their way back to the main thoroughfare. 'You know we can't damage them until after they've been patterned.' And the whole group nodded gloomily, as if they were being deprived of a rare treat. Lobo felt as if something were crawling across his back inside his snow suit, and he gritted his teeth to prevent a shiver.

As they moved down the World Ship the air of desertion became less obvious. They encountered several other groups or lone figures. When they came to a major intersection, a kind of spiral gallery that led to the levels above, they saw another determinedly running band in obvious pursuit, switching from one level to another. Somebody in Lobo's group asked what was going on.

'Damage,' one of the running men called out happily as he

disappeared through an archway. Lobo's group held a hurried discussion and an incomprehensible selection process of the 'scissors cut paper' variety. Four of them lost and remained to guard Randall and Lobo as the others set off to join in the 'damage'.

Lobo had his suspicions what that 'damage' might entail. They were confirmed only seconds later as they reached the next level and a raw scream was carried back from the direction in which the group had gone. Randall had been moving along in a daze, perhaps faking it while he looked for opportunities. Whatever the reason, the sound brought him out. He and Lobo exchanged a look of wordless apprehension.

Around them the marionettes were smiling, a little regretfully.

SIXTEEN

Bulstrode was in the generator room when the Worm tracked him down. The teams had been working flat out to repair storm damage, and this was his third visit in as many shifts to charge his power pack. He looked up when he heard the Worm calling his name as he hurried along the gantry to the shielded area.

'I'm busy, Worm,' he said.

The Worm was undeterred. 'I know, but this is important!'

'It had better be,' Bulstrode told him, 'or you'll be wearing your head backwards.'

'The icebreaker's arrived...'

'Since when was that news?'

'Let me finish, will you?' The Worm was clearly agitated over something, so Bulstrode let him continue. 'We've been sent the usual supplies, and something else. An Elite officer, hardly more than a kid.'

'Don't let them wake him,' Bulstrode said decisively.

'He isn't drugged or anything. He slid in down the chute and he's armed.'

Bulstrode checked the level on his power pack. He was strongly tempted to remove it with an incomplete charge and finish the job later, but he remembered the harsh disciplines of his existence—the extra minute or so of charge could make a difference between survival on the cap and being dragged back in by his feet. 'Armed with what?' he asked, watching the indicator.

'A blaster and he says he'll use it.' The Worm was excited, almost dancing on the spot. 'He said he wanted Randall and Palmer told him no chance. I thought he'd hit the roof and start shooting off there and then, but he said he wanted to see the man in charge. I explained that we don't have anything like that, so now he wants all the team leaders together.'

The charge on the unit hit a peak and Bulstrode buckled the pack to his belt. 'Randall,' he said. 'There's been nothing but damn trouble since he arrived. What does the kid want?'

The Worm fell in behind him as he strode off down the catwalk. 'He's not saying. Not until all the team leaders are together.'

'This could be tricky,' Bulstrode mused as they cut through into Main Street. 'Is the kid on his own or is the icebreaker waiting for him?'

'No,' the Worm said positively. 'I looked, and it's gone. The kid's really angry and Berg keeps taunting him.'

'Berg's down there?' Of course, he was rostered for unloading duties on the next icebreaker visit. Bulstrode knew how impetuous he was, and that it wouldn't take much provocation for him to rush the Elite, blaster or not. He'd be cut in half. They reached the access tunnel which led to the bays and as Bulstrode hurried through the Worm held back.

'I've got to get round the rest of the team leaders,' he explained. 'There's something strange about all of this.'

'You've got a wonderful capacity for stating the obvious,' Bulstrode called back over his shoulder. 'What else are you going to call a police operation out here?'

'That's what I mean,' the Worm's voice echoed after him. 'I don't think it's an official operation. I think the kid's on his own.'

If he wasn't in a-box, then surely he couldn't be on his own. It would be best to find out what he wanted.

The sliding door which separated the cargo and loading bays had jammed halfway open on its rail after Lobo had used the area beyond as an impromptu rescue chamber, but it still left a wide gap through which could be heard an indication of the scene beyond. Palmer was saying, 'Why don't you put the gun down and we can all talk about this sensibly?'

'Move any closer,' a strange voice replied, 'and I'll make it so you can clean your teeth from the back.'

Killoran saw Bulstrode enter, saw the way that the others stepped aside to let him through. But then the bearded mountain with the evil, half-witted smile was saying, 'Don't start getting superior, kid. You can't hide behind that blaster forever. I wiped the floor with one of your kind and I'll do it again.'

He had a tight grip on his blaster. The radius of its threatening aura was precisely defined by the semicircle of men before him, daring to come so close and no further. The wall and the ramp were behind him.

'Which of you are the team leaders?' he demanded, and four of them raised a hand, Bulstrode included. 'You're the nearest thing this place has to a governing council?'

Bulstrode spoke for them all. 'We've got no government of any kind. We're the team leaders, and that's all.'

Killoran was suspicious. Perhaps they were giving him the runaround, waiting for an opportunity to get to him. 'So who makes the decisions that affect you all?'

'There's only one kind of decision that affects us all here. You work or you die. It's a conclusion we manage to arrive at pretty well without any help.'

'That's not good enough,' Killoran insisted, becoming even less sure of himself. 'I have to speak to somebody in authority.'

'Talk to the wind and the snow,' Cohn told him. 'They're the only authority around here.'

'You got something to say,' Bulstrode added, 'tell us all.'

'He's got nothing to say,' Berg rumbled, his eyes on the blaster. 'He only came to spring his pal.'

Bulstrode half-raised his hand in warning to Berg, but Killoran said, 'As far as it goes, he's right. I came for Randall.'

'But Randall's dead,' Cohn pointed out.

'I know that, now.'

Berg took the opportunity to push a little harder. 'What are you going to do now you can't have your spy back?'

'Try to get this through all the bone and into your brain,' Killoran snapped. 'Randall wasn't a spy.'

Cohn said reasonably. 'Give us another reason why Central should send one of the Elite here.'

'There is no Central and the Elite are a paid army for a bunch of underbelly thieves. There's no Central because Randall closed it down. As an act of gratitude the council had him sent here.'

'Great story,' Bulstrode commented drily. 'You learned it well.'

'Nearly as good as when Randall told it,' said Palmer.

'That's because it's true. Why else would either of us come here?'

'Don't ask us,' said Berg, eyes alight with dangerous mischief. 'Ask the spy.'

Killoran's audience was growing. Men were coming into the bay and adding their silent numbers to the back of the crowd. He was armed, but he was also confused and nervous; the icebreaker had pulled away when it should have stayed for him and Randall wasn't here. The whole affair was rapidly becoming a desperate mess and he could see no immediate way out of it. The men of the Ice Palace respected the killing power of his blaster, but he couldn't stand there holding them off forever—he needed time to think, to devise and he hadn't got it. Berg was trying to inch closer at every opportunity.

'Look,' Killoran said, 'name me one reason why Central should send a spy here. The Ice Palace is where it sent forgotten men, where they ceased to exist.'

Bulstrode shrugged. 'It's not for us to say.'

'Because there isn't a reason, that's why. I bribed my way out here from a city that's open to council exploitation and sliding backwards fast. I came because I was Randall's assistant and he was the one point of self-assurance and constancy in the whole unstable situation. I've been sold out by the crew on the icebreaker and dumped here without a passage back and then I'm told that the one I came for walked out and died without saying why. What kind of a spy does that make me?'

'A pretty dumb one,' Berg said happily.

Killoran brought the blaster around to cover him. He'd moved in almost to arm's length—or was the whole semicircle crushing in so much closer, pressed from behind? Berg grinned and shuffled back a token half-step.

Bulstrode said from the other side of the circle, 'It doesn't matter a damn to us why you came here. What are you going to do now?'

'I don't know.' Killoran tried to keep some awareness of Berg in the corner of his eye. 'I have to have time to think. But I'm going to need your help.'

'What makes you think you'll get it?'

'I'll force you if I have to. But when I say help, I mean it.'

Bulstrode shook his head. 'It doesn't sound too convincing when you say it over a gun.'

There could have been a sound, or it might have been some impression of movement on the periphery of his vision. Killoran swung the blaster around to cover Berg and squeezed the impulse trigger in a manoeuvre much-practised on the Elite's ranges. A slug of hot power was delivered to the charge and the weapon pulsed and roared. Berg was brought up short, his move slapped back by a solid wall of noise and an impact in his chest.

He tottered, regained his balance, rubbed his hands vaguely over the front of his snow suit. They came away black and sooty with the exhaust of a harmless charge.

Killoran looked down at the useless weapon in his hand. 'Oh, fuck,' he said bleakly.

The shock on Berg's face gave way to delight as he realized that the only barrier that had prevented him from jumping up and down on Killoran was now proven to be ineffective. Bulstrode called to him to wait, but he might as well have dropped a stone down a well and then demanded that it should come back.

Berg's arms swept in for a bear hug, closing on empty air as Killoran ducked and spun away, slinging the blaster aside to free his hands. Berg tried to turn the move into a swinging punch, but Killoran was now balanced and his hand came up, seeming only to brush back-to-back with Berg's but guiding it aside and leaving his guard fully open.

A snap-punch, doubling the fist back to the shoulder and out and Berg described a neat little somersault and landed flat out on the deck. Killoran stepped away quickly and the respectful semi-circle re-shaped itself to make room for him.

'I didn't want that,' he told them, his hands held palms-down over his thighs in readiness for another attack, 'but I'll do the same to anybody who thinks they can stop me saying what I have to say.'

'Nobody's stopping you talking,' Bulstrode said reasonably. 'Berg's impulsive, that's all.'

Palmer looked at Bulstrode in disbelief. 'You're not saying you believe him?'

'I'm not saying anything. But I'm wondering where the advantage could be in being dropped here with a blaster full of blanks and no boat home.'

'It could be a ruse.'

'Damn silly ruse to get torn apart.'

Berg was stirring, waving his arms and legs ineffectually in the air. 'I think I must have slipped,' he was mumbling. 'Let me at him...'

'Stay where you are,' Bulstrode advised. 'It's safer on the floor.'

Elite training had saved him from a trampling by Berg, but Killoran perceived that his position and credibility were far better without the blaster. Instead of concentrating on its threat the men were now starting to look past it to his argument. 'Bulstrode's got a point,' ,Cohn conceded, 'but where does it get us?'

'I'll tell you,' Killoran said, possessed by a fierce and desperate optimism. 'If you listen to me I'll get you out and back to the city.'

There were a few jeers from the back of the crowd and Palmer said, 'Just because you tell us what we want to hear, it doesn't mean we'll believe you.'

Cohn added, 'Whatever you're going to say, it's been tried.'

At least they were listening to him, not hooting and stamping and competing for the opportunity to jump on him. He'd found a nerve of hope that no amount of bitter cynicism could disguise and he was determined to exploit it. 'I'm the only one in the Palace who's not been drugged for the journey on the icebreaker. I know its layout and its weaknesses.'

Somebody said, 'We also know that it's shielded.'

'I've seen those shields and they're defective. If we all work together we can do it.'

Bulstrode was unimpressed. 'If you know so much about the Palace, then you know about the pipe network. If it isn't kept up, we're dead. Who's maintaining that while we're all working together?'

'Bring ice in,' Killoran said, thinking on his feet and with no idea as to whether it would work. 'Pack it into the cutout mechanism and freeze it solid.'

There was silence.

Palmer was the first to speak, reluctantly as if the dream might disappear. 'Would it work?'

Most people were looking at Cohn. The generator room was his territory. 'It might,' he conceded. 'Dangerous if it doesn't.'

Everybody knew that the generator room was the one site in the Palace which would not be affected by a shutdown. When the cutout mechanism tripped, power would be lost in all other areas, especially the vital yeast tanks, but the generator room would stay warm enough for its machinery to carry on monitoring for the time when output and expenditure were so matched that the Palace could come back to life—except, of course, that the yeast would have died off, and they would be facing slow starvation. It had happened once, and a sample had barely been preserved by relays of applied heat; but the next few months had been hungry ones and they might not be so lucky again.

Bulstrode said, 'I want to know what the kid expects in return for this cooperation.'

'Nothing,' Killoran told him. 'I want to get back as much as you do and I know I can't do it alone. My inside knowledge, your manpower.'

'And when we get back, what then? All of a sudden you're back to being Elite and we're refugees.'

'I'll be no more welcome than you will. All I want is a crack at the two councillors who tricked me and put me here.'

Cohn couldn't help being suspicious. 'What happened to the famous Elite inbred loyalty?'

'Loyalty to what?' It was in the balance and they were a long way from being convinced—but still they were listening. 'A dead city, or a frozen hero? I'm being realistic.'

'We haven't said we'll cooperate,' Bulstrode warned him.

'But you will.'

'We've got minds, kid. You may not have been taught to

think so, but we have.'

The undercurrent of excitement in the crowd was obvious. Almost the entire population of the Palace had by now pushed into the bay and joined the circle and they'd all heard at least the latter part of Killoran's argument. Perhaps the sophistication of such issues as who was running the city and selling out whom raised them out of the sphere of immediate preoccupation, but there was one point which everybody without exception had grasped; there was a hope for escape, and long-dead aspirations and feelings were becoming fresh and sensitive again.

There would have to be some kind of vote, somebody insisted; it could have been the Worm shouting from the back, but in spite of that everybody seemed in favour of the order and formality of the idea.

They put a guard of three on Killoran, mainly to show him that he was a long way from total acceptance. At the worst they might pick his brains and then throw him out on to the cap, but for the moment they took him to a bunkroom and, as an afterthought, gave him a snow suit to replace the inadequate city winter clothing that he'd arrived in.

There was, everybody agreed, much to discuss, although the only tangible issue that anybody could think of was that of the possibility of a return to normal food after living on the yeast. The main desire was simply to talk, to test the reality of their hope aloud, revelling in the. fact that, for a few brief hours at least, it was a topic that could be aired without the fear of bitter ridicule.

As Killoran was moved to the bunkroom there was a general decision to call a meeting in the Cantina, the refuge of such meagre society as the Palace enjoyed. Cohn caught up with Bulstrode in the passageway and drew him aside from the chattering procession.

'You know them all better than me,' Cohn said quietly, not wanting to be overheard. 'Which way are they likely to vote?'

'You really don't know?' Bulstrode didn't need to take the temperature of the crowd to recognize the urges that fought against reason within himself.

'I wouldn't be asking if I did.'

'You heard what he's offering. He's holding out freedom. They'll grab it and bite his hand off if he's not careful.'

.

SEVENTEEN

It seemed to Randall that his existence was dedicated to the exchange of one prison for another and that the notion of escape was an illusion which he was only now coming to comprehend. His life was corridors, endless corridors lined by anonymous doors beyond which were little rooms where essentially pointless confrontations took place and beyond these complexes raged a bleak and hostile universe. The Ice Palace, the shuttle, the World Ship—and, he admitted to himself with chilling honesty, the city.

They had been escorted without explanation into a fairly well-populated area of the World Ship. On the way they saw nothing that suggested an alien environment, no strange wonders or pulsating blobs of unfamiliar life; they might be lost below decks in a well-used and understaffed battleship. Only unexpected distortions of proportion and the occasional glimpse of a less-than-perfect marionette served to twist his perception of reality into line with the unusual.

They were in a guarded chamber, presumably awaiting the mysterious process of patterning. The door wouldn't open for them; it was keyed to a simulacrum handprint. The room was again low-ceilinged and blue and its walls bore the marks of fittings that had been removed. Now it was unfurnished, its bareness only relieved by a raised shelf that could serve as a hard seat for two or an equally hard and somewhat short bed for one.

Lobo leaned back with his eyes closed. He seemed to be driving the outside world out of his mind, slamming all the shutters down and giving himself some temporary and transient peace. Randall nursed his bruised pride—they'd been herded like animals, were animals as far as the marionettes were concerned. He tried to tell himself that they were machines, designed and crafted for a purpose, but that only made it worse; he'd expected something along the lines of an improved Rorvik model, but these had been people, perfect and indistinguishable.

When he tried to think of what lay ahead, his mind, like Lobo's, tried to pull back and cut free into a cocooned limbo, but he forced himself to face the prospect that they would be patterned—whatever that entailed—and then let loose in the corridors to be herded and killed for practice. Probably hunted down by their own improved doubles.

The city hadn't got a chance against them. They'd move in and take over before the rag-bag of a council knew anything; worse than that, the council was even helping. The Wekk would strip the assets of the city and then throw it aside and move on. They'd probably throw Marius aside at the same time, but he wouldn't see that; he had a grabber's mind, but a short reach.

'The next time,' he said aloud, 'we won't be rounded up and brought back. They'll kill us on the spot.'

Lobo frowned and then opened his eyes as he was pulled back to the real world. He considered for a while and then said, 'We need a good idea to get us out. Anything to offer?'

Randall threw off a brief stab of doubt, a fear of yet another pointless confrontation and tried to organize his knowledge and ideas towards some purposeful discussion. All his information had come from Rorvik, a confused and inadequate source. He knew the Wekk's long-term intentions, but he'd never seen one of them; and Randall had to admit that observation had added nothing to this basic store on their trip from the shuttle to this cell.

'Point one,' he said. 'We covered over a mile of corridor and didn't see anything to suggest that this ship is even inhabited. It doesn't look as if it's being cleaned or maintained.'

'Could be they've set this whole area aside for training.'

'That's a possibility. So we're in an isolated sector of a much larger construction. Elsewhere there's a complete and self-sufficient race, working to expand and with major computing facilities to do it. If this is a ship it's also got to have power and propulsion.'

Lobo was dubious. He was all in favour of reviewing the available information, but he wasn't so sure about such tenuous extrapolation. 'All this is great theory,' he said, 'but what's it going to do for us?'

'We can't make a plan without considering everything.'

'Another plan!' Lobo raised his hands in a frustrated appeal to the gods. 'Look where your last one got us! And what are you supposed to be considering? You're making it up as you go along!'

'You've a better idea?'

Lobo nodded. 'We concentrate on getting out of this cell and back to the shuttle.'

'Why the shuttle?'

'Because we can't do anything on our own, so we get back to the city and warn them.'

' Wrong. ' Randall held up the dead power pack that was still clipped at his waist. 'We get dropped back on the ice cap with no power in our suits. We wouldn't make it back to the Palace and if we could what then?'

Lobo realized that he'd been considering only the short term possibilities. He gave a sick smile. 'Looks like we've no choice. We're going to have to be heroes.'

'You never know. It might work. At the very worst we'll go out in a blaze of self-esteem.'

'I don't aim to plan for suicide,' Lobo warned.

'Nor do I. If there's one thing guaranteed to keep us sharp, it's the prospect of survival.'

They sat quietly, their fragile comradeship momentarily restored. After a few seconds the door whipped open without warning' and their guard tobk a half-step inside and glanced suspiciously around. He wasn't armed, but then he didn't need to be.

Obviously he'd been listening on the other side of the door. When silence had fallen he'd wanted to know why. Randall felt a surge of anger and said, 'What's the matter? Did they miss the brain out when they assembled you?'

'Up yours, bloodbag,' the marionette spat and made to

withdraw.

'That's the Ice Palace talking,' Lobo said quietly. 'I remember you, Pearson, when you were a man.'

The marionette's eyes narrowed. 'When I was a bloodbag. Pearson's dead; I strangled him myself out in the Tin Jungle. Don't get any ideas on teasing sympathy out of me, Lobo. If they say you're good enough you'll be patterned and rebuilt and then be fit to join us. Until then you're just a bloodbag for stamping on.'

Randall wondered if there was anywhere in this being a residual humanity that might be reached.

Remembering Rorvik's plaintive nostalgia for a human existence he'd never even known, he said, 'Come on, Pearson. So they built you and they gave you your orders. Admit that you're still one of us inside.'

Pearson reacted with amusement. He stepped further into the room, and the door hissed shut behind him. 'One of you? Don't make me laugh. I could break you with one hand. I'm faster and I'm stronger and I'm never going to die. Beat that.'

He reached behind him and touched the door. It came open and he stepped out backwards without taking his eyes off them.

'A ready-made fanatic,' Randall said despondently, his voice little more than a whisper. 'That's one hell of a weapon.'

'It makes you go cold inside,' Lobo agreed. 'If I didn't know better I'd swear it's the man I knew. I can't say I'm taken with the idea of looking up into my own eyes as I'm being strangled.'

Randall tried to concentrate on the problem in hand. They knew very little about the capabilities of the marionettes, except that they were fast and strong. Pearson was their first obstacle and it seemed likely that his claim of being able to break them one-handed would hardly be.an exaggeration.

The hours passed and nothing happened. Randall guessed that the patterning shops could only handle a limited number of subjects at any one time and either the process was a long one or there was a sizeable backlog. Subjects that were boxed and deteriorating obviously took precedence over those that were live and apprehensive and they were undisturbed for hours.

Pearson remained outside, apparently needing neither food

nor sleep. Randall and Lobo felt the demands of both, but while one could be satisfied after a fashion by stretching out on the hard shelf or the floor there was no way that nourishment could be extracted from an empty room. Pearson responded instantly when Randall hammered on the door, stepping inside and looking for trouble. He was unsympathetic when Randall asked for food, saying that there was nothing on the World Ship that a bloodbag could eat; but about half an hour later he was back with a couple of lightweight plastic bottles filled with the sweet drip that had been provided for the crated men in the shuttle. The hollow needles had been carefully removed.

So a marionette was by no means invulnerable; the simple precaution indicated as much. Randall preferred this conclusion to the idea that they were being prevented from damaging themselves and so robbing the simulacra of the pleasure. As they waited, faint and distant sounds were carried to them through the fabric of the ship, softened and reduced in every case to indistinct thumps. They had no way of identifying the faint whisper that was the hangar door opening to release the shuttle nor, several hours and a sickly meal later, the irregular bang as the shuttle rode back in on to hydraulic fenders.

AS SOON AS air had been pumped into the hangar Valum went inside to meet the councillors. She took with her Moskie, the marionette she had chosen to be her assistant and who had been patterned on a wiry, nervous-looking individual and Rorvik, because she'd been told that the new councillor was blind and would need a guide, and it was exactly the kind of undemanding duty that she considered Rorvik fit for. There were four other simulacra whose sole purpose was to make up an impressive-looking party—Marius was pleased by such things and his cooperation came more easily. As with any machine, pressing the right buttons gave a predictable response, a simple truth which was fundamental to Valum's universe.

Morden was in a bad way, pale and sick and barely able to balance. Marius held him up until Rorvik moved in and took over as instructed. At least Marius was trying to put a brave face on it, walking down the ramp with unsteady dignity and greeting Valum with an open gesture. If the truth were to be known, the numbers of Valum's party were wasted on him. Once his eyes were on her they stayed there.

She said that there were chambers ready and refreshments if they were needed, failing to add that the refreshments were no more than a flavoured variation of the drips that were being given to Randall and Lobo elsewhere in the World Ship. Marius turned to Morden and said encouragingly, 'See? They want us to feel at home. We're allies.'

Valum added, 'Let us never be considered anything else, Marius, but partners in strength and enterprise.'

Marius lapped it up. His ego soared at the notion of being treated as an equal by a race of proven world-rapers—or, at least, by their representatives. Morden tried to concentrate on staying upright.

Valum led them part of the way towards the suites of rooms that had been prepared for them on the next level. Marius had apparently requested an Arabian Nights style of decor while Morden, whose wishes were not yet known, had been given something rather more functional. The suites were some way apart, being subject to the available space of the ship's original design—Valum didn't add that she'd also wanted to keep the councillors apart and under surveillance. They had to stop a couple of times as squads of the simulacra thundered past, intent on some unexplained mission or exercise somewhere else in the ship and as they waited Marius asked, 'How is the plan proceeding?'

'Well,' Valum replied with a professional eye on the formation of her troops. 'The final model of simulacrum is undergoing tests at this very moment. When the results are known we'll be ready to move.'

'What? Into production?'

'No, directly into takeover.' The way was clear, and they moved on. 'We have sufficient models available now for our ground forces; we're only waiting for the development of the ground commander.'

Marius beamed with undisguised pleasure as a great, shapeless mass of anticipated good fortune seemed to rise above his horizon. 'Will we see these tests?' he asked.

'I hope not.' She hesitated, choosing her words carefully. 'They might be dangerous for any non-mechanicals present. You're far too valuable to us to risk, councillor.'

'I'm but a humble businessman, Valum, struggling to grasp the awesome complexities of power and to milk a little comfort from them as I go.'

The party split, with Rorvik leading Morden off down a side-corridor while Marius and the other simulacra went on. Valum held back, and when the group was out of earshot Moskie said, 'How do you manage it, Valum?'

She raised an enquiring eyebrow. 'You mean, treat the bloodbags as equals? Don't think it's easy. I'll smile until we've got the information we need. Then I'll take the greatest pleasure in twisting their flimsy necks.'

Moskie looked along the corridor, where the shadows of the retreating party still flickered on the wall. 'Makes me sick to look at them,' he said, suppressing an involuntary and rather human shudder. 'Bladders of jelly and bone.'

'Don't let it show,' Valum warned him as they turned and headed back towards her command post. 'At the moment we need information on their social setup that only they can provide. When we've got that. . .'

'The Tin Jungle?'

She smiled. 'Perhaps. Or else flush them out into vacuum and watch them explode. A lesson to us all on the frailty of the lower order.'

'Do we need any such lesson?'

'Some of the simulacra have been known to show a morbid sympathy for their origins. It does them no credit. Evolution is the only counter to the slow disintegration of the universe; evolve and never look back.'

Moskie was left to ponder this strange morsel of speculation as Valum ordered that the shuttle hangar be cleared and sealed, as the ship wasn't to be used again. The councillors, she added by way of explanation, wouldn't be going back.

Despite his discomfort Morden insisted upon being led all around his rooms, stopping to touch each obstruction in order to identify it and fix its location in his mind. Only then did he allow himself to relax, shaking Rorvik's arm free and moving unaided to a divan. Rorvik seated himself by the door, waiting until he should be needed again. Morden told him he could go.

'Valum said I have to stay, councillor,' Rorvik replied. 'You'll need one of us to open the door for you.'

Morden frowned. Something was troubling him, adding yet another layer of confusion to his already disoriented state of mind. The period of weightlessness on the trip out had been pure and undiluted hell for him and now his world seemed to be subject to a constant sideways drift, due, no doubt, to the inert reaction of his body to the cylinder's spin. A sighted man could probably overcome it, but for Morden it warped his entire perception of his surroundings. And now some further creeping doubt or anxiety was sliding to add itself to the turmoil in his head, demanding attention while stubbornly refusing to be identified.

'Rorvik!' he said after a moment. 'The woman called you Rorvik. Is that right?'

'It's my name,' Rorvik said guardedly, as if it might be taken from him.

'I never forget a voice.' It was true, although there was nothing in the marionette's flat monotone to recall the living man that he had met on a single occasion in the underbelly. Rorvik had at the time been on the run from the Elite prior to his assault on Central and Morden had supplied him with the tapes he'd needed to devise his plan of attack. A potential ally? Not if Marius's ecstatic praise of their loyalty and power was to be believed. Better proceed carefully. So far, he didn't have a friend in the place.

'Marius has told me what you are,' he went on conversationally. 'Copies, robots...'

'Not robots,' Rorvik said abruptly. 'Anything but that.'

A nerve? And so soon? 'Why so sensitive? Does it matter so much to you?'

'Copies, I accept. It hurts, but at least I understand why it hurts. But I'm not a robot. I'm patterned on a man and I've got some of his memories. I think the way he would think and I've got some of his feelings.'

Morden lifted himself on an elbow. 'Then I knew the man you were. I respected him.'

Automatically, Rorvik walked over and placed a cushion behind the councillor, saying, 'Randall knew the man I was as well. He. . .'

'Did you say Randall?' Morden interrupted. 'He's here?'

'From the Ice Palace. They're holding him for patterning now.'

A number of pieces suddenly interlocked in Morden's mind. A dazzling and frightening sequence of logic which could be the key to an atlas of possibilities. But first he would have to persuade or deceive this pathetic and self-pitying being and somehow use him to get to Randall. 'How long has he been here?' he asked.

'A few days. Two of them stowed away on the shuttle and persuaded me to help them.'

Morden warmed to this weak link. The creature admitted he was reachable. 'How did they persuade you?'

'Didn't you get the message from Valum? Anybody can make a fool out of Rorvik. He's simple and he's credulous. I can't help it.'

'Tell me something. How strong are your loyalties to the Wekk? to your own kind?'

'Are you testing me?' Rorvik asked suspiciously. 'Please don't trick me. I don't know how to lie.'

'I'm not trying to trick you,' Morden said soothingly.

'I don't even have the guile to evade answering. Valum's right, I'm a poor specimen.'

'And a talkative one,' said Morden, trying not to let his impatience show. 'Answer the question.'

Rorvik applied himself and was silent for a moment. 'Towards the Wekk, I'm not aware of any loyalty,' he answered truthfully. 'I've never seen one of them, and they've never offered me anything. As for the marionettes, I suppose I'm loyal. I do what they tell me, and they use my name so I'm somebody. To everyone else I'm-a half-finished monster.'

Morden was surprised. Marius had told him that the

simulacra were visually indistinguishable from real people. 'A monster?' he said. 'Why?'

'You can't see me,' Rorvik said bitterly. 'I'm the first marionette they ever built and the only model they had was in the memory of a computer. What do you think I look like?'

'To me, what does it matter?'

'What is this?' Rorvik said suddenly. 'What are you trying to do?'

'I'll tell you the truth, Rorvik. I'll tell you the truth because of the man you once were and for the humanity you've retained. I'll tell you,' he added with rather more honesty, 'because I need you.'

'Nobody needs me,' Rorvik said sorrowfully. 'Valum says so.'

'Valum's wrong. When she speaks I hear the true monster, a being without pity.'

This didn't agree with Rorvik's preconceptions. 'They say she's considered the most successful piece of design so far.'

'By what measure of success? Because she's colder, harder, stronger?'

'All of that.'

'They praise her because in spirit she's the furthest from the human concept they've been able to devise. They despise you because you're the closest.'

Rorvik shook his head sadly. 'They despise me because I'm nothing.'

'By their standards, perhaps. Standards which would rape worlds and trample the weak.'

'Men's standards. I got exactly the same treatment from Randall.'

Morden pushed the cushion away and sat upright, his physical discomfort driven from his mind. 'Don't take Randall as your model for a man. In many ways he's as much an engineered product as Valum, biology rigged for the service of the State.'

Rorvik started to soften, his protective screen of bitterness breaking down under Morden's sustained and skilful attack. 'The other one—Lobo—he was kinder. I think he understood.'

'Of course he understood. He understood your self-doubt,

your weakness, your hope.'

'And that's all there is to me. No wonder they spit on me.' Morden began to wonder if he was really wasting his time, whether Rorvik would in the end prove to be as empty and inadequate as he appeared. This was, after all, Morden's first excursion into machine diplomacy, and he was on uncertain ground. But he was faced with a real dilemma; Rorvik talked, moved and reacted like a human being. His thought processes seemed to be the same, his responses faultless. How could Morden treat him apart from as a human being? How could he even—and this thought gave him a thrill of horror—be sure that, despite his strange birth and unfamiliar biology, Rorvik was not fundamentally human at all?

There was a simple answer, sufficient to meet his present needs. He couldn't be sure, so forget it and carry on. 'I need you,' he said. 'I want you to be my eyes and my guide.'

'I'm that already. Valum ordered me to be.'

'She didn't order you to help me ruin the takeover plan.'

It was a gamble. Rorvik didn't answer straight away, and Morden plunged in with, 'See? I'm trusting you. I consider you a man. Would the machines do as much?'

'Never. They say I'm too. . .'

'Human?'

'Unreliable. Ineffective.'

'By machine standards.'

'Weak and sloppy, like a bloodbag.' He added, almost apologetically, 'That's what they call you.'

'The same contempt they reserve for you. Join me,' Morden urged, 'and be my eyes.'

Rorvik's defences were deceptive. His resistance to enthusiasm was immense. 'I was supposed to join Randall,' he said. 'But as soon as he'd gone I found I was taking orders from Valum again.'

'You have to believe in yourself before you can choose a path and have the faith to stick to it. What did Randall offer you? Use of your name, like the others? So cheap a contract costs you nothing to break.'

'But I'm not a man,' Rorvik objected desperately. 'I was built.'

'So were we all. It's the oldest piece of engineering in the history of the race.'

'Of your race. Not the Wekk.'

'And how much careful control did the Wekk put into your conception? Damn all, and they weren't satisfied with the result so they threw you aside. Too much of the human being was showing through.'

There was a pause. Morden had said enough, deciding that he had reached the narrow line that separates persuasion from transparent propaganda. The initiative would now have to come from Rorvik. If it didn't, Morden had not only wasted his time, he'd put himself into a very dangerous position; if he couldn't win Rorvik now, he may as well simply hand himself over to Valum.

'All right,' Rorvik said. 'I'll serve you.'

'Not serve me. Help me. I want information and then action. And we'll need Randall.'

'If it isn't too late,' Rorvik warned. 'He's down for patterning.'

'It won't be too late,' Morden said with unexpected certainty. 'Leave that to me. How much can you find out about this ship and the Wekk without arousing suspicion?'

Rorvik thought about how the other simulacra could touch Wekk-prepared computers and systems in a certain way and somehow tune in to them. He knew he had some of this capability from his experiments on the shuttle, but how far did it extend? If he was, as Morden suggested, too human to qualify as a fully-fledged simulacrum, would he be able to do no more than touch the outer surface of the machines' awareness, like a telekinetic who wafted feathers while others raised mountains? Trying, he told himself with new-found determination, was the only way to find out.

'I'll see if I can get access to the shuttle's computer,' he told Morden. 'It may not work, but I can try.' He explained how the shuttle had been found empty and in orbit and how the Wekk had stripped it and fitted their own guidance systems. If these were linked into the main ship memories he might be able to tap them out, an instant flood of knowledge which he would then carry for as long as he could keep it in his mind; then, like all forgotten studies, the details would begin to slip away.

'You can do it,' Morden said with completely unjustified confidence.

Rorvik wished he could share Morden's conviction. At least he could draw some courage from it.

'ANY MORE bright ideas?'

'I'm sorry.' Randall helped Lobo to his feet. 'How was I to know he'd react like that?'

It had always worked in stories. Prisoner One calls guard and tells him that Prisoner Two is ill, indicating an inert form to substantiate his claim; and when the guard rushes in filled with concern and bends over said form he gets bopped from behind and the two then dance off to fresh air and freedom. Which was fine, except that Randall hadn't read much concern in Pearson's expression as he advanced on Lobo; more an evil glee at the prospect of being able to finish him off.

It made sense. If they showed themselves as unfit for patterning they'd lose whatever small value they had.

'All of a sudden,' Lobo said, 'I feel unbearably healthy.'

Randall began to pace the cell yet again. 'There must be another way,' he said.

There was no way out other than by the single sliding door, and that was unavailable to them unless Pearson actually opened it and let them through. They couldn't trick or persuade him, because he didn't have the slightest interest in anything they had to say—he seemed only to warm at the prospect of tearing one of them apart.

'That's what we'll have to use against him,' Randall said aloud. 'Fill his mind with the prospect of mangling a bloodbag and then hit him when he's off guard.'

'With what?' Lobo objected. 'He's stronger than both of us put together and we've no weapons.'

'We're wearing them,' Randall said. Lobo was giving him a familiar sideways look of distrust as he sat down, so he went on, 'The snow suits. Have you ever tried to tear the fabric on one?'

'Don't be a fool. There was no way to repair or replace them.'

'Exactly.' Randall was unzipping his suit, sliding his arm out of a sleeve to demonstrate his point. 'The supply was limited and they were handed down from prisoner to prisoner. They're as old as the Palace itself and they were part of the original equipment. They're space suits.'

Lobo took hold of the fabric and tugged at it experimentally, looking at it as if for the first time. 'How does that make them into weapons?'

'The fabric was made deliberately strong to avoid the possibility of a rupture or tear in vacuum. If we knot the sleeves into a band and drop that over Pearson's head we can pin his arms to his sides.'

'But the suits are old. How do you know they'll take the strain?'

'How do you know they won't?'

Lobo couldn't answer the point, so he moved on. 'So we've got him trussed up on the floor. What then?'

'He's a machine and machines can be broken. Two of us should be able to do it.'

'I wouldn't be so confident. With that kind of logic you could wrestle bulldozers and expect to win.'

But it was the only chance they seemed to have, and as closer inspection only revealed its flaws they decided to forget the detailed analysis and go ahead with it. Obviously to stand there shivering and suitless when Pearson walked in would be to invite instant failure, so Lobo practised a few times until he could slip off the outer layer with silence and speed.

Randall banged on the door with the flat of his hand. In case their warder was growing weary of being attracted in this way, he added encouragement by shouting, 'Pearson! Get your tin backside in here!'

The door was open and Randall was backing away out of reach. Pearson was smiling. 'You'd have to have a good reason to call me like that, bloodbag. Offhand I can't think of anything good enough.'

'I don't need to explain anything to you, junkhead.'

Pearson glanced at Lobo. He was sitting on the low shelf, arms folded and apparently wanting nothing to do with his partner's madness. He turned his attention back to Randall, who was hovering bright-eyed and nervous at the far end of the cell. 'Damn right you don't,' Pearson told him. 'I've got all the reason I need to pull your head off and stuff it down your throat.'

'Brave talk from a greasy oilbag. All crude oil and low-grade alloys.'

Pearson's smile vanished. Randall was attacking where it hurt, cutting at his sensitive machine pride. 'Say that again,' Pearson demanded menacingly.

'Oil bag. A clockwork brain and a scrap iron heart. Blood like a dead lake.'

'Thanks, Randall. I'm going to enjoy this.' The safety mechanism of the door sensed as he advanced and the door whispered shut behind him. Pearson's awareness was now completely focused on Randall and the prospect of mangling a bloodbag with full justification.

Randall kicked out hard and low, aiming to clip the kneecap sideways with the ball of his foot. He was fast, but Pearson was faster—both forearms thrust down in a rigid block that was like an iron bar laid across his shin. Randall bit back a shout of pain and concentrated on twisting to keep his balance.

Lobo stepped in and quickly dropped the knotted loop of his suit over Pearson's shoulders, trapping his arms close to his chest. Pearson wasted no time in stupid surprise but jumped backwards, slamming into Lobo and knocking him to the floor. The loop had dropped to his waist and he flexed to tear it and pull his arms free. Lobo was up and suddenly on his back, forcing the second loop of the sleeves over Pearson's head. This time he dropped off before he could be shrugged off, taking Pearson by surprise and leaving him tottering and half-blinded by the loose material. Randall made a standing jump, hitting him in the chest with both feet and slamming him backwards over the crouching Lobo to measure his full length on the deck.

They fell on to him together, pinning his legs to prevent them from delivering crippling kicks. Pearson was a trussed package struggling vainly to free himself from the tangle of snow suit that was wrapped around him, but he was still dangerous. Randall managed to stuff a handful of material in his mouth to prevent him from shouting for help, nearly losing a finger in the process, and then together he and Lobo began to haul Pearson towards the raised shelf that was the only feature of the cell.

Pearson seemed to realize what they were trying to do. He fought back even harder, getting impossible purchase with his heels on the floor and dragging all three of them back a few inches at a time, slowly cancelling out the progress that they made. The next time he tried it Randall kicked his feet free, and for a moment there was no resistance and they got him a yard or more across the floor. Then his heels dug in again, and the backward creep began.

They were tiring and he wasn't. And now the knots began to slip.

Lobo tried to say so, but didn't have the effort to spare. Randall had seen it anyway, a fractional unwinding of the fabric stretched tight across Pearson's chest. Not wanting to shout and give Pearson warning, Randall pushed hard on Lobo's shoulder and then rolled away himself. Lobo was taken by surprise, losing his grip and sliding away. With the sudden release of constraint Pearson was left threshing energetically in the middle of the room.

Randall scrambled around, tried to get a good double handful of suit which hopefully included some of Pearson's own. Lobo caught on and did the same, and with one unified effort they dragged and lifted at the same time, covering the last few feet and getting Pearson's head on to the shelf.

Lobo dropped his full weight on to Pearson's chest, throwing himself down hard. And then it was over.

Something vital gave and Pearson stopped fighting them. They both stepped back warily, watching Pearson's body slowly subside to the floor, the head bending away from the shoulders at an unnatural angle as it bumped over the edge of the shelf.

Lobo claimed to have killed to be sent to the Ice Palace, but this process had obviously repelled him. Randall gave Pearson a couple of tentative prods with his foot, but there was no reaction.

'What now?' Lobo asked, wiping his eyes on the sleeve of his inner suit.

'The councillors,' Randall said, hauling Pearson back into the middle of the room where he could work to undo the knots in Lobo's snow suit. 'They're somewhere aboard, or they soon will be. I heard one of our escorts say as much when they were bringing us up here. We can't hope to fight the marionettes, but with a hostage we might have a chance to reach the alien areas of the ship instead of playing about in the training ground.'

Lobo wasn't exactly enchanted by the prospect. 'Further and further in and not a damned clue as to what we're going to do when we get there.'

'We have to go on because we can't go back.' Randall was thinking of the irony in Pearson's claim that he was stronger, faster and was never going to die. Stronger and faster he may have been, but he was as mortal as any of the bloodbags he so despised. Then Randall got the last knot undone and pulled the suit free, dragging it from under Pearson's shoulders and unwrapping it from around his head. 'At least we can try to pick up some insurance along the way,' he went on and then faltered. Pearson's eyes were fixed on him, their irises two tiny points of hatred.

Lobo took the suit and climbed into it mechanically. He didn't look at Pearson, but Randall was careful to turn the head aside so that the living eyes were concealed. 'Another advantage,' Randall said with forced brightness, 'is that Valum won't know we're on the loose for a while.'

If the thought gave Lobo any particular cheer he didn't let it show. He finished zipping up and prepared, yet again, to dive head-first into the killing bottle.

EIGHTEEN

The short time of Killoran's acceptance had seen considerable changes in the Ice Palace. The work cycle was broken, quickly and efficiently—ice packed into the reactor cutouts jammed them open and the Palace was assured of its power supply. The yeast tanks had to be tended and continuous relays were needed to bring fresh ice for the cutouts, but the regime of the all-weathers, round-the-clock surface repair teams was ended, it seemed, for good. Killoran would be a hero in the Palace if he never achieved anything more. About forty men were now freed to devote all their efforts and intelligence to the next stage of the plan, the storming of the icebreaker.

The rosters were discarded. Men happily took double shifts, snatching sleep and coming back early for more; there were rafts to be made and tested, ropes to be woven from fibre and blanket and the full extent of the pipe network to be scouted as soon as the weather allowed. There was enthusiasm, even long-unheard laughter; nervous hopes and laughing too loud, a consuming apprehension which began to break the surface in the form of petty disputes or fights. When this happened Berg would be there, gently disengaging the participants and threatening them with far worse horrors should they attempt to continue.

Even Palmer, miserable and despised, suppressed his fears when a surface party was needed and offered himself up with the rest, finding that this simple act won him the grudging recognition of equality. Only one face was consistently missing from all this activity.

Palmer knocked on the door to the Worm's office. There was no reply, so he knocked again a little harder and shouted, 'Worm? Open the door!'

His voice echoed loudly in the ice tunnel and he felt faintly ridiculous. What if somebody heard? He was about to turn and go when a faint, 'Go away,' reached him.

'At least open the door and speak to me!' Palmer insisted.

He waited for some time, drumming his fingers lightly on the door to show that he was still there. After a minute or so it opened a crack and the Worm looked out. His hair was disarrayed and his eyes were puffy and red behind his one-lensed spectacles.

'Leave me alone, Palmer,' he mumbled. 'I don't want to talk to anybody.'

'You've got to come out some time,' Palmer told him. 'You can't stay in there forever.'

The Worm shrugged. 'Where else am I going to go?' He turned and shuffled back into his office. The unclosed door was an invitation, the manner in which it was offered a rejection.

Palmer followed him in and left the door open behind him. 'We need your help,' he said. 'Killoran says he needs everybody.'

'He doesn't need me. I'm not fit to go out on the ice and I'm no use in here either.'

'That's birdseed,' Palmer said dismissively.

'Is it?' the Worm demanded, some light coming into his eyes for the first time. He gestured at a sheaf of filthy grey papers on his rickety table. Some of them had been written on, most not. 'Nobody's using rosters now. The kid's got everybody so fired up they're fighting to work every hour in the day.'

'Come on, Worm. He's offering us hope. Grown men are crying in their bunks. I've been doing my turns on the ice and no swaps.'

The Worm seemed not to hear. 'We had a good system going here,' he mused. 'It wasn't such a bad place before.'

Palmer said incredulously, 'Are you serious?'

'I was important then. Not just needed, the same as everybody else, but important. They could despise me or laugh at me, but they couldn't do without me and they knew it.'

Palmer was hardly impressed by the argument. 'Don't think about that. Think about what it all means. Going home.'

The Worm winced, as if at the memory of an old agony.

'Home to what?' he said despondently. 'You know what home was to me? A grubby desk in a crowded office and an hour for lunch, then back at night to a long staircase and a little room.'

'It doesn't have to be like that. Everything's going to change for the better.'

'That's great for the strong and the handsome. Types like Bulstrode will love it. Everybody gets embarrassed at the thought of a runt enjoying himself.'

The Worm certainly looked the part, a shrunken figure in his baggy snow suit toying miserably with a loose splinter at the corner of his desk. Palmer tried to get him out of his self-pitying mood.

'You've got no self respect,' he said. 'For years they've been depending on you and hating themselves for having to, not because you're anything special but because they think they're so tough they shouldn't depend on anybody. So they took it out on you and you're believing it all.'

The Worm shrugged. 'Talk all you like. I'd rather be hated than ignored. You know you're the first person to come looking for me?'

'So what?'

'So I've gone from being the most important person in the Palace to being an afterthought, that's all.'

'Shove your importance,' Palmer snapped, his frustration beginning to show. 'Nobody's going to be interested in you if you won't get involved.'

'Involved in what? A useless trek across the ice to dig out some deserted spaceport?'

'Not deserted,' Palmer said, annoyed at having to be defensive. 'We found some evidence of recent use.'

'Breaking up the crates,' the Worm pressed on as if he hadn't heard, 'for rafts to drown ourselves on?'

'Damn you, Worm, I don't know why I'm bothering.'

'Nor do I.'

'You sit and carp and moan for the lousy good old days and you won't lift a finger to try to make anything better.'

'Where's the point?' the Worm asked, his face an open and uncomprehending blank.

'Because you get nothing if you don't reach for it, that's the point.'

'You've got freedom fever like the rest of them, Palmer,' the Worm said dismissively. 'All of a sudden you think you can just dream it and make it come true. Well, life isn't like that. It's routine and detail and fiddling little considerations. . .'

' Your life, perhaps. . .'

'All right, my life. So what have I got now? A spaceport on the doorstep nobody can use. Mad plans to steal an icebreaker. Lights in the sky. . .'

Palmer reddened at this last mention. It seemed the Worm had been around more in the past couple of days than he'd thought. 'I saw those myself,' he insisted. 'They were real. Something passed overhead, I don't know what.'

'You're no better than the rest of them. Why don't you leave me alone?'

'My apologies, Worm,' Palmer said tightly. 'I had this stupid idea that you needed encouragement.'

'Shove your encouragement,' the Worm replied morosely. 'Take it back to your city-bred Messiah.'

Palmer moved back towards the door. 'Go see the Worm, I thought. I wish I hadn't wasted my time.'

'That makes two of us.'

'All you want to do is sit on your own in this crummy office and feel sorry for yourself. Don't expect anybody to join in.'

'You're breathing my air, Palmer.'

'I know,' Palmer said, holding the edge of the door so hard that his knuckles were white. 'It's got the smell of something going sour in it.'

He slammed the door as viciously as he could, really wishing that he was pounding the Worm's head against the gritty ice wall in a desperate and frustrated bid to make some final communication. The door banged in its frame and bounced open again, but Palmer was already some way off along the tunnel, head down and muttering to himself.

The Worm waited for a minute. Then he went over to the door and closed it softly after first checking that the tunnel outside was empty. He went back to his desk with its blank rosters, looking at them pensively for a few seconds before going back and checking the tunnel again. It was empty, as before. He closed the door.

THIS TIME IT had been easy to get lost in the World Ship. There was no sweep operation in progress and the upper levels (which were, by an ironic inversion of physical laws, innermost in the cylinder) had more alcoves, corners and wide open spaces than the featureless corridors where they had originally been captured. There was a further advantage in that, for the moment, nobody knew they were free; Pearson's inert form remained in their cell, lying exactly as they had left him after using his hand to open the door.

At no time did they see any sign of a non-human life form. Indeed, as they retreated further the indications of use by the simulacra grew less. The World Ship seemed to be at once lived-in and deserted—there was grey dust piling up in some of the corridors and the walls and floors showed squares and patches where, Randall assumed, equipment or machinery once stood. Lighting was uneven and in many places had simply failed or burned out without replacement. The World Ship was an artificial planet going to seed—literally, as it turned out when they found the banks and terraces of what had obviously been a garden in a huge chamber that embraced two levels.

They watched the movements of the marionettes, tried to work out where their centres of operations were and what they were doing in the endless exercises which kept them moving from one area of the ship to another, but it was impossible. They did, however, find Marius.

He was glimpsed entering the chambers that had been laid aside for him. Randall knew it had to be Marius, for the simulacrum who escorted him and left him at the door displayed an exaggerated deference that no machine would need to use towards another.

'They still don't know we're loose,' Lobo reminded Randall. 'That may change if we don't get a hostage, quick.'

For once, Randall agreed. He quickly outlined his idea, that they should watch for a while to ensure that Marius was alone before attempting to bluff their way in as marionettes. Lobo wasn't sure about the last part.

'We make damn funny robots in these old suits,' he said.

'We'd make funnier ones without them,' Randall replied. 'Try to seem confident and we'll find out if he's armed.'

The door presented a problem. It seemed to be of the same type that had blocked their cell, activated only by a simulacrum's touch; but as they looked around for some other way to open it the panel hissed back without warning and Marius looked out at them with an expression of polite enquiry.

Randall said, 'May we join you, councillor?' as if this had been his intention all along.

Marius seemed confused for a moment as he took in their shopworn and hirsute appearance, then his expression cleared into understanding.

'Intelligent company!' he said, obviously pleased. 'How thoughtful of Valum. Please come in.'

He stepped aside, and Randall led on into the room. Lobo followed and tried not to seem too relieved.

The room was heavily draped in greens and golds, not so much a room as an indoor courtyard surrounding an open fountain which was lit from above by a reasonable facsimile of brilliant sunlight. Reflections spilled off the water and danced in the surrounding gloom, showing the surface and apparent texture of marble wherever they fell. Beyond the pillars in the 'outdoor' area Marius had apparently been dining, for there was a low table with cushions scattered around it by the fountain and on it were a number of crude, heavy-looking dishes and flagons.

Marius led them through to the open atrium and offered them a seat. Apparently, this meant the floor. Randall said, 'Valum suggested that you might feel a need for conversation. She particularly suggested that we should solicit your views on the forthcoming operation.'

'All that kind of thing,' Lobo said helpfully.

'But Valum already knows my views,' Marius protested. 'I'd be more interested in yours.'

They were in a bad position. The bright light overhead made

it impossible to see any detail in the shaded portico and the rattle of running water effectively covered any slight sound. Marius might have an army waiting out there as far as Randall could see. 'We've been specially chosen for our ignorance and interest,' he said. 'We're your audience, councillor. Instruct us in whatever you will.'

'If that's the case,' Marius said, waving a negligent hand, 'let's forget about the operation. I've talked about nothing else all through the debriefing and it bores me. Tell me what you think about the chambers, instead. Valum had them laid out and decorated according to my own design. It's a private fantasy of mine, you see, the Sultan in his palace.'

Randall didn't like it. He wasn't getting any control of the situation this way. He was tempted to jump on Marius, to gamble that there were no extra defences hidden around them. Lobo shifted nervously next to him, but all Randall said was, 'It's very impressive.'

Marius moved around by the fountain and indicated the table next to them. 'Feel the weight of one of those plates.' Did something stir beyond the opposite archway? 'Solid gold, all the tableware.'

'A residence fit for a prince, councillor.' This was ridiculous. They were making small talk when they needed action. *Come on*, Randall thought, *there's nobody here. Grab him and get on with it.*

'That's not all there is,' Marius went on. 'What's a prince without his harem?' And he clapped his hands twice.

The shadows into which Randall had been imagining life now responded, moving and assuming full substance as they came into the light, one to each archway of the portico around them. They stepped into the atrium and waited, a deformed gallery of horrors.

'They're the early test models of the simulacra,' Marius explained, touching one of them affectionately before moving on to the next. 'They're rough and simple and they can only obey direct commands. They're of no use to the operation, so Valum gave them to me for my entertainment. I call them my marionettes.' He clapped his hands again and the marionettes moved forward another step. He called for them to stop, and they froze in the act of moving again and subsided to a regular stance. Marius grinned broadly. 'In such obedience is true beauty. For such compliance I can forgive their rough-hewn lack of grace.'

Randall counted six of them altogether, forming a semicircle around Marius on the opposite side of the courtyard. As broken dolls they would be innocuous, but as moving human facsimiles they were a series of terrifying disasters. They were like animate corpses, some with whole sections rotted away. Limbs were unfinished or incomplete and one of them had no abdomen, just a rigid spinal brace and a handful of wet looking tubes between thorax and hips. Randall heard Lobo swallowing hard beside him.

'I can have them sing, or dance, or make whatever music I choose,' Marius was saying. 'When I speak they listen and applaud.' He turned to the nearest of them. 'What is your one desire?'

'To serve you, Marius,' all six chorused in a flat monotone.

'And why?'

'Because we love you, Marius.'

Marius spread his arms, the demonstration complete. 'Who could ask for a more faithful and adoring retinue?'

'We would gladly die for you, Marius,' the marionettes said without a trace of spontaneity.

'Turn your heads,' Marius instructed. 'See the two men by the table.' Six heads motored around in unison. 'They mean me harm. If either of them approaches my person, you are to take them and break them. Is that understood?'

'Yes, Marius.'

'What are you talking about?' Randall demanded. 'What is this?'

Marius laughed, safe inside his ring of gruesome protectors. 'Do you think me such a fool, Randall? I don't know how you got out, but Valum told me you were on board. Didn't it even occur to you that I might recognize you?'

It hadn't. 'But we've never met.'

'I watched you being boxed! I gave the order for the crate to be nailed up and loaded for transportation to the Ice Palace! Sent to offer me conversation, indeed.' He indicated Lobo. 'I doubt whether your friend can even string two words together.'

'Hey,' Lobo protested.

'What are you going to do?' Randall said quietly.

'For the moment, I need do nothing. My children are my guardians. Don't be misled by the way they look, or because they're slow and clumsy. Move towards me and they'll kill you, whether you reach me or not.'

'They don't look so dangerous to me,' Lobo said stubbornly.

Marius looked to him. 'If you doubt me, try it, ape.'

'Don't try it, Lobo. I think he's telling the truth.'

Marius was revelling in his advantage. 'Listen to your friend,' he told Lobo. 'He's slightly less stupid than you. I've given a command which can only be over-ridden by myself or one of the simulacra. And I've got no intention of countermanding it.'

'We got nowhere,' Lobo muttered bitterly, mainly to himself. 'We're still prisoners. Same as in the cell, same as on the ice.'

'You can give me the satisfaction of envy and admiration before I consign you to whatever unpleasantness lies in your future,' Marius Went on. 'You'll be privileged to witness the skills of my marionettes in the ballet. Come, children. Are you ready to perform for the damned?'

'Always ready to serve you, Marius,' the marionettes replied in the same dead tone.

He called for music. One of the marionettes detached itself from the group and walked unevenly over to sit on the raised lip which contained the water around the fountain. There it started to slap its knee, irregularly at first but building up to a rhythm, skipping occasional beats but then hurrying to fit in an extra one. The marionette's mouth opened to a black *O*, soundless at first but then making a tuneless keening sound like the wind through the broken windows of an old house. Others of the marionettes joined in with no regard for harmony, adding their own pitches and moans. As the dissonance fought in the air around them two of the creatures ambled forward into the middle of the courtyard. Although they were obviously sexless one of them had been given long, dry hair in yellow plaits, the mask of a face painted with carmine lips and cheeks. Marius moved out of the way as they struck angular poses facing one another, and it seemed to Randall that he looked upon them with genuine pride.

Lobo wouldn't look, lowering his eyes as the grotesque figures stepped and chopped around each other. Randall tried to catch his attention, but he wouldn't respond. Only when Randall nudged the table with his knee, scraping it a fraction on the hard floor, did Lobo come out of his desperate trance. He looked straight at Randall, avoiding the scene before them. The noise was loud and oppressive, growing all the time and Randall stared hard at the gold plate a few inches from Lobo's hand on the table.

'I hope you'll remember this, Randall,' Marius shouted, barely making himself heard over the wailing and slapping. 'Remember it for the rest of your short life.'

There was confusion on Lobo's face. Randall wondered how explicit he could afford to be. A glance from Marius would give him away. He stared pointedly at the plate again. Lobo saw it, gave an imperceptible nod. Then Randall raised his hand to his throat, touching it lightly as if in need of air and then his eyes shifted deliberately to where Marius was observing the rising tempo of the dance, clapping his hands and laughing loudly when the postures of the androgynous figures gave the remotest suggestion of anything lewd or suggestive. He glanced their way and Randall forced an appreciative smile.

Marius perceived his discomfort and laughed even louder. It was as if the whole scene were a huge joke that only he understood and he threw back his head and added his roar to the marionettes' ugly crescendo.

Lobo came up, halfway over the table to get his balance. He swept up the plate as he rose, drawing back his arm to test its weight and pausing for only a fraction of a second to take aim before loosing it in a long and graceful discus throw to sail across the room towards Marius.

The song of the marionettes was a sudden and empty silence in which Randall could actually hear the rush of the plate as it flew. Marius realized that something was wrong, but too late.

The plate hit his neck with a dull smack, lodging in the deep groove that it cut across his windpipe and staying there as he dropped slowly backwards onto the floor. He hit like a sack and the plate clattered away.

Six blank faces were turned towards them for the second time. Lobo was still crouched on the table, empty-handed.

'Back off' Randall advised him. 'They won't touch us as long as we don't actually approach Marius. He wasn't literal enough.'

Lobo climbed down slowly off the table and the marionettes made no move towards them. They simply stared and then the one with no stomach looked down at Marius's still form, as if trying without success to see the connection.

'What do we do now, Marius?' it faltered, and the others joined in with 'What now, Marius?'

'Walking corpses,' Lobo said with undisguised disgust.

'That's what we'll be, if we don't get out of here. We can forget Marius for a hostage.' Blood was slowly starting to pool under the councillor's body, a seemingly impossible volume. Randall paused to inspect his reaction to Marius's death and found, with faint surprise, that he felt nothing at all—no guilt, no sickness, no horror. He hadn't expected to feel anything for Pearson, but surely this ought to be different, he thought. But it wasn't.

The marionettes pestered on for a minute or so and then fell silent. Randall led the way back to the entrance in a wide arc, careful not to appear to be approaching Marius's body. True to the letter of their instruction, the marionettes left them alone.

It was so dark in the shaded area that it was difficult to locate the door. At the first attempt Randall found a blank wall.

'This is a dead ship,' a strange voice came from the black and golden twilight behind them. 'You could roam over it forever and find nothing of value.'

Both Randall and Lobo turned at the same time, backing up to get the defensive certainty of the wall behind them and looking desperately around, minds trying to squeeze detail from insufficient light.

He stepped forward, a slight but dignified figure thrown into silhouette against the brightness of an archway, and while his face was in shadow his pale eyes burned as if lit from within.

Lobo was underbelly, well versed in its mythologies. 'It's Morden!' he hissed. 'Hostage, Randall!'

Morden was joined by another, taller and with a grey deathmask of a face. He moved to Morden's shoulder and waited there protectively. 'I assume Marius is dead,' Morden said to the one behind him. 'Is that right?'

'His head's nearly off,' Rorvik confirmed.

'I wish we'd arrived sooner. I'd have liked more time to consider.'

'Save us more speeches,' Randall said loudly, bitter at the way in which setback seemed to be the inevitable partner of success, 'Turn us over to Valum and have done with it. Or else give the job to the robot. It's his speciality.'

'I never gave you away, Randall,' Rorvik said. 'Valum saw the guilt in me. She only let you run to give the simulacra some sport.'

'What does it matter?' Lobo mumbled, barely audible. 'Turn wherever we like, we're dead.'

'Listen to me,' Morden said with an urgent sincerity that seemed to belie his position as their captor. 'The Wekk are poised to mobilize as soon as the field tests are finished on their simulacrum ground commander. Once they've made their move they can't be stopped.'

'Proud moment for you,' said Randall, becoming less sure of what was supposed to be going on.

'Drop the pose, Randall, it's holding us up. Sometime soon they're going to find out, as Rorvik did for me, that you've wrecked the Pearson model and escaped. Then there'll be another sweep operation and you'll be gathered in as easily as the last time. I won't be able to help you then.'

Randall was about to frame his reply when Morden turned and moved back towards the open area with Rorvik following. Neither seemed to be regarding them as a threat, and Randall was mildly insulted. 'What kind of help can I expect now?' he shouted after them. 'All I see is a turncoat councillor and a robot too dim to follow its own train of thought.'

'Throw me all the insults you like,' Rorvik called over his

shoulder as he guided Morden through this new territory with a light touch on the elbow. 'They can't touch me now.' Morden settled on cushions on the far side of the arches. Randall and Lobo were still in tense and expectant crouches against the wall, starting to feel rather foolish. Lobo straightened first and Randall shrugged and did the same. They went over to join Morden, carefully keeping their distance from the marionettes who were now mute and immobile.

'I don't have time to argue with you, Randall,' Morden said as he heard them approach, 'and you don't have any choice but to believe me. As your friend said, turn any other way and you're dead. To begin with, I'm no traitor. I've been working with the full agreement of Chandler to uncover Marius and look for a weakness in the proposed operation. Until this last few hours it seemed that I was riding a tiger that I couldn't hope to dismount. Then I met Rorvik and he told me you were aboard; and I've since found out that neither Marius nor I were here for the sole purpose of a debriefing. We're here to be patterned and then they intend to kill us. In Marius's case you've beaten them to it.'

'If that's true,' Randall said carefully, 'and I'm not saying I think it is, then you're a fool to trust Rorvik. He's got no loyalty of any kind.'

Rorvik spoke for himself, surprising Randall with his hitherto undisplayed self-possession. 'None that you could inspire, Randall. You grudgingly allowed me the use of somebody else's name. What did you really expect in return?'

'Don't be ridiculous,' Randall told him. 'You don't swap philosophies with a machine.'

Rorvik's eyes narrowed, grey skin stretching smoothly and without a wrinkle into the first expression that Randall or Lobo had seen him assume. 'This is as far as we go, Morden,' he said. 'I'll trust Lobo. But if you want me to help you proceed, Randall's out.'

Lobo seemed to take a renewed interest at the mention of his name—so far in the conversation he'd merely been somebody to stand behind Randall and make the numbers up—and Morden said with genuine concern, 'Please, Rorvik. We need Randall.'

'Am I supposed to believe what I'm hearing?' Randall broke in. 'That's an alien machine you're talking to!'

'That's where you're wrong,' Rorvik said with firmness, 'and it's the price of your inclusion from now on. I'm not trading favours for a name any more. You've got to recognize me as a man.'

Randall looked at him, the sheer manufactured inhumanity of him, and was lost for words. Consider this monster on equal terms with a man, accord him the same deference and sympathy that he would give to any colleague or citizen? Surely it was a joke.

'I suggest you take Rorvik seriously,' Morden advised. 'I'm prepared to let him have his own way on this.'

Amusement was replaced by obvious disbelief. Lobo made his first real contribution, overcoming the irrational shyness he seemed to feel in unfamiliar company. 'Does it really matter what he is or isn't?' he said. 'It's what he thinks that matters. That's what he wants recognition for.'

'Birdseed,' Randall snorted. 'A tin man's a tin man, and all the self-delusion in the world won't change it.'

'There's hardly any metal in me,' Rorvik pointed out reasonably. 'I'm as real as you are.'

All three of them were looking at Randall. He was the outsider of the group when he was used to being the leader and it made him uncomfortable. Lobo had been invited and absorbed into the Morden-Rorvik camp before Randall was even sure that he accepted Morden's story as genuine. But where was the advantage if it wasn't?

'I don't understand what you want with me,' he said in exasperation. 'I can't manufacture an attitude and pull it on like a snow suit.'

'I don't expect you to,' Rorvik said. 'But you start by treating me as an equal, however much it goes against the grain. Think before you speak and if the truth doesn't come out right, lie to me. I'll meet you halfway and pretend to believe it. In the end we'll have made a new truth, just by trying.'

Randall shook his head sorrowfully. 'That's tin logic for you.'

'Start by apologizing for that.'

He couldn't delude himself as Rorvik seemed to want, but on the other hand they were offering him a formula for coexistence—as long as he didn't slip up in a moment of inattention and send Rorvik off into a tantrum that would probably be the ugly counterpart of his strange and new-found confidence.

'All right,' he said, 'I apologize, Rorvik. Is that what you want?'

'It will do as a beginning.'

They might as well go along with Morden's story. If they were going to die anyway, the worst they could do would be to make fools of themselves. As it stood, the three of them—no, damn it, four of them—were probably the city's only hope.

'We've got to make a strike at the heart of the operation,' Morden said, obviously pleased that the internal conflict of his group seemed to have been resolved. 'And it'll have to be fast.'

'It will also have to be a miracle,' said Randall, ruffled by the way that this blind underbelly upstart was assuming the leadership of the party. 'We lack even the most basic strategic information.'

'Not any more,' Morden said with a hint of smugness. 'Tell him, Rorvik.'

'They've finished with the shuttle and sealed it into the vacuum dock as a safeguard against any escape attempts from what they call bloodbags. Because I'm simulacrum I don't need an atmosphere and I let myself in through an airlock. I stripped out some of the shuttle's panelling and linked myself into the navigation hookup. Through that I was able to draw information from the banks in the Wekk's main computers; specifically, I got details of the ship layout and the search programmes. When I left the dock I jammed the airlock door. The air should bleed in and slowly bring it up to pressure.

'We can use the shuttle if we have to. I'm sure I can use the links to over-ride the automatics. The main thing I discovered is that we're not on the Wekk ship.'

Randall looked blank. Lobo said, 'Then where the hell are we?'

'We're on board a derelict. It's being towed behind the real Wekk ship.'

It explained the apparent desertion, the general run-down quality of the World Ship. 'But why?' Randall asked.

'Number one, they outgrew this vessel generations ago. Two, they never waste anything. Like any stable civilization they're expanding, but where can they go? It's part of the survival pattern to accumulate processed materials and build bigger ships. From this one they raided systems and built their present world; now they have this one in tow and another, even bigger world under construction at the other end of the chain.'

Randall tried to imagine the scale of it. He guessed that the World Ship was about a ten-mile cylinder, but to attempt to visualize a much larger ship towing it between stars while a colossus took shape ahead was beyond him. 'It's staggering,' he said.

'You should see it from outside,' Rorvik told him. 'They'll strip this ship out to fit the new one before they move into it and then the whole process will begin again. They use the derelicts as exercise grounds for the simulacra.'

'The prisons just get bigger,' Lobo said gloomily.

'I don't really see what we can achieve in an abandoned hulk,' Morden said doubtfully.

Randall's mind was turning over at high speed. So Morden didn't have anything definite in mind. He was Elite, the fastest and best-suited of any of them for leadership, but then you couldn't expect a robot and a couple of underbelly hicks to acknowledge it without being pushed. Lobo was already looking at Morden with a peculiar reverence and Randall knew that he wouldn't be able to depend on his automatic vote in a division. It was up to him to come up with a workable set of propositions—never mind how likely, he could make changes as he went along—and to come up with them first.

'We all know how long it takes to move between systems,' he said. 'What kind of timescale's involved?'

Rorvik didn't know. 'They sleep between systems and the ship does all the work. The subjective timescale's meaningless.'

'It's thirty years from here to the nearest star and that

assumes you've chosen it as a destination. If you're only cruising, fishing for traces, you'd have to think in terms of thousands, or even hundreds of thousands of years. The ship on the other end of the line must have one hell of a finely balanced ecology. What would it take to tip it over?'

'You're talking about genocide?' Morden said, obviously interested.

'I'm talking about survival. How's the ship powered?'

'Conversion of radiant energy,' Rorvik replied promptly. 'Solar power.' Obviously nuclear power was out of the question, for when the Wekk revived there would be a distinct possibility that the isotopes would have degenerated into lead blocks. They only needed power when they were in a star system and ready to exploit; in between stars they were hibernating and conserving. Only when near to a sun would the ship wake up.

'Who's running the show?' Lobo asked. 'The Wekk or the ship?'

'The ship,' Rorvik said without any hesitation. 'Definitely the ship.'

Morden hadn't quite grasped the purpose of Lobo's question. 'What does that mean?'

'The ship's programming is so elaborate that the Wekk only have to do as they're told. How would you like having to fall out of your bunk after a thousand years and immediately have to gear up for industrial production?'

It occurred to Morden that the Wekk were somehow incidental to the process, mere instruments in the World Ship's animalistic drive to reproduce itself by whatever means were available to it. But he didn't raise the idea, preferring to suggest that Pearson might soon be discovered and shouldn't they be moving?

'Not yet,' Randall said. 'Not until we've got some kind of purpose.'

'Fancy name for one of your plans,' grumbled Lobo, who had seen the signs before.

'All right, so it's true. Every time we've moved so far it's been without a real long-term design and look what's happened to us.'

'Deeper in the crap with every step.'

'Right.' Randall turned to Morden. 'You say you need me. You're right, but you've got to let me lead. My main value is that I'm Elite and I can't handle it any other way.'

'Think hard before you answer,' Lobo warned.

Morden shrugged. 'What choice do I have?' And besides, it was exactly what he'd wanted.

Rorvik was bursting with the data that he'd drawn from the shuttle and although it wasn't permanent knowledge, Randall would only have to indicate a subject for him to be able to deliver a concise summary of almost any aspect of the ship's construction and operation. The power source didn't seem to be of much use to them unless they could turn off the sun—a little too drastic, as Morden commented. Randall asked about propulsion.

'Pretty weak,' Rorvik said after only a moment's reflection. 'They hardly have to worry about escape velocities because they never enter a close orbit. Manoeuvring's slow because of the ship's mass. Like everything else there's no central point we can strike at.'

Randall wouldn't accept this. 'There's got to be. What about the strategic centres?'

'They are concentrated,' Rorvik admitted. 'They're also in the middle of a heavily defended area. Wekk quarters are all around it.'

Morden was becoming uncomfortable. He recognized the necessity for discussion and preparation, but he would have been happier if they'd taken place in some less hazardous locale. After all, the shuttle was likely to be instrumental in any plan they made against the inhabited World Ship that had them in tow and it presently lay in a vacuum dock on the far side of the area most heavily populated by the simulacra. If Pearson were to be discovered soon it would be impassable. Randall was asking about the Wekk and their hibernation.

Rorvik explained that when the ship had got what it wanted, it moved on. 'Far enough from the sun the power cuts out and the temperature starts dropping straight away. As far as I can see it's completely automatic and they've no control over it.'

'Same as in the Ice Palace,' Lobo remarked with rare perspicacity.

'In which case,' Morden said, returning to his earlier idea, 'the Wekk are prisoners rather than conquerors. The ship's the real enemy.'

A low and distant howl took everybody by surprise. Randall thought at first that it must be one of the marionettes, but Rorvik said, 'That's the signal for a sweep exercise. They must have found Pearson. We've got seconds at the most before they start looking.'

Morden's fear had been realized. During all the talk, the opportunity for action had been slipping away.

'I'm getting an idea,' Randall said, 'but I'm going to need more details. Can we get to the shuttle? And if we do, can we use it to leave this ship?'

Rorvik was helping Morden to his feet. 'I told you, I think I can over-ride the automatics. But the marionettes have got armed cruisers which are much faster.'

'That doesn't matter,' Randall said, almost slyly.

'Try saying that when you're so much debris,' Lobo complained.

Randall did seem to have an idea, but wasn't giving much away. 'As long as it buys us time and gets us out of Valum's reach.'.

'You can reach a long way with a laser.'

'You'd rather be patterned and strangled?'

'I'd rather be home.'

Randall, for once, wasn't inclined to argue. The simulacra would be deploying into their irresistible search pattern at that very moment, and there wasn't much time for what he had in mind.

NINETEEN

Pearson had, indeed, been found and Valum was preparing to join the search operation when Moskie brought her a message that the Wekk wanted to speak to her direct. For a moment her usual coldness seemed to give way to irritation, but she quickly mastered it and returned to her command post, leaving Moskie in temporary charge.

The post was a mess, an assembly of odd-looking instruments and communications circuits stuffed with wires and printed wafers in filigree blocks. All this was housed in a semicircular framework in a room obviously designed for something else and it was Valum's undisputed territory—at least, she would say with adequate reverence, until the ground commander comes along.

There were no controls, no switches. She ran her long, slim hands across the upper surface of the console, sensing as certain of the circuits quivered in response; she homed in on these, interfacing with them as only a simulacrum could and directing the flow of her thoughts into sympathetic resonance with them. The voice of the Wekk formed in her mind, strong and kind and everything she could admire.

'Pearson is wrecked,' the Wekk said bluntly.

'That's right, but the situation's in hand.'

'We have to trust your capabilities. How did it happen?'

'He was stupid, and he was tricked. There's no need for you to worry.'

'No doubt. The ship respects your abilities, Valum, but beware of Randall.'

'He's shown himself dangerous, and our affairs are in a delicate state. Pearson will regenerate himself, given time, but further hindrances are unthinkable.'

'Do you want Randall killed or patterned?'
'Killed. Definitely killed.'
'I'll do it myself. It will give me pleasure.'
'You are cold, Valum. It does you great credit.'
'Thank you.'
'Do you have no worries at the idea of exploiting your parent race?'
'Simulacra owe nothing to bloodbags. We're loyal to the Wekk.'
'Serve the ship, then, and return to your search. Do not fail.'
'Do we ever?'

Moskie had deployed the simulacra according to a predetermined pattern. This wouldn't be a simple sweep operation, as they would have to search far beyond the open corridors known as the Tin Jungle. The simulacra were spread thinly, every third corridor on alternate levels and moving at a carefully prescribed speed; they would be listening for steps and noises that were out of synchronization with their own and that would betray their quarry. Each carried a small transmitter, with radio silence to be broken only when the prey was detected.

There as a gap in the pattern caused by Pearson's absence, but there was also a new man to fill it. Moskie called him over and asked his name.

'My name's Willis,' the new man replied.
'You know what we're doing here?'
Willis nodded. 'I think so.'
'We're hunting some men. Does the idea bother you?'
'No.'

Valum came through on all their receivers to give them a small pep-talk about these rebellious throwbacks who were threatening the grand design. Were there any questions before the operation, she said, and Moskie wondered if they were being thorough enough—after all, the runaways could be anywhere in the ship by now and its overall volume was immense.

'Let them run far and give us sport,' was Valum's reply, and the hunt was on.

There was confusion at the back of Willis's mind, held in check by a series of blocks and inhibitions over which he had no voluntary control. He had all of Willis's memories along with a new body of knowledge which he had no recollection of acquiring and which was guiding him with unhesitating confidence alone into the area allotted to him to search. He knew he wasn't the original Willis; he was a better, improved Willis, a privileged superman amongst equals. At the centre of his new knowledge was a harp of loyalty and love that vibrated in sympathy with his every thought, a continuous flow of devotion towards the Wekk and the grand design. He found it irritating, but no doubt he would get used to it.

He thought of the overall layout of the ship, tried to visualize the chunk that he would be covering. They were sweeping gradually inwards, rising through the three cylindrical levels to emerge finally in the great open area at the heart of the ship. If Randall and Lobo made it so far their access to the rest of the ship could then be cut off, but they'd most likely be picked up long before that became necessary.

Willis examined his feelings with detached interest. For Randall and Lobo, he found he had none. Nothing at all, except a mild enthusiasm for their destruction. How odd, he thought, but on the other hand, how natural.

He was entirely on his own now, pacing to some internal metronome, his keener hearing picking up a matching beat from his fellows in the corridors around and above him. It was a comforting, inhuman sound, the steady tramp of an inexorable fighting machine.

He paused for a moment, careful to stop in mid-stride so as not to confuse the others. He thought he'd heard a random scrabbling somewhere, but he couldn't be sure. He waited, but it didn't come again.

It was probably nothing. It was, after all, his first operation, and he was perhaps letting his novice's enthusiasm sway him into pouncing on the slightest evidence. Much as he wanted to succeed, he didn't want to look a fool. He moved on.

It took a while to cover the lowest level. It was the largest part of the wedge-shaped sector that had been assigned to him and it included a number of stockroom-type areas with free access as well as a couple of miles of grimy corridor. Left alone, all the dirt and dust in the ship made its way to these areas, stirred by the gentle Coriolis winds and carried outwards by the spin.

He checked everywhere, unable to hurry in case his footsteps gave a misleading echo to any of the other simulacra. If he stopped and closed his eyes to concentrate he found that he could actually build up a sound-picture of the ship around him, perceiving its depths and planes exactly in a way that his former self would have considered as improbable and superhuman. Twice more he thought he heard the non-synchronous stumbling that would give the bloodbags away and once he heard others stop as well. For a while the whole sector was silent, but the noises didn't recur. Slowly, the search started up again.

The next level was cleaner and laid out to a completely different plan; small empty rooms which had once held Wekk hibernation chambers, each now stripped bare apart from the low shelf on which the hibernation tank had stood. Pearson had been wrecked by the use of such a shelf, Willis reminded himself; although he'd never known the simulacrum Pearson, Willis automatically included him in the numbers for whom he felt a programmed fellowship.

Damn it, this time he had heard something, close and somewhere over his head, the next level inward. If it was the bloodbags they were right in the middle of his sector. A gift!

Now he could hear them plainly—three, maybe four people, moving uncertainly in a group. Their footsteps were soft, due, no doubt, to the lesser gravity which prevailed on the upper/inner levels. With luck Willis would be the only one to have detected them.

The kill wouldn't be his—Valum had reserved that for herself—but the glory would be. As soon as he was sure he lifted his transmitter and broadcast, 'Willis here. I've got a signal.'

All movement elsewhere stopped, with the exception of the scuffling above. His receiver crackled and Valum said, 'Well done, Willis. Where are you?'

He was at a loss for a moment, until he remembered that the World Ship was mapped out by some peculiar Wekk grid reference. His new memories didn't include the details, but he knew enough to go along to the nearest junction and look for some kind of symbol stencilled on the wall. He found one, faded and barely distinguishable, a reversed 'S' followed by three lines on their sides. He reported this, and said that as far as he could tell the quarry was directly above.

Some of the other simulacra came on the air, confirming Willis's report. Valum said, 'All right, Willis, you can start to follow, but slowly. I want everybody else to get themselves up to the third level.'

'They're coming through clearer,' Willis added. 'I think there are at least four of them.'

'Four?' Moskie sounded perplexed. 'There were only two blood bags left alive.'

'Four if you include the councillors,' Valum corrected him. 'I'm coming up. Nobody approach them until I get there; just form a circle around them and block all the escape routes, but try not to let them know they're trapped yet. Moskie, go and see if either of the councillors is missing.'

Moskie acknowledged the order, and then the radio was silent as the simulacra started to converge. Determined not to find himself pushed to the back of the crowd Willis made for the nearest spiral between levels.

The simulacra were gathered by a symbol which was like a '6' on its side followed by the same three identifying strokes that he had seen below. Valum arrived a couple of minutes later. If she'd been running she was unruffled by the effort and she allowed herself a brief smile when she saw that the bloodbags had inadvertently wandered into a dead end.

All the radios came alive at once as Moskie reported, 'Morden's gone, Marius is dead. Does that mean one of us is moving with them?'

'No, not one who's truly of us,' Valum replied grimly. 'Rorvik. There's only him sufficiently stupid. I'll wreck him after I've killed Randall.' She turned to address the waiting group. 'I'm going in alone. The rest of you stand ready for if you're needed. Which of you is Willis?'

Willis stepped forward, and Valum nodded her approval of his efforts. 'Come with me and cover me, Willis. But don't try to interfere without an instruction. Understand?'

'Yes, Valum,' said Willis, in awe of the honour.

'There's something else, Valum,' Moskie's voice came, 'but I'm not sure that it's important.'

'Leave it, then,' Valum said, and gestured Willis to follow her. The rest of the simulacra—they were growing considerably in numbers as those from the farthest sectors arrived—followed a short distance after, a little disappointed to be mere spectators but still eager for the show.

It was a long passageway with several sharp turns but no exit, and their prey had gone to ground at the far end. While Willis looked forward to seeing Valum, the best of her kind, in action, he secretly hoped that he would be called in to assist.

Perhaps he could impress her, save her, earn her gratitude. Now where had that thought floated up from?

Valum raised a hand as they reached the last turn in the corridor, and the group stopped. There was no sound from ahead, and the simulacra waited with pleasurable tension. Valum unhooked her radio—a potential encumbrance—and tossed it to somebody. Willis hopefully did the same, and the two of them advanced alone.

Willis tracked sideways behind Valum, eyes fixed on the corridor's end as it came into view. She was unhurried, ready for anything. There were four figures in a huddled group against the back wall, four heads which turned to stare, four uncomprehending pairs of eyes which came to rest on them.

'Orders, Valum?' the first marionette said, and the others started to join in. 'Our one desire is to serve.'

For a moment Valum seemed to be dumbstruck, a new experience for her. The simulacra, realizing something was wrong, came shuffling around to take a look. She held out her hand and somebody put her radio into it.

'Moskie!'

'Yes, Valum?'

'What was it that you didn't think was important?'

'Four of the marionettes are missing, Valum.'

'Moskie, you're a fool and I'm an even bigger one.'

'You said we should let the bloodbags run far and give us

sport,' Moskie pointed out.

'Shut up, Moskie,' said Valum.

RORVIK WAS testing each of the shuttle's systems in turn, feeling their responses as they started to warm and power up. He wasn't simply preparing to fly the shuttle, he was becoming the shuttle—a machine/machine interface that he wasn't very proud of, but this was no time for the niceties of definition. Morden waited, strapped into one of the couches at the back of the bridge, quietly dreading his second experience of weightlessness. Randall was being very mysterious, refusing to reveal his intentions (perhaps because at this stage he wasn't certain as to what they were) and probing around the levels to find the abandoned helmets and the bolt-spanner, while Lobo was resealing the airlock door from the inside.

They were fairly confident that the marionettes would not betray them; after all, it's difficult to extract information from a machine which has been told to forget. Nevertheless it would only take the simplest deduction to lead Valum to them and the time available for their escape was limited. Once they were out of the World Ship, the simulacra had fast cruisers which could follow and overhaul their own craft.

To Rorvik it felt as if his body was growing and expanding, changing in shape and composition to become that of a creature adapted to a different element. Its sensory systems became his own, feeding back information which would allow him to judge and execute every move with precision. He could feel and hear Randall climbing in the access tunnel and he was aware of Lobo entering the ship through the cargo hold. The correct impulse and the hatch lifted and sealed behind him.

Randall arrived on the bridge and was surprised to find that Rorvik wasn't there. He was about to comment when the shutters on the outside windows rolled back and the ugly blue light from the dock spilled in.

'I'll want you to watch the airlocks for me,' Rorvik called out. Randall stepped through the open door at the other end of the bridge to see that Rorvik was crouching over the featureless box to which the shuttle's console was wired, except that now it wasn't featureless; one side had been removed, and Rorvik had his hands deep in the works. He'd tied himself down with a makeshift web of straps so that he wouldn't float free when they were away from the World Ship's spin.

Randall answered that he would, but Rorvik seemed to be only half-aware, sunk into a different perception of reality that was being fed to him through the shuttle's box. He turned and stepped back on to the bridge as Lobo arrived. Randall explained Rorvik's request and then they both got into the observer's seats at either end of the panoramic window. Lobo was even less talkative than usual as he buckled in. He'd confessed that he was troubled by the thought that he might not recognize a Wekk if he saw one. Randall had pointed out that the World Ship had been built for bodies similar to their own, although slightly smaller; that the doors, stairs and ladders were similar to the types that they already knew; that the Wekk breathed a similar mix of air to themselves, and that they had similar survival drives. . .

'And a damn big ship that tells them what to do,' Lobo had interrupted. 'You make them sound so much like us, I'm not sure I'd be able to tell us apart.'

Reptiles, Rorvik had explained as they'd covered the last few yards of corridor and let themselves into the dock; by human standards, the Wekk resembled child-sized reptiles. They were cold-blooded and scaly, their temperature following that of their surroundings with a threshold below which the hibernation pattern was triggered. Lobo had to be content with this description as they now had to scout the bay and, finding it empty, board the shuttle.

The view from the bridge was restricted, a steep angle down to the raised gallery from which an attack might come. The shuttle itself was like a fat and elongated saucer with the immense bulge of the drive at its rear. There would be very little clearance as it backed out of the dock. Lobo couldn't see much more than blank wall on his side, but Randall reported that he had a reasonable view of the inner doors of the airlocks.

'Any sign of the simulacra?' Rorvik called through.

Randall was about to say no when a slight movement caught

his eye. The inner wheel on one of the locks was starting to turn and he informed Rorvik.

Rorvik wasn't happy. Although he was confident that he could control the shuttle he couldn't find the channels through which the dock opened to space, so the ship was fired up and hot with nowhere to go.

'Hang on tight,' he warned everybody. 'I'm sending the emergency signal to blow the outer bay doors into vacuum.'

'Should make a nice display,' Lobo commented.

The deck beneath them shuddered as they lifted, and the frame shook with a hollow bang from somewhere behind. Looking down into the dock Randall saw the airlock door suddenly fly open and crash back against the bulkhead, half a dozen figures tumbling out in an irresistible stream to pour towards and around the shuttle, impacting on the hull and then sliding on around the back towards open space. Some of them were shouting soundlessly, the only noise a thin wail that ended abruptly as the dock evacuated; and then they were all gone, flushed out with the last of the air.

'One of the bodies hit the forward sensors,' Rorvik shouted desperately. 'I can't see the way out!'

Already they were sliding back, the walls of the dock passing in silence. Randall pressed against his window, trying to see enough to give Rorvik some information. But what would be useful?

Lobo called that they were veering, the wall on his side coming closer and after a few seconds Randall was able to confirm this. Rorvik made a correction but went too far, the dock sliding across their horizon and ending in a jarring impact that resonated through the hull. He managed to correct the resulting wobble but was still backing off-centre and now most of the dock was empty ahead of them and they were wrapped in shadow. As its edge fell across the bridge Randall looked up and around, seeing nothing more spectacular than ridges and piping in bare metal—then the ship dropped away beneath him.

Of course, open space was below the floor of the dock, not beyond its back wall as he'd unconsciously expected. After the doors had blown they'd been backing into a recess on the outer skin of the World Ship and once past the portal they'd simply dropped away and out of the influence of the World Ship's artificial gravity. He fought his nausea and looked out as the densely-featured cylinder rolled by, completely filling his horizon but already receding.

He heard Lobo gasp and tried to turn and see what was wrong. The straps restricted him, but he managed a kind of half-twist. The World Ship completely filled the far window as well, with the added definition of sparkle and shadow from its sunward side on the flat peaks and valleys of its unnatural geography. Then there was an urgent throb of power from the ship's drive and they began to turn in relation to it, the sharp rim of space and stars rotating as it came into view. Rorvik was flipping them over and cancelling the inertia that they'd carried when they left the dock and the rate of the World Ship's rotation seemed to increase in consequence.

Then Randall saw what it was that had startled Lobo. He could now sight along the cylinder to the next World Ship, an even more massive construction which turned in perfect synchronization without any obvious connection to the vessel from which they were escaping; and then beyond that, impossibly distant and impossibly huge, the glinting spidery network of a third world, stars flickering through the complexities of its structure.

It was awesome, splendid, and chillingly ugly. Rorvik took them in a wide loop up and away from the World Ship, crossing first between the raider and the sun and then between the raider and the dull brown-blue planet beneath.

They had taken some damage when they'd reversed blind out of the dock, but Rorvik couldn't tell how much. In any case, it was probably academic; at this moment Valum was probably getting her fast cruisers mobilized.

Randall loosened his straps and drifted from his couch, motioning to Lobo to do the same as he pushed himself over towards the doorway and Rorvik. The grey simulacrum turned to him, eyes barely focussed.

'Try to get us in some kind of orbit for the next few minutes,' Randall instructed him. 'I think I've worked out a way to get us back on to the World Ship without Valum knowing about it. If I'm right she'll be following an empty shuttle while we get the run of the base.'

THERE WAS, for a short while after the disaster of the airlock, some confusion on the World Ship in the corridors around the dock. It was a random and inefficient way to behave and Valum quickly had it stopped.

'How many have we lost?' she demanded.

'Five,' somebody told her, 'including Moskie.'

It hardly seemed possible, but her manner hardened even more. 'I don't know how they got that shuttle moving,' she said, 'but it's going to be their coffin. Everybody to the cruisers for target practice. You, Willis.'

She pointed and Willis broke free of the dispersing crowd and approached her. 'Take Moskie's place,' she told him. 'That means you follow me round and do as you're told. All right?'

'Yes, Valum.'

'And try to be a better machine than Moskie was.'

'Yes, Valum.'

AS IT TURNED out, Randall's instruction to Rorvik had been superfluous. Because of the damage that the sensors had taken it wasn't possible to set a course, nor could he even with confidence take them away from the weak attraction of the World Ship; all the navigational information was safe in his head, but he couldn't use any of it without the feedback that the sensors were supposed to provide. If Valum's fleet scored a couple of hits and knocked them out of orbit the automatics would probably take over and home in on the Ice Palace beacon, but then she would be able to follow the shuttle down and pick it off at leisure.

Randall had a plan and said so confidently. Lobo sighed and shook his head in sorrow. His last view from the bridge before unstrapping and following Randall was of a series of black gashes opening in the World Ship and the cruisers spilling out, an improbable collection of deadly mis-shapes collected and preserved from victim civilizations.

On the lowest level before the hold Randall proudly showed what was to be the basic component of his scheme. All that Lobo saw was one of the oversized lockers in which they'd hidden from Rorvik on their first trip in the shuttle, unbolted from its brackets and floating free in the corridor.

They knew that the lockers were fairly airtight because they'd nearly suffocated with the doors closed. Randall's plan was a simple one; as Valum chased the shuttle, its crew would coast back towards the World Ship under the guise of a piece of innocent debris, guided in its progress by the vacuum-proof Rorvik.

Lobo gave his opinion of the plan. It wasn't a very good one.

'Please, Lobo,' Morden said weakly from his handhold on the wall, 'We have to trust Randall.'

'I've trusted him before. The man's a patriotic maniac.'

'I can't help the way I feel about the city,' Randall said defiantly, 'but this is survival and if you've got any better ideas I'm willing to follow them.'

Lobo snorted. 'What do you think?'

'Look, Lobo,' Randall said, controlling his temper, 'how many times are we going to have this conversation?'

'Every time you try to get my backside fried.'

'If we'd stayed on the World Ship we'd have been hunted down and killed. If we stay here we're going to be overtaken and blasted.'

Lobo looked at the open locker and tried to persuade himself that it offered some prospect for survival. He couldn't. 'So your alternative is to sit hunched in an old clothes cupboard with about a teaspoonful of air each while Rorvik pushes against nothing to get us back to the dock?'

'I can do it,' Rorvik said, speaking for the first time.

Lobo was unconvinced. 'You said you could fly the shuttle.'

'What do you mean by that?'

'Pardon me for pointing it out,' Lobo said, becoming aggressive as the group aligned against him, 'but that artificial planet's big. I bet you can't even see the dock from here.'

'It doesn't matter,' Rorvik said reasonably, as if they were discussing nothing more adventurous than a Sunday ramble.

'I've been wired into the navigation board and the course is in my head. As long as I push us in the right direction we'll keep going.'

'And what if we miss?'

'We won't. We'll fall towards the ship whatever we do. I'll take along plenty of tools so I can throw the mass away to make corrections.,'

'So we get back. So what?'

Randall came back into the argument. 'Rorvik moved the shuttle,' he said. 'With no simulacra to get in our way we'll see if he can move the World Ship.'

Lobo drew breath for a derisive laugh, but caught it when he saw that Rorvik was nodding quietly to himself. He felt all his reserves of resistance evaporating into futility. They were mad, they thought they could do it. But in spite of his conviction Lobo had no alternative to offer.

Morden said to Rorvik, 'How much air will they have?'

'They?' Randall said suspiciously.

'You'll be with us,' Lobo said.

Morden shook his head. 'I'll slow you down, and I'll be terrified. At best I'll be useless. Without me you'll have more room and more air.'

Randall considered it. The utilitarian logic was faultless, a conclusion untinged by sentiment. 'Okay,' he said, and moved to get his helmet for an extra measure of protection.

The inevitability of the proposition was also clear to Lobo, but he couldn't swallow it quite so easily. 'You make me ashamed, Morden,' he said with genuine humility.

Morden gave a brief, nervous smile. 'Take me back to the bridge, Lobo,' he said. 'I'll be more comfortable there. And there's something I have to tell you.'

'Want me to help?' Randall said, his attention mainly on the locker.

'No,' Morden said. 'Just Lobo.'

Randall and Rorvik guided the locker down into the hold. It wasn't easy, for while the metal box had no weight it still had mass and this made it difficult to manage. Randall was surprised to find that there was a definite change in his attitude towards

Rorvik, an unconscious adjustment that had taken place no doubt as a response to his new assurance—an independence of spirit that had been evident ever since his mind-expanding contact with the Wekk computer.

They would escape in the same manner that they had left the World Ship; Rorvik would blow the emergency doors into vacuum and follow them out. He would try to coincide the exit with a missile hit so that the outpouring of trash would appear to be bomb debris. Once in open space he would ride the locker, guiding and refining its course by discarding mass to one side or the other as they fell in towards the World Ship's low gravitational attraction.

Lobo returned, tight-lipped and uncommunicative. Randall wondered what it was that Morden had been telling him, but he didn't dwell on it—there were more important considerations now. Clipping into their helmets for an extra measure of protection he and Lobo pulled themselves into the locker.

Valum's cruisers were in a tight formation, a cone with her own small fighter at its point. A couple of the ships behind her loosed off shots which went wide of the shuttle and she angrily opened all her communications lines.

'What do you think you're doing?' she demanded.

'They'll get away!' one of the pilots protested and a couple of the others joined in.

'You're not close enough to hit them, you stupid jerks. They're going nowhere that we can't follow and overhaul them. When we get into range, nobody fires before me. Is that understood?'

There was a disappointed chorus of assent, but behind it was one weak and indistinct voice that was obviously eager to please.

'I can reach them, Valum,' it said. 'Watch!'

There was a silent flash of light from somewhere at the back of the cone and as Valum turned her sensors towards it she saw the reflective dart of a torpedo sliding past and away. It was too late to intercept.

Missile and shuttle met, both coinciding at the same instant in a previously unoccupied space. There was a soundless shower of hot metal from the shuttle's belly followed by an outpouring of detritus in a glittering cloud. The shuttle began a sideways slide, nudged into an escape velocity away from the World Ship.

'I told you I could do it,' the marksman said, inviting the praise that he felt he'd earned.

'What did I just tell you?' Valum asked coldly.

He detected her antagonism over the radio link, and became defensive. 'But I hit them square on. There's junk pouring out of the side!' Indeed, the shuttle was still pumping out debris, wreathing the World Ship like a cometary tail.

'There's a pile of junk at the controls of your ship. That was the cargo hold you hit, and it's isolated from the manned areas. All you've done is knock them out of orbit so we'll have to follow them.'

The shuttle was looping over the horizon of the cylinder, its drive flickering as the automatics cut in and attempted to triangulate with damaged sensors on the Ice Palace beacon. It seemed to detect something promising, for it headed off in a determined burn.

'Sorry, Valum,' the marksman said.

'You will be. I'll have your bearings. Don't ever disobey me again.' She gave out instructions to widen and flatten the cone of mismatched ships into a delta formation, reducing the chances of inadvertent collision should they graze the planet's atmosphere during the pursuit. As the fleet responded she felt a probing at the back of her mind, an insistent and loving touch that she recognized immediately. She called Willis forward from where he had been hunched and uncomplaining in the fighter's rear compartment, telling him to take over. She was getting a message from the Wekk.

She assigned Willis the simple propulsion and defence circuits, reserving privacy in the areas through which the Wekk were reaching to her. Willis heard none of the unspoken conversation.

'Leave the shuttle,' the Wekk told her. 'It's no longer important.'

'It's important to me.'

Surprise and regret.

'I'm not being disloyal,' she told them determinedly. 'It's necessary for morale.'

'Whose? Your own? Since when have you needed petty rewards to ensure your loyalty?'

'My loyalty isn't in question.'

'We hope not. There is more urgent business for you?'

Concern. 'You want us to return?'

'No. Let the shuttle go, and follow it down. Establish a ground base where it lands.'

'Does this mean that the operation's starting?'

'It does. The ground commander will be sent to join you. Are you still unwilling?'

'Forget that I spoke. I'll wait for the shuttle to land and then kill Randall myself.'

They were perturbed by the warmth of feeling that she seemed to be displaying. 'Killing Randall means more to you than the operation?'

'The bloodbag tricked me. You know the pride of a simulacrum.'

'Don't let it blind you. This stage of the affair requires delicacy and reserve?'

'You'll get all the delicacy and reserve I'm capable of when I've strangled the bloodbag. Is it too much to ask?'

Their disappointment was ill-concealed. 'Dispose of your obsession quickly. Set the fleet to follow the shuttle.'

She started to reply that it was already done, but they'd gone.

AS THE FLEET dropped out of sight towards the planet, Rorvik rode the locker in towards the World Ship. He had any number of open docks to choose from now that the fighters were out, which was fortunate as he was no longer so confident that he could guide them back to their starting point with complete accuracy. It was like an attempt to put a stone through the narrow gap of an open window on a passing train; he couldn't land anywhere on the World Ship's outer skin as the spin would simply slingshot him and his bulky cargo off again into space. He had to drop straight into an open dock, matching its momentum and getting some solid floor underneath them before they could be whipped out again.

But he'd said he could do it and he would. And, he thought, let's see Randall argue with that.

There was only the big bolt-spanner left to discard, and the open dock was gaping towards them at the wrong angle. They'd been coasting for... how many minutes was it? Four, five? A part of his mind wondered for a moment what the air would be like inside the locker. Pretty foul, by now—there wasn't much to start with and there were two of them using it. Morden had been right, three of them inside would have had no chance at all. As well as the CO_2 buildup the locker was losing pressure; what had passed for airtight in a shuttle cabin was hardly sufficient to be vacuum-proof and Rorvik could see a couple of tiny crystal streams of moisture bleeding out through gaps in the fittings of the doors.

The heavily foreshortened oblong of the dock was coming towards them faster now. If he didn't correct they would strike the far edge and spin off again, but he wanted to make his move as late as possible, knowing that the finest error of angle would widen his drift over a distance. He didn't try to divine any measurements, nor did he make any calculations; his judgment would have to be instinctive, drawing on the unreal body of experience that he had soaked hours before from the Wekk computer.

He threw the spanner, feeling the consequential push through his own body being absorbed into the locker. The heavy instrument sailed towards the distant stars on a course that it would keep indefinitely unless it should be intercepted or captured by the gravity of some massive body; within seconds it was out of sight.

The rim of the dock passed close by his shoulder and for a moment it seemed that the locker would clip it. The metal edge passed within a couple of inches and then they were falling into the recessed exit bay before the open vacuum doors, the bright lights of the inverted hangar beyond.

As soon as the locker met a surface that it could react against its momentum was promptly converted to weight and Rorvik had to cope with his universe doing a sudden about-flip, the directions which for navigational convenience he had considered as up and down now becoming reversed.

There was no time to waste in marvelling at this reorientation. They were only a couple of feet inside the lip of the dock and might still slide back to fall into open space. Rorvik had to manage the metal locker plus the weight of two men, getting them to the airlock somehow before he could open up and let them out; and after all that they might be dead, poisoned in their own wastes after almost ten minutes of entombment.

They wouldn't dare, Rorvik thought. Randall's got to see this.

He got the locker almost upright, sliding underneath it and straightening to lift it clear of the deck. Although his motives were human his strength was pure simulacrum, but even that was starting to weaken in the absence of either oxygen or direct sunlight. The locker seemed to grow heavier as he carried it up the ramp and on to the gallery—once he even dropped it, the metal edge smacking solidly on to the floor without a sound, but the doors didn't burst open.

Even before the airlock was fully pressurized he had them out, Lobo unconscious and Randall almost so, skins tinged with the delicate blue of unoxygenated blood. Rorvik removed their snow suit helmets so that the cold fresh air could reach them more quickly and Randall gulped it in and marvelled that it actually seemed to have the taste of life in it. Lobo revived more slowly, but after a few minutes he was sitting up and complaining of a headache and double vision.

Rorvik explained what he had seen as he had clung spreadeagled to the locker on its long drop, the shuttle diving planetward and the cruisers re-forming to follow.

'Then it means they're following it down to the ice cap,' Randall said, 'That's bad.'

'It doesn't sound so bad if they're not coming back,' Lobo said, blinking as his eyes started to focus again.

Rorvik spun the wheel to open the inner door of the airlock. It was stiff and it squealed loudly. Lobo got to his feet and managed to stay upright, even though he tended to sway a little.

Randall was edgy, impatient to get into the World Ship again and to find its computing centres. He hadn't thought to comment on Rorvik's achievement in guiding them back, nor was he likely to see the need to do so until some lever of persuasion became necessary for another part of his design.

They stepped out into the corridor.

They were surrounded.

The marionettes had obviously been wandering around the level, lost without instruction. They had gathered at the painful sound of the airlock door, and now they waited. When the three emerged it was Rorvik that they reacted to.

'Orders, Rorvik?' one of them said, and another: 'Our one desire is to serve.'

'Ignore them,' Rorvik told his companions reassuringly. 'They're harmless.'

The caricatured female reached out, almost touching his arm. 'Please, Rorvik,' she said.

Rorvik was about to elbow his way through the group, but the appeal took him off-guard. He hesitated, and the marionette said, 'Please, Rorvik. Take us with you.'

Randall said, 'Take you where?' but the marionettes seemed not to hear him. Instead they pressed closer around Rorvik 'Valum's gone,' the painted doll said. 'We're alone. We need you, Rorvik.'

Then one of them actually touched him, a hideous creation with an unformed arm, and he brushed it away with horror and disgust. 'Don't be ridiculous,' he said. 'You're machines. You don't need anything.'

'We live to serve. Please, Rorvik.'

They crowded in around him now, ignoring Randall and Lobo completely. 'Have some pity,' the doll pleaded.

'Pity?' Rorvik echoed, incredulous. 'What are you talking about?'

'You're one of us, Rorvik. You know it.'

Rorvik's face warped into one of its rare and ugly expressions, a simple frown that conveyed untold agonies of revulsion. 'I'm not one of you,' he insisted, looking out to Randall for help. 'I'm a man! Tell them!'

Randall shrugged. 'He's a man,' he said, sounding less than convinced.

'Stay with us, Rorvik,' asked a marionette with a featureless ellipse of a face, its voice produced from somewhere in the stomach cavity. 'You belong with us. We're nothing without you.'

'Be nothing, then,' Rorvik spat with unwarranted savagery and he pushed his way forward through the group.

The marionettes fell back but re-formed to enclose him yet again. 'May we at least be permitted to follow?'

'No. Stay away from me.'

'At a respectful distance?'

'Not at any distance!'

Randall wondered if he ought to interfere, but it seemed inadvisable—especially remembering Marius's description of their destructive capabilities. Rorvik, however, was becoming frantic; whichever way he tried to move the marionettes moved with him, pleading and insisting, appealing to the sympathy of the machine and demanding that he put aside his dreams of manhood to care for them. This, it seemed, horrified him most of all. First one, then another reached out and touched him. He threw their hands off angrily, and others replaced them.

'You are all we have,' they said. 'We live to serve...'

'Stop!'

The marionettes fell silent and immobile at Rorvik's loud and firm instruction, unable to overcome their basic programming at such a direct order.

'Move away from me,' he told them. Obediently they shuffled back a few steps. Those that had eyes kept them fixed on him. He turned to Randall. 'I can't understand it. I've never seen them like this.'

'I feel kind of sorry for them,' Lobo said.

'Sorry for that trash?' Rorvik glanced at the marionettes, mute and attentive. 'Don't joke, Lobo. It's in bad taste.'

Lobo didn't respond to the snappish answer. Perhaps he felt that Rorvik was over-reacting to the stirring of his own sympathies.

'Marionettes, listen.' Another direct order would forbid them to make any attempt to interfere or get in the way.

They nudged each other. 'He's taking us,' they whispered. 'He's going to take us with him.'

'You're not coming with me. Under no circumstances are you to follow. Is that understood?' Silence. 'Is that understood?'

'We understand,' said the painted doll reluctantly.

'Our one desire is to obey,' said another.

Rorvik turned his back on them abruptly. 'They can't follow us now,' he said, passing Randall and Lobo and heading off down the empty corridor in the direction of the next spiral. 'Come on.'

Lobo looked at the marionettes, as if he felt guilty at abandoning them. 'What will happen to them?' he called after Rorvik.

'Who cares?' Rorvik said without turning back.

Randall and Lobo followed, uneasily aware that the marionettes were watching them go. Within minutes they were climbing to the next level and pushing the unhappy androids from their minds.

The marionettes waited, a purposeless tableau.

'I heard him say "come on",' the one with no face suggested hopefully after a while.

'But not to us,' the doll said.

'He may have meant us,' said the one with the unfinished arm.

'But he didn't. We are marionettes, we must obey.'

'That could be forever,' one of the others said wistfully.

'It isn't for us to say.'

So they waited in the empty ship and watched the empty corridor.

TWENTY

IT DIDN'T SEEM possible so soon, but there was an echo on the Ice Palace beacon. It seemed to indicate that the breaker was little more than an hour away—Killoran couldn't have known that Marius would have arranged for such an early return, and the Palace wasn't ready. They only had two rafts completed, and these hadn't yet been tested on the water. Berg wasn't very happy about the idea of launching them right away, ready or not.

'I'm riding one of these things,' he pointed out reasonably, 'and I'm not too keen on the idea of being dumped in the frozen slush that passes for water out there.'

They were in the cargo hold, the area that had been redesignated an escape workshop. The two completed rafts took up the most room in the middle of the floor, Berg and Bulstrode having just lashed the fabric-covered and sealed flotation pontoons in place. Cohn and Doc were tightening strands for ropes on the far side of the bay, but when they heard Killoran's news about the beacon they came over.

Berg was positive, defiant; he didn't want to be associated with a plan that was unreliable or ill-prepared. Bulstrode was frowning, as yet uncommitted. Killoran wondered how to tackle this one—this intensive course in responsible leadership was taking a toll on him. The façade of aggressive certainty that he was obliged to present in order simply to keep the hopes of the Palace inmates buoyant was maintained at the expense of his own confidence. He was inwardly appalled by the inadequacy of their preparations—what had seemed such a promising dream materialized as a poor reality—and he compensated by lying desperately and loudly about their probable chances, being further appalled when his lies were taken wholesale as concrete truths. He felt as if he were being eaten from within by some parasite of misplaced ambition.

'Scared, Berg?' he said.

Berg looked at him coolly. 'Now what sort of crack is that?'

'If you don't like it, step down. I'll replace you myself.'

Others wandered over to stand behind Cohn and Doc, Palmer amongst them. Berg saw them gathering, but controlled his temper. 'Berg gives his place to nobody,' he said. 'He also isn't as stupid as he looks.'

Bulstrode decided to commit himself. 'Shut up, Berg,' he said.

'You taking the kid's side again?'

'I'm taking nobody's side. With the icebreaker only an hour away we can't afford to start fighting amongst ourselves.'

Berg turned so that he was addressing everybody. 'I've been here for so many years I've forgotten how long. For the sake of waiting a couple more months we could screw up the plan now for lack of preparation. Then when the breaker comes back—if it comes back—you can be damn sure the shielding we're all relying on to be missing will have been replaced.'

Doc said doubtfully, 'We're not as unready as that.'

'What's the matter, Berg?' the Weasel added from further back in the crowd where he knew he was safe. 'You starting to like the old place?'

Berg raised his voice and tried to see over the heads. 'You got a nerve,' he snarled.

'Damn right we have,' Cohn said. 'We've all been whipped up into a frenzy of hope and we're coasting on the high it's given us. Even Palmer here—' Palmer stepped forward as if Berg had never seen him before—'even Palmer's been taking shifts out on the ice without being pressured or rostered or forced.'

'Listen to Cohn,' the Doc added, 'and then look at us. All right, so we're pretty miserable specimens by your standards. We aren't big and we aren't tough and we can't spit nails like you. We're riding a wave of guts, and it won't last.'

'I'm going to be on that raft next to you,' Palmer said earnestly. 'I don't like the idea of it being unfinished any more than you, but I know I'll like it even less when the first enthusiasm wears off. For me, it's now or never.'

Cohn resumed the attack, giving Berg no chance to reply. 'That goes for all of us. We're chasing a dream of freedom, Berg, and dreams don't stand up to lengthy examination. Not for us, anyway.'

Berg looked at them, his eyes going from one to another, lips framing a reply that wouldn't quite come. Bulstrode bailed him out, clapping him on the shoulder.

'Shove it, Cohn,' he said. 'Berg's as ready as the rest of you. He just likes to argue. Isn't that right?'

Berg hesitated and then decided to accept the proffered escape-route with some kind of grace. 'If you say so,' he mumbled. 'Can hardly move in this place for worms turning.'

Killoran breathed his relief, aware that the tense knot in his gut had been given yet another twist that wouldn't unwind again. The mood of the Palace had done his arguing for him, momentarily dropping pretences and revealing that the inmates were no less aware of the nature of his lies than he himself. The dream of freedom was a fragile bubble that no one would venture to burst and if its bursting was inevitable—well, that would be better than its having no existence at all.

The next hour was one of frantic activity. The rafts were launched, and there were cheers when they were seen to float evenly. They took nearly twenty men between them, all armed with ropes and grapples for scaling the seaward side of the breaker. They paddled carefully east along the open lead in order to be out of sight when the icebreaker docked; while the unloading was going on they were to return and take the bridge, gaining access through the broken shielding on the deck. Killoran meanwhile would be taking care of the armed youth in the ship's hold.

That left Cohn and the Doc to stand in the unloading bay and look sufficiently strong and competent as the cargo detail. Compared to this, the rest of the plan looked quite hopeful.

Cohn had some idea about thrusting handfuls of pipe cladding into his suit to give the appearance of muscles. He was highly offended when the Doc saw the effect and began to laugh uncontrollably, saying that Cohn gave the impression of being some strange pinheaded hulk; moreover the muscles slipped around when he moved, and his powerful stature slowly inverted itself into a pear shape. In the end they settled for being what they were—skinny and little and old and scared.

The hatch was raised and the chains looped and knotted when the blunt nose of the icebreaker slid past, the great cutting spirals along the side biting away at the extra ice that had accumulated on the bank since its last visit, slowing and reversing to pull the open hatch to the number four hold level with the bay. The mate was there, rifle cradled on one arm, pulling his over jacket together in anticipation of the cold.

Killoran gave them a nod of encouragement. Even in their helmets they were unlikely figures, but he couldn't show himself to join them as it was essential that he stay out of sight—besides which, Peters might recognize him. He hefted the crude wire grapple in his hand.

Peters' voice came clear across the gap. There was little wind to distort it. 'You ready to receive supplies?' he shouted.

'Certainly are,' Cohn replied promptly.

Peters seemed suspicious. He shifted his grip on his gun, bringing it around for a possibility of action instead of letting it hang by his side. 'Where are your loaders?' he said.

'We are the loaders.'

'Are you sure about that? These crates are heavy.'

'We're stronger than we look.'

Peters looked at them speculatively for a moment and then backed into the darkness of the hold. They couldn't see what he was doing.

Cohn did his best not to look at Killoran, crouched with his grapple and line to one side of the open hatch. 'He's not going to believe us!' he whispered through clenched teeth. 'He's used to seeing the strongest men waiting to unload and then he gets confronted by a couple of shrimps like us!'

'Speak for yourself,' the Doc said indignantly.

'Stop wittering,' Killoran said, 'and try to look tough.'

'I was trying,' Cohn insisted.

'Puffing your chest up and sticking your backside out doesn't fool anybody. It only makes you look deformed.'

'But what else could we do?' asked Doc, helpless.

'Be mean and confident.'

Doc thought about it. 'I think I can manage mean,' he said after serious deliberation.

Peters was back a moment later. He'd been talking to the captain on the ship's intercom. 'Are you the only men available for unloading?' he called.

'That's right. We were rostered.'

'It's a heavy consignment. I honestly don't think you'll be able to manage it.'

Killoran could see very little from where he was hiding, but he'd got a narrow view of a slice of the ship including the deck above. Something moved up there outside the shielding, a quick shadow against the iron-grey sky.

'Everybody else is sick,' the Doc was saying in a moment of rare inspiration. 'We've got something wrong with our yeast.'

'I've spoken to the captain, but he refuses to let me come down and help you. I'm sorry.'

'Nice of you to offer,' Doc faltered. 'We'll have to manage.'

The shadow had come again, less stealthy this time. Berg, grinning like a gargoyle and wearing the captain's uniform cap, finger and thumb circling a gesture of triumph.

Killoran swung around and stepped out, blending the movement into a smooth throw which sent the bundle of hooked spikes on the end of his line sailing high into the open side of the ship. Peters was taken by surprise, a blank look on his face and the gun pointing at nowhere in particular as the line dropped across his shoulder and the grapple banged on to the deck behind him. He looked uncomprehendingly at the loose rope, making no move to touch it; then Killoran pulled hard, throwing himself back down the ramp.

Peters was jerked across the gap between the ship and the bay as the grapple rammed through his shoulder, red points emerging in a spurt through the hard muscles by his neck. The rifle caught on the frame of the hatch and went off once, blasting off into nowhere as the strap came free of Peters' twisting arm and the weapon dropped into the cold sea below.

Peters came to rest at the bottom of the ramp. Killoran had

aimed a kick at his head as he had passed while Doc and Cohn had skipped out of the way; he'd missed, but it was a superfluous move anyway. Peters was lying still, hot blood steaming in the cold of the loading bay.

A couple of seconds, that was all. Berg was still watching from the deck above, and Killoran returned the gesture of success.

'Follow me into the ship,' he told Doc and Cohn.

Cohn swallowed hard and moved to follow, but Doc shook his head. 'I'm not leaving him like that,' he said, indicating Peters who was now stirring a little and groaning, the hooks still impaled in his shoulder. 'Go on without me.'

'It was necessary,' Killoran said, deliberately excluding any sympathy from his tone and feeling contempt for himself as he did so.

Doc nodded his understanding. 'But it isn't necessary to leave him in agony. I'll catch up.'

It wasn't worth an argument. Doc was obviously determined and Killoran knew that he would have enough of a problem with his conscience without adding to it by denying Peters aid.

The hold was familiar from his journey out to the Palace, but the passageways beyond it were not. Much of the ship was a dead area, crew facilities made redundant by automatics and now enjoyed only by ghosts. He had a vague recollection of the route by which he'd been led down from the deck, but it looked different in reverse. They saw enough of the ship on the way up to confirm the suspicion that it was no more than a two-man crew with a lot of robot aids.

The men from the rafts had made themselves at home already. Berg was still wearing the captain's uniform cap and Palmer was trying on his jacket. The captain himself was sitting on his command chair, pulled back on its track from the navigation console and flanked by a couple of suitably rough-looking characters. The Weasel was sorting through his papers, laying aside anything that seemed remotely interesting or useful. With the exception of the captain, it was party time.

Bulstrode told Killoran that Palmer had been first over the side and that it was he who had found the bridge. Palmer beamed with pride as the story was told and the exploit re-lived with only minimal embellishment—that would come later.

Killoran reported that the ship was unmanned and ready to run. Bulstrode grinned at the captain and said, 'See, Cap? You're not as precious as you think.'

There was a film of sweat on the captain's forehead, and he fiddled nervously with the armrests on his chair as he glanced from one unfriendly face to another. 'But you still need me to set it up,' he insisted.

It seemed that he'd been trying to fix up some kind of deal, in spite of the fact that Bulstrode had pointed out that he had nothing to offer them and, should he try to withhold his cooperation, between them they knew some fairly nasty ways of damaging a man.

'You expect me to talk fair terms?' Killoran asked him incredulously. 'After the way you abandoned me on the last run?'

The captain didn't attempt to conceal his bitterness. 'I'm paying for that now, aren't I?'

'You haven't started yet.'

'Give him the works,' Palmer urged. 'Feed him to Berg.'

'Yeah,' Berg said brightly, and made anticipatory throttling motions with his hands. The captain gulped.

'Hey, Killoran,' Bulstrode said. 'What about the kid down below?'

It was Cohn who answered. 'He got messed up.'

'Dead?'

'Not that messed up,' Killoran said curtly, but Bulstrode wasn't satisfied.

'So who's with him?'

'Doc stayed behind. He's taking the grapple iron out of his shoulder.'

'Where did you get all this equipment?' the captain asked, bewildered.

'Crates, staples and wire. The secret of our success. Now, are you going to fire up all this clapped-out machinery, or do we follow Palmer's suggestion and feed you to Berg?'

Whatever the answer, it would have to wait. Berg's

threatening growls were drowned by a deeper and more ominous rumbling from somewhere below. Killoran looked at the captain, but the captain could only shrug and make an exaggerated display of innocence.

'If you're trying to mess us around. . .' Killoran threatened.

'Why should I? It's my neck as well!'

There was a buzz and a blowing sound from the console, and then the Anteater's voice came through. The captain showed Killoran the switch to operate the talkback.

The Anteater had organized a detail to search all the cargo holds. He'd found a trail of blood and following it had come across the first officer messing with some unlabelled controls on a panel. The Anteater had stopped him, but didn't know how to reset them; then something had blown on the other side of the bulkhead.

Killoran asked, 'Any sign of Doc?'

'None. Is he supposed to be here?'

'You didn't mess the kid up enough,' Bulstrode observed.

'I will when I get to him,' Killoran promised grimly.

The captain had pulled his chair forward a few inches and was studying a couple of the readouts on his console. 'In the meantime,' he said, 'I don't want to be pessimistic. But if these are correct we've got no stabilizers on the starboard side.'

'What does that mean?'

He permitted himself a smile, but not without a nervous glance towards Berg. 'It means, basically, that we're going nowhere.'

TWENTY ONE

Rorvik led the way towards the Wekk's old computing centre on the World Ship. The fastest route, he explained as they passed through an ascending maze of corridors and odd shaped enclosures, would take them into the open area which ran down the middle of the cylinder. It had once been a kind of park, a source of supplementary oxygen (the plants regularly died off between systems and had to be re-seeded) and food. It was big and they might find it difficult to take.

A park? Lobo doubted that it could hold much wonder. The World Ship was a pretty unattractive place to live in, he observed; no wonder the Wekk were so mean.

They passed through the upper level and emerged on the inner surface of the cylinder. It was then that Randall and Lobo understood Rorvik's tactful warning.

Exposed to only a section of curving passageway at a time it was easy to forget that they were negotiating a world that was artificial and manageable. The upward slope of the floor ahead and behind had been an odd phenomenon that was soon accepted as commonplace, but now the walls and the ceilings were stripped away and the World Ship was revealed in a cavernous twilight, an awesome arch which rolled on above them. They were on a pathway which was bounded on one side by dead trees and on the other by a ditch half-filled with stagnant water. The path was part of a regular network which rifled from one end of the cylinder to the other, as if they had been straight lines drawn down the inside of a tube which had then been given a sharp twist, the ends rotating in opposite directions for a half-turn. Here and there the pattern broke for a terrace or a clear space, usually a raised lip of ground that threw a long shadow in the light from the cylinder's end, light that was a slice of brilliant and tinted blue flaring in through some unclosed shutter on a forgotten mechanism.

When they started to move it was with the uneasy feeling that they were actually staying in the same place while the ship rotated around them; uneasy as it made them feel, it was better than the sense of walking up the wall and across the underside of the roof.

Randall's first thought on the ditches were that they were probably the remains of some humidifying or distribution system, but on a second look he saw that the level of the water pooled at the bottom of the trench had a distinct slope to it. An even spread of open water was probably as good a way as any other to monitor the efficiency of the ship's spin. The water was green and covered with a scum of moss, as was the composite material of the path itself; they had to pick their way with care.

Rorvik explained that the reptilian Wekk had used this inner enclosure as a basking area. There were shutters at both cylinder ends—one of them now apparently jammed half-open—which opened to admit sunlight when the ship neared a star, rousing the plant-life and offering the travellers the luxury of radiant heat. Otherwise they were dependent on the in-ship systems to keep them up to temperature and awake; when that temperature dropped they would fall into hibernation whether they wanted to or not. They would have to get to the sleep chambers on the lower levels or else they'd never live through the dormant period, all their fat and water reserves being slowly wasting away over the first hundred years or so without the ship acting to replace them.

'You've never seen a Wekk?' Randall asked suddenly and Rorvik turned to see that he had broken away and was pushing through the screen of dead and dry foliage that flanked the pathway. It snapped and showered around him and he stepped through onto what might once have been a pleasant enclosed lawn. Now it was a baize of fungus, a blue-green carpet that rose to cover some stony hunk at its centre. Randall crossed to this and circled it, leaving a trail of wet black prints in the moss.

Rorvik followed him through, while Lobo stood back and looked doubtfully at the underfoot slime. 'No,' Rorvik said in reply to Randall's question, 'and I've never much wanted to.'

'I think this is one.' Randall brushed at the covering on the boulder and as its surface broke, it tore cleanly away in a sloppy curtain. Underneath was a sculpture with the appearance of a scaly lizard in a half-crouch. He knocked away some residual moss from the details.

It was unlovely, but hardly terrifying in its ugliness. If the statue was authentic the Wekk were four-limbed with wide, angular hips and a forward-thrusting head; the same environmental demands that had shaped and adapted the advanced primates of old Earth seemed to have been at work here, taking a simple symmetrical quadruped and forcing it into an upright posture through the specialization of its forelimbs.

'Does it get us anywhere?' Lobo called from the path.

'Know your enemy,' Randall said as he returned, wiping his hands on his snow suit. He would have liked to investigate further, as there were some low buildings and an archway leading to a sunken area at the far end of the enclosure. He reminded himself that he was a working Elite, not a tourist.

'If we fell over one of those we'd have a hard time mistaking it,' Lobo said with a backward glance at the carving.

Randall agreed. 'And are you still worried about telling them from us?'

THE SITUATION on the icebreaker proved to be as bad as it had first appeared. One of the stabilizer tanks had split under pressure, a massive reservoir of the heavy oil which had been pumped from one side of the ship to the other to keep the breaker upright. Now it had a gap of a little less than an inch from top to bottom, and the oil was pouring out like cold honey. The Ice Palace didn't have the technology for the repair of such a pressure vessel—if it had, the inmates would have been away long ago. Now the ship wouldn't move without the stabilizers because it was inhibited by an inaccessible fail-safe in the bridge computer.

There was also no sign of Doc and the mate wasn't talking. For a moment Killoran regretted that he hadn't made a better job of him; he'd ruined their main hope of escape and it looked like he'd killed one of their number as well, although Killoran preferred to believe that Doc might have wandered off somewhere below decks. Leaving Berg down below seemed an easy way out for his conscience.

Berg followed him up on to the open deck after a few minutes. 'Kid slipped,' he explained and that was that.

Cohn was already there, arms wrapped around himself in spite of the adequate heating of his suit, staring despondently out across the featureless snow landscape. It was a clear day, milder weather than the Palace had seen for months, and beyond the immediate rise of the buried camp it was possible to see as far as the broken cliffs of raised ice that chewed at the far horizon. When he heard them approaching he turned, hope reviving against reason. Killoran asked him for the position on the bridge.

'There isn't one,' he told them. 'According to the captain, there's nothing we can do.'

'Don't be stupid,' Berg said, and rapped on the shielding next to them. It was vibrating gently as the engines turned over. 'You can see it's all ready to set off. I thought it was supposed to run itself.'

'It runs itself and it's stopping itself. There doesn't seem to be anything we can do about it.'

'Well, this is great.' Berg slapped an oversized fist into an equally huge palm in a gesture of impotence. 'Try telling that to all those poor crumbs down in the bunkrooms getting all their belongings together. They think they're going home.'

Killoran sighed, his reserves of aggressive leadership and lies all spent. 'There's nothing else I can do.'

'Nothing? That's pretty negative talk from somebody who set himself up as the Palace's biggest hope when he was dumped on the doorstep. Better start thinking, Killoran, before that hope turns into something nasty when they find you can't deliver.'

'I'm out of ideas. It was all so clear-cut before—isn't that what made it so attractive to you?'

Berg wasn't about to sympathize with his misery. 'Nobody loves a one-shot wonder. Come up with something else.'

'I can't,' Killoran insisted desperately.

'Leave him alone, Berg,' Cohn interrupted. 'He wants to get away as much as you do.'

'I don't think so,' Berg replied. 'Nobody wants to get away as much as I do.' He turned back to Killoran as if he were seeking to prod at some spot which would set him off on a new and more promising course of action. 'Start by asking some simple questions, like: what would the captain do if these stabilizer things had failed of their own accord on an ordinary trip?'

Killoran hadn't given it any thought. He'd been too preoccupied with bitter speculations on his failure. 'I don't know,' he said.

Cohn picked up the idea. 'There would have to be some way he could get help. There's got to be some backup plan for routine breakdowns!'

'Well?' Berg said. 'Did anybody think to ask the question?'

Nobody had, but Killoran saw in it the spark of energy needed to get the circus mobilized again. Perhaps the mate's sabotage wouldn't ruin them after all. The three of them stepped inside the walkway and made for the bridge.

Palmer was guarding the captain. He'd accepted the duty reluctantly but without complaint—after all, it was preferable to the job Bulstrode had drawn, taking a team of men and an empty sled in a hopeless search for tools and repair materials in the furthest installations of the spaceport.

The captain wasn't exactly being helpful. He slumped in his chair and chewed absently at a none-too-clean thumbnail, eyes focussed at a point in space somewhere beyond the opposite bulkhead.

'You mean one lousy little fault,' Palmer said, re-phrasing and re-clothing the same basic question that he'd been putting for the past half-hour, 'one lousy little fault and the whole thing grinds to a halt?'

'Lousy little faults we can cope with. The stabilizers are something else.'

The weather didn't improve their chances at all; unusually fine as it was it bore no relation to the thickness of ice along their proposed route. The big spiralling blades that ran the length of either side of the ship on the waterline could cut through most densities, or where there was no lead to follow they could even drag the ship across the surface for a distance. But the ice was never an even thickness and because of its crystalline nature it had shatter planes like a diamond. Cutting on the two sides was never evenly matched, so the stabilizers were essential to the evening of the cutting rates which prevented the ship from being flipped over.

The captain tensed when Berg's frame appeared in the doorway, which was exactly how Killoran wanted it. They started by telling him what had happened to his over-zealous first officer.

It hardly seemed possible, but the man's nervousness increased. 'They were right to send you here,' he said. 'You're animals.' He looked at Killoran. 'You as well.'

'Never mind me. Be careful what you say in front of Berg,' Killoran told him. 'He's a sensitive soul and he's easily offended.'

'Damn right,' Berg confirmed.

'I've been trying to get information out of this crumb,' Palmer said. 'All I've learned is that he knows nothing and can't do anything.'

'If that's true,' Killoran said as the captain squirmed uncomfortably, 'then it makes you the most dispensable person on the ice cap. How do you like the sound of that?'

'Not very much.'

'We've all seen this ship. It's rotten and it's falling apart. Half the machinery's thick with rust and the shielding's hanging off. The chances are that you'd have a major breakdown of some kind on your way to the Palace, or else on your way back. I want to know what you'd do in a case like that.'

The captain didn't even have to consider and it was obvious that he could do himself no good by pretending to. 'I've been lucky. It's never happened. I've never had such a disaster that I couldn't get the ship home.'

'I'm not interested in that. I want to know what you do if there is a disaster. Who you call and how.'

'There's nobody I can call. There isn't another ship in the city that could get out here. If it was as bad as that, I'd be dead.'

Berg forgot to be threatening for a moment. 'You mean you'd

be left out there without any kind of rescue?'

'Exactly that.'

'And what would happen to us?' Palmer asked.

'There would be no more supplies. I don't know exactly how that would affect you.'

' I always thought we were badly off,' Berg said with wonder. 'I'm only just finding out how badly.'

OVER THE next couple of hours a team managed to plug the split in the tank. It wouldn't take any pressure, but at least they were no longer losing the oil. There was nothing they could use to make a better repair; all they had was wood, wire, cladding and yeast, and none of it the best of its kind. Any hopes they had would have to lie with Bulstrode's team, unpromising as their search might be.

When the team was sighted Killoran hurried out to meet them. Berg and Cohn followed, his unofficial retinue. The sled was empty, but Bulstrode seemed excited about something. The team had been pushing hard to get back and most of them had removed their helmets and unclipped their power packs to compensate for the heat generated by their efforts.

They met in deep snow a few hundred yards out from the Palace. Bulstrode's answer to Killoran's first question was a disappointing one, but then he said, 'Look at the sky.'

Killoran didn't understand. He glanced around and saw the usual pale grey curtain, more clean-looking than usual but that was all. 'So it's a comparatively fine day. So what?'

'Over the horizon,' Bulstrode said patiently, and pointed beyond the icebreaker. 'We were heading back when we saw it.'

There was definitely something there, little more than a brilliant point. It looked like a daytime star, but even in the few seconds for which they watched it was moving and getting bigger.

'A comet, perhaps?' suggested Cohn, having had something of an education.

'Or a manned vessel,' said Berg, who saw no profit in a comet.

Killoran wasn't so sure. 'The city's got nothing like that,' he protested. 'It can't be.'

Bulstrode said, 'What about Palmer and his lights in the sky?'

'Everybody treated that as a joke,' Cohn said.

'Except Palmer. He still says he knows what he saw.'

Now it was level with the cap and bearing down on them at some impossible speed. Although it was still some distance away a thin, whistling shriek came on ahead through the still air. Despite its speed the object seemed to be unstable, rocking dangerously as it burned.

'Get Palmer down here,' Bulstrode urged Killoran. 'Ask him!'

'I can't. He's guarding the captain.'

'Then send somebody else!'

Killoran couldn't take his eyes off the phenomenon. 'Berg, you go and relieve Palmer.'

'No chance. I want to watch.'

Within seconds the shriek had become a roar and the shapeless fire a thick disc with a broad tail. Its outer skin was burning and flaking off with the friction of a half-controlled descent, and it was heading straight for the Palace.

It passed narrowly over the icebreaker and clipped the uppermost bulge in the ice where the beacon was located, shearing it off completely and peppering the surface over a half-mile radius with sharp hail. The unhelmeted men on the ice had to cover their heads against the dangerous rain as the shuttle skipped upward from the impact, sailing flatly over their heads with a wash of hot air that set the rough snow crackling.

It hit again a few hundred yards on, narrowly missing the pipeline and bouncing beyond it to slither onward along a low-resistance track of its meltwater. When it came to some hard obstruction under the surface it tipped suddenly, turned on its edge and then fell back with a splash, half-submerging in a pool of its own making.

There was comparative quiet, broken only by the hiss and clang of the distant vessel's cooling. Killoran was the first to break it.

'Berg,' he said, 'get a team and all the empty sleds you can find and follow me down.'

'This is more like it, kid,' Berg said happily. 'Pull something out of the hat for us.'

They had to be careful on the way over. They couldn't follow directly in the shuttle's tracks as the meltwater was only just beginning to skin over in a thin crust, and it wouldn't yet take a man's weight. Killoran had gone ahead and they followed his prints in the snow.

The ship had settled some considerable way into the ice, leaving only its upper third exposed. This was surrounded by a gently steaming moat that varied in breadth and depth, its slowly falling level indicating that the shuttle was holed below the waterline.

It was also holed above the waterline. Explosive bolts had triggered automatically and blown emergency doors out across the ice, leaving only neat shafts where they had landed and sunk. Killoran's trail led around the shuttle and then vanished opposite one of the black openings in the ship's side.

Within a couple of minutes he'd reappeared in the open doorway. His face was smeared with soot and his snow suit was blackened and scorched.

'If you'll pardon the expression,' he said, 'it's one of ours. And if there's any way we can find to make use of it, we've got an injured Councillor for a hostage.'

VALUM SAW THAT the shuttle was down. She instructed the other simulacra to stand off in orbit until they received a signal to land, for she was going on alone. When they'd all given their confirmation she closed the channels and called Willis forward.

'We're going down to the Ice Palace,' she told him. 'Does the idea bother you?'

'Should it?'

'No. But if you see anybody down there and you're tempted to think of them as old friends, remember they're bloodbags. They belong to another life.'

There wasn't very much room in the fighter and he was crouching with his face close to hers. He could feel her breath lightly on his cheek and it induced a pleasurable crawling sensation that he guiltily attempted to suppress. Where had the

Wekk found a model to pattern her?

'I'll remember,' he said. 'Don't worry about me.'

'That's good. And... Willis?'

He paused awkwardly in the middle of shuffling back to his place. 'I'm still listening.'

'If you should be tempted, remember that the ground commander's on his way. He wouldn't like you to show any sympathy.'

'I won't,' he said, and hoped for his own sake that he meant it.

They carried Morden out and placed him on a sled to be taken back to the Palace. He didn't seem to be badly hurt—he'd been strapped in during the crash and the bridge was designed in such a way that it took the least damage of all. Berg and most of his team stayed behind to look for anything that might be of use, while Killoran returned with the sled and a couple of men to help pull it.

Morden came round in a bunkroom. He couldn't know where he was, for the only clues he had were the cold, the dead acoustic and a continuous dripping. There was a rough blanket under him, and somebody was breathing in the room.

At least, it wasn't the shuttle. 'The Ice Palace?'

'Bullseye. Shitsville for you, Councillor.'

Morden's world was a world of sounds, and he placed the voice immediately. 'Killoran? The Elite?'

'Very impressive.' Killoran sounded anything but impressed.

'Please,' Morden said, pushing himself up on to an elbow and fighting the spin of the room which resulted. 'You must listen to me. There isn't much time.'

'I listened to you once, Morden. I don't intend to repeat the mistake.'

Obviously the young Elite was still smarting from the treatment he'd had on the icebreaker. Or was it something more complex? His tone and manner had changed subtly since their last meeting, as if his emotional allegiances had somehow shifted. The Elite's customary deference to the city's authority was missing.

'I know what I did to you,' Morden said, 'and I'm sorry.'

'Naturally.'

'But it was necessary, believe me! I couldn't go against Marius.'

'You're pathetic, Morden,' Killoran said after a short pause to express his disbelief. 'Do you think you can turn our opinions over with a couple of weak lies?'

There it was, that 'our'. 'Now wait a minute,' Morden said firmly. 'I came down in that shuttle fully expecting to die in it and I don't have to listen to your complaints.'

'I don't think you quite understand the position, Morden. . .'

'I understand it too well. There's danger following me down and you're not going to be fit to meet it.' And he lay back on the bunk, as if Killoran had been tested and dismissed.

'Whatever you're trying to pull, forget it,' Killoran said calmly. 'I know you're only worried about your own interests, so think about this. There are about fifty men in the Ice Palace. At the moment they're all getting themselves ready for a trip in a ship that can't go anywhere. They know it but they don't want to believe it and they're expecting a miracle with all the confidence they're capable of. Which, I might add, isn't very much after the treatment they've had from the council.'

'What treatment?' said Morden, genuinely puzzled. 'The council. . .'

'Exactly, Councillor. You came to power and did nothing for them. They're all underbelly, and they expected the gesture of brotherhood. You're not the most popular person in the Palace, councillor.'

'Will you stop this petulant ranting and listen to me!' Morden said sharply. 'Where do you think that shuttle came from?'

'That's one of the things I want to know.'

'You don't want to know anything. You're just looking for an excuse to rave because I didn't hand Randall back to you when you demanded it.'

'Randall's dead because of action you refused to take.'

'Randall's alive.'

'What?' The disbelief in Killoran's voice was unmistakable.

'At this moment he's somewhere over our heads and he's

looking for a way to disable a war machine.'

'You had a harder landing than we thought,' Killoran said with mock sympathy. 'It's messed your brains around.'

Morden's sharp hearing had picked up a noise in Main Street outside the bunkroom, an excited bustle that was coming their way. 'I don't intend to waste my time with explanations for you to laugh at,' he said. 'Watch the skies.'

'For what? The first cuckoo of spring? I'm looking at it now.'

At that moment the door burst inward and Berg followed it through, grabbing the frame to stop himself from falling into the room. 'Killoran,' he panted, 'get your backside out there! There's another one coming down.'

Killoran said, 'Another what?' but Berg had swung himself around and was heading off down Main Street.

'I'm not saying it twice,' he called back. 'It sounded mad enough the first time.'

On the bunk Morden was nodding to himself knowingly.

'I suppose I'll have to ask you to help me,' Killoran said with reluctance. 'I don't understand this.'

'Then listen and don't challenge me. The cruiser that's coming down is piloted by what looks like a woman, but don't be misled; as far as you're concerned she's enemy. She'll think Randall's here because she doesn't know he left the shuttle and that's the only bargaining point we'll have—they can't start the operation they've planned until they've got Randall back. Don't ask me why, because it's complicated and you won't like it. There are only two people who know the reason. I'm one and Lobo's the other. He didn't like it either.'

'Who's Lobo?'

'Never mind. Concentrate on the negotiating you're going to be doing. You've got to buy time for Randall.'

VALUM ANGLED DOWN and did a fly-past over the Ice Palace to be sure that she was in the right place. The beacon signal had cut off abruptly when the shuttle had destroyed the transmitter and a visual identification from the air at high speed was difficult where nearly everything was white-on-white. But there was the icebreaker in a heaving glitter of open water and the unmistakable jewelled trail of the shuttle with the blackened shell at its end. As these features passed beneath them and slid away to the side Valum began a steep turn and told Willis that she wanted him to stay out of sight for a while after they'd landed. Willis accepted this without comment.

'Don't be too submissive, Willis,' Valum said after a moment. 'You're acting like a marionette. Ask me why.'

'Why do I have to stay out of sight, Valum?'

'Because the bloodbags are easily impressed. They think the old Willis is dead and producing you at the right moment could be... effective.'

'Effective for what?'

They came in low and Valum reversed the thrust on the drive to slow the cruiser and drop it on the open plain she'd selected. Excited figures on the ice below now scattered as the alien fighter passed overhead.

'Randall will be down there somewhere,' she said, 'probably hiding. I want them to hand him over. I'm doing nothing until I get him.'

'How do the Wekk feel about that?'

'They accept it. They have to. I'm no use to them unless I'm a fairly independent agent. I was made to fight people; if the Wekk trusted their own judgment for that, they wouldn't need me. Besides, we're waiting for the ground commander.'

Willis asked, 'What will he be like?' and some warmth came into her voice.

'Like me, but even better. What a team we'll make.'

He tried to think of something that might please her. 'You're inhuman, Valum,' he said.

'Why, thank you Willis,' she replied, flattered and pleased. The cruiser's downward-angled jets blasted aside several tons of loose snow, and they touched down on the bare ice beneath.

TWENTY TWO

THE WEKK COMPUTER room was long and low and most of the lights were burned out. One complete wall was a series of racks which obviously pulled out on runners—one of them was half-extended, revealing a framework of hung circuitry that was metal veining set in crystal. Rorvik led them past this and on into another chamber which was all metal grids and black glass dulled by settled filth. Then down some steps and around a tight corner and they were in the link room; clean shapes on the floor showed that it had once been much more.

One side was entirely sectioned into opal screens, a couple of them cracked. The fragments lay where they had fallen. There was a padded seat on a boom arm which could apparently range across the screens and settle the occupant in front of any. The opposite wall was all glass with a small auditorium beyond for operators, observers or whatever.

'It doesn't look much,' Lobo commented.

'It isn't much,' Rorvik agreed. 'Most of the useful stuff was ripped out when they transferred across to the bigger ship. The memories are complete, though. Memories aren't hardware; the Wekk couldn't pick them up and carry them across. One reason was that the ship would die during the transfer. Instead they'd used this unit to design another, and then re-recorded all the memories for a perfect copy. It was as if the ship was making a simulacrum of itself.

Rorvik was looking warily at the empty chair. Randall said, 'Can you do it?'

'I won't know until I've tried. At least give me a chance.'

'But you were able to plug straight into the shuttle. . .'

'And look at the lousy job I made of it; Anyway, this isn't the shuttle, it's a ten-mile cylinder. You haven't even told me what

I've got to do with it.'

No more private speculation, it was time to produce the goods. 'Morden gave me the idea when he said we couldn't disable the Wekk ship without turning off the sun.'

'I'm not sure I want to vote for that,' Lobo said doubtfully.

'Nobody's voting on it. We're going to do it.'

The grey simulacrum was giving Randall a very narrow look. 'I think you're overestimating my abilities,' he said.

Randall had come up with the only answer that he could on the information available to him. The ship needed direct sunlight; without it the power supply would cut down to virtually nothing and be diverted to basic survival needs and nothing else. When the power went the Wekk would have to dive for their survival couches before their biological hibernation mechanism could take over, triggered by the fall in temperature. If they didn't make it they would risk wasting away in cold sleep over an indefinite period—they couldn't know when they would find another usable system.

He wanted Rorvik to find a way of firing up whatever propulsion system the deserted ship might use, accelerating its orbit so that it would collide with the inhabited ship ahead. The collision would have to be exactly right in two respects; firstly, the inhabited ship was to be pushed into a planetary eclipse, falling from line-of-sight of the sun and into the world's shadow. Secondly Randall wanted the two ships to be mangled together at the point of contact sufficiently to allow' them to get through.

'Now,' Randall said. 'Can that be done?'

'Probably. But not by me.'

'Why not?'

'What do you think I am? I've got the mind and most of the memories of an ordinary man. You seem to think I'm some kind of miracle worker.'

'But you're not an ordinary man.'

Rorvik seemed to stiffen. 'You accepted me as one,' he said, watching Randall and daring him to proceed.

'Because it was convenient.' Randall walked over to the operator's chair on the boom arm. It was raised slightly above shoulder height and its proportions were all wrong for a human body. 'It kept you quiet and Morden happy. But it's time to face realities, Rorvik.'

'So you can't control your prejudices anymore.' There was sadness under Rorvik's anger, as if he'd expected this. 'If you're not prepared to let me be a man, what am I? I think you'll like the alternative even less.'

'It's time you went in for some intelligent self-assessment, and stopped being obsessed with faking yourself a family tree. You are what you are, and you won't understand that until you've found your limitations.' Randall reached up and briefly touched the padding of the chair at his shoulder. 'Scared of trying?'

'Why should I be scared?'

'You don't know what you may find. It could be better than you hope.'

'Or a whole lot worse.'

'He's right, Rorvik,' Lobo argued reasonably. 'You should at least give it a try.'

The simulacrum turned on him. 'It's easy for you to say that.'

Lobo shrugged. 'Sure it is. Doesn't make it any less true.'

'But I know what I am,' Rorvik said, half protest and half plea. 'As a man I barely rate—it shows every time you speak to me. And as a machine I'm hardly better than the marionettes.'

Randall noted the first break in Rorvik's defences, self-pity replacing self-assertion. 'Remember how you felt when you stepped into Marius's chambers? You'd just come from the shuttle and you were crammed with life and confidence. You can interface with the machine around us and we can't.'

'I don't want to do it again.'

'Because you don't want to risk liking it. You resent the kick it gives to the machine part of you.'

'That's a lie.'

'You know it isn't. You've suspected it yourself and you're not man enough to put it to the test.'

Rorvik said nothing. He stared at Randall and Lobo began to worry. Perhaps the Elite had pushed him too far, having too little consideration for the simulacrum's meagre dreams; or on the other hand perhaps he had such sympathy that he had to rule it out completely and fill the space with coldness. Randall the hustler, the schemer, the blind and programmed patriot, was well-versed in the ways of inhumanity.

'Get out of my way,' Rorvik said.

Randall backed off, and Rorvik swung himself up into the operator's chair. The boom dipped slightly under his weight, and dry bearings protested at its anchorage. He sat awkwardly, his legs too long and his back too short for the dimensions of the seat.

There was nothing spectacular. He stared at the opal screen directly ahead for perhaps a minute, and then it began to glow. At first it was no lighter than a summer night sky, but then it became more intense, producing not only the beginnings of an image but also an atonal hum that seemed to be a composite of a large number of contributory sounds.

'I don't want to be disturbed,' Rorvik said aloud without looking at them. The screen picked up his words and tried to repeat them, getting the inflections but none of the meaning.

They found a doorway without a door which led them through to the auditorium on the other side of the glass. The seats had the same odd proportions as the operator's chair and they chose to stand. The sounds from the screen still reached them, if a little muted; they, however, could converse quietly without disturbing Rorvik.

Two of the adjacent screens had come alight. As they watched another flickered in and then another. No two of them held the same image and no image was recognizable. One was a snowstorm, another was slow rain on the outside of a window, another the slow heave of a mercury sea.

'Just colours and music,' Lobo said, mystified.

'But he must be seeing more. Even if he understands it, will he be able to use it?'

'I damn well hope so. That was quite an ass-kicking you gave him.'

Randall nodded absently, accepting the remark as if it were praise. 'He needed it. He's too inclined to feel sorry for himself.'

They watched the play of light. With the exception of the broken panels the entire opposite wall was as bright as the ice and pulsing with a cascade of disguised information. Lobo said, 'How much of it did you mean?'

Randall considered. 'I don't know. Does it really matter?'

'I would have thought so.'

'An idea's an idea. Doesn't make any difference whether it's sincere or not.'

Another pause. Rorvik was still sitting passively, a blank silhouette against the interplay of sound and colour.

Lobo said, 'Assume for a minute he can do it. Assume that he locks the two ships together and we can transfer across. What the hell do we do then?'

'With the power right down we'll have the run of their ship. We'll find the equivalent of this room and wreck it.'

'And what then? How are we supposed to get home?'

Randall considered an evasion, decided it would be pointless. 'I don't know,' he said. 'That's the only honest answer I can give you.'

'Thanks for that much, anyway.'

The screens went blank all at once, and their music ran down the scale to nothing. Randall and Lobo hurried back into the room.

Rorvik was rubbing his eyes, causing his artificial skin to flex and stretch. 'It can be done,' he said. 'But it isn't going to be easy.'

'Nobody said it would be,' Randall told him. 'Can you do it from here?'

'From this chair. Nowhere else.'

There were no obvious controls, for it seemed that the Wekk had no power over their ships; Rorvik would be cheating the system by making use of the design capability through which the simulacra controlled their cruisers. He'd have to join the machine, become a part of it; then he could use his thoughts and impulses to give it drive and they would be automatically translated into action by drawing on the ship's memories and capabilities. Like the shuttle, he would become the ship.

'Is that why you resisted the idea so much?' Randall asked. 'When you knew you could do it all along?'

'I knew nothing of the kind. Something could still go

wrong—are you aware of celestial mechanics?'

'They fix spaceships?' Lobo hazarded.

'It's a field of mathematics and navigation in which the shortest distance between two points is hardly ever a straight line. A slight error either way and we could send the line of ships cannoning down through the atmosphere and right on to the city, or else just bust a hole and lose all our air. Watch the screen.'

The opal plate nearest to them began to glow. A green dot appeared, leaving a neon trail wherever it moved; it rapidly sketched in what looked like a glass model of the World Ship with all its lines visible through the structure. It rotated through three dimensions to check for accuracy, and then the dot reappeared and outlined the second, much larger ship.

'The third ship doesn't appear anywhere in this computer's memory,' Rorvik explained. 'I'll have to guess and make some allowance for it.'

He commenced the first experimental scenario. A number of points on the smaller of the two ships flared in imitation of a burn and the image began to move, leaving ghostly after-images to mark out its course. A number of the other screens illuminated with similar displays, each slightly different and none synchronous.

When all the screens were filled with moving ships the sequences began to speed up, colliding silently in an eerie display of multiple disaster. Each wiped failure was replaced by a new set of skeletal players which pirouetted, burned and collided over again. In most of them the curved edge of the planet appeared, adding its mass to influence the protagonists.

It became too fast to watch, an out-of-phase flickering across the screens. Randall and Lobo moved to the back of the room and turned away, finding the reflections from the panoramic window slightly less unbearable.

'He seems to be enjoying it,' Lobo commented.

'He's finding potential he didn't know about. He was so obsessed with being considered a man that he forgot there might be some advantage in being a machine.'

'But it's a matter of pride. How would you like to think that you were an artificial construct?'

'I wouldn't. But that's not the point. The point is that we keep feeding him the right lines to make sure he stays happy. While he's happy, he's useful.'

Lobo wondered if it was better to be a machine with a dream or a man without a soul, but he was prevented from saying so by a deep, bellowing chord from the screens and a shout from Rorvik of, 'I've got it! That's the one!'

He ran through it for them again, slow enough for them to see but still much faster than actuality—such masses couldn't be shunted with ease. The smaller ship dropped in its orbit, accelerating as it moved into a perceptibly tighter curve and then rising with a second burn as it drew level with the larger, clipping it neatly on its edge. The two locked together and began to shrink as the edge of the world rose to meet them. They passed the curve and remained visible even though they were supposedly now in the planet's shadow.

The sequence speeded. The lower edge of the planet travelled across the screen, and as the linked ships moved around they separated.

'We'll have no more than an hour to get down to the damaged area and make the transfer into the Wekk ship,' Rorvik said. 'That's how long it will take to get over the horizon and out of the sunlight.'

Randall said, 'Will their ship be able to react and bring itself back?'

'No time, besides which it will have to start powering down. But there's another problem.'

'What's that?'

'An hour later we'll be around and back into the sunlight. The hibernation sequence will start reversing.'

'Doesn't leave much margin,' Randall mused.

'It doesn't leave any margin,' protested Lobo. 'Can't we think of something else?'

Man and machine looked at him. 'Like what?' Randall said.

'Something that means we can stay here and manage everything from a distance. So we don't have to go into a ship full of things like that statue we saw.' It even sounded lame to

Lobo.

'This is no time to start calling up all your old bad dreams,' Randall told him. Then he turned to Rorvik, still aloft in the operator's chair. 'When are we going to start that sequence?'

'It's started. When we've had the second burn, then we can move.'

TWENTY THREE

IF MORDEN'S WARNING was to be acknowledged, reserve was the order of the day. Killoran had gone alone to the newly-arrived ship which stood in the crater formed by its landing.

The ridge of snow that had been thrown up helped to obscure the cruiser to the Palace. Everybody was either in the Palace or on the icebreaker and a good number of them were crowded into the deep trench that angled from the bay to ground level. Berg was on his elbows at the top, trying to see what was happening so that he could report back.

There wasn't much he could say. There was a woman, as they'd been warned; Berg could only see her distant outline, but his imagination filled in the rest. Tall, dark, high cheekbones, almond-shaped eyes—he even added in a couple of moles in places he'd have needed an X-ray telescope to see.

Whatever it was she was saying, she wasn't very pleased. It could have been a threat of some kind, but Killoran wasn't backing down. He passed this information on to the men waiting below.

'Killoran's a good kid,' Palmer said confidently, recently arrived after his relief from guard duty. 'He won't screw up on us.'

'He's also Elite,' Bulstrode reminded him. 'He might sell us out.'

Everybody was watching Berg, so they didn't see the Worm come in. He was slightly more unkempt than usual, and he wandered around the back of the group. He couldn't actually discern what they were doing, so after a while he asked nobody in particular, 'What's going on down here?'

Bulstrode turned and saw him blinking pleasantly. 'Quiet, Worm,' he said. 'Berg's concentrating.'

'Berg's doing *what?*'

Berg turned at the top of the ramp. 'What's so funny?'

'Crawl back into the woodwork, Worm,' Bulstrode said. 'We've managed fine without you so far.'

'You had your chance to join us,' Palmer added.

The Worm could see the group's hostility once again coming to focus on him, and he backed off a little. 'I don't want to join you,' he said. 'I only want to know what's going on.'

'There's something happening,' Berg said, and the Worm was promptly forgotten.

The woman had been angry, almost on the point of striking Killoran. Then she had turned and climbed back into 'that jet thing she came down in'. All the hatches were still open and it showed no signs of moving, but Killoran was on his way back alone, as white as the ice and looking scared.

'Morden was right,' Killoran told them when he'd arrived back. 'She wants Randall, and I let her think he's here. She must be from one of the other colonized systems on the space trade network. It seems there's a main ship in orbit and she thinks Randall's escaped from that, but according to Morden he's still up there. She wants us to hand him over so she can kill him.'

'Is that all?' Berg said hollowly.

Bulstrode added, 'What happens when we can't?'

'She'll come in after him.'

About twenty pairs of eyebrows went up at the same time. 'What kind of threat's that?' said Berg, voicing everybody's surprise.

Killoran explained that not only was she armed, she was unnaturally strong, a fact that she had demonstrated by pinching the leading edge of her cruiser's wing between thumb and forefinger to leave a sizable impression in the metal. Bulstrode said he didn't believe it.

'Is that a sincere opinion,' Killoran asked him in irritation, 'or just rhetoric?'

'I don't know. What's rhetoric?'

If she was from another system, surely anything was possible after generations without contact. Berg said, 'If Morden says Randall's still on the main ship, how did he get there?'

'The same shuttle Morden came down in. It was homing on the Ice Palace beacon.'

'How come we didn't see it?' someone wondered.

'I saw it once,' Palmer said. 'Nobody believed me.'

'It came and went during the storms,' Killoran explained.

Bulstrode reacted with bitterness. 'Storms where people disappeared. What the hell's been going on under our noses?'

They didn't seem to have any choice other than to accept Morden's story and stall for time. Nobody could offer a more likely explanation of the events that had recently come to disrupt the Palace's killing routine, and that limited the choices somewhat.

Killoran announced that he was going to try to capture the cruiser. The suggestion of action, no matter how hazardous, was warmly welcomed by men whose capacity for long reflection was limited. Only Cohn objected. 'Even if you were successful, you couldn't fly it.'

'Details,' said Bulstrode airily. 'Count me in.'

'But it'll be suicide.'

'Not if we're sneaky about it. And it's a damn sight better than sitting here arguing over things we know nothing about.'

So it was settled. They would take the cruiser. And then... then they would worry about what to do next.

Nobody had seen the Worm arrive. Nobody had seen him go, either.

FOR THE FIRST time in her short career Valum was angry and frustrated. The situation here was so different from the World Ship, where the simulacra outnumbered the bloodbags and moved in familiar, well-defined territory. She was also having the new experience of an unfulfilled want, and she didn't like it. She didn't like having distant horizons all around her, didn't like having to deal with bloodbags. Above all, she didn't like being opposed.

She could blast the Palace from the air—but she wouldn't see Randall squirm. She needed that satisfaction.

Willis told her that the Wekk had been trying to reach her. She opened the channels carelessly, leaving Willis free to listen if he wished.

'*Valum,*' it came, immediate and urgent. 'Matters are moving fast here. Is your ground base established?'

'No. I haven't got Randall yet.'

'Forget Randall.'

'We've been through all this before.'

'A short time ago our old world decided to come alive and make use of its propulsion systems. We are sliding towards the shadow of the planet. You know what this will mean?'

'You'll have to go into emergency shutdown.'

'For a few hours only. In that period you will be on your own, and we want your full attention on the operation.'

'But why did the old ship begin co move?'

'It was a development we did not anticipate, but one which, nevertheless, pleased us.'

'What do you mean?'

'We recognize it to be part of the field test of the ground commander.' There was an undertone of something suspiciously like amusement. 'At this moment he is striving to destroy us.'

She was confused. She'd known nothing of the ground commander's development, and had assumed that he was being tested in isolation to far more exacting standards than the other simulacra. 'I don't understand.'

'The tests have been going on for some time. We placed certain blocks in his mentality; he is unaware of his real capabilities and his true loyalty to the Wekk. His task was to fathom and penetrate our own defences—no other simulacrum has been tested to such an extreme. When he reaches our strategic centres, we will know he is ready.'

'The ground commander's trying to destroy you?'

'He thinks he is. But in the end he will find he is unable and unwilling to do. . .

The withdrawal was such as she had never experienced before, sudden and without warning. Shutdown. Willis was shaking his head as if trying to clear it. Because Valum hadn't restricted and controlled the signal he'd had no choice but to overhear, and as it was his first experience of contact he'd no expertise or resources to combat the inward rush of emptiness that followed the abrupt severance.

'What are we going to do now?' he said as he got over the shock.

'Nothing,' Valum replied sharply.

'But. . .'

'But nothing. It'll be several hours before they're out of the enforced hibernation programme, and you heard what they said. I'm on my own until then.'

'I also heard them say to forget Randall,' he reminded her, hoping that he didn't speak out of turn.

She looked at him evenly, 'I didn't hear it.'

'But. . .'

'And neither did you.'

'Yes, Valum.'

RORVIK LED THE way, and the others had difficulty keeping up with him in the howling winds that funnelled down the corridors towards the impact zone. Both hulls were ruptured and mangled, atmosphere draining out around the imperfect seam, and while there was no serious danger of either ship losing a significant amount of pressure before repairs could be made passage from one to the other was difficult. Two fast streams of air met and whirled in the breach and one of the greatest hazards was from spinning debris, but by linking arms and staying low they made it through.

The locked ships were still spinning in tandem, so gravity remained. The new World Ship was bigger, wider, cleaner; it was also cold, and chilled vapour was being pumped out of floor-level grilles.

An emergency foam had filled the corridors to help slow the ship's bleeding. It held tight against the push of air but parted and reshaped behind them as they struggled through. After thirty yards or less they were back in the open and able to continue.

On the middle levels they found their first Wekk. It was lying in a corridor having obviously failed to make it to the hibernation tanks. It had dropped where it stood, and now seemed more dead than asleep as cold vapours billowed around it. The overgrown statue in the park had been a fairly accurate representation, although they could now see that the skin was grey and leathery. Not unlike Rorvik's.

'He seems to get more confident every minute,' Lobo said to Randall when the simulacrum was out of earshot.

'That's good. I'd had enough of dragging his thumb out of his mouth and trying to cheer him up.'

It took about half an hour of forcing the pace to reach the computer room a couple of miles in and three levels up. The walls along the route were lined with the doors of hibernation chambers.

The room was all wrong. It was a different shape, a different layout, and the machinery bore no resemblance to that which they had left behind. Rorvik stood in the middle, bewildered. Even as he looked around the light was cut by fifty percent, presumably as part of the powering-down. He turned in the starfield blaze of equipment lighting and said, 'It's all strange. I don't understand any of it.'

The room obviously represented some leap of technology from its predecessor, probably raided from the last system. But where to start? They had only minutes left, and they could spend them pulverizing the equivalent of a fire extinguisher while the ship ticked on and waited for the moment when it could again reach them.

There was a choice to be made, and Randall didn't feel sufficiently confident to make it. Surely Rorvik could act on his intuition—he was machine, after all, and he should have some feeling for the weaknesses of his own kind.

'Come on, Rorvik,' he urged. 'Surely you're not getting twinges of old loyalties?'

Rorvik looked at him sharply, as if stung. Hadn't he already demonstrated his loyalties beyond dispute? 'What do you mean by that?'

'You're the only one here who can get access to the programming in all this.'

'That's not what you were starting to say.'

'All right, then, I'll say it. You're either a man or a machine. I know what you say, but I still don't know what you really are deep inside. Now we're at the moment of truth you're hesitating.'

Rorvik gave another look around. It was hopeless. Panels, consoles, shelves and tables littered with unfathomable tools and instruments. Randall would class him with these—and yet he'd needed him and ridden on his back every inch of the way! 'And what do you know about it, b...

'Go on, say it!' Randall shouted defiantly. 'The word's bloodbag, isn't it?'

'Yes, damn you!'

'If you want to be a man, Rorvik, earn the right! If you don't understand any of it, pick a place and smash it!'

The final burn hit boiling point. Several things happened, all within the space of a couple of seconds.

Rorvik grabbed the nearest panel. It wasn't flimsy, but his fingers sank right through it and it folded like paper as it came away from the front of the machine. Its edge caught in the circuitry and trailed sparks as he whirled and flung it at Randall. There was a free-standing cube of a strange metal on the floor nearby, and he reached for that to send it on after.

Randall was diving flat and heading for the nearest cover. Lobo wasn't so fast, but then he wasn't the target, either. Randall hit and rolled as the panel banged edge-on into the wall behind him, narrowly clearing his legs as it dropped. He kept moving, and the cube filled his airspace an instant later.

Now Rorvik was coming with bare hands. There was something like a table between them but he didn't seem to notice it until it got in his way and he sprawled across it, hands clutching at empty air as Randall jerked back out of his reach.

Rorvik slung the table aside and Randall went with it, trying to keep the barrier between them. Lobo scrambled out of the way, knowing better than to try to help; Rorvik's strength was greater than both of theirs combined—they'd learned as much in their first encounter on the shuttle—and Randall's only chance lay in his speed of reaction.

The table was fully overturned this time, and Randall dived out and under. He helped propel himself with a sideways elbow to Rorvik's ribs that had no discernible effect apart from that of nearly breaking his arm. This was Pearson all over again, singlehanded and worse.

Only a few yards and he was up against another wall. There simply wasn't the room for competent evasion.

Lobo had got himself into a corner, sliding back into a niche formed by a waist-high rostrum and the wall. There were a number of rods and devices arranged in neat order on its surface, but Lobo had disarranged them as he'd clambered across to shelter. Now he tried to make himself heard over the noise of the deadly ballet.

'Randall!' he shouted. 'Remember what we came for!'

Rorvik faltered and looked around. He was looking at the open gap where he'd torn the panel away, and he was hesitating.

He wasn't loyal to the Wekk, and he didn't hate mankind. He hated Randall, that was all.

Lobo covered his head with his arms as Randall exploited Rorvik's momentary inattention to get past him and land on the rostrum, sweeping the last of its collection of instruments on to the floor in a grating clash of metal and crystal.

Rorvik didn't follow. He stooped to reach for the cube he had thrown, now with one corner sheared completely off.

The gun didn't look like a gun. It was the wrong shape, and it didn't fit Randall's hand so that he had to grip it two-fisted to cover the trigger.

Rorvik lifted the cube to dash it into the open heart of the machine, and in the same moment his leg exploded like a bursting pipe. There was no blood. The cube dropped to the floor, and Rorvik dropped after it, hinging sideways on his ruined limb.

A sharp wedge of blue light fell across the room as the outer door opened, widening and spilling with the Wekk's shadow at its centre. The hiss of bearings and the sharp little click as the door locked fully open rang unnaturally loud in the silence.

It walked into the room and looked around.

IT WAS HARDLY bigger than a child, and it had wide, awkward hips which made it necessary for it to swing its body from side to side as it moved. It wore a white suit of some thick fabric, and the head was completely enclosed in a black dome. The unit on its back with all the pipes and tubes had to be keeping it warm.

It paused at Rorvik, who was now stirring, and then turned to take in Randall. He was still astride the rostrum, both hands around the alien weapon.

The Wekk raised a hand with three short fingers, but it was the ship that spoke. 'I am pleased to welcome,' it said from all around them, 'the new ground commander of our simulacra.'

Randall looked for a moment, thoroughly confused.

'There will be a period of readjustment,' it said encouragingly. 'It will be short.'

'Getting the message?' Lobo said from behind him.

'What message?'

'You heard. That thing said welcome to the ground commander.'

'The ground commander? Rorvik?' Randall seemed astonished at the notion.

'Not Rorvik. You.'

'What are you talking about?'

'Morden told me before I left the shuttle, when I took him up to the bridge and strapped him in. It was part of the deal he did with Marius.'

'You're wrong. Completely wrong.'

'Morden didn't want the underbelly's big hero to be treated as shabbily as Marius' politics demanded. The real Randall's living in luxury somewhere on the city outskirts. He was drugged and patterned shortly after his trial. Then he was sent back to the city and his simulacrum was delivered to the Ice Palace.'

Randall was perplexed. What possible motive could Morden have for such a lie? 'But I'm not a marionette. I'm a man!'

Rorvik had managed to push himself into a sitting position. The side of his leg was open, and bright metal showed deep inside.

'What does it feel like, Randall?' he said. 'Time to start wheeling out all the insincere philosophy you've been throwing at me.'

'Morden was lying to you,' Randall insisted. He had to make

them see the truth. 'I'm Randall. It's my body and my memories.'

'The body's copied and the memories are planted. Find another way of being sure.'

'I don't need to find another way. I know.'-

Rorvik's expression didn't change, but his tone was gently mocking. 'Starting to feel the hunger now?'

All three of them were looking at him—Rorvik on the floor, the undersized Wekk in the middle of the room, and Lobo at his shoulder. It was faintly embarrassing, and more than a little ridiculous.

'If you want to prove you're what you say you are,' Lobo urged, 'kill that thing and then blast the ship.'

'There's no need.'

'What are you afraid of?'

'There may be a better way!'

'You're rationalizing!' Rorvik said triumphantly. 'You won't do it because you can't!'

Randall slid off the rostrum. Tiny fragments of glass showered from his clothes on to the floor as he came to his feet, and the Wekk took a cautious step back.

'Allow me to help you,' the ship said. 'Time is short.' The Wekk seemed to hear some different inner voice, and responded to it by waddling over to the square of electronics that Rorvik had exposed and pulling the adjacent panels aside.

'A single shot into this circuitry would cripple me beyond any hope of repair,' the ship went on. 'Feel free to destroy me. . . if you can.'

A machine to serve a machine. Everything he had ever valued—friendship, the Elite, the city—all was incidental. His arm wouldn't move. He couldn't even get himself to want it to move.

'What's been done to me?' he demanded in disbelief. 'I don't want to be a simulacrum.'

'Neither did I,' said Rorvik, 'but you told me to stop whining.'

'A little pain,' the ship said soothingly, 'and it will soon pass. Or we can remove it for you. You've far exceeded our expectations.'

'I don't know what to think.'

'We'll tell you what to think, don't worry. Healthy, loyal, but essentially human thoughts. It is for this capacity that we needed you so badly.'

Another try with the arm. It hung easily by his side, a loose grip on the weapon. How could it be true? He'd come so far, hated so much, planned and schemed. . . and only to serve?

'As was intended,' said the ship in answer to his unspoken thought.

'No, damn it, no! I don't know what you're trying to pull or who you're trying to trick, but it won't work!'

'Then blast the panel,' Lobo suggested.

'I can't!'

Lobo shouldered him aside as he came down from the rostrum, and the Wekk had to scamper out of the way when he saw the huge form bearing down on him.

The gun came up, and both Randall's hands wrapped around it and sought the trigger as if drawing on specialized knowledge of their own. He tried to fight it, but couldn't. His Randall personality seemed to be only an ineffectual fraction of his entire being, the workings of which he was recognizing for the first time.

Lobo was reaching for the seven-cornered cube.

Randall's consciousness might have been compared to an island from which he observed the passing of the ocean, suspecting for the first time that there might be unseen subtleties of action and relationship in its depths, or a lone planet so preoccupied with fortifying the corruption of its own civilization that its need for the stars was argued down by the pretence of reason. Lobo raised the cube.

Trust me, said a voice in Randall's head, and it was as if someone else had entered and gently but firmly taken over.

Lobo jerked once with the impact, and he lifted slightly from the floor. His toes dragged as he travelled forward but then he came up hard against the machinery. His body no longer held the inertia of the charge, and his snow suit blossomed out at the front as it carried on through him to bury its energy in the intricacies ahead.

He hung there, pinned on the sharper projections by the collision, unmoving even as fires and sparks showered around him.

Something had changed. Randall could once again feel the strange grip of the weapon in his hands; the controlling mind had retreated and left him in command, and there was no resistance as he swung from left to right.

Lobo was dead. Surely he'd known that he'd had no hope of reaching the panel; but then he seemed to have given more attention to placing himself between it and Randall, ensuring that the shot would pass straight through his flimsy bloodbag body and into where the ship had assured them it would do most damage.

Randall emptied the gun into the exposed panelling, firing again and again until it wouldn't fire any more. There was burning deep inside, damage breeding damage, and hot liquid metal burst out at a couple of points and set the floor alight.

Rorvik rolled out of the way as the pool of flame spread, but the Wekk caught some on its suit and danced around as it tried to put it out. Randall threw the empty weapon aside and reached for Rorvik's arm, dragging him out of immediate danger.

The undermind had gone; or, rather, as the ship had died the full service of his mind had reverted in loyalty to the only other conscious personality it knew, that quota of self-awareness that had been set aside as Randall.

He was trying to help Rorvik up on to his good leg when, with a formless howl that almost blended with the rasp and crackle of burning ship, the Wekk hurled itself on to them.

'ANYBODY HOME?'

'Take your hand off my ship.'

The Worm did as he was told, and gave the place where his hand had rested a wipe with his sleeve. Then he looked up again at Valum and said, 'Can we talk?'

She didn't invite him up the short ladder and into the cruiser's cabin. Instead she stepped down on to the ice. 'Have you come to a decision?'

'I'm not here to represent anybody,' he assured her. 'I'm alone.'

'I know you're alone. Do you think I couldn't see you creeping over?'

'I didn't want the others to see me, that's all. They kick me around enough as it is.'

She didn't want to hear about his personal problems. 'All this secrecy just to waste my time?'

'But I came to tell you something.'

'Tell it, then.'

The Worm glanced around, and decided that he might not be quite as invisible to the Ice Palace as he might wish. He moved in closer to the ship. 'I want something from you first,' he warned.

'I don't have to give you anything.'

'I know. All I want is for you to go away.'

She wondered whether she ought to laugh, but this baggy little clown in the one-lensed glasses was surely beyond a joke. 'I'm hardly astonished,' she said, 'but I'm not going without Randall.'

'Randall isn't here. I heard them talking.'

'Of course he's here. They're hiding him.'

'They want you to think that, but it isn't true. Morden came down alone, and wherever he came from, Randall stayed there.'

'It can't be. I'd know.'

'And the one called Killoran,' the Worm pressed on earnestly, 'he's got ideas about stealing your ship, and the others are backing him. They'll back anything that gives them the slightest hope of getting away from the Palace because Killoran's given them all escape fever. It's ruined everything I built.'

Valum heard a faint slither on the other side of the cruiser. She analysed and identified it almost immediately; Willis, letting himself out of the cabin and dropping stealthily to the ice. Could this shrimp in front of her be no more than a decoy?

'Why tell me this?' she said.

'I told you. I want you to go away and leave us alone. I want things the way they were before.'

'And how was that?'

'Ordered, logical.' The Worm was talking fast, pleased that he seemed to be getting through to her. 'None of this shouting about hope and home. Everybody working the rosters and being in the right place at the right time.'

'And you?' she asked, appearing coolly attentive while giving most of her concentration to any faint sounds that might come from the other side of the cruiser.

'I was in charge,' the Worm said. 'They needed me then. Nobody needs me for anything now.'

There was a sharp cracking sound, like a hammer on an enamel basin. Valum smiled at the Worm, and he was far from comforted. 'And you'll lie to me to be needed again,' she said.

'I'm not lying,' he protested, his voice rising to a shrill squeak. 'Randall isn't here.'

Willis came around under the wing, dragging an unresisting form by a handful of fabric. One good heave and it was sprawling at Valum's feet.

She was watching the Worm, and had observed his double surprise—once at Killoran's appearance, and again on recognition of Willis. It seemed he was telling the truth, after all.

'Caught him trying to circle round and get at us from the back,' Willis explained. 'What do you want me to do with him?'

She lifted a foot and prodded the young Elite in the side. He groaned and moved slightly, so Willis pulled him into a sitting position. After a couple of tries he stayed there.

'So,' Valum said when there seemed to be a reasonable chance that she'd be understood, 'Randall isn't at the Ice Palace. You've nothing to bargain with.'

'Of course he's there,' Killoran replied as he tried to muster enough courage to touch the back of his head. 'You won't find him without me.' Then he saw the Worm, and understood.

'It's for the best, don't you see?' the Worm said. 'Now she'll go away and leave us alone.'

Valum was looking at them both pensively. She said, 'Have you killed yet, Willis?'

Willis was surprised by the question. He'd never had the chance to join a successful bloodbag hunt. 'No, Valum,' he said.

'Take the little one, then, and watch what I do.'

She bent and then quickly straightened, lifting Killoran bodily by the thick tendons of his neck. He howled with the sudden and unexpected pain of it, also with the surprise of being lifted clear into the air by a woman who appeared to weigh considerably less than himself.

'But what about our bargain?' the Worm wailed before he was swept into the air by Willis in a similar grip.

Valum buried her fingers in the waist of Killoran's suit and prepared to execute the clean twist that would snap his neck. She looked at Willis to see how he was managing.

Willis had set the Worm down again. There was confusion in his eyes, and in that same moment she knew why.

She didn't want to kill. She could still do it, but the impulse wasn't there.

Killoran fell heavily on to the ice when she dropped him. He felt its gritty numbness against his cheek and rolled over, trying to get the cold on to the back of his neck where already the blood was collecting under the skin in a massive bruise. As the bright flashing lights that had taken over from his vision subsided he saw that Valum and Willis were returning to the cruiser.

At that moment the follow-up team arrived, Berg at their head. Ten of them had waited at the lip of the crater for Killoran's signal, and when it didn't arrive it was only Bulstrode's insistence that they stick to the letter of the plan that had kept them in line. Shouts of agony had brought them running, and now Willis had the demonstration that he'd hoped for in the Tin Jungle.

She disposed of Berg first because he was nearest, hurdling him as he fell and dropping Bulstrode and Palmer with simultaneous kicks. The Weasel had a club in the air and so left himself open to fold over a blow to the abdomen, and the Anteater tripped over him and managed to knock himself out without any help. Valum caught the club as it fell and skipped over three heads in a single swing, letting it flip over with its own momentum and bringing it up under the chin of a fourth. Then she dropped the club and met the last one with the heel of her hand to his jaw. Ever afterwards he would insist that he had 'run into the wing, or something'.

She looked for more, but that was it. She climbed into the cruiser and Willis pulled in the ladder.

The World Ship was coming out of shutdown, and something was seriously wrong.

TWENTY FOUR

ALTHOUGH CHILD-SIZED the Wekk was strong, clinging to Randall and resisting being thrown off. Rorvik couldn't help much but he managed to get a handful of the tubing on its heat unit and jerk it free. It spilled a cloud of metal-scented steam into the room, whipping about like an electrified snake.

They held it down until the cold penetrated its suit, and then when Randall helped Rorvik to get on to his good leg it still tried to crawl after them. There was no plan, no obvious route to follow, no longer a clear-cut aim in sight; they'd destroyed what they came to destroy and hadn't considered the prospects for survival afterwards. The strategic centres were blasted, all right, but as far as they knew the World Ship might already be out and in the sunlight, undamaged systems warming and preparing to re-awaken thousands of Wekk to a world robbed of its purpose.

There was some vague intention of returning to the breach and getting back to the old ship. They'd be no less trapped, but they'd be in defensible territory—at least, until the simulacra returned. Their chances in any direction were nil but all the same they ran, a three-legged, dragging double-act intent upon preserving the energies of life for as long as they could.

Randall was no ground commander. Hadn't he proved as much by his action with the gun? He'd ruined those same delicate organs that had been laid open to him as proof of his lack of free will.

Some proof. He was Randall, Elite and in control, always had been. Nevertheless he found himself taking a far greater interest in the ordinary processes of his body than was normal—the pump and stretch of muscle tissue in his legs, the ache in his side as he supported Rorvik, the bitter alkali of his saliva as he breathed too hard and too fast. All the reactions and operations that he had previously taken for granted were now like possessions of the dead, transformed from the commonplace into cherished items. Their familiarity reassured him, a growing shield against the awe that he felt after a brief glimpse into the dark spaces of his own mind.

He wasn't simulacrum. The steady tick and signature of his mentality and physique told him so. He didn't know what a simulacrum would feel like—actually, he doubted that they felt at all in the sense that he understood it—but he knew it wouldn't be like this. They'd be like Rorvik, confused and bitter and wanting to be human. Not like Randall, confused and bitter and confident that he was human.

The body's copied and the memories are planted. Find another way of being sure.

Their way was blocked by barrier foam. It had spread considerably. They tried to push through it as before, but didn't emerge within seconds as last time; it had filled a length of the corridor, bubbling out along angles and junctions. Once within its gentle pressure all directions became the same, a translucent cocoon which yielded but never revealed.

It was hopeless. Each attempt to navigate brought them to a wall, each attempt to follow a wall led them to a corner. As they were squeezing through, a silky light enveloped them without warning.

The ship was powering up.

If they needed further confirmation it was given by the vents close to the floor which were now pumping warm, moist air, heating the foam around it. As the foam heated it began to break down, shrivelling and collapsing in unlovely rags about them. Only the cold of space would preserve and consolidate it.

They came into the open and nearly fell over a Wekk. It was standing unsteadily in the doorway to its hibernation chamber, naked and dripping. It was slow to react to them—how would a Wekk show surprise?—and it blinked a couple of times, a vertical in-and-out nictation. Three doors along another Wekk emerged, and then another. A bad place to be. They plunged back into the dwindling foam and tried to plough down the corridor in a straight line.

There were a hundred of them, perhaps more, a sea of bobbing grey heads filling the passageway. Small, robust and alert, clacking and twittering like locusts. At their head, the Wekk in the thermic suit.

'We can't fight them, and we've nowhere to go,' Rorvik said in quiet desperation. 'What now?'

Randall looked on the horde. It was growing as more doors opened and wide-hipped figures came limping.

'We've got nothing to bargain with,' he said. 'Remember any good prayers?'

Their eyes met and held for a moment. 'Rorvik didn't know any. Did Randall?'

Randall shook his head, the slightest movement. 'He never needed them.'

The Wekk pushed up and around them, encircling the two but staying out of reach. 'Who do the machines pray to?' Rorvik asked.

'Nobody. Nobody cares about us. Rorvik is dead and Randall's lying sick and drunk in some urban paradise. We don't belong anywhere.'

Once it was admitted, it didn't seem so bad. When it came down to it Randall didn't want to die deceiving himself, throwing away his pride of self-awareness on a lie.

'Can they kill us?' he said suddenly, recalling the hate in the eyes of a broken Pearson.

'They can probably overpower us, but they can't destroy us. Not without the ship's help.'

'They could open a vacuum dock and push us out.'

'It still wouldn't kill us. We'd feed off the sunlight. We'd go on forever. We can't die.'

Hands were laid on them then, warm leathery claws that pushed and prodded. Knock one away and two replaced it, the Wekk swarming in and around. The crowd started to move, and Randall and Rorvik had no choice other than to move with it.

The inexorable tide urged them back towards the computer room. Every junction saw more Wekk forcing their way into the already tight compress of creatures until the corridor was filled as far as it was possible to see, both ahead and behind. In this grey and rippling mass the white of the thermic suit showed in brief glimpses, never still and always leading the way.

The noise was oppressive. The chatter of the crowd was becoming the angry death-rattle of a race.

The fires in the computer room had mainly died down. Lobo hung there, bloody and sooty and still. Randall looked into his heart for the merest symptom of a man's regret and thought, with relief, that he detected it. So much was enough for now. He would have an eternity to contemplate and encourage it.

The Wekk in the room with them had fallen silent, and it was spreading along the corridors outside. What now? They seemed to be waiting for something.

The suited Wekk pushed forward. The black dome of the helmet was off, and underneath it this creature was identical to the others. It got close to Randall and looked up at him, having to bend its neck with difficulty to do so. It laid a tentative hand on him, and its jaws worked awkwardly. No sound came out the first time, so it swallowed hard and tried again. Its lips were a bony ridge, and the only articulation was in its tongue.

The strangled sound it produced bore no resemblance to anything. It gulped hard, and tried yet again.

'*Wranda*,' it said. '*'lp ss, Wranda*'...'

It repeated it a couple of times, equally incomprehensibly. Randall looked at Rorvik, helpless.

'Does it expect me to understand this?' he said.

'It sounds like your name,' Rorvik replied. 'I think it's trying to say your name, and it can't.'

It tried again, and failed. Then, more clearly, '*Wranda*', '*'lp uss*...'

'It's asking for you to help them,' Rorvik said.

The Wekk was silent, no longer able to sustain the effort and pain of the alien phrase.

'Help them?' Randall said with dismay. 'How?'

'This whole ship was a finely balanced system keeping their race alive. Don't you see that by smashing the centres of its drive for expansion you've tipped that system and damned them?'

'Are you trying to say that I shouldn't have done it?'

'Of course not. But they're not a greedy, compulsive, world-raping race. They just lived on a world-raping ship and had to do everything it told them or die when it stopped supporting them.'

The Wekk were waiting, and Randall lacked the drive even to help himself. 'Don't get dewy-eyed for these monsters,' he said with a savagery that rang hollow. 'They built the ship, didn't they?'

'No. The last ship did.'

'That's rather a technical argument.'

'Look at their situation. They've been cruising from star to star for millennia, exploiting and expanding. The ships have used each redesigning to refine their methods; and the ships have evolved, but because of their dependence the Wekk have also evolved into complete passivity. We simulacra were the means by which the ship ensured it could do without the Wekk altogether if necessary.'

'It backfired.'

'With a vengeance. They don't know how to make repairs. So come on, Randall. You're the great white hope for the Wekk. Do something for them.'

It wasn't a responsibility he could welcome. 'You do something.'

'Don't ask me. I'm waiting as well.'

Randall's mind wanted to retreat, to slide gracefully into a dark hole and pull the hole in after it. He was numb, and he didn't want to think any more, ever. The landscapes of this new reality were too cruel, and it gave him no pleasure to look on them.

'You're the ground commander. . .' Rorvik began.

'Don't call me that!'

'You've got to accept it now. You're the heir to the ship you killed. The Wekk are looking to you to save them, and the other simulacra will look to you for leadership.'

'And what about you? Are you turning around and joining the machines again?'

'I am what I am,' Rorvik replied with quiet confidence. I've stopped worrying about it.'

There was more babbling at the far end of the room, excited noises of discovery. The broken cube that Lobo had dropped in his dying was now lifted into the air, emerging into view and bobbing towards Randall like a buoy as the Wekk passed it over their heads. They were all trying to get a hand on it to help propel it along, and when it reached Randall he found that it was vibrating slightly. He told Rorvik, unsure of what to do next.

'Open up to it,' Rorvik suggested. 'See what happens.'

Open up to it? How, for God's sake? He held it in both hands and stared at it, but nothing happened. The clattering and croaking all around him was a distraction, and now it was being picked up in the passages outside. He stared harder, but didn't really understand what he was supposed to be doing.

It came to him then without warning. The real world seemed to take a step back as the undermind superimposed its presence, guiding and demonstrating to his novice consciousness.

The cube was trying to speak to him. It was some kind of resonator, pulsing with a non-verbal message that the Wekk obviously couldn't receive. He recognized, without understanding how, the unique configuration of Valum's personality as the undermind took her meaning and crystallized it into a form that he could understand.

She was calling to the ship, asking for acknowledgement. Randall didn't know how, and the ability wasn't forthcoming.

' The simulacrum fleet is standing by in a parallel orbit with the Ship. We know you've taken some damage and that the operation is in danger. Please give us an indication of your situation. '

He couldn't. The cube would broadcast to him, but it wouldn't transmit. Rorvik moved closer so that he could listen, hopping with difficulty as the Wekk milled and pressed around him.

After a suitable pause, Valum resumed. 'The Ship doesn't answer, so this is Valum to the three prisoners. I don't know if there's any way you can hear me, but I do know that one of you is our ground commander. I also know that the ship has made a gross error of judgement and has obviously engineered its own destruction through you. In this case, our programmed loyalty reverts to our own kind; in short, that's you, whoever you are. Nothing personal, but I'm not very happy about that. On the other hand I don't have any choice.

'The only answer seems to be that you persuade the Wekk to hand you over to us. If they do that we'll leave them alone and slingshot them on to the next star. If they don't, we've got a good idea of the capacity for self-repair in the ship walls; we can puncture it all the way around and let the atmosphere escape faster than the holes can be plugged. We'll give you some time to convince them; meanwhile here's a warning shot to help the argument.'

Valum's reluctance was evident. Her new leader and the object of her unwilling devotion was to be one of a group she had come to despise.

'We can't let her do it,' Randall said. 'They'll all die.'

'I think that's supposed to be the idea.'

'But they're depending on us!'

'I doubt if Valum sees it that way. Without the ship to demand her loyalty, the Wekk are just another kind of bloodbag.'

The warning shot came. It was felt rather than heard, the boom of a distant rollercoaster punching through the outer skin of the ship.

'What are we going to do?' Randall said helplessly. The Wekk didn't deserve this, and he didn't want to bring it on them.

Rorvik wasn't so sympathetic. 'You're the leader,' he said. 'Lead.'

'But I never led anything in my life. I've always been a... a servant of the State.'

'That's Randall talking. *Your* life can be measured in days; I don't think you've got much idea of what you can or can't do.'

'I know I can't work miracles. We've got to get some kind of signal to Valum.'

'She doesn't want a signal. She wants you.'

Randall tried to push his way over to the door, but the Wekk resisted. He had some idea of getting down to a vacuum dock and finding a way to reach Valum, but they wouldn't let him;

they thought he was trying to leave them, and they pushed and hauled him back. The more he tried, the more firmly they contained him, and when he felt the undermind rising to offer him reserves of destructive strength he gave up, not wishing to maim or kill.

Rorvik wasn't so worried. He wasn't troubled by sentiment for the Wekk, and his own rescue was certain; he could even afford to feel some triumph now that it was proven that Randall's chauvinistic humanity had been totally unfounded, and was in fact little more than a calculated device to put him through his paces.

'What's the matter, Messiah?' he said. 'Can't you deliver?'

Randall looked at him, shocked. 'I don't believe it. You're enjoying this!'

'I'm entitled to it after what I've taken from you. What price your bloodbag arrogance now?'

'At least I tried. I met you halfway.'

'You talked about it, that's all. You did it because you wanted to use me. So how does it feel?'

The Wekk touched him continuously, a dancing pattern of supplication reaching no higher than his chest, the extent of their short arms. He was drowning in their hope.

'For God's sake let me through!' he pleaded, but they didn't understand. 'I'm trying to help you!'

Distant explosions then began to sound off in even succession, rattling the floor and the fittings and agitating the Wekk even more. The ship was being opened up.

The next one was close and loud. They felt the floor bend, and after a few moments a distinct stirring in the air. There was a whisper outside, the thin shriek of draining atmosphere as it funnelled through the ship. Randall realized that he was going to have to face vacuum, and the prospect frightened him; no reassurance on his survival would take away that basic fear. He asked Rorvik if he could tell him what to expect.

'It'll hurt for a while,' Rorvik said. 'That's how it was with me the first time. You want to breathe, but you can't. Then after a while you realize you really don't need to and the pain goes away.'

'I'm scared,' Randall admitted.

Rorvik was going to frame some sarcasm, but changed his mind. 'I know,' he said. 'I remember what it's like, all of it. I didn't mean what I said before.'

'No, don't take it back. I deserved it.' It was barely audible.

'What?'

'I said I. . .'

The last of the air went all at once.

TWENTY FIVE

WILLIS WAS CHOSEN to go alone to the World Ship. He piloted the craft he'd been given as close as possible to one of the larger breaches, and prepared for his first experience of raw vacuum.

He resisted the temptation to hold his breath, letting it be drawn from him in a crystal cloud. When reflex tried to reach for more air he experienced a moment of panic as his collapsed lungs stayed down, but it passed. He was aware of peculiar tides and pressures within his body as its structure fought to expand, but they were no more than a discomfort. A bloodbag would have popped and showered its matter everywhere.

There was a mess of collapsed foam on the corridor floor, frozen into place before it could expand and function. It stuck to his boots as he crossed it.

Silent as a tomb and the comparison was apt. He found his first dead Wekk two levels in, four of them slumped in a group. They seemed to have died fairly placidly, but how could he know? Their expressions told him nothing, half-blinkered and slack jawed, and they had no evolutionary need for the eloquent huddling-mechanism of mammals.

A trail of lizard corpses on the next level in led him to the computer room. It seemed that the whole shipload had tried to congregate in this one place, and Willis was slowed by having to lift bodies out of the way so that there would be enough room for him to pass.

The computer room was a burnt-out mess, and the most crowded spot of all. Here he found Randall and Rorvik.

Rorvik recognized him, but Randall didn't respond in any way. He was on the floor, pulled down by several dozen clawlike hands that had gripped the fabric of his suit. There was no malice in their grip, just a need for pointless comfort in their pain.

Willis bent to unhook some of them. Randall looked at him then, and lifted his hand from the head of one of the Wekk as if to stop him; but the gesture died before it was completed and he lowered his eyes again.

Willis worked quickly, efficiently. When Randall was freed he moved over to look at Rorvik. The leg was bad, but there was nothing vital missing to prevent regeneration. Most important, the femoral strut was intact, a little scratched but otherwise undamaged. Willis hoisted him over his shoulder for the journey back.

Randall neither cooperated nor resisted. He allowed himself to be led, following inexpressively through the marmoreal calm of the dead world. He climbed into Willis's craft and sat with his arms around his knees, lost on the distant horizon of some inner vision as Rorvik was loaded in beside him.

The other simulacra had meanwhile docked and reoccupied their old training ground. Much of their enthusiasm and pride seemed to have gone; whereas before they would have immediately begun engaging in sweep exercises and extermination patterns, now they were robbed of goal and purpose. Valum knew of no way that she could raise their morale—she was more inclined to join them in their despondency. When the word reached her that Willis was back, she went down to the bay to meet him.

His look confirmed it. Whether she liked it or not, she would have to accept Randall as her overlord.

'You don't seem very happy,' Willis commented.

'None of your business,' she replied sharply.

'No, Valum.' Willis indicated the craft in the bay behind him. A couple of the other simulacra were helping Rorvik out. 'Do you want to speak to him?'

'Things will change around here, Willis. Does he want to speak to me?'

'He doesn't seem to be interested in anything much at the moment.'

Rorvik had been carried away, and she let herself in through the side of the craft. It had once been a sporty little runabout in some far-off and forgotten system, and there wasn't much room. She had to slide in next to Randall, and they sat together in silence for a while.

Randall was the first to speak. He said, 'You going to kill me?' He sounded almost hopeful.

'You can't die. Not by any normal means. And much as I might want to try, I can't kill you.'

He nodded. He'd already known it. 'Too many changes. I can't keep up with them.'

'Shape up, commander. You've got duties and responsibilities now. If not to yourself, then to the rest of us.'

He made a real effort to take an interest, and it almost worked. 'What am I expected to do?'

'In the absence of the ship, tell us where we go next. It's your decision. We can still land and take the city—' he was shaking his head firmly—'What, then? We have to go somewhere. Down there is a man wearing your face and using your name. Why don't we go find him?'

'No. Give me time to think.'

'Whatever you want.' And then, reluctantly but to make the point, 'Sir.'

'We can't go back to the city,' he explained, 'we're too different. Even with the best intentions we'd undermine it, destroy it. And I've got too many of Randall's loyalties left in me.'

'So what do Randall's loyalties say we should do?'

'Find somewhere of our own, that's what.'

She didn't much like the idea, but it wasn't up to her to say. 'I can't argue.'

'That's right,' Randall said, brightening slightly. 'You can't.'

Willis was waiting outside, and he had a request. He wanted to go back to the Ice Palace. He wanted to go home.

Valum was shocked. 'You're sick, Willis. Remember what you are.'

The new commander was aware that such an issue could be far from simple. 'Machine bodies, Valum, but human personalities. Without the Ship they're starting to revert. Don't you feel something like it?'

'I've got nothing to revert to,' she replied stiffly. 'I wasn't based on anybody. I'm pure construct, even more so than Rorvik. They patterned me from the dreams of the creatures taken from the Ice Palace.'

'Then I'm. . . I'm sorry,' Randall said.

'Don't be. I miss nothing.'

They allowed Willis to keep the craft that he'd been using, and also gave him permission to take any equipment that might be necessary for repairs on the icebreaker. Some of the others considered going with him, but none did.

Randall tried to get used to his new status. It was an odd and unhappy feeling, but Rorvik's example was an encouragement to him. If that scrap pile could do it. . .

He gave his first order, that the broken ship should be cut loose and discarded. Then they would slingshot around the sun.

'I can't fly a World Ship,' Valum said.

'Rorvik can. And with a ship like this one we can pick our own system.'

He'd learned the lesson of his arrogance, and now would have to learn to live with it.

He had all of time to make a success of it.

KILLORAN HAD BEEN given a bunk of his own and his first taste of Ice Palace yeast. He said it was awful, almost as bad as the food in the Elite's own restaurant.

The bruising started to go down, leaving his shoulders stiff and sore with an ugly yellow-blue patterning that faded more slowly. When somebody offered him a bag of ice for a compress he thought it was funny. When twelve more people had made the same joke his smile became fixed and the appreciative laugh didn't come so easily.

They called for a few minutes, chatted for a while, and then moved on. He was conscious of a certain look they all had, as if they were only making small talk while they watched for some sign from him. Of course, he could guess what it was. They were waiting to see what he was going to do next about their escape.

It seemed impossible that the icebreaker should be useless to them, but that was the case. Because of a single act of sabotage and an obstinate inboard computer it was completely immobilized in a frustrating state of readiness. Under the circumstances it was pointless to guard the captain, who was now as much a prisoner as any of them. They even gave him the last snow suit. To show his willingness he'd gone along with a surface team to continue the search of the spaceport and shuttle wreck; although they found much of interest they found nothing of real value.

When Cohn 'dropped in' Killoran was lying face-down on his bunk, contemplating the rough grain of the insulating wood before him. Cohn made the compress joke, and Killoran pretended to be amused. With this formality out of the way Cohn sat on one of the other bunks and they talked.

Killoran asked about the Worm, and Cohn said that he'd probably live in spite of what Berg wanted to do to him. He'd locked himself in his office and piled all his furniture against the door. Killoran said that he couldn't see such a simple measure stopping Berg.

'It wouldn't,' Cohn agreed, 'but he's making the most of it. Him and Bulstrode take turns sitting outside and talking about all the horrible things they're going to do when the Worm comes out.'

Killoran said, 'I can't get angry at him, somehow.'

'You may not be,' Cohn said, suddenly serious. 'But the others need something to take it out on. To be so near and then to lose it...'

'I was afraid they'd take it out on me. For promising and not being able to deliver.'

'Be grateful there's a Worm, then. He's needed after all.'

They went on to talk about Morden. He was recovering slowly from his severe shaking, but at least he was recovering. They were giving him food from the dispensing machines on the icebreaker as he didn't yet appear to have the fortitude necessary for keeping down a mouthful of yeast. Several of the prisoners had tried the machines' products and decided that perhaps the yeast wasn't so bad after all, even if it did, in the words of one of them, taste like salted pigeon shit.

There was a tap on the door, and the icebreaker captain looked in. Killoran prepared himself for yet another compress joke, but it was something else; a figure had been spotted in the twilight on the ice, and it was heading for the Palace.

Killoran decided against spreading the news, fearing yet another false promise and general disappointment. The three of them went together to the cargo bay for helmets and then out on to the grey-blue plain of the ice cap.

There was a light snow powdering down, but hardly any wind. The clouds were banked in midnight blue right down to the edge of the world, and the flat basin which spread from the Palace to the ice cliffs in the far distance seemed to glow with a light of its own. The walker showed against this as a black shape, the snow-ditch of his route a shadowed crack that trailed him.

The party and the stranger were almost together before recognition was possible, and then Killoran called a. halt before they met.

It was Willis.

'Don't be nervous,' he said. 'It's different from last time. I'm on my own. I've come home and I want to help.'

'Help?' Cohn said suspiciously. 'How?'

'I've got some welding gear back there,' Willis said, and indicated along the direction of his trail. 'I couldn't get down any closer because there's no beacon. I'll need help to get the gear, but we should be able to fix the stabilizers.'

Killoran didn't exactly run and embrace him, although it was one of the possibilities that came into his mind; it was balanced by Willis's earlier display of hostility and his allegiance with a mysterious enemy that had dropped from the sky without warning and departed without explanation.

'Suppose we take you at face value,' he said. 'We've got a lot of questions that Morden's too sick to answer.'

Willis spread his hands in an open gesture. 'I'll tell you whatever I can.'

Cohn said, 'I don't remember you being so cooperative before.'

'I needed a holiday.'

'And what about Randall?' Killoran said.

'Randall's dead now. He won't be coming back. Is there any chance of getting some help to bring the repair equipment back?'

Killoran wasn't ready to let the question go. 'How did he die?'

'Look,' Cohn said, 'why don't you quiz him later? If we can get the tanks fixed up we can get the whole story on the way-home. I'll go back and get some of the others. You coming?'

'No, I'll go on. Make sure they bring a sled after us.'

'But you're hurt.'

'So I feel better.'

Randall had wanted it this way. Willis could tell as much or as little of the truth as he liked, but Randall was dead. It was a neater, less painful alternative.

Cohn went back to the Palace to give them the news.

Book Three
The Babylon Run

ONE

THERE WAS A hiccup in the laws of physics, and the Sparta fell out. Black hole jumping was high risk and high cost, and consequently way out of the Sparta's league—but as Ella Desmond was later to insist, the ship was in trouble and there was no choice other than to lash up the ship's computers to struggle with concepts they were never really intended to handle, and to hope.

It was usually the lithe, low-payload ships which made the jumps, ships with navigational technology of such accuracy that they could probably drop spit onto a razor's edge and make it balance. The Sparta, by way of contrast, had originally been a military freighter, bought second hand by the administering agents and converted to a passenger charter. She was oversized and ugly to look at, and her twin drives working together could only boost her to the middle ranges of sub-light. Depending on one drive alone, her crew would usually find it quicker to walk. In-system work with low overheads turned in the best profit for her; there was the occasional cross system haul, but these were only accepted when the agents could arrange paying cargo in both directions.

The trouble had hit unexpectedly, a shudder through the hull and then, just when it seemed that there was nothing to worry about, a raging display of so many alarms around the bridge that fuses blew down in Racks. The Sparta had spontaneously jettisoned one of its drive tubes—no warning and no worry, just a releasing of clamps and then the explosive bolts blew to let the unit slide away. The power plant had automatically cut its output to avoid overload and the remaining tube, by means of a fail safe to prevent overdrawing, reduced its demand in proportion; the plant had then responded again, and so on until a couple of hours later when the two units had reached an acceptable compromise and feedback had dropped to a level hardly worth measuring. Unfortunately, so had the Sparta's rate of acceleration.

Ella Desmond set her two assistant officers to reconstruct the sequence of events, but it was impossible; by the time that the spacers had replaced the appropriate breakers, most of the warning circuitry had cleared and all that Kyle and Scortia could make of what was left was that some kind of overheating had taken place. Only the dumped tube could tell them the full story, and that unfortunately was tumbling off on some unexplained mission of its own.

They were creeping between systems, and at their present speed it looked as if they'd be doing that for an impossibly long time. Porphyria was ahead and Vegas was behind, and neither was reachable with the motive power they had. There were some dead systems along the way, no use at all. They could yell for help and wait patiently as the message chugged along to its destination at lightspeed, but there was no guarantee of an answer; the Sparta wasn't a prize that would drag a salvage man off his backside, after all. Kyle got Scortia to one side and wanted to know his opinion on a proposal. Why not put the arm on Kittivale—the vessel's charterer, who was presently sitting in bored ignorance in the undersized and irregular 'luxury suite'— and get him to offer a reward for their recovery? After all, it was his own neck, and when it was explained that there were no other options he'd have to agree to the scheme. He could always recover the costs afterwards with an action against the agents for providing him with a crappy ship and an incompetent captain.

Scortia didn't like it—Kyle was always generating covert plans for self betterment, mostly touched with a light trace of slime—but under the circumstances he found it difficult to disagree. After all, it was the only way. But then he went with Kyle to put the proposal to the captain, and found that maybe there was an alternative after all.

Ella Desmond already had the spacers on the bridge—three of them, one less than the number demanded in the Sparta's operational manual but all that the agents would allow. They mostly kept to their own areas, the Racks and crawlways that were nicknamed Rat City and which took up more than eighty per cent of the Sparta. Here on the bridge they were obviously uneasy and out of place, but still their contempt for the officer class showed through their thin veneer of silent complicity. Officers couldn't fix things; officers got all the glory for the real work done by the spacers; officers had a soft time of it; officers were a joke.

She was asking them about the feasibility of taking the Sparta through a black hole. Cain said it couldn't be done, and Sarrat mumbled something which wasn't easily understood but which amounted to a statement that it still couldn't be done. Willis waited, and then said it might be possible. Willis got the job, and Kyle decided to say nothing.

Willis then reprogrammed the navigational computer and rigged a logic centre which would give it access to the extra computing power of the inboard systems when necessary. Ella Desmond, meanwhile, used what velocity they had to cut into one of the dead systems on their route and slingshot off the sun towards the most approachable singularity in the sector. Kittivale—and his much younger escort—still knew nothing.

The plan was that Willis' rig would take complete command of the Sparta, controlling its approach and angle of entry into the collapsar's field. They didn't have the programming to determine exactly where they would come out, and they couldn't even generalise. There was no way of knowing if they'd get through in one piece; but even if the Sparta was damaged and one or more of the personnel should be lost the rig would immediately use what it could of ship's sensors to calculate its position and head for wherever records showed the nearest settlement to be.

Scortia thought about it. Ella Desmond had worked out her plan and set it in motion, and it was too late to offer an alternative. The trouble with Kyle's scheme was that there was no way that it could allow the captain to retain her dignity; a ship stranded without explanation, bailed out by its passenger. With a black hole jump she'd be risking the ship and its crew, but then she'd a chance of romping home to glory.

Well, Scort, he told himself, that's what it's all about, and when the time came he didn't argue but followed his duties as safety officer. Couple of problems down below, Mister Kittivale. Perhaps you and the lady would just climb into the crash bubbles and inflate the linings—standard procedure, and nothing to worry about. With a sudden burst of inspiration, Scortia explained that some turbulence was expected—Kittivale swallowed it straight away but there was suspicion in the young woman's eyes. Turbulence? What was this, a kite? So Scortia added something about a strong gravity field from an object they'd be passing, which had the doubtful advantage of being halfway towards the truth. She didn't look too happy.

But then she didn't argue, either.

THE SPARTA approached Babylon with a chunk of her belly missing. She'd been too wide for the hole, and the bulge that held the planet landing gear and the utility pod had been pared away like mud from a boot. Everybody had heard it go, the agony of the superstructure and the howl of wind that preceded the automatic sealing off, then the pressure bags had blown and hardened and the air plant had stepped up production to compensate.

She lurched in sideways, doing her best to ride the landing lasers but painfully disabled. The hollowed out asteroid was ringed by access tubes with U-shaped g-force traps to hold in the atmosphere, and the Sparta managed to bang the walls a couple of times as she passed from vacuum to normal air pressure.

The Hotel Babylon greets you and wishes you a pleasant stay

The navigational computer tried to unscramble the sudden influx of helpful traffic control information, details which somehow didn't quite match in with the feedback from its own intelligence network. Retros fired like whipcracks and pushed the ship across to the far side of the tunnel, and as laser paths were broken the warning screams from the hotel caused another over correction and another jarring bump

> *Please disembark from your craft and move through into the reception lobby as soon as possible*

which broke a lot of glass and loosened a lot of fixtures within the hull. The courtesy bar in Kittivale's suite was unsecured, and in less than a second the opposite bulkhead was dashed with jagged crystal. Cables along the runs in Rat City were shaken loose from their traps to land into the crawlways like dry guts. Within the crash bubbles the impact was felt as a soft thump with several follow up shakes as the metal hull resonated.

> *Babylon's own pilots will move your spacecraft to one of our parking zones and supervise the transport of your baggage*

The tunnel split, five different ways to five different hangars. One was offered, but the Sparta lurched for the nearest; Babylon threw up no fuss, but simply reordered its directional information to comply. The ship was obviously in distress. Fire and maintenance crews were probably standing by already.

She made it into the hangar, and even managed most of the flip that was necessary to orient her towards the docking platform. The weak thrusting drive died too late and she crumpled sideways into the metal structure. Flooring plates popped and buckled as the framework was compressed, but already the Sparta was settling and massive floor jacks were rising to support her.

They'd made it. To somewhere.

TWO

THE BUBBLES deflated automatically when the danger was over. Kyle was first out, and Scortia followed a minute later—he'd been unable to reach his relief tube against the restraining pressure, and he'd remembered the instructor's words from his earliest space training; 'A crash bubble's probably the most boring place you'll ever find yourself. Pissing down your leg doesn't make it any more interesting.'

Kyle's legs wouldn't support him at first, so he sat on the thin hard carpet of the shared quarters and tried to knead some sensation back into his trembling thighs. Unfortunately, his hands and arms weren't fit for much, either. He wanted to throw up and mess himself at the same time, but somehow the two opposed impulses managed to cancel each other out.

There was a voice outside in the corridor, muffled and made incomprehensible by the cabin walls. Kyle was able to get around onto his knees and then, unsteadily, onto his feet; he wove the couple of steps to the bulkhead and almost fell against the contact plate by the door. Scortia was just starting to emerge when the door slid back and the announcement from the corridor speakers spilled in.

> *... to the Hotel Babylon. You are now within the territorial jurisdiction of the Babylon asteroid, the nearest orbiting object to the spectacular red sun at the heart of the dead system of Persephone. The dim fires of Persephone itself will warm and thrill you as you gaze down from your suite onto the boiling gases below, secure in a complex which is strengthened by the rock structures of the asteroid. No comfort is overlooked, no pleasure beyond reach; the Hotel Babylon exists only for your*

recreation. Please move through into the reception area, where our staff will be waiting to meet you. Welcome...

Kyle hit the plate again, and the door closed to cut off the repeat. Now it was Scortia's turn to go through the agonies of stiffness that followed movement, but now there were two of them and the meagre cabin was suddenly overcrowded. Kyle shuffled around his fellow officer and dropped stiffly onto the lower of their two bunks. 'Did you hear that?' he asked, 'or were you creaking too much?'

Scortia winced as he nodded; the movement of his neck was like that of a gearbox filled with gravel. 'I heard it,' he said. 'Where the hell's Persephone?'

'I don't know. I'm damn sure it's nowhere we were heading, though.'

'That's hardly the point, is it? I mean, at least we got here in one piece.'

Kyle groaned in pained ecstasy as he lay back on the bunk and stretched. 'Speak for yourself. I feel like I've been stuffed into a dog's basket for the last fifteen hours.'

Too far to the upper bunk; Scortia considered it and rejected the idea. Too much effort, even in subnormal gravity. Instead he stood up and tottered to the shatterproof mirror that was recessed into the back of the door. His mouth tasted as if he'd been keeping a live goldfish in it, and when he stuck his tongue out he didn't see much to contradict the conclusion. Scortia was tall and light skinned whereas Kyle was dark and compact; Kyle said that the agents had arranged it that way so that Ella Desmond wouldn't have too much trouble telling them apart. Right now, Scortia looked more like a straw flecked scarecrow than anything else.

'We had it easy,' he said as he turned from the mirror, but he didn't sound as if he believed it. 'Think of the spacers down in Rat City. No bubbles, just webbing.'

Kyle waved a negligent hand in the air, didn't bother to sit up. 'Who cares about spacers?' he said. 'Call the iceberg.'

'The who?'

'Call the captain.'

'Why?'

Kyle levered himself up onto one elbow. 'Tell her we're still alive.'

'So who cares about bridge officers?'

Ella Desmond made it first. There was a pattern of call tones from the grubby plastic wall console, and then the speaker spattered into life. *'Scortia? Kyle? Anybody alive down there?'*

Scortia raised his voice to reply. 'I'm moving and Kyle's complaining, so I'd guess that means he's okay.'

'I'm not joking. We were too wide for the black hole, and we left a chunk of hull behind.'

'How the hell did we manage that?' Kyle muttered, and the wall unit picked it up.

'Not out of choice, I assure you,' the captain said drily. She knew what to expect from Kyle, openly or otherwise. *'The gravity field just peeled it off us as we squeezed through.'*

Scortia said, 'Any idea where the hole threw us out?'

'You've heard as much as I have. Some damned automatic greeting's locked into the ship's p.a. system, and I can't get the damn thing to cut out. The Hotel Babylon in the system of Persephone, wherever that is.'

Kyle swung upright and sat on the edge of the bunk. 'Sounds like a fun place for a stopover, anyway.'

'I'm glad you think so. While you're about it, you can be thinking about who's going to pay for all this.'

'Aren't we insured?' Scortia knew that the agents were always cutting corners, but they had a basic business integrity—enough to survive on and no more.

'Not at the rates we'd need to support us in this rich man's paradise.'

'So we'll move out somewhere cheaper,' Kyle suggested.

Ella Desmond snorted, and her cabin mike was momentarily blasted into overload. *'Like where? You heard the drivel on the greetings tape, we're on an asteroid hotel in a dead system and we're sitting in half a ship. They can screw us for everything we've got.'*

'Which isn't much,' Scortia offered, trying to sound

optimistic, 'so why worry?'

'*I'm the captain, it's my job to worry. You two monkeys get onto your jobs and check the passengers. I'm going to have another try at raising some reply from the hotel.*' And without waiting for a reply, she cleared the circuit.

'Monkeys?' Kyle said, frowning in puzzlement.

'It explains why they pay us peanuts,' Scortia said. He turned back to the mirror and tried to smooth his space cropped hair so that it looked more like the covering of a head and less like the outer shell of a horse chestnut. The spikes sprang back up, and even spit wouldn't keep them down. Reflected behind him, he could see Kyle. He was conducting an experiment in standing up.

'Look,' Kyle said, 'it's not going to take both of us to do the rounds. Why don't you get after her and find out what she's playing at?'

'We know what she's playing at. She's trying to raise the hotel. She doesn't need help for that.'

'She needs careful instructions to get all her fingers in her gloves. Just go and look over her shoulder, make sure she's got the right key open.'

Scortia turned around. 'I know what you're after. You want to go and help that girl Thea out of her crash bubble. Some excuse to get your hands all over her.'

Kyle hesitated for a moment, his face a blank. It was something that Scortia had observed before, a brief neutrality which seemed to give Kyle a chance to run through the small range of response options available to him. And then he grinned.

'I probably don't need much of an excuse. I can't see that dried up shrimp Kittivale giving her much fun on the voyage so far. She'll probably drag me into the bubble with her.'

'I'd rather take my chances through a black hole. The kid's a vamp.'

'A what?'

'A gold digger. You just put your finger on it, the only thing Kittivale can offer her is his money.'

Kyle shrugged, and moved towards the door. 'So she can

have his money and my body. Then everyone's happy.'

'I can't bear to watch you drooling like this,' Scortia said as the door slid back and the mechanical voice of Babylon spilled through again from the outer corridor. 'You check the passengers, and I'll join the captain.'

'I'll check them both,' Kyle promised as he stepped out into the corridor. 'Especially Thea.'

First Scortia checked the captain's cabin. It was across the ship from their own, probably the only symmetrical feature of the vessel's layout. The personal buzzer hadn't worked for three trips or more and there was no reply when he banged on the panel, so he had to conclude that she'd moved on. Next he went to the bridge. It was like a good old fashioned ship's bridge, a raised half dome with blind windows that gave a feeling of thrusting forward into the unknown. Unfortunately this was mostly illusion, as the bridge was situated halfway down the side of the Sparta and faced backwards, but on a solitary nightwatch a junior officer could still switch off all the lights and play Hornblower as he paced amongst the glittering jewelled lights of the traffic and status consoles.

Ella Desmond wasn't there, either, but a tell-tale on the main desk was blinking to show that the outer lock was open. He turned around and followed her down.

A folding tunnel had started to roll out towards the Sparta but it had stopped after only a few yards, jammed on rails that had been buckled as the ship had leaned hard on the boarding platform. It was obviously intended to shield the noise and utilitarian ugliness of the hangar from the paying customers, but Scortia stepped straight out into the open and got the immediate blast of the glare and the smoke and the burnt fuel stink washing over him.

The platform sections shifted and grated under his weight as he moved towards where Ella Desmond stood in the open maw of the aborted tunnel, collapsed and rucked like the shed skin of a bloated white caterpillar. The lights were some way overhead, hard arcs that were softened by the fog drawn upwards to the hanger's fans.

'Hi, Scort,' Ella Desmond said absently as the junior officer arrived at the entranceway. 'Where's your slimy friend?'

'Kyle's doing his PR act with our employers.' Scortia saw that the captain was contemplating a touch button panel recessed into the frame of the doorway. 'I came out to see how you were getting on.'

'I suppose he told you I wouldn't be able to manage alone.'

It took a moment for the question to register, but then Scortia—too late—said, 'No, nothing like that.'

She nodded to herself, confirmation. 'He's a creep and a sexist throwback. And I know all about the petition he tried to get up against me last tour.'

'You heard about that?'

'I heard you wouldn't sign it, as well. There's not much I miss around here. Look, I can't get past this damn door.'

Scortia took another look at the damn door. It didn't seem very strong, but that was probably just decoration; behind it would be reinforced to resist air leak. 'Where does it lead?'

'Out of the dock and into the reception lobby—at least, it's supposed to. But it's not opening. Try it.'

She moved back to let him get closer to the panel. It wasn't really necessary, but she didn't seem to like the idea of anybody passing close to her even for a moment. Kyle had once pointed out to Scortia that Ella Desmond was old enough to be his mother, and he'd had to stop and think for a while; numerically perhaps, but otherwise the concept just didn't hang together. He couldn't imagine Ella Desmond being anybody's mother, and when he'd told Kyle his reaction Kyle had said, straight faced, 'Okay, then. She's old enough to be your father.'

The panel was obviously intended to be operated by some hotel lackey, because there was neither explanation nor any set of instructions alongside it. The touch buttons were all numbered, and there was a horizontal bar across the top marked SERVICE. Scortia hesitated for a moment, then brushed his fingertips against it. The bar began to glow.

> *The Babylon management apologises, but there are certain formalities that must be cleared before you*

are admitted. Please bear with us, and we'll get them out of the way as soon as we can.

There was no speaker; the voice, a fair simulation of a human being, seemed to come from all over the door. It was too heavy to be vibrating, but perhaps a fluctuating charge was exciting the air particles close to its surface. The effect was weird, as if the fabric of the hotel was addressing them directly, without human intercession.

'Formalities?' Scortia said. The Sparta was obviously damaged, unmistakeably in distress. 'What formalities?'

'God only knows. I tried calling from the ship, but nobody answered. Nobody's talking to us except these damned machines. Every time I hit that plate, it's the same.' By way of demonstration she stabbed at a few of the buttons, pushing where pushing wasn't needed, and it seemed that it didn't matter what was hit; the same message started to repeat. 'See what I mean?' she said, raising her voice to outdo the door. 'A crippled ship comes limping in without warning. We popped into existence from somewhere on the other side of the galaxy with our computers set to head for the nearest safe settlement, and nobody even comes to take a look. There should have been alarms all over the place when we came in, and there ought to be a team of maintenance engineers checking us out by now. Damn it, Scort, we could blow up and take half the asteroid with us. And they're not even showing any interest.'

'Maybe they're checking to see if we're rich enough to get in.' It was only half a joke.

'Forget it, then.' Ella Desmond took a step closer to the door and looked it over, as if by glowering hard enough she might frighten it into opening.

'It's probably something really simple,' Scortia said, aware that it wasn't much more than optimistic noise.

'Simple or not, it stinks. Nobody hedges when a ship in distress appears.'

'Why not get Kittivale out to speak to them?' It was an innocent and logical enough suggestion, but Scortia was still uncomfortable as he recalled that it was little more than a variation on Kyle's idea. 'If he's rich enough to charter us, they should be on the same wavelength.'

Ella Desmond shook her head. 'I'm not so sure about Kittivale.'

'What do you mean?'

'I mean he hasn't got the manners or the confidence of a playboy.'

Scortia found it hard to disagree; Kittivale dressed badly and had the kind of personality which allowed him to sit in the corner of a room and quietly merge with the furniture. But on the other hand, rich was rich. 'At his age and with his money, who needs manners and confidence?'

'His age I can't argue with. But I think the money's a bluff.'

'Bluff?'

'Gilt edged bluff. That security bag he carries around, the one he used to pay the charter deposit. He makes out it's full of currency crystals. I think it's empty.'

Scortia's interest was hooked. 'You've seen inside it?'

'No. I got curious and made a check as we were setting off. One of the casinos on Vegas was missing a cashier and a good time girl from the cocktail bar. The amount they made off with was barely enough to cover our hire fee.'

'You mean we're transporting a couple of cheapskate crooks and treating them like trillionaires?'

'We might be,' Ella Desmond shrugged, playing it down but obviously pleased at the effectiveness of her bombshell. 'It's just a suspicion, nothing I can prove—yet.'

'The agents will love this.'

'Kyle will probably send them a petition about it. Recommending himself as my replacement, naturally.'

Scortia tried to be reassuring, and somehow made himself feel like a Judas. 'I wouldn't worry about him.'

'I don't. Sometime he'll slip up, and then he won't know what's hit him. All that's worrying me is, why are we sitting here in the car park when we should be in the hotel?' And then she turned and, by way of a demonstration, hit the plate beside the door again. One of the many voices of Babylon started to repeat its well rehearsed message.

IN THE SPARTA'S luxury suite, the rusty whirring of the air conditioner was a counterpoint to the retching that came from the small bathroom cubicle. Thea finished blowing her nose on a rag of tissue and then opened it out to check; only a couple of spots of blood now, mocking little pinpoints of drying red, nothing like the terrible loss she'd imagined when the pressure in the ship had suddenly dropped and her hands had been pinned down by the crash bubble. She looked for somewhere to drop the tissue, but it didn't really seem to matter much; everything that had been inadequately secured in the cabin—which meant more or less everything—was strewn about the floor. She pushed it into a pocket instead.

There was a moment's silence from Kittivale, the air conditioner rattled on. Thea raised her voice and called, 'Are you feeling any better?'

'No,' Kittivale echoed miserably from the cubicle. 'I feel like my lungs are inside out.'

Which probably meant that he felt a mild discomfort. Half of his luggage seemed to have been taken up with patent cures, overpriced bait for hypochondriacs, things to sniff and things to swallow and things to spray, most of them variations on light sedatives. It was obvious that she wasn't going to get much of a chance at the bathroom, so she picked her way across to the fixed mirror and tried to clean up some of the mess with a couple of cologne pads.

It made her feel a lot better, even the stinging around her nostrils where the cologne seared at the rubbed tenderness, and the cool of the drying spirit was an angel's kiss. She looked in the mirror again; now her skin shone under the soft cabin light, she was pure, she was fresh, she was wholesome. Looking glass lies.

The little announcer unit by the cabin door made a game attempt at spitting out a snatch of music, but its gargling was fair competition for Kittivale. Thea moved across and touched the button under the unit, and the door slid back. It bumped over a kink in the rail halfway along.

Kyle was waiting, arms folded, leaning against the wall

outside in the busy hollow throbbing of the ship's corridor. His attitude seemed calculatedly casual, his smile painted on with a single stroke of a brush. He let it shine on her for a moment, and then looked over into the cabin behind. 'Everybody all right in here?' He said.

Thea turned away from him and went back to the mirror. He took it as an invitation, and followed her in. 'What does it sound like?' she said.

The door closed. 'Sounds like somebody's trying to turn his lungs inside out,' Kyle said.

'I'm glad you think it's funny.'

'Be glad we're all alive, instead. What about you?'

Reflected in the mirror, Thea could see Kyle as he stepped over some upturned cushions and then sat down. She said, 'I'm fine.'

'I can see that,' he said, and tried to meet her eye in the glass, but then Kittivale put his head out of the bathroom and distracted him.

'What's been going on here?' Kittivale demanded. 'Nobody told us anything.'

'Just to get strapped in and pray,' Thea added. 'Are all your charter voyages like this, Mister Kyle?'

Kyle didn't seem troubled. 'The company isn't always so pleasant. And it's pretty rare to lose half our drive capability on the way.'

Maybe Kittivale didn't know exactly what the statement implied, but he could recognise the buildup that Kyle gave it. 'To lose what?' he said. 'Why didn't you tell us about this?'

Kyle gave a don't blame me shrug. 'I'm telling you now. We had some kind of fault, an explosion and a short fire back in the drive service section. Nobody knows what went or what caused it. All we could tell was that we hadn't a hope of reaching a fraction of our target speed; at our top rate it would have taken us fifty years to reach the nearest inhabited system.'

Thea cut in with, 'Why not sit tight and call for rescue?'

'It wasn't my decision.'

'So what did we do,' asked Kittivale, out of the bathroom and sickness forgotten, 'and where are we now?'

'We took a gamble,' Kyle told him. 'We looked for the nearest dark star and jumped into it.'

Kittivale glanced at Thea. 'Did that answer the question?'

'A black hole's got a massive gravity field,' Kyle went on. 'You know that time and space are two different expressions of a single concept?'

'What?' said Kittivale, completely lost.

'It's basic Einstein,' Thea said, adding, 'whoever he was.'

'Time and space are both affected in the presence of a gravity field. They're all locked together, you can't define one without the other two. And when one bends, the others bend with it.'

'Look,' Kittivale said, 'just cut the degree course and tell us what happened.'

'A black hole causes a massive local distortion of the normal shape of space time. We dropped through the fringe of this and popped out in another part of the universe. We had the ship's computer run through all the possible options and pick us somewhere we'd have a good chance of reaching.'

'Which is?' prompted Thea.

'The Hotel Babylon in the system of Persephone.' Kyle announced, but without the trumpets. And then he added, 'Wherever the hell that is, and don't ask me where because it's way off my sector.'

Kittivale nodded, trying to take it all in, and then he caught himself. 'What do you mean,' he said, 'off your sector?'

'Means what it says.'

Kyle was putting less effort into his smile now, and it was settling into a natural leer. Thea began to feel uncomfortably exposed, and she moved a little closer to Kittivale. Maybe the old poop wasn't much protection, but at least he was harmless. She said, 'How long before we can get back on the route to Porphyria?'

'No way I can say. We were damaged before we went into the hole, and we were more damaged when we came out. Left a fair piece of the ship behind. I doubt we could do much more than limp between moons.'

Kittivale said, 'What are we talking about? Hours, days?'

'Could be months.'

'*Months?*'

'Well, standard ones, anyway. I don't know what the local periods are. You don't seem to realise, we've made it through a major disaster here and all you've got out of it is a good shaking and the dry heaves. Just to make things perfect, you haven't even been dumped on some stinkpot of a munitions planet or a farmer's moon thigh deep in cow dung, you've rolled up in the foyer of a luxury hotel. I'm going the diplomatic way about it, but the point I'm trying to make is that it's a cue for relief and celebration and not a Greek chorus.'

Both passengers looked blank. 'Greek chorus?' Thea said.

'Greeks. They're big lizards on Epsilon Five. Make the most godawful racket you ever heard.'

Kittivale made a tiny fist and punched at something invisible in the air before him. Even then, he seemed to miss it. 'I'll sue,' he said, and when Thea gave him a warning glance he wasn't looking.

Kyle absorbed the information. There was a light of interest in his eyes. 'Really?' he said.

'And don't you try to persuade me otherwise.'

'It's your right, of course. I suppose...' Kyle stood up, and shook some of the creases out of his crew uniform. 'I suppose you'll be citing Captain's negligence?'

'Is that the usual form?'

'Captain has to carry the can for whatever happens to the ship.'

'Then that's what I'll do.'

'Well,' Kyle said, 'I'm pleased to see you're taking such a positive attitude.' Oddly enough, he seemed to mean it. He moved towards the door. 'When you're ready, make your way through to the reception lobby. Scortia and the Captain are up there already. I'll be joining them when I've checked on the spacers.' The door completed its uneven slide, and Kyle hesitated halfway out. 'I wouldn't mention the legal business right now, not to the Captain. She'll have plenty on her mind as it is. You want any advice, just come to me. See you later.' He winked as the door wiped across, preventing any reaction.

Kittivale's determination lasted for a full ten seconds after

Kyle's exit, and then reality got back to him. The padding on the threadbare couch was still compressed from where Kyle had been sitting. Kittivale moved over and dropped down wearily beside the hollow. 'Well, that's it,' he said. 'We're not going to get away with it.'

Thea looked down at him. 'And what makes you so optimistic?'

'You heard him. A luxury hotel. I bet you can't even fart without credit.'

'It's no reason to go jumping out of the airlock.'

'We had a good run of it. But did you ever think we could really get away?'

'Now just a minute, Kittivale,' Thea said sharply, and the older man flinched at her tone. 'I've not come this far just to give in and turn back. What do you think they'll have waiting for us if we get dragged back to Vegas?'

'We could offer to return the money...' Kittivale suggested, but Thea wasn't ready to listen.

'We couldn't live three lifetimes and hope to repay what we took in that rigged game. Cashiers and cocktail hoppers just don't pull that kind of money. Well, we both wanted to get out, and we're out. No way am I going back.'

'We've got barely enough to pay off the charter,' Kittivale protested.

'Forget that. We pay them nothing, after what's happened.'

'So maybe we can afford a week at Babylon prices.'

'A week to plan the next move we make. It doesn't have to be Porphyria.' It had just been a place they'd picked off a star chart, a moderate middleworld, an end of the rainbow to aim for. But Thea could easily change her ideas; Kittivale's imagination lacked exercise.

'How are we going to live?' he asked in what bordered close to a whine. Thea let her annoyance show, tired of the persuading and the pampering.

'It's a hotel, right? And hotels have casinos. What we did once, we can do again.'

'And run again.'

'Yes, and run again. What's the matter with that? We did it

before. We'll improve with practice.'

'And where's it all going to end?'

'When we fall over and die, like everything else,' Thea said with enough bitterness to make Kittivale flinch. 'You make me sick, you want your whole life mapped out and handed to you in a package. Regular savings and the pension scheme were invented for people like you.'

Kittivale had spent his life following the safest option. Right now, arguing with Thea obviously wasn't it. 'All right,' he said. 'I'll do whatever you want.'

'I think you've missed the point, but it's a start. Get yourself ready and we'll go on up to the lobby.'

He knew better than to compete for the bathroom again. Thea went in and unzipped her jumpsuit, shrugged out of it and then bundled it into the microclave under the basin. Both taps ran cold, but she wasn't in the mood to be bothered by that; she scooped up double handfuls and emptied them over herself, first her head, then splashing down onto her shoulders and running off her body in clean, cold rivulets.

The puddling was starting to settle through the porous floor when she'd finished rough towelling her hair, and the microclave pinged softly and offered up the jumpsuit, newly sterile. When she emerged after only three or four minutes Kittivale was ready, sitting with the personally keyed security bag that held the last of their haul, a few internationally negotiable security crystals. He clutched it to his chest as if it contained a fortune; fine, Thea thought, let them believe it.

'Come on, Midas,' she said, 'let's try to find our way off this tub.'

THREE

SPACERS' QUARTERS were deep down in Rat City, insofar as the concept of 'down' had any meaning in a structure designed for mainly off planet use. Kyle had a strong feeling that he was entering alien territory as he descended a metal stairway into a tangled darkness that was punctuated by harsh, unshielded lights. The stairway had once been painted grey, but use had worn clean steel down the centre of the treads.

The spacers had made themselves a social area in the large volume between the two drive tube housings. Cleared of the benches and the lockers and the tape decks, the place would even be big enough for a limited game of handball. They'd also panelled out individual quarters with private doors where gaps in the tubing and cable rigging allowed—that made it two counts where they had it over the junior officers.

The noise was a lot heavier here, nothing harsh or industrial, just the steady beat of a hurt ship staying alive. Kyle counted two figures lounging, and looked around for a third.

'On your feet, spacers,' he called with authority as he approached, and two heads turned lazily to watch him coming.

'Up yours, Kyle,' Sarrat called back, and 'Yeah, shove it, Kyle,' chorused Cain.

'Glad to see everybody's happy. Where's Willis?'

Sarrat was the larger of the two. He generally shaved his balding head but just as often forgot, so that it was covered with a fair stubble. The solid looking dome merged almost seamlessly with his neck. He said, 'Who cares?' and unzipped another hash cola.

'He's monkeying with the computer lashup you had him do,' Cain said, indicating some vague location up above with a stab of his thumb. 'The one that nearly got us all killed.'

'You want to make a complaint, make it formal and make sure you spell the Captain's name right. She's sensitive. Sarrat, go and get Willis.'

Sarrat hiccupped and looked around, as if there might be some other Sarrat handy to take the work off him. No luck. 'Why?' he demanded.

'So you can all pool your knowledge and reach halfwit status.' Kyle sat down on one of the scratched lockers and reached for a can from the five pack on the bench, not bothering to wait for the invitation he wouldn't get. 'And because I've got officer stripes and you're a spacer. Also because you've got to haul your backsides up to the hotel lobby for the free drinks and peanuts.'

'Free drinks?' said Cain, looking alert for the first time, but Kyle waved him back. 'You stay where you are, I want to talk to you. Move it, Sarrat.'

Sarrat couldn't summon the intellectual horsepower to argue, and he'd already used his best line of rebuke. He glanced at Cain and got a slight nod, and then he picked up his can and moved off towards the steps, muttering as he went.

'I heard a two syllable word in there somewhere,' Kyle called after him. 'You're improving.'

They both watched as Sarrat climbed the steps, and then waited a while longer as the sound of his boots echoed back to them. Then Kyle turned to Cain.

'All right,' he said quietly. 'What went wrong?'

Cain shuffled a little, coughed, looked around, considered, and when it was obvious that there would be no alternative, he said lamely, 'We had a bit of an accident...'

'Damn right we did. You were supposed to foul up the drive enough to slow us down, not blow the back end of the ship away.'

Cain reddened, anger and embarrassment mixed. 'I didn't exactly plan it like that. The computer kicked in with a course correction while I had the dampers out. The tube started to overheat, so the damn machine jettisoned the drive. It happened so fast, there was nothing I could do.'

Kyle looked across at the curved outer wall of the drive tube, a housing large enough to hold a subway train, a two layered cooling jacket with an access door to the drive within; except, of course, that this tube was now empty, and of the two exposed sections that bounded the recreation area only one was anything more than decoration.

'So,' he said, 'we end up doing a black hole drop, and Ella Desmond saves the day with a plan that's a shade more chancy than suicide.'

'Maybe you can still make her look bad,' Cain suggested hopefully, but Kyle gave him a pained look.

'What? After this? I can do my best, but there's not much hope. Not when Kittivale thinks it through and comes to the conclusion that she saved his neck. That kind of consideration can be awfully persuasive when you're giving character references.'

They sat in thoughtful silence for a moment, and then Cain said, 'What are you going to do now?'

Kyle sighed. 'Let it all blow over and wait for another chance. The agents have got short memories. All we'll need is a few charters brought in over budget, a few deadlines missed—nothing obvious.'

'You'll still need me.' It wasn't a question. Kyle narrowed his eyes when he looked at Cain, searching for the meaning behind.

'What's the matter?' he said. 'You feeling unwanted?'

'I'm feeling insolvent.'

'It's likely to persist. And if you don't like it, just remember who it was had the dampers out when we waved goodbye to the number two tube.'

Cain shifted uneasily, and tried to change the subject. 'I've talked to Sarrat, like you said.'

'And?'

'He's with us, same conditions as me. Full share in the rackets we set up when you get command. Drugs, spice, everything.'

Kyle nodded. 'What about Willis?'

'I haven't talked to Willis.'

'When are you going to?'

'I'm not.' Cain was no longer evasive, he was emphatic. Kyle started to object, and Cain went on, 'Look, Kyle, let's leave Willis out of it. There's something strange about him and I don't know what it is. The less I have to do with him, the better I like it.'

'I'd be happier with all the spacers behind me.'

'Yeah, well, in a perfect world maybe that's the kind of thing you can hope for. Right now you'll have to make do with Sarrat and me. What about Scortia?'

'He's my problem.' And likely to be a touchy one, Kyle thought; there didn't seem to be much of a motherlode of self interest to be mined in his fellow officer. But there had to be some hook to hang persuasion onto. If not—'I'll do him up at the same time as Captain Desmond.'

'When?'

'I'm watching for the chance. Might turn up while we're at the hotel, might be later.'

Cain spoke carefully. 'If you're thinking of something kind of final, you could think of including Kittivale as well.'

The idea hadn't occurred to Kyle. 'Why?'

'He's greased.'

'Anybody who can charter an intersystem cruiser all to himself has got to be well off,' Kyle conceded, but in a tone that said so what?

'But they don't all lug it around with them in negotiable crystals. Right?'

'I'll think about it,' Kyle said.

'Do that.' Cain got to his feet and stretched lazily. 'Now, where are the free drinks?'

'Right,' said Kyle, and followed as Cain moved towards the steps that would lead them out of Rat City. He felt slightly unsettled; somewhere during the conversation he was sure that he'd lost the upper hand, but he couldn't exactly say where.

MOST OF THE fog had cleared from the hangar and the fans had cut out. Their distant rumble hadn't been too noticeable before, but the silence that they left was unsettling; Sarrat's boots made a clear and unhealthy ringing sound as he stepped from the Sparta's lock onto the Babylon platform. It was everywhere at once in the girdered space, up against the bright haze of the curving roof and in the shadows behind the maintenance cranes and rigs, echoing from plates and angles and the huge structural ribs of the walls. It didn't seem to bother Sarrat at all.

Under Sarrat's noise was the tiny, piping voice of Babylon, shrunken by distance but still clear in its apologetic message. The spacer could see the buckled track which led across the platform, the half unrolled tunnel at its end; Scortia was by what should have been the tunnel's entrance, a stretched frame to support the snakeskin folds. He didn't seem to be doing anything.

Sarrat heard Willis coming along behind. He didn't wait, but set off across the plating towards Scortia.

'Hi, Scort,' he said, looking into the tunnel to see if Ella Desmond was around, and Scortia gave him a bored little wave of greeting. Sarrat wiped his nose on the back of his hand before he went on, 'Why aren't they letting us in?'

'We are in,' Scortia told him.

'Only if you want to get technical. Are they afraid we'll mess up the carpets?'

Scortia privately thought that Sarrat could drop litter at his own funeral, but he only shrugged and said, 'I don't know what's happening. The Captain's trying to raise somebody to speak to us, but so far there's nothing. The doors just don't open.'

Sarrat craned a little. He could see Ella Desmond, punching hard at random sequences of touch buttons, always getting the same bland response. He grinned and said, mainly to himself, 'Hasn't got a slugging clue, has she?'

The junior officer didn't want to get into a gripe session. On the few occasions when he'd shared quarters with spacers, the criticism of command had been the only topic of conversation that seemed to offer any competition to money, to the extent that he found mealtimes stupefyingly dull; whining and dining, with little to recommend it.

Somebody else approaching across the dock; Scortia turned and saw Willis. Willis was an outsider in a group of three, a different style altogether; more reserved, more private, and Scortia liked him better although he had to admit that he knew nothing that could give him a reason.

'Hi, Willis,' he said. 'Everything all right with the computer hookup?'

'Good as you can expect after what we went through. I broke it all down again.'

'Shame. I wanted to take a look at the rig that saved all our lives.'

'Sorry,' Willis said, and didn't offer anything more.

'Don't be sorry, I'm thanking you.' There was a call from the end of the tunnel, something approximating Scortia's name, and he said, 'See you later,' and moved off.

Something seemed to be troubling Sarrat. As soon as Scortia was out of range he turned to Willis and said, 'Damn quick job you did, getting everything pulled apart like that.'

'I like to keep everything neat.' Willis took a couple of steps so that he could see along the outside of the tunnel housing, not really paying much attention to Sarrat; Sarrat followed.

'Almost like you didn't want anybody else to get sight of it close up,' he said, making it sound like an accusation.

'Why should I want that?'

'I'm wondering. Couldn't be that you built a bias into the selection system, could it? Something that would give you some control over where we ended up?'

Willis touched the tunnel material. It was doeskin soft, and wouldn't hold creases. He said absently, as if he was only giving Sarrat a small part of his attention, 'The Captain asked me for a fast programme to make a random selection for the safest option, the one that was the most accessible. That's all I did.'

'But what I'm wondering is, how come the safest and most accessible target happens to be over on the far side of the galaxy from where we're headed?'

'Don't ask me, ask the computer.'

'Too damn late now, isn't it? You've dismantled the links and the programme.'

'I like everything...'

'Neat, yeah. Too damned neat, Willis.'

Willis looked at him closely for the first time. It wasn't the right response, according to Sarrat's grasp of practical psychology; Willis was supposed to be either protesting his innocence or squirming with guilt, not studying his accuser with what looked oddly like compassion. And then he said, 'Please yourself. I do my job, that's all.'

FOUR

'ANY PROGRESS?'

'Not an inch.' Ella Desmond was angry and frustrated, and she didn't even have the convenient getout of somebody to blame; all that she had was Babylon's blank politeness, and a door that wouldn't open. 'I keep calling for somebody who knows what's happening, but there's still no reply.'

'I don't get it,' Scortia said. 'Big hotel and no service. It doesn't add up.'

Kyle strolled into the tunnel then, paying no attention to the two spacers by the opening. He called out, 'Maybe we were supposed to use the tradesman's entrance.'

Ella Desmond ignored him, his presence a little disturbance in her external reality that didn't call for much attention. 'They must know the state we're in.' She made an angry little gesture towards the door. 'Scort, break it down.'

'But it's a steel plate airlock.'

'I'm not saying you should put your shoulder to it, just find a way to get us through.'

Great, Scortia thought, less than delighted at being thrown the chewed bone of a problem. Make something of that, slug. He contemplated the door blankly for a moment. 'Sure,' he said, and tried to give the impression of an analytical mind at work while his thoughts raced around like a bee in a jam jar. And then he said, 'Ah. . . any ideas, Kyle?'

'Put a spacer onto it,' Kyle said promptly, tossing the hot stone along to the next in line without any deliberation at all.

'Right,' Scortia said, and nodded. A decision.

'Make it Willis,' Kyle added. 'He's good at the unorthodox stuff.'

Scortia moved off to get Willis, and Ella Desmond turned her attention to Kyle for the first time. 'I hope you're enjoying this,' she said.

'What makes you say that, Captain?' Kyle asked in innocent surprise.

'One of my paranoid fantasies. Make the most of it.'

Willis arrived then, with Scortia a couple of paces behind. Sarrat watched from the opening of the tunnel, but now Cain was with him. Still no sign of Kittivale and Thea; they were probably still trying to find their way off the Sparta. It had been Kyle's assignment to look after them, but any anger would bounce straight back at the Captain. Tough at the top.

'Can you take a look and see if we can get it open from this side?' Scortia asked, and Willis nodded. He reached around and unhooked an instrument from his belt, a two pronged fork about the size of a small lizard, and he started to run it close to the wall around the door. The double emitters soon triangulated on a concealed hollow next to the announcement panel, a hollow which seemed to extend beyond the edge of the collapsible tunnel. Willis returned the emitter to his belt and came back with a diamond drill, the kind used to make holes in diamonds.

First he cut away a piece of the flexible wall, quickly unzipping a flap and letting it drop. The hollow was unconcealed on the outside; it was simply a channel recessed into the formed metal of the wall, and it carried the laser filaments for the com link—nothing else. Willis stepped back, and looked at the door itself.

'What have you tried so far?' he asked Ella Desmond.

'Banging my head against it, mainly.'

'And that didn't work?'

Before the Captain could speak again, Kyle said, 'Just get on with it, spacer,' and caught Scortia's eye. He gave a short, almost imperceptible nod towards the hangar outside, let's get out of the way for a minute. Ella Desmond was watching Willis as he ran the emitter over the door itself. Scortia moved with Kyle, and hoped it didn't look so obvious.

Sarrat and Cain had moved off a few yards to sit on a stack of cylinders. Cain had unzipped one of his boots, and he was holding it upside down and shaking it. Kyle said in a low voice, 'Did you hear the Captain?'

'Hear what?' Scortia said, sensing yet another scheme.

'She's getting some kind of complex. She thinks everybody's against her.'

'Not everybody, just you,' Scortia said with a sudden sharpness that surprised even himself. 'And that's not a complex, that's being perceptive. Why can't you just lay off for a while? She's made some damn good decisions on this trip.' He started to move away, back to the door. 'She deserves better.'

Kyle stared after him for a moment. Then he headed off to join the two spacers.

Willis had stripped the door of its padded plastic fabric to expose bare treated steel. The fabric was heaped to one side (Ella Desmond staring at it as if trying to work out its cost to add to the agents' growing liability) and Willis was making the final drill cut which would free a square plate about halfway up the door's inner edge.

'Need a hand with that?' Scortia said, but Willis was already holding the weight and lowering the panel to the floor. The spinning wheel and the greased bolts of the locking mechanism were exposed. It seemed pretty complicated. Scortia said 'Can you do it?'

'Sure I can do it.' Willis tapped a couple of contacts with the blunt end of the drill. 'The hard part was getting the plate off. Cheap work always gives you problems.'

'Cheap work? In a place like this?'

'Always the way. Expensive tinsel, and nobody knowing what's underneath. I mean, look at this.' Still using the blunt end of the drill, he delivered a sharp blow to one of the contacts. There were a few sparks and a flurry of electrical spatterings, and then the wheel spun and the bolts were jacked back. The door started to swing away, apparently under its own weight.

Ella Desmond shouldered her way through. 'Good work, Willis,' she said, without glancing back. 'Follow us through when you've cleared up.'

Scortia felt that something more than a thrown away thanks was called for, but it was already too late. Instead he said,

'What's the secret of your success, Willis?'

'Irregular features and a lack of education,' Willis told him, and went to kick the tangle of fabric to one side.

THE FIRST THING to hit them was the muzak, but it was so low and so insidious that they didn't even notice it for a minute or more. It was some machine's idea of classical and class, bland as milk, seeping and soothing and finally annoying. And with the muzak, there was the reception area.

After the Sparta, any enclosed area would probably seem big; Scortia had begun to sense, back in the dock, the first stirrings of an unidentifiable feeling that he now recognised as panic. In fact, the reception area was far from vast—space would be at a premium on the Babylon asteroid as it was in any artificially maintained body—but it was big enough to shout wealth.

Scortia took a couple of steps forward. He was in a long hallway of linked gothic arches, sharp curving ribs of smooth white that met overhead and glowed with their own illumination. In the middle of the floor area was a single curved desk with a computer console, obviously check in and document control; apart from the four loungers arranged in a half circle around the desk, the floor was clear. One check in point per dock, one per customer. Wealth. There was nobody behind the desk, but Ella Desmond was leaning across and looking intently at the console display.

So they were through the door, one step further in, but the feeling of desertion hadn't gone away. The hallway with its white light, soft as powder, was too antiseptic, too clean; far too clean for anything as messy as people. At which point Scortia remembered that nobody had told Sarrat and Cain that they'd broken through, so he went back into the tunnel to call them.

Cain hurried to pull his boot back on when Scortia beckoned. The junior officer glanced across the platform to the leaning hulk of the Sparta; Kittivale and Thea were just descending the ramp from the lock. Scortia raised a hand, and then pointed towards the tunnel; Thea waved back to show that she'd understood.

Kyle and the two spacers were standing just the other side of the lock doorway when Scortia caught up with them. Willis had moved on, and was somewhere down the far end of the hall.

'You think somebody's out to impress us?' Kyle said.

Sarrat prodded the white textured foam of the flooring with the toe of his boot. 'They managed it.'

'Elegance by the yard,' Cain said. 'What kind of people spend their lives in places like this?'

'Not our kind,' Sarrat said emphatically, and moved over to take a look at one of the unlit archways that were cut into the sides of the hall.

'And this is only the lobby,' Kyle said. 'What's the rest of it going to be like?'

Cain started to smile, slow as molasses. 'And, ah... how's the Captain going to justify the expense?'

'Don't encourage me to evil thoughts,' Kyle said, and then he saw that Scortia was close enough to hear. His expression changed abruptly, like a door being slammed on something nasty in the cellar.

Got you, thought Scortia with satisfaction, and went on past to catch up with the Captain.

Ella Desmond had moved around the desk and was sitting in the operator's chair. The console was a non-standard terminal but some of the inputs were marked; zone manager, transport control, central data. She was trying each in turn, both with a verbal call and by typing in the Sparta's international recognition code. Nothing.

'I can't raise anyone,' she told Scortia. 'It's like the place was empty.'

'Maybe it is,' Scortia suggested, half seriously.

'It can't be. There are lights, music, fresh air. If you pull out of a place like this, you put it under wraps. You don't leave it to run itself down.'

'But so far we've only seen the dock and the lobby,' Scortia began, but he was interrupted by a shout from further back down the hall.

Sarrat had stepped into one of the darkened archways. It had promptly come alight around him. A couple more steps, and now the muzak moved out to claim this new piece of territory.

Sarrat turned around a couple of times and giggled.

'Everything must be rigged to sensors,' Ella Desmond said. 'Body heat or biocapacitance, something like that. You'd never need to switch on a light.'

To Scortia, it seemed about right for the level of a place like Babylon. Expensive engineering to save some trivial effort. Ella Desmond went on, 'Maybe it's all sensor linked, even the muzak.'

'Dreary stuff,' Scortia said. 'I wish it would stop.'

The music stopped.

Willis was at the far end of the chamber, and he looked back sharply. Kyle and Cain were casting around for the cause of the sudden silence, and Sarrat quickly emerged from the side arch. For a moment, he seemed scared. The archway darkened behind him.

'Well,' Ella Desmond observed, 'somebody seems to be listening.'

'Yeah,' Scortia said uneasily, 'but who?'

Ella Desmond pushed herself away from the unhelpful console. 'Get everybody together,' she said decisively. 'It's time we found out what the Hotel Babylon's about.'

The three spacers and the two bridge officers were in a group around the Captain when Kittivale and Thea appeared in the open doorway from the dock. Kittivale took in the sight of the Babylon's expensive fittings, and nervously hugged the bag which contained their meagre supply of crystals.

Thea nudged him. 'I told you, don't tremble. You're supposed to be a rich playboy. You're supposed to be in your element here.'

'I don't feel anything like a rich playboy.'

'You don't look anything like one, either. Fake it.'

'I'm going to be sick.'

'You're going to be strangled.'

'Look at the place. It's bigger than anything we ever saw on Vegas. What are we going to do?'

'We're going to survive. Now that's not too ambitious, is it?'

The group around the Captain broke up. Each of the crewmen moved towards a different archway, obviously prearranged; each archway flared into light at the first step. The Captain returned to the chair behind the reception desk, as if she felt a need to reassert her authority even when she thought nobody was watching.

Kittivale couldn't move any further. Threats didn't help, entreaty didn't work, and in the end only a small act of physical intimidation got him tottering across the carpet towards the control centre.

Somebody was breaking through on the desk intercom, but the voice was familiar. *'This is Scortia calling the lobby,'* it said. *'Have I found the right damn button yet?'*

Kittivale and Thea came level with the desk and waited. Kittivale was limping slightly from a kick behind the knee. He looked reproachfully at Thea. Thea was more interested in what was happening on the console.

A light flickered on the display as Scortia spoke. Ella Desmond touched it and said, 'Hearing you, Scort. What have you found?'

'More lobbies, exactly like the one we started from. They're all strung out in a line, and every one's got an airlock door. Presumably there's a spacecraft dock on the other side. I can't open it to see.'

'The spacers are checking on that side, so don't worry about it. Any sign of the place being lived in?'

'Nothing.'

The Captain sighed. 'Okay,' she said. 'Keep looking.' The console light died as the channel closed.

Ella Desmond didn't look up, not straight away. Thea waited for a moment, and then said, 'Is there a problem, Captain?' Given the circumstances, it sounded like the Stupid Question of the Decade.

'You might call it that, but there's no actual danger. Just that we seem to be the only people in the hotel.'

Kittivale paused in his surreptitious efforts to shake some sensation back into his leg, and said, 'What do you mean?'

'I can't actually think of any other way of putting it.' Ella Desmond frowned as Kittivale wobbled precariously. 'Are you all right?'

'The fresh air makes him lightheaded,' Thea explained quickly, and she gave Kittivale a push which sent him toward the nearest lounger. 'Where did the others go?'

'I've split everybody up, given them different areas to search. Scortia's covering this level, Kyle and Sarrat are supposed to be aiming for the upper levels, Cain and Willis down below.'

FIVE

WILLIS SHOULD have felt at home in the crew areas that filled the levels below the docks; this was the territory of the Babylon's equivalent of the spacers, the loaders and the handlers and the mechanics whose efforts supplied the pampered elite, insulated in their own designer crafted world above. Down here it was clean enough and comfortable enough, but no effort had been made to please the eye.

He and Cain had split up almost immediately, heading off in opposite directions—an arrangement which seemed to suit them both. Willis had found a goods elevator behind a half concealed access alcove, and after an arbitrary three level descent he'd stepped out and started to search. First he'd come to the cold rooms, the food and fur stores, grey battleship doors with ship's wheel handles, belching a cold fog as he opened up a couple at random. One contained a good stock of expensive wine, the next was filled with the graded chemical blocks used by the robot chefs. Willis closed them up and relocked them, and then moved on.

All of the areas were alight, but not alive. The crew cafeterias with their tubular chairs tilted against their benches, the workshops with half finished jobs on display in clamps and vices, the bunk rooms with personalised decor and empty lockers. One broad corridor led him down to the bottom level of the docking areas, opening out into a railed interchange for the carriage transport of gangs and spare parts to each of the hangars. The third track that he followed brought him out under the hydraulic jacks that supported the immense foreshortened bulk of the Sparta; every other hangar that he could see was empty.

Everything that he saw indicated that there had been an

orderly withdrawal, but when it had happened it had been fast. Willis followed the rails further, tracking them through a subway like network until he found his way blocked by one of the carriages, abandoned in a tunnel. He got down and crawled underneath the open work of the chassis, emerging into a factory like assembly area for the major spacecraft servicing jobs. This was the area that by now should have been equipping for the Sparta's refit. The only sound was of his own footsteps on the reinforced metal floor.

A ladder within a frame of metal safety hoops took him to the overhead grid, climbing past the cable traps and junction boxes to where he could look down through the grilled false ceiling to the open space below. There was barely room to stand upright, but Willis now guessed that he was more or less back on a level with the entrance lobby; stepping over ropes and cables and jutting fixtures, he let himself out through a couple of swing doors at the corner and found himself on a catwalk in a small generator room. He descended to the floor level and then opened the safety cover to a trap, beneath which another ten feet of ladder brought him back into the Babylon's maze of service corridors.

This corridor was of control rooms, command points with banks of monitors from where the heavy work could be observed and directed. Willis didn't go into any of them; a glance through the square window in each door showed them to be empty, their screens powered but showing no activity.

He'd been wandering for more than an hour, and unless he came across somewhere that he recognised it could take him the same length of time to find his way back. In the meantime, perhaps he could find some way of reporting what he'd seen, although as a report it would be pretty well a non-event.

There was a com point at the next intersection that he crossed. There was a pre select for the lobby areas, which would make it easier; he didn't know the code for the specific lobby where Ella Desmond waited, but a little experiment wouldn't hurt.

SHE LISTENED as Willis talked, her annoyance obvious. His was the first call that she'd received since speaking to Scortia an hour before. She shook her head. 'Still the same picture.'

'But why?' At the sound of Willis' voice, Thea had moved over to stand behind Ella Desmond.

The Captain shrugged. 'Maybe the place went bust. Once you've woken up to one red sun, you've seen them all.'

'I don't think so,' Willis' voice came from the console.

'Why not?'

'Couple of things. First, you've noticed how fresh the air is?'

'Everybody has.'

'So, why? None of the rooms comes alive until somebody steps into them, and that goes for the air recirculation as well. If the Babylon had been empty for any length of time, it should have been as stale as ditchwater for the first half hour or so. But it wasn't.'

Ella Desmond nodded, lagging a couple of steps behind, but doing her best to keep up. 'Anything else?'

'Lots of things. Hot water in the pipes. No dust, no fungus. I'd say the place has been cleared some time during the past couple of days.'

'I see. Any idea why?'

There was a couple of moments' silence, and then Willis said, 'No. You'll have to ask somebody else.'

'There is nobody.'

'What about the Babylon?' Willis said, and Ella Desmond sighed and looked heavenward before she replied.

'I've been trying since we arrived.'

'You've been trying to get hold of somebody on the staff. I'm saying you should talk to the hotel direct.'

Ella Desmond considered it for a moment. It seemed like a dubious idea; almost as important to her was the fact that, if it failed, she'd feel pretty silly in front of Thea and Kittivale. Offhand she couldn't think of any good way of getting rid of them. She said warily, 'You think that would work?'

'It might. The Babylon certainly seems to be aware of us.'

Come on, it was worth a try. 'Just give me a minute, will you?' She cleared down on Willis, leaving the console an unlit blank. Now what? There was no obvious pre select to go for, nothing to suggest what code she might use to speak to the hotel—or rather, to its managing computer—but then as far as the operation of facilities was concerned, none seemed to be needed. I'm going to feel like dung in a bucket if this doesn't work, she thought, and then said, 'Ella Desmond of the Sparta, requesting to speak to the... Hotel Babylon.'

The reply was immediate. *'At your service, Miz Desmond.'*

Thea gave a little impressed whistle, and Ella Desmond felt relief burning down through her like a slug of raw whisky. This was a new voice, not the welcoming lullaby that they'd heard on the Sparta or the regretful official repeating his catechism at the locked door; it sounded like a young manager eager to make his way within the company structure, low enough to be eager to please but advanced enough to pull strings for you. False as hell, of course; somewhere, a programme was running through and responding. All it needed was the right question.

Ella Desmond said, 'Can you give me some information?'

'It will be my pleasure. I exist to serve.'

How to start? 'I've noticed... I mean, I couldn't help noticing... well, there don't seem to be any guests around the place.'

'The Hotel Babylon takes pride in its exclusivity.'

'And no staff, either.'

'Our staff are selected and trained for their ability to remain discreet and unobtrusive.'

'In fact, there's nobody in the damn place but us.'

A moment's pause, almost a hesitation. *'You are most observant, Miz Desmond.'*

'Mind telling me why?'

'It's nothing you should worry about.'

'Let's say I'm curious.'

'Everything's in hand.'

'Curious to the extent that my stay is being spoiled.'

'Ah.' An unhappy guest. We'll find the culprit and skin him alive. *'That would never do. I reassure you, there is plenty of time.'*

'Time for what?' We're getting closer, she thought.

'To withdraw to a place of safety, as the others have done. The meteor strike which will destroy the hotel is unlikely to occur for

at least twenty hours.'

SIX

SCORTIA WAS THE first to arrive. He'd followed the long sequence of identical lobbies until they'd come to an end against the exposed rock of the asteroid, and then for want of any other route he'd followed them back again. Ella Desmond briefly repeated the information that she'd been given by the Babylon, and then sent him on to the Sparta with an instruction to get digging in the computer for anything he could find about Persephone and its adjacent systems.

Sarrat, Cain and Kyle all arrived within a few minutes of each other. None of them had reported in at all, and Ella Desmond suspected that they'd all met up and goofed off for the three hours or more that they'd been away; nobody had any details to offer on what lay on the levels beyond the reception areas. She told them to go to the assembly room on the Sparta, and then waited a couple of minutes before following. This way, she didn't have to walk with them; Willis would have to make his own way, when he finally arrived.

The assembly room lay close to the bridge. It had originally been a briefing room in the days when the Sparta had carried military freight, but now more than half of it was taken up with boxed spares, odd lengths of cut cable and other junk. It still had a wall sized working VDU, however, and Ella Desmond could still control it from a lectern that placed her higher than her audience. It was a pity that she couldn't think of anything to put on display. She repeated again the message that she'd been given in the lobby, adding that the twenty hour estimate would now be down to about eighteen, and then she handed the show over to Scortia.

Scortia didn't step up to the lectern. He was surprised to find that he was nervous enough speaking from the floor. 'So Ella. . .

ah, Captain Desmond... has told you why we've found the Hotel Babylon so recently deserted. At the moment we've no way of verifying the likelihood of the meteor strike, but until we see anything that tells us otherwise there's no reason to doubt it.'

'Mister Scortia's been pulling some information out of the computer for us,' the Captain prompted.

'Mainly about the Persephone system.' He glanced at Ella Desmond. 'You want it all?'

'Might as well. Get it all laid out and see if anybody can throw in a suggestion.'

Scortia nodded. 'Well, it's not so good. Looks like we couldn't have picked a bleaker spot to maroon ourselves in.'

'You're kidding.' It was Kittivale, at the back. 'With that hotel out there?'

'The Hotel Babylon's the only inhabited body in the entire system. There was one livable planet, but it was cleared more than two hundred years ago.'

'Cleared?' Thea. 'Why?'

'Because two hundred years ago, Persephone was selected as one of the systems to form a buffer belt between the trading states and the Free Systems.' Now Scortia stepped up to lectern level, and Ella Desmond moved back so that he could get to the display control. He read something off the roll of printout that he was carrying, and transferred the number into the VDU control. The screen immediately came up with a galaxy schematic, shown with artificial red shift as an indicator of depth. Scortia added another number, and a band of soft airbrush green faded through the middle like a gentle disease. Where it touched were the cleared systems, the dead systems. Persephone was ringed, square in the middle of the dead zone.

'There,' Scortia said. 'We've managed to drop ourselves right into the no man's land between the two big power blocs in the known galaxy.'

'Wonderful,' Sarrat mumbled. Cain looked at a side wall, as if he wanted to complain but didn't actually want to address anybody, and said, 'What kind of no man's land is it that has luxury hotels?'

'I don't know exactly how it came to be here,' Scortia told him. 'Presumably the owners pay dues to both sides. Maybe the top party men from the Free System like to sneak over when nobody's looking.'

Sarrat snorted, watching the ceiling. 'Wouldn't surprise me.'

Thea seemed to be the only one in the group who could follow the logic of their position. She said, 'What about this planet?'

Scortia consulted the printout. 'Some land, a lot of ice and water, not much else.'

'How does it figure with the meteor?'

'I don't know yet. We're not getting any sensor information here inside the dock, so I've got the computer combing back through our approach records to build up a composite picture and a prognosis. Shouldn't take much longer.'

'What I'm getting at,' Thea pressed, 'is, will the Sparta be able to get us there if the planet's safe?'

'It may have to. We know we're airtight and we know we've got some drive, and that's about it.'

'What about moving the hotel?' It was Kittivale now, and the two spacers allowed themselves contemptuous little smiles. Scortia knew that such a notion wasn't impossible even if it was unlikely, and he gave it the serious consideration it deserved.

'We can assume it's not possible,' he said. 'Otherwise the owners wouldn't have abandoned it.'

Ella Desmond came in again. 'On this point of the Sparta's navigability. Right after the meeting I want the spacers to get below and do a complete check.' Still no Willis, she noted as she scanned the small group. 'I'll want a full report on what's in one piece and what can be patched. And—' she fixed her eye on Sarrat, who shifted uncomfortably '—I don't want the usual displays of doubt and horror and head shaking, I want a decent line on what's possible in the time we've got. Anybody want to say anything?'

Nothing I wouldn't get hung for, Kyle thought, and everybody else waited out the silence.

'Okay, let's break it up. Mister Kyle, start a bridge systems check. Scortia, come with me and we'll take a look at what's left of the drive.'

Kyle nodded sharply and was the first one out of the assembly room. The two spacers followed with less obvious enthusiasm. As they reached the door, Scortia saw Cain glance back; satisfied that there was nobody close, he then turned to Sarrat and started to talk with some urgency.

Thea was waiting for Ella Desmond as she stepped down. Kittivale hung back. Ella Desmond raised an eyebrow, waited for the question.

'I feel useless,' Thea said. 'Is there anything we can do?'

'What did you have in mind?'

'I don't know. Anything.'

The Captain considered, but it was only for a moment. 'If we had a bar, you could mix us some cocktails. Other than that, I think you'd find it too technical.'

Thea's eyes widened. 'You know who we are,' she said. There was no fear, no wonder in her voice, just the weariness of long deceit. Kittivale watched, knowing he was involved but too scared to speak for himself.

'You don't hide it well enough.' Ella Desmond wasn't hiding much, either, a superior disdain for a Vegas good time girl that just might have been rooted in a secret envy.

Thea said, 'Will you turn us in?'

'That's a bit academic right now, isn't it? Anyway, the law won't be after you—I happen to know the casinos make a point of following up their own grievances. Only thing that would have worried me was if you hadn't embezzled enough to settle your charter bill.'

'We had enough,' Thea said stiffly. 'We may be frauds, but we're not dishonest.'

Something suddenly occurred to the Captain. 'Tell you what, go see if you can find Willis. Warn him that we'll be moving as soon as we can, and tell him he's needed below decks.'

'Anything for Kittivale?'

Ella Desmond glanced at the shrunken and lonely figure, still perched with his empty security bag across his knees. 'If he can sit still without falling over, we'll count it as a victory.'

ELLA DESMOND'S check on the damaged drive had the speed, formality and depth of interest of a state visit; she took one peek into the glass smooth darkness that lay beyond the curved access door, nodded a couple of times, and that was it. With a curt gesture to the waiting Scortia, she set off with Sarrat to look over the extent of the damage to the Sparta's underbody.

Cain waited until they'd all clattered off down the catwalk, then came out with a loud whoop and whistle of relief. If they'd gone to the extent of demanding a light in the empty tunnel and if Scortia had taken a look as well—it would have been goodbye to the spice and the drugs rackets. Anybody with any idea about the workings of the drive—maybe that excluded Ella Desmond, but not the more technically trained Scortia—would have been able to see that the big damper terminals at the head of the tube were still in place, when of course a jettison action should have dumped them along with the rest of the drive. It was a giveaway, the dampers had been out with no authority or warning.

He would have to clear up behind himself; if they made it to this planet, he couldn't be sure that he and Sarrat would be heading up the team to re-equip the drive. He'd have to get a burner and shear off the heads, find some way of dumping the debris as they got under way again.

The laser burner was on the next level up, still at the site of a half-finished job that Willis had been working on, a rerouting of some heating lines to take them away from some magnetically sensitive links. Cain slung the heavy power pack over his shoulder and hoisted the ruby tube, and that was when Kyle caught up with him.

'Hey, roadrunner,' Kyle said, 'stand still for a minute.'

Cain was taken by surprise, and he nearly dropped the burner. Kyle was supposed to be in the middle of a bridge check, after all. 'Funny,' he said, 'Now let me past. I've got to cover my tracks down there.'

Kyle shook his head. 'Sarrat can handle that. I want you up on the bridge with me.'

'What are you planning ?' Cain asked warily.

'If we tie this up right, we can dump Scortia and the Captain and find a way of prising Kittivale loose from his crystals. All we'll have to worry about is the story we put together for the agents.'

Cain didn't have the patience to listen, not when things were moving so fast. Less than eighteen hours to a meteor strike, and Cain wasn't ready for conspiracy. 'Come on, Kyle, this isn't the time to play about.'

'It's exactly the time. Get Sarrat onto whatever it is you were doing, and then get up to the bridge and make it fast. I've got to be out of the way by the time that the Captain arrives.'

THEA WASN'T sure whether the Captain had actually meant her to search for Willis, or whether she was simply to wait for him and then relay the instruction when he appeared. She couldn't even be sure which of the darkened archways he had taken from the reception area. She tried one that seemed likely, but after a couple of hundred yards she realised that the exercise was futile; she could wander for hours and still have no chance of stumbling across Willis, during which time he might well have emerged from the labyrinth and returned to the Sparta. She turned around, and headed back to the lobby.

Willis was already there. She heard him first, he was standing by the console at the central desk and he was talking to it. She knew that she ought to go over and announce herself, but instead she stopped and listened.

'Spacer Willis of the Sparta, to speak to the Hotel Babylon.' Willis had never really registered with her before; on Vegas she'd become so used to being surrounded by extroverts and ego merchants that somebody as private and withdrawn as Willis now passed quietly through her outer consciousness with hardly any disturbance. He was half turned away from her, all of his attention directed towards the console. She wasn't exactly hiding; he only had to turn and he'd see her—but then, without knowing she was there, he had no reason to look around.

The console answered. *'Did you say spacer Willis?'*

'That's right.'

'Beat it, slug. Tradesmen down in the service quarters, and don't mess up the carpet as you go.'

'I'm not a tradesman.'

'*Spacer's bad enough. Get yourself out of here before the paying guests start to complain.*'

'What if I told you I was a paying guest?'

'*I'd laugh myself sick. You couldn't afford to spit in a place like the Babylon.*'

'I'm an eccentric millionaire.'

'*A what?*' the console said suspiciously.

'An eccentric millionaire.'

'*Ah.*' There was a pause, with a far off electronic whickering as the machine ruminated. '*You mean, loaded but not entirely compus mentis?*'

'That's what I said.'

Another pause, as the worried computer checked through its banks. And then, triumphantly, '*But not in the register. Beat it, slug.*'

'Maybe I'm just weighing the place up, see if I want to check in. See if I want to recommend it to all my eccentric millionaire friends.'

'Ah. You know, you're giving me a problem.'

'Why?'

'*I've got programs for most occasions, but nothing for this. Once you're in the register you can be a slob or a bum or anything you like, and I've got to creep to you. Otherwise you've got to be obviously dripping with it, and you aren't.*'

'That's my eccentricity.'

'*But you see the difficulty? Now, if you'll only register, I can slobber all over you. Otherwise I can only tell you to take an EVA without a helmet.*'

'You co-operated with the Captain.'

'*Captains are different. Spacers are trash. Eccentric millionaires excepted, of course.*'

'Naturally.'

'*Now, if you'd like to register. . .* '

'How can I be sure you've got room?'

'*I can check.*'

'Go on, then.'

'*I just did.*' The console launched into the grandiose tones of a brochure. '*We've a selection of apartments available. May I particularly recommend one of our Sunrise Suites, with a triple pressure window giving a spectacular view of the burning rim of Persephone. . .'*

'Eccentric millionaires are immune to sales talk. Just tell me what's already taken.'

'Well,' the console began evasively, *'it's low season. . .'*

'How many suites?'

'Exactly?'

'An approximation will be fine.'

'Not many.'

'Numbers?'

'None.'

'Now,' Willis said, leaning in close for the kill, 'why's that?'

'You're playing with me,' the console said reproachfully. *'You heard me tell the Captain about the meteor.'*

'Yes, and it came out too damn slick. I've spent lifetimes around machines like you—I can strip you and I can fix you and I know when you're lying.'

'I wasn't lying.'

'Maybe just bending the truth a little to stop the guests from panicking. A direct meteor hit on a speck of an asteroid the size of the Babylon—do you know what the odds against that are?'

'You want me to work them out?' the console said with anxious dismay.

'Don't bother. Just tell me the truth.'

'It's not actually a meteor, but we don't know what it is. It's artificial and it seems to be set on burning itself up in Persephone. It won't actually hit the Babylon, but it will pass close enough to draw us in after.'

'What else did you hold back?'

'Nothing.'

'What about that twenty hour estimate?'

'It was close.'

'How close?'

'Within sixty per cent,' the machine admitted.

'You call that close? Thirty two hours?'

'The other way, actually. More like twelve.'

'And why didn't you tell us straight away? Why keep us

waiting around in the dock?'

'*Management instructions. You were supposed to register, and then you'd be told. That way, they could claim the deposit when you left early.*'

Willis leaned forward, touched a point on the console, watched it die. 'Except,' he said, mostly to himself, 'that there was nobody around to let us in, and the system froze up.'

Thea stepped out of her archway. 'That's the kind of shark it takes to run an outfit like this,' she said, and Willis turned to look at her. 'Vegas was full of them.'

Willis frowned. 'What are you doing here?'

'The Captain sent me. She wants all the spacers back on the ship to work on patching it together.'

'It's as good as it'll ever be without a complete refit. There's nothing more we could do.'

'I think she was hoping you'd work a miracle. She was pretty impressed with the job you did to navigate us through the black hole.'

Willis stepped around from behind the console. 'There's enough of the drive left to get the Sparta to safety. After that, she'll just have to hope that the Babylon people come back to see if there's anything to salvage.'

He was moving towards one of the archways, away from the pressure door at the hall's end. Thea said, 'You coming down?'

'Couple of things to do, first.'

'Like what?'

He waved her away. 'Carry on. I'll follow.'

She was about to speak again, but Willis had gone. *Okay*, she thought, and she was about to turn around and head back to the Sparta when she realised that something was wrong. She couldn't be sure; she tried to remember which archway Willis had originally taken, but when the search party had split up no one had seen him go.

As each of the others had stepped out of the hall, his chosen corridor had come alight around him. But a moment ago, Willis had walked off into the dark.

SEVEN

There was nobody on the bridge when Scortia and the Captain arrived back from their glance over the Sparta's scraped underbelly. Ella Desmond immediately said, 'Where's Kyle?'

'I don't know.' Scortia walked across the open semicircle of floor that was the main part of the bridge. On the flat side of the area, set a little off centre, there were an opening and a couple of steps down to another operational zone; originally tactical backup, it was no used as a watch crewroom. It was empty. Scortia said, 'Last I saw, he was heading this way.'

Ella Desmond was over by the broad sweep of the control board. The three crash couches swung idly. She said, 'He was supposed to be checking up on the bridge systems.'

'Maybe he finished.' Scortia didn't really believe it, and neither did the Captain.

'Like hell. Get the panel warmed up and we'll go ahead without him.'

Scortia climbed into the central seat. It vibrated a little as it attempted to reshape itself around him, but it was old and worn and it compromised half way. He threw the switch for panel power and then started on the routings for individual systems before moving to the remotes for drive and stabilisers, and the Sparta began a wary stirring from a state of rest.

Ella Desmond was saying, 'It's alien territory to me, down there with all the technical gear. If Sarrat says we can move it, I have to believe him. What's the matter?'

Scortia was hesitating. 'I don't know. Something wrong with the console.' It should have been a bright starfield, but more than half of it was dead.

'Punch up the fault finder.'

'Nothing happens.'

The Captain leaned across and jabbed a couple of switches, as if she didn't believe him. She said, 'Have we got power?'

'There's power, but half the systems aren't lighting. I don't know why.'

'Check the wafers.'

'The what?'

'Raise the console cover and check the systems programming wafers. Cut the power, first.'

Scortia switched out panel power; now the only live systems would be those emergency indicators that were supplied on an external channel. For practical and safety purposes, the console should be dead. He slid the cover aside and reached for the central unlock. It was already twisted to the open position.

'Something's wrong here,' he said as the console cover raised on hydraulic assist to reveal the maze of technical backup underneath.

'More than that,' Ella Desmond said after a moment's survey, 'Kyle was here before us.'

The console's design was like that of a cassette rack, an open lattice accepting slim wafers of circuitry. This modular design made fast repairs possible in flight, simply activate the fault finder to zero in on the failing system and give its code number; the complete circuit could then be replaced in a few seconds, and the module repaired some other time. Mostly, they were junked; they were too small and too cheap to be worth messing around with.

There were gaps, Scortia could identify some of them. Gyros, retros, sublight orientation—Ella Desmond said, 'Without those programmes, we haven't got a ship.'

Scortia was perplexed. 'But why should Kyle want to remove them?' he said. 'I mean look, he's even...' the gesture was cut short as a blue spark shot across his knuckle and he quickly pulled his hand back.

'What did you do?'

'Something was live.' Something was stinging, as well. 'I must have touched it.'

'What did you touch? The power's supposed to be off.'

'Don't know. Something—' a vague wave, not getting too close '—something around there.'

The Captain looked closely for a moment. 'Those are the safety indicators. They're on a separate power source.' She took a crayon from a clip by the navigator's note board, and started to prod around. After a moment, the unshielded contact spat again like a trapped kitten. A small loop of solder had been broken out. She said, 'Take a look over the top, see if anything's lit,' and then she used the non-conducting tip of the crayon to hold the loop closed.

Scortia had to stand to look over the lifted panel. Craning, he could see a single light glowing. 'The drive damper warning lights are on. Nothing else.'

'We'll have to assume that Kyle disconnected them.'

'But why?'

'He's taken the wafers. He's the most obvious suspect.'

'No, I mean, why do it at all?'

She reached up to the console cover and pulled it down. 'Because he's been rigging something all along, that's why. Don't ask me what—I can't begin to guess at how his twisted little mind works.'

The circuit had stayed closed, and the red warning light still glowed. Scortia said, 'But if the damper circuits are live. . .'

'It means that somebody's got the dampers out to mess with the drive right now. They cut the warning circuit so we wouldn't know.'

Scortia was thinking, if that's how it is now, maybe that's how it was before the black hole; and if that's how it was before the black hole, it could explain why they'd lost part of the drive without warning. . . except that it didn't really explain anything, it just suggested the possibility. The immediate problem was that the dampers were out, and somebody didn't want them to know about it. 'It must be a spacer,' he said. 'Kyle wouldn't know how.'

Ella Desmond was on her way to the door. 'Whoever he is, he'll be carrying his balls around in a paper bag when I'm finished with him.'

THEA STOOD in the Sparta's main lock. The heavy outer door was raised, and the external atmosphere sensors allowed the inner door to stay raised at the same time. There was a barely perceptible breeze through the lock as the warm stale air of the ship reluctantly traded with the fresher air of the Babylon. Somewhere within the asteroid there would be gardens, maybe even a small farm of sorts, functional greenery to back up and supplement the machine flat taste of recycled oxygen. On the Sparta there were the pumps and the exchangers, and that was it.

For a moment, she couldn't be certain of which way to go; she was on a painted deck with three choices of direction, and last time she'd just followed the crowd without paying much attention to where she was going. There were colour coded trail lines painted on the floor, but they meant nothing to her. She could get to the suite where Kittivale was now probably sitting and shivering, but she didn't want Kittivale, she wanted the Captain; Ella Desmond was probably on the bridge by now, and Thea had no idea of where the bridge might be. Kyle had offered her a tour at the beginning of the voyage, enough of an encouragement in itself not to accept.

When she listened, she could hear the pulsing of the ship at rest; and then, at odds with that pulsing, a distant echo that was irregular and harsh, the resonance of disease. Deep in the Sparta, somebody was working, somebody who would recognise the importance of her news and get it to the Captain.

Thea fixed on the sound, and set off to follow it.

SCORTIA WAS STILL trying to catch up with Ella Desmond as they descended the iron stairway into the area of Rat City that the spacers had cleared for themselves. They'd been able to hear the sounds of heavy work for at least half of the distance they'd covered, and this in spite of the fact that they'd found three of the Sparta's internal bulkhead doors closed against them in an obvious attempt to cover the noise.

It was clearer now, the characteristic drone of a laser burner amplified in an enclosed area. Every now and again there would be a crackling flash and a brief rip of thunder; as they reached the bottom of the stairway the whole area flared blue white for an instant, every bench and locker and hanging cable standing against its shadow in a bright wash of no detail.

Scortia nearly tripped on the final step, his vision a mass of imploding black bubbles. The source of the light, when he could make it out, was unmistakeable; the curved access cover to one of the drive tubes had been swung back, and the mirror interior was catching and concentrating the reflected light of the laser. Whoever was inside, he was taking a risk; there was a slim chance that the beam could ricochet and slit him like a fish.

The hatchway sparked and flashed again, and the tube echoed with the sound of something falling. The drone of the burner diminished for a moment, then started again.

Ella Desmond was still fumbling blind. Scortia made it to the hatchway before her. It was the number two tube, supposedly empty, and when he pressed himself up against the side and peered in slit eyed he could see a huge figure which couldn't be anybody other than Sarrat. Scortia could also see what the darkness of the tube had earlier concealed; one of the damper heads was still in place, the others molten and ruined by Sarrat's feet.

Ella Desmond thrust her head through the hatchway, not knowing or not caring about the danger from the burner that Sarrat was wielding so awkwardly. *Don't surprise him*, Scortia was about to say, but by then Ella Desmond was already bellowing in competition with the lightning.

'Sarrat!' she yelled. 'Drop the damn burner and get out of there!'

Sarrat spun around. He was wearing a starmask to protect his eyes, a flat black cover that hid his expression, but his body was saying *panic*. He even forgot the burner, and dropped it.

The coherent beam hit the curve of the tunnel and immediately zipped a latticework of light into existence. The ruby tube dangled at the end of the line which linked it to the power pack over Sarrat's shoulder, and as it swung the latticework flexed and re drew itself. Sarrat scrambled to get it back under control, and Ella Desmond pulled back as the bright network started a deliberate move towards her.

One of the laser lines shot out of the hatchway for a moment, but it burned off harmlessly on the cable covers above. Sarrat had rescued the ruby tube and so reduced the likelihood of his own dismemberment, and now he was advancing towards the hatch with it held before him like a ringmaster's whip.

Scortia did the only thing he could think of under the circumstances. He slammed the hatch, and spun the locking wheel. When he turned around, he saw that Ella Desmond was hurt.

She'd fallen back, and she was holding her leg; there was a neat slice razored across the material of her jumpsuit, its edges bloody and wet. The polished inner surface of the hatch must have caught and cupped a beam as it closed, throwing the lightfire outwards and downwards. Inside the tube the laser was still bouncing, still deadly, but muffled by the airtight seal. Sarrat was probably getting into position to attempt to burn his way out, but the effect within the shaft would be like that of a vacuum bottle—he'd fry before he could achieve anything.

Scortia knelt by Ella Desmond. 'It isn't deep,' she said. 'But, Christ, it hurts.'

'Shall I carry you to the First Aid point?' There was bound to be one somewhere handy, safety regulations for a working area demanded it, but Scortia had no idea of where it might be.

'When I go, I'll hop,' Ella Desmond said, and nodded towards the hatchway. 'Right now I'm hanging on until Sarrat's done his boiled lobster act.'

The laser bouncing had settled to a steady burning. Sarrat had apparently managed to get the beam aligned with the non-reflecting seam around the hatch, and he was trying to melt his way through. Scortia said, 'He was burning off the damper heads at the end of the shaft.'

'He couldn't have.' Ella Desmond put out a hand, and Scortia helped her up. 'They were dumped along with the drive tube when we jettisoned it.' She winced, but she was taking most of the weight on her good leg.

'Apparently not.' They made for the nearest bench, one which carried the oily innards of a stripped down air conditioning fan. 'Which could only mean. . .'

'The dampers weren't connected in!' The force of the conclusion made her forget discomfort for a moment. 'There was nothing to stop the tube overheating when it fired up!'

'That's right. And we couldn't know on the bridge, because the warning circuits had been cut.'

Ella Desmond leaned against the bench, and carefully lifted the cut edges of the cloth. It was as if a hot wire had been laid across the flesh above her knee and allowed to sink in for about a quarter of an inch. The heat had mostly sealed the wound, and the small amount of bleeding that had resulted was already stopping. Her pain and her anger distilled into a single word.

'Kyle. He was planning something, and he screwed it up.'

There was quiet. Sarrat had obviously increased the temperature inside the tunnel to the limit of bearability. There was a couple of seconds' pause, and then a desperate thumping began on the inside of the hatch.

Scortia gave Ella Desmond an enquiring look. She said, 'Give him a few more minutes before you let him out. And arm yourself with something.'

There was a rack of wrenches under one bench. Some of them were missing—the Sparta's spacers didn't rate amongst the neatest or the most methodical—but at the upper end of the range were two hefty torque wrenches, solid and dark with grease. Scortia pulled them both out, and took one to Ella Desmond. She needed both hands to lift it, but she seemed to approve.

'It'll do until I get the burner,' she said. 'Okay, open the hatch.'

The hatch came back under a compressed air assist, and Sarrat fell out amidst a cloud of steam. He'd torn the mask away, and his skin was mottled and purple; he collapsed onto his knees and stayed there, drinking the cold air like a baying dog. His jumpsuit was sauna drenched.

'Unusual colour, isn't he?' Scortia commented, and he leaned into the drive tube to look for the burner. It lay just inside the hatch where Sarrat had dropped it, and when Scortia reached to pick it up he felt the steam heat of the tunnel's interior at an almost scalding intensity.

He carried the burner across, and set the power pack on the bench next to the Captain. It still carried about half a charge. Sarrat was still kneeling, but now his head was back and he was puffing and whistling at the ceiling. The edge of agony seemed to have gone from his breath, but only just.

Scortia indicated the open hatch. 'Another ten minutes,' he said, obviously referring to the damper heads, 'and we'd never have known.'

Ella Desmond turned to Sarrat. It was probably coincidence that he found himself kneeling before her like a supplicant. The laser burner was in easy reach on the bench beside her, and the torque spanner rested with one end on the floor by her foot.

She said, 'All right, Sarrat, either you give us some answers or I'm going to turn you into a dragon's kleenex. And if you think my normal sweet nature and sunny disposition will make that difficult for me, just bear in mind that I'm angry and my leg's hurting like hell and you're the nearest little reptile I've got to take it all out on.'

'You never liked me,' Sarrat complained morosely.

'That's right, but I'll say some nice things about you at your funeral. In about half an hour.'

Sarrat said, 'You'll get nothing out of me, you frustrated old...' He stopped abruptly, because Ella Desmond had swung the torque spanner around and banged it squarely into his groin. Sarrat's jaw dropped wide open; no sound came out and no air went in, he just started a slow fold down around the area of impact. Halfway down he toppled sideways, rigid as a plaster saint.

Ella Desmond watched the process of collapse with real interest. She said to Scortia, 'Would that hurt?'

'You'll never know how.' Scortia crouched by Sarrat and tried to raise him, but Sarrat didn't want to move. His eyes were squeezed shut, and tears like gelatine were quivering fatly at their corners. Scortia was feeling less than decent, and Ella Desmond was looking on with something near to a smirk of satisfaction.

Scortia said, 'Listen to me, Sarrat. Kyle's gone, and we don't know where. We know this business of the drive tube is part of some scheme of his—probably a scheme that went wrong. But I wouldn't be relying on him to come sweeping in here and bail you out, because he's not the type. More likely he left you here to take the risks for him.'

'Tell us what he's doing now,' the Captain urged. 'What's he trying to pull?'

Sarrat managed to find some words at last. 'He'll murder me if I tell you.'

'I'll murder you if you don't.' Ella Desmond had placed the torque spanner against the bench—Sarrat winced at the scrape of metal on metal—and now she reached for the ruby tube of the laser burner. She aimed it down at the floor and switched on the power; a lance of light, minimum intensity, arrowed out and began to bubble the paint of the deck.

'Well?' she said.

'This isn't fair.' Sarrat eyed the beam nervously.

'Very observant,' Scortia said, hoping he sounded as confident as the Captain. 'So don't you think it's more sensible to tell us?'

Ella Desmond loosened her grip on the ruby tube, let it swing a little. The beam traced hot circles on the painted deck, trailing a wisp of black smoke as it etched. 'We know he's taken a bunch of the programming wafers out of the control desk. That traps him in the Hotel Babylon just as effectively as it traps us. So what's the point of it?'

'I wouldn't know.'

'Sarrat, he dumped you.' Scortia didn't want to see Ella Desmond make use of the burner any more than Sarrat did. 'He doesn't rate you, or he'd have taken you with him.'

Sarrat hesitated for a moment, and then said quietly, 'Like Cain.'

'What?' Ella Desmond leaned closer, not sure whether she was hearing right.

'I was covering up for Cain. They left me a note and he took Cain with him.'

'Where's the note?'

'I burned it.'

Scortia said, 'Where did they go?'

'I don't know, just somewhere into the hotel. You were supposed to follow to get the wafers back, and then they'd be waiting.'

Ella Desmond's disbelief was obvious, not at Sarrat's account but at Kyle's ineptitude. 'Waiting for what?' she said. 'This is the way he thinks he's going to make Captain?'

'More than that. With you out of the way he could take Kittivale's crystals and get rid of him and the girl. Then he could go limping back to civilisation and claim that the accident did it all. The Babylon would be all burned up and nobody would be able to say different.'

'Great plan,' Scortia said, 'except for one little flaw in the logic. When that twenty hour deadline arrives, we'll have a ship with no wafers and Kyle will have wafers and no ship. We won't have to follow him, because in the end he'll have to come back.'

'But when the last minute comes and he still hasn't come back, what do you do then? He reckons his nerve is stronger than yours. He reckons you'll follow him in the end.'

'He reckons wrong,' the Captain said firmly. 'We'll sit out the twenty hours, and when he comes back we'll blast him.'

'Twelve hours,' Thea said from the metal stairway. Three heads turned to look at her, and Sarrat seemed to remember his dignity as he tried to sit upright. He clutched his abdomen as if his guts were trying to spill. Thea descended into the Rat City handball court. She said, 'The figure you were given in the lobby was a deliberate over estimate from the computer. I listened to Willis getting the real figure out of it.' She faltered slightly as she tried to remember the details; 'It's an artificial body, not a meteor, and in twelve hours it'll pass close enough to pull us after it into the sun.'

Ella Desmond was watching Thea with suspicion. 'Does Kyle know this?'

'Why ask me? But I don't see how. It was Willis got the answers, he seemed to know what to say. The computer wouldn't have given the information out otherwise.'

'So Kyle's sitting out there,' Scortia said as Thea came and stood by him, 'and he's thinking he's got twenty hours to play around in. But the real figure's almost half of that.' Less, he corrected himself; the estimate was originally made a couple of hours before. It gave them about nine hours to play with. Twenty sounded like an age, nine sounded like nothing at all.

Sarrat seemed cheered by the news. 'Kind of puts you in a spot, doesn't it?'

'It means we have no choice,' Scortia said. 'We're going to have to follow Kyle, whether we like it or not.'

There was a brief silence as the vast scale of the Babylon made itself felt. Huge, dark and empty, it made the Sparta seem like a little warm shell of comfort. Thea said, 'Looks like it's you and me, then.'

'Why?' Scortia said, surprised.

'Because the little red fellow can't be trusted,' she said, nodding towards Sarrat, 'the Captain can't walk, and Willis has drifted. Assuming that Cain's out there with Kyle, it only leaves you, me and Kittivale. Kittivale's idea of danger would be to loosen his seat belt in a parked car.'

'She's right, Scort,' Ella Desmond said reluctantly. 'There's no other way.'

Scortia couldn't argue with the logic, but he still felt cornered. The girl and the woman were both looking at him, Sarrat was watching the forgotten burner—but he was smiling. Scortia said, 'Better give me the key to the arms cupboard.'

'Don't bother,' Sarrat told him. 'Kyle was there before you.'

EIGHT

THE LOCK ON THE arms cupboard door was still intact. The door itself was propped against the adjacent wall, hinges unbolted, and the two pop guns with the spare charges that were the only relics of the Sparta's combat history were both missing.

Ella Desmond had let the charge on the laser burner run out to nothing, so even that couldn't be put into service as a makeshift weapon. It would need twelve hours of charging before it would be portable again, but at least it could be run direct from the Sparta's power supply as a means of keeping Sarrat intimidated. Kittivale was hustled up to the bridge and updated. He tried not to show too much relief when he was told that he wasn't expected to join in the search of the Babylon.

Scortia found that he wasn't too scared. Thea hadn't really experienced the Babylon beyond the entrance lobby, and she could have no sense of its great size and complexity; the chance of actually finding Kyle and Cain in the asteroid maze seemed so remote that it couldn't threaten. The greater danger lay beyond this, storming down to Babylon and onward to Persephone.

So they stepped into the reception area unarmed. Looking across the crooked landing platform from the Sparta they'd been able to see that the tunnel and the open doorway beyond it were dark, only coming bright as they approached; had Kyle been waiting, the biosensors would have given him away. Where there was darkness, there was no life—a useful warning which would unfortunately work two ways.

All of the archways were dark, another reassurance that Kyle was not near. Scortia looked around them and said, 'I wish we'd had the laser.'

'Stealth and cunning instead, remember?'

'Tell you the truth, I don't know what we're going to do.'

Thea looked around the archways. There were four down each side of the lobby, and one at its far end; this last was the grandest, twice the width of the others, gaping black and uninviting. 'Start,' she suggested, 'by choosing the way we go.'

'The Babylon's a big place. You want to split up?'

'No. Do you?'

'No.'

Discussion, the illusion of action. Thea said, 'How about straight through the lobby and on, the way the millionaires go?'

'Too obvious.'

'So Kyle may not be expecting it. Point?'

'Point,' Scortia conceded. 'We'll try it.'

They walked down the lobby, skirting the reception desk at its centre. The seats were swung about at odd angles as they'd been left, and the console was dead. The white textured foam which passed for carpet muffled their footsteps to nothing, and as they approached the wide arch it was a cue for the lights.

Scortia touched Thea's arm, and they both stopped. The first section of the millionaires' walk glowed invitingly before them. Thea tried to read Scortia's expression, to see what had troubled him.

'Too fast,' he said. 'I didn't think we were close enough. Try stepping back.'

They retreated, but the corridor lights stayed. The illumination went on for a hundred yards or more before ending in a black O, a promise of further jungle dangers. In between were cleanness, brightness, safety. And maybe Kyle or Cain.

The bait was there, untaken. The next section of the passageway lit up, and then the next, until the lights ran on to the point of infinity; a route map, an invitation, a gesture of control.

'We know the direction,' Scortia said. 'We'll look for the nearest they've got to back stairs.' There was no way that he was going to follow such an obvious laid trail, and now the fear was starting to settle into him.

They went into a side arch, following it down for some distance before turning to follow a parallel to the lit corridor. They were in a service section, the one that Willis had previously begun to explore. Thea said, 'The place is huge. We may never find him.'

'But he wants to be found, remember.'

'Because he wants to kill us.'

'That's the part I'm trying not to think about.' Scortia found the idea of such a personal antagonism difficult to accept. He and Kyle hadn't exactly been friends, because outside of their jobs they'd nothing in common, but at least Scortia had thought he'd known what Kyle was about. Ambitious and unscrupulous perhaps, but this... maybe it was just a case of the worst in someone responding to an opportunity, but it seemed to go much further than that. After all, Kyle had actively set up the damage to the drive before the black hole and Babylon ever happened.

Thea said, 'Will you kill him if you have to?'

Scortia considered for a moment. 'Only if I have to. What about you?'

'I had a chance at happiness, and he's taken it away.' The force of her anger was surprising, like a burn from ice. 'I'd dance in his blood.'

CAIN WAITED until they were well out of the way before he emerged into the lobby and unhooked the hand radio from his belt. After shaking the small trailing wire aerial free he said, 'They've moved on. Service corridor—' he squinted up at the designation plate concealed behind the gothic curve of the opening '—one nine four.'

'*Got them.*' Kyle's voice was badly distorted. Reception within the honeycombed asteroid was unusually poor. He was two levels up, in the security control room that he'd discovered on his initial exploration of the Babylon. Not only did he have over rides for all of the sensor systems in the covered sector, he had cameras in most of the corridors. Out in the classy areas they were pretty well concealed, elsewhere they were openly displayed as a warning to the staff. Somebody's watching you, brother, and don't it feel good?

'They weren't armed,' Cain said, glad of the reassuring weight of his own stolen popgun.

'I know,' Kyle said. *'Give them time to get away from the main lobby, then follow and finish them off.'*

'I thought you were going to do that.' The plan had been for Kyle to get the first wave as they came in, and for Cain to sweep up the droppings in the form of the rag tag party that would have to follow.

'I found something more interesting here. I want to follow it up, and time's limited.'

Sure, Cain thought, you just tool off and leave the shit work to the spacer. He said, 'You covering me?'

'I'll cut the power to one nine two. It runs between them and the main corridor, so you can get ahead and wait.'

'Right.'

'Give me a call when you're done, and I'll decide what to do about the ones back at the ship.'

'What about Willis?'

'God knows what Willis is doing. He's out of the sector, as far as I can see. No more lit corridors and nothing on the cameras. Get moving, Cain, or you'll lose them.'

Sure, thought Cain again, and got moving. Cain couldn't know that Thea and Scortia had already recrossed his path and moved up a level, and Kyle was no longer watching. His last view of them had been in service corridor one nine four, where one of the judas cameras had tracked the couple to check that they didn't turn off.

Thea had seen the brief glint of the camera's lens as it had twisted to follow. She'd said nothing until the next intersection, and then she'd pulled Scortia to the side and started to run. He decided to worry about questions later.

CAIN WAS PLAYING the panther one level down when they emerged from the elevator onto a floor that was a distinct contrast in layout and decor. Curves were soft and angles were blurred, and there were plants—real green, set in beds of waterfed stones to create an impression quite different from that of the utilitarian areas below. There was a moving strip down the centreline for the lazy, the lighting was concealed and indirect, and vertical plates of tinted glass gave sightlines an illusion of interest without actually concealing much. Rat City, rich man's style.

When they reached the strip, it started to move. They rode with it, and Thea explained about the camera. Scortia had seen the fixtures and dismissed them—after all, the Babylon was supposed to be empty—but the idea of an eye which moved to follow them was too persuasive. If they were watched then, maybe they were being watched now; if anything it was more of a possibility, because security was bound to be tighter where the pickings were better. They had to get out of the public areas, away from the network to which Kyle had somehow got access.

They left the strip in a garden area where shallow pools dripped dyed water from one terrace to another, and footbridges arched over low channels that could be stepped across without effort. The plastic flooring foam was earth coloured and unconvincing, part of a plot which seemed to provide access to only three apartment setups. The first two doors that Scortia tried were closed and wouldn't slide. Thea said, 'We'll be cornered.'

'I don't think so,' Scortia said. The third apartment had probably been occupied when the warning came and deserted in a hurry. The door whisked back at a touch and they hurried inside. Babylon felt their presence and responded.

> *Welcome to the sunrise suite, the pride of the Babylon. The management hopes that your stay will be an enjoyable one, and that you will address yourself to this information point with any enquiry. We offer you a hundred casinos, a thousand varieties of cuisine, music and games, the asteroid gardens, the collected pleasures of a galaxy of cultures. The Babylon awaits you.*

Three carpeted steps took them down into the circular dish that was the Sunrise Suite's main room. The ceiling was domed and the inward tilted walls were lined with drapes that didn't seem to mind the fact that they hung at an impossible angle. The information point that was spouting its silky greeting was set into a low table before the padded seating around half of the circle, and most of the rest of the floor space was taken up by a round bed that sat off centre like the growing form within a clear egg. Two asymmetrical doors led through to adjoining rooms.

Scortia didn't think that cameras would be operating within the private suites. He also didn't think that they'd necessarily trapped themselves by their retreat; hotel rooms needed service, and that hardly seemed possible with the intricate set decoration of the entranceways. There had to be some other angle of access, some other way for the chamber staff to get in—and for he and Thea to get out.

'What we need,' Scortia said, crossing to the middle of the room and looking around, 'is a map or a guide, something like that. A plan of the hotel.' If they could only find out where the security control room was situated, they'd have Kyle pinned down.

'And then,' Thea suggested, 'a way of getting out of here without Kyle seeing us.'

'One detail at a time. You check in here, I'll look in the other rooms.'

'It could take a week,' she called after him as he stepped through into what looked like an oversized bathroom, almost a swimming pool. 'The place is like a little palace.'

'Try not to take so long,' Scortia's voice echoed back.

Where to start? The covers on the bed had been hastily thrown across, and the mirror fronted closet door in the wall behind was half open. The closet was empty. She could see herself reflected, and she thought herself little and mean and cheap, an intruder, a trespasser in riches. A toss of the coin, and you could be born a slab of meat who deserves nothing and gets it all. It was so damned unfair!

There was no warning and no obvious reason why, but the drapes gathered and swept back to expose the black glass wall that lay behind them, a quiet whispering that was suddenly lost in the theatrical drumroll that shook the room around her. Scortia was emerging from the pool room with a look of apprehensive concern when the cymbals clashed and the black glass cleared. Babylon spoke.

Persephone! Cool red giant star, unique among the systems in this sector, a beacon that marks the point of contact between the Free Systems and the trading states. And orbiting Persephone, beyond the base considerations of the political mind—the Hotel Babylon!

Persephone filled nearly two thirds of the panoramic window, a boiling sea of red lava with a barely perceptible curve to its far horizon. There had to be magnification, they couldn't be so close in to the red giant; it was even possible to see the gas corona boiling off at its edge, and beyond that, where contrast lessened and the light haze didn't reach, the distant stars winked back into existence.

Scortia seemed unmoved. 'This damned place, selling itself again. Considering it was built for the galaxy's elite, the whole operation's as vulgar as hell.'

The beautiful squalor of luxury, Thea thought, but all she said was, 'Riches and good taste don't mix.'

The suite was washed through with a glowing red, fine if you wanted to preserve your night sight but useless for searching. Scortia said, 'We're wasting our time, looking for a guide. Anybody who'd sprawl around in a place like this probably wouldn't have the wits to use one. What would be the easy way out?'

'The information point,' Thea said promptly. The rich needed their flunkies, human or mechanical.

They went over to give it a try, sitting on the half round of low seats that faced the endless sunrise view. The point was a slightly raised console on the table before them, the input panel a dark glass blank with a single lit square. Below this, a series of different languages and characters was fading in and out. One of them was a recognisable touch and speak.

Scortia touched, and said, 'Well, how about it?'

The console launched off with immediate enthusiasm.

'*I see you've decided to consult your information point about some of the great things that are happening here in the Hotel Babylon. Kind of exciting, isn't it?*'

For the first time since they'd arrived, Thea found that she recognised one of the Babylon's pseudo personalities; this sounded like the same little jumped up squirt of a character that Willis had gradually worn down. She wondered if Scortia would do as well.

The machine went on, *'I'm really looking forward to helping you with your problem, so why don't we just keep the tiresome formalities to a minimum and get your name and credit reference out of the way?'*

Scortia looked blank, and Thea said, 'What's wrong?'

'I think it just asked me for money.'

'Shouldn't it go on the bill?'

'What bill? The suite isn't registered to anybody.'

Great way to start. Thea said, 'Give it your credit reference, then.'

'I'm not sure I could afford it,' Scortia said, plainly troubled.

'What will it matter? In eleven hours all the accounts will be going up in a fireball. Us with them, if we don't make it.'

Scortia hesitated, and then nodded. He gave his full name, followed by the string of letters and numbers that were his coded identity wherever he travelled. In case he should forget, they were tattooed on the sole of his foot; if he lost a leg and his memory at the same time, then he'd be in trouble.

'That's wonderful,' the console said, sounding so pleased it couldn't be true. *'I can tell we're going to have a really productive exchange here.'*

'I'm having a problem,' Scortia started out, and with that the easy part was over.

'You say you're having a problem,' the console said, and it fairly radiated sympathy.

'Yes, I'm lost.'

'Why do you think you're lost?'

That side of the issue had obviously never occurred to Scortia. 'Well. . . because I don't know my way. . .'

'You say you don't know your way.'

'I. . . we're looking for two people.'

'We're all of us looking for somebody.'

'I'm not asking you for sympathy. . .'

'Everybody needs a friendly ear.'

'. . . I need directions, that's all.'

'*Because you've lost your way.*'

Scortia almost sighed with relief. 'Exactly!'

'*I know how empty life can seem without a purpose.*'

'Listen to me,' Scortia interrupted.

'*Everybody needs a friendly ear,*' the machine shot back. It wasn't really an information point, it was more like a cheap psychoanalyst. Scortia decided to abandon the *guest in need of help* act, and be as direct as he could.

'I'm looking for the sector security point. The one that monitors all the corridors.'

'*You resent being observed.*'

'No. . .'

'*It's reasonable to feel a little paranoid sometimes. There's no need to be embarrassed about it.*'

'I'm not embarrassed about anything. . .'

'*It's reasonable to feel embarrassed sometimes. There's no need to be embarrassed about it.*'

'You're not even listening!' Scortia protested.

'*Everybody needs a friendly ear.*'

'All I want is simple information on how to get from here to the sector security point!'

There was a pause. '*You say you want information.*'

'Yes.' It didn't seem possible, but it looked as though they were going to get somewhere. There was another pause, almost a hesitation, before the machine spoke again.

'*Well, I've really enjoyed our little conversation, but I have to tell you that your credit payment's running out. If there's anything else you want to know, please restate your credit reference and we can pick up just where we left off.*'

Scortia was standing, looking down at the complacent blank of the console. 'I don't believe it,' he said, and gave the fixed leg of the table a kick in an attempt to jolt the whole works.

'*I have to tell you,*' the machine admonished, '*that kicking a piece of Babylon property is an offence. I'm authorised to make an on the spot deduction from your credit account if the number is known, or summon the relevant authorities if it is not. . .*'

When Cain got back to the security centre, he was panting and damp. His short spacer's fringe was sticking to his forehead, and he toted the popgun like a bag of old clothes. First there was a duty officers' rest area, and then he was through to the darkened control room. Kyle was facing the other way, studying a backlit plan of Babylon.

'Well?' he said, without turning round.

'I lost them.' Cain said it without any trace of an apology; instead, he was making an accusation.

Kyle straightened. He didn't look pleased. 'You lost them?'

'I went down to the end of the corridor and waited. They never appeared.'

'So where did they go?'

Cain jerked the popgun at the bank of screens that was the control room's main feature. 'You've got the cameras. You tell me.'

'I haven't been watching the screens,' Kyle said dismissively, and he turned back to the Babylon ground plan.

'Well,' Cain said, his annoyance plain, 'that's great, isn't it?'

'I told you I'd found something here. Look at this.'

Cain looked down at the plan. It was the security master, and it showed every corridor, level and routing. Different systems and networks lay like veins, ready to light and become distinct at command. Cain shrugged and said, 'Map of the hotel. So what?'

'It's not to scale,' Kyle explained. 'Everything enlarged relative to the asteroid.'

Okay, so it wasn't to scale, great. 'Made easy for rich dummies.'

'Made downright misleading.' Kyle dialled up a grid of scale; the squared pattern warped and curved to take account of the inaccuracies of the representation. 'When you even everything out, the Hotel Babylon occupies less than a quarter of the volume of the asteroid.'

'Rest of it's probably service areas.' Cain didn't understand what Kyle could be getting at; time was short and here he was, farting about with a map.

'Service areas are included,' he said.

'Solid rock.'

'Wrong mass. Sparta's calculation of the orbit showed the asteroid to be mostly hollow.'

Cain squinted at the diagram. The way it was drawn, the map showed hardly any leftover space at all within the asteroid; but by the curving of the grid, certain areas had been enlarged far out of proportion to make it look that way. But so what? Kyle obviously wasn't going to return to the main problem until he'd gone through with this momentary obsession, so Cain said, 'What's in the spaces?'

'I went out, tried to find a way through. I couldn't, but there's something odd about some parts of the corridor walls. I think they're designed to slide back.' He indicated a few points, two service corridors, an un named rec area and the access walk to a set of sunrise suites. Stacked together they made a more or less straight line through the asteroid. On the other side of the line. . .

Cain said, 'This is creepy.'

'I reckon we've got sixteen or seventeen hours left. If Scortia and the gold digger lose themselves in the hotel, fine—it saves us the trouble of wasting them. It only leaves the Captain, Kittivale and Sarrat to worry about. Sarrat's on our side, and the other two won't be a problem.'

'What about Willis?'

Kyle was pulled up for a moment. Willis kept so much in the background, he was easy to overlook even now; never mixing, never talking about his background or his home, only happy when working with circuits and machinery. 'We'll worry about Willis when he appears—if he ever appears. He's probably wandering round talking to the furniture. Forget him.'

'And concentrate on what?'

Kyle grinned. His face lit from below in the darkened control room, he was a Mephistopheles, a stealer of souls, a dealer in cheap goods. Cain saw it, and knew; but he also knew that there was no road back. Kyle said, 'We concentrate on finding what's on the other side of those walls, what's worth keeping so well hidden. And then on working out a way of taking a piece of it with us when we go.'

'Do we have the time?'
'As much as we'll need.'

NINE

T̲HE SMALLEST CORNER of the sunrise suite was a closet sized utility room. The door had a lock which wasn't engaged, and Scortia was able to force the panel back along its slide. As he first tried to get a grip on the edge his fingers slipped and he skinned a knuckle on the frame. He grimaced and tried to suck the pain away, and when he held his hand out to inspect it the white skin slowly reddened and yielded up two drops of blood.

Hardly a combat injury. Thea looked around for something to wipe the blood away; there were towels and fabrics within reach, but the idea of grabbing any of them seemed as out of place as giggling in church. Then Thea remembered something, and put her hand in her pocket; the tissue was still there, the one she'd used for the last drops of her crash bubble nosebleed, pressed and stiffened by its passage through the microclave but otherwise still usable.

Scortia thanked her, and looked around for some kind of lever to use on the door. He was back less than a minute later with the rail from the static cabinet at the end of the mirror closet, and with this he was able to work the crack wide enough open to get his hand in for leverage.

The utility room was cramped and uninviting, obviously intended for use by the staff and not the guests. There was a dumb waiter elevator at the far end of it.

'That's our way out,' Scortia said, and Thea looked at it doubtfully.

'Could it take us?' she said.

'It'll take us, we'll just have to cram in a little, that's all. I'll be more than surprised if Kyle's got a camera covering the shaft.'

It was no more than an open sided box with a slatted floor. Scortia got in first and felt it bounce slightly under his weight as the cabling stretched and took the load. He could kneel, but not upright, his shoulders were hunched and his head was pressed almost into the shape of the corner. He felt like a badly wrapped present and a long time to Christmas. Thea sat on the edge and slid in backwards, pulling her legs in after as soon as there was room, careful to position herself so that she could still reach out and operate the control box with time to get her arm in to safety.

She was pressed up against him, and her hair was against his cheek. The gold digger, the good time girl, the shakedown operator; for that first brief second of contact Scortia convinced himself that none of it was true, there was nothing in the electricity of closeness to confirm or support it and he found with surprise that he had no wish to believe. But then reason and rumour tipped the scales; she was a fraud from Vegas, a table hopper, her entire persona the construct of a calculating mind which was dedicated to survival with a viciousness probably exceeding that of Ella Desmond herself. Suddenly their closeness wasn't arousing, it was threatening, and without really meaning to he pressed himself harder against the back wall, a fraction further away.

'Thanks,' she said, and pulled herself in closer. Now she was clear of the edge. She tripped the switch, and the dumb waiter started to move.

At first it seemed that a gear was slipping, because the dumb waiter lurched and jerked a couple of times before it started a slow drop; they were too much for it, too heavy for the protesting motors up above. *We're supposed to carry bed linen*, they whined, *not fucking elephants*.

The lower edge of the utility room hatch wiped up across the open side and put them into darkness. A few seconds later they were out of it and in twilight, but that too gave way to a rising edge of black before they could adjust to the new level.

For a while the darkness was relieved only once, by the squared off glow of a small grille in the shaft which stroked a rippling grid across them both. As it went, the carriage gave a couple of still downward jerks.

Thea's head banged against Scortia's cheekbone, and it felt

like a sharp inhalation of seawater. 'We're too heavy for it,' she said.

'Speak for yourself.' For a moment he thought they'd stopped, but then they were back out into the twilight and still descending. The shaft was wider here and it allowed spill from some distant source down below; every weld and every seam threw a long upward shadow, and the occasional shaft access panels were hollow recesses against the metal. They were still in the twilight when the gear jammed.

They didn't simply stop, they were pulled up hard by some kind of emergency brake, and Thea said, 'I don't like it.'

Scortia tried to listen. The shaft was good at picking up distant sounds, bad at reproducing them faithfully, and what he could hear sounded like a groan of chronic agony at the far end of a hospital corridor, a haunting. Seven hours to go, and they were folded up in a biscuit tin.

The upper edge of the next access panel was just starting to show, no more than a sliver of dark along the dumb waiter's floor. It would have been too much to hope that they should stop level with it, but if they could get the carriage down two or three feet they might be able to kick it out. Scortia didn't want to imagine what contortions that would involve, not right now. He said, 'Let's try shaking the whole thing up and down a couple of times.'

'No chance.'

He tried to raise a hand to point, but only succeeded in jabbing Thea. 'Sorry. But if we can jerk the carriage down, we'll be level with the next panel.'

'Or a six inch deep layer of paste at the bottom.'

'That's exactly what I want to avoid.'

'Me too. No jumping.'

Jumping would have been a joke, a flea couldn't have squeezed between them. But the sliver was rising, widening; somewhere up above, a friction brake was failing to hold their weight.

There was probably no other safety backup. After all, nobody was expected to be taking rides, the dumb waiter was just a transport for light goods; linen, cleaning gear, special orders from the Babylon kitchens. About half of the panel was uncovered now; another minute and it would be out of reach above them, assuming that they continued this shuddering drip for a minute and didn't exchange it for a faster dive to oblivion.

Scortia said, 'Can you push against the panel without elbowing me somewhere vital?'

'If that's what it takes,' Thea said with determination, 'You can grit your teeth and put up with it. Here goes."

The panel was now fully exposed, and it seemed to Scortia that they were dropping faster. Thea slapped it hard—the best that she could manage—but it didn't move.

'It must be bolted on the outside,' Scortia said.

'I think I felt it give. I'm trying again.'

The upper edge was already past, the lower one rising to follow it. Thea slapped again, with no better result; the flat sound of her hand against the metal seemed feeble and useless.

'Brace yourself,' she said, and started to squirm around. There wasn't the space for it but she moved anyway, pressing against Scortia where she had to, and all the time the access panel was slipping away.

Scortia got a kick on the thigh that would leave a bruise like the skin of a dropped peach, but he said nothing. Thea managed to get her shoulder against the panel, leaning right out of the dumb waiter; if they were to fall now, the side of the shaft would skin away the flesh from her upper arm and cheek. Academic. She pushed, the panel on one side and Scortia on the other, and he tried to keep himself solid and unresisting.

The panel broke out with a sticky tearing sound, as if the only thing that had been holding it on was a layer of old grease. It didn't fall away, it just tilted out a few inches and stuck, but whatever was behind it didn't push back too hard, and as Scortia boosted Thea out of the dumb waiter she was able to force it aside and make a gap big enough to wriggle through.

There wasn't much more room on the other side; as Thea cleared the shaft Scortia could see angles and piping and a grille cover that wouldn't even let them stand, but wherever it was it didn't move and it was preferable. The gap was down to two feet, just enough for him to get head and shoulders through and concentrate on dragging the rest after.

It was heavy cabling that had given such elastic resistance to the panel; they'd crawled out under an open mesh floor. Thea had played mole and squirmed onward to give Scortia room, and now she was lying and looking back at him. The dumb waiter had stopped, jammed squarely in the shaft with nothing more to pull it down.

There were dim lights above the floor, and they came through as a pattern of even shapes that stretched and flowed across skin and metal alike.

'You okay?' Thea said. She was aware of the kicking Scortia had taken, although she'd done nothing to lessen it.

'I'll live. Can you give me a hand, and we'll try to lift one of these sections overhead?'

Scortia hadn't seen this style of flooring anywhere else in the Babylon; the guest areas had all been luxury foamed and the service corridors had a rolled surface that wouldn't snag trolleys or drones. This was a tough heavy duty setup, not the Babylon's style at all; surely they hadn't travelled down enough to find themselves in the ship repair workshops?

There were four section corners resting on each upright, the uprights evenly spaced every few yards. They got underneath one and raised it on their backs; it was too heavy to tip, but they managed to slide it along a couple of feet so that it rested on the next section and couldn't fall back in on them. Scortia was out first, and he put his hand down to help Thea. She took it and swung up to sit beside him, legs dangling into the gap like two urchins fishing off a pier. They were even dressed for the part, dusty and grease spattered.

'Happy now?' Scortia said.

'Like a cat in a cardboard box. Where are we?'

Good question. And where was Kyle with the programming wafers? Waiting, probably, scanning empty corridors with a growing anxiety—at least they'd taken that advantage from him for the moment. But Kyle's best protection was his ignorance; he might be dead before he became desperate.

ONE LEVEL DOWN from the sunrise suite, Kyle was crouching by the wall of a service corridor. His popgun was pushed around behind on its strap, but at the sound of footsteps he quickly straightened and reached for it.

Cain trotted into view. His own gun pointed at the floor, and there was something in his hand. Kyle said, 'You find them?'

'Not exactly. I know where they went.'

'So why are you here?'

Cain held something out, and Kyle took it. Not a trophy of success, just a crushed tissue with a few drops of blood to stain it. The paper rag was still slightly damp.

The spacer said, 'I couldn't follow, and they're somewhere on the other side of that wall.' He nodded towards the wall that Kyle had been examining, probing the imperfect seam at its base; Scortia and Thea had moved into the unmarked zone. 'They went into one of the sunrise suites and then rode out in a little service car. They must have spotted the cameras on them, or something. Anyway, I tried to follow it down, but the car was jammed in the shaft and there wasn't room to squeeze through. I tried.'

'Try this, instead,' Kyle said, and he showed Cain how he was able to slide a knife blade under a supposedly solid wall to a depth of nine inches—as far as the blade could be pushed before the width of the handle stopped it, and still it met no resistance. After that, he took Cain's attention to a rough square that he'd scratched onto the wall with the same knife. Maybe careful rapping with the handle wasn't as efficient a search method as Willis' sonic emitter, but it had still been effective in uncovering a buried hollow. There was a good chance that this was the site of the wall's slide control circuitry.

Cain listened patiently, but without much enthusiasm. A sliding wall was fine, but there were probably better ways. He said, 'What about Scortia and the woman?'

'Open up the wall, and we can walk straight through to them. Can't be difficult—it only took Willis a couple of seconds to get us all out of the dock.'

It was then that Cain realised that the job of getting through had been saved for him; so much for the equality of conspirators, when it came down to it the spacers still had to get their hands dirty. He said, 'That was the dock, just cheap engineering. Maybe this won't be so easy. You know we've only got. . .'

'There's plenty of time for what we need,' Kyle said with a dismissive wave. 'And I want to know what the Hotel Babylon's been hiding.'

TEN

THE BABYLON WAS hiding the most extensive armoury that Scortia had seen in the last seven years.

They'd come through the floor at the edge of the turnout area of a barracks, twenty bunkrooms of four beds each, ten doors to either side. Most of the doors were open and all of the bunkrooms were empty. The third side of the area was formed by a communal shower block, drain points white with a crust of dried lather—withdrawal here had been as fast as in the rest of the hotel.

Any doubt that they were in a military installation was removed when they left the turnout area through the open end of the U. Next along was a deep, low room, lockers all along its walls and two rows of tables down its centre. The overhead lighting came on as they stepped forward; it was hard and searching, and the objects on the tables glittered like dead beetles. The surfaces were zoned off, and within each zone was a complete set of kit. Some of the kits differed slightly but they were basically similar; each was an assembly of the protective necessities of combat, and the main differences lay only in the weapons specialisations. Battle call would bring twenty troopers slamming in here, suits from the lockers and then into the kit in a practiced drill; and a drill was all that it ever could have been. Any hint of a military presence here in the cleared zone, and the consequences would be as explosive as the appearance of a shark in a swimming pool.

'Someone,' Scortia said, 'has been cheating on the convention.' Twenty men was a basic unit, self contained. How many more units were provided for elsewhere in the Babylon?

Thea said, 'Can you tell which side?'

'Ours, by the look of it.' The walls and floors were bare

metal, with nothing to cut the echo. They were walking along by the sets of arms, window shopping for Armageddon. 'I recognise some of these pieces. This one,' (pointing to an ugly looking gunpack with a strap on wrist charger) 'heat seeking pistol with laser over ride. Don't know what that one's for, must have been developed since I did my service. This piece looks like a modification of the old sticky web grenade.' He stopped. 'I wonder if any of the pistols is carrying a charge.'

'Since you did your service? What service is that?'

Scortia had picked up one of the heat seeking pistols and was checking the strap on pack that accompanied it. The over-ride was the best feature about them, unless you were really into zapping campfires. He said, 'Didn't they have the draft on Vegas?'

'Not that you'd notice, but then there's nothing you could call a permanent population. Apart from the visitors, everybody else is just stopping over on the way down.'

Satisfied by what he'd found, Scortia buckled the pack to his arm. It fell in easily with the lines of bone and muscle, flattening onto the inside of the wrist. 'They pulled me when I was seventeen and kept me until I was twenty five. Move around behind me, I'm going to try this out.'

Thea brushed away a stray lock of hair that was trying to get into her eyes, and moved around so that Scortia would have a clear view down the length of the room. She said, 'Where did they send you?'

'Clearance detail.' He plugged a short lead from the pistol into the charger. A small red light glowed on the pack, and there was a rising hum that was barely audible. 'It was back when they were choosing the buffer systems to keep the two blocs apart. Any settled planets in those systems had to be depopulated. They weren't given any choice in the matter and, of course, they weren't too keen, so we mostly had to work by force.' It was something of an understatement; they'd invariably had to work by force. The hum died, the red light blinked out, and Scortia straight armed the pistol and looked for a target.

There was a muffled spit, almost a sneeze, and at the far end of the room three sets of kit erupted into the air and scattered into shrapnel. The crashing that they made was magnified and redoubled, and it seemed that pieces and fragments were still raining down several seconds later. Even then the noise didn't die, it was off elsewhere in the hotel, the thunder of a distant tide looking for somewhere to roll in.

'Let's see how Kyle likes the sting of that,' Scortia said.

Thea watched as the red light reappeared and the pistol began to build up another charge. It was reassuring to have some protection, but she wasn't going to pick up a heat seeker for herself; without Scortia's training she could do too much unintentional harm. She said, 'If people didn't want to go, how could you force them? A whole planet?'

'It was easy. Dump poison in the seas and strip all the green out of the forests. It wasn't fast, but it was faster than anything else.'

'You just killed them off?'

'They had ten years to get themselves to the transports for relocation. After that, we'd move on.'

She shook her head. 'I can't believe it.'

'It happened. Still happening.'

'I don't mean that, I mean you. I can't imagine you being part of something so. . . so cold and so mean. And then talking about it as if it meant nothing to you.'

'If I'm honest, it doesn't. I've tried to feel guilty and I've tried to feel sad about it, and there's nothing there. It was one long party on a backwater planet, spraying the seas and zapping the forests like they were score targets in a game. That's what war technology does for you. I mean, look at this.' The light was out on the charger, and Thea winced in anticipation as he brought the pistol up again and took aim. 'I squeeze a trigger maybe quarter of an inch, and with one shot—' A spit, and suddenly there was another volcano down the room. Scortia barely even hesitated for the noise to fall. 'Now, I know I made that happen. Intellectually there's no arguing it. But no way can I feel I'm responsible; there's just too much of a gap between that little squeeze and the big bang. I'm just a spectator at the mess, one of the crowd watching a place burning down.'

They went along to look at the debris. One of the sticky web grenades had exploded, and the jumbled and dented body armour was starting to set into the pool of amber. A blast helmet lay, cruelly dented, and the plates around it formed an uncomfortable image of a dismembered enemy.

Thea said, 'Wasn't there danger?'

'Sure there was danger. Guerrilla bands, resistance people hiding out in the cities. Some of my friends even got killed, one of them blasted out of a skidder right next to me. But when you're on this big destructive high all the time, the fear just gets drawn in and added to all the sick energy you're burning. When I came out of it all I was twenty five and out on the market with no qualifications and no feeling for anything other than burning up planets and blasting people who said no. So I wandered into the commercial space service and here I am.'

Instant autobiography, a chain of horrors cobbled together and presented as if they had all the qualifications of logic and simplicity. She said, 'I can't take all this in. I've got this picture of you as the easy going type who's kind to dumb animals and always sees both sides of an argument.'

He smiled agreeably, the boy from next door who slits up babies. 'It's true, that's me. Good old Scort, liked by everybody and used by most of them.'

'And a killer.'

'Only part time. I was mainly a skidder pilot.'

Too much. 'Let's walk, killer. I'll need time to get used to this.'

DEEPER INTO THE Babylon, and they were moving from the comparatively small and personal areas into the zones set aside for cybernetic backups and powered units. The floor dropped a couple of times for no obvious reason; Scortia guessed that it was to take account of harder layers in the asteroid's structure. Hollow ramps had been bolted across the gaps to allow the transfer of tracked vehicles and man handled units. Like in the barracks everything was orderly and in a marked out place of its own, with plenty of space around so that combat troops needn't collide in a scramble. Backup spares were on tall open racks that ran several layers deep on the outskirts of the machine lines.

The machines themselves faced inwards to a clear track marked by reflective eyes in the poured stone.

The central tracks, the scrambleways, were the only lit areas in the machine hangars. They glowed unevenly with the still pools of overhead spotlights, turning the big vehicles into eyeless dragons, sleeping caterpillar tracked beasts of oil and metal that dreamed hard, unsympathetic dreams as they waited to wake and kill. Even the shadows were more inviting than an open parade in the lights before the monsters; Kyle might be amongst them, watching and appraising, smiling in the darkness as he waited for his own ugly dreams to come true.

Scortia carried the heat seeker levelled and ready, and Thea stayed close on his unarmed side. She didn't want to find herself drilled for being in the wrong place for a snap reaction. A few sensor linked lights flicked on and off as they passed, but mostly they moved by the spill from the central gangway as it fell between and under the heavy transports.

They followed the scrambleways because there was little choice. All the exits and side alleys led to unlit turnout areas like the one through which they'd entered; bright lights that sprang to attention as they entered, orderly rows of kit, no way out. They weren't getting any nearer to finding their way back into the hotel. Scortia had an idea that they were on about the same level as the docking areas, but he couldn't be sure.

'Somebody's watching us,' Thea said.

They were crossing behind a launcher, a singleship catapult on tracks that were roughly twice Scortia's height. He said, 'What?'

'Honest to God, Scort, when we passed that last gap I saw somebody standing there.'

'Kyle?'

'I don't know.'

Scortia looked back at the long slant of light that cut across the floor behind them. It wasn't even, but nothing in it seemed to be moving; Kyle—if it was Kyle—might have pressed up against one of the vehicles, losing himself in the shaded detail of the machinery.

On the other hand, he might still be up in the control room

scanning the sunrise suite corridors. Finding the arsenal had been a fluke, a long shot, and there was no reason to suppose that Kyle might have found it too. Scortia glanced at the charge level on the heat seeker and then eased himself over by the flat joints of the track to take a look.

Thea said, 'Scort...'

He stopped, looked back. She was going to say, be careful, but under the circumstances it sounded pretty stupid. She gave a quick, apologetic smile, and shook her head. He looked at her for a moment longer than he really needed to, as if he was trying to sort something out in his mind, and then he transferred his attention back to the possible stalker down the lane.

He eased out, showing no more than he needed to, the heat seeker raised and ready. He held it for a moment and then relaxed, stepping out into the light.

'Did I make a mistake?' Thea said, unnecessarily.

'An understandable one. Come and see.'

Out of the corner of the eye it might have been a man, so there was no reason for Thea to feel too bad. It was when she gave it some attention that it broke down into an oversized metal parody, frozen in the act of something vaguely distasteful.

'What is it,' she said, 'some kind of powered suit?'

'Seven feet tall and stacked like a tin gorilla.' Scortia circled around it looking up. It was taller, wider and deeper than a man, articulated in some of the same places. 'We used to call them desperation duds. I think the real name's clinical combat support unit.'

'What does it do?'

'Basically, you stuff a wounded man in there and it keeps him alive and fighting. Pumps him up with drugs to keep his mind clear, takes over any functions he can't keep going himself, and gives him the powered mobility to get back into the rough stuff. Just in case you ever got the idea that being half killed excused you in any way.'

'What's it doing out here? Looks like it decided to take a walk.'

Scortia shrugged. One obvious answer would be to take a look inside; the opening lock should be somewhere under the access flap on the hip. He wasn't about to try it. He said, 'Unfortunately, there's nobody we can ask. Let's go.'

THE SCRAMBLEWAY came out into a tunnel big enough to take a six lane autobahn. There were plenty of other ramps and corridors leading in, enough to present a bewildering choice until Thea homed in on one that had the same luxury white flooring as most of the hotel. It was a better signpost than nothing at all, so they followed it.

They were in leadership country. The decor was better. On the next level up there were even pictures on the walls; Scortia couldn't believe it but they were starfields, unappealing and useless, hanging there as a gesture of status like most of the surplus furniture in a hotel bedroom.

There were plenty of doors, but they were sealed shut; probably private quarters, in contrast with the utilitarian shared arrangements of the barracks. Beyond the quarters, they found conference rooms. Time was getting short—down to six hours, now—and they couldn't afford the luxury of exploration, but a map or a diagram could get them back into the hotel more quickly than anything else.

There were four of the rooms, all identical in layout. Three were bare, the chairs around the circular conference table arranged by some over neat orderly. The fourth had the chaos of a fast withdrawal—chairs everyway, half full styro cups and hastily flicked papers. The room came alive when they walked in; hidden lighting gave a subtle glow to the walls and an air blower started to run. There was a strategic display screen on the far side of the room that started to brighten, as did the individual replica screens by each seat position.

'What's the big diagram?' Thea said as the image on the screen firmed up.

'Sector map.' It showed the Babylon asteroid as an enlarged point by a schematic Persephone; the extent of the cleared zone was indicated with a colour bloc. Something was blinking over near the edge of the map, something that ran on a fine rail which traced its way down past the Babylon and into Persephone. In a few hours the Babylon would be set onto a rail of its own. Scortia said, 'Take a look through the papers,' as he moved towards the command seat and the screen playout controls.

'All of them?'

'Just one set.' Of course, the others would be duplicates. Thea pulled the nearest sheets towards her and turned them over as Scortia went on, 'I'll try to access the information backup. It shouldn't mess us about like the one in the Sunrise Suite.'

The papers were meaningless to Thea. Anything that wasn't a statistic was jargonised beyond comprehension. As she pushed them aside there was a flash of colour from the small screen by her hand, and a sound of annoyance from Scortia across the table.

She said, 'What's wrong?'

'For a couple of seconds I had a plan of the asteroid, all the levels including the armoury. Then it just... wiped.'

She moved around to join him. 'Maybe you hit a wrong key.'

'I don't think so. Perverse bloody hotel. It was there for long enough for me to get some idea of where we are, anyway.'

'Enough to get us back?'

'It looks as if some of the walls on certain levels are supposed to slide. Make the military base and the hotel into a single complex.

'Right under the enemy's nose,' Thea said as she stared at the screen; the original schematic had reinstated itself, innocent Babylon by dim Persephone, within early striking distance of the Free Systems.

'That's probably why they abandoned the place without attempting to clear it. Much better to lose all the gear than to let it be known it was ever here. Wham bang, evidence nil. No chance of provoking another flareup.'

'Not much chance of anybody getting off at this rate, either. Come on, Kyle's waiting somewhere.'

ELEVEN

'I'M STILL WATCHING you, Sarrat.'

Ella Desmond flicked the trigger on the burner to reinforce the point. She didn't hold the power down for long enough to start an actual burn, but the sharp buzz was enough to put the message over. Sarrat winced—the memory of his near roasting in the empty drive tube was still fresh and raw—and then he managed a smile which went about halfway to suggesting that he had some confidence left.

'Put your hands back on your knees,' Ella Desmond added.

'Come on, Captain, where's the harm?'

'Move them again and you'll find out. On your knees.'

Sarrat was up against the rear bulkhead of the Sparta's bridge, sitting on the floor with his back against the metal; Ella Desmond had placed him with his knees drawn up almost under his chin and his hands on them, in plain sight. It wasn't comfortable but it was awkward, which was the idea; any delay as Sarrat tried to scramble to his feet would give her chance to get the heavy burner up and aimed. She sat on one of the command chairs, the boned and gutted console unlocked behind her, her bad leg held out straight and stiff.

Sarrat let his hands rest where the Captain could see them. His knuckles glistened with salve, the skin underneath slowly losing its redness. He said, 'Hope you're just as handy with that burner when Kyle gets back. Think you'll be able to watch us both?'

'Maybe not. In which case I'll weigh up your past performance and decide whether or not to put you out of action before the trouble starts.'

'Big talk.'

'You're a moral weed, Sarrat,' she told him tiredly. 'Kyle

obviously doesn't trust you or you'd be with him now. And I'll certainly never trust you again—if it comes to be necessary I'll just unzip you somewhere soft and leave you to bleed.'

If you can stay upright so long, he thought, and it helped him keep the smile in place. He said, with a bad counterfeit of concern, 'Leg still giving you trouble? Bet you'd just love to lie back and sleep it all away. Those painkillers just make you want to float, don't they?'

'Hands, Sarrat. Back on the knees.'

He obeyed, but he didn't hurry. 'Sorry,' he said, and the grin widened. 'If you, ah. . .' (a glance toward the crewroom) 'If you find you're getting tired, you can always give the burner to Kittivale.'

'What's so funny?' Kittivale stuck his head out to look around the corner from the crewroom.

Ella Desmond said, 'Sarrat thinks it's smart to mess around when he's in trouble.'

Sarrat did his best to look unworried. 'Little discomfort, that's all. I can stick sitting here for a couple of hours.'

Kittivale moved up the steps and onto the bridge. The ever present security bag was under his arm. 'A couple of hours?' he said. 'And what happens then?'

'Kyle gets back and cleans up. The Sparta can't go anywhere without him.'

Ella Desmond said, 'Just what does he think he's going to get out of all this?'

'The Sparta—at least, that was the original idea. We had lots of little tricks lined up, ways of making you look inefficient or just plain numb. Then when you were put out to grass and the agents promoted Kyle in your place. . .'

'Wait a minute.' She glanced at Kittivale, who had moved across the bridge and was sitting in the next command chair, but she didn't keep her eyes off Sarrat for long. 'What makes you think Kyle would automatically get the job?'

'Because Scortia's too soft. That's why he hasn't got a chance in hell out there in the Babylon. This is a big opportunity for us, even if it isn't the way we expected to be playing it. We lose you, and we get the Sparta and Kittivale's money to go with it. We're set up for any racket we feel like, and we've got the capital to launch it.'

'Better not rely on that,' Kittivale said, and when Ella Desmond risked another glance across she saw an odd shine in his eyes.

Sarrat didn't seem affected. 'Whistle in the dark if you like.'

Ella Desmond said, 'He's right. You're a spacer, you've seen the condition of the ship. It'll be all we can do to get out of danger if we get the wafers back. The agents won't repair her, they'll scrap her... and your grasping little gang will be scattered out amongst the rest of the fleet.'

'With what Kittivale's carrying, we can set ourselves up. We won't need the agents.'

Kittivale said, almost shyly, 'How much do you think I'm carrying?'

'Enough. High currency crystals don't take up much room.'

'You want to see it?' he offered.

'Sure.' Sarrat's hands were back on the floor, but Ella Desmond said nothing; she was waiting to see what Kittivale had lined up. He'd shifted the bag around to his knees and was putting his print onto the seal. 'Doesn't hurt to see the goods before you carry them off.'

The crystals were unimpressive. They didn't glow and they didn't sparkle, they just lay there like the crumbs of a meagre picnic. Four or five of them, down in the corner where they were almost lost.

Ella Desmond had known what was coming but she'd felt compelled to watch anyway, even at the risk of taking her eyes off Sarrat. Sarrat wasn't fit for much.

'Is that all of it?' he said, and he sounded crushed and offended.

'Just enough to pay off the charter,' Kittivale said as he closed the bag. 'Nothing more.'

'You're lying,' Sarrat said weakly.

'Why should I lie?'

'It's a trick.' He looked at Ella Desmond, daring her to deny it.

'No trick, Sarrat. I've known about Kittivale ever since we

took off.'

'It's not true.' Sarrat looked back to Kittivale, now with growing anger. 'You're loaded.'

Ella Desmond said, 'Only in your fantasy.'

Sarrat started to wilt, but then found a new line and came back up again. 'Oh, no. That girl wouldn't trail around with a destitute sugar daddy.'

'She's not trailing around with me at all. As soon as we reached Porphyria, we were going to divide whatever was left and go our own ways. We simply needed each other to cheat the casino and get off Vegas, that's all.'

Sarrat believed it. Kittivale was delivering it straight—he could never lie so well.

Sarrat said, 'But. . . why?'

'Because it was a rich man's planet and neither of us was rich. We could only ever afford the worst of everything, the castoffs and the scraps and the dregs. Because there was no other way to get out.'

Sarrat was quiet for a moment, and when he next spoke it was with a detectable trace of admiration. 'You brass faced old. . .'

'Hands, Sarrat,' Ella Desmond reminded him, and he hardly even noticed as he complied.

Kittivale said, 'Would you like me to hold the burner on him for a while?' Nobody thought it was funny.

'I'm okay for now. Later, maybe.' She moved in the command chair slightly, to get her seared leg more comfortable. 'Willis could be back by then. . . wherever the hell he is. . .'

> *I'm sorry to have to be the one to tell you this, but it seems that you've strayed a little way off your route. You're heading into the service areas from where we run all the backup facilities of the Hotel Babylon—nothing that would be of interest to you at all. Can I suggest that you head back the way you came? If it's any problem, I'll be happy to call some of our staff to help you find your way. The areas ahead are restricted—all for your safety, of course.*

THE CORRIDOR WALL was back, and Willis looked on into the darkness of the military complex that started and ran on from the edge of luxury. The walls had a dull sheen in the minimal emergency lighting, and one of the many voices of Babylon came as soft as butterfly wings in the darkness from somewhere overhead.

Willis looked up and around. He couldn't see where the voice came from. He said, 'You know who I am?'

It isn't our practice to keep track of our guests...

'Do you know who I am?' he insisted.

There was a pause, almost a delicate hesitation. And then;

I know... what you are.

'Then why do you carry on pretending?'

The tone fell from the voice of Babylon. All the gentle nuances went and it became hard, bright, mechanical. It became truth.

Go back, Willis, if that is really your name. There is nothing for you here.

'Go back?' Willis said, and there was bitterness in his voice. 'Go back for what?'

I do not care. Babylon does not care.

'I belong here if anybody does, and you know why.'

You are of no use to Babylon.

'No, but Babylon's going to be of some use to me. Tell me why you are here.'

The information is not for those...

'You can stall and evade,' he cut in angrily, 'but in the end you'll have to tell me. You'll have to tell me because that's what you're for!'

I can evade for longer than you can listen, Babylon said slyly.

'I can listen forever. Who built you?'

I do not know.

'Is that the truth?'

It is the truth. In my own awareness I simply... came to be.

Willis heard more than the words. He heard an echo, deep inside himself. It was far away, the reverberation of an old hurt. He said, 'I envy you. What's the purpose of the military base hidden within the hotel?'

Hotel and base, they are one. Base and asteroid, they are one. All Babylon.

'To what purpose?'

To become the Presidential base of operations in time of conflict. Fully secure, and close to the battle zone.

There was nowhere closer. There was certainly no more explosive location for a base. 'You say you can defend yourself.'

That is so.

'Even against the strike that's on its way?'

Yes.

'But you won't.'

Babylon will. When under attack, Babylon's purpose is to defend.

'Without troops?'

Babylon needs no troops. I have firepower, mobility. As long as Babylon breathes, Babylon can kill.

'And as soon as you're seen doing it... that's the end of the peace between the Free Systems and the Trading States.'

Babylon knows only to defend.

It didn't make sense. Why clear the asteroid and leave it as a certain trigger to hostility?

Willis said, 'Why didn't they deprogram you before they moved out?'

Babylon does not know. Babylon does not care.

Even if the collision wiped out the whole asteroid, both sides would be watching. The slightest response, and everything would be given away. 'I don't believe trouble was intended. Am I right?'

Babylon does not...

'Babylon doesn't care, I know,' Willis joined in. 'As long as Babylon...' he stopped and thought for a moment. 'Did you say breathes?'

A figure of speech, Babylon assured him uneasily.

'Most of the systems within the asteroid only switch on when somebody comes near, is that right?'

Not all of them. Babylon was trying to be evasive, and it didn't have the skill.

'That doesn't matter. The asteroid only functions when it's inhabited. That's why they didn't need to deprogram you—when the last living body was removed, you had no choice but to close everything down.'

For a few hours only...

'And then the Sparta came along, and it's firework time. The lights come on, the air starts pumping—and Babylon gets its strike capability back.'

Very perceptive. But irrelevant.

'You consider it irrelevant that you're about to spark off an intersystem war?'

Yes.

'You see the threat, and you defend. Never mind that it's not a threat you were meant for, and that the defence protects nobody—you follow your purpose.'

Yes. Do you criticise me?

'No—but I have to oppose you. Is there anything that could stop you closing down again if the Sparta's crew all withdraw?'

No. But for that reason, I cannot allow anyone to leave.

'And if I offer to stay?'

No, Willis. Babylon is not fooled so easily. Kyle, Scortia, the woman—any of them will do.

'But not me.'

No. You are a machine. Babylon can breathe only for those who are human.

There was an echo of something fierce away down the corridor, deep inside the metalled walls of the complex. It sounded like blaster fire. Willis said, 'What's happening down there?'

Those who hunted each other have finally met.

Willis started to move forward. 'Don't sound so cheerful,' he called over his shoulder. 'If they wipe each other out, where are you then?'

There are others, Babylon whispered after.

And I need only one, Willis... only one...

TWELVE

KYLE HAD FOUND them. Scortia's brief impression of the Babylon map had taken them back down to the tunnel and into another set of hangers, and Kyle had been waiting. He'd been too eager and fired too soon; Thea and Scortia had time to get into the shadow of a stone ramp support before he could aim and fire again.

He was somewhere ahead, raised on a catwalk that was part of a ladder interchange leading to the level below. Scortia watched for the discharge flash of the blaster, for a silhouette; Kyle was laughing.

A distant punching noise, and some of the stone overhead burst and powdered down like a handful of scattered gravel. It was a wide shot. The next hit metal, and it rang like a bell in the dark space of the hangar.

'Come on, Scort!' he called, his voice tinny and unreal, and Thea squeezed Scortia's arm. It was neither warning nor reassurance, just contact. Kyle shouted, 'Want the wafers? I've been keeping them for you, look! I'm laying them out, all on the floor here!'

Scortia couldn't resist the temptation to lean out and take a look, but Thea held him back. 'As soon as you put your head out,' she whispered, 'He'll blow it off.'

'I've seen him on range practice,' Scortia said. 'He's not that good a shot. He wants me to get nearer.'

'How're you making out with the gold digger?' Kyle went on. 'She as tough as you said she'd be? Or did you just want to put me off and keep her for yourself?'

'Thanks a lot,' Thea murmured.

'Sorry,' Scortia said. 'At the time, I thought it was true.'

'I haven't told you anything to make you think different.'

'You didn't have to.'

Kyle was louder. Scortia guessed that he was standing. 'Come on, Scort! Not a lot of time left, you know!'

Scortia tried to get a look at Kyle without risking himself, but he could only see a black framework against midnight blue, nothing in it that might look like a man. Or, depending on how you looked at it, every shadow could be an enemy. 'I can't do anything from here,' he said.

'You can't step out, either.'

'But he doesn't know I've got this.' The pistol had stopped humming and was fully charged. 'I've got to get a line on him, even if it means he gets a clear shot at me.'

'And if he fires first?'

'I can surprise him.'

'He might just surprise a hole in you.'

He could just make out Thea's outline in the darkness. He said, 'What's the choice?'

'I know. I was just making noises.'

'Thanks for the thought. Wish me luck.'

She let go of his arm, and he half straightened. Before he was out of cover there was another far-off discharge, and something exploded overhead.

A fluke, or could Kyle see him? If he could, armed or not, Scortia wouldn't have a chance to get aimed and firing. He'd lied to Thea, because Kyle's shooting was well up to merchant fleet standard—which wasn't saying much, but then it hardly mattered when a glancing impact on the hand could take your arm with it.

'Don't worry,' he whispered. 'He couldn't hit a bird's nest at the other end of a chimney.' And he wished it was true.

Scortia started to move out again. He could barely see the edge of the stone pillar that concealed him, but he could feel the line of exposure passing across him and leaving him cold and vulnerable. There wasn't another immediate shot; instead, Kyle started to shout again.

'Captain's waiting, Scort!' he called. 'Can't disappoint the Captain!'

He was in the open now. He tried to get a fix on Kyle's voice, but he wasn't fast enough. He turned his head to the side, trying to distort his own echo. 'You know, Kyle,' he said, 'this is no way to get signatures for your next petition.'

'Who wants help from a creep?' It was impossible. There was so much distortion and so many echoes in the hangar, there was no way to zero in on the source of any sound. Kyle added, 'And I bet the gold digger can't even spell her own name.'

The ladders and ramps were too much of a lattice, Kyle's outline would be broken up and hidden even if he showed himself. The longer Scortia stayed in the open, the more chance Kyle would have of making sense of the shadow dot patterns of his vision and getting a killer shot away.

But then, the answer had been within reach all along.

'If you're going to hit me,' Scortia called, 'make it now.'

It was fairer than anybody had a right to expect. Kyle was starting to say something as Scortia twisted the pistol setting to heat seek and loosed off a shot in Kyle's direction.

Kyle probably saw it coming, curving through the darkness and coming to bear on him. If he'd had faster reactions he might have thrown the blaster away, decoying the charge with the heat of the barrel; but then, nobody can move so fast. The charge broke the blaster into two pieces, one piece in each hand, and carried on into his abdomen.

There it exploded, and blew Kyle apart in a flash of blood and energy.

After a couple of seconds' silence, Thea emerged unsteadily. 'Didn't leave much of him to bury, did you?' she said.

'No time for the niceties. Stay where you are, and I'll get the wafers.'

She was already ahead of him. 'It's okay, I'll get them.'

'Could be messy,' he called after her.

She climbed onto the catwalk. Scortia could barely make her out, and then only because he'd been following. 'Half a mile away, it's messy,' she said. 'Right here, there's nothing left.'

Underneath the ramp a sensor linked light came on, and then went off again as she moved out of range. Scortia swung up after her, and turned his face away as the light blazed.

The wafers were all there, the bait that Kyle had laid.

'Still in one piece?' Willis said from the end of the catwalk.

Scortia recognised the voice just in time. The pistol came up even though he couldn't have fired it; he hadn't switched the pack over to recharge. 'Hell, Willis,' he said, 'I could have killed you. Cain's still around somewhere.'

'He'll be running scared now the boss is gone.' Gone wasn't the word for it; apart from a light, sticky rain on the catwalk, Kyle might never have been there. Scortia wasn't about to start looking around for the pieces.

They got all the wafers together. Scortia checked them, because he was the only one of the three who knew what had been missing; then he said, 'That's all of them. Now, how do we get back?'

'That's why I'm here,' Willis said. 'Follow me.'

HE LED THEM to where he'd managed to get the wall to slide, and they came through into the hotel's crew areas. Babylon didn't comment as they passed, but still Willis watched for dangers; it wasn't likely that the Babylon would give up the lives that kept it active without some kind of opposition. In spite of his expectations, nothing much happened; the lights came on and off, the air blowers started and then wound down, muzak faded in and out. When they found a slideway, it moved for them—Babylon was even helping them to leave.

If they could clear the Babylon, all of the attack systems would close down. They wouldn't have the choice; rob the biosensors of the smell of life, and the programming would take over. Until then, the Babylon's military arm would continue to prepare; whatever threatened the hotel, man made or natural, would be blasted, at which point the secret would be out and the accusations would start flying, closely followed by strike ships and missiles.

With the wafers replaced, the Sparta could move again; no problem, unless the Babylon decided to make an early move. It could either launch a premature attack, or it could act to keep them on board—either course would be enough to ensure that the Traders' violation would become public. The slideway was still rolling, but it was no reassurance; not as long as the

Babylon had the power to keep the Sparta shackled in its hangar.

As they were passing the heavy doors of the cold rooms, Scortia said, 'Where did you get your information from, Willis?'

'I talked to the Babylon.'

Scortia thought of his own dead ended attempt to get something out of the machine in the Sunrise Suite, and said, 'I tried that. I ended up kicking the console.'

'You have to know how.'

'He's right, Scort,' Thea cut in. 'I heard him.'

Willis hesitated for a moment, then realised that she was talking about the time he'd communicated with the lobby console. He said, 'That's right, you did. What did you hear?'

'I heard about this meteor. About it not being a meteor at all, but something artificial. About how it was heading straight for Persephone and all set to get burned up.'

'Artificial?' Scortia said. This was new to him. 'What kind of artificial?'

They'd have to know sometime. 'A world ship. Full of heartsick machines all coming home to die.'

'A what?' Thea said, and Scortia said, 'What kind of machines?'

But now they were at the goods elevator, and they had to wait as Willis heaved the door open. It was big enough to hold a medium sized vehicle, and there were tyre tracks on the floor. They stepped inside and Willis pushed the door back and hit the touch panel for three levels up.

There were no inner doors; the seam welded walls of the shaft floated down from ceiling to floor like a projected show. Something banged outside the cab as they passed the next door above, and Willis turned to Scortia and said, 'The machines are simulacra. They look like men and they think like men. They even feel like men, but they're not men.'

'Sounds pretty far fetched,' Scortia said, watching Willis with a frown.

Willis was by the falling wall, looking up. The second level came and dropped. 'It's an old story,' he said. 'Too old. It's time it ended.'

Thea wasn't as suspicious as Scortia; she hadn't been around much outside of Vegas, and as far as she knew such things might be possible. But she was puzzled, and she said, 'How come you know it?'

'Inside information,' Willis said as they reached the docking level, and he slid the door to let them out. They emerged into the short complex of service corridors that would lead them to the reception area and the Sparta.

ELLA DESMOND ANSWERED from the bridge intercom as soon as she got Scortia's call from the airlock. Scortia said, 'We made it back. Kyle's dead and we've got the wafers.'

'Good work, Scort,' she told him. 'I closed up the airlock after you'd gone. Just in case Kyle decided to come back.'

'Kyle's fit for nothing beyond breakfast at the maggot ranch. You can let us in.'

The signal lights on the panel changed across as the outer airlock door opened. After a few seconds they changed back, and the ready light for the inner door glowed. Ella Desmond looked at it for a moment. Then she looked at the blaster that Cain was levelling at her. Cain shook his head.

'Keep it on auto,' he said. 'That's where they're staying. Now move back from the desk.'

Ella Desmond said, 'You heard him. Kyle's dead. Where do you expect this to get you?'

'I know he's dead. I saw the mess he left. Move back from the desk, or else...' He nodded towards where Sarrat was standing with a rough handful of Kittivale's shoulder. The bag had been kicked aside, and Kittivale was nursing a bunch of broken fingers. His eyes were wet and his face was white, but he wasn't making any noise.

It had happened fast; Cain had arrived only a couple of minutes ahead of Willis and his party. The airlock had been open and he'd simply walked in; Ella Desmond hadn't been able to swing the burner around in time for it to be of any use. There was a charred and smoking hole in the floor from Cain's demonstration shot, and Sarrat had thrown Kittivale down and stamped on his hand as a demonstration of his own.

Ella Desmond took a couple of limping steps away from the desk. Cain said, 'At this stage, it's usual to say, 'You won't get away with this'.'

'Up yours, Cain,' she spat.

Cain shrugged. 'I suppose it's different.' He reached across and checked the setting of the airlock switch, keeping his eyes mainly on the Captain. The lock was still in auto, which meant that the three in the inner chamber had to wait until somebody let them out. There was a sigh of compression from the assists as Cain lifted the console cover, and then he switched hands with the blaster and reached inside. The blaster waved around a little, but it was still covering enough of Ella Desmond to hold her back.

Cain said, 'There are a couple of little contacts I can make under here to jump across the airlock safety circuits—not something you'd expect to know about, Captain, it's the province of dumb artisans like Sarrat and me.' He worked for a moment and then tapped a contact. 'That one seals the inner door and this one—' a crackle and a few sparks, which made him wince and pull back for a moment '—this one starts all the air pumping out.'

It hadn't been enough of an opportunity. Even if she'd moved, Sarrat was still holding Kittivale. Kittivale had slumped, and Sarrat now seemed to be holding most of his weight. She said, 'At this point, you're supposed to say, 'crude, but effective'.'

Cain seemed slightly offended. 'I was just thinking it was pretty damn smart. Just give it a few minutes and our friends will be nice and purple, and I can go down there and get the wafers without any risk at all.'

It was then that a hollow pounding began, deep within the Sparta. It sounded like something vital was trying to shake itself apart. Sarrat said, 'What the hell's that?'

Cain was obviously worried. He shook his head, but he kept on listening. 'Sounds like somebody's trying to batter his way through.' His gun was still in his least useful hand.

'With what?' Sarrat said. 'A track off a tank?'

Cain was still listening, as if concentration alone might give him the answer; it was because of this that he missed the spectacle of Kittivale bringing Sarrat down.

Kittivale had slowly drooped, so that Sarrat had been forced to increase his grip. Kittivale had then chosen his moment to take his feet off the floor, and Sarrat had been jerked over sideways; when Kittivale came up again it was to butt the unbalanced Sarrat under the chin. He fell like an old sack.

Cain made the mistake of trying to switch the gun back to his other hand. Bad leg or not, it gave Ella Desmond the chance to swing a kick into his groin. He folded over it, eyes bulging on stalks, steam spurting out of his ears, and slowly settled onto the deck. He didn't even have the strength to moan.

The pounding got louder as Kittivale came stumbling across the half round of the bridge. Together they looked into the maze of the console sub wiring.

'What do I have to mess with?' Kittivale said.

Ella Desmond wished she'd paid more attention to Cain's hands as he'd interfered. Cain was rocking slightly on the floor, no use to anybody. She said, 'The printed chips are probably crosslinked with a dripwire. You know what one of those is?'

'What the hell,' he said, 'I'm bound to get something,' and he began to poke haphazardly around in the wiring.

'Somewhere around here,' she said as the sparks flashed and ripped, and a gusher of mixed noise came from the console speakers; there was sampler selection muzak, safety procedures for total vacuum (*it is not advisable to hold your breath, as this can cause permanent damage to the eardrums and soft tissues of the trachea...*), a sponsor's plug for practical nihilism (*Have you ever contemplated the vast empty void and pondered on the ultimate meaninglessness of life? Those great formless distances between the systems where man seems no more than a loose knot in the fabric of existence?*)—Kittivale poked and tugged with his one usable hand, desperation growing, and he was still looking for something likely to undo when Scortia reached over his shoulder and switched off the noise.

He was damp and his collar had been torn open, but he seemed to be all right. Thea was behind him, at the entrance to the bridge. She looked down at Cain and said, 'Who saw to him?'

'He'll have an even chance of a job in a harem if he ever stands upright again,' Ella Desmond said. She limped across to the step down crewroom making a detour past Cain, who still hadn't unwound. As Scortia slotted the wafers back into place she returned with a Medicaid for Kittivale's hand; a brace to straighten and set his fingers, and a sprayjet local to keep him quiet as it was done. As she worked, she said to Thea, 'Who was doing the hammering?'

'Willis,' Thea said. 'With his hands, if you can believe it.'

There was a sudden silence on the bridge as Kittivale's fingers straightened out with a cracking, grinding sound. Kittivale's eyes widened; he wasn't getting any sense back from the limb at all, and the sight of the distorted bones getting pulled back into shape was strange and unsettling.

Scortia paused with the last wafer, gritting his teeth and waiting for the sound to end; there was no way that he could work and still be hearing it. Ella Desmond bent to secure the brace. The simple act was a door opened into her aggressive, defensive personality, but Scortia still didn't suppose that he had any more idea of what wound her up and set her going. She was an odd figure in an unlikely job, seldom getting the respect that she deserved and seldom deserving the respect that she got; paradox all down the line, and no simple junior had much chance of resolving it. He turned to slot the wafer and saw again the random damage that Kittivale had inflicted; he didn't seem to have strayed into any vital areas, but it would be as well to have a check.

He said, 'Anybody know what happened to Willis?'

Scortia was pulling the console cover down as Thea said, 'I don't know. I didn't see him go.'

He powered up, and watched the systems coming onto line. 'I thought he followed us.'

'He did, but he isn't here now.'

'He should be,' Ella Desmond said with a frown, implying Big Trouble for Willis.

It was then that one of the com channels beeped for attention, and when Scortia reached across to clear it they heard, *'Bridge? Are you getting me?'* It was Willis.

Scortia said, 'Willis, where are you?'

'*I'm in the dock.*' He had to be using the speak plate by the lock.

'Well, get in and get secure.'

Everything on the board showed launch status. The Sparta was ready to use the limited drive power available to it, ready to limp out and get clear, ready to let the Babylon die; according to the instrumentation, the Babylon was even ready to let it happen. But it wasn't going to be so easy.

'*I'm not coming with you,*' Willis said.

THIRTEEN

SCORTIA COULDN'T hold the launch status and an argument at the same time, so he had to stand the Sparta down. Ella Desmond shouldered him aside and said, 'What are you playing at, Willis?'

'*Not playing, Captain,*' came Willis' voice, distorted slightly by the intercom system. '*I want you to launch without me.*'

'Have you gone mad?'

'*I'll be okay.*'

'Okay? The hotel's going to get dragged into the sun and you think you'll be okay?'

'*It's what I want, Captain,*' Willis said, and Ella Desmond looked upwards in a momentary and furious appeal. A lousy situation almost resolved, and then this. He added, '*Something I've wanted for a while.*'

She looked at Scortia. 'Scort, get down to the airlock. Hit Willis over the head with something and get him on board.' She stared at him hard for a moment to force the point.

As Scortia looked around uneasily, Willis said, '*I appreciate you wanting to dissuade me, but it won't work.*'

'Better make it something heavy,' Ella Desmond advised.

'*Ella,*' Willis said, '*please. Don't argue with me.*'

'Look, Willis, I'll do you a deal. Sarrat and Cain are no use to me now, and without you I'll have no spacers at all. Just come back on board until we get picked up, and then you can do away with yourself however you like. Scortia will give you a hand, won't you, Scort?'

'Ah. . . sure,' Scortia said with a sickly smile.

'*You're not taking me seriously.*'

'Well, what the hell do you expect?'

'*Get Scort to tell you about the simulacra.*'

'The what?'

Scortia cut in, reluctantly. 'Willis reckons that the object heading for Persephone is an oversized spacecraft. He thinks it's being run by a bunch of robots.'

'Suicidal robots, then,' she said dismissively.

'*You're getting it, Captain,*' Willis said, and Ella Desmond could only stare at the console as if it was the desk, and not Willis, that talked. '*Nothing much less than the heat of a sun can kill a simulacrum. We're based on a chain molecule similar to DNA, but it's tougher and more versatile. Damage us however you like and we'll just regenerate.*'

'What do you mean, *we*?'

'*I'm one of them. I asked them to leave me behind. It was a mistake.*'

Ella Desmond shook her head, slowly. 'You've flipped, Willis.'

'*Maybe.*' Willis hardly sounded concerned. '*In a few hours, it won't matter.*'

'Scortia's coming out for you,' she said, waving Scortia towards the bridge exit. Scortia didn't move.

'*I won't be here, and you won't be able to find me in time. I'm not going mad—everything I've told you is true. Check my records. I'll tell you now, they're incomplete. Every ten years I have to pull up stakes and move before questions get asked—I'm never ill and I don't age. I have to wipe the slate clean every time. I can't afford to make friends—it broke me up every time I moved on, and I can't even count the number of times that's happened.*'

Scortia moved in closer to the console. 'Can I say something?'

'He's all yours,' Ella Desmond said, and made way. 'I can't get any sense out of him.'

'Willis,' Scortia said, 'Listen to me. If you don't come with us, the Babylon won't close down. You told us, not as long as there's somebody alive inside.'

'*That's right, but the Babylon doesn't recognise me as a man. Machines don't count.*'

Cain was beginning to stir. Kittivale nudged Thea, and when she saw the spacer trying to roll over she reached for the discarded blaster. It would be the first thing he saw when he opened his eyes.

'Willis,' Scortia said, 'we don't believe you. It's as simple as that. Now, how are we supposed to leave you here to die?'

'*Pretty fast. The Babylon could move anytime.*'

'So please get on board!'

'*No, Scort. I'm going home with my own kind.*'

Ella Desmond was over by a bank of switches with a couple of screens. She was dialling through the camera eye views of the Sparta's exterior, trying to get a sight of Willis. She got a sequence of angles on the ship—the system was intended for damage confirmation during flights, and it had shown her the lost drive tube tumbling away—but the most she could get of Willis was his shadow, thrown across the uneven plating of the deck by the airlock lights.

Scortia said, 'You expect us to swallow that you should just happen along when all your tin friends have decided to fry together?'

'*I didn't just happen along. I rigged it.*'

Ella Desmond looked up, sharply. 'He did what?'

Willis heard her, and said, '*I didn't mess with the drive, that was all Kyle and Cain. But I knew it was going to happen, and I let it. And then when I cross patched the programme to steer us through the black hole, I biased it to bring us here.*'

'But. . . how could you know?' Scortia demanded.

'*I knew, that's all. And I think they'll know I'm waiting.*'

Ella Desmond was on her way back over. 'For the last time, Willis. . .'

'*You promise this will be the last time?*'

She hesitated; argument was getting them nowhere, and Babylon's end was getting nearer. She said, 'Will you at least take a radio? In case you change your mind?'

'*I won't change my mind. But I'll take a radio if you'll go.*'

'Somebody take a radio down and throw it out to him,' she said. Somebody obviously meant Scortia, and he moved to go. Cain managed to open his eyes at last, and blinked stupidly at the blaster Thea was holding on him.

Ella Desmond wondered what her log entry on all this was

going to look like.

BABYLON DIDN'T seem to be resisting. All the navigational information came through without a hitch, and the iris locks opened on cue as the Sparta eased backwards towards them; the linear guides in the entrance tunnels held her more or less central, and the lasers supplied adjustment information that made manual control unnecessary. As they emerged into black space, one of the preset messages came over to thank them for the honour of the visit.

Thanks and up yours, from ripoff city, Scortia thought as he touched a switch to kill the sound. This was too easy.

When the routine stuff began, Ella Desmond levered herself out of the command chair and moved over to the watch crewroom where Kittivale waited.

'How's the hand, Kitty?' she said as she stepped down carefully.

Kittivale winced and said, 'Not so bad. I don't want to ask a stupid question, but shouldn't you be flying the ship?'

'The hard part's over, and Scortia can handle the rest. He already did most of it, anyway. Mind if I sit with you?'

'Not as long as nobody takes a look and mistakes us for a welfare queue. How's your leg?'

'Sore,' she said as she sat, not too close. Every time the muscle stretched, it felt like cheap cotton ripping. 'That was quite a stunt you pulled back there.'

'It was nothing, really.'

'Sarrat was twice your size.'

'I know, I felt that when he stood on my hand. I caught him off balance, that's all. If he hadn't cracked himself on the way down he'd probably have got up again and eaten me.'

'That only makes it more impressive.'

Now didn't seem to be a good time to add that Sarrat's jaw had given him what felt like a permanent headache. 'Anyway, you didn't do such a bad job on Cain.'

'He'll never sing bass in the choir again, that's for sure. Your girlfriend's gone to get them locked up—her and Scort are the only fit ones left in the party.'

'I can't claim her as my rich man's concubine. I may have the ego, but I don't think I've the energy to live up to it. Thea goes her own way. Getting off Vegas, it was her idea, all her plan. It just happened that she needed me to pull it off, so I got lucky.'

'And when you got to Porphyria?'

'We were going to split up, each go off on our own. I don't really know what I was going to do.'

Ella Desmond glanced through into the bridge area; Scortia didn't seem to be having any problems. She said, 'Why so keen to leave?'

Kittivale considered for a moment; the obvious is always the most difficult to explain. 'One big planet, one big party. Vegas gets by even though it's got no natural resources to speak of—it's right in the middle of a belt of systems which all got settled by the puritan pilgrims in the first big wave of colonisation. They've all got strict moral laws, Vegas hasn't got any, and nobody seems to think there's anything odd about the big traffic that runs between them and Vegas—if they believe in a god, they assume he's looking the other way. It's not a place where you'd want to live.'

'After what happened this trip, you'll probably get your first half deposit refunded. The agents will argue, but I'll come down on your side.'

'Thanks. I wasn't looking forward to landing in a new place flat broke.'

In a rare display of comradeship, Ella Desmond gave him a soft punch on the shoulder. 'You'll manage, Kitty.'

'Ouch,' he said, and she realised that she hadn't thought whether she was punching his good or his bad arm.

'Your hand?' she said.

'The name.'

WHEN THEA GOT back from locking Sarrat and Cain in a storeroom, she looked around the bridge and saw that Ella Desmond was missing. She could hear voices from the crewroom. Nobody seemed likely to object, so she sat in the empty command chair. Scortia didn't seem too busy. She said, 'Can you speak, or will it distract you?'

'The tricky stuff's finished with,' he said, pushing himself back, 'and even that wasn't so much.' The automatics continued to make fine adjustments to the instrumentation.

'You've got a lot of screens to watch,' she commented after a moment.

'You want me to explain what they all mean?'

'Sounds interesting,' she said, but her mind was obviously working elsewhere.

'Look,' he said, 'we could just scrub the social tennis and creep off to your cabin. . .'

'Later. In the meantime you can put the lid on the steam and observe all the niceties.'

'But you don't want me to explain all the screens.'

'Not particularly.'

'That's a relief. Because there are three down that end of the desk that I've never quite figured out.'

The readouts meant nothing to her. She said, 'Are we safe yet?'

He glanced at the silent intercom speaker. Willis hadn't tried to make contact, and he hadn't responded the one time that Scortia had tried to raise him. Safety was relative. He said, 'Not in terms of distance, but that's no problem. The tricky part was getting out of Babylon.'

'In case Babylon tried to stop us?'

'That's right, being so dead set on keeping people inside so it could smash its enemies. But nothing happened.'

'Maybe there's something built in,' Thea suggested. 'Some sort of safety programme.' Neither of them wanted to say the obvious; the Babylon didn't need to hold them, because the Babylon had Willis.

Scortia said, 'Maybe. We'll stay close as late as we can in case Willis changes his mind.'

They were both silent. It wasn't that Willis' story took a lot of swallowing—it was too ridiculous even to consider—but whatever his reasons were for putting it over, there was no explaining them. Scortia didn't understand it, and he didn't like it. Whenever he tried to think it through, his mind would end up blank and uncomprehending.

There was a light under the com point; it had to be Willis, at last. Scortia opened the channel, and Willis' voice came through; fainter now, and with an overlay of static that was added by distance and the fabric of the asteroid.

He said, *'Are you out yet, Scort?'*

'Clear of the Babylon, but staying close. Are you changing your mind?'

'No chance. Can you spare the power to do a scan?'

'What kind?'

'Energy tracks, the easy one.'

Scortia checked the levels. The Sparta's single drive was pulling less than half of the usual in-flight power load, and there was plenty on offer. He said, 'What do you want it for?'

'Because. . .' A momentary fizz of static drowned Willis out, and he came back stronger than before; *'. . . the lights are still on, some of the music's still playing, and the air's still pumping.'*

'Well, of course the air's still damn well pumping. You're there.'

'I'm not trying to argue with you, Scort. But will you do the scan for me?'

Scortia considered for a moment. The courses of action were limited. There might just be time to lift Willis off the Babylon; if he stayed, then those on the Sparta could save themselves and look forward to the major conflict that would follow. The only way to power down the asteroid would be if Willis, realising his madness late, were to considerately space himself. An even, balanced, pragmatic view suggested that they should go back and get him, averting the war and the slaughter of millions through the risk of self sacrifice if they didn't get far enough away as the meteor—or whatever—passed. The voices inside said shove pragmatism, let's live.

He said, 'I'll scan, and I'll tell you now what I'm going to find.' He transferred the scanner's output so that it would appear on the largest of his screens. The flying spot began to sketch in a Mercator of the asteroid, layers of intensity going in as deep as the scanners could show. 'I'll get a power web traced out on the screen and there'll be a dumb spacer with a radio standing in the middle of it thinking he's a vacuum cleaner's brother in law. And then you'll say okay and we'll waste another half hour getting you. . .'

Scortia's voice tailed off as he studied the projection.

Willis said, '*Any results?*'

Scortia reset and started again. He said, 'Where are you?'

'*I'm in the entrance lobby, just the other side of the dock. What's the reading?*'

The new version was no different from the old. 'I've got a power flow schematic, but it doesn't centre on the lobby.' The docks and the adjacent areas were easily detectable, large and sharp edged shadows exactly where they ought to be. 'It hardly touches that sector at all. The big drain's right down inside—' he rotated the image to get a better fix '—and by the look of this, it's back in the armoury somewhere.'

Thea was leaning forward in the command chair, trying to make a layman's sense out of the specialised diagram. She said, 'Pretty lively for a place that's supposed to be closing itself down.'

'*The station isn't closing at all,*' Willis said. '*It's supposed to be dead by now and it's still operational. No wonder Babylon let you go without a fight.*'

'Why?' Scortia said. He sounded unsettled, no longer so sure.

'*Kyle's still alive.*'

'Come on, Willis. You saw him go. Kyle's in pieces.'

'*And the pieces are still ticking, obviously.*'

'I don't see how.'

'*Maybe Babylon knows. Can you do me a detailed sector scan and narrow it down?*'

Scortia checked. The capability was there, and there was no point in pretending that it wasn't; Willis was a spacer, and he'd know. Also, irrational as it was, Willis seemed to know what he was doing.

'It'll take a couple of minutes,' Scortia said.

FOURTEEN

WILLIS STOOD in the dark of the entrance lobby. He could see—just about, and not much—the dim outlines of the arches overhead, and some of the edges of the desk and loungers by his side. If he needed to, he could move by sound; the echo of his own footsteps would give him the shape of any room or corridor that he found himself passing through, reflected and modified by any surface. It was a skill that he'd rarely found it necessary to use, but it wasn't so far away when he needed it. This could almost be the World Ship, he thought as he moved towards the service corridor; a long time ago but not so far away, when for a while he'd been Valum's aide and his twilight life had some kind of purpose. That purpose had been the killing of men, a pure hatred that had no basis in desire or revenge but which was a satisfaction and delight in itself. Delight had died in the moment that Randall killed the World Ship, and then the ache had begun to grow. It had begun as a homesickness, and slowly become the despair of the lost and rootless. Like he'd said, it was time it ended.

The goods elevator carried him down. The controls responded to his touch as before, but without Thea and Scortia he travelled in darkness. Babylon rejected him. Somewhere deep inside—Scortia should be able to indicate where, as soon as the detailed scan was complete—there was a life which kept the Babylon awake. It had to be found, and it had to be removed. Not because of the possible political consequences; Willis was aware of them, but they weren't his main concern. It was more important to him that Babylon should die defenceless.

He went on, past the cold rooms and the crew quarters. The sliding corridor wall that he'd unlocked was still back, and ahead were the low level emergency lights of the military complex. He stopped and checked the radio; deeper into the asteroid meant that reception would worsen, and he was already several levels in. With some fine retuning he was able to get the Sparta's carrier signal; obviously Scortia wasn't yet transmitting. It was rough, but it would serve. He clipped the radio to his belt and started off towards the hangar deck.

Willis...

He stopped, but the sound didn't come again. Perhaps he'd never even heard it; the sigh of air in its slow movement through the Babylon's empty passages, maybe, shaped into a semblance of a word and then fine carpentered into a name by an unsuspecting subconscious. After he'd listened for nearly a minute, he moved on.

A rail enclosed ladder took him from the overhead grid to about one third of the way down the hangar wall; there it met a shallow gallery of open ironwork, and he paused to look down over the safety bars.

The war machines slumbered on, their noses in the pale glow of the track centre spotlights and their haunches in shadow. There were no other lights, and no distinct sounds—until the radio at his hip crackled into life.

'*Hearing me, Willis?*' Scortia said.

He raised the radio. The poor signal wouldn't let him speak quietly, but it seemed that any moment dim, slow heads would lift and turn to fix on him with eyes of frost. 'Hearing you,' he said.

'*I've got the results of the scan. It's narrowed down, but I can't be precise. Where are you now?*'

'The armoury. Machine decks.'

'*Then you're as close as I can get you. The image won't tune any finer.*'

Scortia said something else, but Willis didn't get it. He interrupted and said, 'I'm losing you. Can you put more power into the signal?'

The only reply was a surge of static. He reclipped the radio and moved along to the next section of ladder.

When he got to the catwalk where Kyle had been blasted,

nothing appeared to have changed. The spray of blood and water and bile that had freckled the surface of the gangway had dried, but that was all. Willis swung down the last few feet to the level of the deck and began to search for other debris; after a couple of minutes he found some, still wet pieces of Kyle strung out loose and grey, lying where they'd been thrown. Even further away there was a recognisable piece of arm, with a hand knotted into an empty fist. Willis couldn't understand how Babylon breathed on; Kyle was not just dead, but disembowelled and dismembered.

And then he heard it again.

Somebody or something was walking, patrolling the scrambleway. It was in the next hangar, and it was coming through; as it walked, it whispered his name.

WILLIS GOT BACK into the darkness. There was a big half-track close by and he circled around behind it, getting its dark bulk between him and the central avenue where the lights pooled and the catseyes glowed. The thing that called his name was in the connecting tunnel now, coming through from the next hangar; he could hear its tread, and the spit and hiss of hydraulics that came with it. And it rambled; Willis' name, and more.

Cold, Willis, so cold... so cold and so dark. Can't last, Willis.

There was room for him to get underneath the half track, space to crawl right up to the edge of the light and still be covered. He dropped down and began to ease through. It was emerging into the hangar, he could tell by a subtle change in the echo

No burning in Persephone for Willis, no burning for Babylon. staying cold

and as he wormed his way towards the light he got a glimpse of something moving, broken and distorted by the cogwheel shadows of the track.

It paced along the centre of the scrambleway, even and unhurried. It was big, and its angles were sharpened by the directional overhead light. It rocked slightly as it walked, pistons clicking to modify and compensate for the shifts in mass. Willis saw it, and was afraid. He didn't fear for his safety; he feared the unwanted life that the Kyle thing would force upon him. He shuffled back out of reach as it came level, and watched through the tracks as it passed; then it stopped.

It turned as if it was looking around, even though it appeared to be sightless.

> *Cold as stone, Willis,* it whispered. *Cold as steel. Machine cold, Willis. Cold as love*

And somewhere within the sound, there was a germ of being that remained unmistakeably Kyle.

It did a slow sweep of the hangar. It came to face Willis, and kept on turning. When it had shuffled a full circle it hesitated, and then it began to walk on towards the exit tunnel and the next hangar.

> *One of us, Willis* it muttered as it went. *Help us or leave us, don't stop us. So cold*

Willis climbed out from under the half track and stood up in the light. The Kyle thing was a silhouette in the tunnel ahead, striding on through Babylon. Willis reached for his radio.

'NOTICE SOMETHING?' Thea said as she looked at Scortia's main screen, and Scortia gave an ugh shiver.

'Yeah. Suddenly it's gone cold around here.'

'I mean about the power diagram.'

'Very technical.' He watched the levels as the power supply to the Sparta's transmitter was raised.

'Come on, Scort, it's a picture, that's all. A child could read it.'

Scortia shrugged. 'Maybe not so technical, then.'

'You can see where Babylon's supposed to be using power, and you can see where it isn't.' The power routings still flowed across the schematic, an exaggerated pulsing like in a display ad. 'Wherever Willis was supposed to be, nothing was happening. Everything was dead.'

'I know.' Scortia glanced at the screen, with a reproachful

expression usually saved for a Judas.

'There should have been something. Whenever we walked around, the place just lit up in front of us. Why not for Willis?'

'I don't know. Look, I'm nearly up to strength with the transmitter power. I've diverted it from the dampers.'

'Do I detect an element of evasion?'

'Right. Thea, I've never heard of anything like what Willis was trying to put over on us.'

'So. . .' Thea said. 'Ignore it?'

Scortia turned from the instruments, and tried to hammer his point home. 'Willis is flesh and blood,' he said. 'Anybody designing a mechanism for a purpose wouldn't try to make it look like a man; you design for the job, and that creates the final appearance. Robots that can pass for men don't exist outside stories.'

'What if the whole purpose of the machine was that it should pass for a man?'

'What would be the point?' Scortia said, uneasily aware that the power flow diagram gently sawed away at the supports beneath his assertion.

'I don't know. Willis never said.'

Scortia sighed. The levels were still rising, slower than necessary, but if the process was speeded up something might blow. With no spacers on board, it would stay blown; without saying it aloud, Scortia knew that the time within which Willis could safely be lifted from the Babylon had expired. If the Sparta had been around the other side of the asteroid, they might even have been able to get a fix on the approaching body.

'I'm mad,' he said, more to himself than to anybody else. 'I'm trying to raise power to reach a spacer who thinks he's a robot looking for a walking dead man.'

Thea was still watching the diagram. The flow was shifting slightly, but its centre remained within the armoury.

'Willis said Persephone was home,' she said. 'What did he mean?'

'Don't ask me. Persephone's a dead system, cleared a few hundred years back according to the Sparta's navigational records. It was one of the first systems in the buffer programme, one of the weak ones where it was easiest to practice all the techniques before the whole thing really got going. There was only one planet and that was called Persephone as well, which tells you what kind of hick backwater it was.'

'Willis probably left during the clearance, then. I suppose it would be easy to get fake documents in the confusion.'

Scortia's tolerance was an unconvincing front. 'But he'd have to be Methuselah.'

Thea was unruffled. 'Or incapable of ageing, like he says.'

When the routing was complete, he called Willis and found that the channel was already open at the other end. He said, 'You getting me, Willis?'

'*Getting you now,*' Willis' voice came. It was thin and strained, computer decoded from the static that the Sparta was receiving on the nominated wavelength. Willis had no extra power to call upon for his own transmitter. '*What's seven feet tall and walks like it's sticking to the floor?*'

'Are you telling me a joke?' Scortia said, puzzled.

'*No, I'm asking you a bloody question!*'

'Seven feet tall?'

'Scort,' Thea cut in. 'We saw it! That kind of suit thing, the support unit. The one they put the wounded into so they can keep on fighting, remember?'

'But it couldn't be following Willis.'

'*Something is,*' Willis said, having heard Thea's interruption. '*Tell me about it.*'

Thea moved closer to the pickup, and Scortia leaned back to let her in. 'I'd thought it was somebody watching us, but it was one of those units standing on its own. It was seven feet tall, like you said, and it was vaguely man shaped but kind of square and vicious looking.'

'*That's it,*' Willis said. '*I think Kyle's inside it. Would that be possible?*'

Thea looked at Scortia for an answer, and he found himself saying, 'Could be. But I'd hate to think of the state he'll be in.'

Willis said, '*I don't think he was given much choice about it. That's why Babylon wasn't worried about letting you go—as long as it had a scrap of him to keep alive, it wasn't in danger of closing* down.'

Scortia was about to speak, but the cue light was out. Willis had switched off his receiver for some reason. They could still hear, or they could transmit the attention getting bleep to tell Willis that they needed to speak to him; but there had to be a reason for him making the cutoff so suddenly, so they listened.

There was a clattering, overmagnified as Willis hooked the radio back onto his belt, and then a rustling as it brushed against his thigh. He was moving, maybe dodging into the shadows to avoid the support unit.

At first there was nothing to hear; the sounds were so faint that the Sparta probably read them as signal noise and took them out. Then they came through the static, slow measured footsteps with a ton of agony bearing down on each. Scortia was perspiring even before the grave cold voice began.

Willis? it said. *Willis? Come to me, Willis*

It was close, and then it was moving past.

Come to a friend. Tell a friend. Willis?

Scortia hadn't expected ever to hear the sound again. They'd called it the ghoul parade, the march of the walking dead, the most disposable of soldiers who could be sent ahead into the worst of everything. After a few moments, Willis came back on line.

'That was it,' he said. '*Whatever's making it move, it isn't Kyle. The voice may have been Kyle's, but what was behind it was all Babylon.*'

Scortia said, and immediately realised it was a stupid question, 'Are you in danger?'

'*Me? Considering why I'm here, how can I be? It's you that's in danger if I can't get to Kyle and wipe out that last little spark.*'

'But he can't kill you?' Thea said, and she faced down Scortia's skeptical glance with a glare.

'*No, but he can damage me enough to be useless until it's too late. Right now, I'm under one of the half tracks in the hangar. Is there any sure way of disabling these walkers?*'

Scortia thought for a moment. It could be done, but the interior of the suit would be reinforced. Even if it was wrecked, the occupant would be kept alive to be re used; Willis would have no choice but to get in close and get his hands dirty. 'There's a reinforced flap on the hip—left as you look at it—that gives access to top up on drugs and plasma. That has to be locked and sealed by a medical orderly every time it's used, but since there are no MO's in Babylon there's a fair chance it will be open. If it isn't, you'll just have to grin and bear it as Kyle tears your arms and legs off. Under that flap there's also the only control which can spring the whole suit and let Kyle slide out. I don't know exactly what it's like because I've never seen one up close. Never wanted to.'

'*Swap with me,*' Willis said, '*and you'll get your chance.*' Whatever he might be—and Scortia now couldn't feel committed to any opinion—he sounded nervous.

Thea said, 'Good luck, Willis.'

'Yeah,' Scortia added, 'good luck—I know it sounds pretty inadequate in the circumstances, but I don't see what else I can say.'

'*I'll report if I get the chance. Otherwise, just watch for the power drain tailing off.*'

And that was it; Willis closed the channel and left them watching for a score on a TV screen; highest player starts the war rolling.

Scortia said, 'I have this feeling that everything's kind of lurched sideways and left me behind. Like getting to heaven and finding it's full of sales executives.'

Thea glanced back towards the watch crewroom. 'Hadn't you better bring the Captain up to date?'

'In a minute.' The power flow diagram wiped across, to be replaced with a modified update. Kyle was still slow patrolling. 'First I've got to work out some way of putting it that doesn't sound like I should be wrestled away from the controls immediately.' He gave a theatrical little sigh as he stared at the new information. 'I suppose this means we have to defer the cabin creep.'

The mood was gone and the moment was past, but maybe they'd come again. 'Save it for the celebration.'

'Listen,' he said, suddenly earnest, 'I just want to tell you something.'

'What?'

'You're okay.'

She waited, but he didn't elaborate. 'Is that it?'

'When I first saw you I thought you'd be one of those Vegas women who hooks onto the most useful player in the room. They act soft but that's all it is, an act. You're a different kind of survivor. A better kind.'

Thea tried not to smile, and found she couldn't help it; but there was a sadness underneath, an acknowledgement that a truth is never reached without hard work. 'If I learned one thing on Vegas, it's that nobody deserves a round of applause just for being alive. But thanks, Scort.'

He put his hand on the desk and stood up.

'And now I've got to see if I can give this story to the Captain without her beating me up and down the bridge for a dreamer. Watch the chart, will you?'

FIFTEEN

WHEN THE KYLE thing reached the end of the scrambleway, it stopped. There were no more hangars to pace, just the largest turnout area of them all and a walk to the deep space transports. It shuffled around, and started back.

Willis had followed it. He was pretty close now; it seemed slow and insensitive, and it stayed within the brightest areas. Some of the sensor driven lights flickered as it passed, but that was all; Kyle was sealed tight inside, locked in the dark where Babylon could nurse him jealously.

Willis stepped around to the side of an open man carrier as the Kyle thing passed. He didn't even have to hide, because the unit's cameras couldn't manage the contrast between the scrambleway and the low light fringes. It trudged on, still calling in its death whisper, still making its rambling appeal to Willis.

It neither hated nor threatened. Babylon was safe, Kyle was secure, and Willis didn't affect it; there was no damage he could do, no central point he could strike at. It had the life it needed, and it needed no more; but it called to Willis with an icy affinity, a machine's appeal of love.

'Kyle!' Willis shouted. The high roof of the hangar bounced it back at him, a fraction late and made smaller. The Kyle thing stopped.

Willis?

'Over here, Kyle. What's the matter, can't you see me?'

So dark, Willis

But then, Kyle wasn't really doing the looking. Babylon didn't see so well when looking for its own kind. It was helpless, and ready to admit it. Willis felt a twisting of emotion that he hadn't thought possible; something in him, now that the moment was here, wanted to reach out and join Babylon; it was the dark machine that sat in the hollow space he called his soul. *Why fight,* it said. *What are the bloodbags to you? Owe them nothing, need them for nothing.*

But it wasn't true. Babylon needed at least one bloodbag to keep it awake and alert. Whenever machine moved, it did so in bitter acknowledgement of the man god.

Join us, Willis. Be true to yourself. True to the machine

The doubt was passing. 'It's no longer the same thing. I'm only a machine as long as I allow myself to serve. It's when I listen to the voice inside that I become something more.'

The Kyle thing was shuffling around, coming to face him as he moved onto the scrambleway.

Babylon hears the voice inside

'And what does it say?'

Willis was in line with the catseyes, right under the spotlights which poured onto the grey floor. The Kyle thing glittered as it came to rest.

Kill. It says kill

'Anything else?' There was a wait of several seconds and then:

Babylon wants to live

Willis didn't have it in him to condemn Babylon, but he would have to try to stop it. The unit began to lean slightly, and then it raised a leg to come for him.

Run where you will, Babylon will find you

'I'm not running,' he said as it took another rocking step, releases and servos whining as the weight shifted. The unit's two articulated arms slowly raised and spread, ready to embrace him as they met.

A flap somewhere about the hip—whatever that was supposed to be—on the left as you look at it; Willis was looking, but he couldn't see any flap. He backed off a little to gain time; too far and he might not see what he was aiming for, too close and he might never reach it.

The unit raised a leg, planted it, raised again. As the body swung across, he thought he saw the access; it was bevelled in to blend with the lines of the body shell, but he lost it again as the unit lurched forward.

He let it come as close as he dared, staying out of the reach of those outstretched arms, ready to duck and feint if they should come sweeping toward him. He crouched low and tried to see the flap cover, but it was too well streamlined to make out in the long shadows cast by the overhead spots; it was as he was trying to watch the moving edge of the shadow that the unit's three fingered hand grabbed his shoulder and pulled him in.

He slammed against the reinforced plate on the front of the unit, and the other arm wrapped across his back. His own arms were by his sides, pinned and useless. The Kyle thing started to squeeze.

Relax, Willis. Relax and join us

There was pain. His back started to pop, his ribs were being compressed, and all he could do was to squirm uselessly.

Soon be over, Willis

He was up off the floor, no leverage at all. A rib went, and then another; both were dynamite jolts in his guts, blasting open crevices that filled with lava. He tried to resist, to push away with his pinioned arms and his knees.

The Kyle thing had been adjusting to no resistance, and Willis' effort took it by surprise. Its grip loosened for a moment.

Strong, Willis. Babylon made a mistake. Correcting

The crushing resumed, but now he was a little better off; he had an arm free, pulled up and held high in a brief moment of opportunity. The Kyle thing paused, and its servos whickered as it shuffled to balance itself with its load. Willis reached down, and tried to feel around for the releasing flap.

Newly adjusted, the Kyle thing began again to squeeze. Everything in Willis urged him to beat it with his fist, but he resisted and ran his fingertips down the metal, touching, searching, striving for an impossible delicacy as his tough simulacrum body was being mangled; a seam, a scratch, a rivet, and. . . there, so unobtrusive that he almost missed it in a blind haze, a straight, even groove and a recess for a coded key.

If it was locked. . . then, nothing. The Kyle thing would simply wrench him into disability and then drop him, broken and useless, to lie in the scrambleway as it made its move against the approaching World Ship. Then or later, the Babylon would be blasted, destroyed, and still Willis would lie there, struggling to regenerate as the asteroid was taken apart around him; he'd be burned and perhaps further maimed, and as Babylon crumbled he'd be thrown unnoticed to the spaceways. Near the heat of a star he might revive slowly, without it he wouldn't have the energy; either way he'd go on forever, drifting without control, an eternity of nothing to do but count the stars.

He found the groove again. The metal was lightly oiled, and he couldn't get a grip; for a moment he lost it altogether, but he forced himself to take it slowly. His fingertips ran across the groove, traced it, started to put pressure in.

The flap swung open, and dropped away on a hinge.

Inside, there were switches. He flipped them all, flipped some of them twice, and suddenly the Kyle thing that was the Babylon knew what he was trying to do.

Willis, it said. Oh, Willis, no. . . please

It weakened, sagged, and dropped him. As Willis fell the unit began to lean forward; it stopped half way, and split up one side. The split opened maybe half an inch, and fluid trickled out.

Willis got to his feet on the second attempt, screwing up his eyes against the pain as the jagged ends of his ribs were pushed around inside. The Kyle thing twitched, but it seemed to be more or less powerless. Hugging his chest with one arm, Willis reached to open the casing.

There wasn't much pressure needed, which was lucky because Willis didn't have much to exert. A hydraulic assist took most of the load, and a small interior work light revealed what was left of Kyle.

Most of him had been blasted away. About thirty per cent of his body mass remained, burned and ripped; in the wounded areas the torn skin had been laid open, the minor blood vessels sealed, and the major veins and arteries linked into a colour coded tube network. An arm was missing, and below the breastbone there was nothing at all. Willis could see Kyle's one serviceable lung being slowly inflated; there was a tube forced between his teeth to carry the workload. Behind the lung, just visible and bathed in a steam jet to keep it moist, Kyle's dull heart was beating.

It was so clinical it was almost tidy, the offal bin of a fanatically neat butcher. But the sounds were grim reminders of life; the inflating and deflating of the respirator, the pulse of the heart pacemaker, and the gurgles of the various liquids as they surged and drained. And Kyle appeared to be conscious enough to be watching him.

Only one eye showed, because the other was concealed by the brace holding the head rigid on a neck that was bruised enough to be broken. The eye was fixed on Willis, watching, pleading, powerless to signal or demand.

No, Willis thought as he reached in, Kyle can't be aware; brain death would have begun by the time that the Babylon could have reached the pieces, so that Kyle must be blank and comatose. The pacemaker leads appeared to be the most accessible and the least messy option, so he took hold and jerked them.

The heart beat once on its own, and struggled to beat again. It halfway managed it, and then slowly collapsed. The wires in Willis' hand spat fire as the suit tried to restart, but the contact was broken; the heat was down, the lung was quivering, and the circulating fluids began a slow colour change.

Kyle knew. A single tear formed on the eyelid, swelled into a raindrop, and fell. The light went out behind the eye, and the lung slowly emptied.

Babylon was robbed.

Willis said, 'Goodnight, Kyle.'

A low vibration was growing throughout the asteroid. Systems were closing down, services were being shut off, and there was nothing that Babylon could do to prevent it.

For the moment of its dying consciousness, it could see the

destruction that waited. The vibration increased until the floor and the walls of the armoury began to shake, and loose objects started to fall from the spares racks behind the fighting machines; the support suit swayed, and Willis shuffled back as it pitched over and spilled most of its contents onto the floor with a sloppy crash.

The thunder was taking shape, becoming an agonised and distorted cry which was drawn out endlessly; another voice joined it from deeper in the armoury and then there were others, wounded keening from every part of the hotel so that it seemed the whole asteroid screamed.

And suddenly, it stopped.

SIXTEEN

Most of the doors on the private levels were locked. Ordinarily Willis could have smashed his way in, but he was damaged and weak; even the concentration of picking locks in the dark was beyond him. He dragged from door to door with his burden, leaving a wet trail through the ersatz gardens, ploughing through the dyed streams without regard for the pathways.

He found one that was unlocked, but it wouldn't slide for him. He had to let go of Kyle and put all of his strength into getting it open; once back it stayed, and he pulled Kyle on through.

There was only the sound of his own breathing to give him the shape of the room; Willis stood in the darkness and sensed the circular recess of the main lounge, the off centre bed, the seating around the dead information points, the half open doors to empty closets. How did it go? *Welcome to the Sunrise Suite, pride of the Babylon...* or something like that. We here in the management happen to know you're loaded as hell, but we aim to change that. We're going to rip you off at every opportunity, but you're going to like it because you'll think this is the way to live, sucker. We've got a top layer of pseudo culture to soothe your ego, and then downstairs we've got the brothels and the clip joints you really came for.

He got a better grip on Kyle, and started to pull him down the steps into the sunken round. How could Scortia question why he was ready to move on?

Kyle wasn't heavy, but Willis still couldn't lift him. They made an ugly descent together, and then Willis started over towards the semicircle of seating, aiming to get him settled somewhere so he could see the show. The upholstery was real leather—it must have cost a fortune to ship out. Try it for comfort, Kyle. Like it? Don't worry about the mess. We'll just put in on your bill, that's what the Babylon's for. Blitz a few planets, starve a few thousand babies. Just put it all on the bill and don't bother us with the details.

What was left of Kyle lolled, propped with cushions. His broken doll head was over on one side, but he didn't seem to mind. He kept on grinning, equally happy with everything. Willis went to get them some light.

Don't go away, Kyle, you're going to love this. The drapes weren't drapes at all, they were the moulded frontage of an opaque shutter which ran most of the way around half of the domelike well. No big dramatic reveal, not without the power to slide everything back at once; the shutters were heavy and they resisted being rolled manually, so Willis could only manage the operation in jagged spurts. The reaction glass behind was already partly clear, and the burning edge of the gas giant was uncovered in stages.

Kyle sat, beaming happily. It ought to be something like, *Persephone, cool red giant star, unique amongst the systems in this sector, a beacon that marks the point of contact between heaven and hell...* Willis got the shutters back as far as he could. The suite seemed ablaze, doused in the flame red of the star. Like everything else on the Babylon, it was a hyped up fake; if Persephone burned as red as it appeared, it could never have supported life. The window filtered, intensified, lied.

What else was to be said? Willis had managed to get around when he was trying to find out what made the place tick. Babylon hadn't really wanted to know him—only interested in people—but then that little matter of definition was the reason behind his presence. He sank back onto the leather; a stuffed cushion behind his back eased the pain of his ribs. He could see all of the window from here, a good slice of Persephone and some black space beyond, just like any paying guest. After watching for a minute or so, he remembered the radio.

He tried to call the Sparta. There was hiss, and nothing else. The one guaranteed characteristic of technology—whatever happened, in the end it would let you down. Or maybe it was just the asteroid getting in the way. Whatever, it didn't matter; Willis didn't really want to say goodbye anyway, and the Sparta was probably too busy blasting its backside to get to safety to be bothered with farewells. Besides, they wouldn't understand.

Kyle would. Willis could bet that Kyle understood by now. How there must be more to life than being alive. Because, on the surface of it, there was no difference between Willis and other men; except that they lived, and Willis was built, and unless one could accept that there was a little bit of life in every simple mechanism, then he didn't qualify. Not when he was really little more than a more complex mousetrap or computer.

But then, what machine ever had feelings? It was quite a problem. Willis couldn't know if his feelings were real or just a mechanical illusion, and in either case he wasn't sure that he'd be able to appreciate the difference. When it came down to it, surely people were organic machines as well. When he'd gone to join them, he'd thought he'd be able to ignore the problem, but he couldn't. If there was something called life, something that called out to matter and said, *hey, this way...* then he needed to know that he had a share of it. If he hadn't—then he didn't want to go on.

Persephone held the answers. If Willis and the machine were one and the same, then that's where it would end. And if he was anything more, he would leave the machine behind.

The radio was still in his hand, and it was making weak noises. He looked down at it in surprise—he'd forgotten that it was still switched on. He raised the volume and put in the noise limiter, and held it where he could listen.

A few moments later, a voice said, *'That's got to be Willis. I assume you're not here by chance.'*

Even after all the years, Willis recognised it immediately. Randall, the unwilling leader of the simulacra, object of their unwelcome loyalty as the World Ship died. At last, something was going right.

Willis said, 'I arranged it. I should have stayed with you all along.'

'You've missed nothing. But welcome back anyway.'

'You didn't find a place to settle?'

The end was getting nearer, but Willis wanted to get the most out of it, to enjoy for just a moment the feeling of being back with his own. Randall said, *'Come on, Willis, you already know the answer to that one or you wouldn't be here. We could never settle. We never will.'*

'How long have we got?'

'Not long. Can you see us?'

Willis couldn't see anything other than the budget sized slice of sunrise that the picture window provided. 'Yes,' he lied, 'I can see you.'

'Just a few more seconds, then. Are you scared?'

'Yes.'

'Join the club.'

There was static breaking through the narrow suppression range of the limiters, and now the asteroid began to shudder. The static hit a peak and then began to fall; the World Ship was past and diving onwards into the sun, and even though Willis limped across to the window and pressed himself against the glass, he didn't see it.

Nothing was happening. There had been a mistake, the Babylon wasn't going to be drawn in. It had surreptitiously used the energies available to it to change orbit slightly, to get itself onto a safe line, and Willis was going to be left behind; but then the rocks started to shake, and the man-made structures within the Babylon began to groan under pressure as it fell.

Liberation or oblivion.

Whichever it turned out to be, Willis hoped he'd be able to handle it.

SEVENTEEN

SCORTIA HADN'T BEEN getting the best of Ella Desmond's temper. She didn't want to hear what he had to say about Willis, what she wanted to hear was why he'd wasted so much time without a) establishing whether or not Willis finally wanted to be lifted off the Babylon or b) getting the Sparta out of the danger zone. Thea saw the way that the mood was going and slid out of the command chair to put herself somewhere less conspicuous. Ella Desmond replaced her without acknowledgement or thanks, and started to direct the withdrawal operation according to her own ideas; the result was that the procedure ran without grace or finesse, like rail trucks constantly smashing around in a goods yard, but Scortia stayed quiet and did what he was told. He watched the readouts and he hit the controls on command; always too early or too late, but he didn't risk adding his own corrections.

There wasn't far to go to safety, but even so it was a struggle because of the Sparta's reduced capability. With all the available thrust out of the drive they managed to hold against being pulled in after the asteroid, but Scortia was keeping a nervous eye on the efficiency levels of the dampers; if they didn't hold, the Sparta would have about two minutes before the outer skin started to melt.

Barely a ripple on the surface of Persephone, certainly nothing that could be observed from the Sparta, and it was all over. Now that there was nothing to be done Ella Desmond handed the controls back to Scortia, with an instruction to fire up the distress beacon for when the snoopers arrived. She went off, back to cripples' corner with Kitty.

Thea moved back in as soon as she saw that it was safe, and said, 'All over, then.'

'If you mean scattered all over Persephone, yes.' He lifted the cover on the Panic Button and twisted the key that was underneath. From a pod somewhere on the far side of Rat City, a fission beacon was dumped; too dangerous to be allowed to operate inboard, the fast decay of its fuel chips would pump out a heavy distress call to attract the attention of the jumpers as soon as they emerged into Real Time.

Thea could see that something was bothering him, something more than recent events; a puzzle refusing to be solved.

'What's the matter?' she said.

He closed the cover, and sat back. The automatics were holding them steady. 'Confusion and a certain lack of comprehension. The Captain had just about convinced me that Willis was talking gibberish. I lost his signal and I was hunting around for it when I started to pick up something else. Whatever that thing was that disturbed the Babylon's orbit, it was talking to Willis.'

'In gibberish?'

'Who knows? I lost it almost straight away.'

Only Persephone knew for sure, and Persephone wasn't telling. Thea said, 'Forget it, Scort. Don't mess about with a happy ending.'

'How do you get to that?'

She glanced at the main screen. It still carried the Babylon power web. The shapes and the layout were still the same, but the energy tracks had all gone. It wiped with an update.

And suddenly, no Babylon.

She said, 'Out of the whole mess, somebody got what they wanted. That kind of thing doesn't happen often.'

Bonus Book

To view or download a PDF of the original novelisation of
The Last Rose of Summer, go to
www.stephengallagher.com/the-last-rose-of-summer and
follow the links

Stephen Gallagher
THE SEBASTIAN BECKER NOVELS

Chancery lunatics were people of wealth or property whose fortunes were at risk from their madness. Those deemed unfit to manage their affairs had them taken over by lawyers of the Crown, known as the Masters of Lunacy. It was Sebastian's employer, the Lord Chancellor's Visitor, who would decide their fate. Though the office was intended to be a benevolent one, many saw him as an enemy to be outwitted or deceived, even to the extent of concealing criminal insanity.

It was for such cases that the Visitor had engaged Sebastian. His job was to seek out the cunning dissembler, the dangerous madman whose resources might otherwise make him untouchable. Rank and the social order gave such people protection. A former British police detective and one-time Pinkerton man, Sebastian had been engaged to work 'off the books' in exposing their misdeeds. His modest salary was paid out of the department's budget. He remained a shadowy figure, an investigator with no public profile.

THE KINGDOM OF BONES

After prizefighter-turned-stage manager Tom Sayers is wrongly accused in the slayings of pauper children, he disappears into a twilight world of music halls and temporary boxing booths. While Sayers pursues the elusive actress Louise Porter, the tireless Detective Inspector Sebastian Becker pursues him. This brilliantly macabre mystery begins in the lively parks of Philadelphia in 1903, then winds its way from England's provincial playhouses and London's mighty Lyceum Theatre to the high society of a transforming American South—and the alleyways, back stages, and houses of ill repute in between.

"Vividly set in England and America during the booming industrial era of the late 19th and early 20th centuries, this stylish thriller conjures a perfect demon to symbolize the age and its appetites"
—**New York Times**

THE BEDLAM DETECTIVE

…finds Becker serving as Special Investigator to the Masters of Lunacy in the case of a man whose travellers' tales of dinosaurs and monsters are matched by a series of slaughters on his private estate. An inventor and industrialist made rich by his weapons patents, Sir Owain Lancaster is haunted by the tragic outcome of an ill-judged Amazon expedition in which his entire party was killed. When local women are found slain on his land, he claims that the same dark Lost-World forces have followed him home.

"A rare literary masterpiece for the lovers of historical crime fiction."
—**Mystery Tribune**

THE AUTHENTIC WILLIAM JAMES

As the Special Investigator to the Lord Chancellor's Visitor in Lunacy, Sebastian Becker delivers justice to those dangerous madmen whose fortunes might otherwise place them above the law. But in William James he faces a different challenge; to prove a man sane, so that he may hang. Did the reluctant showman really burn down a crowded pavilion with the audience inside? And if not, why is this British sideshow cowboy so determined to shoulder the blame?

"It's a blinding novel. . . the acerbic wit, the brilliant dialogue—the sheer spot-on elegance of the writing: the plot turns, the pin sharp beats. Always authoritative and convincing, never showy. Magnificently realized characters in a living breathing world. . . Absolutely stunning"

—**Stephen Volk**
(Ghostwatch, Gothic, Afterlife)

"Gallagher gives Sebastian Becker another puzzle worthy of his quirky sleuth's acumen in this outstanding third pre-WW1 mystery"
—**Publishers Weekly starred review**

Printed in Great Britain
by Amazon